I0585701

Teaching Fairy Tales

Series in Fairy-Tale Studies

General Editor
Donald Haase, Wayne State University

Advisory Editors
Cristina Bacchilega, University of Hawai'i, Mānoa
Stephen Benson, University of East Anglia
Nancy L. Canepa, Dartmouth College
Anne E. Duggan, Wayne State University
Pauline Greenhill, University of Winnipeg
Christine A. Jones, University of Utah
Janet Langlois, Wayne State University
Ulrich Marzolph, University of Göttingen
Carolina Fernández Rodríguez, University of Oviedo
Maria Tatar, Harvard University
Jack Zipes, University of Minnesota

A complete listing of the books in this series can be found online at wsupress.wayne.edu

TEACHING
FAIRY TALES

Edited by
Nancy L. Canepa

Wayne State University Press
Detroit

Copyright © 2019 by Wayne State University Press, Detroit, Michigan 48201. All rights reserved. No part of this book may be reproduced without formal permission.

ISBN (paperback): 978-0-8143-3935-0
ISBN (hardcover): 978-0-8143-4569-6
ISBN (ebook): 978-0-8143-3936-7

Library of Congress Control Number: 2018965006

Published with the assistance of a fund established by Thelma Gray James of Wayne State University for the publication of folklore and English studies.

Wayne State University Press
Leonard N. Simons Building
4809 Woodward Avenue
Detroit, Michigan 48201-1309

Visit us online at wsupress.wayne.edu

Contents

Teaching Fairy Tales

AN INTRODUCTION

Nancy L. Canepa

Fairy tales are among our most beloved and ubiquitous narrative proto-types; from their characteristic chronotope that evokes times long past and places remote, to their reassuring "happily-ever-afters," they con-stitute an easily recognizable and nearly universal form of tale-telling. Fairy-tale types such as Little Red Riding Hood, Cinderella, and Snow White, in one or another of their countless versions, are indeed among the few narrative forms of which we can confidently assume a common shared knowledge. On the first day of one of the courses I regularly teach, "Literary Fairy Tales," I introduce a mini–case study on Little Red Riding Hood by asking how many students have read, heard, watched, or otherwise experienced some version of this tale; it is rare that 100% of hands don't go up. I follow this up with similar questions on the *Odyssey*, the Bible, *Hamlet*, or other canonical Western texts, with (in many cases) barely a 50% success rate.

In his classic definition of 1946, the folklorist Stith Thompson tells us that the fairy tale is a narrative "involving a succession of motifs or episodes. It moves in an unreal world without definite locality or defi-nite characters and is filled with the marvelous. In this never-never land humble heroes kill adversaries, succeed to kingdoms, and marry prin-cesses" (Thompson, 8; cited in Haase, 1: 323). How have such "simple" stories situated in "never-never land" come to wield such cultural power?

If the fairy tale is as alive and well today as it was 500 or 1,000 years ago, this has to do with the way it has transformed, adapted, and been continually reconceived as an expression of both collective aspirations and individual sensibilities.

Many studies have been dedicated to the style and structure of the fairy tale, to its characters and settings, but just as many have looked at the treatment, within its magical frame, of real personal and societal issues in their multiple temporal and spatial configurations: "Fairy tales register an effort . . . to develop maps for coping with personal anxieties, family conflicts, social frictions, and the myriad frustrations of everyday life" (Tatar, "Introduction" [1999], xi). Whether in oral or literary form, fairy tales have and always have had social functions—to entertain, to acculturate, but also to grapple with and question dominant values and ideologies. As Donald Haase points out, "The fairy tale . . . fulfills a sociocultural purpose, whether that is satisfying the audience's need to see its wishes realized or confirming a society's structure of status and power" (Haase, 324). Through fairy tales human beings transpose their own worlds and reimagine new worlds, just as the stories that fairy tales tell can be creatively integrated into our own real-life trajectories. "Stories animate life," in the words of Arthur Frank. "Stories do not just have plots. Stories work to *emplot* lives: they offer a plot that makes some particular future not only plausible but also compelling" (Frank, 3, 10). Organizing our experience into words and stories is an essential human activity that gives life meaning, and perhaps no other genre illustrates this narrative reciprocity as well as the fairy tale. We fashion our lives into stories, and in the process come under the transformative magic of already-existing stories.

The systematic study of the fairy tale is a relatively recent phenomenon. Although folklorists have been collecting and analyzing fairy tales for nearly two centuries, only in the immediate past have scholars engaged in pioneering critical reinvestigations of the fairy-tale tradition. This activity has resulted in the publication of a wealth of materials and resources and, in the words of Don Haase and Anne Duggan, "the international institutionalization of folktale and fairy-tale studies."

> Whether we label the production and reception of the fairy tale in the last four decades of the twentieth century a "vogue," an "obsession," a "golden age," or a "growth industry," one thing remains certain: an enormous amount of cultural energy and creative, intellectual, and economic capital have been invested internationally in the folktale and fairy tale—and this continues to be the case mid-way through the second decade of the twenty-first century. (Duggan et al., xlii)

We have seen an outpouring of editions, re-editions, translations, and anthologies that have reconsidered canonical works by, for example, Charles Perrault, the

Brothers Grimm, and Hans Christian Andersen. But of equal importance have been the excavations, translations, and editions of lesser-known fairy-tale texts that were previously unavailable or inaccessible in English, such as tales from the earliest history of the European fairy tale or unfamiliar versions of the best-known tale types. At the same time, books and articles that offer innovative critical perspectives on the forms and functions of fairy tales have proliferated, and original theoretical approaches to fairy tales continue to evolve. These works, together with monographs on single authors or conglomerations of authors, edited volumes, and compilations of tales and critical materials for use in the classroom have been published in new book series (such as the Series in Fairy-Tale Studies at Wayne State University Press) and in the many academic and commercial presses that have welcomed scholarship in fairy-tale studies. Important reference works published in the last decades include the monumental (and ongoing) *Enzyklopädie des Märchens* (initiated by Kurt Ranke, 1975–); the *Oxford Companion to Fairy Tales* (edited by Jack Zipes, 2nd ed., 2015); Hans Jörg Uther's *Types of International Folktales* (2004), a revision of the older Aarne-Thompson tale-type index; and the four-volume *Folktales and Fairy Tales: Traditions and Texts from Around the World* (edited by Anne Duggan and Donald Haase, with Helen J. Callow, 2nd ed., 2016). Over this same period journals focusing on folktales and fairy tales, such as *Fabula* and *Marvels & Tales*, have reached international prominence; in addition, websites and electronic databases aimed at gathering resources and facilitating research have proliferated (*SurLaLune Fairy Tales*, *Endicott Studio*, and *D. L. Ashliman's Folklore and Mythology: Electronic Texts* are just a few), and conferences and conference sessions dedicated to fairy-tale topics have become ever more numerous.

All these developments have contributed to the solid establishment of the field of fairy-tale studies. This area of study, which brings together and takes advantage of the expertise of folklorists and literary scholars but also of experts from disciplines such as social and cultural history, gender studies, film studies, and psychology, has concentrated on exploring both Western and non-Western traditions of fairy tales and on considering the fairy tale as a genre distinct from other narrative forms. Literary fairy tales have often been the primary focus, though discussions about the complex and dynamic relationships between literary and oral traditions have also thrived. Much scholarship has centered on the repetitions, revisitations, subversions, and, in general, the reverberating dialogues that have endured over the course of the history of the fairy tale; by showcasing such intertextuality, this work complements and ultimately moves beyond both the focus on specific collections of tales or national traditions and the ahistorical discussion of universal fairy-tale "archetypes." At the same time as they have offered sophisticated models for reading fairy tales, scholars have shown how an integration of fairy tales into the teaching of literature and culture can encourage us to widen the parameters of how and what we think and do as educators and scholars. Indeed, courses on fairy tales have also seen a boom in popularity in the past several decades and today are regularly taught in a wide range of college and university departments: at the undergraduate and graduate levels, as courses that fulfill general education requirements, and as advanced foreign-language courses or upper-division seminars.

In the classroom the fairy tale becomes a unique vehicle for introducing compelling discussion topics and for developing students' critical skills. The status of the fairy tale as a basic narrative whose structures and content have influenced many other genres provides a wonderful starting point for an overall discussion of narrative, even with the most inexperienced students. The question of how we may better understand the development of the fairy-tale tradition leads to the larger examination of how a genre evolves over time and, more generally, of the relationship between literature and history, art and society. Consideration of the social and cultural contexts in which fairy tales have been created and received, as well as the role of fairy tales in acculturation, informs the sociohistorical approach, which perhaps more than any other has shaped the field over the past decades, and students generally find this approach relevant and stimulating. Feminist scholarship in particular has not only offered groundbreaking readings of canonical tales and led to the "rediscovery" of tales by women but has also produced stimulating exchanges regarding canon formation and the ideologies involved in anthologizing, editing, and translating. Investigating the influence of the fairy tale on other narrative genres and art forms, both in and outside the West, has opened up broader reflections on the relationships among the arts and on questions of interdisciplinarity and cultural exchange. In other words, all these approaches implicate both the specific genre at hand—the fairy tale—and larger issues of literary and cultural history, transmission, and interpretation, making courses on the fairy tale an ideal entryway to the humanities overall.

The essays in this volume aim to offer teachers a variety of approaches, informative materials, and instruments for navigating the central issues of fairy-tale studies and for creating and teaching meaningful and innovative course or units on the fairy tale. The fairy-tale traditions, predominantly but not exclusively of Western Europe, investigated by the contributors range from the Greco-Roman "prehistory" of fairy tales to the first appearance of postclassical authored tales in sixteenth- and seventeenth-century Italy and France, to both renowned "classics" (the Brothers Grimm) and lesser-known tales of the nineteenth century, to turn-of-the-century original works informed by fairy-tale motifs (such as

J. M. Barrie's *Peter Pan*), to twentieth- and twenty-first-century experiments in refashioning the classic fairy-tale canon, including the revolutionary adaptation of fairy tales into animated cinema and the use, by writers of adult fiction and poetry, of fairy-tale structures and contents in works that take on the most contemporary of social and political issues.

Teaching Fairy Tales

Some years ago I organized the two-day colloquium "New Critical and Pedagogical Perspectives on the Fairy Tale." The first day consisted of papers on recent critical developments in the field. On the second day, using a workshop format, participants shared syllabi, methodologies, and classroom activities that they had successfully adopted in fairy-tale courses. What struck many of us was that, whereas the first day's proceedings were extensions of the ongoing conversations in the field that regularly take place at conferences and in the pages of journals, the concrete discussions dedicated to pedagogical strategies were unique. And yet translating the advances in fairy-tale studies into concrete and practical ideas for bringing fairy tales into the classroom with intellectual rigor and creativity is not always a simple matter; teaching fairy tales presents both distinct organizational questions and exciting opportunities for rethinking conventional pedagogical approaches. How do we structure courses on fairy tales? When designing a seemingly straightforward "survey" course on the European fairy tale, do we opt for a traditional chronological organization with its panoramic historical overview, on the model of some literature survey courses? Or might we choose an organizational model based on "case studies," in which we read multiple versions, old and new, of a tale type in order to highlight the parallel tracks of tradition and innovation that the fairy tale has ridden since its inception? How do we integrate innovative theoretical approaches into our courses on fairy tales? And how do we fruitfully incorporate fairy tales into courses on other topics, such as surveys organized by national literature or period, genre courses (the novella, fantastic literature), and courses on folklore, children's literature, or gender studies? How do we work with national traditions of fairy tales in foreign-language courses or study fairy-tale production across the arts? And, because fairy tales always seem to inspire great inventiveness in students, how do we introduce tale-telling activities into the classroom, link these activities in meaningful ways to course content, and, in doing so, develop new critical and creative competencies? How do fairy tales adapt as online courses? Lewis Seifert's essay in this volume, "Fairy Tales in the Classroom" (Part II), surveys possible answers to these sorts of questions, just as the contributors address many of them in greater detail.

The contributors to this volume approach fairy tales from diverse angles, yet all would concur, I believe, that students' classroom encounters with a genre they were most likely exposed to from a young age can be a wonderful opportunity not only for developing essential skills in critical reading and textual analysis and promoting cultural and linguistic competencies but also for revisiting the assumptions, interpretive stances, and emotional and intellectual constructions that govern their everyday lives and their shared cultural heritages. In the classroom it is hard for students to remain impassive in the face of the stories that fairy tales tell, for even today these stories structure our cultural expectations and encourage the most productive sort of blending of the personal and the cultural. As Maria Tatar notes, "Fairy tales, rather than sending messages, teaching morals, or constructing lessons, get conversations going. Piling on one outrage after another, they oblige us to react, to take positions and make judgments, enabling us to work through cultural contradictions using the power of a symbolic story" (Tatar, "Introduction" [2015], 3).

A number of the contributors provide step-by-step models for the reading of a particular tale or the implementation of a classroom activity; some do this in the context of the discussion of a particular critical approach or a specific type of course. Many of the contributors consider the fairy tale's "natural" intertextuality and the fascinating and multiple ways in which fairy tales transform over time and space, adapting to changing desires and needs, and explore "how fairy tales affect the making of who we are and of the world we are in" (Bacchilega, 3). They—as well as most of the other contributors, I suspect—would agree with Cristina Bacchilega when she maintains that "thinking about transformation—within the tales' storyworlds; in the genre's ongoing process of production, reception, reproduction, adaptation, and translation; in the fairy-tale's relation to other genres; and more generally as action in the social world—offers a spacious and productive way into that exploration" (Bacchilega, 3). Yet other contributors promote experiential engagement with fairy tales in the form of, for example, storytelling or organizing an exhibition of fairy-tale illustrations. The 27 contributors, though mainly hailing from literary studies, represent a diversity of fields and disciplines, institutional affiliation, and perspectives on and experiences with fairy tales, making for a rich, eclectic volume. There are essays to engage educators who are just embarking on their teaching careers and beginning to get their bearings in the field of fairy-tale studies and essays that will offer new insights to more seasoned educators (I can attest to this!).

The first section, "Foundations of Fairy-Tale Studies," engages with many of the big questions that stand at the fore of fairy-tale studies: How do we define the fairy tale? Were there ancient narratives akin to what we consider fairy tales today? When and how did the fairy tale evolve in Europe? What is the "classic" fairy tale, and does it even make sense to talk about a fairy-tale canon? Some of the ideas contained in the essays of this section are readily available elsewhere, yet having them compiled in one place and as an overture to the pedagogical essays that follow offers a useful orientation for readers new to teaching fairy tales; these essays might also be fruitfully adopted as introductory readings for students. In the opening essay, "What Is a Fairy Tale?" Maria Tatar considers why this narrative form has been with us for so long, reflecting on how fairy tales are "stories that dispense with extraneous details to give us primal anxieties and desires" and that "use magic, not to falsify or delude but rather to enable counterfactuals, to move us to imagine 'what if?' or to wonder 'why?'" Graham Anderson begins his essay, "The Prehistory of Fairy Tales," by answering the question of whether there were fairy tales in the ancient world in the affirmative. He then accompanies us on an excursion through various recognizable ancient analogues of common fairy-tale types, including Cinderella, the Sorcerer's Apprentice, Snow White, and the Pied Piper. In "The Evolution of Folk- and Fairy Tales in Europe and North America," Jack Zipes outlines the diverse forms and functions of oral and textual narratives and the complex dialogues among them that arose as the literary fairy tale came into being, offering a survey of the genre from its inception in Renaissance Italy up to Disney fairy-tale films. In the final essay of this opening section, "The Fairy-Tale Canon," Donald Haase reviews "the relations between the canon, fairy-tale scholarship, and teaching," underlining how our choices of primary and critical materials as we design courses inform the way our students rediscover fairy tales but also encourage them to reflect on the idea of a shared culture. Finally, Haase asks whether the concept itself of a canon may or may not be helpful in investigating this genre.

The essays in the second section, "Teaching and Learning with Fairy Tales" (the main body of the volume), are organized by chapters titled "Fairy Tales and Tale Types" (Chapter 1), "Fairy Tales in Context" (Chapter 2), "Teaching New Scholarly Approaches to Fairy Tales" (Chapter 3), "Fairy Tales in the Foreign-Language Classroom" (Chapter 4), "Fairy-Tale Activities and Projects" (Chapter 5), "Fairy-Tale Courses: Sample Syllabi" (Chapter 6), and "From Teaching Fairy Tales to Creative Tale-Telling" (Chapter 7). Lewis Seifert's opening essay to this section reviews various types of courses and pedagogical strategies and concludes with what might serve as the final "moral" of this volume: "As we have much to learn from each other across the disciplinary spectrum that makes up fairy-tale studies, so too sharing and comparing pedagogical objectives and activities can benefit us all."

The contributors to Chapter 1, "Fairy Tales and Tale Types," outline close readings of tales, usually a number of variants of a tale type, in order to contravene notions of the fairy tale as a simple, moralizing, and/or static narrative. Anne

Duggan, for example, in her discussion of monster bridegroom tales, especially "Beauty and the Beast," considers adaptations of ATU 425A–C from Apuleius and Straparola to Cocteau and Disney in terms of how each "supports or undermines the ideological underpinnings of marriage practices, female agency, and sexuality within a specific sociocultural context." Victoria Somoff, in her discussion of four variants of the tale type "The Fisherman and His Wife" (ATU 555), often considered for its supposedly "transparent didacticism," gives a "step-by-step account of one pedagogical attempt to 'subtract' morality from fairy tales," instead focusing on how these tales "stretch the fairy tale's generic boundaries to an extreme" and "emerge as meta-fairy tales: examples of the genre that lay bare some of the major principles of its poetics." Gina Miele, in her analysis of a tale with a number of embedded narratives, demonstrates how fairy tales can embody complex narrative strategies such as framing, as well as promote an ethics of narration that underlines the life-changing power of storytelling.

The contributors to Chapter 2, "Fairy Tales in Context," zero in on essential moments and documents in fairy-tale history, investigating how through fairy tales we can gain unique perspectives on cultural history. Linda Worley discusses how in her course "Fairy Tales in European Context" students learn to use various critical "keys" or perspectives to develop their understanding of "the ever-changing cultural positions and array of meanings generated by fairy tales in the past and as they are being retold in the present." Allison Stedman demonstrates what two early modern tales, one French and one Italian, can reveal about the larger cultural climates in which they were produced—in this case, the centralization of courts in the seventeenth century and the response to it by marginalized intellectuals and aristocrats. Faith Beasley also considers early modern French tales, but in their relation to the collective practices and "social networking" that informed salon culture. She argues that "resurrecting these texts and the female-dominated salon culture that nourished and produced them allows students to reflect on the broader questions of canon formation and publication politics." The last essay in this section, by Jennifer Schacker, examines the paratextual material of L. Frank Baum's introduction to *The Wonderful World of Oz* as a way "to challenge students to examine the interpretive frameworks within which tales are and have been located: analyzing and historicizing the metacommunicative dimensions of tales."

The contributors to Chapter 3, "Teaching New Scholarly Approaches to Fairy Tales," argue that encouraging students to read fairy tales critically, through either well-established lenses or newer ways of thinking about fairy tales, enables them to engage more actively with material that can otherwise seem overfamiliar to them. Charlotte Trinquet du Lys outlines a women's studies course in which early modern French tales are read from a feminist perspective, in the context of the overall European tradition. Maria Nikolajeva models a cognitive-affective critical approach to fairy tales, one that focuses on "how texts stimulate recipients' perception, attention, imagination . . . and other cognitive activity through recognition of recurrent patterns." She argues that how we engage with fictional characters, and the inferences we make and the empathy we feel for them, may have relevance in real-life situations, and she convincingly demonstrates the surprising ways in which this approach opens up the seemingly flat characters of the fairy tale. Ann Schmiesing analyzes fairy tales from a disabilities studies perspective, showing how this approach helps to "enrich students' understanding not only of sociohistorical constructions and representations of disability (and the marginalized identities of gender and race with which disability so frequently intersects) but also of key conventions and patterns in the fairy tale as a genre." The last two essays read individual tales or groups of tales as elements in larger webs of signification and relation. Cristina Bacchilega takes a transnational and comparative perspective as she discusses folk- and fairy tales in relation to other traditional genres, in the specific context of two of her courses, the undergraduate course "Fairy Tales and Their Adaptations" and the graduate course "Folklore and Literature: Questions of Adaptation and Translation." Both courses encourage students to "approach folktale and fairy-tale translations and adaptations as sociohistorically and ideologically situated and to approach the fairy-tale web as participating in a larger network of genres and people moving and adapting across cultures." In a related vein, Suzanne Magnanini asks how to most fruitfully put to use in the classroom the concept of fairy-tale networks—how "to transform our own students into active collectors and spinners of tales and webs"—by tracing the phases of a project in which students expand their work on one tale type to create their own Prezi web.

The contributors to Chapter 4 focus on fairy tales in the foreign-language classroom. Maria Kaliambou describes activities that she uses in her Modern Greek language classes, in which folk- and fairy tales are used to reinforce the four basic skills and as catalysts for developing vocabulary, grammar, and cultural proficiency. Christine Jones discusses a "grammar in culture" bridge course that she designed around French and Francophone folk- and fairy-tale history, in which tales are studied in terms of their language, poetics, and intertextual allusions. Through her analysis of the nineteenth-century Louisiana writer Sidonie de la Houssaye's children's tale "Une poupée d'autrefois" (An Old-Fashioned Doll), Jones invites students to hone their interpretive techniques and cultural proficiency as they consider the "difference in the repetition" in fairy tales and the cultures that produced them. Cristina Mazzoni models ways in which fairy tales lend themselves to continued language study even in the most advanced literature and culture courses, focusing on variants of the popular Mediterranean tale type ATU 408, "The Three Oranges." She too stresses how "the repetition of themes and even, in some cases, of a basic plot eases students into the reading of potentially difficult texts, allowing them to focus on details that might otherwise go unnoticed."

In Chapter 5, "Fairy-Tale Activities and Projects," contributors share experiences of successful hands-on classroom work with fairy tales. Elio Brancaforte takes us through the various organizational phases of an exhibition that his students at Tulane University organized in 2013, "Once Upon a Canvas: Exploring Fairy Tale Illustrations from 1870–1942." William Moebius describes a series of activities he has developed over nearly 40 years of teaching the course "Myth, Folktale, and Children's Literature." In the activity outlined in Benjamin Balak and Charlotte Trinquet du Lys's essay, students discover "surprising parallels between . . . fairy tales and the history of economic thought" that "[foreground] the important pedagogical role of interdisciplinary liberal arts education." Julie Koehler tells of the special challenges and opportunities involved in converting a successful fairy-tale course into an asynchronous online format, and in particular, the re-creation of the rich classroom discussions in which students from different backgrounds engage with fairy-tale tradition. In the last essay in this section, I outline projects developed in a variety of courses, which include teaching language and culture through fairy tales in a beginning foreign-language class, using fairy tales as a springboard to oral storytelling in an advanced foreign-language literature course, exploring the history and the materiality of print fairy tales through activities in the special collections library, creating original fairy-tale videos, and visiting a local elementary school for a fairy-tale unit created by students.

Chapter 6 offers a sampling of syllabi from a range of courses that incorporate fairy tales. Although many of these syllabi center on the European tradition, their focuses vary, demonstrating how the study of fairy tales can be used to address a broad spectrum of questions related to cultural history.

Many of the contributors make reference to how they have incorporated creative work into their course activities; the two essays in Chapter 7, "From Teaching Fairy Tales to Creative Tale-Telling," both by storytellers, invite students to reflect more explicitly on the construction and transmission of narrative and to become tale-tellers themselves. Kay Stone's essay outlines a possible course in which students prepare two traditional tales for performance, "using practical, imaginative methods for bringing stories to life." Gioia Timpanelli outlines the creative process by which she was inspired by a short Sicilian folktale, "St. Peter and the Old Man," to write her original tale, "Do Angels Like Potatoes?" In doing so, she provides an evocative model for reflecting on, living with, and participating in the never-ending transmutations of story. As she reflects, "When one finds a story that has wonder and wisdom, is measured with poetry, and balanced by common sense and good judgment, then one can join the line of tellers who went before and will come after and tell that good story."

In my experience, and I suspect those of others, courses in which we teach fairy tales are a consistently sure draw, generally attracting more students than we can accommodate. From a practical (and institutional) perspective, this is in itself a valid reason for teaching such courses. At a moment of declining enrollments in humanities courses, teaching fairy tales is a way to get a large number and a wide variety of students into our classes. Yet even more important is what happens after they are in: students rediscover their connection with narratives from their own earlier lives and in the process rekindle an appreciation of the riches of narrative that may lead them to enroll in other literature or culture courses. Fairy tales evoke memories of personal childhoods and communal traditions; fairy tales were as comfortable in oral spinning circles and in chapbooks as they are in advertisements for prom dresses or luxury cars in the popular culture of today. As such, they are a wonderful tool for reflecting on how the past continues to live in the present—or better, how we cannot understand the present without remembering the past. Finally, fairy tales prove irresistible because, in the words of Jack Zipes, they suggestively "test the correlation between real social practices and imaginative possibilities that . . . are thwarted in our everyday interactions. . . . Fairy tales as socially symbolic acts enable us to intercede in civilizing processes that deny the ethical fulfillment of the meaning of humanity" (Zipes, *Fairy Tales*, xiii). But most of all, they are "survival stories with hope" (Zipes, *Why Fairy Tales Stick*, 27). Especially in these times, we surely need to teach, hear, and tell more of these stories, both in the classroom and outside it.

Bibliography

Bacchilega, Cristina. *Fairy Tales Transformed: Twenty-First Century Adaptations and the Politics of Wonder*. Detroit: Wayne State University Press, 2013.

Duggan, Anne E., and Donald Haase, eds., with Helen J. Callow. *Folktales and Fairy Tales: Traditions and Texts from Around the World*, 4 vols., 2nd ed. Santa Barbara, CA: Greenwood/ABC-CLIO, 2016.

Frank, Arthur W. *Letting Stories Breathe: A Socio-Narratology*. Chicago: University of Chicago Press, 2010.

Haase, Donald. "Fairy Tale." In *The Greenwood Encyclopedia of Folktales and Fairy Tales*, 3 vols. Ed. Donald Haase. Westport, CT: Greenwod Press, 2008. 1: 322–25.

Tatar, Maria. "Introduction." In *The Cambridge Companion to Fairy Tales*. Ed. Maria Tatar. Cambridge, UK: Cambridge University Press, 2015. 1–10.

———. "Introduction." In *The Classic Fairy Tales*. Ed. Maria Tatar. New York: Norton, 1999. ix–xviii.

Thompson, Stith. *The Folktale*. New York: Dryden Press, 1946.

Zipes, Jack. *Fairy Tales and the Art of Subversion*. Oxon, UK: Routledge, 2012.

———. *Why Fairy Tales Stick: The Evolution and Relevance of a Genre*. Oxon, UK: Routledge, 2006.

PART ONE

FOUNDATIONS OF FAIRY-TALE STUDIES

WHAT IS A FAIRY TALE?

Maria Tatar

Our associations with fairy tales remain impaired by a variety of cultural vectors, ranging from the misleading name given to the genre to the twentieth-century Disneyfication of canonical stories. Frivolous, juvenile, shallow, and inconsequential—all those connotations are captured in the dismissive phrase, "That's just a fairy tale."

The term *fairy tale* has not served the genre well. The sprightly supernatural creatures featured so prominently in the name rarely make an appearance in representative stories. There are none in "Little Red Riding Hood," "Jack and the Beanstalk," or "Beauty and the Beast." And although there may be enchantresses or fairy godmothers in "Cinderella" and "Rapunzel," they bear no resemblance to the woodland creatures found frequently in British and Celtic lore.

It was the French, more specifically Madame d'Aulnoy, who gave us the term *conte de fées*, leading us to frame the stories as though they turn on the lives of diminutive folk rather than ordinary people. In English the term was first used in 1749, casually by Horace Walpole, and with self-conscious purpose when Sarah Fielding called a story embedded in her children's novel *The Governess* "The Princess Hebe: A Fairy Tale." The German term *Märchen* more accurately points to the origins of the stories in the notion of news, reports, tall tales, rumors, and gossip—all part of a vernacular discourse that channeled social exchanges long before print culture entered the picture.

There is magic in fairy tales, and the presence of enchantment is perhaps the defining feature of the genre. As Stephen Swann Jones puts it, "Fairy tales depict magical or marvellous events or phenomena as a valid part of human experience" (Jones, 9). We are not so much in the realm of fairies as in the domain of what J. R. R. Tolkien refers to as *Faërie*, that "Perilous Realm" where anything can happen. Rumpelstiltskin spins straw to gold; Hansel and Gretel discover in the woods a cottage with a roof made of bread and windows of spun sugar; a skull lying on the forest floor begins to talk; a boy sails down the river in a peach. Again and again we witness transformations that break down the divide between life and death, nature and culture, animal and human, or self and other. Metamorphosis implies magic, and presto! we can see the clear link between two defining features of the fairy tale.

Fairy tales take up deep cultural contradictions, creating what Claude Lévi-Strauss called miniature models: stories that dispense with extraneous details to give us primal anxieties and desires—the raw rather than the cooked, as it were. They use magic, not to falsify or delude but rather to enable counterfactuals, to move us to imagine "what if?" or to wonder "why?" And that move, as both Plato and Aristotle assured us, marks the beginning of philosophy. While fairy-tale heroes and heroines wander, we track their moves and wonder, in both senses of the term, at their adventures. It is no surprise that the term *wonder tale* has been proposed and embraced as an alternative to the misleading *fairy tale* (Warner, xxii).

Fairy tales, both those from oral storytelling cultures (*Volksmärchen*, as the Germans call them) and those from literary cultures (*Kunstmärchen*), create secondary worlds with an ontological grounding that accepts the supernatural as part and parcel of reality. No one is astonished when magic happens, in part because the secondary world is clearly cordoned off from reality with the classic opening, "Once upon a time." That phrase signals what Jessica Tiffin calls "a precise relationship with reality which makes no pretense at reality, but which is continually aware of its own status *as story*, as ritualized narrative enactment" (Tiffin, 13). In other words, fairy tales demand a willing suspension of disbelief, a recognition that the story about to unfold is a product of human invention—a thought experiment, the goal of which, in the end, is not only to entertain but also to get us thinking, thinking more, and thinking harder.

In *The Social Conquest of Earth* E. O. Wilson tells us that humans were able to become the dominant species on the planet, for better or for worse, when they started building campsites, making nests near them, and collaborating to promote the chances of survival. In communal settings they not only passed on wisdom but also began to tell stories that encapsulated something more than practical knowledge. Those first stories may have been something along the lines of "Little Red

Riding Hood." What could have been more important than the predator-prey relationship, and what better way to capture its perils than a girl, a wolf, and an encounter in the woods?

We will never be able to identify the exact moment or inflection point when one set of stories branched off from straightforward reporting to a fractured version of reality. But imagine a time before electronic entertainments, with long dark nights around campfires and other sources of heat and light, and it is not much of a challenge to realize that human beings, always quick to adapt, began doing more than exchanging information, trading wisdom, and reporting gossip.

"Literature," Vladimir Nabokov tells us, "was born on the day when a boy came crying 'wolf, wolf,' and there was no wolf behind him" (Nabokov, 5). In other words, literature does not represent reality but deliberately bends the truth, misrepresents it, giving us fabrications, deceptions, and lies. Fairy tales are what Zora Neale Hurston calls "big old lies," valued as fabrications that give us higher truths (Hurston, 8). On the surface of these stories we have what a character in Milan Kundera's *The Unbearable Lightness of Being* calls "an intelligible lie." Beneath lurks "something different, something mysterious or abstract," what could be called an "unintelligible truth" (Kundera, 63). The genius of storytelling lies in its double nature as artifice that reveals as it conceals, satisfies our curiosity as it arouses it, and talks to us in order to get us thinking.

What differentiates fairy tales from legends, myths, novels, and other narrative forms? As we have seen, magic and metamorphosis are distinctive features of fairy tales, the one relevant to causality, the other to capturing its effects. We can add to this list by including what Max Lüthi calls "depthlessness," or a focus on surfaces fueled by plot-driven accounts (Lüthi, 11). If novels probe motivation and explore the inner lives of characters, fairy tales do not let us read the minds of their figures. And that is precisely why C. S. Lewis embraced the form, for its "brevity, its severe restraints on description, its flexible traditionalism, its inflexible hostility to all analysis, digression, reflections, and 'gas'" (Lewis, 46). Philip Pullman favors referring to fairy-tale figures rather than characters, for Snow White, Rumpelstiltskin, and Hop o' My Thumb carry too little psychological baggage to be full-blown characters (Pullman, xiii). They act and react but rarely pause to reflect, unless they are directly in front of a mirror.

Fairy tales are worldly, oriented toward routes, odysseys, and voyages, and they are anything but wordy. The economy of the style is inversely proportional to the magnitude of the many jolts and shocks we experience on the narrative ride. With a few swift strokes, children are left to starve in the woods, a girl is locked in a tower, or a woman slams the lid of a trunk on her stepson, decapitating him. Fairy tales instinctively take up cultural contradictions, stripping them down to their core and then enacting those abstractions in fairy-tale plots. And here we come to a second point made by Max Lüthi about fairy-tale style: its tendency toward abstraction, a formal feature to which Claude Lévi-Strauss added anthropological content.

As noted, Lévi-Strauss has argued that myth gives us miniature models of cultural contradictions. Stripped of complications, myth enacts abstractions, such as the relationship between predator and prey, hostility and hospitality, compassion and cruelty, or self and other. In "Little Red Riding Hood," for example, the predator-prey relationship is mapped onto the question of innocence and seduction in ways so provocative that they produce a cultural repetition compulsion as we try in vain to get that story right. These miniature models, primal and mythical, are generative, getting us to talk in the same ways that headlines do their cultural work today. Like African dilemma tales, which give us extreme situations (a boy is given the choice of executing his cruel biological father or his kind adoptive father—now you decide which he should slay), fairy tales make us wonder as we wander through their storied precincts. It becomes all the more logical that Einstein, in several reported conversations that may be apocryphal but that ring true nonetheless, told parents, "If you want intelligent children, read them fairy tales. If you want more intelligent children, read them more fairy tales."[1]

Unlike the literary fairy tales of, say, Hans Christian Andersen or Oscar Wilde, the fairy tale in its folkloric inflection knows no stable form. For nearly every tale type, we have hundreds and in some cases thousands of extant versions. Soon after the term *folklore* was coined by William Thoms and the field became established as a scholarly discipline, folklorists set themselves the task of collecting and classifying the vast array of materials that constituted their domain. *The Types of the Folktale* (*Verzeichnis der Märchentypen*), a landmark study of 1910 by the Finnish scholar Antti Aarne, set up a classification system of tale types that, despite criticism of its premises from various quarters, remains an obligatory first stop for fairy-tale researchers. In its most recently updated and revised iteration, *The Types of International Folktales*, edited by Hans-Jörg Uther, fairy tales are broken down into their constitutive plot units and bibliographical references are provided for variants. The tale-type index is supplemented by Stith Thompson's *Motif-Index of Folk-Literature*, a six-volume reference work that classifies the basic elements found in the plots of traditional literature from around the world.

It may seem astonishing that Aarne and the succession of scholars who revised his work countenanced the idea of limiting the number of tales to roughly 2,500

---

1. en.wikiquote.org/wiki/Albert_Einstein#Disputed (accessed March 29, 2018).

types, but by contrast with the calculations of their Russian colleague Vladimir Propp, that number seems downright astronomical. In *The Morphology of the Folktale*, published in 1928, Propp declared that "all fairy tales are of one type in regard to their structure" (Propp, 23). Rather than classify tales by themes (a "dangerous" move), the Russian folklorist preferred to show how the building blocks (he identifies 31 functions and 7 spheres of action) of all fairy tales remain constant and help us understand the predictability of fairy-tale plots.

How do we then identify a "Donkeyskin" variant or recognize that Little Red Riding Hood is lurking somewhere in the shadows of a story? Is it the structure that somehow shines through or tropes that flash out at us? When Carrie loses a shoe in the television series *Sex and the City*, has she turned into Cinderella? When the narrator of Neil Gaiman's *Ocean at the End of the Lane* drives down a road flanked by brambles and briar roses, is he reenacting the journey of the prince in "Sleeping Beauty"? The question of adaptation has been taken up productively by Cristina Bacchilega, who writes about a fairy-tale web (using a metaphor drawn from discourses about the connectedness and interdependence of fairy tales in general) and the "multimedial or transmedial proliferation of fairy-tale transformations in recent years" (Bacchilega, 16). She is concerned with how stories "mingle with, influence, anticipate, interrupt, take over, or support one another," how they engage in reciprocal intertextual exchanges that cannot always be neatly identified and mapped.

Despite the kaleidoscopic twists that reanimate stories such as "Tom Thumb" or "Snow White," we cling to the idea of an "original," a primal narrative that exists only in our imaginations. The terms we use to describe reinvented fairy tales—fractured, adapted, varied, and rescripted—imply some kind of pure and culturally innocent master narrative. In fact, when we want to understand contemporary mash-ups such as the musical *Into the Woods* or ABC's television series *Once Upon a Time*, we should be focused less on folkloric and literary antecedents than on folkloric DNA, strands of information and instruction, densely packed and organized with fairy-tale memes.

Today, our portal to fairy tales is Disney Studios, and stories such as "Sleeping Beauty," "Beauty and the Beast," and "The Little Mermaid" have real cultural traction because of those feature-length animated films. The films often nod to the authority of the spoken and written word, opening with a sequence in which a disembodied voice reads from a book. Today we probably imagine the author of those stories as the Brothers Grimm.

Jacob and Wilhelm Grimm held all the aces when it came to the right surname for collectors of fairy tales. Their *Children's Stories and Household Tales*, published in two volumes in 1812 and 1815, branded the stories in what soon became global terms (though only after their deaths). Unlike Giambattista Basile in Italy, Charles Perrault in France, or Alexander Afanas'ev, who contributed much to what has become the modern canon, their winning last name compactly captured the dark side of fairy tales. It was almost too easy to call the NBC crime series inspired by a phantasmagoria of fairy-tale tropes *Grimm*, plain and simple.

The Grimms' two volumes of fairy tales became the gold standard by which other narratives were measured. And presto! the tales moved from oral storytelling cultures into a library of books, with improvisational energy and antic variation shut down, not for good of course but at least slowed down. Removed from Tolkien's cauldron of story (where they had simmered away with successive generations adding new ingredients) and Salman Rushdie's ocean of the stream of stories (with its swiftly moving rainbow currents), the Grimms' stories enshrined a standard version that made variants deviations from the norm rather than unique reinventions.[2] That canonical version is nothing more than a fiction propping up our faith in defunct archetypes. In one of the stories from Franz Xaver von Schönwerth's *Turnip Princess*, it is the prince who has to kiss the frog; in another a princess demolishes the Cinderella stereotype when she turns out to be a failure in the kitchen, burning every dish.

"Make it new" was never a piece of advice you had to give storytellers spinning yarns at communal gatherings. They were always making it new—shamelessly cutting and pasting but always improvising as well—so that their stories would tick and whirr just as smoothly as the ones told the night before. The most skillful raconteurs were the iconoclasts. They were able to preserve the tales and keep them alive precisely because they were constantly trying to undo them or blow them up.

Today, "Cinderella," "Sleeping Beauty," and "Jack and the Beanstalk" keep coming back, always inflected in new ways. On screen they trumpet their genealogy in such titles as Tommy Wirkola's *Hansel and Gretel: Witch Hunters* or Tex Avery's *Red Hot Riding Hood*; but even more often they conceal their affiliations, as in Steven Spielberg's *Jurassic Park* (remember those female raptors in the kitchen, eager to make a meal of Lex and Tim?) or David Slade's *Hard Candy* (with Ellen Page sporting a red hoodie and, for a change, stalking the wolf).

Fairy tales seem to have a built-in refresh button, inviting us to adapt and repurpose as they migrate into new scenes of storytelling and make themselves at home in new media. In the 1940s the Bluebeard story set up shop in Hollywood, and

---

2. Tolkien writes about the cauldron of story in "On Fairy-Stories" in *The Tolkien Reader*, and Rushdie refers to the "ocean of the stream of stories" in *Haroun and the Sea of Stories*.

screenwriters dropped subtle hints about their folkloric point of reference with oversized house keys, forbidden chambers, and marriages haunted by the threat of murder. The vogue was brief but intense, with Cukor's *Gaslight* (1944), Hitchcock's *Notorious* (1946), and Fritz Lang's *Secrets Beyond the Door* (1947) among the most prominent examples.[3]

Along came Anne Sexton, with her smart, sassy poems updating the Brothers Grimm in *Transformations*, and Margaret Atwood, who described the Grimms' fairy tales as the "most influential book" she had ever read, as well as Angela Carter, who made it her business to "demythologize" fairy tales. Never mind Disney Studios, which began monetizing fairy tales back in 1937 with *Snow White and the Seven Dwarfs* and continues today with the wildly successful *Frozen*, inspired by Hans Christian Andersen's "Snow Queen." *Frozen* works because it has been stripped of religious orthodoxies and infused with new, culturally relevant messages about the value of empathy, solidarity, and finding your identity.

How do we make it new today? What is the secret sauce for successful fairy-tale adaptations? Poe's Imp of the Perverse often steals into fairy-tale territory to animate reinventions. Snow White luxuriates in her coffin and becomes a vampiristic ghoul in Neil Gaiman's "Snow Glass Apples"; Sleeping Beauty becomes a willing sex slave in Anne Rice's quartet of Sleeping Beauty novels; Rumpelstiltskin is ready for a killing spree in John Katzenbach's *The Analyst*. Our adult entertainments demand fictions larger than life and twice as unnatural.

Fairy tales are encoded with enigmas, provocative puzzles charged with existential mysteries. Magic has a "high coefficient of weirdness," as Bronislaw Malinowski tells us, and that can make for riveting stories (Malinowski, 220). Hansel and Gretel, forced to leave home, face down a demon who embodies warmth and hospitality—offering the children comfort food and a soft bed—but turns murderously hostile, fattening them up for a feast. Beauty is turned over to Beast in a story that tests the limits of compassion and empathy in the face of monstrosity. Briar Rose invites riskless voyeurism in scenes that feed our desire for beauty's protection against mortality, corruption, and decay. The constant in these stories is less character than abstract concepts, always reshuffled and reinvigorated by the values of the next generation of tellers.

Fairy tales deliver not only the shock of beauty, as Max Lüthi puts it, but also jolts of horror, rewiring our brains and also charging them up, challenging us to think more and think harder about the harsh realities exposed in them. The pleasures of the genre arouse curiosity about the world around us and provide social,

---

3. For the cinematic variations, see Tatar, *Secrets Beyond the Door*.

cultural, and intellectual capital for navigating its perils. For that reason, fairy tales have been credited with an insurrectionary and emancipatory potential that goes against the grain of conventional wisdom about fairy tales as trivial pursuits. Jack Zipes tells us that fairy tales are "informed by a human disposition to action—to transform the world and make it more adaptable to human needs, while we try to change and make ourselves fit for the world" (Zipes, 2). As the philosopher Ernst Bloch puts it, fairy tales hold forth the utopian promise of "something better" or a "more colorful and easier somewhere else," over the rainbow, east o' the sun and west o' the moon, in the land of milk and honey (Bloch, 168).

BIBLIOGRAPHY

Aarne, Antti. *The Types of the Folktale: A Classification and Bibliography*, 2nd ed. Trans. Stith Thompson. Helsinki: Academia Scientiarum Fennica, 1961.

Bacchilega, Cristina. *Fairy Tales Transformed? Twenty-First-Century Adaptations and the Politics of Wonder*. Detroit: Wayne State University Press, 2013.

Bloch, Ernst. "The Fairytale Moves on Its Own Time." In *The Utopian Function of Art and Literature—Selected Essays*. Cambridge, MA: MIT Press, 1988.

Hurston, Zora Neale. *Mules and Men*. New York: Harper Perennial, 2008.

Jones, Stephen Swann. *Fairy Tales: The Magic Mirror of Imagination*. New York: Routledge, 2002.

Kundera, Milan. *The Unbearable Lightness of Being: A Novel*. New York: Harper Perennial, 2009.

Lewis, C. S. *On Stories: And Other Essays on Literature*. New York: Houghton Mifflin Harcourt, 2002.

Lüthi, Max. *The European Folktale: Form and Nature*. Bloomington: Indiana University Press, 1986.

Malinowski, Bronislaw. *Coral Gardens and Their Magic*. New York: Dover, 1935.

Nabokov, Vladimir. *Lectures on Literature*. Ed. Fredson Bowers. New York: Harcourt Brace Jovanovich, 1998.

Propp, Vladimir. *Morphology of the Folktale*. Trans. Laurence Scott. Austin: University of Texas Press, 1975.

Pullman, Philip. *Fairy Tales from the Brothers Grimm*. New York: Viking, 2012.

Rushdie, Salman. *Haroun and the Sea of Stories*. London: Granta Books, Viking Penguin, 1990.

Tatar, Maria. *Secrets Beyond the Door: The Story of Bluebeard and His Wives*. Princeton, NJ: Princeton University Press, 2006.

Thompson, Stith. *Motif Index of Folk-Literature*, 6 vols., rev. ed. Bloomington: Indiana University Press, 1955–1958.

Tiffin, Jessica. *Marvelous Geometry: Narrative and Metafiction in Modern Fairy Tales*. Detroit: Wayne State University Press, 2009.

Tolkien, J. R. R. *The Tolkien Reader*. New York: Ballantine, 1966.

Uther, Hans-Jörg. *The Types of International Folktales: A Classification and Bibliography*, 3 vols. Helsinki: Academia Scientiarum Fennica, 2011.

Warner, Marina. *Once Upon a Time: A Short History of Fairy Tale*. Oxford, UK: Oxford University Press, 2014.

Wilson, E. O. *The Social Conquest of Earth*. New York: Liveright, 2013.

Zipes, Jack. *The Irresistible Fairy Tale: The Cultural and Social History of a Genre*. Princeton, NJ: Princeton University Press, 2013.

THE PREHISTORY OF FAIRY TALES

Graham Anderson

Anyone who sets out to study ancient fairy tales can expect to encounter a measure of surprise. The first reaction is likely to be "ancient *what*? Were there really fairy tales in the ancient world?" The trouble is that we expect Romans and especially Greeks to have more serious things on their minds and better things to do than to tell fairy tales. Or worse, we might be tempted to ask why ancient storytellers should tell fairy tales when there were so many myths and legends to be going on with: Why tell "Snow White" when there is "Jason and the Argonauts"? We also think of fairy tales as somehow "ours"—Western European and recent—yet at the same time somehow "timeless"; only a spoilsport would try to relocate them elsewhere. We can begin by attempting a definition of fairy tale that might serve to apply to ancient and modern examples alike. We might offer a narrative that treats romantic, fantastic, and magical themes in a strongly moral framework while admitting that an element of flexibility might be needed to cover every conceivable example that has ever been regarded as fairy tale. If we allow a measure of development, it might be in the increasing access to a younger audience. We might also note the fondness for catchphrases in the telling of popular stories: "All the better to see you with." "Who's been sitting in my chair?" "Mirror, mirror on the wall." I propose to look briefly at four fairy-tale-type narratives to establish a case for recognizing familiar fairy tales as ancient. It will then be possible to ask questions about whether or not they are distinctively different from the fairy tales we now tend to take for granted.

"CINDERELLA" (ATU 510A)

Let us begin with "Cinderella," perhaps the world's best-known fairy tale. We all know the version from Charles Perrault in the 1690s—glass slipper, pumpkin coach, rat coachman, fairy godmother, ugly sisters. Almost everything about Perrault's version has since become proverbial, even "You *shall* go to the ball." Can we presume to claim that a story with none of these features can possibly be an earlier form of "Cinderella"? It is time to look at a story surviving in Greek from the Augustan age.

> They tell the fabulous story (*mytheuousi*) that while Rhodopis was bathing, an eagle seized one of her shoes from her maid and brought it to Memphis, and while the king was dispensing justice in the open air, the eagle arrived over his head and threw the shoe into his lap. The king was aroused by the *rythmos* of the sandal and the strangeness of the event, and sent all around the country in search of the woman who wore it. When she was found in Naucratis she was brought up country to Memphis and became the king's wife. (Strabo 17.1.33, 1st century BCE/CE)

This version, with much detail that is different and which is a generally bare outline, does serve to draw attention to what is in fact the most distinctive motif: the slipper test that will bring the couple together. It is also a reminder that the material of the slipper, the mode of transport, and the rest are so much decorative detail. Other differences relate to social custom: there is no such institution as a West European ball possible in ancient Egypt; and the fact that the couple do not set eyes on one another at all before the slipper test hints at a strictly segregated society. The fairy godmother and the animal helper are here combined into a supernatural agent who just happens to be a bird. But where are the heroine's humble occupation and hearth connections? We find these, too, in an earlier version of Rhodopis's story, as told by the historian Herodotus (2.134f.), in which the protagonist had been a slave and then a courtesan, roles appropriate to a persecuted heroine; and the author singles out a telling and exceptional detail: "She spent a tenth of her wealth on making a great many iron roasting-spits and sent them to Delphi." Now, an offering would have been usual after finishing a previous occupation and suggests previous kitchen tasks beside the hearth. We have no sibling rivals this time around, but we have more than enough detail to confirm that this is indeed a Cinderella tale, some 17 centuries earlier than the example we tend to think of as "the first."

At this point it is useful to take note of other versions that have appeared earlier than Perrault but later than the ancient example offered. The ninth-century Chinese tale of Yeh Hsien does give the Cinderella girl a sibling rival and sets the slipper event at a drama festival; and a Neapolitan version by Giambattista Basile in the early seventeenth century offers no fewer than six rival stepsisters. Moreover, the Chinese and Neapolitan versions have a development that is missing in our other two versions: A ball gown is provided by a magic tree planted by the heroine. Clearly we are not looking at a simple lineal descent here but rather the possibly tangled branches of a thematic tree, where we do not have a clear view of the roots. But we also have enough information to enable us to ask, What does a Cinderella story have to be "about" if it is to apply to all four examples? We might provisionally suggest that it is about a marriage brought about by a "bride show" test; the later three versions at least contain a suggestion that the inherent qualities of the heroine have been responsible for her success in marrying the prince.

"THE SORCERER'S APPRENTICE" (ATU 325)

So much then for the prospect of a romantic tale developed through magical or quasi-magical means. Let us now look (in summary) at a story where magic alone carries the momentum of the action.

> A rich young man called Eucrates is finishing off his education with a grand tour of Egypt; he meets a native Egyptian holy man called Pancrates and attaches himself as a companion. He finds that the Egyptian performs magic on domestic implements so that a bar, broom or pestle can be made to do household chores. When the master is away, Eucrates tries his hand, having overheard half the spell; he animates a jar and pestle, but does not know the rest of the spell, so that he is powerless when they flood the house with water. The Egyptian returns and puts matters to rights, before disappearing for good. Eucrates cannot demonstrate his magical powers for fear of flooding the house once more. (Lucian, *Lovers of Lies*, 33–36, 2nd century CE)

Here we have a cautionary tale revolving round the use or misuse of magic. In this case we have a channel of transmission at a sophisticated level: Goethe popularized Lucian's story in his *Zaubererlehrling* before it was taken up as a symphonic poem by Dukas and as an episode in Walt Disney's *Fantasia*, with Mickey Mouse cast as the sorcerer's apprentice!

Thus far we see a literary line of transmission, crossing over into other media altogether. But there are also modern popular versions of the story over a cross-section of the European oral tradition. They usually involve a magician who has a magic book. By opening the book, the apprentice releases fairies or demons who demand tasks; they cannot be put to rest until they are given an impossible task, such as twisting a rope of sand. Often, as in our ancient version, the magician figure is a specifically named individual, such as a legendary local figure with occult powers. As in the case of "Cinderella," we are able to suspect continuous transmission from antiquity.

"THE EMPEROR'S NEW CLOTHES" (ATU 1620)

In both the "Cinderella" and "The Sorcerer's Apprentice" cases we could say that the story, ancient and modern, is perfectly recognizable despite small differences of detail across the centuries. Often, however, it can be rather more difficult to adjust our angle of vision to spot a familiar fairy tale in ancient guise. Take the following outline:

> There was once a king of Epirus called Pyrrhus, who was a famous general. Because of that he looked up to Alexander the Great, and fancied that he was the spitting image of Alexander. It wasn't long before his courtiers realised that the way to flatter him and win his favour was to agree with him: if he showed them any portrait of Alexander, they learned to say that Alexander looked just like him. One day an old woman arrived from Larissa, up country in Thessaly; Pyrrhus showed her busts of famous generals, including Alexander, and asked which he most resembled. After some hesitation she said "Batrachion the cook." And there was indeed a cook of that name in Larissa, who did indeed look like Pyrrhus (both of them in fact were very ugly). So the old woman was proved right, and the flatterers at court were shown up as what they were. (Lucian, *Against the Ignorant Book-Collector*, 21, 2nd century CE)

We seem to be looking here at a different version of "The Emperor's New Clothes." The essence of the tale is often something rather different from the most memorable detail. If pressed for that detail, we might be tempted to say that it is the fact that the king has nothing on; but this version is really the same in essence and structure: It is a tale about how flatterers are found out by the one person who has nothing to lose by speaking out and describing the evidence in front of his or her own eyes.

Again there are two pathways of transmission. In one we have stories of the naked king (from the medieval Spanish collector Juan Manuel onward); in the other we have stories where the rogues are not weavers of invisible cloth but instead painters of invisible paintings (as in Chapter 27 of the German version featuring the celebrated trickster Till Eulenspiegel). Our ancient version is, if anything, closer to the invisible painting than to the naked king. We should note that there is actually nothing magical about any of the versions. The magic is simply in the mind of the dupe betrayed by his own vanity. There is some variation in the choice of whistle-blower (a Negro slave in Juan Manuel's version, an innocent child in Hans Christian Andersen's). Indeed we might argue that the story is only accidentally a fairy tale through its inclusion in Andersen's collection, a fairy tale by association. But the repertoire readily expands to include it.

"RIP VAN WINKLE" (ATU 766)

It may prove difficult to separate fairy tale from miracle story, as in the following example:

> Epimenides of Crete was serving as a shepherd. While he went to look for a lost sheep he went into a cave and fell asleep. When he awoke and could not find the sheep, he went home and found someone else in his house; only his brother, now an old man, was able to tell him that he had slept for fifty-seven years. (Diogenes Laertius 1.109)

The story in this form belongs to the third century CE. It is, as far as it goes, the story of Rip van Winkle. Do we call it historical legend because the person to whom the experience is attributed in this case actually existed and the location is precise? Or do we call it fairy tale because of the element of the supernatural involved? Comparison with "Rip van Winkle" may help: there are no funny little men to ask a favor of him in this ancient version, as there are in Washington Irving's story, and no suggestion of the Otherworld as such; nor are we told of any dream during the interval. But this may be because Diogenes Laertius saw the story as biographical legend (from Theopompus); he may well have abridged precisely the decisive fairy-tale element out of the tale. We should unhesitatingly include the story as it stands in an anthology of ancient fairy tale, but with these reservations duly expressed. It seems as clear a take on "Rip van Winkle" as we shall get and proves that there was an almost fully developed version of this story in classical times.

SOME OTHER CASES

Not every case is as easy to isolate or as clear-cut as the previous examples. If anyone asks, "Was there a Pied Piper story in the ancient world?" our instinct is to presume not, as the action is traditionally located in the medieval German town of Hamelin. Until, that is, we remember what the essence of the story actually is: A town's rulers commission a task for a fee, and the task is performed by an oddly garbed outsider who is also a musician with a power over rodents. After the task is completed, the rulers refuse to pay. The mysterious stranger takes the town's children instead and causes them to disappear.

Let us compare this outline with the following:

A ruler Laomedon commissions two gods to build the walls of Troy, and he refuses to pay; one of the two sends a sea-monster which demands sacrifice, including that of the king's daughter; the other girls of the town are sent away. The king asks Heracles to kill the monster, and again refuses to pay. This time Heracles kills the males, and only one, the future king Priam, lives to tell the tale. (Servius, on *Aeneid* 1.550; Strabo 13.1.48)

The basic motif is clear enough: Refuse to pay and your town will lose its children (one way or another). One of the gods is Apollo, who builds walls to the music of his magic lyre and has a connection with mice, not rats; he also seems to have a hint of some kind of rainbow garb. Here there are three creditors, different kinds of tasks, two sets of young people, and insufficient detail about Apollo's background; the story is also less easy to grasp at a hearing. But in the end the mosaic of sources does establish the outline of the same story.

In a number of other instances we are tempted to pass over fairy tales or fairy-tale elements because the generic labeling encourages us to look for something else. The episode of Polyphemus in Homer's *Odyssey* presents us with a tale of a "stupid ogre" figure (9.105–566). In fact, there is nothing magical or extraordinary about the story at all, other than the amazing strength of the cannibal giant; but the context in the *Odyssey* encourages us to see a hero tale in the context of an epic narrative rather than a trickster tale that is likely to have been independent of the story of Odysseus in the first place. The story of Circe, the witch in the wood who turns passing sailors into swine with a magic potion and is only stopped by Odysseus with his magic antidote (10.203–396), once more suggests fairy tale, and not even one with a quick-witted hero falling back on his own cunning, because he has only to carry out the instructions of the trickster-god Hermes to secure a result. Both Polyphemus and Circe could belong to the canon of Greek mythology, which is capable of laying claim to all traditional tales down to the end of the Trojan War; and we can raise the question, Is there any real difference between myth and fairy tale? Can fairy tale be projected back into the extant corpus of Greek mythology? If there is merely a difference of perspective, how can we account for it?

At the outset we might be tempted to test a fairy tale and a mythical version of what appears to be the same story. Here are two takes on "Snow White":

Snow White has a rival, the queen, who tries to have her killed in the forest. She is looked after by dwarfs, giants, bandits, or other outsiders. The queen finds she is alive and makes three attempts on her life, disguised as an old woman: with too tight a bodice, with a sleeping draught, and with a poisoned apple or pin in her head. She is left for dead in a glass case but revived by a kiss from the prince. (after the Brothers Grimm)

A girl called Chione (Snow-girl) is so beautiful she has a thousand suitors; both Apollo and Hermes fall in love with her at first sight. One rapes her by disguising as an old woman; the other rapes her by putting her to sleep with his magic wand. She bears two children, but is killed by Artemis with a dart for boasting she is more beautiful than Artemis herself, and (irreversibly) cremated. (Ovid, *Metamorphoses* 11.295–345)

Three murder attempts in the modern version, two rapes and one murder in the other. What has happened? The story seems to have been expurgated. The means of rape, the disguise as an old woman, and magic sleep have been recycled into two more murder attempts. We might be tempted to account for the drastic divergence in ending through supposed generic differences between myth and fairy tale; the fairy tale goes almost inevitably for the happy ending, whereas the myth presents the story as a cautionary tale in which the gods punish what they regard as impiety. In other words, the rules of the game have changed. But it does not follow that the story would have developed one way in antiquity and a different way in modern tales. We know of an ancient novel on the Chione theme; it would have been expected to have a happy ending, though we do not know for certain from the few fragments that it did. But Ovid has rather a propensity to select versions of myths that turn out ominously for the humans involved, though not invariably. On balance, we cannot insist that myths and fairy tales are generically different. Both are simply tales with a variety of options available.

"Cupid and Psyche" (ATU 425B)

The culmination of ancient fairy-tale telling is "Cupid and Psyche," a long Latin tale from the mid-second century CE, told in the middle of a picaresque novel, the *Metamorphoses* or *The Golden Ass* by Apuleius. It is told as a consoling tale by an old woman to a young female captive in a robbers' den—just the sort of context we need for an *anilis fabula*, an old wives' tale.

A beautiful princess with two less attractive sisters is forced by an oracle to marry a mysterious husband she is not allowed to see. They make love in the dark, and she is allowed the free run of his magic palace. Her envious sisters persuade her to break the taboo on the grounds that she is married to a monster who wishes to devour the child she is expecting. Her husband turns out to be none other than the god Cupid, who promptly takes his leave the moment she contrives to see him by candlelight. Cupid's jealous mother, Venus, persecutes Psyche, setting her typical folkloric tasks, which she accomplishes, sometimes with the help of sympathetic animals. Cupid rescues her from a near fatal sleep at the end of her fourth task, and all the parties are reconciled, as Psyche is properly married in heaven, to general rejoicing. (Apuleius, 4.28–6.24)

The tale has been convincingly related to the modern folktale "The Search for the Lost Husband"; there were some 1,200 modern folk versions collected up to the 1950s. It has also been argued that "Cupid and Psyche" is a synthetic myth made up by Apuleius and watered down into a folktale from a much later summary of his own text (Fehling); or that the tale is a Platonic-style allegory of the soul (*psyche*) contrived to fit the rest of Apuleius's story (e.g., Thibau); or that it is an Eastern myth prettified into an ornamental literary tale (Reitzenstein). But whatever the origins, the overall ethos is clearly enough that of a literary fairy tale, and one close in character to the French fairy tales produced from the late seventeenth century onward by such female French writers as Madame d'Aulnoy or Mademoiselle L'Héritier to appeal to French court tastes. The detail is quite rococo, as in the description of Cupid's magic palace. We can see a number of motifs that can easily be related to the modern canon of fairy tale itself: sibling rivalry, as in Cinderella's two ugly sisters; the monster bridegroom, fleetingly suggested by the sisters; the tasks involving grain sorting, wool gathering, and the like, suggesting the housekeeping tasks of the young bride; and the fatal sleep broken by the kiss of the prince, as in "Snow White." We are very much here in the world of "our" fairy tales, even if Psyche's pregnancy suggests that this is not a tale for the nursery.

The characterization is also familiar enough in the modern fairy tale: The vindictive older woman rival, so familiar from the queen in "Snow White," is played out here by Venus; the heroine is (for the most part) the epitome of young female innocence and indeed embodies the virtuous obedience so characteristic of the didactic element in modern fairy tale. We are tempted to ask whether this is a unique experiment on the part of Apuleius or simply a reminder of how much of ancient literature is lost to us. Once more, we can note that the identities of the tale as a myth (featuring gods and goddesses) and as a fairy tale (featuring supernatural beings) do not really get in each other's way. There is no reason why it should not be both or why they should be distinguished.

FAIRY TALES AND THEIR CONTEXTS

I should note the seemingly chance contexts from which I have drawn these examples. Of the initial sample, "Cinderella" comes from a work on learned geography; "The Sorcerer's Apprentice" from a satire on philosophers' superstitions; "The Emperor's New Clothes" from a rhetorical invective; and "Rip van Winkle" from a philosophical biography. Only "Cupid and Psyche" comes from a work of narrative fiction and from the context of an old woman telling a diversionary story to a frightened young adult. This might prompt us to note that many of our tales surface accidentally in literary or scholarly contexts, whereas their normal milieu would have been the nursery, told to children by nurses or old women to frighten or reward their charges. The tales themselves would have been frowned on in polite or educated circles. The appeal of such tales is not too difficult to account for: "Cupid and Psyche" and "Cinderella" embody life aspirations—social advancement and a good marriage (in "Cupid and Psyche" in return for obedience and domestic skills). Most often the human ambitions are given the accelerant of a magic object, such as magical servants to do the housework. And the moral tone is never too far away: The wicked sisters in "Cupid and Psyche" meet their deaths at the hands of their own ambitions to take Psyche's place; the incautious apprentice is found out; the pompous king is exposed to ridicule. Epimenides' story offers none of these, though Washington Irving's take attempts at least some of them.

CONCLUSIONS

There can be no doubt that fairy tales did indeed exist in the ancient world, whatever their context. I have chosen to confine examples to the relatively well-charted world of Greco-Roman antiquity, where we can point to complete examples; those from the ancient Near East tend to be much more fragmentary and so less easy to present for teaching purposes. It should be clear from even such limited soundings that the potential for development of such stories existed in the ancient world; "Cupid and Psyche" alone demonstrates the capacity of one tale for rhetorical development, for pathos and verbal wit, and for the emergence of gender stereotyping and family tensions. We are left as so often with the frustration that so much literature and subliterature from antiquity is no longer available and that there may have been much more.

BIBLIOGRAPHY

Bilingual editions of Apuleius, Diogenes Laertius, Herodotus, Homer, Lucian, Ovid, and Strabo (of varying age and quality) are available in the Loeb Classical

Library series. Discussion of fairy-tale-type narratives in the context of the ancient world is often incidental, where it occurs at all. Jack Zipes's *Oxford Companion to Fairy Tales* (Oxford, UK: Oxford University Press, 2000) appeared too early to take account of my *Fairytale in the Ancient World* (London: Routledge, 2000), which I summarized in H. E. Davidson and A. Chaudhri, *A Companion to the Fairy Tale* (Cambridge, UK: D. S. Brewer, 2003), 85–98. There is a much more comprehensive treatment in William Hansen, *Ariadne's Thread: A Guide to International Tales Found in Classical Literature* (Ithaca, NY: Cornell University Press, 2002), which also covers analogues in fable and folktale under the broader banner "international tale."

Apuleius. *Cupid and Psyche*. Trans. E. J. Kenney. Cambridge, UK: Cambridge University Press, 1990.

"Chione." In *Ancient Greek Novels: The Fragments*. Ed. Susan A. Stephens and John J. Winkler. Princeton, NJ: Princeton University Press, 1995. 289–313.

Fehling, D. *Amor und Psyche*. Wiesbaden: Franz Steiner, 1977.

Manuel, Juan. "The Emperor's New Clothes." In *The Past We Share: The Near Eastern Ancestry of Western Folk Literature*. By E. L. Ranelagh. London: Quartet Books, 1979. 19.

Oppenheimer, P., ed. and trans. *Till Eulenspiegel: His Adventures*. Oxford, UK: World's Classics, 1995.

Reitzenstein, R. *Das Maerchen von Amor und Psyche bei Apuleius*. Leipzig: B. G. Teubner, 1912.

Servius. *Servianorum in Vergilii carmina commentariorum editionis Harvardianae*. Ed. E. K. Rand, J. J. Savage, H. T. Smith, G. B. Waldrop, J. P. Elder, B. M. Peebles, and A. F. Stocker. Lancaster, PA: Lancaster Press, 1946–1965. [Known as the Harvard Servius.]

Thibau, R. "Les Métamorphoses d'Apulée et la théorie paltonicienne de l'Eros." *Studia Philosophica Gandensia* 3 (1965): 89–144.

Yeh Hsien. ["The Story of Yeh Hsien (as Told by Tuan Ch'eng Shih)."] In *The Cinderella Story: The Origins and Variations of the Story Known as Cinderella*. By N. Philip. London: Penguin, 1989. 18–20.

The Evolution of Folk- and Fairy Tales in Europe and North America

Jack Zipes

During its long evolution, the literary fairy tale has distinguished itself as a genre by "appropriating" many motifs, themes, signs, and drawings from folklore, embellishing them and combining them with elements from other literary genres; it became gradually necessary in the modern world to adapt a certain kind of oral storytelling that dealt with miraculous and magical transformation to standards of literacy and make it acceptable for diffusion in the public sphere. As Pertti Anttonen remarked in his superb essay "Oral Traditions and the Making of the Finnish Nation," this appropriation led to the "textualization" of oral tales "that were transformed through textual documentation and representation into literary imitations of their original performances and their orality" (Anttonen, 325). The term *textualization* refers to

> the ways in which oral performances and orally expressed utterances are transformed into literary representations of orality. When we textualize oral expressions, we do not merely document them by writing down words that were sung or uttered. We create artefacts that function as representations of the original oral utterances. In addition, these artefacts by their very existence as written documents enter literary culture in the accomplishment of their representation of orality. In this respect, to textualize

also means to "literalize," that is, to transform oral utterances into literary representations that are to be read, interpreted and analyzed through reading, and by extension,
to be preserved as textual documents that call for further reading as well as cultivation
as specimens of cultural history and heritage. (Anttonen, 325)

The fairy tale is only one type of textual and literary appropriation of a particular oral storytelling tradition related to the oral wonder tale, often called the
Zaubermärchen or the *conte merveilleux*, which existed throughout Europe in many
different forms before the Common Era and during the medieval period. As more
and more wonder tales were written down and printed from the fourteenth to
the eighteenth century—often in Latin—they constituted the genre of the literary
fairy tale that began establishing its own conventions, motifs, topoi, characters, and
plots, based to a large extent on those developed in the oral tradition but altered to
address new reading publics formed by the aristocracy, clergy, and middle classes.
Although slaves, peasants, women, and children were marginalized and excluded in
the formation of this literary tradition, their material, voices, style, and beliefs were
incorporated into the new genre during this long period of gestation.

What exactly is the oral wonder tale? This is a question that is almost impossible to answer, because each village and community in Europe and North America
developed various modes of storytelling and different types of tales closely connected to their customs, laws, morals, and beliefs. But Vladimir Propp's now famous
study, *The Morphology of the Folk Tale* (1928), can be somewhat helpful here. Using
about 100 texts from Aleksandr Afanas'ev's *Russian Folktales* (1855–1863), Propp
outlined 31 basic functions that constitute the formation of a paradigmatic wonder
tale, which was and still is common in Russia and shares many properties with wonder tales throughout the world. By functions, Propp means the fundamental and
constant components of a tale that are the acts of a character and are necessary for
driving the action forward. Consequently, most plots follow a basic pattern, which
begins with the protagonist confronted with an interdiction or prohibition that he
or she violates in some way. This leads to the banishment of the protagonist or to
the assignment of a task related to the interdiction or prohibition. The protagonist
is marked by the task, which becomes his or her assigned identity and destiny.
Afterward the protagonist has encounters with all sorts of characters: a deceitful
villain; a mysterious individual or creature who gives the protagonist gifts; three
different animals or creatures who are helped by the protagonist and promise to
repay him or her; or three different animals or creatures who offer gifts to help the
protagonist, who is in trouble. The gifts are often magical agents, which bring about
miraculous change. Because the protagonist is now endowed with gifts, he or she

is tested or moves on to deal with inimical forces. But then there is a sudden fall in the protagonist's fortunes that is generally only a temporary setback. A wonder or miracle is needed to reverse the wheel of fortune. The protagonist makes use of endowed gifts (and this includes magical agents and cunning) to achieve his or her goal. Often there are three battles with the villain, three impossible tasks that are miraculously completed, or the breaking of a magic spell through some counter-magical agent. The inimical forces are vanquished. The success of the protagonist usually leads to marriage and wealth. Sometimes simple survival and acquisition of important knowledge based on experience form the ending of the tale.

Propp's structural approach to the wonder tale, though useful, should be treated with caution because innumerable variations in theme and plot types can be found throughout Europe and North America. In fact, the wonder tale is based on a hybrid formation that encompasses the chronicle, myth, legend, anecdote, and other oral forms and constantly changes depending on the circumstances of the teller. If there is one "constant" in the structure and theme of the wonder tale that was always passed on to the literary fairy tale, it is *transformation*, to be sure, miraculous transformation. Everybody and everything can be transformed in a wonder tale. In particular, the social status of the protagonists changes. For the peasants, slaves, and serfs who constituted most of the population before and during the Middle Ages, the hope for change was embedded in this kind of narrative, and this hope had nothing to do with a systematic and institutionalized belief system (see Fordsdyke; and Reichl). That is, the tales told by the peasants were secular, and the fortuitous changes and happenings that occurred in the tales could not be predicted or guaranteed.

Rarely do wonder tales end unhappily in the oral tradition. They are information about daily life and wish fulfillments. They are obviously connected to initiation rites that introduce listeners to the "proper" way to become a member of a particular community. In many ways, one could say that wonder tales serve a function in the civilizing process of all societies. The narrative elements issue from real-life experiences and customs to form a paradigm that facilitates recall for tellers and listeners. The paradigmatic structure enables teller and listeners to recognize, store, remember, and reproduce the stories and to change them to fit their experiences and desires because of the easily identifiable characters who are associated with particular assignments and settings. For instance, many tales concern a simple fellow named Jack, Hans, Pierre, or Ivan who is so naïve that he seems as though he will never do well in life. He is often the youngest son, and his brothers and other people take advantage of him or demean him. However, his kindness and naïveté eventually enable him to avoid disasters. By the end of the tale he generally rises in social status and proves himself to be more gifted and astute than he seems.

Other recognizable characters in wonder tales include the Cinderella girl who rises from the ashes to reveal herself to be more beautiful than her stepsisters, the faithful bride, the loyal sister, the vengeful discharged soldier, the boastful tailor, the cunning thief, devious robbers, ferocious ogres, the unjust king, the malicious magician and rebellious pupil, the queen who cannot have a child, the princess who cannot laugh, a flying horse, a talking fish, a magic sack or table, a powerful club, a kind duck, a sly fox, treacherous nixies, and a beast-bridegroom. The forests are often enchanted, and the settings change rapidly from the sea to glass and golden mountains. There are mysterious underground realms and caves. Many tales are about the land of milk and honey, where everything is turned upside down and the peasants rule and can eat to their heart's content. The protagonist moves faster than jet planes on the backs of griffins and eagles or through the use of seven-league boots. Most important are the capes or clothes that make the hero invisible or the magic objects that endow him with the power to transform himself. In some cases there are musical instruments with enormous captivating forces, swords and clubs capable of conquering anyone or anything, or lakes, ponds, and seas that are difficult to cross and serve as the home for supernatural creatures.

The characters, settings, and motifs are combined and varied according to specific functions to induce *wonder*. It is this sense of wondrous change that distinguishes the wonder tales from such other oral tales as the chronicle, legend, fable, anecdote, and myth; it is clearly the sense of wondrous change that distinguishes the *literary* fairy tale from the moral story, novella, sentimental tale, and other modern short literary genres.

Wonder causes astonishment, and as marvelous object or phenomenon, it is often regarded as a supernatural occurrence and can be an omen or portent. It gives rise to admiration, fear, awe, and reverence. In the oral wonder tale listeners are to ponder the workings of the universe, where anything can happen at any time and these happy or fortuitous events are never explained. Nor do the characters demand an explanation—they are opportunistic. They are encouraged to be so, and if they do not take advantage of the opportunity that will benefit them in their relations with others, they are either dumb or mean-spirited. Only the "good" opportunistic protagonist succeeds, because he or she is open to and wants a change. In fact, most heroes need some kind of wondrous transformation to survive, and they indicate how to take advantage of the unexpected opportunities that come their way.

The tales seek to awaken our regard for the marvelous *changing* conditions of life and to evoke in a religious sense profound feelings of awe and respect for life as a miraculous process that can be altered and changed to compensate for the lack of power, wealth, and pleasure most people experience. Lack, deprivation, prohibition, and interdiction motivate people to look for signs of fulfillment and emancipation. In the wonder tales those who are naïve and simple are able to succeed because they are untainted and can recognize the wondrous signs. They have retained their belief in the miraculous condition of nature and revere nature in all its aspects. They have not been spoiled by conventionalism, power, or rationalism. In contrast to the humble characters, the villains are those who use their status, weapons, and words intentionally to exploit, control, transfix, incarcerate, and destroy for their benefit. They have no respect or consideration for nature and other human beings, and they actually seek to abuse magic by preventing change and causing everything to be transfixed according to their interests. The wondrous protagonist wants to keep the process of natural change flowing and indicates possibilities for overcoming the obstacles that prevent other characters or creatures from living in a peaceful and pleasurable way.

The focus on wonder in the oral folktale does not mean that all oral wonder tales, and later the literary fairy tales, served and serve a liberating purpose, though they tend to maintain a utopian spirit. Nor were they subversive, though there are strong hints that the narrators favored the oppressed protagonists. The nature and meaning of folktales have depended on the stage of development of a tribe, community, or society. Oral tales have served to stabilize, conserve, or challenge the common beliefs, laws, values, and norms of a group. The ideology expressed in wonder tales always stemmed and still stems from the position that the narrator assumed and assumes with regard to the developments in his or her community, and the narrative plot and changes made in the tale depended on the sense of wonder or awe that the narrator wanted to evoke. In other words, the sense of wonder in the tale and the intended emotion sought by the narrator is ideological. The oral tales have always played some role in the socialization and acculturation of listeners. Certainly, the narratives were intended to acquaint people with learning experiences so that they would know how to comport themselves or take advantage of unexpected opportunities. The information and knowledge imparted by the oral wonder tales involves a learning process through which protagonist and listener are enriched by encounters with extraordinary characters and situations.

Because these wonder tales have been with us for thousands of years and have undergone so many different changes in the oral tradition, it is difficult to determine clearly what the ideological intention of the narrator was, and if we disregard the narrator's intention, it is often difficult to reconstruct (and/or deconstruct) the ideological meaning of a tale because the textualization of an oral tale adds other historical, social, and ideological factors that need to be taken into consideration. In the last analysis, however, even if we cannot establish whether a wonder tale is ideologically conservative, sexist, progressive, liberating, and so on, it is the celebration of wondrous change and how the protagonist reacts to wondrous occurrences that account for the tale's major appeal. In addition, these tales nurture the imagination with alternative possibilities to life at "home," from which the protagonist is often banished to find his or her "true" home. This pursuit of home accounts for the utopian spirit of the tales, because the miraculous transformation involves not only the transformation of the protagonist but also the realization of a more ideal setting in which the hero/heroine can fulfill his or her potential. In fairy tales home is always a transformed home that opens the way to a future or destiny that is different from what the hero or heroine had anticipated.

Ultimately, the definition of both the wonder tale and the fairy tale, which derives from it, depends on the manner in which a narrator/author arranges *known* functions of a tale aesthetically and ideologically to induce wonder and then transmits the tale as a whole according to customary usage of a society in a given historical period. The first stage for the literary fairy tale involved a kind of class and perhaps even gender appropriation. The voices of the nonliterate tellers were submerged, and because women in most cases were not allowed to be scribes, the tales were scripted according to male dictates or fantasies, even though many were told by women. Put crudely, one could say that the literary appropriation of the oral wonder tales served the hegemonic interests of males in the upper classes of particular communities and societies in Europe and North America, and to a great extent, this is still true if we examine carefully who dominates the media networks and the culture industry in America. However, such a crude statement must be qualified, because the writing down of the tales, their textualization and re-creation, has also preserved a great deal of the value system of those deprived of power. And the more the literary fairy tale in the different cultural textualization of Europe and North America was cultivated and developed, the more it became individualized and varied by intellectuals and artists, who often sympathized with the marginalized in society or were marginalized themselves. The literary fairy tale allowed for new possibilities of subversion in the written word and in print, and therefore it was always looked upon with misgivings by the governing authorities in the civilization process.

The literary fairy tale is a relatively young and modern genre. Although a great deal of historical evidence shows that oral wonder tales were told and written down in India, Mongolia, China, Persia, Turkey, Egypt, and Morocco[1] 3,000 or

---

1. For an interesting study of how strong the storytelling tradition in Northern Africa was, see Hamilton.

4,000 years ago, and although all kinds of folk motifs of magical transformation became part and parcel of national epics and myths throughout the world, the literary fairy tale did not really establish itself as a genre in Europe and later in North America until some new material and sociocultural conditions provided fruitful ground for its formation. The most significant developments from approximately 1450 to 1700 include the standardization and categorization of the vernacular languages, which gradually became official nation-state languages; the invention of the printing press; the growth of reading publics throughout Europe that began to develop a taste for short narratives of different kinds for their reading pleasure; and the conception of new literary genres in the vernacular and their acceptance by the educated elite classes.

Literary fairy tales were not at first called fairy tales, nor can one say with certainty that they were simple appropriations of oral folktales that were popular among the common people. Indeed, the intersection of the oral tradition of storytelling with the writing and publishing of narratives, which I have referred to as textualization, is definitely crucial for understanding the formation of the fairy tale, but the oral sources were not the only ones that provided the motifs, characters, plot devices, and topoi of the genre. The early authors of fairy tales were generally extremely well educated and well read and drew on both oral and literary materials when they created their fairy tales. Graham Anderson argues in *Fairytale in the Ancient World* and other works (including the essay in this volume) that many myths were essentially fairy or wonder tales (see Anderson, *Fairytale*; and Anderson, *Greek and Roman Folklore*). For example, one can readily see strong fairy-tale elements in Apollonius's *Jason and the Golden Fleece* (fourth century BCE) and in Apuleius's fairy tale "Cupid and Psyche," part of *The Golden Ass*, which appeared in the second century CE. The fairy tale gradually distinguished itself from myth and other tales of the oral tradition in the early medieval period through carefully constructed plots, sophisticated references to social norms, religion, literature, and customs, embellished language that signified the high civilized status of the writer, and linguistic codes that were informed by a particular civilizing process and carried information about it (see Ziolkowski).

Contained in chivalric romances, heroic sagas and epics, chronicles, sermons, poems, lais, and primers during the European Middle Ages, the fairy tale was often a story about miraculous encounters, changes, and initiations illustrating a particular didactic point that the writer wished to express in an entertaining manner. It was often written in Latin, Middle English, or some old high form of French, Spanish, Italian, or German. For the most part, these early literary fairy tales were not intended for children. In fact, they were not intended for most people because most people could not read. The fairy tale was thus marked by the social class of the writers and readers, and because the clerics dominated literary production in Latin up through the late Middle Ages, the "secular" if not hedonistic fairy tale was not fully acceptable in European courts and cities, and it was certainly not an autonomous literary genre. Oral wonder tales and songs uttered and sung in the vernacular continued to thrive in the Middle Ages and the early Renaissance period. Their influence can be seen in whatever materials were selected for textualization.

In the late thirteenth century the anonymous collection *Novellino* (*The Hundred Old Tales*), with its fantastic themes, unusual medieval exempla, and fables, indicated along with other medieval marvelous tales and reports that new literary genres were about to flower, and in the fourteenth century such writers as Giovanni Boccaccio (*The Decameron*, 1349–50) and Geoffrey Chaucer (*The Canterbury Tales*, 1387) helped prepare the way for the establishment of the fairy tale as an independent genre. Although they did not write "pure" fairy tales per se, many of their stories—and these were not the only writers who influenced the development of the fairy tale—have fairy-tale motifs and structures and borrow from oral wonder tales. Moreover, the frame narratives—a device that can be traced to ancient India and was common in the Middle East long before Europeans appropriated it—that they created allowed for the introduction of diverse tales told in different modes and styles, and it is the frame that became extremely important for Giovan Francesco Straparola in his *Le piacevoli notti* (The Pleasant Nights, 1550–1553) and for Giambattista Basile in *Lo cunto de li cunti* (*The Tale of Tales*), better known as *Il Pentamerone* (1634–1636), because they used their frames to collect, revise, and produce some of the most illustrious literary fairy tales in the West that were to influence major writers of the genre from the sixteenth to the nineteenth century.

In many ways the tales of Straparola and Basile can be considered crucial for understanding the rise of the genre. Straparola wrote in a succinct Tuscan or standard Italian, and Basile wrote in a Neapolitan dialect marked by an elaborate baroque style with striking metaphors and peculiar idioms and references that are difficult to decipher today. Although all their fairy tales have moral or didactic points, they have little to do with official Christian doctrine. On the contrary, their tales are often bawdy, irreverent, erotic, cruel, frank, and unpredictable. The endings are not always happy; some are even tragic, and many are hilarious. Some tales are short, but most are somewhat lengthy, and they are all clearly intended to represent and reflect the mores and customs of their time, to celebrate the value of storytelling, and to shed light on the emerging civilizing process of Italian society. From the beginning, fairy tales were symbolic commentaries on the mores and customs of a particular society and the classes and groups in these societies and how their actions and relations could lead to success and happiness.

Although other Italian writers such as Giulio Cesare Cortese and Pompeo Sarnelli created fairy tales in the seventeenth century, the conditions in the different reading publics in Italy were not propitious for the genre to allow it to take root. The oral tradition and the "realistic" novellas and stories remained dominant in Italy. This was also the case in Great Britain. Although there was a strong interest in fairy lore in the 1590s, as indicated by *The Faerie Queene* (1590–1596) written by Sir Edmund Spenser, who was influenced by Italian epic poetry, and although Shakespeare introduced fairies and magical events in some of his best plays, such as *A Midsummer Night's Dream* (1596) and *The Tempest* (1610–1611), the trend in English society was to ban the fairies and make way for utilitarianism and Puritanism. There were, of course, some interesting attempts in poetry by Ben Jonson, Michael Drayton, and Robert Herrick to incorporate folklore and fairy-tale motifs in their works. But the waning interest in fairy tales and the obstacles created by censorship undermined these literary attempts. Fortunately, oral storytelling provided the refuge for fairy beliefs (see Davies).

It was not until the 1690s in France that the fairy tale could establish itself as a "legitimate" genre for educated classes. It was during this time that numerous gifted female writers, such as Madame d'Aulnoy, Madame d'Auneuil, Madame de Murat, Mademoiselle L'Héritier, Madame de la Force, and Mademoiselle Bernard, introduced fairy tales into their literary salons and published their works, and their tales, along with those of Charles Perrault, Eustache Le Noble, and Jean de Mailly, initiating a mode or craze that prepared the grounds for the institution of the literary fairy tale as a genre. First of all, the French female writers baptized their tales *contes de fées*, or fairy tales, and they were the first to designate the tales as such. The designation is not simply based on the fact that there are fairies in all their tales but also on the fact that the seat of power in all their tales—and also in those of Perrault and other male writers of the time—lies with omnipotent women.

Similar to the tales of Straparola and Basile, whose works were somewhat known by the French, the *contes de fées* are secular and form discourses about courtly manners and power and they rely on motifs, characters, and plots of oral tales. The narratives vary in length from 10 to 60 pages, and they were not at all addressed to children. Depending on the author, they are ornate, didactic, ironic, and mocking. Between 1690 and 1705 the tales reflected many of the changes that were occurring at King Louis XIV's court, and Perrault wrote his tales consciously to demonstrate the validity of this "modern" genre, as opposed to the classical Greek and Roman myths. Many of the tale types can be traced to the oral folk tradition, and they also borrow from the Italian literary fairy tale and numerous other literary and art works of this period.

In addition to the accomplishments of the first wave of French authors, mention should be made of Antoine Galland and his remarkable translation of Arabic narratives in *Les Mille et Une Nuits* (The Thousand and One Nights, 1704–1717). Not only did Galland introduce Middle Eastern traditions and customs to Western readers, but he also imitated the Oriental tales and created his own—something hundreds of authors would do in the centuries that followed. Galland's translations and his own creative inventions are clear examples of textualization and are crucial for understanding how the oral and literary are not opposed to one another but are fused with one another and foster fascinating hybrid tales.

By 1720, at the latest, the fairy tale as a genre that encompassed the oral and literary forms was being institutionalized as a genre, and the paradigmatic form and motifs were becoming known throughout Europe and later in North America. This dissemination of the tales was due in large part to the dominance of French as the cultural language in Europe. But there were other ways that the French tales became known and set a pattern for most fairy-tale writers. It was during this time that chapbooks or "cheap" books were being produced in such series as the *Bibliothèque Bleue*, and the books were carried by peddlers from village to village to be sold with other goods. The "sophisticated" tales of the upper-class writers were abbreviated and changed a great deal to address other audiences. These tales were often read aloud and made their way into or back into the oral tradition. Interestingly, the tales were retold innumerable times and circulated throughout diverse regions of Europe, often leading to some other literary appropriation and publication. In addition, there were numerous translations into English, German, Spanish, Russian, Greek, and Italian.

Another important development was the rise of the literary fairy tale for children. Already during the 1690s, François Fénelon, the important theologian and Archbishop of Cambrai, who had been in charge of the Dauphin's education at King Louis XIV's court, had written several didactic fairy tales to make the Dauphin's lessons more enjoyable. But they were kept for private use and were printed only in 1730 after Fénelon's death. More important than Fénelon was Madame Leprince de Beaumont, who published *Magasin des Enfants* (1756), which included "Beauty and the Beast" and 10 or so overtly moralistic fairy tales for children. Like many of her predecessors, she used a frame story in which a governess engages several young girls between age 6 and 10 in discussions about morals, manners, ethics, and gender roles that lead her to tell stories to illustrate her points. Madame Leprince de Beaumont's utilization of such a frame was based on her work as a governess in England, and the frame was set up to be copied by other adults to cultivate a type of storytelling and reading in homes of the upper classes that would reinforce acceptable notions of propriety, especially proper sex roles. It was only as part of the civilizing process that storytelling developed in the aristocratic and bourgeois homes in the seventeenth and eighteenth centuries, first through governesses and nannies and later in the eighteenth and nineteenth centuries through mothers, tutors, and governesses who told stories in separate rooms designated for children called nurseries.

Toward the end of the eighteenth century, numerous publishers in France, England, and Germany began serious production of books for children, and the genre of the fairy tale assumed a new dimension, which included concerns about how to socialize children and indoctrinate them through literary products that were appropriate for their age, mentality, and morals. The rise of "bourgeois" children's literature meant that publishers would make the fairy-tale genre more comprehensive, but they would also—along with parents, educators, religious leaders, and writers—pay great attention to the potential of the fantastic and miraculous in the fairy tale to disturb and/or enlighten children's minds. There were numerous debates about the value of the fantastic and the marvelous in literary form and their possible detrimental effects on the souls of readers in many European countries. They were significant and interesting, but they did not have any real impact on the publication of fairy tales. Certainly, not in France. Indeed, by 1785 Charles Mayer could begin producing his famous forty-volume *Cabinet des fées*, which was completed in 1789 and contained the most significant of the 100-year mode of fairy tales that paved the way for the institution of the fairy tale in other countries. From this point on, most writers in the West, whether they wrote for adults or for children, consciously held a dialogue with a fairy-tale discourse that had become firmly established in Europe and embraced intercourse with the oral storytelling tradition and all other kinds of folklore that existed throughout the world. For instance, the French fairy tale, which now included *The Arabian Nights*, had a profound influence on German writers of the Enlightenment and Romantic era, and the development in Germany provided the continuity for the institution of the genre in the West as a whole.

Perhaps the most significant publication at the beginning of the nineteenth century that indicated how interwoven the oral tales had become with the literary narratives through textualization was the first edition of *Kinder- und Hausmärchen* (Children's and Household Tales) published in 1812–1815 by the Brothers Grimm. It is well known that in the centuries before the Grimms produced *Kinder- und Hausmärchen*, the literate people of Europe had generally ignored or looked down on the stories of the common people. Ironically, these were the tales with which they had also been raised, but it was not until the end of the eighteenth century and beginning of the nineteenth century, when nation-states were being formed, that their attitudes toward history and national identity changed and led to a "romantic" rediscovery of oral wonder tales and literary fairy tales and other short genres, such as animal stories, legends, humorous anecdotes, riddles, and witch and ghost stories. For many German Romantic writers, whom the Grimms knew, there was a tendency to idealize the past. Many of them—for example, the great poet Novalis and the fabulous writer E. T. A. Hoffmann—believed that the essence of the golden age could be found only through the fairy tale, and to a certain extent there was something utopian and romantic in the quest of pioneer European folklorists who began seeking to understand and redefine their present through collecting "common" tales of the past that became cultural treasures.

This is the reason I consider the period from 1812 to 1912 the golden age of folk- and fairy tales in Europe and North America. It was during this period that hundreds of educated European and American collectors, who called themselves at first antiquarians, philologists, traditionalists, and later folklorists, began taking an intense interest in the tales of the folk, which included people from all social classes, and gathering all sorts of oral stories, writing them down, and publishing them so that they would not perish. Textualization, they strongly believed, would strengthen and preserve communal and national ties.

The Grimms were not the first scholars to turn their attention to folktales, which they considered gems of German culture, relics that needed preservation. But they played a significant role in a widespread cultural trend and set high standards for collecting folktales that marked the work of most European and American folklorists through the twentieth century. In fact, their long-term scholarly investigation of narratives from all parts of Europe was a direct or indirect inspiration for philologists, collectors, and translators of tales. At one point in his foreword to Kurt Ranke's anthology *Folktales of Germany* (1966), the notable American folklorist Richard Dorson remarked how the Grimms had exercised a great influence on early antiquarians and writers in Great Britain and then added:

> As with Britain, so with the countries on the continent. The brothers corresponded with, encouraged, stimulated, admired, and were admired by collectors from France to Russia and from Norway to Hungary. Their links with the giants who followed them are direct and clear. They exchanged letters with Asbjörnsen and Moe in Norway, with Emmanuel Cosquin in France, with Vuk Karadzic in Serbia, with Elias Lönnrot in Finland—all hallowed figures performing Grimm-like services for their countries. Aleksandr Nikolaevic Afanas'ev, called the "Wilhelm Grimm of Russia," lavishly praised the *Volksmärchen* of

the brothers as a model for presenting the folk literature of his own country. As a result of the Grimms' prodigious and timely influence, scholars in one country after another utilized folklore as a vehicle to promote a national language, literature, history, and mythology. (Ranke, xiii)

A good example of the breadth and depth of the Grimms' influence in the nineteenth century is the work of Johann Wilhelm Wolf (1817–1855), founder of the *Zeitschrift für Deutsche Mythologie und Sittenkunde* (Journal for German Mythology and Customs) (see Fränkel). He came to embody what the Grimms had projected as the exemplary collector of tales: Wolf became the ideal field worker and collected tales, sayings, proverbs, superstitions, and artifacts directly from the mouths of the folk; he also wrote erudite and theoretical commentaries. Aside from his important collection *Deutsche Hausmärchen* (1851), his founding of the *Zeitschrift für Deutsche Mythologie* in 1853 contributed to the development of folklore in Central Europe. Although the journal lasted only four years and Wolf died after the second issue was published, this journal served briefly as one of the most central contact points for the best German-speaking scholars in Central Europe: Ignaz and Joseph Zingerle, Adalbert Kuhn, Ernst Meier, Heinrich Pröhle, August Stöber, Karl Sinnrock, Franz Josef Vonbun, Reinhold Köhler, Wilhelm Mannhardt, and many other leading folklorists of the time. They contributed and commented on legends, puzzles, superstitions, nursery rhymes, children's games, folktales, animal stories, proverbs, and myths that they had discovered in countries from France to Russia and in every region of Germany and the Hapsburg Empire, including Switzerland. Most of these men did original fieldwork. Most transcribed their tales from different dialects, although some published dialect versions. What is perhaps most important is that the folklorists took great care in designating the regions where they collected their tales and contextualizing them. That is, their focus was on a particular region, not on a nation or a nation-state. Most of them also produced books and collections of stories, often with subtitles such as "gathered orally from the folk" or with dedications to the Grimms. In this respect, these scholars validated the process of textualization and provided material for creative writers to conceive their particular fairy tales.

In mid-nineteenth-century Europe the typical collection of tales was generally published in the standard or high language of the country. Therefore any story collected orally would be transcribed or translated into a literary language or the dominant vernacular, and although most of the folklorists tried not to add phrases or hone their tales, they all more or less touched up the "raw" language in which they had heard the tale. Many of the tales were heard or read in one language and then written down in another. For instance, this type of transcription/translation can be seen in Laura Gonzenbach's tales, told in Sicilian dialect by rural women and then written down in high German, and in Rachel Busk's translation of Roman dialect tales into English; in addition, Robert Bain and W. R. S. Ralston translated tales from Russian into English, Johann Georg von Hahn and Bernhard Schmidt from Greek into German, Wentworth Webster from Portuguese into English, and Albert Henry Wratislaw and Jeremiah Curtin from Slavic into English. It was not until the latter part of the nineteenth century that folklorists began publishing dialect tales without translation. Here the works of Giuseppe Pitrè, Vittorio Imbriani, François-Marie Luzel, Achille Millien, Victor Smith, and Carolina Coronedi-Berti are important. And of course, the founding and remarkable growth of folklore journals enabled folklorists to provide all kinds of source materials and essays on customs and beliefs as well as historical articles that traced the origins of the tales and their motifs. Aside from Wolf's *Zeitschrift für Deutsche Mythologie und Sittenkunde*, some of the other important journals that were founded in the latter half of the nineteenth century are *Revue Celtique* (1870), *Alemannia* (1873), *Romania* (1872), *The Folk-Lore Record* (1878), *Mélusine* (1877), *Archivo per lo Studio delle Tradizioni Popolari* (1882), *El Folklore Andaluz* (1882), *Revue des Traditions Populaires* (1886), *Ethnologische Mitteilungen aus Ungarn* (1887), *Journal of American Folklore* (1888), and *Schweizerisches Archiv für Volkskunde* (1897).

Thanks to the journals, private correspondence, and books, almost all the leading folklorists in nineteenth-century Europe and North America were in touch with each other's works and were all familiar with the Grimms' *Kinder- und Hausmärchen* and their scholarly work in philology and linguistics. What is significant, however, is that most folklorists after 1850 became more precise and more thorough than the Grimms in collecting and publishing their tales; they paid more attention and respect to the tellers of the tales, the regional relevance of each tale, the linguistic peculiarities, and the significance of the tales in the sociocultural and historical context. It is here that the tales must be understood as part of the nationalist trends and the formation of new nation-states in the latter half of the nineteenth and the early part of the twentieth century.

Collecting folktales was a social and political act of some kind—and it still is. Not only did educated middle-class collectors give voice to the lower classes, but they also spoke out in defense of their native languages and in the interests of national and regional movements that sought more autonomy for groups with particular interests.[2] For instance, Norway separated from Denmark in 1814 and

---

2. See Del Giudice and Porter; Schacker; Leerssen; and Baycroft and Hopkin.

became an independent state with its own language and dialects. There was a tendency, therefore, to shake off the Danish yoke. Jørgen Moe and Peter Christian Asbjørnsen regarded themselves in the 1830s and 1840s as defenders of the Norwegian language and customs by collecting diverse types of folk songs, legends, and tales in dialect and then transcribing them (see Hult). In contrast to the Grimms, Moe and Asbjørnsen traveled to different regions of Norway and stimulated other collectors to write down local tales. Indeed, the collecting throughout Scandinavia had strong nationalist and regional aspects (see Kvideland). Denmark also manifested signs of Romantic nationalism. As Reimund Kvideland points out, "The struggle against German influences in the southern boundary region created a nationalistic atmosphere in Denmark which promoted interest in folklore. Svend Grundtvig, who was working on a major publication of Danish ballads, made a public appeal for the collection of folktales" (Kvideland, 160). In Russia the great collector Alexander Afanas'ev also realized that his collections of tales in the 1850s and 1860s might assist the numerous ethnic groups in Russia to become more aware of the virtues of their different languages and customs (see Riordan). Many French collectors, such as Luzel, Sébillot, and Cosquin, took pride in the regional traditions that they sought to keep alive, and of course, after the defeat of the French by the Prussians in 1872, a strong element of regionalism and nationalism animated their collecting, whether they were liberals or conservatives (see Hopkin).

At the same time that textualization engendered the rise of folktale collecting in the nineteenth century, we must not forget the significance of Romanticism for the rise of the literary fairy tale and how hybridization was common in both folk- and fairy tales. Most important at the beginning of the nineteenth century was the contribution of German Romantic writers. Wilhelm Heinrich Wackenroder, Ludwig Tieck, Novalis, Joseph von Eichendorff, Clemens Brentano, Adelbert Chamisso, Friedrich de la Motte Fouqué, E. T. A. Hoffmann, and others wrote extraordinary and highly complex metaphorical tales that revealed a major shift in the function of the genre; the fairy tale began to address philosophical and practical concerns of the emerging middle classes and was written in defense of the imagination and as a critique of the worst aspects of the Enlightenment and absolutism. This viewpoint had clearly been expressed in Johann Wolfgang Goethe's bluntly titled classical narrative "The Fairy Tale" (1795), as though it were the fairy tale to end all fairy tales. Goethe optimistically envisioned a successful rebirth of a rejuvenated monarchy that would enjoy the support of all social classes in his answer to the violence and destruction of the French Revolution. In response, Novalis wrote a long, elaborate fairy tale in *Heinrich von Ofterdingen* (1798) called "Klingsohr's Märchen" that celebrates the erotic and artistic impulses of revolution and emphasizes magical transformation and flexibility.

The Romantics did not intend their fairy tales to amuse audiences in the traditional sense of *divertissement*. Instead, they sought to engage the reader in a serious discourse about art, philosophy, education, and love. The focus was on the creative individual or artist, who envisioned a life without inhibitions and social constraints. It was a theme that became popular in the romantic fairy tales throughout Europe and in North America. In contrast to most folktales or fairy tales that have strong roots in folklore and propose the possibility of the integration of the hero into society, the fairy tales of the nineteenth and twentieth centuries tend to pit the individual against society or to use the protagonist in a way to mirror the foibles and contradictions of society.

This conflict between the "heroic" individual (often identified with Nature or natural forces) and society (understood as one-dimensional rationality and bureaucracy) became a major theme in British Romanticism. At the same time, the Romantics also sought to rediscover their English, Scottish, Welsh, and Irish heritage by exploring folklore and the history of the fairies, elves, leprechauns, and other "little people." Here, prose (Sir Walter Scott, James Hogg, Allan Cunningham), poetry (Samuel Coleridge, Robert Southey, John Keats, Percy Bysshe Shelley, Tom Moore, and Thomas Hood), and folklore and fairy-tale studies (Scott, Thomas Crofton Croker, Thomas Keightley) paved the way for an astounding production of fairy tales in the second half of the nineteenth century.

The function of the fairy tale for adults underwent a major shift in the nineteenth century that made it an appropriate means to maintain a dialogue about social and political issues within the bourgeois public sphere—and this was clear in all nations in Europe and North America—but the fairy tale for children was carefully monitored and censored until the 1820s. Although there were various collections published for upper-class children in the latter part of the eighteenth century and at the turn of the nineteenth century along with numerous chapbooks containing classical fairy tales, they were not regarded as prime and "proper" reading material for children. They were not considered "healthy" for the development of young people's souls and minds. For the most part, publishers, church leaders, and educators favored other genres of stories, more realistic, sentimental, and didactic. Even the Brothers Grimm, in particular Wilhelm, began to revise their collected tales in *Kinder- und Hausmärchen* (1812–1815), making them more appropriate for children than they had done in the beginning and cleansing their narratives of erotic and bawdy passages. However, the fantastic and miraculous elements were kept so that they were not at first fully accepted by the middle-class reading audiences, which only began to change their attitude toward the fairy tale during the course of the 1820s and 1830s throughout Europe.

Aside from the gradual success that the Grimms' tales had as a children's book, the publication of Wilhelm Hauff's *Märchen Almanach* (1826), containing Eastern-flavored tales for young people, Edgard Taylor's translation of the Grimms' tales as *German Popular Stories* (1823) with illustrations by the famous George Cruikshank, and Pierre-Jules Hetzel's *Livre des enfants* (1837), which contained 40 tales from the *Cabinet des fées* edited for children, indicated that the fairy tale had become acceptable for young readers. This acceptance largely resulted from the fact that adults themselves became more tolerant of fantasy literature and realized that it would not pervert the minds of their children. Indeed, middle-class attitudes toward amusement began to change, and people understood that children needed time and space for recreation themselves without having morals and ethics imposed on them and without the feeling that their reading or listening had to involve indoctrination.

It is not by chance, then, that the fairy tale for children came into its own from 1830 to 1900. The most significant writer of this period was Hans Christian Andersen, who began publishing his tales in 1835, and they were almost immediately translated into many different languages and became popular throughout the Western world. More and more, the fairy tale of the nineteenth century became marked by the individual desires and needs of the authors who felt that industrialization and rationalization of labor made their lives compartmentalized. As daily life became more structured and institutions more bureaucratic, there was little space left for leisure, hobbies, daydreaming, and the imagination. It was the fairy tale that provided room for amusement, nonsense, and recreation. This does not mean that it abandoned its more traditional role in the civilizing process as agent of socialization. For instance, up until the 1860s most fairy-tale writers for children, including Catherine Sinclair, George Cruikshank, and Alfred Crowquill in England, Carlo Collodi in Italy, Comtesse Sophe de Ségur in France, and Ludwig Bechstein in Germany, emphasized the lessons to be learned in keeping with the principles of the Protestant ethic: industriousness, honesty, cleanliness, diligence, virtuousness—and male supremacy. However, just as the "conventional" fairy tale for adults had become subverted at the end of the eighteenth century, there was a major movement to write parodies of fairy tales, which were intended for both children and adults. In other words, the classical tales were turned upside down and inside out to question the value system upheld by the dominant socialization process and to keep wonder, curiosity, and creativity alive.

By the 1860s numerous writers continued the "romantic" project of subverting the formal structure of the canonized tales (Perrault, Grimm, Bechstein, Andersen) and to experiment with the repertoire of motifs, characters, and topoi to defend the free imagination of the individual and to extend the discursive social commentary of the fairy tale. The best example of the type of subversion attempted during the latter part of the nineteenth century is Lewis Carroll's *Alice in Wonderland* (1865), which engendered numerous imitations and original works in Europe and America, and Oscar Wilde's *The Happy Prince and Other Stories* (1888), which undermined Andersen's tales and reflected a keen sense of tolerance and justice critical of British norms. Even today, unusual versions of Carroll's and Wilde's works have been created for the theater, television, the cinema, comic books, and other kinds of literature, demonstrating the unusual way that the fairy-tale genre has evolved to address changing social issues and aesthetic modes.

It should be noted that most of the fairy-tale collections and folktales published in Great Britain in the nineteenth century were also produced, if not pirated, in the United States and Canada. At the same time, Horace Scudder, a well-known American writer and editor, championed European fairy tales in the *Riverside Magazine for Children* and published several anthologies, such as *Fables and Folk Stories* (1882), for children between 1860 and 1890; Thomas Frederick Crane, a professor of languages at Cornell and co-founder of the American Folklore Society, translated and edited *Italian Popular Tales* (1885); and hundreds of different types of wonder tales (European, African, and American) were disseminated through word of mouth and in print in the nineteenth century, as William Bernard McCarthy has amply and brilliantly demonstrated in his anthology *Cinderella in America: A Book of Folk and Fairy Tales*.

By the beginning of the twentieth century, the fairy tale had become fully institutionalized in Europe and North America, as indicated by the great success and popularity of L. Frank Baum's *Wonderful Wizard of Oz* (1900) and J. M. Barrie's *Peter Pan* (1904) and their sequels in literature, drama, and film up to the present. The full institutionalization of the genre means that a specific process of textualization, production, distribution, and reception had become regularized in the public sphere of each Western society, and it began to play and continues to play a significant role in the formation and preservation of the cultural heritage of a nation-state. Without such institutionalization in advanced industrialized and technological countries, the genre would perish, and thus any genre must be a kind of self-perpetuating institution involved in the socialization and acculturation of readers. It is the interaction of writer/publisher/audience in a given society that makes for the definition of the genre in any given epoch. This has certainly been the case with the fairy tale. The aesthetics of each literary fairy tale will depend on how and why an individual writer wants to intervene in the discourse of the genre as institution. Such interventions bring about transformations in the institution itself and its relation to other institutions so that the fairy tale today is unthinkable without taking into consideration its dialectical relationship with other genres and media as well as its actual absorption of these genres and media.

Ironically, the most significant revolution in the institution of the fairy tale took place in 1937, when Walt Disney produced the first animated feature fairy-tale film, *Snow White and the Seven Dwarfs*. Although fairy tales had been adapted for film as early as the 1890s, Disney was the first to use technicolor to embrace the Broadway and Hollywood musical as a formula for fairy tales and to print books, records, toys, and other artifacts to accompany his films. Indeed, he spiced up the classical tales with delightful humor and pristine fun that would be acceptable for middle-class families. The commercial success was so great that Disney used the same cinematic devices and ideological messages in his next three fairy-tale films: *Pinocchio* (1940), *Cinderella* (1950), and *Sleeping Beauty* (1959). The Disney formula has not changed much since Walt's death, and even such films as *The Little Mermaid* (1989), *Beauty and the Beast* (1991), *Aladdin* (1992), *Mulan* (1998), *Tangled* (2011), *Frozen* (2014), and *Cinderella* (2015) follow a traditional pattern of a "good" young man or woman finding some magical means to help him or her battle sinister forces. What counts most in the Disney fairy tale is the repetition of the same message: Happiness will always come to those who work hard and are kind and brave. And it is through the spectacular projection of this message and through music, jokes, dazzling animation, and zany characters that the Disney corporate artists have made a profitable business out of the fairy tale. Indeed, the Disney corporation has literally commercialized the classical fairy tale as its own trademark.

This commercialization does not mean that the fairy tale has become a mere commodity, for the conventional Disney fairy tale in film and literature serves as a referential text that has challenged gifted writers and artists to create fascinating critiques of some of the blatant sexist and racist features of the Disney films and the classical canon as well. The works of these writers and artists offer alternatives to the standard formulas that stimulate readers and viewers to rethink their aesthetic and ideological notions of what a fairy tale is. In particular, the period from 1960 to the present has witnessed a flowering of remarkable experiments in the institution of the fairy tale in North America and Europe. In fact, experimentation linked to magic realism and a postmodern sensibility have become the key words in the fairy-tale genre, which pervades people's daily lives in ways that are unimaginable and provides hope that miraculous change can help us survive an increasingly unjust world.

BIBLIOGRAPHY

Anderson, Graham. *Fairytale in the Ancient World*. London: Routledge, 2000.
———. *Greek and Roman Folklore: A Handbook*. Westport, CT: Greenwood Press, 2006.

Anttonen, Pertti. "Oral Traditions and the Making of the Finnish Nation." In *Folklore and Nationalism in Europe During the Long Nineteenth Century*. Ed. Timothy Baycroft and David Hopkin. Leiden: Brill, 2012. 325–50.

Baycroft, Timothy, and David Hopkin, eds. *Folklore and Nationalism in Europe During the Long Nineteenth Century*. Leiden: Brill, 2012.

Davies, L. I. "Orality, Literacy, Popular Culture: An Eighteenth-Century Case Study." *Oral Tradition* 25.2 (2010): 305–23.

Del Giudice, Luisa, and Gerald Porter, eds. *Imagined States: Nationalism, Utopia, and Longing in Oral Cultures*. Logan: Utah State University Press, 2001.

Fordsdyke, Sara. *Slaves Tell Tales: And Other Episodes in the Politics of Popular Culture in Ancient Greece*. Princeton, NJ: Princeton University Press, 2012.

Fränkel, Ludwig. "Wolf, Johann Wilhelm." In *Allgemeine Deutsche Biographie (ADB)*. Leipzig: Duncker & Humboldt, 1898. 43: 765–77.

Hamilton, Richard. *The Last Storytellers: Tales from the Heart of Morocco*. London: I. B. Tauris, 2011.

Hopkin, David. *Voices of the People in Nineteenth-Century France*. Cambridge, UK: Cambridge University Press, 2012.

Hult, Marte Hvam. *Framing a National Narrative: The Legend Collections of Peter Christen Asbjørnsen*. Detroit: Wayne State University Press, 2003.

Kvideland, Reimund. "The Collecting and Study of Tales in Scandinavia." In *A Companion to the Fairy Tale*. Ed. Hilda Ellis Davidson and Anna Chaudhri. Cambridge, UK: D. S. Brewer, 2003. 159–68.

Leerssen, Joep. *National Thought in Europe: A Cultural History*. Amsterdam: Amsterdam University Press, 2006.

McCarthy, William Bernard, ed. *Cinderella in America: A Book of Folk and Fairy Tales*. Jackson: University Press of Mississippi, 2007.

Ranke, Kurt. *Folktales of Germany*. Trans. Lotte Baumann. Chicago: University of Chicago Press, 1966.

Reichl, Karl, ed. *Medieval Oral Literature*. Berlin: De Gruyter, 2012.

Riordan, James. "Russian Fairy Tales and Their Collectors." In *A Companion to the Fairy Tale*. Ed. Hilda Ellis Davidson and Anna Chaudhri. Cambridge, UK: D. S. Brewer, 2003. 217–26.

Schacker, Jennifer. *National Dreams: The Remaking of Fairy Tales in Nineteenth-Century England*. Philadelphia: University of Pennsylvania Press, 2003.

Ziolkowski, Jan. *Fairy Tales from Before Fairy Tales: The Medieval Latin Past of Wonderful Lies*. Ann Arbor: University of Michigan Press, 2006.

THE FAIRY-TALE CANON

Donald Haase

Writing about the term *canon* in 1992, in the midst of America's so-called culture wars, Robert Scholes stated that "in the last decade, literary scholars have come to use the word as the name for a set of texts that constitute our cultural heritage and, as such, are the sources from which the academic curriculum in literature should be drawn. This situation is full of complexities and perplexities" (Scholes, 142). Scholes's description of the canon as understood in the last decades of the twentieth century is an apt introduction to thinking specifically about the fairy-tale canon and its relationship to teaching. In this essay I consider not only the relations between the canon, fairy-tale scholarship, and teaching but also the complexities and perplexities that surround the canon in the study of folktales and fairy tales.

Contemporary fairy-tale studies and pedagogy revolve around the concept of the canon. That might not be obvious if you were to search for the term *canon* or *fairy-tale canon* among the topics in reference works or in the indexes of scholarly books about fairy tales, where the terms only occasionally appear as discrete headwords or index entries. When I googled "fairy-tale canon" on April 30, 2016, I turned up a mere 2,180 hits (along with Google's well-intended question of whether I didn't actually mean to search "fairy *tail* canon," which, for better or worse, produced 11,700 results). Compare that to the 27,400 hits for "fairy-tale adaptations" and the 122,000 hits for "fairy-tale princesses," which are also important concepts in contemporary scholarship and classrooms.

My not-very-scientific Google searches and perusal of headwords and indexes might seem to suggest that the fairy-tale canon holds no interest for scholars and teachers. Far from it. Since at least the 1960s and 1970s, the implicit mission of fairy-tale studies has been to reexamine, challenge, and undermine the fairy-tale canon.[1] The very idea of a canon—that there is a body of exemplary texts so universal and timeless that they naturally embody enduring aesthetic, cultural, and moral qualities that give them a privileged status—was and still is antithetical to the increasingly prevalent view among literary and cultural scholars generally that texts must be understood in sociohistorical contexts and read through the lens of ideological criticism. In 1990, John Guillory observed:

> In recent years many literary critics have become convinced that the selection of literary texts for "canonization" (the selection of what are conventionally called the "classics") operates in a way very like the formation of the biblical canon. These critics detect beneath the supposed objectivity of value judgments a political agenda: the exclusion of many groups of people from representation in the literary canon. (Guillory, 233)

In the case of fairy-tale studies, second-wave feminists not only pointed out that women-authored and women-centered tales were absent from the fairy-tale canon but also faulted canonical tales such as "Snow White" and "Sleeping Beauty" for promulgating repressive gender stereotypes based on a misogynistic patriarchal worldview.[2] Scholars influenced by Marxism and the Frankfurt school argued that collectors like the Brothers Grimm had co-opted the voice of the oppressed, imbued folktales with a repressive nineteenth-century ideology, and forced them into the service of capitalism and the culture industry.[3] Ever since, fairy-tale scholarship and teaching, especially in North America, have reflected, implicitly, if not always explicitly, a fundamental resistance to the male-dominated Western fairy-tale canon and have made efforts to allow other voices to be heard.

Undermining the Fairy-Tale Canon

Jack Zipes, who has done more than anyone to influence the direction of contemporary fairy-tale scholarship and many of the college and university courses it has engendered, opens his 2006 book *Why Fairy Tales Stick* by describing the canon and

1. See Anne E. Duggan and Donald Haase's introduction to Duggan et al.; and Haase ("Challenges," 77).
2. See Kolbenschlag. For a survey of feminist fairy-tale criticism, see Haase ("Feminist Fairy-Tale Scholarship").
3. See Zipes (*Breaking the Magic Spell*; *Fairy Tales*).

the process of canonization, which have been at the heart of his relentless work to understand, subvert, and reclaim the fairy tale's social and political power.

> As is well known there is a classical fairy-tale canon in the Western world that has been in existence ever since the nineteenth century if not earlier. The tales that constitute this canon are "Cinderella," "Little Red Riding Hood," "Sleeping Beauty," "Hansel and Gretel," "Rapunzel," "Rumpelstiltskin," "The Frog Prince," "Snow White," "Bluebeard," "Beauty and the Beast," "Jack and the Beanstalk," "The Princess and the Pea," "The Little Mermaid," "The Ugly Duckling," "Aladdin and the Magic Lamp," "Albi Baba and the Forty Thieves," and so on. In my previous works I argued that these tales became canonized because they were adapted from the oral tradition of folklore for aristocratic and middle-class audiences as print culture developed in the sixteenth and seventeenth centuries and basically reshaped and retold during this time to reinforce the dominant patriarchal ideology throughout the nineteenth and twentieth centuries. Consequently, the most telling or catchy tales were reprinted and reproduced in multiple forms and . . . became almost "mythicized" as natural stories, as second nature. We respond to these classical tales almost as if we were born with them, and yet, we know full well that they have been socially produced and induced. (Zipes, *Why Fairy Tales Stick*, 1)

Zipes goes on to state, however, that he is no longer satisfied with his long-standing argument that "classical tales have been consciously and subconsciously reproduced largely in print by a cultural industry that favors patriarchal and reactionary notions of gender, ethnicity, behavior, and social class" (Zipes, *Why Fairy Tales Stick*, 2). In his book Zipes searches for a deeper explanation of canon formation and the persistent popularity of canonical tales, not by abandoning sociocultural and historical perspectives but by taking an "epidemiological approach" that draws on social biology, evolutionary psychology, and memetics (the theory that "units of cultural knowledge"—memes—are "transmitted from person to person across culture, time, and space"; Magnus-Johnston, 2: 641). Few scholars, however, have adopted this approach to understanding the fairy-tale canon, so the dominant view remains that social and cultural institutions—including editors, authors, translators, publishers, the media, educators, and scholars—have constructed the Western fairy-tale canon to undergird and propagate an ideology that serves society's most powerful players.

Accordingly, the scholars and teachers who subscribe to this view display a keen interest in how canonical, or "classical," tales are produced and received. They seek to demystify the process of canonization by raising awareness of the tales' constructedness and by demonstrating how editors, collectors, translators, anthologists, and publishers have altered and framed tales to make them appear as though they emerged naturally from oral storytellers and were not products of conscious literary creation. For example, the collecting and editorial practices used by the Brothers Grimm in producing 17 different editions of their canonical *Kinder- und Hausmärchen* (Children's and Household Tales) between 1812 and 1858 have received extensive critical scrutiny that has important implications for the existing fairy-tale canon.[4] Together with studies of the reception of the Grimms' famous collection,[5] this research has clearly demonstrated that, although they have been promoted as timeless works of universal meaning, the tales and the collection as a whole were carefully constructed in the context of historically specific social, cultural, and literary ideologies.

Undermined in this way, canonical works—whether individual tales or entire collections—lose their former authority and privilege. That is, they invite, even demand, reassessment and intense critical scrutiny as sociohistorical constructs. Critics have eagerly accepted that invitation by exposing the gender politics, social agenda, and ideology of classical tales wherever they appear in fairy-tale history. No fairy tales have been immune from this critical scrutiny, which has become the default perspective of many fairy-tale scholars. However, Charles Perrault, the Brothers Grimm, Hans Christian Andersen, and Walt Disney have borne the brunt of the critique because of their important roles in producing the texts that have achieved canonical status and in shaping our expectations of the fairy tale as a classical genre.

Mining the Fairy-Tale Canon

Work to undermine the fairy-tale canon finds its counterpart in efforts to mine canonical tales for new meanings and relevance and thereby to reclaim the canon. In other words, scholars have also tried to emancipate tales from the values and ideological constraints of their canonization by undertaking oppositional readings that go against the grain of conventional thinking. These transgressive readings may identify submerged voices of resistance in classical tales or new perspectives that enable interpretations that are antithetical to the sociocultural norms associated with the established canon.

Despite his ideological critique of canonical tales by Perrault and the Brothers Grimm, Zipes himself has consistently tried to reclaim them by uncovering their roots in oral traditions, their concern with "social injustice and possibilities

---

4. See, for example, Bottigheimer; Rölleke; Tatar (*Hard Facts*); Zipes (*Fairy Tales*); and Schmiesing.
5. See, for example, Haase (*Reception of Grimms' Fairy Tales*; "Framing the Brothers Grimm"); and Joosen and Lathey.

for self-determination," and their utopian drive (Zipes, *Complete Fairy Tales*, xxxv). In the early twenty-first century, scholars are also reclaiming classical tales by performing queer readings that, in the words of Lewis C. Seifert,

> work against the expected, the familiar, the predictable—of gender, sexuality, and structures of domination more generally—exposing their unexpected, unfamiliar, and unpredictable sides. This is undoubtedly one of the reasons that queer critical perspectives are only beginning to gain traction within the larger field of fairy-tale studies. Fairy tales—or at least their classic or traditional versions—are among the best known stories in the world, and their plots are anything if not expected, familiar, and predictable. They are obvious givens in cultures the world over, and the same is true for their ostensible representations of sexuality, most often involving normatively heterosexual desires and quests. (Seifert, 17)[6]

As Seifert points out, because "fairy tales have been—and continue to be—used to enshrine normative heterosexual love," queer fairy-tale studies are needed "to show . . . that there is nothing inevitable about the link between the fairy tale and heteronormativity" (18). Because "queer perspectives have the potential to undo or at least unsettle the genre's seemingly self-evident connection with heteronormative desires and structures," they represent an important approach to destabilizing, denaturalizing, and demythologizing the fairy-tale canon (18).

A New Canon

Dissatisfaction with the canon has also generated efforts to supplement, expand, or even re-create the fairy-tale canon with alternative tales. This has not been the work of scholarship alone but has developed since the 1970s in tandem with a flood of new tales and adaptations of classical tales by contemporary writers, illustrators, animators, filmmakers, and other creative artists. Vanessa Joosen has shown how modern fairy-tale scholars and postmodern creative writers and illustrators have been engaged in a symbiotic intertextual dialogue in which creative adaptations of canonical tales feed on the findings and perspectives of fairy-tale studies; and, in turn, fairy-tale studies find examples and confirmation of the anticanonical project in these subversive adaptations. The contemporary production of countless new fairy tales and adaptations that do not take conventional wisdom about classical tales for granted, in tandem with plentiful critical fairy-tale scholarship on their

---

6. See also Turner and Greenhill; and essays in the section "Regendering Cinderella" in Hennard Dutheil de la Rochère et al.

production and reception, highlights an expanding corpus of accessible and innovative tales in every conceivable medium—from print, illustrations, and graphic novels to film, television, music videos, and more[7]—that not only tests the authority of canonical tales but also competes with them for attention. There are endless examples, so suffice it to say that teachers, students, and other readers need not turn automatically—or only—to the classical version of "Little Red Riding Hood" by the Grimms or Perrault when they can easily experience innovative versions by creative writers and filmmakers such as Angela Carter, Tanith Lee, Neil Jordan, David Kaplan, or Matthew Bright, or the 52 international versions with 36 color and 61 black-and-white illustrations of the tale anthologized by Sandra L. Beckett in *Revisioning Red Riding Hood Around the World*.

Expanding the corpus of tales available to readers also involves identifying overlooked or suppressed tales and traditions that implicitly or explicitly challenge the values and representations of the Western fairy-tale canon and that surprise us or challenge our expectations as readers. Some scholars and translators address the telling deficit of non-Western tales in the canon by drawing attention to undeservedly lesser-known tales that can complement or compete with the usual Anglo-European narratives. As Lee Haring states in his collection of folktales from the Indian Ocean in 2007, "The broadening of the literary canon requires a massive program of retrieval, to which this book contributes" (Haring, xii). Other scholars are recovering literary tales, especially those by women, that for decades or even centuries had stood in the shadows of a male-dominated genre and remained undervalued or unknown.[8] Still others draw attention to historically important tales and collections, some from the early modern period, that present us with versions of otherwise well-known tales that are significantly different from the canonical versions of Perrault and the Grimms.[9] Previously unavailable in English or available only in outdated translations, tales by writers such as Giovan Francesco Straparola (sixteenth century) and Giambattista Basile (seventeenth century) and by nineteenth- and twentieth-century collectors such as Laura Gonzenbach and Giuseppe Pitrè, for instance, now appear in excellent translations with up-to-date introductions and notes.[10] In his English-language anthologies *The Great Fairy Tale Tradition* and *The Golden Age of Folk and Fairy Tales*, Jack Zipes provides, alongside classical tales from the Brothers Grimm, a diverse corpus of European fairy tales published by writers from the sixteenth to the nineteenth century and by

---

7. See the corresponding entries in Duggan et al.
8. See, for example, Jarvis; Jarvis and Blackwell; and Seifert and Stanton.
9. See, for example, Canepa (*Out of the Woods*; *Court to Forest*); and Harries.
10. See, for example, Straparola; Basile; Zipes (*Beautiful Angiola*); and Zipes and Russo.

nineteenth-century folklorists whose works have not enjoyed the fame or canonical status of the Grimms.

COMPLEXITIES AND PERPLEXITIES OF THE FAIRY-TALE CANON

It might seem perplexing that Zipes, who has challenged the alleged timelessness and authority of the constructed fairy-tale canon, has published anthologies that invoke affirmatively the language of canonicity. Titles such as *The Great Fairy Tale Tradition* and *The Golden Age of Folk and Fairy Tales* validate the special status of tales previously considered canonical and confer it upon lesser-known tales. Zipes refers to the nearly forgotten tales collected by Laura Gonzenbach as a "buried treasure" (Zipes, *Beautiful Angiola*, xi) and calls them, in the subtitle of his translation, *The Great Treasury of Sicilian Folk and Fairy Tales*. Similarly, he regards Pitrè's folktales as both a "great cultural treasure" and "a timeless treasure" (Zipes and Russo, 1: 32). As paradoxical as it may be, this recourse to the language of canonicity is not a regression to the prescriptive orthodoxy of the fairy-tale canon but a validation of neglected collections and collectors; it is also a way of reclaiming classical tales and the terminology of canonicity itself for a new era and new interpretive possibilities.

Consider *The Annotated Classic Fairy Tales*, Maria Tatar's anthology of tales by canonical Anglo-European authors and collectors. Beautifully produced by W. W. Norton and Company as a richly illustrated large-format tome, *The Annotated Classic Fairy Tales* conveys the canonical status of its contents both in its title and in its physical appearance (and in the publisher's text on the front flap, which characterizes the volume as a "treasure trove"). Noting that "fairy tales have become a vital part of our cultural capital," Tatar values these tales not for their timeless authority but for their giving readers the opportunity to "reinvigorate them" by "reclaiming them, turning them into *our* cultural stories by inflecting them in new ways and in some cases rescripting what happened 'once upon a time'" (Tatar, *Annotated Classic Fairy Tales*, xix, xvii).

If, as Robert Scholes observed, the canon is considered "a set of texts that constitute *our* cultural heritage" (emphasis added), it is not the canon Tatar has in mind when she refers to classical tales as "*our* cultural stories." Scholes is describing (and critiquing) a concept of the canon as an authoritative body of texts whose values are universal and timeless, reflecting the aesthetic, moral, and ethical standards of a culture whose core values remain fixed and static, a culture that perpetuates itself. In contrast, Tatar's classic tales have no inherent authority; they are universal and timeless only in the sense that narrative itself—storytelling—is universal and timeless, that *homo narrans* gives them life across time in infinitely variable readings and retellings. "The stories," Tatar writes in the introduction to *The Annotated Classic Fairy Tales*,

> are irresistible, for they offer opportunities to talk, to negotiate, to deliberate, to chatter, and to prattle on endlessly as did the old wives from whom the stories are thought to derive. And from the tangle of that talk and chitchat, we begin to define our own values, desires, appetites, and aspirations, creating identities that will allow us to produce happily-ever-after endings for ourselves and for our children. (Tatar, *Annotated Classic Fairy Tales*, xix)

To call classical tales "*our* cultural stories," as Tatar does, is not to affirm the canon as an authoritative source of common cultural values and identity but as a source of infinite opportunities for reinvention—of the stories and of ourselves. *Our* is not collective; it signifies instead each person's individual ownership of the recurring tales that we "reinvigorate" and turn into "*our* cultural stories" when each of us experiences or retells them.[11]

The idea of the canon as the repository of a shared cultural heritage—"our cultural heritage"—has been criticized for ignoring the fact that canonical texts have been overwhelmingly the products of white male Anglo-Europeans. The traditional fairy-tale canon has certainly been vulnerable to this complaint, which has triggered efforts to diversify it, as noted earlier. The problem and its complexity increase, however, when the fairy tale is produced and received in transnational and global contexts, as it is today. The complexity pertains not just to the problems inherent in speaking about "our cultural heritage" when the very idea of a homogeneous culture is in question. It also pertains to the inclusion of culturally diverse texts in the fairy-tale canon itself and to the idea of reading as reclamation. What happens and what ethics are involved, for example, when North American readers approach non-Western tales as irresistible opportunities to reinvigorate those newly available texts with new meaning and turn them into "*our* cultural stories"? Questions of this nature are not settled and constitute complexities that scholars, teachers, and students will need to confront.

Questions about the generic and textual identity of canonical tales are also unsettled, compounding the canon's complexity. Despite at least 200 years of interest in the fairy tale among folklorists, literary scholars, philologists, and others, there is no consensus about its definition and generic identity.[12] Whereas some

---

11. See also Haase ("Yours, Mine, or Ours?").
12. See Haase ("Fairy Tale").

understand the fairy tale as a discrete narrative genre with an inherent set of definitive characteristics, others see it as a broad category, like "folktale," that embraces diverse but related genres such as animal tale, humorous tale, cautionary tale, and formula tale. Contemporary scholars tend not to take a prescriptive approach to the fairy tale as a genre but recognize it as a moving target, a protean phenomenon that is prone to transformation. The generic identity of the classical fairy tale has been destabilized and complicated in particular by the flood of new fairy tales and adaptations in diverse media—from animation, live-action film, and television series to graphic novels, interactive websites, and computer games, to name just a few examples—that challenge the generic, aesthetic, and cultural norms of the originally verbal narratives.

The multimedial production and reception of fairy tales in today's globalized culture is the subject of Cristina Bacchilega's *Fairy Tales Transformed? Twenty-First Century Adaptations and the Politics of Wonder*. Bacchilega demonstrates how contemporary adaptations not only decenter canonical tales but also transform their generic and textual identity. Her analysis of fairy-tale films, for instance, focuses specifically on those films that rely on the fragmentation of canonical tales, which they repurpose by remixing their fragmented motifs and narrative elements with other genres. Bacchilega focuses on this kind of "generic complexity" (Bacchilega, 112) not because it is new but because it is important to recognize that fairy tales are produced and received in a vast web of tales and other genres to which they are linked. Reutilized fragments of classical tales may invoke their canonical source, but they do not affirm its authority, exclusivity, or privilege. Instead, they exist in manifold relations to other intertextual elements, all acting as hyperlinks to other tales, motifs, and genres in the fairy-tale web.[13] The idea that the canon is composed of a stable corpus and a cultural core cannot be sustained in a globalized culture where classical tales have been reduced to fragments and there is no defined center. The infinite fairy-tale web overwhelms and displaces the fairy-tale canon.

If the canon constructed in the nineteenth century originally comprised verbal texts—especially published texts, bound between the covers of a book and exuding an aura of stability and permanence—the relentless dissemination and consumption of fairy tales in diverse media in the twentieth and twenty-first centuries have made a print-based canon consisting of individual texts unsustainable. In fact, it is questionable whether the classical fairy tale is even a text at all. To say "Sleeping Beauty" has canonical status is not necessarily to identify an actual text. We

---

13. See Bacchilega for a thorough discussion of the fairy-tale web and the hypertextual nature of fairy-tale adaptations. On the hypertextual nature of print editions and their place in the contemporary fairy-tale web, see Haase ("Hypertextual Gutenberg").

might reasonably think of the Sleeping Beauty tales by Perrault and the Grimms as belonging to the traditional canon, but for all their similarities, these are two distinctly different tales, distinctly different texts—different thematically, stylistically, and aesthetically.

During America's culture wars, when E. D. Hirsch Jr. listed Cinderella, Little Red Riding Hood, Sleeping Beauty, and Snow White in his book *Cultural Literacy: What Every American Needs to Know*, he did not specify which of the many versions of those tales he meant. He did not specify because it did not matter. Many a classical tale is not a unique text but a *tale type*. As understood by folklorists, "A tale type is not itself a tale but instead merely an ideal construction that is common to and abstracted from different versions of a narrative" (Uther, 3: 999). The tales Hirsch found worthy of knowing and classical tales generally exist in multiple versions or variants. If the fairy-tale canon is supposed to identify and privilege narratives with moral, aesthetic, or sociocultural norms, canonizing tale types instead of fixed texts of exemplary value seems like a sloppy way of doing so. Of course, given their interest in variation and nonelitist culture, folklorists are not prone to canonizing. So it is perplexing that tale types, which resist hierarchies and elitist canons, became the cornerstone of the fairy-tale canon.

Final Thoughts

In one way or another, the canon seems always to be with us. Some might argue that the traditional fairy-tale canon became a victim of the culture wars. If so, its ghost still haunts us, perplexing us and complicating our understanding of the elusive genre. Long after its apparent demise, twenty-first-century fairy-tale scholars and creative artists remain focused on subverting, expanding, rereading, reconceiving, replacing, or displacing the canon. Resistance to the canon inspires the production of new editions, anthologies, and textbooks, as well as new ways of thinking about the fairy tale and our responsibilities as scholars and teachers. In that respect, our struggle with the fairy-tale canon has served us—and continues to serve us—well.

The canon is dead! Long live the canon!

Bibliography

Bacchilega, Cristina. *Fairy Tales Transformed? Twenty-First Century Adaptations and the Politics of Wonder*. Detroit: Wayne State University Press, 2013.

Basile, Giambattista. *The Tale of Tales, or Entertainment for Little Ones*. Trans. Nancy Canepa. New York: Penguin, 2016 [2007].

Beckett, Sandra L. *Revisioning Red Riding Hood from Around the World: An Anthology of International Retellings*. Detroit: Wayne State University Press, 2014.

Bottigheimer, Ruth B. *Grimms' Bad Girls and Bold Boys: The Moral and Social Vision of the Tales*. New Haven, CT: Yale University Press, 1987.

Canepa, Nancy. *From Court to Forest: Giambattista Basile's* Lo cunto de li cunti *and the Birth of the Literary Fairy Tale*. Detroit: Wayne State University, 1999.

———, ed. *Out of the Woods: The Origins of the Literary Fairy Tale in Italy and France*. Detroit: Wayne State University Press, 1997.

Duggan, Anne E., and Donald Haase, eds., with Helen J. Callow. *Folktales and Fairy Tales: Traditions and Texts from Around the World*, 4 vols., 2nd ed. Santa Barbara, CA: Greenwood/ABC-CLIO, 2016.

Guillory, John. "Canon." In *Critical Terms for Literary Study*. Ed. Frank Lentricchia and Thomas McLaughlin. Chicago: University of Chicago Press, 1990. 233–49.

Haase, Donald. "Challenges of Folktale and Fairy-Tale Studies in the Twenty-First Century." *Fabula* 57 (2016): 73–85.

———. "Fairy Tale." In *Folktales and Fairy Tales: Traditions and Texts from Around the World*, 2nd ed. Ed. Anne E. Duggan and Donald Haase, with Helen J. Callow. Santa Barbara, CA: Greenwood/ABC-CLIO, 2016. 1: 319–22.

———. "Feminist Fairy-Tale Scholarship." In *Fairy Tales and Feminism: New Approaches*. Ed. Donald Haase. Detroit: Wayne State University Press, 2004. 1–36.

———. "Framing the Brothers Grimm: Paratexts and Intercultural Transmission in Postwar English-Language Editions of the *Kinder- und Hausmärchen*." *Fabula* 44 (2003): 55–69.

———. "Hypertextual Gutenberg: The Textual and Hypertextual Life of Folktales and Fairy Tales in English-Language Popular Print Editions." *Fabula* 47 (2006): 221–30.

———, ed. *The Reception of Grimms' Fairy Tales: Responses, Reactions, Revisions*. Detroit: Wayne State University Press, 1993.

———. "Yours, Mine, or Ours? Perrault, the Brothers Grimm, and the Ownership of Fairy Tales." In *The Classic Fairy Tales*. Ed. Maria Tatar. New York: Norton, 1999. 353–64.

Haring, Lee. *Stars and Keys: Folktales and Creolization in the Indian Ocean*. Trans. Claudie Ricaud and Dawood Auleear. Bloomington: Indiana University Press, 2007.

Harries, Elizabeth Wanning. *Twice Upon a Time: Women Writers and the History of the Fairy Tale*. Princeton, NJ: Princeton University Press, 2001.

Hennard Dutheil de la Rochère, Martine, Gillian Lathey, and Monika Woźniak, eds. *Cinderella Across Cultures: New Directions and Interdisciplinary Perspectives*. Detroit: Wayne State University Press, 2016.

Hirsch, E. D., Jr. *Cultural Literacy: What Every American Needs to Know*. Boston: Houghton Mifflin, 1987.

Jarvis, Shawn. "Trivial Pursuit? Women Deconstructing the Grimmian Model in the *Kaffeterkreis*." In *The Reception of Grimms' Fairy Tales: Responses, Reactions, Revisions*. Ed. Donald Haase. Detroit: Wayne State University Press, 1993. 102–26.

Jarvis, Shawn C., and Jeannine Blackwell, eds. and trans. *The Queen's Mirror: Fairy Tales by German Women, 1780–1900*. Lincoln: University of Nebraska Press, 2001.

Joosen, Vanessa. *Critical and Creative Perspectives on Fairy Tales: An Intertextual Dialogue Between Fairy-Tale Scholarship and Postmodern Retellings*. Detroit: Wayne State University Press, 2011.

Joosen, Vanessa, and Gillian Lathey, eds. *Grimms' Tales Around the Globe: The Dynamics of Their International Reception*. Detroit: Wayne State University Press, 2014.

Kolbenschlag, Madonna. *Kiss Sleeping Beauty Good-Bye: Breaking the Spell of Feminine Myths and Models*. New York: Doubleday, 1979.

Magnus-Johnston, Kendra. "Meme." In *Folktales and Fairy Tales: Traditions and Texts from Around the World*, 2nd ed. Ed. Anne E. Duggan and Donald Haase, with Helen J. Callow. Santa Barbara, CA: Greenwood/ABC-CLIO, 2016. 2: 641–42.

Rölleke, Heinz. *Die Märchen der Brüder Grimm: Quellen und Studien—Gesammelte Aufsätze*. Trier: Wissenschaftlicher Verlag, 2000.

Schmiesing, Ann. *Disability, Deformity, and Disease in the Grimms' Fairy Tales*. Detroit: Wayne State University Press, 2014.

Scholes, Robert. "Canonicity and Textuality." In *Introduction to Scholarship in Modern Languages and Literatures*. Ed. Joseph Gibaldi. New York: Modern Language Association of America, 1992. 138–58.

Seifert, Lewis C., ed. "Queering Fairy Tales." Special issue of *Marvels & Tales* 29, no. 1 (2015).

Seifert, Lewis C., and Domna C. Stanton, eds. and trans. *Enchanted Eloquence: Fairy Tales by Seventeenth-Century French Women Writers*. Toronto: Centre for Reformation and Renaissance Studies, 2010.

Straparola, Giovan Francesco. *The Pleasant Nights*, 2 vols. Ed. Donald Beecher. Toronto: University of Toronto Press, 2012.

Tatar, Maria, ed. *The Annotated Classic Fairy Tales*. New York: Norton, 2002.

———. *The Hard Facts of the Grimms' Fairy Tales*, 2nd ed. Princeton, NJ: Princeton University Press, 2003.

Turner, Kay, and Pauline Greenhill, eds. *Transgressive Tales: Queering the Grimms*. Detroit: Wayne State University Press, 2012.

Uther, Hans-Jörg. "Tale Type." In *Folktales and Fairy Tales: Traditions and Texts from Around the World*, 2nd ed. Ed. Anne E. Duggan and Donald Haase, with Helen J. Callow. Santa Barbara, CA: Greenwood/ABC-CLIO, 2016. 3: 999–1002.

Zipes, Jack, trans. *Beautiful Angiola: The Great Treasury of Sicilian Folk and Fairy Tales Collected by Laura Gonzenbach*. New York: Routledge, 2004.

———. *Breaking the Magic Spell: Radical Theories of Folk and Fairy Tales*. Austin: University of Texas Press, 1979.

———, trans. *The Complete Fairy Tales of the Brothers Grimm*, 3rd ed. New York: Bantam, 2003.

———. "De-Disneyfying Disney: Notes on the Development of the Fairy-Tale Film." In *The Enchanted Screen: The Unknown History of Fairy-Tale Films*. By Jack Zipes. New York: Routledge, 2011. 16–30.

————. *Fairy Tales and the Art of Subversion: The Classical Genre for Children and the Process of Civilization*, 2nd ed. New York: Routledge, 2012.

————, ed. *The Golden Age of Folk and Fairy Tales: From the Brothers Grimm to Andrew Lang.* Indianapolis: Hackett, 2012.

————, ed. *The Great Fairy Tale Tradition: From Straparola and Basile to the Brothers Grimm.* New York: Norton, 2001.

————. *Why Fairy Tales Stick: The Evolution and Relevance of a Genre.* New York: Routledge, 2006.

Zipes, Jack, and Joseph Russo, trans. and eds. *The Collected Sicilian Folk and Fairy Tales of Giuseppe Pitrè*, 2 vols. New York: Routledge, 2009.

PART TWO

TEACHING AND LEARNING WITH FAIRY TALES

Fairy Tales in the Classroom

Lewis C. Seifert

Over the past 30 years, as the field of fairy-tale studies has come into its own and expanded, courses devoted to the fairy tale have become more and more common on college campuses. This is hardly a coincidence, of course. As more scholars have been drawn to the field, they have created courses reflective of their own scholarly interests and approaches. And so, for the future vitality of this field, it is imperative that we scholars and teachers of fairy tales develop responsible pedagogical practices—that is, courses and classroom strategies that represent the most salient questions of our evolving field. Naturally, the same is true of teaching in any field of study. But I would argue that it is particularly crucial for the field of fairy-tale studies, a relative newcomer to the academic scene. To promote a better understanding of the genre and train future generations of fairy-tale scholars, it is incumbent upon us to think collectively about *how* we teach *what* we teach. Saying this, I recognize that we will not arrive at anything like a consensus on a single or preferred pedagogical model. Nor should we. Our field is simply too diverse (in terms of disciplinary focus and thus the sorts of courses taught) for that to be possible or even desirable. Still, just as we have much to learn from each other across the disciplinary spectrum that makes up fairy-tale studies, so too sharing and comparing pedagogical objectives and activities can benefit us all. In the following pages, by surveying some possible types of courses on the fairy tale and then sampling classroom strategies, my aim is to stimulate further discussion and innovation.

Types of Courses

The topics, objectives, and structure of courses devoted in part or in whole to the fairy tale vary greatly depending on the academic discipline in which they are taught.[1] But the following types of courses or course units are readily adaptable to a variety of disciplines: introductory or survey courses, courses on fairy-tale adaptations in film and television, courses on specialized topics, and units on fairy tales in other courses.

Introductory or Survey Courses

Introductory or survey courses are aimed at exposing students to a range of fairy tales and critical approaches to the genre, and they can be designed in many different ways depending on the target audience and the instructor's preferences and/or expertise. Historical surveys of the fairy tale that present its chronological development from some point in the past to the present give students a sense of the long history of fairy-tale motifs and structures and their changes over time. Among the challenges instructors must address is how to balance breadth versus depth. The primary aim of these courses is to allow students to discover a broad selection of tales, organized chronologically, but they might also incorporate units on specific tale types, with versions from different historical periods. Thus, a course retracing the development of the Western European fairy tale might sacrifice strictly chronological organization to introduce a unit on versions of "Cinderella" by Basile, Perrault, d'Aulnoy, and the Grimms. The Norton anthologies by both Maria Tatar and Jack Zipes, organized around tale types and story cycles, lend themselves well to such comparative units.

One of the first considerations when constructing such courses is the balance between classic and other fairy tales. The canonical fairy tales of Charles Perrault, the Grimm brothers, and Hans Christian Andersen are central texts in any introductory or survey course on the Western fairy tale, to be sure. But it is important to give students an understanding of the many retellings and rewritings this canon has inspired across national traditions, especially because the history of the fairy tale is precisely one of adaptations. And so, to help students understand this feature of the genre, introductory or survey courses might have students do comparative readings of selected "canonical" tales and more contemporary rewritings (e.g., reading Perrault's "Blue Beard" followed by Angela Carter's "The Bloody Chamber").

Geographic range is another consideration for historical surveys. Although some courses might concentrate on a specific national tradition (e.g., fairy tales of France

---

1. See the sample syllabi included in Chapter 6 of this volume.

and the French-speaking world or Spain and Latin America), because of the trans-regional and transnational character of the fairy tale, even these courses can (and arguably *should*) be constructed to include relevant versions from other traditions, using available translations. For instance, a course on the history of the German fairy tale might include relevant stories from Straparola, Basile, and the seventeenth-century French vogue, as appropriate. To give students a sense of the global reach of the fairy tale—over and beyond the Western European and North American tradition—it is illuminating for students to read selected tales from other, non-Western traditions. As a starting point, instructors might consult the relevant tales included in Tatar's Norton anthology or Christine Jones and Jennifer Schacker's *Marvelous Transformations*.

Finally, introductory or survey courses can profitably incorporate units devoted to critical approaches to the fairy tale, which can even be used as the organizational structure for part or all of a course, with units devoted to structural, psychological, sociohistorical, and feminist approaches, among others. When including such units, instructors must consider how to present the history of the genre, which might be covered in a shorter introductory unit or through versions of a single tale type to illustrate the particular approach studied. For courses organized around the historical development of the genre or a national tradition, critical approaches might be presented instead through essays devoted to specific tales, without disrupting the chronological or geographic focus. Whatever the organization of the introductory or survey course, some attention to critical approaches is crucial, not only for an understanding of the fairy tale and the field of fairy-tale studies more generally but also for the development of students' critical reading skills. Introducing these approaches can and should be a primary objective for courses devoted to the fairy tale, which lends itself well to illustrating the methods and the stakes of various critical perspectives.

Courses on Fairy-Tale Adaptations in Film and Television

Studies of fairy tales in film and television have become an important subfield in fairy-tale studies, and courses devoted wholly or in part to fairy tales in film and/or television have made their appearance in colleges and universities. The rapidly expanding body of scholarship devoted to film and television adaptations of fairy tales is invaluable for both instructors and students in these courses.[2] Unless conceived as part of a sequence, with a prerequisite (such as an introductory course on the fairy tale), these courses should ideally cover some basics (the definition of the

---

2. See especially Greenhill and Matrix; Zipes (*Enchanted Screen*); Greenhill and Rudy; and Zipes et al.

fairy tale, a brief history of the genre, essential concepts of film or television studies) before proceeding to in-depth study of films and/or television series. The study of canonical or adapted print versions alongside the film and/or television series is also a fruitful exercise. And, when possible, the comparative study of multiple filmic adaptations of a single tale type or fairy tale has benefits akin to those of the comparative analysis of multiple text versions I mentioned previously. Requiring less specialized knowledge are units devoted to fairy tales in film and television in other courses, including introductory and survey courses. In the latter, for instance, a unit could focus on one or more films, or else a film (or films) could be integrated into a comparative study of a tale type, alongside print versions. Given the importance and the popularity of the mediums of film and television for the fairy tale as a genre, it is crucial that students learn to think critically about them, and every course on the fairy tale can benefit from at least some attention to film and/or television.

Courses on Specialized Topics

The possibilities for specialized courses on the fairy tale are seemingly limitless and can encompass courses on specific periods (such as the Victorian fairy tale), specific authors (e.g., the Brothers Grimm), a specific tale type or tale cycle (such as "Cinderella"), or a particular theme or topic in fairy-tale studies (such as "Folklore and Literature: Questions of Translation and Adaptation," a syllabus by Cristina Bacchilega included in Chapter 6), among others. Depending on the preparation of the students, some preliminary coverage of key concepts of the field (including the history of the genre and an overview of critical approaches) is likely necessary. And attention to comparative versions of tale types across periods and geographic regions provides students with a fuller grasp of both the specific topic at hand and the diffusion of the fairy tale globally. Obviously, courses with an overarching theme need not be specialized, and introductory or survey courses on the fairy tale can be organized around a specific topic. Also possible are hybrid courses, in which part of the course covers general information (basic concepts, history of the genre, critical approaches, etc.) and the other part focuses on a specific topic or topics. As the field of fairy-tale studies evolves, the range of topics will certainly also expand.

Units on Fairy Tales in Other Courses

Units on fairy tales can be integrated into courses across a wide variety of disciplines—folklore, literature, film, and gender studies being only the most obvious. They can also be used in composition and foreign-language courses, with special attention to narrative structure and language. Although the objectives of these units will vary according to the courses in which they appear, some attention to the definition of the fairy tale and the history of the genre is useful, indeed necessary. In addition to illustrating the thematic, narrative, or linguistic elements relevant to the course, the tales chosen can and should be used to discuss the specificity of the genre, if only briefly.

PEDAGOGICAL STRATEGIES
Defining the Fairy Tale

Courses on the fairy tale enjoy wide popularity among students. Yet some of the very reasons they are drawn to these courses present instructors with notable challenges. Based largely on their childhood experience with the genre, many students have what they think is a deep familiarity with fairy tales. But because the stories they know best are usually limited to those by Charles Perrault, the Grimm brothers, Hans Christian Andersen, and the Disney retellings, they often have many misconceptions that need to be dispelled. A few of the stereotypes that students may bring to the classroom are that fairy tales were originally intended for children, that they are always "compact" narratives, that they are simple and straightforward, that they always feature fairies, princes, and princesses, and that they inevitably reinforce conservative social structures.

A particularly vexing challenge is the affection many college students continue to have for Disney fairy-tale films along with their reluctance to examine them critically. So, from the beginning of a course or unit on fairy tales, instructors are immediately confronted with the task of demystifying students' conceptions of the genre. Helping them understand that what they *think* they know about fairy tales and what fairy tales really *are* are likely two very different things. In my experience, this can be the most important and ultimately most rewarding task of teaching a course on fairy tales, which requires a range of pedagogical strategies throughout the entire course. Rather than giving students a prepackaged definition at the outset, instructors might ask them to share their own definitions of the fairy tale and then have them compare those definitions against examples of lesser-known tales and discuss which aspects are valid and which are not. It is obviously necessary to have some sort of working definition before the unit or course can proceed, but it is also useful to keep this definition loose enough to allow for analysis of narratives—in text, film, graphic novel, among others—that may not be readily classified as fairy tales.[3] For instance, stories that draw on fairy-tale motifs, structures, characters, and themes are not necessarily fairy tales; still, one of our central pedagogical objectives should be to give students

---

3. Marina Warner proposes a useful and flexible definition in her recent *Once Upon a Time*.

a sense of how readily fairy-tale elements have been and continue to be adapted by other, non-fairy-tale forms. At the same time, we should encourage students to settle on a capacious definition that allows for the hybridity of narrative forms on the one hand and the genre's adaptability to new contexts and media on the other.

Understanding the Appeal of Fairy Tales

Linked to the definition of the genre is consideration of the appeal of fairy tales across time and cultures. Why fairy tales "stick" (to quote the title of a book by Jack Zipes)—why they are passed down from generation to generation and why they travel around the globe—is a question that is not easily answered. Students should certainly be made aware of various theories about the persistence and diffusion of fairy tales (including Zipes's theory of memes, for instance), but more immediately relevant—and less speculative—is a reflection on the meaning and resonance of fairy tales for our present. This is a fruitful question to ask in light of the recurring popularity of fairy-tale films and television series, but it is also one that can be considered when studying contemporary adaptations of tale types. It goes without saying that there is much to be gained from having students reflect on the appeal and meaning that fairy tales have in the present. But a similar exercise for fairy tales in the past and/or in different cultures is equally beneficial, even if it requires detailed contextual information, whether provided by the instructor or researched by the students themselves. In this approach, fairy tales might even become the medium for highlighting and studying specific topics in the past or in a different culture.

Reassessing Childhood Experiences with Fairy Tales

As a general rule, college-level humanities courses aim to move beyond subjective responses to the material studied. Yet subjective responses need not obviate rigorous analytical reflection. For my students one of the most rewarding experiences of taking a course on fairy tales is the opportunity it provides to reflect on their own childhoods—their recollections of storytelling, their feelings then and now about specific stories, and the influence fairy tales had and continue to have on them. Unlike defining the genre or understanding its appeal and meaning, this reflection is likely to be less a discrete moment in a course and much more an ongoing and recurring discussion. Different fairy tales and themes speak to students in different ways, and so it is useful to return to this question frequently and in a variety of contexts.

Students often express surprise, if not shock, at encountering unadulterated versions that contrast sharply with the innocuous fairy tales of their childhood. This reaction can be channeled toward a discussion of the ideological motivations subtending adaptations of fairy tales and children's literature generally. Students are usually also eager to share what they were drawn to and/or repulsed by in fairy tales, after which they can be asked to reflect on the socializing and acculturating influences fairy tales had on them personally. Positive, negative, and ambivalent feelings toward characters or plot twists are all fruitful for classroom discussion, particularly when students recall different childhood reactions. It can also be productive to ask students whether their reactions have changed over time—especially after their experiences in a course on fairy tales—and, if so, how they account for this change. In particular, students' evolving thoughts about Disney fairy tales make for a compelling and important topic of discussion, particularly when these films are compared with other versions. In sum, having students confront their childhood memories of fairy tales with specific versions illustrates for them how critical reflection can benefit them personally, even if that involves discomfort and questioning.

Close Reading

The rigorous critical reflection we scholars and teachers of fairy tales want to encourage in our students requires attention to close analysis of the texts, images, and films we include in our courses. Depending on the approach adopted and the medium studied, specific terminology and concepts will need to be stressed. But, in the end, whatever the terminology and concepts we present, the goal remains the same: providing students with the tools to reflect on the meaning of fairy tales. Even if this goal seems no different from that for courses on other genres, fairy tales present a special challenge, I would argue. In their classic (compact) form, they are characterized by a deceptive simplicity of style, characterization, and narrative structure. And yet this apparent simplicity calls for careful and meticulous attention to detail, all the more so when encountering versions of well-known fairy tales. For instance, when teaching Perrault's prose tales, I draw students' attention to the complex relationship between the narratives and the final versed morals. Rather than reiterate the ostensible "lesson" of the narrative, the morals more often than not formulate a logic that contradicts it, sometimes even calling into question the efficacy of the genre itself (see, for instance, the versed morals at the end of "Blue Beard"). Having students observe how Perrault uses irony, metaphor, and allegory (among others) in his morals leads to reexamination of specific details of the narrative and, ultimately, to a broader reflection on Perrault's multifaceted uses of the fairy-tale form in the *Stories or Tales of Past Times*.

Close analysis of Perrault's morals and of his narratives also requires consideration of contextual references, and the same is obviously true for all other fairy tales, of whatever tradition. When available, annotated critical editions are invaluable for providing otherwise elusive cultural and linguistic allusions. But more contemporary fairy tales, with familiar cultural references, are often more accessible to students, in which case the challenge is to make students sensitive to the function of those references. Whether through literary, filmic, linguistic, or cultural features, fairy tales lend themselves readily to the acquisition of close reading skills, and this is surely one of the strongest arguments we can use to advocate for the study of the fairy tale.

Comparative Readings

As a field, fairy-tale studies is necessarily comparative in scope because the fairy tale, as much scholarship has shown, is the product of exchanges and borrowings across geographic, ethnic, and linguistic boundaries and of adaptations for specific audiences. Accordingly, students have a lot to gain from comparisons of different versions of fairy tales, which permit them to trace the historical development of specific tales and grasp what is at stake in contemporary adaptations of classic tales. Comparisons can also enhance close reading activities by focusing on moments of significant differences among versions of the same story.

Yet another goal for comparative readings might be a reflection on how varying conceptions of the fairy tale are manifested in specific versions. For instance, beyond obvious plot differences, Perrault's "Little Red Riding Hood" differs from the Grimms' version in tone. Perrault's narrator is an ironic parody of oral storytelling, and the moral is an overt allegory of erotic seduction. The Grimms' version, by contrast, strikes a more didactic note that students might overlook by directing their attention to the miraculous rescue of Little Red Cap and her grandmother by the huntsman. When more contemporary adaptations are juxtaposed to classic versions, it can be tempting for students to overlook the complexity of the older versions in favor of the perceived relevance of the more recent versions. In such cases we should endeavor to help students grasp the stylistic and ideological density of both the classic versions *and* their adaptations so as to acknowledge the continuities as well as the differences between them. However conceived, comparative readings should allow students to grasp the complexity of the fairy tale and to arrive at more questions than answers.

Cultural Uses of the Fairy Tale

References to fairy tales are ubiquitous across a wide range of cultural discourses and illustrate in striking fashion the profound, if not visceral, appeal of the genre. In academic discourse, advertising, journalism, online venues, political rhetoric, and social commentary (among many others), *which* fairy tales are referenced, *how* they are cited and transformed, and *why* are but a few of the questions that should be considered. In our teaching, examples of these references make for fruitful illustrations for lectures or discussion prompts when studying specific tale types or features of the fairy tale as a genre. (For instance, the abundant allusions to "Little Red Riding Hood" in contemporary print and television advertisements often foreground eroticism, and in particular female sexual assertiveness. Having students contrast this representation with the naïveté of the heroine in the classic versions by Perrault and the Grimms leads them to grasp the story's adaptability to vastly different cultural contexts and its uses to reinforce and/or contest gender and sexual stereotypes.) Beyond the classroom, giving students the opportunity to research the uses of specific characters and motifs in selected cultural discourses is an excellent assignment for individual or group projects.

Creative Projects

The study of fairy tales readily opens the way to a wide range of creative projects. Whether the disciplinary focus is a foreign language, writing, literature, film, folklore, or something else, creative assignments provide students with the opportunity to illustrate their understanding of the genre in ways that are personally meaningful and to do so while working toward a specific pedagogical objective. The possibilities for such projects are numerous, depending on the focus of the course and the interests of the students. Having them write their own fairy tale(s) has obvious benefits in foreign-language and writing courses, but this exercise can also be readily incorporated into introductory or thematic courses. Students with artistic talents might illustrate selected tales, and those with expertise in web design might create a website. Groups of students can undertake more ambitious projects, such as writing and performing a fairy-tale play or musical or making a film. In courses where the central focus is the fairy tale, it can be useful to have students include a self-assessment in which they explain the objectives for their project, their creative process, and their overall evaluation of the final result. However defined, assignments that give students the freedom to express themselves creatively have the potential to transform the fairy tale while enacting its transformative power. Putting into practice what they learn about the genre in our courses, students can contribute firsthand to the continued vitality of the fairy-tale tradition.

BIBLIOGRAPHY

Greenhill, Pauline, and Sidney Eve Matrix, eds. *Fairy Tale Films: Visions of Ambiguity*. Logan: Utah State University Press, 2010.

Greenhill, Pauline, and Jill Terry Rudy, eds. *Channeling Wonder: Fairy Tales and Television*. Detroit: Wayne State University Press, 2014.

Jones, Christine A., and Jennifer Schacker, eds. *Marvelous Transformations: An Anthology of Fairy Tales and Contemporary Critical Perspectives*. Peterborough, Canada: Broadview Press, 2013.

Tatar, Maria, ed. *The Classic Fairy Tales: Texts, Criticism*. New York: Norton, 1999.

Warner, Marina. *Once Upon a Time: A Short History of the Fairy Tale*. Oxford, UK: Oxford University Press, 2014.

Zipes, Jack. *The Enchanted Screen: The Unknown History of Fairy-Tale Films*. New York: Routledge, 2011.

———, ed. *The Great Fairy Tale Tradition: From Straparola and Basile to the Brothers Grimm*. New York: Norton, 2001.

———. *Why Fairy Tales Stick: The Evolution and Relevance of a Genre*. New York: Routledge, 2006.

Zipes, Jack, Pauline Greenhill, and Kendra Magnus-Johnston, eds. *Fairy-Tale Films Beyond Disney: International Perspectives*. New York: Routledge, 2016.

CHAPTER ONE

Fairy Tales and Tale Types

Marriage, Female Agency, and Sexuality in Monster Bridegroom Tales

Teaching "Beauty and the Beast"

Anne E. Duggan

With the popularity of Walt Disney Studios' *Beauty and the Beast* (1991) among our present generation of students, the unit on "Beauty and the Beast" tales in my "Understanding the Fairy Tale" course is particularly successful. As in the case of other familiar fairy tales, students often take for granted the ways in which "Beauty and the Beast" tales communicate historically and culturally specific notions about marriage, female agency, and sexuality. They are often fascinated by the fact that the tale has its own historical development. They come to appreciate that the classical version is the result of a series of adaptations of monster bridegroom tales that can be traced back to the Latin "Cupid and Psyche," is mediated through sixteenth- and seventeenth-century Italian and French variants, and culminates in Jeanne-Marie Leprince de Beaumont's version, the main source for twentieth-century adaptations.

"Understanding the Fairy Tale" is an intermediate-level general education course. Each course unit of about three weeks is organized around textual and filmic versions of (1) "Little Red Riding Hood," (2) "Beauty and the Beast," (3) "Cinderella" and "Donkey Skin," (4) "Bluebeard," and (5) *The Arabian Nights*. I use Maria Tatar's *Classic Fairy Tales* (1999) as the main textbook and post several tales, articles, and films on Blackboard. Most units move from Italian, French, and German variants to English, American, and filmic versions, concluding with discussion of a scholarly article relevant to the tale type. For each unit, students must write a paper that brings together at least two written versions and one filmic adaptation of a tale and includes at least one secondary reference. Except for its emphasis on the French tale tradition, the section on "Beauty and the Beast" illustrates the ways in which the other units in the course are organized and culminates in an organized class debate about whether Disney's *Beauty and the Beast* is a feminist or sexist adaptation of the tale.

During the first two weeks of the semester, students develop a historical and theoretical framework for understanding the genre of the fairy tale, which helps them situate tales within specific sociocultural and ideological contexts. We begin by looking at the different settings for the writing of fairy tales, reading Ruth Bottigheimer's article on tales by the Italian Giovanni Straparola, Jack Zipes's overview of the 1690s French tale tradition ("Rise of the French Fairy Tale"), and Zipes's overview of the work of the Brothers Grimm ("Two Brothers Named Grimm"). For an introduction to approaches, I provide students with Robyn McCallum's "Approaches to the Literary Fairy Tale," in Zipes's *Oxford Companion to Fairy Tales* (2000), and terminology from Haase's *Greenwood Encyclopedia of Folktales and Fairy Tales*, including *contes de fées*, fairy tale, folktale, märchen, motif, monogenesis, polygenesis, and tale type. With respect to monster bridegroom tales, students can draw from this overview to consider the ways in which Italian and French versions differ from German adaptations. They also learn to use relevant terminology in their discussions and papers to be able to analyze recurring motifs in variants of monster bridegroom tales and consider their diffusion over space and time.

In the unit on "Beauty and the Beast" tales, we focus on marriage practices in different sociohistorical and cultural contexts in conjunction with an examination of female agency and sexuality, which are central themes in each variant. We begin with Apuleius's second-century Latin "Story of Cupid and Psyche," viewed by scholars as one of the important source texts for "Beauty and the Beast" tales, and then examine Straparola's sixteenth-century Italian "The Pig King," which was a second important intertext in the development of French variants of monster bridegroom tales. After providing some background on the 1690s French *conteuses*, we examine French versions of "Beauty and the Beast" by Gabrielle-Suzanne Barbot de Villeneuve (1740) and Jeanne-Marie Leprince de Beaumont (1757) and the Grimms' "The Frog King, or Iron Heinrich" (1812). After discussing the classical tradition, students turn their attention to Angela Carter's revision of the tale in "The Tiger's Bride" (1993) and two filmic versions: Jean Cocteau's *La Belle et la bête*

(1946) and Disney Studios' *Beauty and the Beast*. Through the study of these variants, students are able to understand the different ways in which each adaptation supports or undermines the ideological underpinnings of marriage practices, female agency, and sexuality within a specific sociocultural context.

For Apuleius's "Cupid and Psyche" and Straparola's "The Pig King," I provide students with a study guide that is used as support for class discussion (Appendix A). Questions related to Apuleius's story encourage students to think about the themes and structure of the story and relate these to the situation of the female characters. We break the story into three main "episodes": the prelude, centering on Venus's jealousy of Psyche; Psyche's flight to Cupid's palace, which foregrounds her sisters' jealousy; and Psyche's ordeals and quest to regain Cupid. Through our reading of Psyche's initial submission to Cupid and the reasons behind her sisters' jealousy (both are unhappily married), we examine the plight of women in a society that sacrifices them on the marriage market to men who often dominate them. Students then apply Algirdas Greimas's actantial model, which they learned in a previous unit, to the analysis of the structure of "Cupid and Psyche."[1] Interestingly, this model suggests at least two possible readings of female agency in "Cupid and Psyche": one in which Psyche functions as the object, sent by her parents and Apollo to Cupid, who has agency in the story; and a second in which Psyche is the agent of her desire, seeking to regain her lover Cupid, the object of her quest (Appendix B).

Such a structuralist analysis suggests a complex reading of the tale, in which a virginal heroine is sacrificed to a patriarchal society but gains agency over the course of the narrative, in part through disobedience.[2] I then introduce students to three approaches that can build on this initial analysis (Appendix C): psychological, focusing on women's fears about marriage and sexuality and on relations between female siblings and between mother and daughter-in-law; Jungian, through which we can read the tale in terms of Psyche's initiation into womanhood and her sisters' malice as the resistance of feminine nature to a patriarchal society; and sociohistorical, examining the tale as a representation of actual marriage practices in Roman North African society. For the last approach, I provide students with basic information from Josiah Osgood's informative article, which closely examines the

---

1. In *Structural Semantics*, Algirdas Greimas proposes a dynamic structuralist model that is useful in teasing out the ideology of a tale. It is based on six "actants": the *subject*, who is sent on a quest by the *sender* to recover an *object*, often supported by a *helper*; the *receiver*, who is the individual or entity that benefits from the recovery of the object; and the *opponent*.

2. Psyche is unaware of the identity of her husband, who forbids her to look upon him, although he visits her bed each night. Urged by her jealous sisters, Psyche disobeys, which leads to Cupid's flight and Psyche's quest to recover him.

relation between the tale and Roman marriage laws and practices. By introducing students to the specific sociocultural references in the tale, they gain new insights into a genre often viewed as pure fiction or fantasy; at the same time, they can begin to conceive of the monster bridegroom tale as a means to reflect on a particular society's perspective on marriage practices and female agency.

As a way to segue into the classical French versions of "Beauty and the Beast" and to emphasize the choices authors make in their adaptations, students study Straparola's "The Pig King." The study guide (Appendix A) asks students to find links between the Latin tale and the Italian tale, which leads to discussion of such themes as the monster bridegroom, forced marriage, female agency, and sexuality. Students are able to see that the figuratively monstrous nature of Cupid takes concrete material form in Straparola's pig, anticipating the figure of the Beast in what has become the classical form of the tale. We can view the sisters who eventually are killed in Straparola's tale as having affinities with Psyche's sisters in their resistance to patriarchal practices: Just as Psyche's sisters deplore their horrible husbands, Meldina's sisters resist being forced to marry a filthy, cruel pig, and the eldest even plots to murder her monster bridegroom. For her part, although Meldina willingly agrees to marry the pig king, her wedding night often surprises students in its rather perverse and explicit representation of sexuality. The morning after the wedding celebration we see Meldina "lying in the bed, all defiled with mud as it was, and looking pleased and contented" (Tatar, 46). As in the case of "Cupid and Psyche," in which Psyche gains agency over the course of the tale, thus complicating a reading that views the heroine only in passive terms, Straparola's tale presents contradictions in the figure of Meldina: The apparently submissive and obedient daughter becomes the bride who appears to engage in bestiality.

In anticipation of students' reading of Villeneuve's and Leprince de Beaumont's versions of "Beauty and the Beast," I discuss the monster bridegroom tales penned by *conteuses* such as Marie-Catherine d'Aulnoy and Henriette-Julie de Murat. I explain that both writers were familiar with Straparola's tale but toned down the bawdy tendencies of Straparola's version to accommodate their aristocratic readership. I note that different class issues change as we move from the urban tales of the Italian writer to the aristocratic court context of the *conteuses*. Straparola's heroine is from a poor, implicitly lower-class family, whereas the heroine in monster bridegroom tales by d'Aulnoy ("The Green Serpent," "The Ram," "Prince Marcassin") and Murat ("The Pig King") is a princess or a young woman from a fallen noble family. In the case of d'Aulnoy's "The Green Serpent," I emphasize that d'Aulnoy consciously posits the equality of the sexes by casting both the heroine and the hero as ugly monsters who will recover their beauty by the end of the tale. This move importantly changes the dynamics of a tale in which, typically, a young beautiful woman must exercise patience and show affection for a beastly male in order to survive. D'Aulnoy herself was wedded to a libertine some thirty years her senior. Her choice to modify the tale to make heroine and hero equally monstrous—thus demanding patience from both characters as they learn to appreciate each other—can be read as a rejection of a narrative that, in the final analysis, condones the inequality between a monstrous (more powerful, ugly, old, abusive) husband and a usually much younger, less experienced wife that was part and parcel of early modern arranged marriages.[3]

The background provided on the 1690s *conteuses* sets the stage for our reading of Villeneuve's version of "Beauty and the Beast." In many respects, Villeneuve's tale marks a transition from the 1690s aristocratic tale tradition to the more sober bourgeois tales penned by Leprince de Beaumont. Although students are not required to read Virginia Swain's "Beauty's Chambers: Mixed Styles and Mixed Messages in Villeneuve's 'Beauty and the Beast,'" I draw heavily from her analysis to guide students through the text. I provide students with discussion questions that again ask them to make connections between Villeneuve's tale and "Cupid and Psyche" and to focus on aspects of the text related to gender and the cultural context of the tale.

First students discuss the questions in small groups; then we come together and begin making connections between Villeneuve's "Beauty and the Beast" and Apuleius's "Cupid and Psyche." Students often note that just as the wind god Zephyr carries Psyche off to Cupid's palace, so a swift horse whose stride is like "the breath of a zephyr" carries Beauty off to the castle of her monster bridegroom (Villeneuve, 165). When Psyche is brought to the cliff where she is to be carried away to her "dreadful wedding," she has the appearance "of a woman going to her grave, not her bridal bed" (Apuleius, 4). For her part, Beauty believes she is going to be killed by the beast, but she is surrounded by "bridal pomp" (Villeneuve, 65). As such, both stories conflate death and marriage. Both stories stage tensions with jealous sisters, and Villeneuve's Beauty sees a young man in her dreams who is "as handsome as any portrait of Cupid" (Villeneuve, 169).

After making connections with one of the source tales, students identify elements in the story that might situate it within a specific cultural context. I point out that the outskirts of the Beast's castle are surrounded by snowy terrain but that orange trees grow on the Beast's land. For an early-eighteenth-century reader, this would have immediately evoked the Orangerie of Versailles, which was designed

---

3. For more on the context of early modern French marriage, in particular, the problematic union of young women emerging from the convent to marry older and more experienced men, see Gibson.

in such a way that orange trees could bear fruit in winter. The Beast's grounds also include a grand canal, another important landmark of the gardens of Versailles. In the castle there is a large room of mirrors—an element that appears in a tale by d'Aulnoy as well—clearly a reference to Versailles's Hall of Mirrors. At the same time that the space of the Beast's castle bears traces of Versailles, the forms of entertainment that the Beast offers Beauty further ground the tale in the aristocratic culture of seventeenth- and early-eighteenth-century France. Beauty is able to watch operas, one of the most popular forms of art in the period, as well as Italian theater and the fair at Saint Germain.

Class discussion leads us to question the ideological underpinnings of the tale. At the same time that Villeneuve's "Beauty and the Beast" seems to celebrate the aristocratic culture embraced by such writers as d'Aulnoy, it also marks a shift away from courtly worldliness to a society that values domestic bliss and in which women appear to lose some of their social and political power. As Swain points out, Beauty initially is pleased by the worldly entertainments offered to her by the Beast. But as the tale evolves, Beauty appreciates these ostentatious forms less and less, which parallels her choice to abandon affection (the handsome unknown in her dreams) for the more solid virtue of gratitude (the Beast).[4] Implicitly, this suggests that Beauty must forgo her own personal desire to "repay" the Beast for not killing her father or herself and for granting her family a newfound wealth. Beauty becomes an object of exchange in a transaction between men, and female agency is further challenged in the tale's secondary story about Beauty's fairy mother. Swain points out that "Beauty's mother abandons the public, powerful world into which she was born and twice confronts death in order to adopt a life centered on her husband and child. . . . If the Beast's Amazonian mother and Beauty's fairy godmother belong to a generation of powerful, independent, and *single* women, the daughters—exemplified by Beauty—are being taught to marry, devote themselves to husbands and family, and be content with their lot" (210).

Not only, then, does Villeneuve's tale mark a transition in the evolution of the tale, bridging the gap between d'Aulnoy and Murat's earlier transformations of "Cupid and Psyche" on the one hand and Leprince de Beaumont's now classical version of "Beauty and the Beast" on the other. Her tale also traces the shift occurring in French society in which the feminocentric spaces of the salon that supported women as authors and as arbiters of culture—and in which the 1690s

---

4. In the tale, the handsome unknown—who will turn out to be the true image of the Beast—comes to Beauty in her dreams. Although she feels affection or desire for him, she feels obligated to the Beast. This tension between the handsome unknown and the Beast comes to incarnate the tension between affection and gratitude; the story's moral demands the privileging of gratitude over affection.

conteuses penned their tales—slowly comes to be replaced by a new locus for female agency: the domestic space of the bourgeois household. Villeneuve's Amazons and fairy queens represent the older generation of women reminiscent of d'Aulnoy and Murat's heroines, whereas her Beauty embodies the rising valorization of female domesticity grounded in a bourgeois model of marriage, which is more solidly exemplified by the more submissive heroine of Leprince de Beaumont's classical version of "Beauty and the Beast."

Upon reading Leprince de Beaumont's version of "Beauty and the Beast," students easily see the modifications that the author made to Villeneuve's tale, most notably with respect to its length but also with respect to style and tone. Whereas Villeneuve's tale is about 76 pages long and is written in the novella-like style of d'Aulnoy and Murat, Leprince de Beaumont significantly pares down her source text to produce a tale of about 11 pages that is written in a much more succinct and less convoluted style. Although Villeneuve's tale is not devoid of moral lessons, these are heightened in Leprince de Beaumont through, first, a frame narrative that presents the tale as a lesson in good behavior, told by Mademoiselle Goodness to the young ladies in her care; and, second, through the emphasis on a Christian morality that underpins her adaptation.[5] Again marking a transition in the story, Villeneuve moves away from the purely aristocratic heroines of her predecessors and leads her readers to believe that Beauty is the daughter of a merchant until the end of the story, when it is revealed that she is in fact the daughter of a fairy and a king. In Leprince de Beaumont's hands, Beauty is squarely and unambiguously bourgeois and manages to marry the beastly prince. Misalliance criticized but averted in Villeneuve's version becomes unquestionably acceptable in Leprince de Beaumont's tale, published 17 years later.

Having the students consider the cultural context of Villeneuve's version, as well as the world of the fairies, helps them see the ways in which Leprince de Beaumont's tale marks a rupture with earlier monster bridegroom tales penned by women writers. Significantly, Leprince de Beaumont's jealous sisters seek to embody the courtly tradition that had been valued by the 1690s *conteuses*, which, at least for daughters of a wealthy merchant, is represented as "bad" behavior. As opposed to her sisters, who enjoy balls and theater—forms of entertainment that Villeneuve's Beauty eventually abandons—from the beginning of the tale Leprince de Beaumont's Beauty prefers "reading good books," a theme that will return in Disney's filmic adaptation. Leprince de Beaumont also introduces into her version motifs taken from "Cinderella." When the family loses its wealth and relocates to

---

5. The frame narrative is now available in English in the fourth volume of Duggan et al.

the countryside, Beauty takes care of all the housework and cooks, her hard work making her "very healthy" (Leprince de Beaumont, 33), while her idle sisters insult her. As opposed to her worldly sisters, Beauty is "not all that attached to life," and indeed she puts herself "in God's hands" (Leprince de Beaumont, 36, 37).

Later, at the Beast's castle, rather than entertaining his Beauty with theater and opera, this Beast provides Beauty with a bookcase, music books, and a harpsichord. As opposed to the opulent room of mirrors in Villeneuve, in Leprince de Beaumont we find only a simple, nonostentatious mirror that allows Beauty to see her father. As such, the symbol of worldliness present in Villeneuve's tale becomes a symbol of domesticity and daughterly devotion. Through such transformations of her source tale, Leprince de Beaumont infuses her adaptation with Christian undertones that we do not see in previous monster bridegroom tales. Indeed, the tale ends by associating the two sisters, about to be turned into statues, with the seven deadly sins: "You can correct pride, anger, gluttony, and laziness. But a miracle is needed to convert a heart filled with malice and envy" (Leprince de Beaumont, 42).[6]

In the end, Leprince de Beaumont gives us a thoroughly domesticated Beauty (even Villeneuve's Beauty did not scrub floors), who is rewarded for her good, self-abnegating behavior of giving herself over to a Beast for the (financial) sake of her family.[7] Leprince de Beaumont's tale became the predominant point of reference for later reworkings of "Beauty and the Beast." Writers such as Angela Carter challenged Leprince de Beaumont's Christian morality and legitimation of the exchange of women on the marriage market. Whereas Leprince de Beaumont's version only suggests an exchange of wealth for the hand of the heroine, Carter foregrounds this aspect of the tale in "The Tiger's Bride," which opens with the line, "My father lost me to The Beast at cards" (Carter, 50).

Although Carter's text can at first be difficult for students, knowing the source tale and reflecting on the modifications Carter makes to it help students understand the complexity and significance of "The Tiger's Bride." Initially I have students get into small groups and simply describe the location of the story, the heroine, the Beast, the rose, and the Beast's palace. Breaking down the complex story into these

---

6. For the sake of thematic unity, I am going to leave out of this discussion my use of "The Frog King" by the Brothers Grimm in the "Understanding the Fairy Tale" course. We do consider the ways in which the Grimms' version in fact grants the heroine more agency than other versions. As opposed to Leprince de Beaumont's Beauty in particular, the heroine of the Grimm tale ends up being rewarded for her disobedience: In casting the nasty frog against the wall in a true gesture of ingratitude, the young princess is rewarded with the hand of a handsome prince!

7. The Beast gives Beauty's father a chest of gold coins at the beginning of the tale, implicitly in exchange for his daughter. In Villeneuve the Beast gives the father two trunks of riches after he delivers Beauty to him.

five simple units makes the discussion of the text less intimidating. With respect to location, we discuss the relation between Carter's tale and the gothic, with its focus on southern European settings. With respect to the heroine, we consider what it means for Beauty's father to refer to her as "my pearl," while the Beast's valet refers to her as being a part of her father's "treasures" (Carter, 54). Such conceptions of Beauty work to commodify her as a token in an economic exchange between men, which indeed happens more elusively in earlier renditions of monster bridegroom tales.[8]

Students also notice that the Beast is more animal-like than in the French versions. His overperfumed body covers up his animal odor; he is at pains to maintain an upright position; and the chairs in his palace are clawed up. Whereas French beasts are monstrous in appearance and often lack manners and polite speech, Carter literalizes the beastliness of her beast, emphasizing his animal nature, and rejects what is implicit in other monster bridegroom tales: that the heroine must patiently tame the manly beast to reach a happy ending. Interestingly, in Carter's tale, the narrative moves from characters attempting to conceal their animality to having them embrace it. Narrating her own story, this Beauty notes that "horses are better than we [humans] are" (Carter, 54), anticipating the conclusion of the tale, in which she lies with the Beast, who licks off her layers of skin—of "civilization" or human society—to reveal her inner animal. In effect, Carter gives voice to her Beauty, who is able to speak about the pain of her commodification, from which she escapes by embracing her animality. Rather than having her Beauty "civilize" a beastly man, Carter's heroine gains agency both by relating her own story and by becoming animal.

Carter's tale is suggestive of a queer—that is, nonheteronormative—adaptation of the tale, given the heroine's bestiality or becoming-beast, but I provide students with some guidelines to read Jean Cocteau's filmic adaptation in more explicitly queer terms.[9] Although Cocteau's *La Belle et la bête* is relatively faithful to Leprince de Beaumont's tale, it is coded as queer in several ways, as I try to show students. Because a queer reading is not an obvious one for first- and second-year students with no background on Cocteau or queer theory, I provide them with a handout of quotes by scholars discussing the queer inflections of Cocteau's film (Appendix D). I explain that Cocteau and Jean Marais, who played the Beast, were partners, and their homosexuality plays out in different ways in the film. I note that critics such as Irène Eynat-Confino have argued that queer directors have often used

---

8. When teaching such texts to an upper-level or graduate class, it would be useful to provide students with Luce Irigaray's chapter "Women on the Market" from her *This Sex Which Is Not One*.
9. For a succinct presentation of queer theory, see Duggan (7–8).

the image of the monster to represent the queer Other, viewed as monstrous by heteronormative society. I draw from Daniel Fischlin to help students consider the ways in which desire plays out in the film between director and star: "From that perspective the film's camera-work becomes a sensuous point of contact between Cocteau and his lover" (80). Finally, we consider the film's ending, when Beauty wonders what has happened to her Beast, seemingly disappointed that he has transformed into a handsome prince. For Susan Hayward, this moment undermines the heteronormativity of the source tale: Beauty appears to prefer a queer relation with a nonhuman animal than one with the obligatory handsome prince.[10]

This unit of the course culminates in Disney's *Beauty and the Beast*, the main source of the tale for contemporary students. Students easily see the ways in which the Disney film draws on that of Cocteau, most notably in the doubling of the Beast (the Beast and Avenant in Cocteau; the Beast and Gaston in Disney). We discuss the ways in which Disney makes much more explicit than other versions the relation between the "beastly" behavior of the Beast and the "civilizing" role of Belle. At first, Belle appears more plucky than the heroines of Villeneuve and Leprince de Beaumont: She constantly resists submission to Gaston; she is an avid reader and is adventurous enough to dream about leaving her provincial town; she goes searching for her father, lost at the Beast's castle; and she disobeys the Beast's order not to go into the West Wing. However, she will play the damsel in distress as well as the woman who will domesticate her man. When Belle is blissfully united with the Beast at the end of the film, one wonders what happened to the adventurous girl we saw at the beginning. As June Cummins argues, "While Belle initially appears spunky, independent, and curious, her surrender to the seduction of sexual difference, like the plot's surrender to romantic closure, denies her that independence and forces her into subjugation" (26). In the end, does she simply serve as a support for male subjects, or is there more to Disney's film than this?

To encourage students to draw more generally from their knowledge about the history and different contexts and meanings of the tale as it relates to marriage, female agency, and sexuality, I organize a class debate about whether the Disney film is a feminist or sexist rendition of the monster bridegroom tale. I put students into four randomly assigned groups and then designate two groups to argue that the Disney film is feminist, and two groups to argue that it is sexist. Each group generates a list of potential arguments and each student in the group is responsible for presenting two or three arguments for or against a feminist reading of the film.

---

10. One could certainly, however, carry out a queer reading of monster bridegroom tales, no matter how conservative they might appear, thus undermining the arguably fragile heteronormativity of such tale types.

I then ask one person in one group to begin, and we move back and forth from the "feminist" groups to the "sexist" groups. The first time I taught the course, students enjoyed the debate so much that they asked if we could do debates in the other units of the course. However, I found that the debate worked best in the "Beauty and the Beast" unit in part because the Disney film is so amenable to both feminist and sexist readings. Because the debate asks students to draw on all their knowledge about "Beauty and the Beast" tales, it prepares them for the paper they write comparing different textual and filmic versions of the tale. (See Appendix E for guidelines for the "Beauty and the Beast" paper.)

In every unit of the course, I try to provide students with the critical support to situate each iteration of a tale within a specific historical, social, and cultural context. In the case of monster bridegroom tales, students come to appreciate the ways in which Roman North Africa, Renaissance Italy, courtly France, and twentieth-century America inflect the tales in different ways, and at the same time they gain a sense of the historical evolution of a tale. Fairy tales are not simply universal innocent tales written expressly for children, and like any other literary form or cultural artifact, they have histories and communicate ideologies, in this case, about marriage practices (as they relate to class and gender) and the agency of women. At the same time, as exemplified here, students learn that sometimes tales are more complicated than they seem. Not all monster bridegroom/"Beauty and the Beast" tales objectify or subjugate female characters in any absolute way, and not all male writers of such tales prove to be more problematic than female ones. One could argue that both Apuleius and Straparola give their heroines more agency and problematize their fate more than Villeneuve or Leprince de Beaumont. Both Carter and Cocteau also point to the queer possibilities of monster bridegroom tales in their rejection of heteronormativity and embrace of alternative sexualities. In class discussions and through the debate and the culminating paper, students learn to work with the tensions present in the texts between agency and objectification, between queer desires and heteronormativity, tensions that cannot be contained by the closure of an apparently happy ending.

APPENDIX A

Lucius Apuleius (c. 124–170), a Berber from Algeria; see "Apuleius" by John Stephens, in Duggan and Haase, eds., ***Folktales and Fairy Tales: Traditions and Texts from Around the World***, 57.

- A rhetorician, satirist, and author of the only Roman novel to have been preserved in complete form.
- Principal work: *The Golden Ass*, also known as *Metamorphoses*.
- The frame narrative relates the story of Lucius of Corinth, who is transformed into an ass and experiences many adventures before being restored to human form after the intervention of the goddess Isis.
- The underlying cause of Lucius's transformation, and one of the central themes of the whole work, is *curiositas* (meddlesome curiosity).
- Curious about magic, Lucius is taken by his lover, Fotis, to spy on her mistress in the act of transforming herself into an owl; Lucius asks his lover to bring him the magic ointment; he transforms into an ass, and before he can eat roses and transform back, he is taken by thieves; his restoration is constantly deferred.
- His original form is restored after he subordinates his appetites and desires to the principles of rationality and order.
- Lucius overhears the story of "Cupid and Psyche," which is commonly interpreted as an analogy for Lucius's own trials and eventual redemption.

Apuleius, "Cupid and Psyche"
- Think of the structure of the story. Arguably, it has three main "episodes." What are the three main parts of the story? Provide a title and a summary for each subsection.
- What are the central themes of the story? How do these themes relate to women?
- Organize the story in terms of Greimas's schema. Fill in each function with a character; more than one character can occupy the same function, and the same character might occupy different functions, depending on the perspective one takes to the tale.

Sender		Receiver
	Subject	
	Object	
Helper		Opponent

Straparola, "The Pig King"
- Explain the ways in which "The Pig King" is similar to "Cupid and Psyche."
- Explain the ways in which Straparola's tale differs from that of Apuleius.
- What might explain these differences, and what might these differences mean? Do they modify the meaning of the tale?

APPENDIX B

Model 1: Cupid as Agent, Psyche as Object		
Sender Apollo (oracle) Parents (send Psyche to "winged pest")		**Receiver** Cupid
	Subject: Cupid	
	Object: Psyche	
Helper Zephyr		**Opponent** Two sisters

Model 2: Psyche as Agent, Cupid as Object		
Sender Pan (sends Psyche to regain Cupid)		**Receiver** Psyche
	Subject: Psyche	
	Object: Cupid	
Helper Ants Reed Eagle Tower		**Opponent** Venus

APPENDIX C
Ways of Understanding "Cupid and Psyche"

Psychological Reading
- Fears about marriage and sexuality
- Sibling rivalry
- Question of relations between daughter-in-law and mother-in-law

Jungian Reading (Eric Neumann)
- Transition maiden-flower to fruit-mother
- Death as symbolic for initiation into womanhood
- Sisters' marriages as symbol of patriarchal slavery
- Sisters represent projections of the suppressed or unconscious matriarchal tendencies in Psyche; they represent the resistance of feminine nature
- "Venus is the archetypal Great Mother; Psyche must differentiate her consciousness and take responsibility for her own actions. Psyche's true act of heroism is to disobey Cupid and look at him by the lamplight" (*Encyclopedia of Psychology and Religion*, 193).

Sociohistorical Reading (Josiah Osgood)
- Readers were Roman citizens like Apuleius who knew Latin.
- The story refers to real legal marriage practices and Roman institutions.
- Reference to Venus's chariot: The chariot was often "the present that Roman grooms sometimes gave their brides—generally before their wedding" (418).
- When Psyche informs her sisters that Cupid divorced her, she uses "a legally binding formula for divorce that went back well into the Roman republic" (422). "Divorce was not a formal ceremony . . . and need not involve written documents. Rather, when one party no longer felt good will toward the other, he or she could notify the spouse (by a messenger, for instance), reclaim his or her property, and then be considered divorced"; "valid marriage to someone else confirmed divorce from a former partner" (423).
- Venus claims that Psyche is her runaway slave. According to Roman law, people could not conceal a runaway slave. The humor: that gods and goddesses respected Roman law.
- Under Roman law, a citizen could not legally marry a slave. Venus's complaint about Psyche's status is very "Roman sounding" (427).

APPENDIX D

Cocteau Criticism

Irene Eynat-Confino (*On the Uses of the Fantastic in Modern Theatre: Cocteau, Oedipus, and the Monster*, 2008).

- "As Cocteau's works repeatedly show, by using the monster as a trope or a concrete supernatural being . . . he was giving voice to an ordeal that he shared with the many whose sexuality was nonnormative and condemned as such by society" (93).
- In the homophobic atmosphere of the 1920s "the identification of the homosexual with the monster had become a staple of popular imagination" (95). Homosexuality was considered a "monstrous" vice and contrary to nature.
- "The assignment of homosexuality to the domain of monstrosity and bestiality has been part of the church tradition in the West" (97).

Daniel Fischlin ("Queer Margins: Cocteau, *La Belle et la bête*, and the Jewish Differend," 1998)

- "The Beast, depending upon the gaze constructing his or her presence, is thus an ambiguous sexual construct, a queer, especially in a reading that incorporates Cocteau's directorial eye into the context of the gaze constructing the beast as an object of desire. From that perspective the film's camerawork becomes a sensuous point of contact between Cocteau and his lover, a way of constructing their queer relationship in a visual code driven by the passion of the lover's gaze. At that level of signification the Beast becomes the very signifier of queer presence in the film, despite the (not quite) conventional heterosexuality figured in the dénouement with which Cocteau was notoriously unhappy" (80).

Caroline Sheaffer-Jones ("Fixing the Gaze: Jean Cocteau's *La Belle et la bête*," 2002)

- At the end of film, Belle sees herself as the monster: "It's me . . . it's me the monster [*le monstre*], my Beast [*ma Bête*]" (366). The notion that the gender of characters is ambiguous: *The Beast* is feminine in French, whereas *monster* is masculine.

Susan Hayward ("La Belle et la bête," 1996)

- "The trick was to pull Beauty, played by Josette Day, along on a trolley, thus giving the illusion that she was floating into her unconscious" (45).

- "It is indeed a film made by a man who never denied his homosexuality and who had an openness that braved the morality of the times." Hayward argues that *Beauty and the Beast* "is a film about homoerotic love" (47).

- "But it is also about attempting to discover a different, non-phallic perception of human relationships. Why, otherwise, is Belle so terribly disappointed at the end of the film when the Beast—*la* Bête, whom she now realises she loves, transforms into Prince Charming?" (47).

- Hayward argues that Belle "wants more from life than a marriage of reason—which is the underlying message from Mme Leprince de Beaumont's eighteenth-century fairy tale—she wants to be 'frightened' ('*J'aime avoir peur*,' she declares)" (47). (Cocteau himself believed that one must fear something every day in order to create the world anew.)

- "The psychology of the unconscious, sexual awakening and the female agencing of desire were images not seen on-screen since the avant-garde cinema of the 1920s. The advocacy of a female subjectivity (the story is told from Belle's point of view) and the notion of equality, so present in this film, ran very contrary to the prevailing message of films dealing with sexual relations in the late-1940s and early-1950s. . . . In France, as in America, the purpose was to get women back into the domestic sphere" (47).

Appendix E
Guidelines for "Beauty and the Beast" Paper

Getting Ready for Paper #2

In all papers, think of using useful terminology such as "tale type," "motif," "function" (of a character, for instance), "structure" (of a tale or film). Also, where possible, think of how to incorporate the sociohistorical background, drawing from Zipes, Bottigheimer, and Shavit.

To include secondary references, think of incorporating them as follows: "According to Jack Zipes . . ."; "For Cristina Bacchilega, the tale means . . ."; "June Cummins argues . . ."; "As Irène Eynat-Confino demonstrates . . ."

Possible Topics

- **Compare Apuleius's "Cupid and Psyche" to another text and one of the films.** Which elements and messages of "Cupid and Psyche" are present in later versions? How do later versions differ from this story?
- **Examine the representation of women and gender.** How is Beauty constructed in the different versions of "Beauty and the Beast"? Is she more passive or active; what is her relation to the male figure in different versions?
- **What does "Beauty and the Beast" say about sexuality?** In all versions of the tale, the (hetero/queer) sexual aspect of the tale plays out in different ways, from "Cupid and Psyche" to "The Pig King" and Cocteau's and Disney's *Beauty and the Beast*. How is sexuality represented? How explicit is the text? What is the importance of the target audience of the tale when taking into account the role of sexuality?
- **How is the pedagogical message of the story foregrounded?** Especially looking at Villeneuve, Leprince de Beaumont, and Disney, what are the pedagogical messages in these different versions? To whom is the message addressed: Beauty, Beast, sisters? Does the sociohistorical context in which the story was produced have something to do with the type of message that is put forward?

N.B.: Students are assessed on organization and analysis.

Bibliography

Apulieus. "Cupid and Psyche." In *Spells of Enchantment: The Wondrous Fairy Tales of Western Culture.* Ed. Jack Zipes. New York: Viking, 1991. 1–27.

Beauty and the Beast. Dir. Gary Trousdale and Kirk Wise. Walt Disney Studios. USA. 1991.

La Belle et la bête. Dir. Jean Cocteau. France. 1946.

Bottigheimer, Ruth. "Straparola's *Piacevoli Notti*: Rags-to-Riches Fairy Tales as Urban Creations." *Merveilles et Contes* 8.2 (1994): 281–96.

Carter, Angela. "The Tiger's Bride." In *The Classic Fairy Tales*. Ed. Maria Tatar. New York: Norton, 1999. 50–66.

Cummins, June. "Romancing the Plot: The Real Beast of Disney's *Beauty and the Beast*." *Children's Literature Association Quarterly* 20.1 (1995): 22–28.

Duggan, Anne E. *Queer Enchantments: Gender, Sexuality, and Class in the Fairy-Tale Cinema of Jacques Demy*. Detroit: Wayne State University Press, 2013.

Duggan, Anne E., and Donald Haase, eds., with Helen J. Callow. *Folktales and Fairy Tales: Traditions and Texts from Around the World*, 4 vols. Santa Barbara, CA: Greenwood/ABC-CLIO, 2016.

Eynat-Confino, Irène. *On the Uses of the Fantastic in Modern Theatre: Cocteau, Oedipus, and the Monster*. New York: Palgrave, 2008.

Fischlin, Daniel. "Queer Margins: Cocteau, *La Belle et la bête* and the Jewish Differend." *Textual Practice* 12.1 (1998): 69–88.

Gibson, Wendy. *Women in Seventeenth-Century France*. New York: Palgrave Macmillan, 1989.

Greimas, Algirdas. *Structural Semantics: An Attempt at a Method*. Lincoln: University of Nebraska Press, 1983.

Haase, Donald, ed. *The Greenwood Encyclopedia of Folktales and Fairy Tales*, 3 vols. Westport, CT: Greenwood Press, 2008.

Hayward, Susan. "La Belle et la bête." *History Today* 46.7 (1996): 43–48.

Irigaray, Luce. "Women on the Market." In *This Sex Which Is Not One*. By Luce Irigaray. Trans. Catherine Porter. Ithaca, NY: Cornell University Press, 1985. 170–91.

Leprince de Beaumont, Jeanne-Marie. "Beauty and the Beast." In *The Classic Fairy Tales*. Ed. Maria Tatar. New York: Norton, 1999. 32–42.

Neumann, Eric. *Amor and Psyche*. 1956. London: Routledge, 1999.

Osgood, Josiah. "Nuptiae Iure Civili Congruae: Apuleius's Story of Cupid and Psyche and the Roman Law of Marriage." *Transactions of the American Philological Association* 136.2 (2006): 415–41.

Sheaffer-Jones, Caroline. "Fixing the Gaze: Jean Cocteau's *La Belle et la bête*." *Romanic Review* 93.3 (May 2002): 361–74.

Swain, Virginia. "Beauty's Chambers: Mixed Styles and Mixed Messages in Villeneuve's 'Beauty and the Beast.'" *Marvels & Tales* 19.2 (2005): 197–23.

Tatar, Maria, ed. *The Classic Fairy Tales*. New York: Norton, 1999.

Villeneuve, Gabrielle-Suzanne Barbot de. "The Story of Beauty and the Beast." In *Beauties, Beasts, and Enchantment: Classic French Fairy Tales*. Ed. Jack Zipes. New York: New American Library, 1989. 153–229.

Zipes, Jack. "Once There Were Two Brothers Named Grimm." In *When Dreams Came True: Classical Fairy Tales and Their Tradition*. By Jack Zipes. New York: Routledge, 1999. 61–79.

———, ed. *The Oxford Companion to Fairy Tales*. Oxford: Oxford University Press, 2000.

———. "The Rise of the French Fairy Tale and the Decline of France." In *When Dreams Came True: Classical Fairy Tales and Their Tradition*. By Jack Zipes. New York: Routledge, 1999. 33–52.

Morals and Miracles

The Case of ATU 555, "The Fisherman and His Wife"

Victoria Somoff

Scholars of folklore have long opposed the persistent attempts of readers and educators to view fairy tales as conveying moral lessons. In her study of the *Nursery and Household Tales* by the Brothers Grimm, Maria Tatar asserts that didactic and edifying messages are alien to the poetics of the folkloric fairy tale and are not found in oral sources but rather have been injected into folk narratives ex post facto, during their transcription and adaptation for literate audiences. Charting the stages in the editorial history of that celebrated collection, Tatar shows convincingly how the Grimms, "ever responsive to the values of their time and increasingly sensitive to pedagogical demands, transformed adult folk material into a hybrid form of folklore and literature for children" (Tatar, *Hard Facts*, xxii). It is not surprising, then, that college students whose experience of fairy tales comes precisely from children's anthologies (as well as and at times primarily from Disney film adaptations) firmly associate fairy tales with morality. The question I pose to students on the first day of my course on Russian fairy tales—How would you define this genre?— invariably produces such answers as "Fairy tales teach moral lessons" and "In fairy tales, virtue is rewarded and vice is punished." In my experience, challenging this assumption in the classroom requires a sustained effort; and even when this preconceived notion is overturned with regard to a particular fairy tale, students' expectations of a morally gratifying story instantly resurface as soon as a different tale is presented for their interpretation. In this essay I offer a step-by-step account of one pedagogical attempt to "subtract" morality from fairy tales, using as my material four variants (German, Japanese, and two Russian) of ATU tale type 555, "The Fisherman and His Wife," which is described by Uther thus:

> A poor old fisherman rescues a supernatural being (magic fish, other animal, divine being, saint, ogre, man in form of animal) from distress (danger of death, imprisonment, transformation). Or the fisherman puts the fish back into the water. In return the magic being grants him (and his wife) that all his wishes will be fulfilled. In the beginning they profit only moderately, but later the wife becomes excessively demanding (e.g., they wish to become noblemen, kings, and finally even God himself). The fish (spirit) takes back his gift and the couple is returned to their former poor condition or punished in addition (transformed to animals). (Uther, 325)

The seemingly transparent didacticism of these narratives makes them particularly advantageous for testing the fairy tale's resistance to a moral reading. The ethical dimension of the ATU 555 tales seems too glaring to disregard; even Tatar, despite her insistence that fairy tales are fundamentally amoral, sees the eponymous German version of ATU 555 as essentially instructional: "'The Fisherman and His Wife' lacks the fairy-tale magic usually associated with the Grimms' tales. Instead, the tale offers a cautionary lesson about the importance of remaining satisfied with your station in life" (Tatar, *Annotated Brothers Grimm*, 93). In our classroom discussion of ATU 555, students are first asked to describe, in analytical detail, the peculiarities of these narratives in relation to other fairy tales they have encountered. At the same time, in the course of our examination of the tales, students conclude that fairy-tale magic is not missing from "The Fisherman and His Wife"; rather, these narratives reveal the *limits* of the miraculous and the internal limits of the fairy tale as a genre. Accordingly, the "unhappy ending" of the ATU 555 tales, atypical for fairy tales, is determined not by the characters' ethical deficiencies but by a rupture in the fairy tale's narrative logic.

Our analysis of the ATU 555 fairy tales begins with a homework assignment. The reading list includes four tales from three cultural traditions: "The Fisherman and His Wife" (German), "The Goldfish" (Russian), "The Greedy Old Woman" (Russian), and "The Stonecutter" (Japanese).[1] By this time in the course, the

---

1. Because the course is taught in English, all texts are given in English translation. Translations from Russian have been adjusted.

students have already mastered the concept of the tale type and studied the volume of Uther's *Types of International Folktales* devoted to "Tales of Magic" (Folklore Fellow Communications, no. 284); they have also read significant portions of Vladimir Propp's *Morphology of the Folktale* and worked extensively with Propp's concepts of "function," "sequence of functions," and "dramatis personae" (Propp, 79). The writing assignment, due on the day of the class for which students have read the four tales, consists of two questions and draws on this previously acquired knowledge. First, students are asked to undertake a comparative analysis of the four tales: What similarities among them account for their attribution to the same tale type? On the other hand, what differences between the four variants of ATU 555 can be observed? The second question has to do with Propp's morphological model, namely, do the ATU 555 tales conform to it? Which of Propp's functions and dramatis personae can be identified in these narratives? Alternatively, do these tales deviate from the fairy tale's structural principles as established by Propp; and if so, specifically how?

Classroom discussion begins with the students' responses to these two questions. I remind the students that variation is a fundamental feature of oral tradition, and I ask them to share their observations of the four tales' similarities and differences—an exercise that tangibly demonstrates that folk narratives exist in multiformity. Among the tales' major similarities noted by the students are the characters' dissatisfaction with their circumstances, the development of the plot as a series of wish fulfillments accomplished with the help of a magical agent, and the characters' ultimate return to their initial state. Before we go around the room listing the differences among the tales, I ask the students to add their classmates' observations to their own in order to compile a comprehensive list, on which we will then rely in the process of interpretation. I point out that such a procedure is crucial to the interpretation of a folk narrative, which, unlike a literary work, has no definitive form but exists in the totality of the variants of a nonextant original source. Students usually notice and comment on the following main differences among the four tales:

1. The tales feature different "donors," or wish-granters: a fish in "The Fisherman and His Wife" and "The Goldfish" (a flounder and a goldfish, respectively); a tree in "The Greedy Old Woman"; and a mountain spirit in "The Stonecutter."

2. "The Stonecutter" features no "nagging wife" or any marital discord; instead, the main character, clearly a bachelor, only thinks to himself, or rather dreams, of improving his lot, with the mountain spirit immediately fulfilling

his silent wish: "He said to himself: 'Oh, if only I were a rich man, and could sleep in a bed with silken curtains and golden tassels, how happy I should be!' And a voice answered him: 'Your wish is heard; a rich man you shall be!'" (Lang, 192).

3. The German and Russian tales feature an explicit social hierarchy: Their characters ascend a societal ladder and then crash all the way back down. In the German tale the wife wishes to become king, then emperor, then pope; in "The Goldfish" the social stations are governor and queen; and in "The Greedy Old Woman" the old man and his wife advance from poor peasants to rich farmers, overseers, nobility, military, and, finally, to royalty (tsar and tsarina). The hero of "The Stonecutter," on the other hand, having become a rich man and then a prince upon the fulfillment of his first two wishes, undergoes a series of nonhierarchical transformations into objects and phenomena of the natural world, turning into the sun, then a cloud, and then a rock.

4. At the end of "The Greedy Old Woman" the characters convert into animals: "When [the tree] heard these stupid words, it rustled its leaves and spoke to the old man: 'You be a bear and your wife a sow bear!' The old man at that very moment turned into a bear and the old woman into a sow bear, and they ran off into the forest" (Afanas'ev, *Complete Folktales*, 120).

5. Whereas at the end of "The Fisherman and His Wife" and "The Goldfish" the characters are reduced once more to poverty and misery, in "The Stonecutter" the hero returns to his initial state voluntarily and is completely satisfied with it: "His bed was hard and his food scanty, but he had learned to be satisfied with it, and did not long to be something or somebody else. And as he never asked for things he did not have, or desired to be greater and mightier than other people, he was happy at last, and never again heard the voice of the mountain spirit" (Lang, 197).

Next, we consider Propp's morphological model and conclude that the AT 555 narratives should be classified as "lack" (rather than "villainy") tales, in which the plot develops as a sequence of multiple lacks and their "liquidations." The German and Russian tales also feature Propp's first donor function (i.e., the hero is tested by a wish-granter) and the receipt of a magical agent. We establish that the tales' most pronounced divergence from Propp's model—and from all the fairy tales we have studied in the course so far—has to do with their finale, in which the characters return to their initial state of lack. In Proppian terms the tales' "unhappy ending" is described as a "lack not liquidated." The students usually comment that in the

Japanese tale the ending is not really unhappy, because the stonecutter is fully sat-isfied with being returned to his original stonecutting self. However, this ending is achieved without the elevation in status requisite for lack tales; rather, the hero recognizes his original status as in fact lacking nothing.

The question regarding the distinctive trajectory of character and plot devel-opment in the AT 555 tale type can thus be formulated more specifically: Lack is typically liquidated in lack fairy tales; why, in these narratives, is it not? To answer this question, students invariably resort to the ethical dimension, formulating moral lessons that, in their view, can be drawn from the characters' failure to rise in for-tunes. Namely, the students deem the characters' return to their initial situation as the deserved consequence of their ethically flawed behavior; representative answers include "They did not value what they had," "This is punishment for ambition," and "They failed to ever be satisfied." As these and similar verdicts quickly accrue, I point out that despite their thematic cohesiveness, they fall into two different groups: One set of answers is organized around the dictum of "be content with what you have" and therefore commends total abstinence from desire, whereas the other implies a warning against only *excessive* wish making, advising moderation and restraint of desire rather than complete renunciation. We agree that these two rules of conduct are sufficiently distinct and decide to consider them in turn.

We begin with the apparently unproblematic and most commonly drawn pre-scription from the ATU 555 tales, that of being content with what you have. I ask students to find the exact descriptions of the characters' initial lack in the German tale "The Fisherman and His Wife" and the Russian tale "The Goldfish." In the former the husband and wife reside in what the original manuscript received by the Grimms called a *Pissputt*, or "piss pot"—a designation that sent the tale's sub-sequent editors and translators on a quest for substitutions that would not offend their readers' sensibilities (Tatar, *Annotated Brothers Grimm*, 94). The Russian tale says that the old man and his wife "lived in dire poverty"; indeed, the wife's first request to the magic goldfish is for bread ("Soon, we won't even have a dry crust; what will you eat then?"), and the second is for a new washtub ("Our washtub broke, I have nothing to do my washing in") (Afanas'ev, *Complete Folktales*, 116). Accordingly, when we draw the "be content with what you have" moral from these tales, we are suggesting that the characters have been punished for their attempt to escape a state of hunger and wretchedness and that they should have been "content" with their sheer deprivation—a conclusion that puts the moralizer in an ethically dubious position (and, as students often elaborate, confines "morality" to epoch-specific propagandizing on behalf of the powerful against any aspirations of the poor).

I suggest interrogating this conclusion further and ask the students why, in their view, the characters' punishment at the end of the Russian tale "The Greedy Old Woman" is configured as a transformation into animals: "The old man at that very moment turned into a bear and the old woman into a sow bear, and they ran off into the forest." In the course of discussion—which typically ranges from the socioethical to the philosophically speculative—the students suggest that the characters are thus exempt from the exigencies of desire once and for all: As animals, unlike humans, they now have no wishes, only instinctual needs. In "The Greedy Old Woman" dissatisfaction with one's parameters of existence emerges as a species-differentiating factor: Animals adapt to their pregiven circumstances (environments), whereas humans strive to exceed them. Accordingly, the "be content with what you have" dictum becomes problematic not only on an ethical level but also on an ontological level, because complete adherence to this dictum can be accomplished only by simultaneously abdicating one's humanity. Seeking further evidence for this thesis, the students often reflect on their earlier observation that "The Stonecutter" lacks a nagging wife persona to play the villain or culprit in the rise of desire; instead, the Japanese tale presents the wish-making process as intrinsic to the human condition, rendering the "be content with what you have" rule of conduct highly problematic.

During such discussions, students often recall another observation made in the course of our comparative analysis. In the Japanese tale, as distinct from the German and Russian ones, the hero ends up being fully content with what he had to begin with, namely, the advantages and the limitations of being a stonecutter: "His bed was hard and his food scanty, but he had learned to be satisfied with it, and did not long to be something or somebody else." According to some students, this suggests that the "be content with what you have" lesson can be drawn from at least this particular version of ATU 555. At this point, I note a complication: How, I ask, did the stonecutter arrive at the state of acceptance of, if not satisfaction with, the conditions that at the tale's beginning he very much wanted to escape? In the course of discussion the students agree that it was only by undergoing a series of diverse and radical transformations—from stonecutter to rich man to prince to sun, cloud, and rock—that the hero was able to recognize his initial state as being "just right." His ultimate liberation from the anguish of wish-making thus results solely from his persistent aspiration to become "something or somebody else"; if he had not ardently engaged in wish-making, he would never have achieved the equanimity that is his final reward. Accordingly, the "be content with what you have" lesson that prescribes renunciation of desire is inadequate to address the character and plot development in "The Stonecutter."

We can then turn to the other, apparently less radical rule of conduct, the one that does not censure desire and ambition altogether but cautions against greed, or *excessive* yearning for material gain and social promotion. Students read the previously mentioned description of ATU 555 from *The Types of International Folktales* that I bring to class, and we observe that the description of the tale type has this lesson already built in: "In the beginning, [the characters] profit only moderately, but later the wife becomes excessively demanding. . . . The fish (spirit) takes back his gift and the couple is returned to their former poor condition or punished in addition (transformed to animals)" (Uther, 325).[2] I ask students whether this compromise formulation suggested by the description of the ATU 555 tale type—in effect, you can wish, but don't get greedy—works for its four variants under discussion. By this point in the conversation, students are usually less willing to let moralizing go unchallenged. They pause to reflect on the uneasiness of determining exactly how much—of either property or societal standing—one "should" ask for. In terms of desire, bound ever to intensify, where does one draw the line between "just enough" and "too much"? In "The Greedy Old Woman," for instance, the wife demands to be made a noblewoman, then a colonel's wife, then a general's wife, and finally the tsar's wife. Assuming that there is a vacancy in the monarchy (in one of the Russian tales, the existing king conveniently dies), is there a nonarbitrary principle according to which we can classify one of these desires as still reasonable and another as excessive?

I bring up another consideration: In lack tales, to which the tales of ATU 555 belong, the functions of lack and corresponding liquidation often snowball: double, treble, or further multiply. In these tales it is common, once the first lacking object is successfully (re)gained, for a new lack to instantly arise. For example, in the Russian tale "Prince Ivan, the Firebird, and the Gray Wolf," which the class has read previously, the hero searches first for the firebird, then for a golden-maned horse, and then for Princess Elena the Fair. Assisted by a "donor," the Gray Wolf, Prince Ivan succeeds in liquidating all these lacks, marries Elena the Fair, and, to top it off, inherits a kingdom (Afanas'ev, *Complete Folktales*, 612–24). In general, the hero in lack tales desires, pursues, and triumphantly obtains all manner of riches, exotic objects, beautiful maidens, and superior social standing, if not rulership; according to Propp, the fairy-tale narrative "reaches its peak" in the function of liquidation (Propp, 53). In this light, the "moral" that one ought to temper one's wants and

2. It is worth noting that the Russian "Greedy Old Woman" contains an ethical gloss right in its title. Earlier in the course, we had discussed type 480, "The Tale of the Kind and the Unkind Girls," where ethical judgment is incorporated, similarly, in the title of the tale type itself; here, too, we had concluded that the opposition between the two "girls" in such narratives cannot be accounted for in ethical terms.

ambitions (even if doing so seems endorsed by the description of the ATU 555 tale type) emerges as incompatible with the poetics of the lack fairy tale as a genre.

The cause of the ATU 555 characters' ultimate downfall cannot consist in the escalation of their desires because, generically speaking, such escalation constitutes the trigger and driving force of the events they experience. Where, then, should we look for this cause? Students notice that in the German and Russian tales, where the characters' return to their initial state of lack is involuntary, events keep unfolding in full agreement with the plot development of lack tales—that is, with the donor fulfilling the characters' wishes, be they for comfort, wealth, or power—right up until the wife's final wish. Thus we might suppose that the characters' downfall has to do not with the emergence of desire or its escalation but rather with this last wish itself. I ask the students to find the formulations of the wife's final wish in the German and Russian tales: "If I can't make the sun and the moon rise, I won't be able to bear it. . . . I want to be like God" (Grimms, 72); "If God wishes, he can send death unto you, and you are put into the damp earth. Go to the tree and ask that it make us gods" ("The Greedy Old Woman"; Afanas'ev, *Complete Folktales*, 120); and "I want to be the ruler of the sea, so that all the seas and all the fishes will obey me" ("The Goldfish"; Afanas'ev, *Complete Folktales*, 118). I ask students why, in their view, the donors refuse to liquidate this particular lack.

Students observe that the wife's final wish is qualitatively different from all her previous ones. She asks not for the satisfaction of her natural (biological) needs or for a still higher place on the social pyramid but for omnipotence and immortality—qualities that would place her outside both natural and human hierarchies altogether. All the wife's previous wishes had been immediately granted, because, however intemperate they may have seemed, they had remained within the parameters of the human world. The Russian tale "The Goldfish" configures these parameters most concretely; in this tale, the wife's final wish is to become "ruler of the sea" and "to command all fishes," that is, to be in charge of the goldfish itself. In Proppian terms the wife here strives to transgress the boundary between the two dramatis personae of the fairy tale: hero and donor. It is at this point that the typical development of the fairy-tale plot, in which liquidation inevitably follows lack, comes to a screeching and irrevocable halt.

The wife's transgression, therefore, is best interpreted not in ethical but rather in structural ("morphological") terms. The fairy-tale event of the miracle presupposes two participants, the recipient and the agent of magic, or hero and donor. In the German and Russian tales the wife attempts to annul this boundary, which leads to a morphological collapse of the fairy-tale narrative. In "The Goldfish" this moment is marked by the breakdown in communication between human and magical worlds. In response to the wife's final wish as conveyed by the old man, "the goldfish did not say anything . . . but turned around and went down to the depth of the sea" (Afanas'ev, *Complete Folktales*, 118).

From this perspective the pronounced incongruity between husband and wife, which is an important aspect of the German and Russian tales, consists not in the ethical dimensions of their worldviews—the wife's unbridled craving for wealth and power versus the husband's placid contentment with the status quo—but rather in their attitudes toward the miraculous. Upon his first encounter with the magic fish, the old man asks for nothing, recognizing the boundary between the human and magical worlds as absolute: "I would have thrown a talking fish back into the water anyway" (Grimms, 65); "I do not need anything from you; go back to the sea" ("The Goldfish"; Afanas'ev, *Complete Folktales*, 116). The wife, on the other hand, attempts to overstep this same boundary and gain control over the magical world in her final wish. These disparate spouses can be seen as two extremes in relation to the typical fairy-tale hero, who readily accepts magical help, uses it freely to pursue the objects of his/her desires, spectacularly rises in wealth and status, and yet always remains on the receiving end of the miraculous.

At the end of the class, I sum up the results of our analysis. Having tested the two moral lessons commonly drawn from the ATU 555 tales, we see that neither can adequately account for the plot and character development in the four versions of the tale type that we examined. We conclude that the fairy-tale magic temporarily enjoyed by these characters is not repossessed because of their greed or refusal to be content; on the contrary, unless desire emerges and intensifies, there is no lack tale plot. Instead, we envision the characters' return to their initial state of lack not as punishment for their ethical flaws but rather as the result of a breakdown in the conditions under which the miraculous works. In this light, the tales of ATU 555, which stretch the fairy tale's generic boundaries to an extreme, emerge as meta–fairy tales: examples of the genre that lay bare some of the major principles of its poetics.

Bibliography

Afanas'ev, Alexander N. *The Complete Folktales of A. N. Afanas'ev*, v. 1. Ed. Jack V. Haney. Jackson: University Press of Mississippi, 2014.

———. *Narodnye russkie skazki A. N. Afanas'eva.* Moscow: Nauka, 1984.

———. *Russian Fairy Tales.* Trans. Norbert Guterman. New York: Pantheon, 1973.

Grimm, Jacob, and Wilhelm Grimm. *The Complete Fairy Tales of the Brothers Grimm.* Trans. Jack Zipes. New York: Bantam, 2003.

Lang, Andrew, ed. *The Crimson Fairy Book.* London: Longmans, Green, 1903.

Propp, Vladimir. *Morphology of the Folktale.* Trans. Laurence Scott. Ed. Louis Wagner. Austin: University of Texas Press, 1968.

Tatar, Maria, ed. *The Annotated Brothers Grimm: The Bicentennial Edition.* New York: Norton, 2014.

———. *The Hard Facts of the Grimms' Fairy Tales.* Princeton, NJ: Princeton University Press, 2003.

Uther, Hans-Jörg. *The Types of International Folktales: A Classification and Bibliography—Based on the System of Antti Aarne and Stith Thompson*, pt. 1. Helsinki: Academia Scientiarum Fennica, 2004.

Italo Calvino's "The Parrot"

Teaching Frame and Embedded Narratives

Gina M. Miele

In Italian literature and culture courses, I teach folktales and fairy tales to demonstrate how they can illuminate post-unification and postwar Italian culture and reflect the sociohistorical, economic, and political currents of an emerging nation. As my students begin to understand these fundamental periods of Italian history from the perspective of the people rather than from historians, they form a more representative picture of the Italian nation and culture. By reading Luigi Capuana's literary fairy tales written just after the unification of Italy or Italo Calvino's fairy-tale anthology published in the decade following World War II, students envision how fabulists seek to foster a sense of community during times of political and cultural rebuilding, both between narrator and audience and in society at large. Given our current political climate, my students readily supply modern examples of how storytelling (in film, television, novel, short story, blog, vlog, and video games) functions as a mouthpiece for national sentiment during uncertain times, often citing, for example, sketches from the most recent installment of *Saturday Night Live*.

In an effort to speak to all Italians, native Sicilian Capuana wrote his fairy tales in the new national language of a Tuscanized Italian, whereas Italo Calvino transcribed folktales from their original dialects to the national language. In my classroom, opportunities naturally arise to evaluate how framing a new nation requires a bit of storytelling, as politicians shape their blueprint of the ideal society, embedding within it anecdotes that help citizens work out fears and concerns and encouraging them to believe that the vision can become reality. Likewise, with its extensive network of characters and settings, the model of frame or embedded narratives can simulate a multilayered social reality that allows for narrative exchange among the figures that represent various segments of the populace and ruling class, while also giving the storyteller the power to intervene in reality or manipulate, instruct, and even indoctrinate young readers.

As my students delve into the Italian tales, we simultaneously interrogate how the evolution of the genre in Italy fits into the long tradition of oral and literary European fairy tales, allowing students to place the Italian tales within the context of fairy tales they may recall from childhood, including those of Hans Christian Andersen, Charles Perrault, and the Brothers Grimm. When I first introduce frame narratives and interpolated tales from the Italian tradition, students are quick to provide modern American examples from television, including the popular series *Grimm* and *Once Upon a Time*, the first episode of which is an effective introduction to embedded narratives. After we view the inaugural episode of *Once Upon a Time*, I ask my students to reflect on the interplay between the frame narrative about Emma and Henry, her son who lives in Storybrooke, Maine, with his adoptive mother, Regina, and the myriad tales that occur in Fairy Tale Land. By the end of the episode, Fairy Tale Land breaks into the narrative landscape of Storybrooke when we discover that Regina is in fact the Evil Queen, Rumpelstiltskin is masquerading as Mr. Gold, and Snow White and Prince Charming have turned up as Mary Margaret and a John Doe comatose patient.

Over the years, my students have enthusiastically extended their research on frames to bookmaking and filmmaking projects that showcase embedded tales they have co-written with peers. One student, majoring in science with a minor in Italian, noted the many times that interpolated narratives power science fiction and hosted a viewing of her favorite episode of *Star Trek: The Next Generation* titled "The Inner Light." In this enchanting episode, Captain Jean-Luc Picard is struck unconscious by an alien probe and lives an entire lifetime as a man named Kamin on a dying planet, all within mere minutes in "real time" on the *Enterprise*. Another student, a math major, discovered and shared parallels between frame narratives and algebraic equations, and two students studying music and dance teamed up to perform Calvino's "The Parrot," accompanied by an original score and interpretive dance.

Although I use Capuana's five fairy-tale collections in my courses, the work I most frequently choose when introducing my students to Italian folk- and fairy tales is Italo Calvino's *Fiabe italiane* (Italian Folktales). A definitive national or master collection of Italian folktales did not exist until 1956, when Calvino published *Fiabe italiane*, a compilation of 200 tales, selected primarily from nineteenth-century tale collections. Shortly after completing the anthology, Calvino wrote in the introduction, "Now my journey through folklore is over, the book is done. As I write this preface, I feel aloof, detached. Will it be possible to come down to earth again?" (Calvino, *Italian Folktales*, xviii). The author's metaphorical journey through "woodlands and enchanted castles" lasted approximately two years, its incipit dating to January 15, 1954, when the folklorist Giuseppe Cocchiara proposed that Calvino write a collection for the Einaudi publishing house of the most beautiful tales of the Italian people (Calvino, *Italian Folktales*, xviii; Lavagetto, xi). Calvino, who had once questioned whether an Italian equivalent of the Brothers Grimm even existed, was soon to embody the very role himself (xv). Representing the twenty regions of Italy and offering examples of every major tale type, often in multiple versions, Calvino's anthology can be used to introduce students of the fairy tale to a host of tale types, motifs, literary devices, and character types.

If instructors have limited time to dedicate to folktales or fairy tales within the larger context of a literature or culture class, I recommend "Il pappagallo" ("The Parrot") from Monferrato (tale 15), one of the most intriguing tales for its plot, structure, and style. The tale exemplifies an Italian folktale, meaning that it is, as Calvino declared, unparalleled in "grace, wit and unity of design" (*Italian Folktales*, xviii). Moreover, it provides students with an example par excellence of a frame tale and embedded narratives. When I teach "The Parrot," I always present first the history of the embedded narrative in literature as a way of contextualizing the tale for my students. The technique of a story within a story is a familiar one both in folklore and in the Italian *novella* tradition. Giovanni Boccaccio's *Decameron* (1349–1350) contains a realistic exterior frame whose characters are also narrators of interpolated tales. In addition, Boccaccio took the device of the story within a story to a third level by having characters in some of the *novelle* narrate tales to other characters. Giovan Francesco Straparola set the varied stories of his collection *Le piacevoli notti* (The Pleasant Nights, 1550–1553) in a "carefully chosen discursive milieu: the conversations of a group of aristocrats, in a rented castle on an island off Venice, telling stories to amuse each other during 'Caresme-Prenant' (the last three days of carnival before Lent)" (Wanning Harries, 105). Fifty years later, Giambattista Basile enclosed his 50 stories of the *Cunto de li cunti* (The Tale of Tales, 1634–1636) in a frame narrative that is an "overarching and self-referential fairy tale rather than the more-or-less realistic conversations that Straparola borrows from Boccaccio" (Wanning Harries, 106).

Perhaps the most widely known example of a story or stories within a story, especially by students outside a traditional Italian language and literature program, can be found in the nightly storytelling of Scheherazade in the *Arabian Nights*. The narrative device of the frame reminds us that some folk stories, in effect, are massive apothecary cabinets, reminiscent of those of the Mago Tre-Pi (an anagram and obvious characterization of the Sicilian folklorist Giuseppe Pitrè) in Luigi Capuana's *meta-fiaba* or meta–fairy tale "Il raccontafiabe" ("The Storyteller"), which store innumerable tales within their countless drawers. Narratives become embedded over time and space, fitting into one another like so many Russian nesting dolls.

Frames have long shaped the viewer's or reader's experience. To emphasize this to my students, I bring them to our university galleries to observe our sculpture garden, permanent collection, and changing exhibitions. We discuss the frames that encase each work of art and how the walls of the gallery are used as a secondary framing device. I ask them how the frame changes the way they understand the composition and if a simpler or more elaborate frame might further affect their interpretation. When possible, I contact the gallery registrar or exhibition designer to request an "unframing" of a work of art. As we look on, the preparator sets a framed piece face down on a table and then lifts the painting or photograph out, allowing my students to physically see the way the image changes as the frame is removed. We wonder whether it is possible to "unsee" the frame once we have seen it, a question worth pondering with frame narratives as well. Can we "unhear" them if we try to read the interpolated tales in isolation?

One illuminating activity that helps students connect to embedded tales is to have them bring frames of various sizes to the gallery and hold them up over detailed images of a larger work. Together we imagine the story taking place within the smaller arrangement and how it relates to the larger narrative. This can also be done with images on a computer screen or in an art book if you do not have access to a campus exhibit. I also recommend showing students paintings within paintings to reflect on the ways stories speak to one another in frame and embedded narratives. There are many examples from which to choose, of course, especially from the Dutch Golden Age, but my students respond favorably to Johannes Vermeer's *The Love Letter*, in which a doorway frames the image of a woman receiving a letter and two framed paintings grace the wall behind her. You might want to separate the students into small groups for this activity and include other paintings, such as Vermeer's *Woman Holding a Balance*, Gabriel Metsu's *Man Writing a Letter* and *Woman Reading a Letter*, and James Abbot McNeill Whistler's *Whistler's Mother*. When I ask them to play detective and figure out what messages the paintings within paintings hold for the viewer, my students research historical details about the period and pen intricate yarns about the figures in the paintings, thus adding yet another layer to the existing story, as all storytellers do. Even Calvino, who, like a parrot, repeated stories in his effort to transcribe and translate from dialect oral tales passed down through generations, imbued them with the life force of the new parent-narrator, taking "the interchangeable ingredients" of folktales and organizing them according to his unique vision (*Italian Folktales*, xxxi).

At the end of our study of art, I suggest that frames, both literal and figurative, serve as a transition from one world to another. In the case of a painting, the frame, matte, and glass provide clues that we must give up our reality in order to enter the narrative space on the canvas. When we return to the classroom, we identify specific markers in our literary works that indicate we are moving from the primary to an embedded tale, as can be seen in Appendix A for Calvino's "The Parrot." Calvino's version of the tale tells of a merchant who is supposed to go away on business but is afraid to leave his daughter at home alone because a certain king has designs on her. Before leaving, the concerned father buys the young woman a talking parrot to keep her company and, after much last-minute advice to her, sets out on his journey. No sooner is the merchant out of town than the king enlists an old woman to bring a letter to the merchant's daughter. In the meantime, the young maiden asks the parrot to converse with her to pass the time.

When the bird begins to tell the girl "a good story," a parenthesis is opened in the narrative framework of the primary tale (designated S1) (Calvino, *Italian Folktales*, 45).[1] The third-person narrator (N1) of the principal tale (S1) becomes mute in order to allow the voice of the parrot (N2) to narrate the substory (S2). The intended audience also undergoes a transfiguration of sorts. The reader of Calvino's transcribed tale (designated as A1), who in essence substitutes for the original "listener" from a preliterate society in which tales were orally disseminated in the various regions of Italy, continues to act as audience to the parrot's tale. However, the parrot's actual listener, the merchant's daughter, is much more specific. Indeed, as we will see, the animal storyteller gears his narrative directly at the young woman, manipulating it when necessary to keep her attention and protect her from danger.

As students who have studied the *Arabian Nights* will note, Calvino's version of "The Parrot" mimics on a smaller scale not only the structure of the *Arabian Nights* but also its frame narrative. In Calvino's story a parrot narrates to a merchant's daughter the trials of a young princess whose father, the king, is killed by enemies while riding in a carriage in the woods. The murderers let the princess go, but in the

---

1. For a diagram of the narrative frame, refer to the appendixes at the end of this essay. Students can be guided along the embedded tales by means of the visual diagram.

confusion, she leaves her favorite doll, an exact replica of herself, behind. Wandering through the woods, the girl comes upon a court of another queen and becomes a favored servant. Consumed by jealousy, the other servants plot her downfall by tricking the young maiden into asking about the queen's son, who has been missing and assumed dead for some time. The queen is enraged at the girl's audacity and consequently shuts her up in a dungeon. At midnight, five men (four sorcerers and their prisoner, the queen's son) enter her prison cell. At this juncture in the narrative, there is an abrupt rupture in the embedded story whereby the internal tale (S2) is quite literally interrupted and the reader is redirected to the events of the primary narrative (S1).

A physical marker, the knock at the door, which eventually becomes almost constant, reinforces the verbal cue of the narrative rupture. By referring to the chart presented in Appendix A of this essay, students can see the pairing of the verbal and physical cues whenever S1 dominates. The knock at the door is symbolic of the desire to break down the barrier between reality and fantasy or to invade the domain of storytelling. To avoid confusion, I refer to "reality" here as the narrative of S1, the tale of the merchant's daughter and the parrot, even though we clearly remain even then within a fantasy realm or fictional space.

During the course of the parrot's tale, the parrot and the merchant's daughter are interrupted three times by a servant who announces first that he bears a letter from the king and then that an old woman, who claims to be the young lady's aunt, wants an audience with her. At the first interruption, the girl, who is "eager to hear what happened next in the tale, which had reached its most exciting part," sends the servant away and begs the parrot to continue narrating (Calvino, *Italian Folktales*, 46). When the servant knocks again, insisting that the girl read the king's letter, she accepts because the tale seems to have reached its conclusion with the imminent marriage of the maiden to the queen's son. With haste, the parrot interjects, "But it's not finished yet, there's still some more to come. . . . Just listen to this" (46). The subtale relates that the maiden, who was not interested in marrying the queen's son, moves on to another city with an ill prince. The maiden, dressed in men's attire and claiming to be a foreign doctor, enters the young prince's room and finds a trapdoor under his bed. Opening it, she sees a long corridor with a burning lamp at the far end. The parrot's narrative is again interrupted by a knock at the door, but the merchant's daughter, completely engrossed in the tale and "dying to know its outcome," tells the servant she will receive no visitors (46).

In the next segment of the parrot's tale, it is revealed that an old woman is boiling the heart of the king's son in an underground chamber in revenge for the execution of her own son. The maiden removes the heart and carries it back to the king's son to eat. When the boy regains his strength, the king promises to make the young maiden the boy's wife and future queen. The reader should not be surprised when, at this point of apparent conclusion, there is another knock at the door, which causes the merchant's daughter to exclaim, "It's a fine story. . . . Now that it's over, I can receive that woman who claims to be my aunt" (Calvino, *Italian Folktales*, 47). Ever the clever and adept storyteller, the parrot claims that "there's still more to come" and manipulates the grand finale so that the maiden in the doctor's disguise again refuses to marry and journeys to yet another city where a king's son is under a spell (47). Midway through the intrigue, in which the maiden finds that two witches are placing a pebble each evening in the mouth of the prince to make him mute, the persistent knocking at the door breaks through the veil of fantasy and transports the reader back to the realm of reality. The merchant's daughter, however, is "so absorbed in the story that she [doesn't] even hear the knock" (47). The parrot continues to spin his tale, weaving into the plot a trick played by the maiden on the witches that frees the prince from their spell. The maiden is named physician to the court just as the knocking begins anew. Wise to the pattern of the tales, the merchant's daughter asks, "Does the story go on, or is it over?" (47). Naturally, the tale goes on to tell of the maiden's journey to a new city, where the king has gone mad after falling in love with a doll he found in the woods. When the girl goes before the king, exclaiming, "That is my doll!" the king sees that she is the doll's living image and makes her his bride (47).

When the dreaded knock on the door is heard again, the parrot is "at a total loss to continue the story," but in a final effort to prevent a complete rupture of the fantasy world, he stutters, "'Just a minute, just a minute, there's still a tiny bit more,' . . . but he had no idea what to say next" (Calvino, *Italian Folktales*, 47). In this moment, the imminent danger of a permanent rupture of the barrier between S1 and S2 materializes. The two narratives inhabit a liminal space for a brief interval. In one final utterance from the parrot-narrator, both the frame narrative and the embedded narrative converge: Upon hearing the voice of the merchant, the parrot recovers, "Ah, here we are at the end of the story. . . . The king married the maiden, and they lived happily ever after" (47). The narrative rupture is fully literalized by the opening of the door and the arrival of the merchant. The inner and outer tales, which are bracketed by a variant of the common "once upon a time" and "they lived happily ever after" frame, conclude, and both audiences (A1 and A2) understand that we are "leaving a narrative world where the supernatural is commonplace, where the rules of our ordinary world do not apply, where wishes can come true" (Wanning Harries, 104).

Each of the internal stories in "The Parrot" has the same protagonist, and therefore they function together as one macronarrative. The repeated knocks at the door create suspense for both the young maiden (A2) and the reader (A1). Although the embedded tale (S2) continues after each interruption, one finds micro-incipits at each juncture, marked by such phrases as "But it's not quite over," "There's still more to come," and "Just listen to this," in which the story begins anew with a different adventure. The parrot must think on his feet to keep the tale going in order to save the girl's virtue from the king, just as Scheherazade ends each evening's tale with a cliffhanger so as to live one day longer. The parrot also has a self-interested motive. He is actually a king (in love with the merchant's daughter) who puts on a parrot's disguise to keep the rival king at bay. When the merchant arrives home, the newly revealed king begs, "Forgive me, sir, . . . I am a king who put on a parrot's disguise, because I am in love with your daughter. Aware of the intentions of a rival king to abduct her, I came here beneath a parrot's plumage *to entertain her in an honorable manner* and at the same time to prevent my rival from carrying out his schemes. I believe I have succeeded in both purposes, and that I can now ask for your daughter's hand in marriage" (Calvino, *Italian Folktales*, 48; emphasis mine).

Clearly the young king's words highlight the dual nature of storytelling: Stories are at once stimulating and cautionary. Cristina Lavinio contends that fairy tales inherently have two functions: the "funzione fascinatrice," or spell-binding function (which in the case of "Il pappagallo" has literally to do with seduction), and the "funzione dilatoria," or dilatory function (tales are narrated to pass the time, while waiting for a dangerous situation to be resolved or changed for the better) (92). In the case of the parrot, his storytelling functions as protector and, ultimately, as savior of the young maiden's virtue. The girl's fascination with the internal tale and her desire to know its outcome prevent her from being ensnared by the rival king. She is at once seduced and restrained by the tale. Her moral character and virtue remain intact, even as she goes through the motions of seduction in the cat and mouse game played by the parrot. At the end of the tale, the merchant returns home and, recognizing the untainted innocence of his daughter, remarks, "Well done, my daughter. . . . I see you've remained faithfully at home" (Calvino, *Italian Folktales*, 47).

Just as Scheherezade's evening ritual of telling a tale without revealing its conclusion prevented her death at her husband's hand, the parrot in our tale averts the maiden's moral death by keeping her enthralled in fantasy. In both cases, by the time fantasy loses its grip and gives way to reality, the danger has passed and the intended victim is saved. For Scheherazade, in the course of the thousand and one nights, she has born King Shahriyar three children and has won his love in revealing herself as clever, kind, innovative, and loyal. In the case of the merchant's daughter, her father arrives at the door in the exact moment that the parrot fumbles to find a new tale to relate.

Students understand from both examples that storytelling is a powerful device that has more than the token entertainment or therapeutic value in its ability to take the reader away from the troubles of reality. In embracing fantasy, the listener is protected from a host of evils until he or she leaves the magical realm. Elizabeth Wanning Harries suggests that in many cases "tale-telling does not merely fill time up but extends it" (105). This is undeniably the case with Italo Calvino's variant of "The Parrot." The parrot-king must extend time to protect the innocence of his intended love and to prevent a transgression on her part.

The tale of the king who puts on the guise of a parrot and tells his beloved tales to keep a rival king away from her is a common tale type in folklore. Sicilian folklorist Giuseppe Pitrè included a version, "The Parrot with Three Tales to Tell," in his 1875 collection *Fiabe, novelle e racconti popolari siciliani*. Recounted to Pitrè by his most gifted informant, Agatuzza Messia, in Palermo, the tale derives from a fifteenth-century Sanskrit collection, *Shuka Saptatit: Seventy Tales of the Parrot* (Zipes and Russo, 16). Pitrè's variant, in which the parrot and his role of tale-teller acquire more sinister undertones, acts as an interesting companion to Calvino's and can be used in class to discuss a contrasting function of narration. In "The Parrot with Three Tales to Tell," the parrot is in fact a notary who lives across the street from a beautiful woman whose husband is away on business. The notary, in competition with his gentleman friend to be the first to speak to the married woman, sells his soul to the devil to become a parrot. Once safely housed in a cage in the woman's home, he narrates three interpolated tales to deceive and manipulate the innocent woman. His friend instead calls on an old crone who, pretending to be her grandmother, thrice visits the woman to bring her to mass. When the young woman refuses to leave the parrot, the old crone cries out, "Oh, you wicked woman! For the sake of a mere bird, you're ready to lose your soul!" (Zipes and Russo, 42). And lose her soul she does, for the parrot uses the art of storytelling to seduce her, ultimately killing her husband, not to defend her innocence and virtue (as does Calvino's parrot) but to steal her for himself. The first- and second-degree narrators (N1 and N2) are thus at odds with each other in a way that they are not in Calvino's tale. Indeed, Pitrè's story presents both a different moral message and model of female behavior than Calvino's, offering, as Jack Zipes notes, "a frank commentary on the amorality of courting, desire and seduction" (Zipes and Russo, 16). Although the parrot has protected the woman from another seducer (his gentleman friend) with his adept narration, he has in effect connived, lied, and murdered, all in the name of winning a contest and a woman. In direct contrast to Calvino's parrot, for Pitrè's parrot "the art of telling stories . . . is more about learning how to survive under harsh conditions than learning to lead a moral life" (Zipes and Russo, 17).

In his introduction to *Fiabe italiane*, Calvino explains why such prominent folklorists as Domenico Comparetti and Giuseppe Pitrè chose to publish this tale within a tale at the beginning of their anthologies as a kind of prologue.

> The parrot, by telling an interminable story, manages to save the virtue of a girl. It is a symbolic defense of the narrative art against those who accuse it of being profane and hedonistic. The suspense of the story keeps the fascinated listener from transgression. This is its minimal and conservative justification, but something more profound is revealed in the very narrative construction of "The Parrot": the art of storytelling which the narrator displays and which is humorously exemplified in the parody of tales that "never end." Therein lies, for us, its real moral: the storyteller, with a kind of instinctive skillfulness, shies away from the constraint of popular tradition, from the unwritten law that the common people are capable only of repeating trite themes without ever actually "creating"; perhaps the narrator thinks that he is producing only variations on a theme, whereas actually he ends up telling us what is in his heart. (Calvino, *Italian Folktales*, xxxi)

At the conclusion of this close reading of Calvino's story within a story, I introduce students to other frame and embedded narratives, including those of Giovan Francesco Straparola, Giambattista Basile, and Ludwig Tieck. Framing devices can also be found in such fairy-tale films as *The Princess Bride*, *Ever After*, and most recently *The Tale of Tales*. Another opportunity to expand students' comprehension is to have them create visual representations of the multiple narrators, tales, and audiences or to find moments in which one tale bursts into the other. Explore the idea of stopping time or prolonging life through storytelling, and ask students to consider where the stories begin and end. Are the tales linear? Do they always circle back to the outermost narrative? My students are eager to discuss why people are attracted to stories within stories and how they personally respond to this structure.

Finally, I deepen their understanding of the literary device of embedded narratives by assigning secondary readings, such as Stephen Belcher's "Framed Tales in the Oral Tradition: An Exploration," Elizabeth Wanning Harries' "New Frames for Old Tales," Bonnie Irwin's "What's in a Frame? The Medieval Textualization of Traditional Storytelling," and Sadhana Naithani's "The Teacher and the Taught: Structures and Meaning in the *Arabian Nights* and *Panchatantra*." For relevant examples of frame stories in literature, film, television, music, theater, and even video games, invite your students to visit tvtropes.org/pmwiki/pmwiki.php/Main/ FramingDevice. As a culminating activity to this study, I invite students to work in groups to come up with other examples of embedded narratives that we then compile into a comprehensive chart. I have never left such a session without gaining new knowledge from my students that furthers my own understanding of what makes frame and embedded narratives so fascinating to readers and listeners alike.

APPENDIX A

Linear Movement of the Primary and Embedded Tales in Italo Calvino's "The Parrot"

S1	"Once upon a time there was a merchant . . ." The maiden: "Talk to me, parrot."	half page
S2	"Once upon a time there was a king . . ."	half page +
S1	"At that moment, the parrot was interrupted . . ." The maiden: "Parrot go on with your story."	5 lines
S2	"In the morning the jailers noticed . . ."	7 lines
S1	"The servant knocked again . . ." The maiden: "Now that the story is over . . ." The parrot: "But it's not finished yet, there's still some more to come. . . . Just listen to this."	3 lines
S2	"The maiden was not interested in marrying . . ."	8 lines
S1	"At that moment the servant knocked . . ." The maiden: "Go on, parrot, go on with your story."	5 lines
S2	"The maiden walked down to that light . . ."	7 lines
S1	"It's a fine story," said the merchant's daughter. "Now that it's over, I can receive that woman who claims to be my aunt." The parrot: "But it's not quite over . . ." "There's still some more to come. Just listen to this."	
S2	"The maiden in doctor's disguise also refused to marry . . ."	6 lines
S1	"Someone knocked on the door, but the merchant's daughter was so absorbed in the story that she didn't even hear the knock. The parrot continued."	3 lines
S2	"The next night when the witches put the pebble . . ."	5 lines
S1	"The knocking continued, and the merchant's daughter was all ready to say, 'Come in . . .'" The maiden: "Does the story go on, or is it over?" The parrot: "It goes on . . . Just listen to this."	2 lines
S2	"The maiden wasn't interested in remaining as physician . . ."	8 lines
S1	"There was another knock, and the parrot was at a total loss to continue the story. 'Just a minute, just a minute, there's still a tiny bit more,' he said, but he had no idea what to say next."	4 lines

S1/S2	"'Ah here we are at the end of the story,' announced the parrot. 'The king married the maiden, and they lived happily ever after.'"	2 lines
S1	"The girl finally ran to open the door." Explanation by parrot: "I am a king who put on a parrot's disguise, because I am in love with your daughter." "Aware of the intentions of a rival king to abduct her, I came here beneath a parrot's plumage *to entertain her in an honorable manner* and at the same time to prevent my rival from carrying out his schemes." The merchant gave his consent. His daughter married the king who had told her the tale, and the other king died of rage.	14 lines

APPENDIX B

Frame and Embedded Narratives, Narrators, and Audiences in Italo Calvino's "The Parrot"

$$[S1 + N1 + A1 \, (S2 + N2 + A2)]$$

where

S1 = Primary tale of merchant and his daughter
N1 = Third-person narrator of primary tale / Calvino / storyteller in oral setting
A1 = Reader of Calvino's tale / listener or audience in oral setting
S2 = Embedded tale of young princess and her travels to different courts and cities
N2 = The Parrot (a king disguised in a parrot's plumage)
A2 = Merchant's daughter

The arrow from A1 to A2 indicates that A1, the reader of Calvino's transcribed tale or the listener in a preliterate society, continues to act as audience (along with the merchant's daughter, A2) to the embedded tale narrated by the parrot.

BIBLIOGRAPHY

Adler, Sara Maria. *Calvino: The Writer as Fablemaker.* Potomac, MD: Porrúa Turanzas, 1979.

Bacchilega, Cristina. "Calvino's Journey: Modern Transformations of Folktale, Story, and Myth." *Journal of Folklore Research* 26.2 (1989): 81–98.

Beckwith, Marc. "Italo Calvino and the Nature of Italian Folktales." *Italica* 64.2 (1987): 244–62.

Belcher, Stephen. "Framed Tales in the Oral Tradition: An Exploration." *Fabula* 36 (1994): 1–19.

Benson, Stephen. *Cycles of Influence.* Detroit: Wayne State University Press, 2003.

Bronzini, Giovanni Battista. "From the Grimms to Calvino: Folk Tales in the Year Two Thousand." In *Storytelling in Contemporary Societies.* Ed. Lutz Rohrich and Sabine Wienker-Piephs. Tübingen: Gunter Narr, 1990.

Byatt, A. S. *On Histories and Stories.* Cambridge, MA: Harvard University Press, 2000.

Calvino, Italo. *Fiabe italiane.* Milan: Mondadori, 1993.

———. "Introduzione." In *Sulla fiaba.* By Italo Calvino. Milan: Mondadori, 1996. 151–56.

———. *Italian Folktales.* Trans. George Martin. New York: Harcourt Brace Jovanovich, 1980.

———. "La mappa delle metafore." In *Sulla fiaba.* By Italo Calvino. Milan: Mondadori, 1996. 135–50.

———. "Il midollo del leone." *Paragone* 66 (1955): 17–31.

———. "Presentazione." In *Sulla fiaba.* By Italo Calvino. Milan: Mondadori, 1996. 95–106.

———. *Sulla fiaba*. Milan: Mondadori, 1996.

———. "La tradizione popolare nelle fiabe." In *Sulla fiaba*. By Italo Calvino. Milan: Mondadori, 1996. 117–34.

Deidier, Roberto. *Le forme del tempo: Saggio su Italo Calvino*. Milan: Edizioni Angelo Guerini, 1995.

Falaschi, Giovanni, ed. *Italo Calvino: Atti del Convegno Internazionale*. Florence: Garzanti, 1988.

Frigessi, Delia, ed. *Inchiesta sulle fate: Italo Calvino e la fiaba*. Bergamo: Pierluigi Lubrina, 1988.

Irwin, Bonnie. "What's in a Frame? The Medieval Textualization of Traditional Storytelling." *Oral Tradition* 10.1 (1995): 27–53.

Lavagetto, Mario. "Preface." In *Fiabe italiane*. By Italo Calvino. Milan: Mondadori, 1993. xi–xlvii.

Lavinio, Cristina. *La magia della fiaba: Tra oralità e scrittura*. Florence: La Nuova Italia Editrice, 1993.

Luthi, Max. *The European Folktale: Form and Nature*. Trans. John D. Niles. Philadelphia: Institute for the Study of Human Issues, 1982.

Murtaugh, Kristen. "Italo Calvino." *Commonweal* 19 (June 1981): 381–82.

Naithani, Sadhana. "The Teacher and the Taught: Structures and Meaning in the *Arabian Nights* and *Panchatantra*." *Marvels & Tales* 18 (2004): 272–85.

Olken, I. T. *With Pleated Eye and Garnet Wing: Symmetries of Italo Calvino*. Ann Arbor: University of Michigan Press, 1984.

Pitrè, Giuseppe. *Biblioteca delle tradizioni popolari siciliane*, vol. 4, *Fiabe, novelle e racconti popolari siciliani*. Bologna: Forni Editori, 1968.

Re, Lucia. *Calvino and the Age of Neorealism: Fables of Estrangement*. Stanford, CA: Stanford University Press, 1990.

Salvemini, Francesca. *Il realismo fantastico di Italo Calvino*. Rome: Edizioni Associate Editrice, 2001.

Wanning Harries, Elizabeth. "New Frames for Old Tales." In *Twice Upon a Time: Women Writers and the History of the Fairy Tale*. By Elizabeth Wanning Harries. Princeton, NJ: Princeton University Press, 2001. 104–34.

Zipes, Jack, and Joseph Russo, eds. *The Collected Sicilian Folk and Fairy Tales of Giuseppe Pitrè*. New York: Routledge, 2008.

CHAPTER TWO

Fairy Tales in Context

Fairy Tales in European Context

READING THROUGH MULTIPLE LENSES

Linda Kraus Worley

Designing a large lecture class on a topic as varied and vast as European fairy tales is a challenging project. Even more challenging is helping students to acquire skills and a knowledge base that they can call on to understand tales—both traditional and retold—after they have left the course. My contributions to the course "Fairy Tales in European Context" (see Chapter 6 of this volume for the syllabus), a popular course at the University of Kentucky that had initially been created by a colleague, stemmed from these challenges and from new demands to restructure the course so that it could fulfill a general education requirement in the humanities and also serve as one of the required courses for a new minor in folklore and mythology.[1] My response to the new requirements was to build from the general education mandate for the course—to focus on critical inquiry—and to make one of the primary organizing principles for the course the ability to apply critical theories. Other organizing principles included grouping tales by themes, national traditions, and chronology. The various iterations of the course have focused more and more on creating opportunities for the students to

---

1. I was fortunate to inherit the course from my colleague Jeannine Blackwell, whose expertise in the early modern era and fairy tales had created the foundation of nuanced investigation of cultural contexts.

learn about, critique, and apply what I term the basic keys to deal with tales. In addition, students work with the intertextual dialogues that take place between and among "classical" tales, criticism, and retold tales since the 1970s. The overriding goal is for students to finish the course with tools that will help them work with "classical" tales, emerging contemporary rewritings, and criticism.

Let me begin my discussion of the course with the parameters of the class, the learning goals, and the syllabus. The course has a cap of 125 students and always has more on the waiting list. The class is drawn from across campus because many students use the course to fulfill one of their humanities requirements. The students purchase two anthologies for the course: *The Great Fairy Tale Tradition: From Straparola and Basile to the Brothers Grimm*, edited by Jack Zipes; and *The Classic Fairy Tales*, edited by Maria Tatar. In addition to two lecture sessions a week, students meet once a week in discussion groups of 25, which either a teaching assistant or I lead. These sessions are an integral part of the course in light of the learning goals, which include students being able to

1. demonstrate a close understanding of fairy tales as a genre;
2. identify and work with the core elements of folktales and fairy tales;
3. place the various tellers, writers, and editors of fairy tales in their historical and personal contexts;
4. outline the historical development of written and collected folklore materials in Europe;
5. demonstrate knowledge of the anxieties and desires of European societies as reflected in the tales;
6. analyze tales by learning about, applying, and critiquing folklore/structural, sociohistorical, gender, Freudian, and Jungian interpretive approaches to texts;
7. analyze images associated with tales using visual interpretive tools;
8. critique the ever-changing cultural positions and array of meanings generated by fairy tales in the past and as they are being retold in the present; and
9. explore the intertextual relationships among "classical" tales, contemporary rewritings, and criticism.

The last four goals will serve as the focus of my discussion here as I detail how I have condensed the dominant critical and theoretical approaches of the twentieth century into what I term three keys that can be used to unlock fairy tales.[2] Because this is an introductory-level course, the aim is to introduce students to various

---

2. The course is divided into six units: fundamentals; social, cultural, and historical interpretations; the family drama and psychological interpretations; themes of the "classical" tales; literary tales of the nineteenth century; and the telling of tales "aslant" in the twentieth and twenty-first centuries.

approaches, recognizing that such a basic introduction will by its nature leave out some critical complexities. The first key comprises approaches that look at the structures of tales and plots (the Aarne-Thompson-Uther classification system; Propp's functions). The second key encompasses various sociocultural critical approaches that concentrate on the individual in society (Darnton; Duggan; Weber; Zipes, *Fairy Tales*); and the third key includes psychoanalytic and psychological approaches (Freud; Bettelheim, *Uses of Enchantment*; Campbell; Gilbert and Gubar). Issues of gender, ethnicity, and class are not separated out because they are interwoven into the explorations of each of the keys.

The best way to demonstrate how critical theories and tools are interwoven into our readings of fairy tales is to share some examples of activities designed to acquaint students with each of the keys and to prepare them for assignments scheduled for later in the semester, in which they are to creatively and critically use the keys to engage with texts. Early in the semester, students complete an assignment designed to inductively introduce them to the Aarne-Thompson categories. Students are given photocopies of the outline of the classification of tales from Aarne and Thompson's *Types of the Folktale: A Classification and Bibliography*, the pages dealing with ATU 500 ("The Name of the Supernatural Helper") and 501 ("The Three Old Spinning Women") as well as a worksheet (Appendix A), which they fill out in the discussion session. I ask them to grapple with the worksheet's questions on their own and then in pairs before we unravel the resource together. This activity asks them to look for facts, figure out how the individual entries for tale types are arranged, and compare the two tale types. We discuss the uses and limitations of the system, including some of the subtle issues of gender.

It can be exciting for students at this early point in the semester to work with one of the basic research tools used by folklorists and to experience critiquing this basic tool. Their critiques of a 50-year-old tool match up quite well with those that Hans-Jörg Uther cites as fueling his recent revision of the system (Uther, "Classifying Tales"). Typical comments from students are that they are at first intimidated when confronted by the task but then recognize that they are able to decipher the organization of the entries. Some remark that they now feel like folklorists. I underscore throughout the semester that this comparative tool, even with all its flaws, allows them to find similar tales and to recognize what might be the core elements of a tale type. As part of the unit on fundamentals, students also read excerpts from Vladimir Propp's *Theory and History of Folklore* and *Morphology of the Folktale*.[3] In small groups they are asked to condense the 31 functions

---

3. Unless otherwise stated, all critical excerpts come from Tatar's anthology *The Classic Fairy Tales*. The Propp excerpts are to be found on pages 378–81 and 382–87, respectively. The excerpts are supplemented with other materials uploaded to a web-based learning management system or in the library.

Propp postulates into what they see as the most important and characteristic functions. We create a class version of about eight functions. Just as we critiqued the Aarne-Thompson system, we also consider the uses and limits of Propp's ideas, in particular how his structural approach is useful in describing, but not in interpreting, tales. The activities are designed to acquaint students with these foundational keys; they also allow them to see that, just as tales change in rewritings and retellings, so too are theoretical texts questioned and modified.

Our early discussion regarding the ATU system sensitizes the students to the fact that the variations among individual tales even in one tale type are so marked that, in order to discern the core of a tale, as opposed to the incidents and details added by a particular teller, editor, or author, several versions must be read. Students learn that precisely the variable details may be important when interpreting a particular tale in its sociohistorical context, with all its ambiguities and intertextual connections. Students become aware of the dangers inherent in making generalized, universal interpretive statements about just one version of a tale. Their work has prepared them to begin to examine the myriad approaches that can be termed sociocultural. The students read and discuss texts such as Darnton's "Peasants Tell Tales: The Meaning of Mother Goose," Eugen Weber's "Fairies and Hard Facts: The Reality of Folk Tales," and Anne Duggan's "Ideology and the Importance of Socio-Political and Gender Contexts." These texts point to the historical contexts—social, political, cultural—in which tales were told and retold as well as received. In addition, I want the students to recognize how dominant ideologies can be at work in multiple ways in texts, conserving as well as subverting power and gender relationships.

One exercise that looks at the reality and image of witches is designed to model early feminist readings that critiqued dominant patriarchal narratives. Students work with a sheet divided into four columns; each column is meant to help them look at the "witch" from different perspectives. The first column is to be filled in with contemporary associations with the word *witch*, the second with notes from my lecture presenting the crimes and characteristics associated with witches from the point of view of Kraemer and Spengler in *The Witches' Hammer* (Institoris). (I sometimes have them examine the table of contents of this book as a pre-lecture exercise.) During the lecture, which is accompanied by many images, I underscore which late medieval/early modern institutions profited from the witch trials, pointing out that *The Witches' Hammer* concentrates on the crimes of women, although historical records of witch trials show that who was accused—men or women—varied greatly by region and era. Students then fill in the third column, which asks them to think about which real-life tasks and roles performed by women might correspond to the second column. For example, the accusations leveled by the inquisitors regarding the killing of children by witches are readily seen as linked to women's roles as midwives. The various accusations related to the impairment of male procreation lead to some interesting discussions when students are thinking of possible real-life scenarios. The final step of the activity is to have students consider what a woman might do and try to be in order not to be accused of witchcraft. This last column then leads to a discussion about the gender traits associated with many of the well-known fairy-tale heroines. The results of this discussion provide a powerful lead-in to our work with "Snow White" and Gilbert and Gubar's seminal essay "Snow White and Her Wicked Stepmother" from *The Madwoman in the Attic*. Students recognize that other ways of seeing tales and their plots are possible by changing perspectives.

Our final critical key for this part of the semester focuses on Freudian and Jungian approaches to tales. "Hänsel and Gretel" and "Snow White," among other tales, serve as the basis for Freudian interpretations. The students hear and read about core Freudian concepts, such as psychosexual developmental stages, projection, the Oedipus complex, and dream work, which have been used, especially, by Bruno Bettelheim in *The Uses of Enchantment* to explicate tales. I model a Freudian interpretation—which includes pointing to the splitting of the father figure in a father-son rivalry—of the set of tales positioned together under the title "Triumphant Apprentices" (Straparola's "Maestro Lattantio and His Apprentice Dionigi," Le Noble's "The Apprentice Magician," and the Grimms' "The Thief and His Master," all found in Zipes, *Fairy Tale Tradition*, 347–60). My reading serves as the basis for an activity that asks students to apply their knowledge of Freudian ideas to Disney's "The Sorcerer's Apprentice." The class views the clip from *Fantasia* in class. Partners are then asked to form a cogent Freudian interpretation, which we then refine together in class. Students readily discern Freudian symbolism in images such as the apprentice's usurpation of the master's pointed hat and the phallic dream of cosmic power. They also recognize the reinstatement of paternal power at the end, a resolution that runs counter to the successful rebellion of the son in the traditional tales of the "Triumphant Apprentices" set. This exercise tends to be a pivotal moment in the semester as students realize that critical tools can lead to radical new insights into Disney films, a genre they had both taken for granted and felt they understood. In this respect, the *heimlich* (the home-like, familiar) becomes *unheimlich* (un-home-like, uncanny).

Having grappled with a sampling of Freudian interpretations, students are well equipped and, indeed, anxious to verbalize some of the gaps and excesses they see in Freudian criticism. In a lecture I point out that many of their doubts were also advanced by Jung, Freud's one-time disciple, especially with respect to Freud's insistence on the centrality of psychosexual stages. In this unit students are introduced to Joseph Campbell's use of Jungian and mythological thought in the development of his ideas explicated in *The Hero with a Thousand Faces*. Students apply the heroic quest cycle to "Iron Hans" as an at-home assignment, which they then refine in their discussion sessions (Appendix B). Many of the students immediately recognize the correspondences between Campbell's schema and Propp's set of functions (as condensed by the class earlier in the semester). Claims by Jungians with respect to universal structures and archetypes are tested by looking at the simpleton/trickster hero in various guises in "Costantino Fortunato," "Cagliuso," Perrault's "Puss in Boots," the Grimms' "Puss in Boots" and "The Brave Little Tailor," both Lang's and Jacob's versions of "Jack and the Bean Stalk," and several of the Appalachian Jack tales published by Richard Chase. Once again, the limits but also the uses of Jung's universalizing gestures are underscored as we look at the various social, cultural, and historical contexts and thematic stresses of these particular tales in light of the broad range of Indo-European variants.

This introduction to some of the leading critical approaches of the early and mid-twentieth century sensitizes students to the power of critical theories, their achievements and limitations. The critical approaches are presented in roughly chronological order. Students become aware that criticism often responds to earlier criticism; they are aware that different sets of questions lead to different answers. They continue to work with the tools gained thus far as the course shifts to an emphasis on major fairy-tale themes and the layers of cultural contexts that formed specific tales in settings such as the French salons or in the Grimms' historical moment. Students continue to write mini-essays that tend to be relatively sophisticated, because of, I suspect, the early exposure to multiple critical approaches foregrounded in the course. Through writing and discussions they also practice becoming proficient readers of illustrations and are asked to recognize an illustration as an interpretation determined by cultural contexts.

One of the major assignments in the course occurs midsemester. Students are asked to write a paper in which they apply a combination of the core structural keys and either psychological or sociohistorical keys to a tale group not dealt with in class. Students help create a set of interpretive questions appropriate to each key, which they then apply to their chosen tale group. There is ample room for revision as they hand in an outline and have a first draft edited by a peer according to a detailed peer-review worksheet I give them.

For the purposes of this essay, I will skip the middle units of the course, which, I suspect, cover familiar pedagogical and thematic territory, in order to focus on the last unit of the course, in which we concentrate on intertextual overlapping among "classical" tales, criticism, and rewritings from the 1970s to the present.[4] Students continue to draw on the various approaches to reading tales that were explicitly practiced at the beginning of the semester as we begin to look at tales that have been creatively retold since the 1970s. In preparation for dealing with tales told "aslant," students are asked to verbalize their ideas regarding the characteristics of "classical" tales, characteristics that are then compared with those posited by Max Lüthi. Students are asked to imagine how these characteristics might be modified in retellings: What might change with respect to the tone of the rewriting, the intended audience, the uses and limitations of the chosen media, the attitude toward the magical second world, the lack of depth of characters, and so on.

The most interesting part of this unit may be when I discuss with students how, in addition to the fact that retold tales are in dialogue with classical tales, they might also be interacting with critical approaches of the twentieth century, such as psychoanalysis and feminism, and with theoretical contexts of the late twentieth and early twenty-first centuries, such as postmodernism or animal studies.[5] Retold tales, for their part, can also lead to new critical insights and to new ways of seeing classical tales. To concretize these intertwinings, the students work with a number of rewritings and re-imaginings of "Little Red Riding Hood," including Angela Carter's "The Company of Wolves," several clips from Neil Jordan's 1984 movie *The Company of Wolves*, the Betty Boop cartoon "Dizzy Red Riding Hood," a Max Factor lipstick ad, Kiki Smith's sculpture *Daughter* (1999), Roald Dahl's "Little Red Riding Hood and the Wolf" and "The Three Little Pigs," and Sam the Sham's "Li'l Red Riding Hood" and the Sham-Ettes' response, "Big Bad Wolf." For each imaginative work we describe what has changed and posit the cultural positions fueling the creative changes as well as our reading, viewing, or listening. For some rewritings the overlap with feminist thought or with psychoanalytic ideas is obvious, whether it is a rewriting that affirms or satirizes the theoretical ideas. For other rewritings we are led to envision new imaginative and critical contexts (Joosen; Zipes, "Hyping").

---

4. Vanessa Joosen provides a wealth of retold tales and illustrations that interact with Marcia K. Lieberman's "Some Day My Prince Will Come," Bettelheim's *Uses of Enchantment*, and Gilbert and Gubar's *Madwoman in the Attic*.

5. I agree with Vanessa Joosen when she states, "Rather than examining the influence of criticism on fairy-tale retellings, I consider the relationship between the two discourses as an intertextual *dialogue* in the truest sense. The implementation, as a metatextual dimension, of ideas that were or would become topical in criticism has made the fairy-tale retelling a relevant source of ideas for subsequent studies. Conversely, some authors of fairy-tale retellings have found inspiration in the scholarship on the traditional tales" (1).

The final assignment of the semester is for students to work in self-chosen small groups for several weeks to prepare oral and visual presentations on three concrete re-imaginings since 2000 of one traditional tale of their choosing. The retellings they discover can be in any medium: film, advertisements, written texts, cartoons, art, and so on. As a group, students describe the retellings to their classmates in the discussion sessions, underscoring the changes (if any) from the traditional tale(s). They are also asked to discern the underlying ideological and critical underpinnings of the rewritings as they interact with their cultural contexts. This final assignment produces thoughtful and entertaining 20-minute-long presentations. Students are graded on the critical depth of their work and on the mechanics of an oral presentation. These presentations take up the last few scheduled discussion sessions.

An overarching goal of the course is to help students become active readers and viewers of tales, both traditional and retold. This exposure to some of the core historical and contemporary critical approaches, minimal though it might be, hits the mark for at least some. Students understand the learning goals of the course and have written in evaluations, "This class is a great class, not only entertaining, but also interesting because of so many viewpoints and perspectives"; "I really liked it all! Learning different theories and views helps me with analysis of all texts, not just fairy tales"; and "I found reading various analyses of different tales very interesting! It was cool to look at one story through many lenses."

APPENDIX A
Exploration of Aarne-Thompson Tale Types and Aarne-Thompson-Uther's Revision

Look closely at the copies you have received from Antti Aarne and Stith Thompson's *The Types of the Folktale: A Classification and Bibliography* (in *FF Communications*, no. 184) (Helsinki: Academia Scientiarum Fennica, 1961), 167–69.

1. Which sections of the AT classification system contain both "Rumpelstiltskin" and "The Three Spinners"?
2. What are the AT numbers for each of these two tales?
3. What are the three basic parts of the plot of "Rumpelstiltskin"?
4. Jot down the number of written variants found in the following cultural groups!
   ___ English
   ___ Finnish
   ___ French
   ___ Danish
   ___ German
   ___ Irish
   ___ Italian
   ___ Hungarian
   ___ Spanish
   ___ Swedish

5. Based on the numbers you found, in which parts of Europe does the tale type seem most prevalent? In the north, west, center, east, or south? What might you hypothesize from a historical-geographic point of view?

6. What is the major variant to the tale type?

7. Compare the plot information given for "Rumpelstiltskin" with that given for "The Three Old Women Helpers." Where do they share characteristics? Where are they different?

8. Look closely at the motifs for "Rumpelstiltskin." How are they organized?

9. Examine the various examples of motifs. Do they match the definition and examples from class?

10. What purposes does the Aarne-Thompson classification system serve? What are some of its limitations?

11. Compare the photocopy of the AT entries with your copy of ATU 500 as revised by Hans-Jürg Uther. Comment on the changes.

APPENDIX B

"Iron Hans": The Hero's Quest

Elements of the Jungian Quest

Match parts of "Iron Hans" with the various stages of the Jungian quest as outlined by Joseph Campbell. Do all of the elements fit? Why or why not?

1. Departure: the separation of a hero from the known world / Call to adventure
2. Initiation
   Journey into an "other world"
   Supernatural aid
   Trials and tests
   Meeting with goddess
   "Ultimate boon"
3. Return to the known world
   Return threshold
   Master of two worlds

How do these stages compare with Propp's functions? Which myths or movies do you know that follow this pattern?

Bibliography

Aarne, Antti, and Stith Thompson. *The Types of the Folktale: A Classification and Bibliography*. *FF Communications*, no. 184. Helsinki: Suomalainen Tiedeakatemia, 1961.

Bettelheim, Bruno. "Hansel and Gretel." In *The Uses of Enchantment: The Meaning and Importance of Fairy Tales*. By Bruno Bettelheim. New York: Knopf, 1976. 159–66.

———. "The Struggle for Meaning." In *The Uses of Enchantment: The Meaning and Importance of Fairy Tales*. By Bruno Bettelheim. New York: Knopf, 1976. 3–8.

———. *The Uses of Enchantment: The Meaning and Importance of Fairy Tales*. New York: Knopf, 1976.

Campbell, Joseph. *The Hero with a Thousand Faces*. Princeton, NJ: Princeton University Press, 1968.

Chase, Richard, ed. *The Jack Tales: Folktales from the Southern Appalachians*. Boston: Houghton Mifflin, 1943.

Darnton, Robert. "Peasants Tell Tales: The Meaning of Mother Goose." In *The Great Cat Massacre and Other Episodes in French Cultural History*. By Robert Darnton. New York: Basic Books, 1984. 9–22.

Duggan, Anne E. "Ideology and the Importance of Socio-Political and Gender Contexts." In *Marvelous Transformations: An Anthology of Fairy Tales and Contemporary Critical Perspectives*. Ed. Christine A. Jones and Jennifer Schacker. Petersborough, Canada: Broadview Press, 2013. 518–22.

Freud, Sigmund. "The Occurrence in Dreams of Material from Fairy Tales." In *Freud: Complete Works*. Ed. Ivan Smith. 2010. 2596–2601. www.freudforscholars.com/Freud_Complete _Works.pdf (accessed February 16, 2015).

Gilbert, Sandra M., and Susan Gubar. *The Madwoman in the Attic: The Woman Writer and the Nineteenth-Century Literary Imagination*. New Haven, CT: Yale University Press, 1979.

Institoris, Heinrich. *Malleus Maleficarum*. Trans. Montague Sommers. London: Folio Society, 1968.

Joosen, Vanessa. *Critical and Creative Perspectives on Fairy Tales: An Intertextual Dialogue Between Fairy-Tale Scholarship and Postmodern Retellings*. Detroit: Wayne State University Press, 2011.

Lüthi, Max. *The European Folktale: Form and Nature*. Trans. John D. Niles. Philadelphia: Institute for the Study of Human Issues, 1982.

Seifert, Lewis C. "Animal-Human Hybridity in d'Aulnoy's 'Babiole' and 'Prince Wild Boar.'" *Marvels & Tales* 25.1 (2011): 244–60.

Tatar, Maria. *The Classic Fairy Tales*. New York: Norton, 1999.

Uther, Hans-Jörg. "Classifying Tales: Remarks to Indexes and Systems of Ordering." *Narodna Umjetnost: Hrvatski časopis za etnologiju i folkloristiku* 46.1 (2009): 15–32. pdfs.semanticscholar .org/3937/5248763ca74025bb8215b59b4a7a99428cf3.pdf (accessed February 20, 2015).

———. *The Types of International Folktales: A Classification and Bibliography, Based on the System of Antti Aarne and Stith Thompson*, 3 vols. *FF Communications*, nos. 284, 285, 286. Helsinki: Suomalainen Tiedeakatemia, 2004.

Weber, Eugen. "Fairies and Hard Facts: The Reality of Folk Tales." *Journal of the History of Ideas* 42.1 (1981): 93–113.

Zipes, Jack, ed. *Fairy Tales and the Art of Subversion: The Classical Genre for Children and the Process of Civilization*. New York: Methuen, 1988.

———. *The Great Fairy Tale Tradition: From Straparola and Basile to the Brothers Grimm*. New York: Norton, 2001.

———. "Hyping the Grimms' Fairy Tales." In *Grimm Legacies: The Magic Spell of the Grimms' Folk and Fairy Tales*. By Jack Zipes. Princeton, NJ: Princeton University Press, 2015. 58–77.

Perspectives on the Civilizing Process

Using Fairy Tales to Teach French and Italian Cultural History

Allison Stedman

I teach Giambattista Basile's fairy tale "The Dove" ("La palomma"; *Lo cunto de li cunti* 2.7 [The Tale of Tales, 1634–1636]) and Marie-Catherine d'Aulnoy's "The Bee and the Orange Tree" ("L'Oranger et l'abeille"; *Les Contes de fées*, vol. 2 [Tales of the Fairies, 1697]) in a lecture-style liberal studies course, "Literature and Culture of France and Italy." Designed as a survey of French and Italian cultural history from the Middle Ages to the nineteenth century, this course investigates what literary texts reveal about the cultural climates that produced them by considering how works from two different national traditions engage with common questions at similar historical moments. Beginning with the medieval ethos of courtly love and ending with the nineteenth-century Industrial Revolution, students compare the way that the same cultural phenomenon is represented in one French and one Italian text from five different historical periods. For our first unit on the Middle Ages, for example, we study courtly love by analyzing how its compatibility with feudalism is represented in Marie de France's 1170 narrative poem "Lanval" and in tales from the anonymous Italian *Novellino* (1281–1300). For our second unit on the Renaissance, we investigate the varying degrees to which relativism operates in French and Italian humanism by comparing stories from Giovanni Boccaccio's

Decameron (1348–1353) with a story from Marguerite de Navarre's *Heptameron* (1558). The literary fairy tales of Basile and d'Aulnoy provide the central texts for our third unit on the seventeenth-century centralization of the royal court, helping students to understand how marginalized intellectuals and aristocrats responded to this phenomenon in early-seventeenth-century Naples and late-seventeenth-century Paris.

Because Basile's fairy tales were written in the 1630s and d'Aulnoy's were written in the 1690s, I begin our unit on the seventeenth century with a lecture on the assigned reading from Christopher Duggan's *A Concise History of Italy*. Students are asked to read pages 60–75 from this work, along with the first four pages of Basile's fairy tale, and to answer the following discussion questions before class, posting their answer to question 3 on our class blog:[1]

1. What is the Catholic Counter-Reformation? How do the ideals of this movement influence visual art and Italian culture in general during the 1500s and 1600s? (Duggan)
2. How does the Italian political structure evolve over the course of the 1500s? Describe how these changes manifest themselves in the political structure of Naples in the early seventeenth century? (Duggan)
3. Nardaniello and Lanval occupy the same rank in the aristocratic hierarchy. Compare these two characters. What do their similarities and differences reveal about their respective authors' opinions of the nobility in the Middle Ages versus the seventeenth century? (Basile)

The lecture is an interactive one. I use the classroom's document camera to project a printout of the discussion questions on the screen behind me, making sure that each question has a large space beneath it to record our answers, which are written out by hand. This format helps students gain a collective understanding of early modern Italy as politically fragmented but culturally integrated, thanks to the work of intellectuals, and helps them become familiar with the cultural trends and signifiers that united Italy during this period. The emergence of a national culture based on humanist values, the establishment of the Tuscan vernacular as the primary literary language, the rise of the Catholic Counter-Reformation, and finally the spread of what Norbert Elias has described as the "civilizing process" compose the four main components of the lecture.

To help students understand the Catholic Counter-Reformation, I provide a short PowerPoint introduction to Baroque visual art, focusing specifically on its

---

1. I am grateful to my colleague Paul Youngman for the idea of a class blog.

militancy and investment in the power of the visual image as a counterstrategy to the austerity of Protestantism. I accentuate the power of the visual image in this type of artistic production by comparing Baroque frescoes and stuccowork with examples of Italian Renaissance religious art from the previous century, focusing in particular on the differences between Michelangelo's frescoes of the Sistine Chapel (1508–1512, 1535–1541) and Giovanni Battista Gaulli's decoration of the ceiling of the Roman Jesuit church Il Gésu (1670–1683). In looking at segments from Michelangelo's ceiling (Figure 1) and from his altar wall's representation of "The Last Judgment" (Figure 2), we discuss how humanist mentalities, being structured by relativism, allowed for the coexistence of Christian and pagan, spiritual and corporeal themes within the same painting. Michelangelo's frescoes, for example, incorporate allusions to classical mythology—including a depiction of the River Styx—into what is otherwise a biblical account of the Last Judgment. And they also prioritize the accurate representation of the nude human body, despite the spiritual nature of the subject matter.

We then compare these images to artistic works produced by Gaulli (Figure 3) and other Catholic Counter-Reformation artists, such as Andrea Pozzo (Figure 4), discussing how this religious movement adopted both Mannerist and Baroque painting styles to create its desired effect. From Mannerism these paintings adopted brilliant colors, swirling compositions, and shallow perspectives; whereas from the Baroque they adopted religious or supernatural themes, artifice, excess, and dramatic, bright polychrony. We discuss the desired effect of Baroque art on the viewer, focusing specifically on its desire to solicit an awestruck, captivated, rapt reaction through the creation of large-scale frescoes and sculptures that incorporate light, excess, movement, and explosivity to the point that frescoes and sculptures alike appear to burst out of their frames. Finally, we discuss the ideological purpose of this art: to seduce and to inspire the viewer into a renewed vigor and oneness with the Roman Catholic faith. We address the cognitive processes that this type of art relies on. In asking the viewer to feel awestruck and overwhelmed, the viewer is ultimately placed in a passive, reactive, even subservient position.

Still using PowerPoint, I go on to present the civilizing process as defined by Elias in broad terms. I explain the phenomenon as a socio- and psychogenetic evolution of human consciousness whereby norms, customs, rules, and etiquette are codified into forms that, when adopted by a particular person, allow that person to appear "civilized" according to Western cultural norms. I let students come up with some examples of what they think makes us "civilized," before filling in some of Elias's own illustrations from his book *The Civilizing Process*, including

Figure 1. Michelangelo, ceiling of the Sistine Chapel (Vatican City, Rome, 1508–1512).

Figure 2. Michelangelo, *The Last Judgment*, altar wall of the Sistine Chapel (Vatican City, Rome, 1535–1541).

Figure 3. Giovanni Battista Gaulli, *Triumph of the Sacred Name of Jesus*, ceiling of the Church of the Gésu (Rome, 1670–1683).

Figure 4. Andrea Pozzo, *Apotheosis of Saint Ignatius*, ceiling of the Church of Saint'Ignazio (Rome, 1685–1694).

general manners, behavior at table, attitudes toward bodily functions, nose blowing, spitting, public posture, and behavior in the bedroom. We talk about how this process played out in aristocratic courts all over Italy before spreading to the rest of Europe, encouraging standardization in dress, deportment, aesthetics, cooking, and manners and ultimately creating an elaborate system of constraints and conventions that relied heavily on ritual and ceremony for reinforcement. I ask students what kind of impact the newly ritualized and codified existence at court might have had on the nobility, asking them to think about their own state of mind when participating in a ritual as opposed to undertaking a creative activity. The goal here is to get students to see an important parallel between the cognitive processes solicited by Catholic Counter-Reformation art and those created by the civilizing process itself: Because both institutions rely on individual capitulation for success, both ultimately seek a passive, complicit response from their interlocutors.

Next, we address some of the specifics of the early modern Neapolitan court. Michele Rak's chapter in the multivolume classic *Storia di Napoli* provides the foundation for our brief discussion of the history of Naples, and Nancy Canepa's introduction to her translation of Giambattista Basile's fairy-tale collection *Lo cunto de li cunti* (*The Tale of Tales*) provides students with an accessible biography of the author and an overview of his literary production. Using this introduction as a point of departure, we discuss Basile's primary political appointment as a courtier to the Prince of Avellino and we assess how the civilizing process affected the role of the courtier, transforming it from a position of serious intellectual engagement to a position designed to facilitate ritual and conventional activities. Although during the 1500s courtiers had been active in making cultural and political policies in dialogue with those in power, during the 1600s courtiers began to be called on to organize ceremonial activities, to supervise the planning of parties, and to engage in technical discussions about literature. I ask students to consider how this change in role might have frustrated and disillusioned an intellectually gifted courtier like Basile.

Our discussion of Basile's fairy tale begins with an overview of *Lo cunto*'s narrative structure, in which 49 fairy tales are framed by a fiftieth. I ask students to compare the structure of *Lo cunto* to the structure of Boccaccio's earlier *Decameron* (in which the clearly demarcated frame narrative constitutes a different literary genre from the interpolated stories) and to some of the Baroque art that we have previously viewed. To help students with this task, I project the table of contents of both works side by side on the document camera and then review slides of the Baroque frescoes we had analyzed earlier. Students immediately notice the Baroque tendency of the fairy tale in *Lo cunto* to exceed limits, producing a narrative in which fairy tales make up not only the interpolated narratives but also the frame of the collection. I read the beginning of "The Dove" to the students in English, Italian, and Neapolitan, placing the texts on the document camera as I read, and we discuss why Basile may have chosen to write the tale in Neapolitan rather than in Tuscan, which had recently emerged as Italy's primary literary language. This discussion helps to establish Basile and his work as embodying innovative cultural change on the levels of language and style as well as on the levels of form and content.

We then move on to the third discussion question, which students had been asked to blog about before class, comparing Nardo Aniello, the prince in Basile's story, to Lanval, the noble knight from a French medieval narrative poem we had studied earlier in the semester. Both Nardo and Lanval are the sons of kings who, at the beginning of their respective stories, find themselves alone in the woods and separated from the rest of their men. At this point, both men encounter beautiful, ethereal women—fairies—with whom they fall in love, overcome various obstacles, and finally live happily ever after at the tale's conclusion. Despite the similarities of the general plot structures, however, the princely heroes manifest strikingly different personalities, personal circumstances, and responses to adversity. Basile's hero, Nardo, for example, meets the fairy Filadoro in response to the curse of an old woman, who condemns him to fall in love with the daughter of an ogress (Filadoro) after Nardo shoots the old woman's bean pot for sport and causes her to starve to death. Lanval, on the other hand, meets an unnamed fairy in the woods as compensation for his humble acceptance of mistreatment by his lord King Arthur, who, despite Lanval's generosity and loyalty to him as a member of the round table, had neglected Lanval when distributing fiefs.

After comparing the details of the two princes' respective situations, I have the class closely read the scenes in which the princes and the fairies meet for the first time, paying particular attention to their manners of speaking, attitudes toward authority, and general comportment. The discussion reveals that Lanval, despite his shortfalls, nonetheless plays an active role in the poem. Regardless of the circumstances in which he finds himself, he ultimately acts in a way that is chivalrous to his lord, courtly to his lady, and courageous, dignified, exemplary, and honorable. Nardo, on the other hand, plays a primarily passive role in the text, behaving self-centeredly, displaying little empathy for others, and being easily manipulated. I ask students to consider the degree to which the civilizing process's emphasis on conformity, superficiality, and ritual may have influenced this shift in the way the seventeenth-century Neapolitan text represents the nobility.

Our next class begins with a discussion of the role of appearances in Basile's text. We focus on quotes in which Nardo is struck by the fairy Filadoro's beauty and by her ogress-mother's ugliness. Students begin to see Nardo as a character who is exceptionally susceptible to visual imagery and who reacts to it in a way that mimics the ideal Catholic subject beholding the inside of a Counter-Reformation church. Even though the fairy that Nardo meets in the woods bears little resemblance to the opulent, seductive, and radiantly beautiful fairy that Lanval had encountered in Marie de France's earlier poem (Filadoro, by contrast, is a simple forest girl who amuses herself by gathering snails and singing childish songs), Nardo is so thunderstruck by her appearance that he becomes completely paralyzed, even temporarily losing the ability to speak.

> When the prince saw before him this writing desk full of Nature's most precious possessions, this bank of the heaven's richest deposits, and this arsenal of Love's most almighty forces, he did not know what had happened to him, and the rays of her eyes, passing through that round crystal face until they reached the bait of his heart, lit him up to such a degree that he became a furnace that fired the stones for the plans for the construction of the house of his hopes . . . [His] heart was immediately pierced through and through, so that each of them used their eyes to beg the other for mercy, and even if their tongues had the pip, their gazes were trumpets of the Vicaria crier that rendered public the secrets of their souls. . . . Both one and the other [stood] there for a long time with sand in their gullets, unable to squeeze out one accursed word. (Basile, 186)

When Nardo finally does muster up the ability to address the fairy, he does so in an excessive, Baroque manner, heaping adulatory clauses one on top of the other to the point that even Filadoro, herself susceptible to appearances at that moment, finds the need to cut him off, exclaiming, "Keep your hands down, my dear knight. . . . I am a woman who knows how to take her own measure, and I do not need others to serve as my ruler" (Basile, 186). We discuss to what degree Nardo's reaction to the sight of Filadoro could be interpreted as a mental state conditioned by the civilizing process, and students begin to see how Basile manipulates the Baroque aesthetic against itself, using outrageous metaphors to exaggerate the prince's visual susceptibility to the point that the excessiveness of such susceptibility becomes exposed.

We go on to discuss Filadoro's role in the fairy tale, comparing her active, creative responses to adversity with Nardo's passive and resigned reactions to the same situations. To facilitate this discussion, I use the document camera to help the students diagram the plot of the fairy tale by hand, organizing it into a sequence of three curses and redemptions and assessing how Nardo and Filadoro respond to each curse before moving on to the next phase of the diagram. First, the curse of the old woman (whose bean pot Nardo had carelessly shattered at the beginning of the tale) causes the prince to fall in love with the daughter of an ogress, who in turn condemns him to a life of drudgery. In response to this curse, Nardo weeps, but the fairy sows the land, chops the wood, and finally digs a tunnel to help them escape. Upon learning of their escape, the ogress puts the fairy tale's second curse on Nardo, portending that upon the first kiss he receives, he will forget Filadoro. Upon his arrival at the court, Nardo receives a kiss from his mother and the curse immediately takes effect, but Filadoro cross-dresses as a scullery boy, makes a cake, and enchants a dove, who reminds Nardo of his obligations to Filadoro—a second sequence of three actions that ultimately undo the ogress's curse and earn Filadoro Nardo's hand in marriage. But just as their nuptials are about to take place, the ghost of the old woman whose pot Nardo had shattered at the beginning of the tale once again appears and curses Nardo with a final anathema: that he will always see the ruined pot of beans before his eyes and that it will bring him misery. In response to this curse, Nardo turns pale, but Filadoro convinces him to trust her ingenuity, saying, "Have no fear, my husband. *Sciatola* and *matola*: if it is a spell, may it not be valid; I'll get you out of the fire!" (Basile, 194).

Curse	Nardo	Filadoro
Nardo to fall in love with the daughter of an ogress (old woman)	Cries	Sows land Chops wood Digs escape tunnel
Nardo to forget Filadoro when kissed (ogress)	Forgets her	Cross-dresses Makes cake Enchants dove
Nardo always to see the ruined pot of beans before him and reap horns from it (shadow of old woman)	Turns pale	Tells Nardo to trust her ingenuity

As a result of this chart, students are able to see the markedly different ways in which Nardo and Filadoro respond to challenges that require creative solutions. We discuss the degree to which the different upbringings of the two characters may have influenced the polarity of their responses. Whereas Nardo has been taught to adopt a passive orientation to external circumstances, following pre-established codes of behavior without questioning them in order to fit in at court, Filadoro has not and thus would most likely not have felt the same effects of the civilizing process.

In our previous class discussions of Marie de France's medieval narrative poem "Lanval," we had examined the similarities of the phrase groups and styles of address that Marie de France uses in the preface to the *Lais* when she addresses King Henry II, comparing them to the way in which the fairy enchantress addresses King Arthur when she arrives at his court at the end of the tale. In this context we had discussed the degree to which the author can be identified with the fairy enchantress. I ask the students if Basile may have embedded similar signifiers in his text that enable him to be identified with Filadoro.

To respond to this question, I have the class return to our earlier diagram of the story's plot, and I ask the students to ascertain which social class Filadoro might belong to by examining her actions. Students generally point out that the first three, which take place in the forest, are acts of manual labor, whereas the second three, which take place on the fringes of the royal court, are more refined. Significantly, at the end of the last sequence, action on the part of the fairy is no longer required. Students generally interpret the evolution of the fairy's actions as reflecting her upward social mobility. The fairy works her way out of the woods as a peasant, appears at court with the clever ruse of a courtier, and finally becomes a member of the noble leisure class. I ask the students to consider an alternative interpretation as well: What if the fairy, as she moves up through society, does not in fact change social identity but rather remains a courtier-like figure throughout, relying on her natural creativity and ingenuity to confront a variety of circumstances? As such, the fairy reveals that access to the court without the sacrifice of individual agency might still be possible for those who embody courtier-like intelligence, versatility, and adaptability—traits that Basile himself had displayed when orchestrating his own upward mobility from a member of the Neapolitan middle class to achieving the rank of count and the title of Conte di Torrone by the time of his death.

In the previous night's blog, I had asked students to analyze the degree to which the ending of "The Dove" can be considered Baroque in terms of language and plot, with respect to the emotional states of the characters and with respect to the kind of response solicited from the general reader. We return to this in class and summarize our conclusions using the document camera. Students generally point out that the Baroque amplification typical of the characters' previous responses to curses is missing from the ending. The lack of Baroque ornamentation in particular leaves the narrative's open-ended conclusion exposed, a conclusion in which

Filadoro obtains not only the highest social status possible but also the prince's eternal dependence on her. Without Filadoro, the prince is left at the mercy of the old woman's final curse; he depends on Filadoro to "get him out of the fire," without knowing when or where this metaphorical fire may strike. As such, the courtier figure in the civilized court of the fairy tale not only is restored to his former position of authority with respect to the prince he advises but also in fact obtains an even greater degree of royal indebtedness and dependence. The civilizing process may have stripped the nobility of its former agency, but this need not necessarily be the case for the courtier, as Filadoro's triumph implies. As such, the tale can be read as embodying an autobiographical wish-fulfillment narrative for seventeenth-century courtiers who, like Basile, sought access to power through merit rather than birth.

We conclude our section on Basile with a comparison of the supernatural forces on the left- and right-hand columns of the tale's plot diagram. Curses, although initiated by individuals, nonetheless ultimately place individuals in passive positions because they require an intermediary to ensure that the curse will be realized. Once the individual's curse is voiced aloud, the ultimate discretion of the heavens is necessary for the curse to take effect, as curses are only initiated in response to an individual's awareness that he or she lacks the necessary physical or intellectual power to obtain retribution independently. As a result, curses place both initiators and recipients in passive, receptive positions similar to those elicited by the Baroque art of the Catholic Counter-Reformation and the centralization of court ritual during the civilizing process.

Unlike curses, which confirm that an individual's agency has reached its limit, fairy magic is a type of supernatural power that works in conjunction with an individual's natural creativity and intelligence and that depends on individual agency for success. Although Filadoro's first acts of fairy magic are largely responsive to the agency of others, the closer she gets to the court, the more she is able to infuse her magic with her own creativity and initiative, using this power in increasingly clever and ingenious ways. The fact that Filadoro's magic is consistently able to diffuse curses initiated by others ultimately projects an ideological victory for the kind of individual agency associated with the Renaissance courtier over the cultural hegemony of the civilizing process and of the Catholic Counter-Reformation. Just as Filadoro manipulates the curses of the old woman and her mother, transforming them into acts of her own creative magic, so also Basile, in his fairy tale, manipulates the Baroque, appropriating the aesthetic incarnation of religious and sociopolitical reform in a creative way that ultimately undermines the hegemony of both.

The representation of the Neapolitan court in Basile's tale provides a foundational point of comparison for the second part of our unit, which concerns itself with the civilizing process's more radical incarnation at the late-seventeenth-century French court of Versailles. To familiarize themselves with the general time period, students read an excerpt from Roger Price's *A Concise History of France* and we discuss the early-seventeenth-century political climate, assessing how instability in both religion and politics contributed to Louis XIV's desire to establish an absolute monarchy in which all elements of society fell under the political and cultural authority of the king. We discuss the ideological incompatibilities of absolutism versus relativism as abstract concepts, and students begin to see that according to absolutist mentalities, the only way to ensure that the two major rebellions of the earlier part of the century would not repeat themselves was by ensuring the continued superiority of one side over the other.

With respect to the tumultuous aftermath of the religious wars brought about by the previous century's Protestant Reformation, Louis XIV ensured the superiority of Roman Catholicism by making it the official religion of France, by adopting a classical Baroque aesthetic similar to the Baroque of the Catholic Counter-Reformation, and by establishing a network of royal academies to ensure that this aesthetic would be respected in all areas of society and culture. In response to the Fronde (an aristocratic uprising that had taken place between 1648 and 1653 during Louis XIV's minority), the king assured the victory of the monarchy over the nobility by forcing the lower nobility into military service, by reinforcing royal authority over the provincial nobility, and perhaps most significantly by building a sprawling royal palace at Versailles and forcing the upper nobility to take up residence there. At Versailles, members of the nobility found themselves alienated from the feudal authority associated with their provincial estates. Their daily existence was monopolized by elaborate court rituals and their previous official responsibilities were replaced by superficial tasks and honorific positions.

We discuss the effect that Louis XIV's expropriation of the upper nobility's free time would have had on the Parisian salon network, a sociodiscursive institution that had previously provided the upper aristocracy with an important cultural and intellectual hub; and we discuss how the loss of noble patronage and prestige would have affected the autonomy of a well-established Parisian salon hostess like Marie-Catherine d'Aulnoy. The exercise helps students to see the degree to which the situations of the early-seventeenth-century Neapolitan courtier and the late-seventeenth-century French salon hostess were similar in terms of the intellectual marginalization that both experienced as a result of the civilizing processes associated with the centralization of the royal court.

Our comparison of Basile's and d'Aulnoy's respective literary fairy tales begins with an analysis of the similarities of the two main characters: the fairy Filadoro and the princess Aimée. Students note that, despite differences in their original social statuses (Filadoro's is unknown; Aimée is inadvertently separated from her royal parents as a baby), both heroines have at least four major things in common: (1) they are raised by cannibalistic ogresses beyond the limits of civilized society; (2) they escape their ogress-mothers following the arrival of an errant prince who unwittingly deviates from the civilized court of his family; (3) they rely on a mixture of fairy magic and intellectual ingenuity to escape the ogresses and to protect their respective princes from being eaten alive; and finally (4) both end up marrying their princes at the conclusion of the tale, presumably living out the rest of their lives at court. As a result of this comparison, students are able to see the similar ways in which the tales portray the effects of the civilizing process. Although the princes who were raised at court are helpless and indecisive when subjected to circumstances that require creative solutions, both Filadoro and Aimée are able to navigate these uncertainties effectively, ensuring survival and prosperity both for themselves and for the princes they protect.

Having established these similarities, I ask students if they notice any differences in the journeys of the respective heroines or in the nature of the fairy magic that the heroines have access to. Students generally point out that, whereas Filadoro's fairy magic is innate, Aimée's is dependent on the possession of a magic wand that rightfully belongs to the fairy Trufio. A diagram of the plots of the two stories side by side reveals that Filadoro's innate magical abilities become increasingly powerful and innovative the closer she gets to court, whereas Aimée's access to fairy magic by means of Trufio's wand is most effective in the liminal space between island and court and weakens the closer she gets to the royal palace, where she loses control of the wand altogether.

"The Dove": Space	"The Dove": Actions Performed by Fairy Magic	"The Bee and the Orange Tree": Space	"The Bee and the Orange Tree": Actions Performed by Fairy Magic
	Source of fairy magic = Filadoro: interior, stable magic		Source of fairy magic = Trufio's wand: exterior, fickle magic
Woods: ogres' realm	Sows land Chops wood Digs escape tunnel	**Island:** ogres' realm	Enchants doe (Tourmentine) Speaks French (Aimée) Enchants escape bean (Aimée)
		Liminal space	Pond, boat, old woman (Aimée) Pillar, picture, dwarf (Aimée) Tub, orange tree, bee (Aimée) MAGIC MOST POWERFUL
Inn		**Linda's court**	Aimée freed from enchantment (Trufio) Aimée returned to court (Trufio)
Court	Bakes cake Enchants dove MAGIC MOST POWERFUL	**Court**	

The breakdown of these differences reveals that, although both Basile and d'Aulnoy create character dynamics in their fairy tales that exhibit fundamentally negative responses to the effects of the civilizing process, only Basile remains optimistic about the possibilities for individuals to overcome cultural hegemony through individual creativity and innovation without exiting society altogether. Filadoro's creative agency cements her elevated social status by guaranteeing the prince's perpetual dependence on her, whereas Aimée's creative agency encounters no such validation; in accepting a life at court, the heroine must also accept that her actions can no longer influence the quality of her identity, a consequence emphasized by the fact that her first-born son, "Faithful Love," soon finds his name buried under so many titles that it is almost impossible to remember the unique and individualistic way his parents fell in love. As such, the endings of the tales reveal an important difference between two prominent early-modern intellectuals who felt themselves marginalized by the civilizing process and who otherwise chose very similar narrative strategies of cultural resistance.

BIBLIOGRAPHY

Basile, Giambattista. "The Dove." In *Giambattista Basile's The Tale of Tales, or Entertainment for Little Ones*. Ed. and trans. Nancy L. Canepa. Detroit: Wayne State University Press, 2007. 184–94.

Canepa, Nancy L. "Introduction." In *Giambattista Basile's The Tale of Tales, or Entertainment for Little Ones*. Ed. and trans. Nancy L. Canepa. Detroit: Wayne State University Press, 2007. 1–31.

D'Aulnoy, Marie-Catherine Le Jumel de Barneville. "The Bee and the Orange Tree." In *Beauties, Beasts, and Enchantment*. Ed. and trans. Jack Zipes. London: Penguin, 1991. 417–37.

Duggan, Christopher. *A Concise History of Italy*. Cambridge, UK: Cambridge University Press, 1994.

Elias, Norbert. *The Civilizing Process: Sociogenetic and Psychogenetic Investigations*. Ed. Eric Dunning, Johan Goudsblom, and Stephen Mennell. Trans. Edmund Jephcott. Oxford, UK: Blackwell, 1994.

France, Marie de. "Lanval." In *The Lais of Marie de France*. Trans. Glyn S. Burgess and Keith Busby. London: Penguin, 2003. 41, 73–81.

Price, Roger. *A Concise History of France*. Cambridge, UK: Cambridge University Press, 1993.

Rak, Michele. "La tradizione popolare: Dialettale napoletana tra la conquista spagnola e le rivoluzioni del 1647–1648." In *Storia di Napoli: Cultura e letteratura*. Ed. Ernesto Pontieri. Naples: Edizioni Scientifiche Italiane, 1980. 7: 419–590.

"The Enchantments of Eloquence"

SALON CULTURE AND THE FRENCH FAIRY-TALE TRADITION

Faith E. Beasley

Early modern France would at first glance seem to have little in common with the world of today's college students. Inhabitants of Louis XIV's France and today's social-media-adept young people do, however, share one passion: social networking. Many of the great works we associate with France's classical canon are products of salon culture, where such interactions took the form of conversation and reigned supreme. The first published French fairy tales emerged out of this vibrant social and literary context, considered a distinguishing characteristic of French culture today as well as 300 years ago. When we interpret these early modern French fairy tales, many of which are familiar to us from childhood, in this unique context, we see these tales in a new light and discover a dynamic fairy-tale culture that was intricately related to salon culture.

The salon context in which French fairy tales were produced accounts for many of the differences one can perceive between these tales and those of other countries. The form, themes, and function of these tales in society have a particular French twist. I have regularly taught the well-known French fairy tales by Charles Perrault, but I also always include tales that are less well-known to a twenty-first-century audience but that were considered by contemporaries to be the primary examples of the genre: tales penned by such women writers as Catherine Bernard, Marie-Jeanne L'Héritier de Villandon, and Marie-Catherine Le Jumel de Barneville, Baroness d'Aulnoy. In French literature survey courses on the seventeenth and eighteenth centuries, advanced French literature seminars, and women's and gender studies courses on the history of feminism, I focus students' attention on the development of the written fairy tale in France, situate the genre in the French literary tradition, stressing its relationship to the novel—also a genre developed and practiced by women in France—and explain how authors used fairy tales for social commentary. Perrault is often the only French fairy-tale writer students can identify, yet between 1690 and 1709 two-thirds of tales published in France were written by women.[1] Presenting the female-authored tales not only allows for a comparison between male and female practitioners but also allows us to ask broader questions, such as why literary history identifies Perrault as the genre's main practitioner in France and why women were drawn to this genre at this particular time.

In a course I have developed specifically on salon culture, I continue this shift away from the content of the tales and focus on their modes of production, stressing how these works emanate from salons and their particular relationship to oral and written narratives. My use of the fairy tale in this context can be fruitfully integrated into a variety of other course settings. I use the example of the fairy-tale genre as it developed in seventeenth-century France to inspire students to reflect in general on how a literary text comes to be and, more broadly, how knowledge is constructed. In our analyses of fairy tales, we identify the genre as a form of collective writing and explore, through class exercises, papers, and our interpretation of the tales themselves, the important effects of collaborative creation. We contrast this view of the literary text with the more conventional, modern view of literature as a product of the singular mind working alone to compose a text and, more broadly, that enlightened individuals create and disseminate the knowledge they produce. We identify early modern modes of production and analyze how they affected the composition of the tales, in addition to interpreting the themes and content in light of the specific concerns of French literary culture of late seventeenth-century France. Like the women's tales themselves, salon culture and its influence on mainstream classical French literature has until recently been relegated to the shadows of French literary history. Resurrecting these texts and the female-dominated salon

---

1. In the Introduction to my *Options for Teaching Seventeenth- and Eighteenth-Century French Women Writers*, I provide a succinct overview of French women writers in the early modern period and explain the context that I use in my classes for the written fairy-tale genre to which women were drawn particularly in the latter part of the seventeenth century. A number of the essays in the volume offer ways to teach these French fairy tales, notably the essay by Allison Stedman.

culture that nourished and produced them allows students to reflect on the broader questions of canon formation and publication politics.[2]

L'Héritier's *Les Enchantements de l'éloquence ou les effets de la douceur* (The Enchantments of Eloquence, or the Effects of Sweetness) is a perfect illustration of the strong and in many ways unique link between the fairy-tale genre as practiced in seventeenth-century France and salon culture. L'Héritier's tale can be profitably used to illuminate literary and cultural history and to highlight characteristics of the fairy-tale genre as developed and practiced in France. Students come to this text toward the end of my salon course, when their grasp of the classical French literary tradition is fairly solid and they have already read a number of other works that I present as products of salon interaction, works such as novels, literary debates, published conversations, epistolary exchanges, and travel narratives.[3] We examine in depth definitions of conversation during this period and analyze the various forms of social interaction and the publics that engaged in intellectual and social networking. Students often have some familiarity with court life and with the development of the French Academy and other official spheres that exerted power over artistic creation, but most have limited knowledge of French salon culture during the classical period, specifically under Louis XIII, the regent Queen Anne of Austria, and Louis XIV. We thus reconstruct this particular milieu, explore how it functioned, and examine its particular interests, its participants, and its influence on and relationship to mainstream culture. Students are often surprised to learn that salons did not constitute a separate sphere but were actually enmeshed in the mainstream French classical culture associated with Corneille, Racine, and Molière.

Considered by many of their contemporaries to be the arbiters of literary production, early modern French women initiated the creation of salons, which united a diverse group of interlocutors—male and female, traditionally educated or intellectually curious politicians, philosophers, and worldly cultural entities—to compose, read, discuss, and critique texts that were then sent forth into the world to nourish other conversations. In class we try to replicate the ambiance of an early modern salon and to re-create the kind of interactions contemporaries might have experienced. For example, I have students read passages from texts aloud to make them aware of how differently texts were received in the early modern period. We examine the *Mercure Galant*, one of the first serial newspapers in

---

2. I address the erasure of the fairy tale and salon culture from the dominant narrative of literary history in my *Salons, History, and the Creation of Seventeenth-Century France.*

3. I discuss the specifics of teaching this course in my *Options for Teaching Seventeenth- and Eighteenth-Century French Women Writers.*

France, identifying the collaborative processes such as epistolary exchanges that resulted in a representation of the world. The first published fairy tales in France were products of these collective reading and writing practices. By having students encounter a tale for the first time in an oral classroom salon setting, students grasp how texts and knowledge can evolve from collective conversations about a work, conversations that in turn engender other texts.

The methodological underpinning of my various courses that incorporate fairy tales is derived from work by cultural historians (e.g., Roger Chartier) who focus on how texts are produced and received during the early modern period. As Chartier cogently reminds us, readers were more likely to encounter texts in a group setting such as salons ("Loisir et sociabilité"). The figure of the solitary reader immersed in his or her own thoughts was exceptional in early modern culture. To further replicate the early modern encounter with texts such as fairy tales, I find that it is also effective to create a virtual salon by posting, for example, the opening paragraphs of two tales and having students comment on them and respond to the comments of their classmates. Through this exercise students learn firsthand how the mingling of diverse voices creates something new; often a novel interpretation of a passage arises from between the lines of multiple individual interpretations. I draw parallels with Facebook and readers' reactions to a posted article in an effort to underscore how ideas are generated through sociability, which was the foundation of the early modern French salon; we create a *salon en papier*, re-creating the *Mercure Galant* newspaper and replicating through the written word the oral context that inspired and generated French fairy tales.

To further emphasize the role of collaboration, sociability, and conversation in early modern knowledge and literary production, I often ask students to write their first paper in the form of a conversation, which was a form often used by early modern French writers from the mid-seventeenth century through the eighteenth century. Students like this approach, especially in a foreign-language classroom, because it allows them to use the familiar conversational register and combine it creatively with conventional textual analysis. I instruct them to be aware of how new interpretations can sometimes arise out of the interplay of voices, even fictional ones.

Armed with a heightened awareness of how the written fairy-tale genre came to be in seventeenth-century France, we turn to the analysis of specific tales and read them as reflecting this unique cultural context but, more important, as the product of diverse voices as epitomized by salon culture. With this new framework in mind, students are able to grasp rather easily how the fairy-tale tradition—and L'Héritier's *Les Enchantements* as the perfect illustration of that tradition—is a product of salon culture and raises all the issues so prevalent in the seventeenth-century French

Republic of Letters in general and in female-dominated salons in particular. In what follows I offer a reading of the tale within this framework to illustrate how a French tale was both generated by and interpreted in its original context.

L'Héritier (1664–1734) was a celebrated *salonnière* and was the first to publish fairy tales and to reflect critically on the genre.[4] She was also Charles Perrault's niece. As Lewis Seifert and Domna Stanton remark, L'Héritier's tales illustrate the impact on literary creation of the art of conversation as practiced in the salons. Her tales, like those of many of her female contemporaries, are often interpolated into novels and recounted by a character. In this way, fairy-tale writers, and L'Héritier in particular, create a *mise-en-abîme* of salon creativity in order to pay homage to the principal genres developed by women in the salons, the novel and the *nouvelle historique*, following the lead of the celebrated novelist Madeleine de Scudéry, who was known for embedding long conversations into her own works. Indeed, at precisely the time that L'Héritier and others were composing their fairy tales, Scudéry was publishing volumes of conversations, some drawn from her previously published novels but many newly composed for these separate volumes.[5]

L'Héritier's *Les Enchantements de l'éloquence* corresponds to the ATU 480 tale type ("The Kind and the Unkind Girls") and expounds on this type to highlight the art of conversation. It can thus be used to provide a perfect illustration of how the French fairy-tale genre was intricately linked to a uniquely French literary and social context and to show how taking this context into account endows this tale with new meaning. The relationship between the tale and its context also illustrates the role that fairy tales were designed to play in French society.

L'Héritier tells the story of Blanche, a beautiful girl whose father remarries after the premature death of Blanche's mother. This stepmother proves to be as unpleasant and uncouth as her daughter, Alix; both women make the Cinderella-like Blanche miserable. Blanche's only respite comes from reading novels, an activity that might appear curious but a specification that can be easily explained when one understands the tale's French context and its relationship to the fairy-tale genre. One day, when Blanche goes to a fountain to get water, she is almost killed by a wild boar. Luckily a prince happens to be in the area; he shoots at the boar but hits Blanche instead. The two speak, and the prince is charmed by her words and not simply by her exceptional appearance. At Blanche's request, he leaves her and she returns home alone. The

---

4. For L'Héritier's biography, as well as those of other practitioners of the genre, see, in particular, Seifert's and Stanton's volume and Seifert's study.

5. There is a strong bond between L'Héritier and Scudéry, who frequented the same salons. In the eighteenth century critics maintained that L'Héritier even took over Scudéry's famous salon, her *samedis*, upon the death of the novelist (Seifert and Stanton, 62n53).

prince discovers that she is in fact of noble blood. He consults a fairy, who creates an ointment that can heal Blanche's princely inflicted wounds. Dulcincula, the fairy, goes to Blanche disguised as an old woman; the narrator underscores that she is as charmed by Blanche's conversation as the prince. Blanche recovers and visits the fountain again, where she meets another fairy, Eloquentia Nativa, who, as a reward for Blanche's genteel way of speaking to her, endows Blanche with the power to have precious gems flow from her mouth whenever she says something. The stepmother sends her ugly daughter to the fountain, hoping that she will encounter the same magic, but Alix verbally mistreats the fairy. Instead of gems, toads, serpents, and spiders come out of her mouth, thanks to the vindictive fairy's spell. The prince then marries Blanche, who, thanks to the fairy, is as wealthy as the king; the whole realm rejoices and Alix dies in a corner. The moral of the tale is that sweet and courteous language trumps material wealth.

L'Héritier's valorization of the art of conversation traverses the entire tale. L'Héritier dedicates the tale to the Duchesse d'Eperon and moves seamlessly from this opening to the tale itself. The author/narrator offers the moral that the tale will exemplify at the beginning, in this opening dedication, instead of at the end, as we see illustrated in Perrault's formulation of the genre. L'Héritier thus initiates a conversation with her benefactor and invites readers to interpret the tale through the lens of salon culture. She announces that she will tell a tale that illustrates the value of the type of social interaction founded on language and on conversation so prized in the salons:

> It would please you, beautiful Duchess, to interrupt your serious and learned activities to listen to one of these stories. . . . A very learned lady . . . told me this story when I was a child in order to impress upon me that good manners [*les honnêtetés*] never hurt anyone . . . and that often courteous and gentle language is better than a rich inheritance.
>
> She tried to prove to me the truth of this very sensible maxim with this marvelous story that I am going to tell you. During the time when there were fairies in France . . .[6]

L'Héritier underscores a particular female oral lineage for her tale, one that is associated with learned women and not the traditional nurses and grandmothers

---

6. "Vous voulez, belle Duchesse, interrompre pour quelques instants vos occupations sérieuses et savantes pour écouter une de ces fables. . . . Une dame très instruite . . . m'a fait ce conte quand j'étais enfant, pour m'imprimer dans l'esprit que les honnêtetés n'ont jamais fait tort à personne . . . et que souvent Doux et courtois langage. / Vaut mieux que riche héritage. Elle s'efforçait de me prouver la vérité de cette maxime fort sensée . . . par l'histoire très merveilleuse que je vais vous raconter. Dans le temps où il y avait en France des fées . . ." (L'Héritier, opening lines).

usually cited as the roots of fairy-tale transmission. The author asks the duchess to interrupt her "learned activities" to listen to a story that she has heard from a "very learned lady." L'Héritier's narrator thus identifies herself with storytellers in the salons as opposed to the peasant hearth, as she characterizes her primary public as learned women of the salons who are knowledgeable about "les honnêtetés" valued in and transmitted by these spaces.[7] This identification is reinforced by the moral that the tale is designed to teach: Polite speech and conversation, hallmarks of salon interaction, are powerful pedagogical tools that create knowledge. L'Héritier's tale reflects the valorization of the word often seen in works by women writers of this period in France, where the ability to control and use language was elevated over conventional feminine qualities such as beauty or other values such as wealth.[8] Fairy tales were thus used to inspire women to take up the pen and have an effect on their world through the written word. This is a quite different objective than entertaining the young minds of children or developing cautionary tales to advance compliance for certain modes of behavior.

Throughout *Les Enchantements* L'Héritier structures her story to highlight the art and influence of salon interactions, especially conversation. The narrator interjects many asides into her narrative, forcing the reader to disengage from her fiction and enter into a conversation with her, much as salon conversants might have done as they were listening to such stories recounted orally in the salons. This style thus concretely illustrates a collective engagement with literature that contrasts with a relationship between a solitary reader and a text.

L'Héritier goes even further in *Les Enchantements* and valorizes the premier genre of literary creation fostered by salon interaction. Her heroine, Blanche, is nourished by novels, the genre whose best practitioners in France were considered to be women. When Blanche's illiterate stepmother tries to prohibit her from reading novels, the heroine's weak father has one glorious moment when he stands up to this domineering, uncultured second wife and defends his daughter's love of novels and the value of reading. He states, "One cannot deny that well-written novels teach about the world and polite language. Blanche already has the disposition to speak

---

7. Much work has been done on what Joan DeJean has termed "salon writing." In seventeenth-century France, collective or collaborative writing was a hallmark of salon interaction. I argue that women not only wrote works such as novels but also critiqued all types of works and thus affected mainstream literary production in ways that have not been recognized in conventional literary histories (see Beasley, *Salons*). I explore further the influence of salon conversation on the history of French thought in my *Versailles Meets the Taj Mahal*.

8. For example, in "Sapho à Erinne," a chapter in her *Femmes Illustres*, Madeleine de Scudéry has Sapho exhort Erinne to turn to writing to inscribe her memory into posterity rather than relying on memories of her beauty (which Scudéry reminds her is ephemeral) or male-authored accounts.

well. I hope that reading these pleasant works will give her the habit of expressing herself politely."[9] He thus defends linguistic competency and mastery and substitutes knowledge and reading for beauty or docility as the prized traits of the model woman. In this tale, it is the stepmother's and her daughter's rejection of this value and their coarse language that identify them as the negative foil to the heroine's goodness. L'Héritier purposefully has the defense of novels and polite conversation spoken by the male authority figure, underscoring that salon culture and its values are not simply the domain of women. Salons were governed by women, but they were far from feminocentric spaces. The mastery of language, associated with the salons, was meant to exert an effect on men and women alike and make society as a whole more civilized. In the same vein, the fictional product of salon culture, the novel, was not considered the domain of women alone and certainly was not addressed solely to a female public. Like novels, the fairy tales coming out of the salons, often embedded in novels, were designed to reach a larger public beyond the walls of the salon, and their lessons were intended to have an impact on society as a whole.

Not content to have her male protagonist defend novels, L'Héritier goes a step further and reaches out to this salon public in her own voice. Immediately following the father's emphatic defense, L'Héritier/the narrator reenters the text and addresses the duchess to whom she dedicated the work, saying, "Perhaps you will find that Blanche's father is a bit too predisposed toward novels." Such interjections underscore how intricately related the fairy-tale genre at this period is to the salons that produced them. L'Héritier constructs a dialogue with the inscribed reader, who is a combination of the Duchesse d'Eperon and an ungendered worldly figure who is well versed in the values and practices associated with the salons. The dialogue between the author/narrator and the duchess symbolizes the larger conversation L'Héritier hopes to initiate between the text and the reading public at large. The form of this tale thus mirrors literary composition and critique in the salons, while the content expresses many of the values advanced by worldly salon participants. This tale and others offer examples of female agency associated with

---

9. "Du moins on ne peut pas nier que les romans bien fait n'apprennent le monde et la politesse du langage. Blanche a déjà assez de disposition à parler juste et j'espère que la lecture de ces agréables ouvrages achèvera de lui en donner l'habitude" (L'Héritier, 247). This passage is quite lengthy and takes up many of the points raised in treatises on the novel. Blanche's father elevates the novel over history, which was a position that generated a lot of discussion during this period. The father states, immediately before the passage cited, "L'Histoire peint les hommes comme ils sont et les romans les représentent tels qu'ils devraient être, et semblent par là les engager d'aspirer à la perfection" ("History depicts people as they are, and novels represent them as they should be, and in this way [novels] seem to entreat people to aspire to perfection").

seventeenth-century French women. Thus they do not enforce the gender stereo-types with which fairy tales are usually identified later in literary history. A useful class activity involves juxtaposing the traits of a female character from one of these lesser-known French versions with the more well-known versions, or even com-paring re-edited nineteenth-century versions of the tales with their seventeenth-century originals.

Blanche succeeds and is rewarded with happiness because she is able to speak well, not because she is beautiful. In the event the reader does not understand that it is words, not physical beauty, that is of value, L'Héritier condemns Alix, the horrible stepsister, to suffer the cruel fate of having toads come out of her mouth every time she opens it. This is considered the ultimate punishment. L'Héritier's elevation of the values advocated by salon culture is unambiguous. She advances that these values are as relevant for seventeenth-century France as for the land of fairies, a lesson that she underscores by weaving the real world into the fairy tale through her narratorial interventions and by eliciting responses from her real-life readers.

French fairy tales such as *Les Enchantements* take up topics of conversation in the salons and echo themes and concerns raised in texts produced in the salons, such as letters, novels, and maxims. Beginning with the Marquise de Rambouillet's famous *chambre bleue* in the 1620s and extending through the early eighteenth cen-tury, many literary works emanating from the salons presented serious challenges to prevailing attitudes regarding women's roles and place in society. Authors and salon interlocutors offered responses to the age-old *querelle des femmes*, addressing issues of marriage, education for women, writing, literary critique, property rights, and power structures. Developed in the salons, French fairy tales at the end of the sev-enteenth century continued to take up such themes begun almost a century earlier. Fairy-tale authors such as L'Héritier and Bernard, who are the second generation of seventeenth-century salon participants and women writers in France, inherited the desire to use literary creation to critique and not just to offer a way to escape reality. They perpetuated the conversations started in the salons and ensured their permanence by inscribing them into writing.[10]

In my class on salons and social networking in the classical period, we thus trace the evolution of conversation and use fairy tales to show how salon conversa-tion, transformed into narrative, results in serious challenges to prevailing attitudes. By placing and interpreting these fairy tales in the context that produced them,

---

10. See Stedman's *Rococo Fiction* for a detailed analysis of the shift from conversation to writing at the end of the century.

students learn to view the entire genre in a new light. Not just texts used to impart conventional, male-authored gender norms to malleable children, French fairy tales of the period are a link in the chain of protofeminist writing.

In addition to L'Héritier's *Les Enchantements*, I include two other tales from this period that also illustrate how French fairy tales are a product of a particular context that placed a premium on female agency and expression; these tales also underscore the need to interpret them in that context to understand their full meaning and function. Perrault's version of "Riquet à la Houppe" is well known, but, as is often the case, the version of the same tale by Catherine Bernard is not usually part of the fairy-tale lexicon and until recently was available only in the appendix of the Garnier Flammarion edition of Perrault's works.[11] Catherine Bernard composed two fairy tales, "Le Prince Rosier" and "Riquet à la Houppe." Both were first inserted into her novel *Inès de Cordoue* (1696). To an even greater extent than L'Héritier, Bernard modeled her works after the first generation of women novelists, specifically Lafayette and Villedieu. She was a member of salon circles and derived her support from this milieu. Unlike many other writers, she earned her living by writing; she never married, and she was cut off from her Protestant family when she converted to Catholicism just before Louis XIV revoked the Edict of Nantes. Bernard was thus conscious of her public as she composed her plays and novels and can be viewed as continuing the efforts of her predecessors to both valorize salon conversation and generate more conversations.

The comparison between Perrault's and Bernard's treatment of the same fairy tale provides a good example of women's efforts to shape the genre to advance their own collective goals. In Perrault's version a queen gives birth to an ugly son, Riquet. A fairy comes to their aid and endows him with so much *esprit*, or wit, that everyone who meets him forgets how physically unattractive he is. A few years later, in a neighboring kingdom, two daughters are born, one ugly and one beautiful. A fairy intervenes and makes the beautiful one as stupid as she is attractive and grants *esprit* to the ugly one. The beautiful one encounters Riquet in the forest; he has the power to grant *esprit* to whoever accepts to marry him. The princess accepts his proposal in exchange for *esprit* and agrees to marry him the following year. At the end of the year she is saddened by the fact that she is about to marry a hideous, albeit witty, prince. Riquet, undaunted, informs her that the same clearly clairvoyant fairy that had granted him the power to bestow wit on someone he loves had given the princess the ability to render the person

---

11. For a succinct biography that situates Catherine Bernard in her literary context, see Beasley, "Catherine Bernard." Interestingly, literary historians often identify Bernard as a cousin of Pierre and Thomas Corneille and as Bernard de Fontenelle's niece, but there is no concrete evidence to support such familial ties.

of her choice handsome if need be. The princess thus transforms him into the most handsome prince in the world, and the two marry and live happily ever after.

Like Perrault's, Bernard's tale posits *esprit* as a desirable characteristic, one that is on a par with the more traditional quality, beauty. But Bernard's tale differs from Perrault's in a few key ways. First, there is no prince; furthermore, the heroine is introduced in the first line as a scourge on the house of a nobleman from Grenada because she is so stupid, so bereft of *esprit*, that she is unattractive despite her incredible beauty. Unlike in Perrault's version, in Bernard's tale a hideous gnome comes out of the ground and offers to endow Mama, the beautiful girl lacking in *esprit*, with this essential trait if she will marry him at the end of a year. Because her lack of *esprit* has made her a pariah, despite her incredible beauty, she accepts the gnome's proposition out of desperation. During her year as a woman transformed by the gift of *esprit*, Mama falls in love with Arada, who is attracted to her because she has been transformed into the perfect combination of beauty and wit. But to keep her gift of *esprit*, Mama must eventually join her hideous gnome husband underground, and she prepares for the marriage promised in exchange for the transformative gift.

In contrast to Perrault's tale, where the ugly husband is transformed into "the most handsome, the most perfectly created, and the nicest man" the heroine has ever seen, Bernard's hapless heroine and the gnome are both miserable as they prepare for life together. The gnome finally reluctantly agrees to allow Mama to break her promise of marriage, but only if she gives up her *esprit*, which she realizes she cannot do if she hopes to keep her lover, Arada. She thus goes ahead with the marriage to keep this essential trait that attracted Arada in the first place and looks for a way to have both happiness and *esprit* in her life underground with the gnome. Mama convinces Arada to join her secretly underground, and each night she puts an herb under her gnome husband's nose to make him sleep so she can join her lover. Bernard, however, makes this happy ending only temporary. The gnome discovers the ruse and transforms the lover into a gnome like himself. The heroine, unable to distinguish between the two gnomes, is forced to live out her miserable life in despair. The moral of Bernard's story is that in the end all husbands become hideous and passion inevitably dies. Love cannot be controlled, especially by women. As is common in novels of the period, passion is a negative, destructive force that is especially dangerous for women, and marriage is a form of slavery that renders women powerless.[12]

---

12. I have often included another tale that has an interesting twist on the traditional fairy-tale "happily ever after plot": d'Aulnoy's "La Chatte Blanche" (The White Cat). Instead of being the reward

Whereas Perrault's tale ends "happily ever after" and celebrates true love and marriage, Bernard uses the same motifs to offer a fatalistic commentary on male-female relationships. A beast remains a beast in her tale, and a wife cannot escape the horrible bonds of a marriage over which she has no control. The dangers of passion and love, especially the undesirable bonds of marriage, were fodder for conversation and narrative throughout the century, with most of Bernard's female literary precursors urging women to value friendship over passion and to avoid the bonds of marriage if they could not reconfigure it. By the end of the century, though, salon culture as defined and created by women earlier in the century was waning, and the learned women who had shaped it were subjected to waves of attack by Molière and Boileau, among others.[13] Bernard's "Riquet" reflects this somber decline. One could argue that Bernard intends for her tale to be compared with Perrault's rosy version in order to generate new conversations.

In my classes I present the two "Riquet" tales as they might have been encountered in the salons: read aloud and discussed in light of the themes that have traversed the works read throughout the term. The full impact of Bernard's subversive rewriting of Perrault's traditional tale is especially apparent when students read the beginning and end of the two tales aloud, as the authors' initial publics would have encountered them. Students easily tease out the difference between the tales and in the discussion that follows explore reasons behind Bernard's transformation as well as the probable effect of this condemnation of marriage, love, and passion. The fairy tale is revealed to be a pedagogical tool used by women to challenge the societal beliefs and mores of their adult contemporaries, not a genre whose primary purpose is to transport children to an idyllic fairyland bearing little semblance to reality.

One final example can serve to solidify the bond that I have been stressing between salon culture and the fairy-tale genre in France: the multi-authored text titled *The Marquise/Marquis de Banneville* (1695).[14] I have taught this text

---

granted by the king to the son who accomplishes the tasks designed to prove his worthiness to rule, upon regaining her human form, the feline female protagonist saves the day and endows each son with a kingdom, saving one for herself and the son she has chosen as her prince.

13. Albistur and Armogathe, in their *Histoire du féminisme*, refer to the end of the century as "le grand renfermement de la femme." There is no doubt that as the first *salonnières* passed away, the new generation of women writers did not find the support their predecessors had enjoyed, at least from part of the public. See Beasley (*Salons*) for a discussion of the difference between the seventeenth- and eighteenth-century salons in France and the role of women in the literary sphere.

14. The MLA has produced a useful pedagogical edition of this text in both French and English, with an excellent introduction by Joan DeJean; see Choisy et al. (*Histoire*; *Story*).

successfully in French literature courses but also in English in a survey for women's and gender studies on the history of feminist thought. Students are amazed by the modernity of this text, so including it has the additional advantage of illustrating just how relevant even works that are centuries old can be.

The inclusion of *The Marquise/Marquis de Banneville* in my conversation course in particular allows me to end the term by re-creating the salon interactions the students have been studying and by highlighting how the values of this milieu found expression through literary production. This text provokes conversation, just as it did in the seventeenth century. Moreover, it was composed collectively by some of the authors who are most associated with the fairy-tale genre during this period, namely, L'Héritier and Perrault, along with the abbé de Choisy. It is possible that more voices were also involved in its composition. The text was originally first published in the *Mercure Galant*. Like the other fairy tales, this text is thus a product of conversation in terms of its form and content.

Unlike many traditional fairy tales, *The Marquise/Marquis* does not resort to magic for its happy ending; nor are fairies even present. In many ways the specialists of the fairy tale, Perrault and L'Héritier, created something that is magical but closely mirrors reality. They use humans, not animals or mythical or imaginary figures, to explore the traditional codes of masculinity and femininity, the roles of men and women in society, and conceptions of beauty—the same issues that surfaced in literary productions and salon conversations throughout the century. But in this instance they push the boundaries even further and interrogate gender norms and the way gender structures society and organizes personal interactions. *The Marquise/Marquis* tells the story of a boy whose mother makes the decision to raise him as a girl to keep him from the perils of the military. The heroine lives her life as a girl, falls in love, and discovers that she is indeed male only when her mother tells her just as she is about to marry her true love. She decides to marry him anyway. As Joan DeJean remarks in the introduction to her edition of this text, "The story's view of gender is anything but normative, prefiguring almost uncannily some of today's most avant-garde thinking about masculinity and femininity as acquired social and cultural identities" (DeJean, "Introduction," xix). In a surprising plot twist, her new husband turns out to be a woman. The two retire to a country estate, have a child, and live happily ever after. This text makes its readers think as well as converse, and in this sense it embodies the rich written fairy-tale tradition as it developed in France at the end of the seventeenth century.

In my experience, reading and teaching these French fairy tales in the context that produced them changes the way students relate to what they first considered an irrelevant, distant past and deepens their appreciation of the various roles literature can play in any society. Reviving the context in which the tales were produced—salon culture—also generates alternative interpretations of the texts and tropes that are familiar to fairy-tale readers. Students' conception of the genre and its purposes is radically transformed. No longer simply sources for the Disney-esque movies of their childhood, seventeenth-century French fairy tales recover their original intentionality, becoming protofeminist vehicles used especially by women to promote social change. Interpreting these tales in the salon context in which they were produced not only alters the way we read individual tales but also offers a new cultural and literary history of the most canonical period of French literary history and inspires students to approach literature differently, to interrogate how texts are produced and to what ends, and to question how and why their meanings have been transformed over time.

Bibliography

Albistur, Maïté, and Daniel Armogathe. *Histoire du féminisme français du moyen âge à nos jours.* Paris: Des Femmes, 1977.

Barchilon, Jacques. *Le Conte merveilleux français de 1690 à 1790: Cent ans de féerie et de poésie ignorées de l'histoire littéraire.* Paris: Honoré Champion, 1975.

Beasley, Faith E. "Catherine Bernard." In *The Dictionary of Literary Biography: Seventeenth-Century French Writers.* Ed. Françoise Jaouën. New York: Bruccoli Clark Layman, 2003. 39–43.

———, ed. *Options for Teaching Seventeenth- and Eighteenth-Century French Women Writers.* New York: MLA, 2011.

———. *Salons, History, and the Creation of Seventeenth-Century France: Mastering Memory.* Aldershot, UK: Ashgate, 2006.

———. *Versailles Meets the Taj Mahal: François Bernier, Marguerite de La Sablière, and Enlightening Conversations in Seventeenth-Century France.* Toronto: University of Toronto Press, 2018.

Bernard, Catherine. "Riquet à la Houppe." In *Contes de Perrault.* By Charles Perrault. Ed. G. Rouger. Paris: Classiques Garnier, 1967. 271–78.

Bottigheimer, Ruth B. *Fairy Godfather: Straparola, Venice, and the Fairy Tale Tradition.* Philadelphia: University of Pennsylvania Press, 2002.

———. *Fairy Tales and Society: Illusion, Allusion, and Paradigm.* Philadelphia: University of Pennsylvania Press, 1986.

———, ed. *Fairy Tales Framed: Early Forewords, Afterwords, and Critical Words.* Albany: State University of New York Press, 2012.

———. "France's First Fairy Tales: The Restoration and Rise Narratives of *Les facetieuses nuictz du Seigneur François Straparole*." *Marvels & Tales* 19.1 (2005): 17–31.

Chartier, Roger. *Ecouter les morts avec les yeux*. Paris: Fayard, 2011.

———. "Loisir et sociabilité: Lire à haute voix dans l'Europe modern." *Littératures Classiques* 12 (January 1990): 127–47.

Choisy, François-Timoléon de, Marie-Jeanne L'Héritier, and Charles Perrault. *Histoire de la Marquise-Marquis de Banneville*. Ed. Joan DeJean. New York: MLA, 2004.

———. *The Story of the Marquise-Marquis de Banneville*. Ed. Joan DeJean. Trans. Steven Rendall. New York: MLA, 2004.

Craveri, Benedetta. *The Age of Conversation*. Trans. Teresa Waugh. New York: New York Review, 2005.

DeGraff, Amy Vanderlyn. *The Tower and the Well: A Psychological Interpretation of the Fairy Tales of Madame d'Aulnoy*. Birmingham, AL: Summa, 1984.

DeJean, Joan E. "Introduction." In *The Story of the Marquise-Marquis de Banneville*. By François-Timoléon de Choisy, Marie-Jeanne L'Héritier, and Charles Perrault. Trans. Steven Rendall. New York: MLA, 2004.

———. *Tender Geographies: Women and the Origins of the Novel in France*. New York: Columbia University Press, 1991.

Duggan, Anne E. *Salonnières, Furies, and Fairies: The Politics of Gender and Cultural Change in Absolutist France*. Newark: University of Delaware Press, 2005.

Goldsmith, Elizabeth C. *Exclusive Conversations: The Art of Interaction in Seventeenth-Century France*. Philadelphia: University of Pennsylvania Press, 1988.

Goldsmith, Elizabeth C., and Dena Goodman, eds. *Going Public: Women and Publishing in Early Modern France*. Ithaca, NY: Cornell University Press, 1995.

L'Héritier de Villandon, Marie-Jeanne. *Les Enchantements de l'éloquence ou les effets de la douceur*. In *Contes de Perrault*. By Charles Perrault. Ed. G. Rouger. Paris: Classiques Garnier, 1967. 239–70.

Robert, Raymonde. *Le Conte de fées littéraire en France de la fin du XVIIe à la fin du XVIIIe siècle*. Paris: Honoré Champion, 2002.

Scudéry, Madeleine de. *Les Femmes illustres*. Paris: Antoine de Sommaville, 1642.

Seifert, Lewis Carl. *Fairy Tales, Sexuality, and Gender in France: 1690–1715*. Cambridge, UK: Cambridge University Press, 1996.

Seifert, Lewis Carl, and Domna C. Stanton, eds. *Enchanted Eloquence: Fairy Tales by Seventeenth-Century French Women Writers*. Toronto: Iter, 2010.

Stedman, Allison. *Rococo Fiction in France, 1600–1715: Seditious Frivolity*. Lanham, MD: Bucknell University Press, 2013.

Storer, Mary Elizabeth. *Un épisode littéraire de la fin du XVIIe siècle: La mode des contes de fées (1685–1700)*. Geneva: Slatkine Reprints, 1972 [1928].

Timmermans, Linda. *L'Accès des femmes à la culture, 1598–1715: Un débat d'idées de Saint François de Sales à la Marquise de Lambert*. Paris: Champion, 1993.

Warner, Marina. *From the Beast to the Blonde: On Fairytales and Their Tellers*. London: Chatto & Windus, 1994.

Zipes, Jack, ed. and trans. *Beauties, Beasts, and Enchantment: Classic French Fairy Tales*. New York: Meridian, 1991.

———, ed. *Don't Bet on the Prince: Contemporary Feminist Fairy Tales in North America and England*. New York: Methuen, 1986.

Long Ago and Far Away

HISTORICIZING FAIRY-TALE DISCOURSE

Jennifer Schacker

University students enter seminar rooms and lecture halls having had a lifetime of exposure to "fairy tales"—some of it guided by adult authority figures, much of it now recalled with nostalgia. Fairy tales seem to be ubiquitous in the childhoods and early educational experiences of my own students; fairy tales also serve as points of reference (if not the focus of study) in a remarkable range of academic disciplines, popping up in history, folklore, literature, foreign-language, education, and library science courses. A number of issues are at stake when designing a course focused on material with which students feel intimately familiar and over which they believe they already have a degree of mastery. One way of encouraging a class to approach the genre with open minds and a fresh critical perspective is to balance the (re)reading of what are now canonical texts with that of lesser-known and obscure tales. Equally important, courses on the fairy-tale genre can challenge students to examine the interpretive frameworks within which tales are and have been located: analyzing and historicizing the metacommunicative dimensions of tales (details that shape or imply a particular reading practice) and related paratexts. Here, I discuss some of the ways I have encouraged student exploration of such matters, drawing on paratextual and metacommunicative features of "texts" (print and cinematic) that students otherwise may be tempted to overlook.

One paratext I use in class—whether teaching a full survey course on fairy tales or a unit on the genre within a course on children's literature—is L. Frank Baum's introduction to the novel he framed as a "modern fairy tale": *The Wonderful Wizard of Oz* (1900). One benefit of discussing this one-page introduction with students is, admittedly, specific to my own research and teaching: I can trace my work on fairy-tale history to the undergraduate honors thesis I wrote on the Oz series in the late 1980s. Baum's introduction to the first and best-known of his Oz books gestures toward an extant history of fairy-tale books, and it was my curiosity about the nineteenth-century precedents for twentieth-century experiments (such as Baum's) that drew me to the study of material from that period—and has sustained my interest ever since.[1] I mention this here because it can be incredibly useful to map out for students the specific and idiosyncratic paths that led each of us into critical study of fairy tales; I suspect that many fairy-tale scholars likewise trace that path back to favorite books or series from childhood.

Whatever the special resonance that Baum's work may have for me, examination of his short introduction to *The Wonderful Wizard of Oz* can highlight a range of ideas and frameworks useful to the development of any course on English-language fairy-tale history. Here are some of the ends to which I have put this particular example to use in my classes.

CRITICAL READING OF FAIRY-TALE DISCOURSE

Baum's introduction itself is somewhat conventional by the standards of turn-of-the-century publishing for children. In it, Baum speaks *of* child readers, not *to* them. Along these lines, I ask my students to look for cues as to the text's implied reader. They often point out that Baum discusses the desires of "the modern child" and his own aspirations to offer "pleasure [to] children of today," suggesting that his concern for and interest in modern children (and their pleasure) is something shared with the reader—with children being objects but not participants in that conversation (Baum, n.p.).

From the outset, Baum establishes the "old-time fairy tale" as the backdrop against which his own new book stands in relief. Before making claims about his own work, Baum asserts an intrinsic link between the genre of the fairy tale and "childhood through the ages" and makes a distinction between old ("historical") fairy

---

1. I recently had an opportunity to revisit my early research on the Oz books in a paper commemorating the thirtieth anniversary of the publication of Jack Zipes's *Fairy Tales and the Art of Subversion*; see Schacker.

INTRODUCTION.

Folk lore, legends, myths and fairy tales have followed childhood through the ages, for every healthy youngster has a wholesome and instinctive love for stories fantastic, marvelous and manifestly unreal. The winged fairies of Grimm and Andersen have brought more happiness to childish hearts than all other human creations.

Yet the old-time fairy tale, having served for generations, may now be classed as "historical" in the children's library; for the time has come for a series of newer "wonder tales" in which the stereotyped genie, dwarf and fairy are eliminated, together with all the horrible and blood-curdling incident devised by their authors to point a fearsome moral to each tale. Modern education includes morality; therefore the modern child seeks only entertainment in its wonder-tales and gladly dispenses with all disagreeable incident.

Having this thought in mind, the story of "The Wonderful Wizard of Oz" was written solely to pleasure children of today. It aspires to being a modernized fairy tale, in which the wonderment and joy are retained and the heart-aches and nightmares are left out.

L. FRANK BAUM.

CHICAGO, APRIL, 1900.

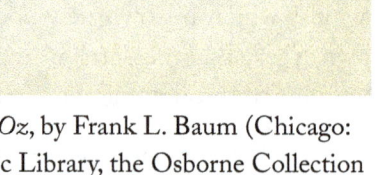

Figure 1. The introduction to *The Wonderful Wizard of Oz*, by Frank L. Baum (Chicago: George M. Hill, 1900, n.p.). Courtesy of Toronto Public Library, the Osborne Collection of Early Children's Books.

tales and new ("modern") fairy tales. Because my students have a chance to study the specific writers to whom Baum refers—the Brothers Grimm and Hans Christian Andersen—they instantly recognize that the Grimms and Andersen were in 1900 anything but ancient forefathers. Tales attributed to the Grimms had been in print in English for about 75 years when Baum penned his introduction, and tales by Andersen had been circulating in English translation for less than 60 years. The question then becomes, What is at stake in Baum's framing of those relatively recent chapters in fairy-tale history as canonical but also old and out-of-date?

Recognizing Intertextual Strategies

The vision of tales such as those of the Grimms and Andersen as connected to or reflective of "old-time" traditions is certainly powerful, and Baum mobilizes it strategically. In fact, explorations of "fairy tales" in my classes—whether we are studying texts framed as literary or texts that claim to represent oral traditions—repeatedly return to discussion of framing and the variety of (inter)textual strategies used to mark specific works as culturally valuable. In some cases, cultural or literary value seems to reside in links to a narrative heritage (what Charles Briggs and Richard Bauman would call the minimizing of intertextual gaps); in other cases—such as the one currently under examination—value resides in distance or departure from narrative precedents (the maximizing of intertextual gaps) (Briggs and Bauman, 149).

What exactly is the vision of the fairy tale against which Baum is seeking to define his own work in *The Wonderful Wizard of Oz* as *departure*? It became conventional in the early twentieth century to refer to a triumvirate of fairy-tale giants as representative of "classic" or canonical fairy-tale writers: Charles Perrault, the Brothers Grimm (two writers so frequently treated as one), and Hans Christian Andersen—or what I have come to refer to as PGA. It can be revealing to *challenge* Baum's characterizations of a portion of that tradition (he names the Grimms and Andersen as icons of traditional or "old-time fairy tales") and his characterization of his own work.

For instance, Baum dismisses the "blood-curdling incidents" and "fearsome morals" of "old-time" fairy tales, but my students often point out that *The Wonderful Wizard of Oz* is remarkably frank and noneuphemistic in its portrayal of conflict, death, and dismemberment: Baum has not dispensed with such things at all, although his calm treatment of potentially horrific narrative elements is worth studying in itself. And although there is little in the way of moralizing narrative intrusion in Baum's Oz books, individual characters do reflect on the implications of their situations and the behavior of those around them—so it seems disingenuous for him to claim that didacticism and moral education have no place in his books. Nevertheless, something important is at stake in Baum's efforts to link his work to a relatively recent history of fairy-tale publication (cast as "old") *and* to differentiate his work from that canon. With this in mind, I suggest to students that it may be less productive (and less interesting) to explore whether Baum's claims about his own distinctiveness are valid than it is to situate those claims in an emergent discourse about the fairy tale and, specifically, the fairy tale for children—one that Baum was able to assume his adult addressees would comprehend and one to which he actively contributed. This discourse continues to resonate today.

Likewise, students who have engaged in historicized close reading of tales from centuries past are in a great position to think critically about the ways in which generalized claims about "traditional" or "classic" fairy tales obfuscate or distort the distinctive character of diverse chapters in fairy-tale history (especially the elements of irony, self-parody, subversion, and playful intertextual reference). Several decades of critical and historical work on the fairy-tale writings of PGA have exposed more in the way of difference than similarity—in terms of respective audiences, cultural status, writing style, political and ideological factors, and so on. But what they do have in common—whether we are looking solely at the Grimms and Andersen (as does Baum) or we include Perrault in the mix (as have so many other twentieth- and twenty-first-century commentators)—is that their work dominated the English print market of fairy tales in the decades preceding Baum's statement, both contributing to and being shaped by emergent generic expectations through the work of various translators, editors, commentators, and illustrators. Although late-nineteenth-century editions of tales attributed to each are highly variable (e.g., neither the social satire of Andersen nor the courtly wit of Perrault is erased across the board, and debates about the appropriateness of each for child readers persist), it seems that the dominant vision of PGA by century's end was that they were of a kind despite their many fundamental differences.

Discussion of Baum's short introduction also offers opportunities for analysis of verbal-visual counterpoint. The page is decorated simply by W. W. Denslow's image of a sitting Toto—attentive, obedient, still—situated at the lower right-hand corner of the box that encloses the written text. Once students warm to the idea that points of harmony and tension between a text's verbal and visual elements are worth our attention, the ideas start to flow. For some, this image of the tame and attentive dog resonates with Baum's discussion of the child reader: children themselves might be seen as creatures that adults seek to tame and train. Or, like Toto, their attentiveness can be seen as a learned, adaptive, but potentially self-serving behavior—pleasing to a "master" but not necessarily a model to which they adhere when master is absent. Wherever students take their discussion of this image of Toto, the introductory page of prose is something that can be seen as self-contained and relatively static, both graphically and in terms of Baum's characterization of "folk lore, legends, myths and fairy tales" as the presumably unchanging backdrop against which his modern creation emerges as new, dynamic, and innovative. Interrogation of Baum's claims in this regard (including what is left implied, unspoken, and assumed about the nature of folklore and fairy tales), and the material form of the page on which those claims are made, becomes an exercise in critical and close reading of fairy-tale discourse. This critical reading practice is central to my teaching of the fairy tale, and Baum's introduction has proven to be a rich and relatively accessible focus for our collaborative close readings.

Of course, one need not cull examples from the history of fairy tales and children's literature to encourage this kind of critical reading practice; examples abound in later twentieth- and twenty-first-century popular culture. In survey courses on the fairy-tale genre (see, e.g., my syllabus in Chapter 6 of this volume), I generally begin in familiar terrain, as with a case study of the story known as "Sleeping Beauty." Assigned readings in this introductory unit can include English translations of Giambattista Basile's "Sole, Luna, e Talia" (1634) and Charles Perrault's "La Belle au bois dormant" (1697), as well as a sampling of Robert Coover's hypertextual experiments in *Briar Rose* (1996); but I also like to encourage discussion of select scenes from the 1959 Disney film, which has had a shaping influence on students' preconceptions of the "Sleeping Beauty" story. Although I encourage students to think critically about the ways in which the Disney animated feature adapts and alters Perrault's tale (to which it explicitly claims indebtedness), I do not spend much class time in plot comparison. Instead, I try to engage students in some analysis of the film's interpretive framing and the ways in which it establishes a horizon of expectations for the viewer of the fairy-tale film, focusing on details that they may have overlooked or forgotten, an exercise in defamiliarization.

Interestingly, Disney's *Sleeping Beauty* opens with images of a book, a sacred-looking and quasi-medieval text, linking the animated feature to a romanticized and wildly inaccurate vision of the tale's print history—and one that stands in stark contrast to the portrait of the genre's past offered by Baum 59 years earlier. The film's opening image of a bejeweled book with the golden inscription of "Sleeping Beauty" on its cover, positioned on a satin pillow as though in a museum or shop window display, opening as though by magic to reveal the elaborately decorated pages within (reminiscent of an illuminated manuscript), the stilted formality of the booming, disembodied male voice—details such as these are ones that my students have been able to identify as significant to the interpretive framing of the film. We discuss the ways in which these images serve to underscore links to print tradition (fetishized and fictionalized though it may be), one imbued with patriarchal and cultural authority.

Students enter seminar rooms and lecture halls having had a lifetime of exposure *not only* to "fairy tales" but also to representations of the genre's history, most of which are as charming, seductive, and misleading as the opening sequence of Disney's *Sleeping Beauty*. It is these elements of fairy-tale discourse that I encourage them to historicize and examine critically. In the case of the opening of *Sleeping Beauty*, close and critical viewing can offer perspectives on the ways in which many children have been introduced to fairy tales in the past 50 years or so: as an authoritative, hegemonic, unchanging, untouchable, precious, even sacred form. By recognizing that this is a powerful and persuasive construction, the product of specific ideological and historical conditions—not incontrovertible "fact"—we are free to spend the rest of the semester examining fairy-tale texts and paratexts in all their stylistic and ideological variability.

BIBLIOGRAPHY

Basile, Giambattista. "Sun, Moon, and Talia, Fifth Entertainment of the Fifth Day." Trans. Nancy Canepa. In *Marvelous Transformations: An Anthology of Fairy Tales and Contemporary Critical Perspectives*. Ed. Christine A. Jones and Jennifer Schacker. Peterborough, Canada: Broadview Press, 2012. 135–38.

Baum, L. Frank. *The Wonderful Wizard of Oz*. Chicago: George M. Hill, 1900.

Briggs, Charles L., and Richard Bauman. "Genre, Intertextuality, and Social Power." *Journal of Linguistic Anthropology* 2.2 (1992): 131–72.

Coover, Robert. *Briar Rose*. New York: Grove Press, 1996.

Perrault, Charles. "Sleeping Beauty." Trans. Christine A. Jones. In *Marvelous Transformations: An Anthology of Fairy Tales and Contemporary Critical Perspectives*. Ed. Christine A. Jones and Jennifer Schacker. Peterborough, Canada: Broadview Press, 2012. 177–84.

Schacker, Jennifer. "L. Frank Baum, Fairy Tale Discourse, and the History of Folklore." *Folklore Historian* 30 (2013): 7–21.

Sleeping Beauty. Dir. Clyde Geronimi. Walt Disney Corp., 1959.

Zipes, Jack. *Fairy Tales and the Art of Subversion: The Classical Genre for Children and the Process of Civilization*, 2nd ed. London: Routledge, 2012.

CHAPTER THREE

Teaching New Scholarly Approaches to Fairy Tales

Teaching Western Fairy-Tale Traditions in Women's Studies

Charlotte Trinquet du Lys

The idea of teaching classic fairy tales with a feminist approach started when I was asked by a liberal arts college in my area to teach a class in the women's studies department. I had already taught a French fairy-tale class at my public institution several times, as a survey of fairy tales from their institutionalization in seventeenth-century France to Disney, and turning this survey into a women's studies class sounded (almost) obvious. The fact that I teach in Florida forced me to incorporate, even from the beginning, Disney's fairy-tale reinterpretations, for socioeconomic reasons: Disney employs about 10% of the greater Orlando workforce, most of which consists of young people on short-term or part-time contracts. When I asked my students at both institutions if they knew any Disney employees, the response was an average of three per student, with about 35% of students themselves employed by Disney.

"Early Modern French Fairy Tales: The Power of Women" is an upper-level undergraduate course taught in English and designed to introduce seventeenth-century classic fairy-tale writing within the larger context of the Western fairy-tale tradition, from both sociohistorical and feminist perspectives. The idea is to equip students with the tools to decode the socially constructed realities from different periods of fairy-tale writing and to give them an understanding of the passage of traditions, knowledge, and cultures in these constructed realities. The main text for the course is the anthology *The Great Fairy Tale Tradition: From Straparola and Basile to the Brothers Grimm*, edited by Jack Zipes.

In this essay I survey the various components of the course. The essay is divided into three sections exemplifying how these components are articulated across the semester: the first week of class, the core body of the classes (14 weeks total), and the final project.

The First Week

The first week of class is spent on an introduction to the history of French fairy tales and on critical approaches that will be used during the semester. It is critical because it establishes the basic knowledge (sociohistorical context, critical approaches) students need to have before the primary materials can be introduced. Seventeenth-century literature and especially the fairy-tale tradition(s) are extremely interesting to study from a feminist angle because they correspond to a period in France when women enjoyed more literary freedom than ever before. When put into historical context, the fairy-tale vogue of the 1690s is part of a vast network of genres created and developed by women; these genres include psychological and historical novels, novellas, memoirs, and epistolary novels. Fairy-tale telling was already part of courtly entertainment in the mid-1670s, as reported by the well-known *salonnière* Madame de Sévigné in a 1677 letter to her daughter, and was therefore part of an oral female literary tradition more than 20 years before publication of the first fairy tale in France.[1] In this letter Madame de Sévigné refers to a new female entertainment at court, called *mitonner* (literally, "cooking up something" or "buttering up someone," in this case referring to tale-telling), which gives historians the first historical account of the structure of fairy tales as they will be published 20 years later (Trinquet, *Le Conte de fées français*, 47).

The fairy tales of the 1690s can be divided into two traditions. The main tradition, in terms of number of tales and number of pages as well as number of authors, which we call the *aristocratic style*, includes all the courtly women living at Versailles or in exile from Versailles, such as Charlotte-Rose de Caumont de La Force and Henriette Julie de Murat, Parisian tellers such as Marie-Catherine d'Aulnoy and Marie-Jeanne L'Héritier, and some male aristocratic writers, such as Jean de Mailly. This style resembles the novellas written earlier in the century by the *précieuses*, and the volumes of fairy tales that adopt this style are usually framed in the tradition of the European novella. When a frame story is used to introduce the fairy tales, most of the time it reiterates what Madame de Sévigné was telling her

---

1. Letter dated August 6, 1677 (Sévigné, 2: 516).

daughter in 1677 and presents the same venues, the same selection of participants, and the same narrative repertoire as described in the letter. Furthermore, the fairy tales written in these volumes also exemplify Sevigné's description of tales and exhibit the same aristocratic characters, settings, narrative structure, and length (about an hour). This *aristocratic style* did not survive in the literary canon after the eighteenth century and was brought back to scholarly light only in the 1920s.[2] Many texts, even though they were translated into several languages and transmitted into folklore through eighteenth- and nineteenth-century European chapbooks, are still unfamiliar to the general public and our students alike.

The other tradition, which resulted in a few fairy tales of the 1690s, could be called the *bourgeois style*. It is characterized by short, to-the-point stories with no frame tale, and the style tries to imitate what we commonly refer to as Mother Goose tales: tales supposedly told by peasant nurses to children and close to what we consider folkloric tales. These are Charles Perrault's classic fairy tales, and the Brothers Grimm after him.[3] This tradition is the only one that has survived in literature.

When speaking about seventeenth-century French fairy tales, we also have to debunk two notions that have ruled for centuries and have become conventional wisdom: (1) that stories told and written at that time came from folklore and (2) that theses stories were written for children. The French corpus between 1690 and 1700 includes 75 fairy tales, of which 37 are considered folkloric because they correspond to a tale type (ATU) and are commonly found in folk repertoires of magic tales that scholars gathered in the nineteenth and early twentieth centuries. However, out of these 37 tales, 33 can be linked to fairy tales already written by Giovan Francesco Straparola and Giambattista Basile. Straparola published *Le piacevoli notti* (The Pleasant Nights) in Venice in the 1550s; it was translated into French in 1560 and enjoyed an enormous success. *Le piacevoli notti* contains 13 fairy tales as well as novellas, moral exempla, and other forms of narrative. Basile's *Lo cunto de li cunti* (The Tale of Tales), the first volume entirely composed of fairy tales (49 independent tales and the frame tale, also a fairy tale), was published posthumously between 1634 and 1636 in Naples, in Neapolitan vernacular. Out of these 63 fairy tales, French authors used 38 tales to write 34 of their fairy tales.[4]

---

2. The first modern thesis on the 1690s vogue is Storer.

3. Giambattista Basile's and Giovan Francesco Straparola's fairy tales, the main sources of the 1690s fairy tales, correspond better to the aristocratic tradition because, even though the stories are on the short side, the authors framed their volumes of tales and their writing style, the characters' backgrounds, and the intended audiences in a way that is closer to the courtly tradition than to Perrault's.

4. One of these tales is not considered folkloric.

This corpus of French and Italian fairy tales includes variants of 24 different tale types.[5]

We can credit Charles Perrault, and after him, the detractor of aristocratic fairy tales L'Abbé de Villiers, with the assumption that fairy tales come from a folkloric repertoire, by way of wet nurses and servants who tell these stories to children. The frontispiece of Perrault's 1697 edition of *Histoires ou contes du temps passé* (Stories or Tales of Times Past) shows a servant telling stories to well-off children in front of a fireplace while she spins in the candlelight. The background includes a poster on which is inscribed "Contes de ma mere loye" (Tales of Mother Goose), the title Perrault chose for his 1695 manuscript of five tales. On the other hand, the idea that the fairy-tale vogue of the 1690s emerged from the storytelling of servants to children of the bourgeoisie was rejected by all the women fairy-tale writers—though L'Héritier stated that some of the tales were told to her when she was young. As exemplified by several of d'Aulnoy's frontispieces and L'Héritier's and Murat's dedications and prefaces, women writers refused to associate their tales with peasant lore and constantly reiterated that the fairy tales they created belonged to the literary tradition. Furthermore, they emphasized their own role in the creation of the literary fairy-tale tradition by calling their tales *contes <u>des</u> fées* (tales of *the* fairies), which has a double meaning: On one hand, it refers to tales about fairies' adventures; and on the other, it refers to tales *written* by fairies, who become synonymous with the women writers themselves (Trinquet, *Le Conte de fées français*, 52–62).[6]

Fairy tales in early modern Europe were not written for children but were part of a long tradition of literary entertainment in the form of short narrative going back to Boccaccio's *Decameron*, Chaucer's *Canterbury Tales*, and Marguerite de Navarre's *Heptaméron*. These stories were written by and for adults belonging to the court and salon societies and were often part of courtly games played by the elite during social gatherings. As shown by Lewis Seifert, it is only starting from Madame Leprince de Beaumont's retelling of Madame de Villeneuve's "Beauty and the Beast" (1756)

---

5. In the system originally designed by Antti Aarne and Stith Thompson to classify and organize tales according to their structure and variants (the ATU system), each tale type has a number and tales are grouped in what is commonly called the tale-type index. This classification was revised and updated in 2004 by Hans-Jörg Uther. See www.mftd.org/index.php?action=atu.

6. It is interesting to have students compare the frontispiece of Madame d'Aulnoy's *Suite des contes nouveaux, ou des fées à la mode* (Following of the New Tales, or the Fashionable Fairies; Paris: Compagnie des libraires, 1711) with Perrault's. D'Aulnoy takes the same frame but changes the night for a day, the bourgeois audience of children for aristocratic adolescents, the cat for a monkey, and the peasant spinner for a reading woman dressed as a Sybil. For more on this comparison, see Verdier.

that we begin to encounter a fairy-tale tradition intended for child readers (Seifert, "Madame Le Prince de Beaumont").

As students familiarize themselves with the background information, they are engaged with a particular critical approach: in this case, feminist theories. Teaching a course on any form of seventeenth-century literature from a feminist point of view presents a first problem with the anachronism of the word *feminism*. Women writers, as we previously explored, were writing for and in a salon society, among and for their peers. Their intent was never to englobe the female gender as a whole, and they had little to do with anyone but women of their class. This is why it is historically inaccurate to place these tales in the modern feminist tradition, and concepts such as Joan DeJean's "feminocentrism" or the notion of "protofeminism" are more correct when we discuss that period. Because of their immense success, however, the messages of the seventeenth-century female writers passed into the folklore of Western civilization, ultimately influencing large parts of modern female behavior. Because they were battling for causes that are fundamental to all women who are subjugated by male-dominant societies, their messages are now universally recognized to encompass all women. Unfortunately, their texts have not survived to the same degree, which is why it is critical to make students understand the connections between the early modern texts and our modern Western society by allowing the writing of women to resurface and by decoding their true meaning.

At the end of the first week of class, and with this background information in mind, students are ready to engage in a personal reflection on the typical ending of a classic fairy tale: marriage. To do so, students are asked to read two peer-reviewed articles. The first one restates the importance of the proto-feminist context that led to the writing of fairy tales: Faith Beasley's "Altering the Fabric of History: Women's Participation in the Classical Age." I ask them to reflect on a series of questions about the article:

According to Beasley, what was the usual marital status of women writers?
What do Scudéry's novels promote for women?
What does the word *feminocentric* mean in the context of women's writing of the seventeenth century?

The second article, "On Fairy Tales, Subversion, and Ambiguity: Feminist Approaches to the Seventeenth-Century French Contes de Fées" by Lewis Seifert, focuses more specifically on fairy tales and feminism. Once again, students have to reflect on their reading. For example, I ask them these questions: Talking specifically about fairy tales, Lewis Seifert explores three topics: personal expression and self, nostalgia, and marriage closure. Can you explain why he chose these topics and why they are important to the study of fairy tales and feminism? These assignments, in terms of Bloom's taxonomy, correspond to the following levels: cognitive 1.2 (comprehension: organizing, comparing, interpreting main ideas) and affective 2.2 (responding: students' active participation in the learning process).[7] Students are thus ready for the next levels.

WEEKS 2–14: FAIRY-TALE CYCLES

Once the sociohistorical background is understood and analyzed, the course is divided into cycles in which several fairy tales corresponding to a specific tale type (ATU) are studied together. For each cycle a different learning paradigm is proposed to broaden students' knowledge but also to give them the tools they will need to complete their final project. In each case students have to read several fairy tales, watch cinematographic versions, and read two to four peer-reviewed articles. The following is a list of the different cycles I chose to study:

The Cinderella Cycle (ATU 510A): "Cendrillon" (Perrault), "Finette-Cendron" (d'Aulnoy), "Aschenputtel" (Grimms), *Cinderella* (Disney). Learning paradigm: decoding fairy tales, proto-feminism, gender writing.

The Power of Love (ATU 310): "Petrosinella" (Basile), "Persinette" (de La Force), Rapunzel (Grimms), *Tangled* (Disney). Learning paradigm: rewriting fairy tales, sociohistorical context, women and power.

The Monster and the Bride Cycle (ATU 433B, 312): "Le Prince Marcassin" (d'Aulnoy), "Le Roi porc" (Murat), "La Belle et la bête" (Leprince de Beaumont), *Beauty and the Beast* (Disney), "La Barbe bleue" (Perrault), *Barbe bleue* (Catherine Breillat). Learning paradigm: gender studies.

The Sleeping Beauty Cycle (ATU 410): *Roman de Perceforest*, "Sole, Luna, e Talia" (Basile), "La Belle au bois dormant" (Perrault). Learning paradigm: feminist approaches.

---

7. See Bloom et al. Bloom's taxonomy was created in 1956 by Benjamin Bloom, Max Englehart, Edward Furst, and David Krathwohl. It consists of a categorization of six major educational goals, divided between cognitive (knowledge, comprehension, and critical thinking) and affective (the way students react emotionally). The cognitive learning levels are represented in the form of a pyramid, where the base is the lower learning level and the top is the highest learning level. The six categories are (1.1) knowledge, (1.2) comprehension, (1.3) application, (1.4) analysis, (1.5) synthesis, and (1.6) evaluation. In 2001 the Bloom taxonomy was revised as follows: remembering, understanding, applying, analyzing, evaluating, and creating. The affective levels of learning are categorized as follows: (2.1) receiving, (2.2) responding, (2.3) valuing, (2.4) organizing, and (2.5) characterizing.

Well/Badly Raised Cycle (ATU 333): "Le Petit Chaperon rouge" (Perrault), "Rot-käppchen" (Brothers Grimm). Learning paradigms: folklore, literature, and pop culture; moralism; education; patriarchal views in literature.

Women Soldiers Cycle (ATU 884A): "Costanzo-Costanza" (Straparola), "La serva d'aglie" (Basile), "Le Sauvage" (Murat), "Marmoisan" (L'Héritier), "Belle-belle ou le chevalier Fortuné" (d'Aulnoy). Learning paradigms: the place of women in European societies, reality versus fiction.

The Fairies Cycle (ATU 480): "Le tre fate," "Le doie pizzelle" (Basile), "Les Fées" (Perrault), "Les Enchantements de l'éloquence" (L'Héritier). Learning para-digms: male vs. female writers, the power of fairies, the power of writing.

To illustrate how I teach these cycles, I focus on the second and third weeks of the semester, the Cinderella cycle, using the tales by Charles Perrault ("Petit Poucet" and "Cendrillon"), Madame d'Aulnoy ("Finette Cendron"), the Grimms ("Aschenputtel"), and Disney's *Cinderella*. Through a series of written assignments, secondary readings, and class and group discussions, students learn to decode fairy tales, understand proto-feminism, and recognize gendered writing. What is par-ticularly interesting about the fairy-tale tradition(s) of the 1690s is the fact that in several cases, as in this one, the tales—taken from the Italians or not—were rewrit-ten by several authors, thus emphasizing the diverse styles of fairy-tale writing and the personal agendas of the writers. After understanding where the seventeenth-century tales are situated in the spatiotemporal history of the tale type, students compare Perrault's versions with Madame d'Aulnoy's (first individual assignment).

Perrault and Madame d'Aulnoy published their tales three months apart, and because, interestingly enough, "Le Petit Poucet" and "Cendrillon" were not part of Perrault's 1695 manuscript, we have to consider the possibility that the tales were written as a friendly (or not) competition. A close reading of the tales reveals that d'Aulnoy had Perrault's version of "Cendrillon" in mind when she wrote her tale. "Le Petit Poucet" and "Cendrillon" are both elevation tales, where the hero goes from rags at the beginning of the tale to riches at the end. Madame d'Aulnoy's "Finette Cendron," however, combines both tales to form a restoration tale, fea-turing a strong female character who loses everything, only to regain it at the end. Both tales are examples of the two styles in which tales were written at the time. We have the short (male) versions with characters coming from a lower social class and making their way to success through industry and wit. The vocabulary and the plot are simple, and although the moral ending of the tale is clearly intended for an adult audience, the tale itself is simple enough that it can be understood by a large audience. This is an example of the bourgeois style I introduced in the first week of class. On the other hand, we have a long tale that introduces many subplots that portray the upper class and their codes of honor and behavior. This style is what I call the aristocratic style and is mostly authored by women, with the exception of Jean de Mailly's fairy tales. Even though the story ends with a marriage, "Finette Cendron" is one of Madame d'Aulnoy's most proto-feminist tales.

Through brain-storming in small groups and class discussions, the students are encouraged to dig deeper, as we add the Grimms' "Cinderella" to the equation. Their first reactions are essentially the same from year to year: Perrault focuses mostly on the physical appearance of his heroine, whereas the Grimms describe her as devout; in both cases, Cinderella is helpless without her godmother, making her a one-dimensional character. As one male student described it, Cinderella is "much more *feminine* and soft in nature and in need of saving by the heroic and noble prince." All students agree that despite the title, male-authored stories offer a bigger, more important role to the male characters by concentrating on their heroic accomplishments, whereas the women are either vile or passive or exist within the realm of the men (i.e., "for their pleasure").

D'Aulnoy, however, gives a voice, a name, and multidimensionality to her heroine. Finette-Cendron is presented as witty, independent, skillful, reliable, grateful, and forgiving. But at this point only a handful of students understand what is mainly at stake in d'Aulnoy's tale: Finette-Cendron, by being given a voice, can negotiate her marriage contract, one of the most important battles for the early modern aristocracy and one that has been portrayed in works of literature such as *Clélie, histoire romaine* (Madeleine de Scudéry, 1654–1660). In this seventeenth-century best seller, the two heroines open a discussion on the value of marriage. Sapho is in favor of women not marrying and therefore staying free, a theory that is also put forth at the end of Madame de Lafayette's first psychological novel, *La Princesse de Clèves* (The Princess of Clèves, 1678). Clélie's point of view differs, however, by accepting marriage so long as women get to write half the contract, which is exactly what happens at the end of Finette's search and her meeting with the prince. In d'Aulnoy's version, Finette not only "writes" her history (by retelling it to her future parents-in-law) but also negotiates her wedding contract—her father-in-law will return the usurped kingdom to her parents (therefore the kingdom will no longer be part of the in-laws' estate and will belong to her when her parents die)—and negotiates marriages that are advantageous to her sisters (Trinquet, "Voix clandestines," 77). D'Aulnoy, in challenging Perrault's "Le Petit Poucet" and "Cendrillon," inscribes herself into the matrilineal and feminocentric culture of her predecessors. Thus her tale cannot be understood unless it is considered in the sociopolitical climate of its creation and within the context of the century-long legal battle for state- versus religiously sanctioned marriages; at the time of the fairy-tale vogue, Louis XIV was finally regaining control of the marriage laws, which had previously been in the hands of the clerical legislature.[8]

Likewise, Disney's version of Cinderella cannot be separated from the time and space of its creation, and when confronted with d'Aulnoy's version, which is the next assigned step, students have a much better understanding of their own sociocultural upbringing. "Cinderella" is no longer a cute movie they saw when they were children but a fundamental step in their own cultural development. After reading two peer-reviewed articles that they select from a list of five, their next group assignment is to dissect the various elements (traits, functions, and motifs) of the versions. Their reaction is interesting; the students (especially the women) get angry when it becomes obvious to them that they have been "cheated" by their own cultural environment into believing that girls should be passive creatures who have to wait politely for their prince. "Cinderella," in this classroom context, acts as their rite of passage into understanding where they come from, something many of them (especially in Central Florida, where Disney's influence is not questioned) never thought about before. For the final class activity, students rewrite "Cinderella" with the elements of the versions they think best suit their own generation(s).

At the end of this cycle, students have completed three individual homework assignments, three group activities, and one class activity; they have read and summarized two peer-reviewed articles (in the form of a quiz), and they have viewed a movie with a critical perspective in mind. They are thus two steps further into Bloom's taxonomy scale: They have broken down the information presented to them and identified and understood key concepts about writing fairy tales and conveying a standpoint (cognitive: 1.4, analysis). Furthermore, they are able to make inferences and judgments about the information they received and to find evidence in the texts to support theories put forth in the secondary readings (cognitive: 1.5, evaluation). By analyzing Disney's *Cinderella* against the background of early modern texts, students can attach value to their own sociohistorical context and associate it with the knowledge they have acquired (affective: 2.3, valuing). Finally, by reassembling the tale according to their own societal expectations, they have learned to compare, relate, and elaborate on what has been learned and are able to put together different values, information, and ideas and accommodate them within their own schema (affective: 2.4, organizing).

---

8. On women and marriage and salon literature, see DeJean; and Beasley (*Revising Memory*).

Every cycle repeats more or less the same formula, each time with a focus on a different critical approach and a variation of group and individual assignments, quizzes, and critical readings and viewings. During these cycles, students are also encouraged to further prepare for the final project by producing their own rewriting of the studied tales, for extra credit and a chance to have their version selected and read on our radio show (*Secrets of the Fairies*, Wednesdays, 9–10 am, WPRK, 91.5 FM).[9] One-third of the way into the semester, they are ready to start their final assignment, for which they will have periods available in class for consultations with me.

The Final Project

The final project, in lieu of a research paper for this class, is a (re)creation of a fairy tale. The goal of this project-based collaborative assignment is to re-create a salon experience in a twenty-first-century community, by reproducing the tale creation that was an integral part of the intellectual life of seventeenth-century literary salons. Students are given the choice between two models of salon creation. The first model, the *Chambre bleue* model, consists of a group of students rewriting or creating a fairy tale together. This common creation of a literary text reflects what happened in the early salons, such as Madame de Rambouillet's famous *Chambre bleue*. In this *ruelle* (the word *salon* is an anachronism; *ruelle* refers to the space between the bed and the wall in the chamber where Madame de Rambouillet received her guests), women and men presented and discussed their literary creations in an amicable atmosphere conducive to collaborative elaboration and publication. The most important collaborative work coming from the *Chambre bleue* is *La Guirlande de Julie*, a compilation of poems created by the salon aficionados and dedicated to Julie d'Angennes, daughter of Madame de Rambouillet. This piece is not only a good example of collaboration but also one of the most prized samples of *préciosité* writing. At the other end of the century, the d'Aulnoy salon model is a little different in the sense that the group chooses a tale type for which every member of the group will create their own version and publish it separately, in a competitive setting, mimicking what happened during the fairy-tale vogue of the 1690s.

Choosing one of these two historical literary models allows tale creation to become interactive: students collaborate with other members of their group (in

9. At Rollins College we have produced a series of local radio shows in which we speak about various topics. I encourage my students to rewrite their tales and present them to me for a live reading on the air. The series is still available at secretsofthefairies.org/.

the class) and also, potentially, with a broader audience (Internet, user fiction, fan fiction, radio show, other courses, etc.), mirroring the literary production of the seventeenth century. Within these parameters, students are completely free to use any tale type, style, technological tool, and all of their imagination. Although they are not assigned a specific critical approach to work with, their reflective statement about the project has to specify from which perspective they have chosen to write their tale. When the projects are finally presented (often to the class and some community members), students have to justify their creation and analyze the others. The final creations range from a classic rewriting to completely new stories and from a storytelling in front of an audience to plays, computer-created cartoons, stop-motion animation (with Lego, modeling clay, hand puppets), puppet shows, and even beautifully handwritten and illustrated manuscripts. They have synthesized an entire semester of lectures, readings, and discussions into a fun and creative project, proving that the famous seventeenth-century motto *plaire et instruire* is more than ever a reality.

In terms of Bloom's taxonomy, at the end of the semester, students have achieved the highest levels in both cognitive and affective areas: They have compiled information in new patterns and found alternative solutions to what they were reading and analyzing (cognitive: 1.5, synthesis); they have presented and defended their opinions by making judgments about the received information and the validity of ideas (cognitive: 1.6, evaluation); and finally, they have developed new values acquired through learning about new cultural contexts. All of this exerts influence on their behavior and is incorporated into the way they learn in the future (affective: 2.5, characterizing). They are leaving the classroom with a new knowledge of the creation, diffusion, and institutionalization of the Western literary fairy tale with an understanding of diverse critical approaches (sociohistorical, feminist/gender studies) and, most of all, with the lifelong skill of being able to read and comprehend socially constructed realities.

BIBLIOGRAPHY

Basile, Giambattista. *Lo cunto de li cunti: Overo lo trattenemiento de peccerille*. Ed. Mario Petrini. Rome: Laterza, 1976.

Beasley, Faith. "Altering the Fabric of History: Women's Participation in the Classical Age." In *A History of Women's Writing in France*. Ed. Sonya Stephens. Cambridge, UK: Cambridge University Press, 2000. 64–83.

———. *Revising Memory: Women's Fiction and Memoirs in Seventeenth-Century France*. New Brunswick, NJ: Rutgers University Press, 1990.

Bloom, Benjamin, M. D. Engelhart, E. J. Furst, W. H. Hill, and D. R. Krathwohl. *Taxonomy of Educational Objectives: The Classification of Educational Goals*. Handbook I, *Cognitive Domain*. New York: David McKay, 1956.

d'Aulnoy, Madame. *Contes*, 2 vols. Ed. J. Barchilon and P. Hourcade. Paris: Société des Textes Français Modernes, 1997.

DeJean, Joan. *Tender Geographies: Women and the Origins of the Novel in France*. New York: Colombia University Press, 1991.

Grimm, Jacob, and Wilhelm Grimm. *The Complete Fairy Tales of the Brothers Grimm*. Trans. Jack Zipes. New York: Random House, 2003.

Lafayette, Madame de. *La Princesse de Clèves*. Paris: Garnier Flammarion, 1980.

La Guirlande de Julie, augmentée de pièces nouvelles publiée sur le manuscript original avec une notice de gaignières et de bure et des notes par Ad van Bever. Paris: Sansot Libraire, 1907.

Leprince de Beaumont, Jeanne-Marie. *La Belle et la bête*. Paris: Poche, 2002.

L'Héritier de Villandon, Marie-Jeanne. *Oeuvres meslees*. Paris: Jean Guignard, 1696.

Mailly, Chevalier de. *Contes galans dédié aux dames*. Paris: Brunet, 1698. Reprinted in *Cabinet des fées ou Collection choisie des contes des fées . . .*, vol. 5 (Amsterdam, 1785); and in *Nouveau Cabinet des Fées*, vol. 6 (Geneva: Slatkine Reprints, 1978).

Murat, Madame la comtesse de. *Histoires sublimes et allegoriques, par Madame la Comtesse D***, *dediees aux fées modernes*. Paris: Florentin et Pierre Delaulne, 1699.

Perrault, Charles. *Contes*. Ed. Roger Zuber. Paris: Lettres Françaises, Coll. de l'Imprimerie Nationale, 1987.

Scudéry, Madeleine de. *Clélie, histoire romaine*. Paris: 1660. Geneva: Slatkine Reprints, 1973.

Seifert, Lewis. "Madame Le Prince de Beaumont and the Infantilization of the Fairy Tale." *French Literature Series* 31 (2004): 25–39.

———. "On Fairy Tales, Subversion, and Ambiguity: Feminist Approaches to the Seventeenth-Century French Contes de Fées." In *Fairy Tales and Feminism: New Approaches*. Ed. Donald Haase. Detroit: Wayne State University Press, 2004. 53–71.

Sévigné, Madame de. *Correspondance*, 3 vols. Ed. Roger Duchêne. Paris: Gallimard, 1972.

Storer, Mary Elizabeth. *La Mode des contes de fées (1685–1700)*. Paris: Edouard Champion, 1928.

Straparola, Giovan Francesco. *Les Facetieuses Nuits de Straparole, traduites par Jean Louveau et Pierre de Larivey*, 2 vols. 1573. Paris: P. Jannet, 1857.

Trinquet, Charlotte. *Le Conte de fées français (1690–1700): Traditions italiennes et origines aristo-cratiques*. Tubingen: Narr Verlag, 2012.

———. "Voix clandestines dans les contes de fées, l'exemple de 'Finette-Cendron' de Madame d'Aulnoy." *Cahiers du Dix-septième: An Interdisciplinary Journal* 10.2 (2006): 65–82.

Uther, Hans-Jörg. *The Types of International Folktales: A Classification and Bibliography*, 3 vols. Helsinki: Suomalainen Tiedeakatemia, 2004.

Verdier, Gabrielle. "Figures de la conteuse dans les contes de fées féminins." *Dix-septième siècle* 180 (July–September 1993): 481–99.

Villeneuve, Gabrielle-Suzanne de. *La Belle et la bête.* Paris: Folio, 2010.

Villiers, Abbé de. *Entretiens sur les contes de fées et sur quelques autres ouvrages du temps: Pour servir de préservatif contre le mauvais goût—Dediez à messieurs de l'académie Française.* Paris: Jacques Collombat, 1699.

Zipes, Jack, ed. *The Great Fairy Tale Tradition: From Straparola and Basile to the Brothers Grimm.* New York: Norton, 2001.

Cognitive-Affective Approaches to Fairy Tales

Maria Nikolajeva

Although fairy tales are frequently believed to be simple and straightforward narratives, on closer consideration they are multifaceted and laden with profound layers of meaning. Yet the various scholarly approaches to fairy tales, including structural, sociohistorical, psychoanalytical, and educational, have one point in common: Fairy-tale characters are not endowed with a rich internal life. They have their fixed roles in the plot, representing clear-cut polarities of good and evil, without further nuances. It is therefore unlikely that readers or listeners engage with fairy-tale agents emotionally, the way we do with novels. Fairy-tale readers are primarily interested in the plot, and the characters are instrumental: We may want them to achieve their goals and for the villains to be punished, but we do not empathize with them; we do not assume that they have consciousness that motivates their actions. Even psychoanalytical approaches deal with symbols rather than actual emotions.

A radically innovative way of thinking about fairy tales, particularly about fairy-tale characters, is found in cognitive criticism, a relatively new direction of inquiry at the crossroads of literary studies and cognitive science. Cognitive criticism examines how texts stimulate recipients' perception, attention, imagination, prediction, retrospection, memory, and other cognitive activity through recognition of recurrent patterns: scripts, schemas, and prototypes. A script is a typical mininarrative; for instance, the hero leaves home, seeks and wins a fortune, and returns home. A schema is a recognizable situation: A hero meets a helper and gets a magical object. A prototype is a recurrent character or object: a hero, a villain, a fairy godmother, a magic wand, or a magic mirror. On encountering these patterns in a story, our brains retrieve stored memories of similar patterns, compare them, reconfigure the information, and store it again.

Existing literary cognitive studies focus predominantly on novels that feature complex, round, dynamic characters with a sophisticated internal life. However, some scholars have also examined popular culture, that, like fairy tales, is repeatedly identified as deliberately lacking psychological depth. As structural approaches demonstrate, the basic structures of fairy tales are universal, including plot and character gallery. The cognitive approach explores how texts evoke recipients' responses through deviations from familiar schemas and scripts, that is, variations in setting, character constellation, the nature of conflict and complications, and the outcome. Thus students acquainted with the best-known version of "Snow White" are surprised by versions featuring warriors, robbers, or dragons rather than dwarfs. They do not expect Little Red Riding Hood to shoot the wolf, to marry him, or to tame him and then return him to his natural habitat, as it happens in some modern retellings. Such deviations demand attention and imagination because the familiar script becomes unpredictable.

Cognitive criticism also explores why and how we engage with fictional characters, in particular, how we use theory of mind, or mind modeling (the ability to understand other people's thoughts, intentions, and beliefs) and empathy (the ability to understand other people's emotions). Although fairy-tale characters are not associated with complex interiority, cognitive criticism demonstrates, with reference to cognitive science, that human brains can, through mirror neurons, respond to fictional events and characters as though they are real and that fiction stimulates such responses through various narrative devices. With empathy and mind modeling as analytical tools, it becomes possible to discern an implicit interiority that explains why we engage cognitively and emotionally with fairy-tale characters at all, even though they obviously have no thoughts or emotions, no intentions, no motivations, and no beliefs or ethical values. However, cognitive criticism does not simply bring back the psychological dimension of fictional characters, dismissed by formalism and structuralism. Instead, it examines the ways that texts invite and sometimes force recipients to use empathy and mind modeling, both with life-to-text projection (i.e., relating fictional situations to their own life experiences) and with text-to-life projection (i.e., making inferences from fictional characters that might prove helpful in real life).

When engaging with fairy tales, we align with heroes merely on account of their being heroes, and we either do not care about or feel aversion toward characters who prevent heroes from obtaining their goals. However, as cognitive critics point out, the attraction of fiction is that it satisfies our curiosity about other people's minds. Paradoxically, whereas the minds of fairy-tale heroes are seldom transparent in the same way that novel protagonists' frequently are, our real-life experience is closer to fairy tales than to novels. Novel characters' interiority is deliberately exposed to readers. In real life, however, we can only make inferences about other people's minds through their direct speech, behavior, facial expressions, or body language. Misreadings can be fatal. The straightforwardness of fairy tales allows us to test mind modeling without running the risk of real-life consequences. This is one of the many possible explanations for why we remain fascinated by fairy tales long after the emergence of the novel. Obviously, we get deeply engaged with fairy-tale heroes, albeit in a different way from how we engage with novel characters. Yet we cannot avoid making guesses about fairy-tale characters' interiority, even though, or perhaps especially because, there are no visible expressions of their thoughts and emotions in the text. Cognitive criticism would claim that fairy tales have a strong potential for creative mind modeling and empathy, even though it may not be self-evident. The cognitive approach prompts questions about interiority that is well hidden beneath the surface.

Suggestions for Teaching Activities

When using the cognitive approach to fairy tales, you want to catch students' attention and shake their preconceptions of fairy tales as straightforward narratives with an action-oriented plot, flat, static actors subordinate to the plot, and clear-cut divisions between good and evil, moral and immoral. Preferably, students should already have been introduced to other approaches. They might be aware that fairy tales reflect the social structures of the times in which they were written, which accounts for the abundance of stepparents or the practice of abandoning infants in the woods during famine. If exposed to structuralist approaches, they will know that fairy tales consist of a limited number of building blocks combined in a particular order; prohibition is followed by violation, pursuit by escape, and battle by victory. Such an approach emphasizes that the actors in fairy tales have their fixed roles and therefore act on the demand of the plot rather than on their psychological traits. The fairy-tale villain is evil because the plot needs an evil actor, not because the actor has evil intentions motivated by external circumstances or internal traits. Likewise, the hero acts the way he does because the plot dictates this; besides, heroes tend to have a supporting team without whose assistance they would not manage their tasks. Heroes are not necessarily brave or smart; they are simply lucky. Finally, students are likely to have been introduced to psychoanalytical approaches to fairy tales—Freudian, Jungian, or both—which view the fairy-tale plot and actor gallery as a reflection of complex processes of the human psyche.

In my experience, students get suspicious when introduced to cognitive-affective methods, because these involve a radically different way of thinking about stories. Today, most students in English departments are trained to consider texts from a hermeneutic perspective, with a task of providing an interpretation. Cognitive-affective engagement with texts suggests abandoning hermeneutic activity, instead focusing on how the text appeals to recipients, on how it stimulates attention, imagination, and memory. Although it may initially feel alien, students find this approach gratifying.

Let us consider the Brothers Grimm's "Snow White" as an example of how a cognitive-affective approach might be used in the classroom. Try to steer students away from interpretation. Instead, focus on the cognitive-affective affordances of the story: How exactly does the story make recipients interested? If students are familiar only with critical approaches like those mentioned, they may be surprised by questions such as: *How does the stepmother in "Snow White" (ATU 709) feel when she orders her stepdaughter to be killed?*

Most students will be perplexed because, in engaging with fairy tales, we naturally and logically empathize with the hero/heroine and do not care about other actors' feelings. However, to amplify the effect, offer a follow-up question: *How does Snow White feel when she realizes that her stepmother wants to kill her?*

Presumably, the students will be at a loss when confronted with this question as well. They have invested in Snow White because she is the main character—moreover, the title character. It is her story, not the stepmother's story (as some contemporary fractured fairy tales rewrite it). Yet students are typically interested in the plot: Will Snow White escape? Where will she go? Whom will she meet? Will the stepmother learn that Snow White is alive, and what will she do about it? And will there be a prince for Snow White to marry? They anticipate this sequence of events because, stored in their minds, they have a script, built on previous stories they have encountered. Any deviation from the script will alert them. Try to ask some of the following:

What if the huntsman follows the stepmother's orders and kills Snow White?
What if Snow White escapes from the huntsman but perishes in the woods of hunger and exposure?
What if the prince never comes along, and Snow White sleeps in her glass coffin for ever and ever?

Such possibilities disrupt the script and affect engagement with the story. The first two options simply do not allow the plot to develop. The last option contradicts the fairy-tale script of a happy ending. A happy ending is, however, not imperative. Some versions use different scripts: In Charles Perrault's "Little Red Riding Hood" the wolf gobbles up the girl, and, according to Perrault and his time, she deserves it. When your students claim that fairy tales always have a happy ending, have some examples at hand to show the opposite. Suggest, as a thought experiment, a version in which Snow White's eternal sleep is a fair punishment for disobedience.

Return to Snow White's ostensible thoughts and feelings. With conventional approaches, either she does not have any or we do not care about them. We are on her side against the evil stepmother; we are invested in the plot tension between good and evil, innocent and guilty. Yet being on someone's side does not automatically mean that we are interested in their interiority; we may simply want the heroine to succeed. A cognitive approach suggests the question: *Does Snow White know that her stepmother hates her?*

When you pose this question to your students, whatever they reply, follow up with: *How do we know it?* That question demands embedded mind modeling: We believe that character A has certain beliefs about character B's emotions and intentions. Ask the students to go back to the story, searching for indications that Snow White is aware of her stepmother's feelings toward her. Snow White is a young child (according to most versions, she is 7 years old when she surpasses the stepmother in beauty), likely to believe that everyone is benevolent, and there are no examples of the stepmother treating her badly—unlike, for instance, Cinderella's stepmother. Snow White has no reference frame to compare her stepmother to her mother, whom she never met; she may know that her mother was beautiful, but so is the stepmother. It is conventional to associate beauty with virtue. Seven-year-old Snow White has no reason to believe that her stepmother dislikes her. We are in a privileged position over Snow White because we know something that she does not know. *Yet how exactly do we know that the stepmother hates Snow White?*

The students might suggest that the stepmother hates Snow White because it is natural for stepmothers to hate their stepdaughters. In this conclusion, they, first, follow a script according to which fairy-tale stepmothers hate their stepdaughters. You may prompt them to recall similar fairy tales: "Cinderella," "Six Swans," "Diamonds and Toads," or "Mother Holle." Tell them, if they have not heard it yet, or remind them, if they have, that fairy-tale stepmothers are circumscriptions of birth mothers and that the stepmother figure was introduced by fairy-tale collectors as less offensive in the rivalry between an older and a younger woman. Looking at the mother-daughter conflict is a psychoanalytical approach, and noting how and why birth mothers were replaced by stepmothers involves sociohistorical models. Second, the students probably realize that the stepmother's hatred is a schema necessary for the plot: She is the heroine's antagonist and thus the plot engine. This is a structuralist approach.

However, from the cognitive-affective perspective, such explanations are inconclusive. Curious about human nature, not least about the perversity of an evil mind, we contemplate the motivations and intentions behind the actors' behavior. The story offers us many clues. The new queen is described as proud, haughty, and vain, traits viewed as negative, if not directly evil. But when the queen hears from the mirror that Snow White is more beautiful, her true nature is revealed: She is envious; she hates her stepdaughter and wants to get rid of her. Such feelings are unequivocally evil and immoral. Ask the students: *Are the stepmother's feelings justified?*

Most of them will argue passionately that they are not. If some believe that they are, it will make a fascinating discussion! In any case, follow up with: *Do you understand the stepmother's feelings?* If they do, they have taken a major step in their cognitive-affective engagement with fictional texts; they empathize with another person without sharing their thoughts and emotions, which in real life is a valuable social skill.

Cognitive criticism emphasizes the difference between empathy and immersive identification, when we acknowledge only those thoughts and feelings that are similar to our own. By applying empathy, students admit that a person can have evil thoughts and intentions, even though these cannot be justified from the social and human point of view. Hatred is a social, or higher-cognitive, emotion corresponding to the basic emotion of disgust, threatening not just our happiness but sometimes our life. Evolutionarily, the purpose of disgust was to help our ancestors avoid being poisoned by unsuitable food. Hatred is caused by a strong belief that another person prevents our well-being. It is every individual's ultimate goal to be happy, and if Snow White is a hindrance to her stepmother's happiness, she must be eliminated. However, building one's happiness on someone else's distress, not to mention death, is ethically dubious. Emotions such as envy and hatred are regulated by social and ethical rules. Although we understand the stepmother's motivations, we do not share her goal. We share Snow White's goal: to be happy. If we are familiar with the fairy-tale script of happiness, we know that her goal is marriage to a prince. Again, the students may feel uncomfortable with this line of argument, but it will govern their thinking in a new direction.

At this point, a new actor is introduced into the plot, the huntsman. He is a marginal character but pivotal for Snow White's fate. In the short episode, a broad range of emotions are easy to miss because of the dramatic external events. Ask the students the following: *Why does the huntsman obey the evil queen? Does he know that he is doing wrong? Why does he change his mind and let Snow White escape?*

The first question only evokes speculations; let the students use their imagination. The huntsman is used to following orders and does not contemplate the consequences. He fears that if he disobeys, the queen will get angry and have him executed (he obviously knows that she has a bad temper). He is secretly in love with the queen (again, a scenario that some fractured fairy tales play on) and wants to win her favor. This is embedded mind modeling again: We think that the huntsman thinks that the queen thinks. . . . The second question, however, connects emotions with ethics. Knowing that your actions are wrong and still acting is an ethical choice that leads to guilt, a social emotion that results from breaking societal rules or practices. The story does not mention that the huntsman feels guilty, but it does say that he feels pity toward Snow White and is relieved not to have her death on his conscience. He believes that she will be killed by wild beasts, but this will not be his fault. The huntsman disappears from the tale, and we do not care about his further emotional issues, although we may wonder how he feels about betraying his queen.

Turn back to Snow White. *What does Snow White feel when she realizes that the huntsman is going to kill her?* The simplest answer to expect is that she is scared. *How do you know that she is scared?* The students probably respond with, Anyone would be scared if someone draws a knife on you. They follow a script, both a real-life script and a fictional script. Few of them, if any, will have been exposed to such danger, but they know, based on the script, that threat causes fear. Do not be satisfied by the answer, but persist: How *scared is she?*

Fear is a basic emotion that includes a wide range of feelings. Being scared of mice or spiders is different from being terrified of imminent and violent death. Ask the students to imagine the scope of Snow White's horror (to be really provocative, suggest that she wets herself). Ask them to think of synonyms for "fear" and "fright" as well as metaphors (such as "petrified with fear"), and discuss the degree and nuance of each. Fear is evolutionarily conditioned because it assisted our ancestors in assessing a sudden unfamiliar situation: flee or fight? Snow White can neither flee nor fight, and she reacts with the only option available to her: She begs for mercy. As it turns out, it is the right strategy, and it helps that she is young and beautiful. But she did not know that for sure.

Further: *What does Snow White feel when she realizes that her stepmother hates her so much that she wishes her dead?* This is yet another example of embedded empathy. If the students previously agreed that Snow White does not know, until that moment, that her stepmother hates her, this is the moment of revelation. The story does not mention how Snow White feels toward her stepmother; it is conceivable that she likes her, maybe even loves and admires her. Realizing that someone whom you love hates you causes utter distress. The story, however, does not mention this strong emotion. Instead, it states that Snow White is scared as she runs through the woods. *Is she more scared than when the huntsman is about to kill her? How do we know this?*

Here is a perfect occasion to bring in film or illustrated versions, with which your students are likely to have been acquainted before they took your course, particularly the Disney adaptation. (A digital version, *Snow White* by Nosy Crow, may offer a good counterbalance to the familiar Disney images.) Snow White's flight through the dangerous dark woods is a gratifying action to represent visually. As already suggested, students are unlikely to have experienced anything near Snow White's horror. However, the imagery of sinister scenery, with dark, gnarled trees, shadows, and shining eyes in the darkness, evokes extradiegetic fear: We get scared of the image as such rather than empathize with the character's fear. This is possible because of mirror neurons signaling danger to the lower, emotional areas of brain, even though the higher, rational parts of the brain "understand" that we are not threatened by fictional images. The visual portrayal of an emotion is both stronger and more immediate than the verbal statement "She was scared." Ask your students to recollect when they first saw, for instance, the Disney version of *Snow White* and to analyze their fears from a critical perspective.

You can stop here or go on to contemplate further emotions and intentions that appear in the plot—for instance, why Snow White trusts her hosts (particularly in versions where they are robbers rather than dwarfs); why they trust and protect her; why Snow White falls for the three temptations; and what her feelings are when her stepmother gets her due punishment. Remind the students that in Perrault's version of "Cinderella" the stepmother and stepsisters are not punished; on the contrary, kindhearted Cinderella arranges attractive marriages for them, which contributes to her image as good and noble. Conclude the session by asking the students whether they feel that the cognitive approach has opened new dimensions in the fairy tale that they had not considered before. If they are unconvinced, here is what you can point out:

- You have doubtless discovered new features of this particular fairy tale and a new understanding of it, even though it may seem a purely academic exercise. It will, however, alert you to aspects of fairy tales that you may not have noticed before.

- You have considered a different way of thinking about fairy tales than the formalist, sociohistorical, psychoanalytical, or feminist. All these different approaches are mutually complementary, and adding another facet is always valuable.
- Fairy tales have an irresistible appeal to us, and a cognitive reading opens a dimension that further explains this appeal. In engaging with a seemingly flat and predictable tale, our brains are stimulated to investigate cracks between the lines into which we can project our empathy, to discover the depth of human relationships and thus the human emotions behind the superficial plot. With this approach, we acknowledge that flat and predictable fairy-tale characters are modeled on real people who are complex and ambivalent.
- Although fairy tales do not directly give us access to other people's minds, they do stimulate our affective responses and make us realize how we think about other people and about ourselves.

This teaching strategy can be transferred to any fairy tale, traditional or modern. Here are some suggestions for opening questions:

What does Little Red Riding Hood's mother think when she sends off her daughter on a dangerous walk through the woods? Does she expect her daughter to obey and keep to the path?

What does Hansel and Gretel's father feel when the (step)mother suggests that they abandon the children in the woods?

Why is Cinderella's stepmother mean to her? (Unlike Snow White's stepmother, she is not envious of Cinderella's beauty.) What is her intention in keeping Cinderella away from the prince?

Why does the princess promise the frog to be his friend if he rescues her ball? Does she intend to keep her promise?

How does Beauty feel about her father sending her to the Beast's castle to save his own life?

What does the little mermaid feel when she learns from her grandmother that she will turn into sea foam upon her death? (This feeling will motivate all her actions throughout the tale until the turning point, when her altruistic love becomes stronger than the selfish fear of death.)

The cognitive-affective approach to fiction is deliberately provocative because it makes us think about literature beyond some of the more conventional directions. In exposing our students to this approach, we not only provide them with yet another interpretative tool but also alert them to textual features they may never have contemplated before. Which is exactly what our brains love.

Bibliography

Evans, Dylan. *Emotions: A Very Short Introduction.* Oxford, UK: Oxford University Press, 2001.

Hogan, Patrick Colm. *The Mind and Its Stories: Narrative Universals and Human Emotion.* Cambridge, UK: Cambridge University Press, 2003.

Nikolajeva, Maria. "Exploring Empathy and Ethics in Fairy Tales About Three Brothers." In *Cambridge Companion to Fairy Tales.* Ed. Maria Tatar. Cambridge, UK: Cambridge University Press, 2014. 134–49.

Oatley, Keith. *Best Laid Schemes: The Psychology of Emotions.* Cambridge, UK: Cambridge University Press, 1992.

Stockwell, Peter. *Cognitive Poetics: An Introduction.* London: Routledge, 2002.

Zunshine, Lisa. *Getting Inside Your Head: What Cognitive Science Can Tell Us About Popular Culture.* Baltimore: Johns Hopkins University Press, 2012.

Teaching Fairy Tales from a Disability Studies Perspective

Ann Schmiesing

Handless maidens, thumb-size boys, blinded stepsisters, one-legged soldiers, and animals born to human parents are but a few of the many physically anomalous characters who populate European fairy tales. Their presence exemplifies what disability studies scholars David T. Mitchell and Sharon L. Snyder have theorized as "narrative prosthesis," a concept that refers to narratives' frequent dependence on disability and related physical or intellectual differences to propel the plot and delineate character. As Mitchell and Snyder explain:

> Since what we now call disability has been historically narrated as that which characterizes a body as deviant from shared norms of bodily appearance and ability, disability has functioned throughout history as one of the most marked and remarked on differences that propel the act of storytelling into existence. Narratives turn signs of cultural deviance into textually marked bodies. (53–54)

Most frequently, disability in fairy tales serves as a narrative-prosthetic mark that further "others" an underdog or evildoer. We have perhaps become so accustomed to this othering function that we might think of disability in literature, if at all, only in metaphorical terms as symbolizing a character's psychic turmoil, aberrant behavior, or underdog status. However, there is a case for considering disability in its own right and interrogating the terms according to which narratives often press it into metaphorical service. In teaching fairy tales, such consideration can enrich students' understanding not only of sociohistorical constructions and representations of disability (and the marginalized identities of gender and race with which disability so frequently intersects) but also of key conventions and patterns in the fairy tale as a genre.

Terminology and Concepts

In "Fairy Tales of Germany," a core curriculum course at the University of Colorado, I include a discussion of disability and related forms of physical anomaly in my teaching of the Grimms' fairy tales (see the syllabus "Fairy Tales of Germany" in Chapter 6 of this volume). I do so principally at two points in the course: first when discussing the Grimms' "The Maiden Without Hands" and later when discussing the attributes of the Grimms' male heroes, many of whom are regarded by other characters as physically or intellectually deficient. Most of my students have not previously discussed disability in an academic context, and few, if any, have heard of the growing field of disability studies. For this reason, I familiarize them with key disability studies concepts and terms when asking them to analyze how disability is portrayed in a particular tale or tales.

Although the explanations in this essay will necessarily be brief, in-depth explorations of the concepts of disability studies can be found in the scholarship to which I refer. A discussion of disability in fairy tales might even begin with a reading from Simi Linton's *Claiming Disability*, Tobin Siebers's *Disability Theory*, or Lennard J. Davis's edited volume *The Disability Studies Reader*. With regard to portrayals of disability in literature, an excerpt from Mitchell and Snyder's *Narrative Prosthesis* could be appropriate, or students could consult an existing study of disability in fairy tales (e.g., Franks; Schmiesing; Yamato; Yenika-Agbaw).

The Americans with Disabilities Act (ADA) defines *disability* as "a physical or mental impairment that substantially limits one or more major life activities, a record of such an impairment, or being regarded as having such as impairment" (see "Disability"). Students accustomed to thinking of disability as including only deaf, blind, mobility-impaired, or intellectually disabled individuals might be surprised to learn that disability under current legal definitions can also include a broad spectrum of diseases, physical conditions, and learning disabilities (Davis, *Enforcing Normalcy*, 8). Indeed, disability studies scholars regard disability as an unstable term, not as an absolute category or set of categories.

In its relatively short history, disability studies scholars have also emphasized disability as a social construct requiring change in the body politic to ensure access (the *social model* of disability) and rejected views of disability as a bodily defect that medical practice must attempt to cure (the *medical model* of disability) (Couser, 112). Whereas *impairment* refers to the physical aspect of, say, being unable to walk, disability refers to the social contexts that make the built environment inaccessible to mobility-impaired people and casts their impairment as a negative. In practice, it is difficult to keep the terms *disability* and *impairment* separate, in part because what is regarded as an impairment might itself be socially determined (Quayson, 4). Without returning to the medical model, some disability studies scholars have argued that the social model might seem to reject medical intervention and that activism and legislation might improve access for disabled people but cannot take away the suffering and pain that impairment itself may cause (Linton, 138). Scholars such as Tobin Siebers have viewed disability in terms of *complex embodiment* (Siebers, 25; see also Shakespeare, 272–73), an approach that seeks to understand how individual and environmental factors affect the lives of disabled people and recognizes that disability may require medical and social interventions.

First and foremost, disability studies rejects *ableism*, the marginalizing of disabled people and the centering of nondisabled views. Ableism can manifest itself in assumptions that all disabled people aspire to a nondisabled norm, that disability determines an individual's characteristics, and that disabled people are inferior to nondisabled people (Linton, 9). Popular representations of people with disabilities often follow one of two ableist patterns: The disabled person is depicted either as an object of pity or as what in disability studies is known as a *supercripple* (or *supercrip*). Narratives depicting supercripples work so hard to depict the disabled protagonist as "normal" that they portray the protagonist "as possessing talents and abilities only dreamed about by able-bodied people" (Siebers, 111; see also Alaniz, 305). An example of a disabled person represented as an object of pity might be a poster child used for a telethon, whereas allegations in 2012 that Oscar Pistorius might have an unfair advantage on his prosthetic legs over able-bodied competitors in the London Olympics exemplify representations of a disabled person as a supercripple. In modern society supercripples often appear in science fiction and pop culture imaginings of cyborgs and other bionically enhanced individuals.

Popular representations of disabled people also frequently reveal a preoccupation with *overcoming* disability. Because in most cases a disability cannot actually be physically overcome, what is overcome is usually social stigma (Linton, 17). An individual who has "overcome" blindness typically has not become sighted but has instead overcome social stereotypes of what a blind person can and cannot do or achieve. Because of the social stigma of disability, some disabled individuals may attempt to *pass* as nondisabled.

Applications

Once students are familiar with some of the key terms and tenets of disability studies, a discussion of disability in a course on fairy tales could begin simply by asking students to prepare a list, before or during class, of the disabled characters who have appeared in the fairy tales they have read so far. Students are usually quite surprised at the number and variety of disabled characters they encounter as they skim through tales. My goal in asking students to consider how many disabled characters appear in fairy tales is not to reduce the study of disability to counting and categorization but to enable students to appreciate the prevalence of disability and to begin to consider its sociohistorical and narratological importance. In my course, students include not only the obvious portrayals, such as the blinding of the prince in the Grimms' "Rapunzel," but also the less obvious, such as muteness in "The Virgin Mary's Child" and Joringel's temporary paralysis in "Jorinda and Joringel."

Brainstorming the many references to disability in fairy tales leads to interesting questions concerning whether and how particular characters and conditions could be viewed in terms of disability: Is Snow White's deep sleep disabling? Is the Dummy or simpleton character actually intellectually impaired or merely regarded as such by those around him? How are disability and physical decline used as markers of old age in depictions of elderly characters? Can wounded soldiers in fairy tales be thought of as disabled veterans? To what extent can we conceptualize monstrous births and transformations of humans into animals or inanimate objects in terms of disability? (For example, the Grimms' Frog King repeatedly refers to what he cannot do in his frog form; similarly, in hog bridegroom tales [ATU 441], such as Straparola's "The Pig King," d'Aulnoy's "Prince Marcassin," and the Grimms' "Hans My Hedgehog," characters frequently comment on what the protagonist is incapable of doing or achieving in his animal or half-animal body.)

As they ponder these and other questions, students appreciate that fairy tales themselves present an expansive and fluid conception of what we today call disability. This in turn clarifies the rationale for applying a twenty-first-century American definition of disability to a fairy tale from nineteenth-century Germany (or Renaissance Italy or seventeenth- or eighteenth-century France). Moreover, once reminded of the complex origins of most literary fairy tales, students understand the futility of trying to diagnose specific medical conditions in disabled characters. Indeed, although Susan Schoon Eberly has asserted that diseases such as Hunter syndrome are represented in folkloric depictions of changelings and hybrid characters, the limited descriptions of such characters and the fact that most fairy and folktales have undergone significant changes as they are told and retold in their various oral and written forms mean that such diagnoses are usually speculative at best and, at worst, might reinforce a medical model of disability and in general result from reading the tales too literally. Instead of having students engage in medical diagnostics, I encourage them to consider the following questions: How does the narrative construct difference as disability, and what implications might these constructions have for the fairy tale as a genre and for how we think about disability and disabled individuals?

As students delve into these issues, other questions will emerge. In how many tales is disability a punishment for wrongdoing (as in the blinding of the stepsisters in the Grimms' "Cinderella"), and in how many is it portrayed as a challenge or trial that a virtuous character must overcome? To what extent does the narrator directly comment on a character's disability, and what bearing does this commentary have on the text? (For example, the narrator of Hans Christian Andersen's "The Steadfast Tin Soldier" directly deems the title character remarkable because he has only one leg, but some narrators refrain from such commentary and instead focus on relating other characters' reactions to the disabled individual.) Are disabled characters initially shunned by one or both parents (as in many monstrous birth tales) or accepted and loved (as in the Grimms' "Thumbling")? How does the binary opposition between beauty and ugliness in fairy tales mirror the binary between able-bodiedness and disability—and how might a disability studies perspective enable us to view "Beauty and the Beast" narratives in a different light by focusing on the experience of the physically different Beast instead of on Beauty? Does society view the disabled or physically anomalous character as a freak, and, if so, how does the protagonist respond to this enfreakment? (In "Thumbling" there is even a reference to the freak shows that were for so long a commonplace in European cities, and students can be shown broadsides advertising the physically different characters on display in such shows, for example, from the volumes published by Ricky Jay and Hans Scheugl.) Is the protagonist viewed as an object of pity or as a supercripple? To what extent is a disability studies interpretation of a tale compatible or at odds with psychological interpretations? Does disability in the tale or tales in question intersect with gender roles or other identities? How so? Does the character remain disabled at the end of the tale, or is his or her disability magically erased? What bearing does this have on the fairy tale's "happy ending"?

These last several questions merit particular attention. In discussing supercripples, students often point out the frequent intertwining of superability with a particular physical vulnerability in popular imaginings of superheroes (e.g., Superman has numerous superpowers, but at the same time exposure to Kryptonite could sicken or kill him). As José Alaniz has pointed out, this vulnerability can be theorized as disability in many portrayals of comic book superheroes (306–7). Similarly, Elsa's inability to control her superability in Disney's *Frozen* becomes in a sense disabling; she cannot use her sense of touch in the manner in which "normal" people can, isolates herself from others in an attempt to avoid inadvertently injuring or killing her sister Anna with her ice-making powers, and attempts to keep her powers secret and thus in effect to pass as "normal." In the Grimms' "How Six Made Their Way in the World," disability and superability are likewise intertwined in the portrayal of the runner; he allegedly detaches one of his legs because on two legs he runs at superhuman speed, but his detachable leg can also be read as a prosthesis worn by an amputee (Schmiesing, 68–69). Just as superability can be intertwined with disability, so too are disabled fairy-tale characters often presented as having an extraordinary ability that surpasses the achievements of the nondisabled characters around them: The Donkey in the Grimms' tale of the same name learns to play the lute like a master, despite being told that his hooves will make lute playing impossible; the Grimms' Thumbling can steer a horse simply by sitting in its ear and telling it which way to go; and Hans My Hedgehog becomes so unusually successful as a swineherd that every pigsty in town must be emptied to accommodate all the livestock he gives to the villagers.

Depictions of disabled characters as supercrips reinforce ableism by imagining disabled individuals as extraordinarily *abled*. A similar erasure of disability appears in the many fairy-tale endings in which the disabled character magically becomes nondisabled. Disability and related manifestations of physical difference often function as the "lack" that, in Vladimir Propp's formulation, must frequently be "liquidated" in fairy tales and folklore (53–55). Jack Zipes insightfully observes that the fairy tale as a genre "presents moral and political critiques of society at the same time as it undermines them and reconciles the distraught protagonist with society" (118). I ask students to apply this observation to fairy-tale portrayals of disability and to trace the manner in which fairy tales simultaneously critique the marginalization of disabled people (by sympathetically portraying disabled protagonists who are unjustly stigmatized and enfreaked by those around them) and then undermine this critique (by so frequently portraying a happy ending as possible only after the disabled protagonist has been magically made "normal"). How do the magical restorations to normalcy that are part and parcel of many fairy-tale endings relate to the popular fascination with "medical miracles" that cure disability or disease? Are there fairy tales in which the reinscription of an ableist paradigm is subverted? I point my students to Perrault's "Riquet with the Tuft," in which the narrator suggests that Riquet's hunchback and limp might not actually have been magically removed and that the princess instead began to see Riquet's physical difference as beautiful.

Just as the fairy tale often enforces dominant constructions of gender norms, so, too, does it enforce social constructions of physical and intellectual normalcy. In tracing narrative prosthesis in a tale or tales, students can consider the intersections of disability and other marginalized identities. In the Grimms' tales, for example, female characters tend to be depicted with disabilities or physical conditions that render them more passive (e.g., muteness, handlessness, deep sleep), whereas disabled male characters most often continue to exercise agency in their disabled state. Students can analyze the differing degrees to which gender and disability intersect in a particular collection or in a particular tale type. For instance, whereas in the Grimms' "The Maiden Without Hands" the handless maiden possesses considerable agency and independence in the first edition of the *Kinder- und Hausmärchen*, in the second and subsequent editions she is rendered much more passive and dependent on others; in contrast to her passivity, Penta in Basile's "Penta with the Chopped-Off Hands" is depicted using her feet to sew, brush hair, and starch clothing.

Students might also consider the extent to which gender plays a role in disability-related punishments, and here Ruth B. Bottigheimer's analysis contrasting muteness as punishment in "The Virgin Mary's Child" with the absence of punishment in "Brother Lustig" is relevant (Bottigheimer, 81–94). How does disability as depicted in fairy tales also intersect with socioeconomic status (beggars, soldiers), age (elderly characters), and skin color? Students are surprised to see that tales in which a human character is depicted with black skin in the Grimms' fairy tales also typically contain references to some form of physical impairment or disability (e.g., "Hans My Hedgehog," "The Prince Who Feared Nothing," "The White Bride and the Black Bride"). Like disability, black skin is presented in these tales as a physical defect that marks a wicked character or that must be cured in a virtuous character. Studying these representations enables students to better understand and deconstruct the "materiality of metaphor" in fairy tales—the manner in which disability, like other physical characteristics, is frequently used to make representations of otherness more concrete in literature (Mitchell and Snyder, 47–48).

Foregrounding disability can also enhance students' critical thinking by enabling them to see the multiple interpretive approaches that can be applied to a single text. I ask my students to consider whether a disability studies perspective is compatible or in conflict with psychological interpretations of various fairy tales. The deficiencies of Alan Dundes's psychoanalytic interpretation of "The Maiden Without Hands," pointed out by Maria Tatar and Jack Zipes, become all the more palpable when considered from the vantage point of disability studies (Dundes, 58–61;

Tatar, 123; Zipes, 172–73; see also Schmiesing, 87–89). Ravit Raufman interprets the tiny body of the Tom Thumb and Thumbling characters as a projection of "maternal-symbiotic needs" and "the experience of maternal immaturity" (49), but students will find that reading these characters from a disability studies perspective, as Betty M. Adelson has, yields a different view (Adelson, 109; see also Schmiesing, 159). Psychoanalytic interpretations can enhance our understanding of disabled characters such as Hans My Hedgehog, whose experience of physical anomaly is intertwined with his Oedipal conflict with his father (Schmiesing, 125). My goal in having students contemplate the materiality of metaphor and the relationship of disability studies to psychological interpretations is not to foster anti-psychological or anti-symbolic readings but to encourage a nuanced understanding of the various interpretive approaches that can be applied to fairy tales.

Conclusion

Although disabled characters abound in literature, disability has tended to receive less attention in literature courses than other marginalized identities such as gender and race. Most of my students have not previously discussed disability in their courses, and many will see disability studies as a new way to think about representations of the body. Their close reading skills are sharpened as they become aware of the tendency to "read over" disability in literature and instead begin to register the significance of disability in narratives. Drawing attention to disabled characters and their narrative-prosthetic functions in fairy tales can enrich students' understanding not only of how narratives construct marginalized identities but also of how fundamental conventions and patterns appear in the fairy tale as a genre.

Bibliography

Adelson, Betty M. *The Lives of Dwarfs: Their Journey from Public Curiosity Toward Social Liberation.* New Brunswick, NJ: Rutgers University Press, 2005.

Alaniz, José. "Supercrip: Disability and the Marvel Silver Age Superhero." *International Journal of Comic Book Art* 6.2 (2004): 304–24.

Bell, Christopher, ed. *Blackness and Disability: Critical Examinations and Cultural Interventions.* East Lansing: Michigan State University Press, 2011.

Bottigheimer, Ruth. *Grimms' Bad Girls and Bold Boys: The Moral and Social Vision of the Tales.* New Haven, CT: Yale University Press, 1987.

Couser, G. Thomas. "Signifying Bodies: Life Writing and Disability Studies." In *Disability Studies: Enabling the Humanities.* Ed. Sharon L. Snyder, Brenda Jo Brueggemann, and Rosemarie Garland-Thomson. New York: MLA, 2002. 109–17.

Davis, Lennard J., ed. *The Disability Studies Reader*, 3rd ed. New York: Routledge, 2010.

————. *Enforcing Normalcy: Disability, Deafness, and the Body*. London: Verso, 1995.

"Disability." *ADA National Network: Glossary of ADA Terms*. adata.org/glossary-terms#D (accessed March 25, 2018).

Dundes, Alan. "The Psychoanalytic Study of the Grimms' Tale with Special Reference to 'The Maiden Without Hands' (AT 706)." *Germanic Review* 42 (1987): 50–65.

Franks, Beth. "Gutting the Golden Goose: Disability in Grimms' Fairy Tales." In *Embodied Rhetorics: Disability in Language and Culture*. Ed. James C. Wilson and Cynthia Lewiecki-Wilson. Carbondale: Southern Illinois University Press, 2001. 244–58.

Jay, Ricky. *Extraordinary Exhibitions: The Wonderful Remains of an Enormous Head, the Whimsiphusicon, and Death to the Savage Unitarians*. New York: Quantuck Lane, 2005.

Linton, Simi. *Claiming Disability: Knowledge and Identity*. New York: New York University Press, 1998.

Mitchell, David T., and Sharon L. Snyder. *Narrative Prosthesis: Disability and the Dependencies of Discourse*. Ann Arbor: University of Michigan Press, 2000.

Propp, Vladimir. *Morphology of the Folktale*, 2nd ed. Trans. Laurence Scott. Austin: University of Texas Press, 1968.

Quayson, Ato. *Aesthetic Nervousness: Disability and the Crisis of Representation*. New York: Columbia University Press, 2007.

Raufman, Ravit. "The Birth of Fingerling as a Feminine Projection: Maternal Psychological Mechanisms in the Fingerling Fairy Tale." *Western Folklore* 68.1 (2009): 49–71.

Scheugl, Hans. *Showfreaks und Monster: Sammlung Felix Adonos*. Cologne: M. DuMont Schauberg, 1974.

Schmiesing, Ann. *Disability, Deformity, and Disease in the Grimms' Fairy Tales*. Detroit: Wayne State University Press, 2014.

Schoon Eberly, Susan. "Fairies and the Folklore of Disability: Changelings, Hybrids, and the Solitary Fairy." *Folklore* 99.1 (1988): 58–77.

Shakespeare, Tom. "The Social Model of Disability." In *The Disability Studies Reader*, 3rd ed. Ed. Lennard J. Davis. New York: Routledge, 2010. 266–73.

Siebers, Tobin. *Disability Theory*. Ann Arbor: University of Michigan Press, 2008.

Tatar, Maria. *Off with Their Heads! Fairy Tales and the Culture of Childhood*. Princeton, NJ: Princeton University Press, 1992.

Yamato, Lori. "Surgical Humanization in H. C. Andersen's 'The Little Mermaid.'" *Marvels & Tales* 31.2 (2017): 295–312.

Yenika-Agbaw, Vivian. "Reading Disability in Children's Literature: Hans Christian Andersen's Tales." *Journal of Literary and Cultural Disability Studies* 5.1 (2011): 91–108.

Zipes, Jack. *The Brothers Grimm: From Enchanted Forests to the Modern World*. New York: Palgrave Macmillan, 2002.

Teaching Fairy-Tale Versions, Adaptations, and Translations

Cristina Bacchilega

Even though I continue to incorporate the study of fairy tales in my undergraduate course "Folklore and Oral Narratives" at the University of Hawai'i, Mānoa, in the last ten years or so, I have been fortunate to design and teach a few upper-division courses devoted entirely to fairy tales: "Fairy Tales and Their Adaptations," "Twenty-First-Century Fairy-Tale Fiction," "Twenty-First-Century Fairy-Tale Fiction and Film," and "Fairy Tales and Social Change." However, for our graduate curriculum, I have continued to teach fairy tales and their adaptations under the umbrella of a "folklore and literature" approach and a "comparative literature" designation. Why? Our graduate program is relatively small, which discourages a narrower focus, but I also believe in the value of considering fairy tales in relation to other traditional genres and of doing so transnationally as well as comparatively. To pursue these goals, in the undergraduate course "Fairy Tales and Their Adaptations" I build on the concepts of version and author-narrator that come from folklore studies, whereas in the graduate course "Folklore and Literature: Questions of Adaptation and Translation"—for which I offer a syllabus (see Chapter 6 of this volume)—I stress the work of translation and also of genre adaptation across cultures.

In what follows, I offer snapshots of what occurred on the first day in these two courses, in 2010 and 2013, respectively, to show how I set up our learning processes; I outline my approach to versions and adaptations in the undergraduate course; and I offer a rationale for starting the graduate course with metanarratives and translations. Because folklore is in the doing or the experience, and so are (narrative) traditions, I particularly enjoy incorporating activities into my courses, which I foreground in this chapter; because such activities change over time as new technologies and publications come into the classroom, I present some of these updates in the notes.

THAWING THE "ONCE UPON A TIME"

Spring 2010. It is the first day of class in "Fairy Tales and Their Adaptations," the large-enrollment undergraduate English course that welcomes nonmajors as well. Sixty or so students are in the room with a master's-level teaching assistant and me, and we start by watching the opening scene of *Shrek* (2001). Reactions: Most students appear engaged, visibly enjoy watching something they are familiar with, and laugh appropriately when it is clear that the scene of fairy-tale reading has taken place in the outhouse. I also show the DVD's beginning of scene 8, where our unpromising hero, Shrek, sets out to rescue the princess in the tower (who, as the audience knows, is already awake) and then enacts with much difference the romantic scene he'd scoffed at when paging though the fairy-tale book. I ask the students, "What are the assumptions and stereotypes about fairy tales that *Shrek* parodies in these scenes?" No pulling of teeth is required to get clear and precise responses to my question:

"Fairy tales come to us from books."
"These books are for children."
"We know fairy tales all too well, and boys tire of them quickly."
"Fairy tales are set in medieval times, 'once upon a time.'"
"The heroine is passive, even unconscious."
"The kiss that awakens her is magic and transformative!"
"Her rescue inevitably leads to romance."
"Fairy tales lie to us and they fool naïve people."[1]

---

1. In August 2011, I began the honors seminar "Twenty-First-Century Fairy-Tale Fiction and Film" by showing four short YouTube videos of Neil Gaiman's fairy-tale poem "Instructions" (2000): Gaiman reads at Cody's Bookstore in Berkeley; Gaiman reads at Yale in 2006; Gaiman reads as part of the animated trailer of *Instructions* as a children's book illustrated by Charles Vess; Gaiman reads as a fan's montage of movie clips interprets the poem visually. In this more advanced and focused course, I steer the discussion to the poem's consistent conjuring up of what makes a fairy tale and how it instructs as well as the fairy-tale poem's varied adaptations in performance and media.

Before going over the syllabus, I announce, "Our goal this semester is to historicize fairy tales so as to liquidate the frozen-like popular culture image of the genre that *Shrek*'s humor playfully took to task."[2] During the last 15 minutes of class, we brainstorm in groups: What is a fairy tale? Each student jots down notes, and the TA and I write key ideas on the board.

I have taught "Fairy Tales and Their Adaptations" two other times and, although my selection of texts varies, the course's structure has remained in place. During the first few weeks of the semester, we read and discuss multiple versions of selected tale types, and I ask students to focus on generic conventions and formulas, themes, power dynamics in the tales, and the tales' social functions in different sociocultural contexts. My aim, as the syllabus states, is to introduce students to "the genre's complex history, multiple social uses, and transformations into literary fiction and film for adults." In 2010—partly because Disney's film *The Princess and the Frog* had just come out—we read the Grimms' "The Frog King, or Iron Henry" first along with Alexander Afanas'ev's "The Frog Princess" and then moved to other animal bride and bridegroom tales, followed by "Cinderella" and "Snow White" tales.

Early in the process, when we are reading "Cinderella" versions, I use the concept of the tale type as a tool, not an end-all but a somewhat stabilizing starting point, to assemble a table that lists, as one set of variables, the ATU 510 tale type's specific plot episodes and Vladimir Propp's character functions and, as the other set, title and relevant bibliographic information for several versions of "Cinderella" that students have read; working in small groups, students fill out the comparative table by identifying the individual tale's specifics and differences.[3] This section of the course leads up to the students' completion of a research-based project involving comparative analysis of a fairy tale of their choice, and their compilation of a similar table for that tale type is part of the assignment.

---

2. One of the taglines for *Shrek* previews specific disruptions of fairy-tale expectations: "The Prince isn't Charming. The Princess isn't Sleeping. The sidekick isn't helping. The ogre is a hero. Fairy tales will never be the same again." This lighthearted self-consciousness opens the way to enjoy both the comedy and the love story, its humor working to reach adults and children in different ways. Part of my goal as a teacher is to make students more critically aware by the end of the semester of not only how different adaptations balance reviving and critiquing the genre but also how they lower or heighten the audience's critical threshold.

3. Sometimes I model the comparative table for them, but in most cases the group exercise is successful and offers them a reading and note-taking strategy as we read more tales. The idea of the tables is hardly original, but students have consistently commented on how they find this table useful as what I would call a heuristic device, and one student, Shelby Giese, effectively adapted it to focus on food in specific tale types in her honors thesis, "Feasting in Fairy Tales" (2014).

Pedagogically, I rely on a "questions for discussion" assignment for students to point to the versions' differences and similarities in relation to their own expectations, and I offer mini-lectures and PowerPoint presentations on Giambattista Basile, French fairy-tale writers, nineteenth-century folklorists, and the Grimms to contextualize our making meaning out of these patterns. In the process I introduce the concept of the "author-narrator"[4] as a conscious intervention in the assumed dichotomy of literature and folklore. This hybrid notion pushes the students to consider fairy tales as "extra-individual" or traditional narratives that are—in oral and print form and in other media—shaped creatively by individuals, who, in turn, are acted upon and respond to the specifics of their traditions and culture.[5] To learn more about the production of tales in specific contexts, each student reads assigned critical essays—in 2010 from Maria Tatar's *Classic Fairy Tales*—and two more about a specific tale for the research project. These projects have been successful for the most part, advancing each student's curiosity about a specific tale, engaging them in basic comparative research methods, and exhibiting their ability to read at least some details in their comparative tables as symptomatic of specific cultural and historical milieu, norms, and debates of the time and individual author-narrator poetics and ideology.

The combination of foregrounding detailed differences, discussing varied experiences students already have of fairy tales, and sketching a history of the genre that is, even in Europe alone, far from unified generally yields good results: Preconceived notions of the genre begin to give, partly because I am not championing one alternative, preset notion myself. As the frozen-like block thaws, I also strive to keep the definition of "fairy tale" active or in the making: I bring in a handout with a number of pithy statements by such scholars as JoAnn Conrad, Max Lüthi, Maria Tatar, Marina Warner, and Jack Zipes; we focus on what kinds of features each scholar identifies with the genre and how they relate to the students' initial definitions; I then ask students to formulate and share with one another their own evolving definitions.[6]

---

4. Author-narrator is not a term much used in English-language studies of folk- and fairy tales, but I draw on Michele Rak's "scrittore-narratore" in his discussion of Basile's *Lo cunto de li cunti* (The Tale of Tales) to foreground how fairy tales in print are not "unique one-offs" (Carter, x) but are produced at an intersection of tradition and creativity that takes into account oral and written versions. The most literal translation of Rak's term is "writer-narrator," but I like how "author-narrator" questions the originality of an "author" in a broadly defined storytelling web (see Basile).

5. For recent and provocative scholarly discussions of authorship, see the short essays by Glassie, Harries, and Maggi. These essays lend themselves well to discussion in an undergraduate course.

6. How this sharing occurs has varied. In a similar lower-division course in Fall 2011, the PhD apprentice in the course took notes on the brainstorming session by using the application MindNode to

Fairy-tale adaptations are our focus in the second half of the semester. Although the question of what a fairy tale is or, better, does remains open-ended all along, I make my definition of "adaptation" available to students right away. Drawing on the work of Linda Hutcheon and Robert Stam, one of my PowerPoint slides states, "We experience 'adaptation' when we recognize a text's close resemblance with, or immediately connect it with another text, at the same time that we acknowledge they are different, whether the change has to do with genre, medium, or audience." I talk about adaptation as the remake of a tale that implies a specific interpretation of it, evokes it in our minds by retelling it with a difference, and changes it in ways that are shaped by medium (film, comics, poetry, blog) and by "filters," such as cultural values, economic constraints, fashionable beliefs, and artist's poetics. This definition is not immediately clear to all, but as we discuss examples and also as students contribute to a growing list of "strategies of adaptation," things click. The reason I offer a definition of adaptation is that I want the discovery and interpretive process to be focused on more specific questions: On which aspects of a fairy tale does the adaptation focus? What is left out? What is the social context or issue that provokes the adaptation into being? To what effects and for whom? What makes this adaptation compelling or not? How does it change our understanding of the tale?

At first, we revisit the "Cinderella" tales from earlier in the semester by reading Emma Donoghue's short story "The Tale of the Shoe"; then, we work our way from Donoghue's "The Tale of the Handkerchief" to the Grimms' "Goose Girl," a story few of the students even know of. Pedagogically, I am extending the heuristic and comparative tools we used in the first part of the course to apply to adaptations, but I aim to raise questions about and address responses to adaptations that are more pointed and ideologically charged. Even though the differences among versions of a tale are meaningful in relation to one another, they are not necessarily motivated; in contrast, a fairy-tale adaptation is a deliberate or purposeful intervention in the discourse of fairy tales: what they are, what they do, and how they matter. These interventions, I stress, are not necessarily progressive or subversive; in fact, often they are commercially motivated, and some only reinforce the assumption that fairy tales are trivial or for children only.

---

visualize an initial collective definition of the genre the first day of class; we stored this first simple "mind map" in our online course site; three weeks later and then at the end of the semester, we went through the same process, resulting in more informed and complex visualizations of what students thought of fairy tales. I have used this application since with success; but I have also had students contribute to a Google Doc, in which case the initial input is individual and we then have to work as a group to see where definitions overlap and which aspects of the genre they privilege.

I work closely in class on reading Emma Donoghue's individual tales in *Kissing the Witch* as adaptations in the framework of questions about the collection as a whole: What do Emma Donoghue's tales reject in fairy tales? Why? What does Donoghue magnify or explore in fairy tales? Why? What does the title *Kissing the Witch* do to our expectations of fairy-tale alliances, scripts, and possibilities? How are her fairy tales addressing young adults, and in the early twenty-first century specifically? How do they relate to conflicts or issues that young adults experience? In the process of our discussions of the what and why of adaptation, I pause for us to take note of how a student's comment might be identifying an "adaptation strategy": updating, relocating, changing the ending, changing the narrative voice, and so on. And to close our discussion of Donoghue's retellings, I offer my interpretation of how some of her strategies of fairy-tale adaptation—transposing elements or reassigning parts, challenging commonly held assumptions of what a girl wants, changing the journey and its motivation or ending—coalesce to a purpose or effect: making visible who or what was excluded from a heteronormative tale and/or giving voice to silenced/vilified characters, which in turn attracts new readers to the genre and potentially empowers them.

Based on the process of connecting the "who, what, how, and why" of adaptation (Hutcheon) that I modeled, students engage in a brief creative exercise and then work on group presentations. The creative exercise asks each group to adapt a tale of their choice for a specific audience and present only in outline form and through sample dialogue the crucial changes they would make and why. This low-stakes, in-class group assignment foregrounds the process of adaptation, allows for playfulness, and demands team or extra-individual negotiation. The tightly structured group presentations have tended to focus on fairy-tale films partly because students are familiar with them already and partly because their competence in decoding filmic language helps them to discuss adaptation strategies not only narratively but also in a medium-appropriate and insightful way. Each student in the group zooms in on distinct fairy-tale elements that the film adapts (plot, ending, characterization; suspension of disbelief and genre mixing; family, class, gender, and other power dynamics; initiation and transformation; narration), whether it is retelling a single tale or not.[7] Complementing my evaluation and the TA's, students fill out

---

7. In the "Fairy Tales and Social Struggles" upper-level course, the assignment is more specific, as each group is tasked with discussing "how fairy-tale elements of the film impact its representation of social struggles and to what effects for the audience." The assignment sheet also includes the following statement: "Approaching a film or any other cultural texts in relation to social struggles may include focusing on the power dynamics and social issues it represents; asking whose perspectives and histories it favors, counters, or forgets; showing how it naturalizes dominant ideologies; analyzing its ideological

a brief form about each presentation they listen to with their takeaways, suggestions, and questions; this feedback goes to the TA and me, but we also share it with the presenters.

What follows in the final weeks varies from semester to semester, but I have included graphic novels (e.g., Willingham's *Fables: 1001 Nights of Snowfall*) and web comics (*Redden* by Maya Kern). Throughout the semester, just before class starts I also offer three- to five-minute "fairy-tale starters" (commercials, cartoons, clips of early fairy-tale films, song videos, or illustrations relevant to the tale of the day) to encourage students to be on time, put them in the mood, and showcase the range of uses this genre is put to in popular culture. My syllabus states, "Fairy tales today permeate contemporary culture in various media, and one of our ongoing projects as a class will be to explore why they 'stick' and how they've changed." By the end, I consider the course to have worked if most students are able and willing to approach fairy-tale versions and adaptations as sociohistorically and ideologically situated and networked, and if they see themselves not as consumers but as active players in this fairy-tale web.[8]

Translating the "Once Upon a Time"

Fall 2013. It is the first meeting of "Folklore and Literature: Questions of Translation and Adaptation" (see the syllabus in Chapter 6 of this volume), an English graduate course that is also expected to have a comparative literature breadth and a good number of pre-1900 texts. I meet with 14 master's and doctoral students from several departments—English, American Studies, and Japanese—and with varied research interests, including linguistics, Pacific and Hawaiian literature, a specific genre of folklore, and popular culture. Before even working our way to introductions and the syllabus, I present the class with two nineteenth-century calls

position in relation to power structures based on its focus/contradictions/absences/tensions/desire axis; asking what the film does to us as audience, how it animates us as social beings; and showing how it makes visible certain injustices and/or makes it possible for the audience to envision social change. At the core of this presentation assignment is the exploration of some questions: Why would a director who wishes to explore a social struggle or issue choose the fairy-tale mode to do so? What does associating a film with the fairy-tale genre make or not make possible for its envisioning social change? How does mixing the fairy tale with other genres affect its circulation and ideological impact? What role does the dominant understanding of the fairy tale as a wish-fulfillment narrative for children play in our reception of films that actively resist that or of films that parody it?"

8. Some students, of course, are attracted to the course because they are already enjoying the multiplicity of fairy-tale versions and adaptations; they tend to be the ones who are more interested in fairy-tale scholarship, history, and interpretation. But this is not the majority, especially in a large-enrollment class.

for preserving traditional narratives through print publication: William Thoms's introduction of the word *folklore* in an 1846 letter to the London literary magazine *The Atheneum* and Joseph H. Kānepuʻu's letter, "Ka poe kakau moʻolelo a kaao paha," published in 1862 on the front page of the Hawaiian newspaper *Ka Hoku o ka Pakipika*. My purpose is to juxtapose these two roughly contemporaneous statements of the urgency to put oral traditions in writing: They not only pose the writers in different relationships to the stories and storytellers but are also symptomatic of divergent—and contextually situated—motivations, methods, and goals.

Thoms enlists readers' help in collecting the quickly disappearing traditions of the British Isles, but he also states that contributions will be "sifted" and "brevity will be recommended." These oral traditions from Thoms's modern-man perspective are valued mostly as archives of British lore; in the name of progress, he accepts that the lifestyle of the country folk telling those stories is almost no longer.[9] Only some 40 years after American missionaries brought the printing press to the Kingdom of Hawaiʻi, Kānepuʻu writes to complain about the newspaper editors' cutting out lines of chants and songs from the *moʻolelo* (Hawaiian stories and histories) they are publishing. His generation was the first to commit these traditions to writing, thus adapting them and creating their national literature. As rendered in scholar Noenoe Silva's translation, Kānepuʻu wrote, "The generations of Hawaiians of 1870, 1880, 1890, and 1990 are going to want [this literature]" ("Nā Hulu Kupuna," 45).[10] The knowledge in and of this literature and language is valued for future use and the survival of a people, not just the memory of them. I do not belabor the point but suggest that preservation and tradition are not the same, just as uses of folklore and literature are hardly static or universal, and adaptation and translation have varied political roles to play in the life of a story.

Then, combining the introduction to the course with personal introductions, I invite students to address in their remarks some aspect of the following questions: What are your thoughts about tradition, storytelling, translation, and adaptation now? What has been most productive for you in thinking about these cultural practices? What kinds of questions interest you and why? (see syllabus in Chapter 6). I find out that students are interested in either adaptation or translation, not so much both; only a few have some previous experience with folklore studies; some are creative writers as well as scholars; some are eager to work on *moʻolelo*, and others on folktales and fairy tales; and although everyone has competence in a second

---

9. Thoms writes of "garnering the few ears which are remaining scattered over that field" where previously one could have gathered a "goodly crop" of traditions. This letter is often discussed as an example of the devolutionary premise of folklore studies even in its very beginnings.

10. See Silva (*Aloha Betrayed*); Nogelmeier; and hoʻomanawanui.

language (French, Hawaiian Japanese, Spanish), the only language we all share is English.

At this point it's time for stories. One is "Lu cuntu di 'Si raccunta.'" I read it out loud from a scan of its 1875 publication in Giuseppe Pitrè's *Fiabe, novelle e racconti popolari siciliani*, the yellowed pages of which I project on the screen. I grew up with Italian, but my pronunciation of the Sicilian is tentative because—I mention—I grew up in Rome and Italian-only public school education sought to eradicate regional dialects in the twentieth century, even Sicilian, which had an early poetic tradition as early as in the twelfth and thirteenth centuries. I suggest listening for rhythm, repetition, and tone to make some meaning of the action represented as well as to recognize some esthetic principle at work in the telling. I read the short tale again, and this time the students have access to a handout with Jack Zipes and Joseph Russo's 2009 translation, "The Tale Told Time and Again." In this tale a young girl finds a promissory note while grooming her chicken's feathers; she then obtains ownership of a rich merchant's shop by winning his wager when she tells him the note's story, without using the formulaic "it's been told time and again." The story she tells involves no magic, but her creative storytelling act brings about an unlikely and empowering transformation. An immediate reaction students have is to contrast the energy of the oral experience, especially the young girl's assertive tone, to the story's scholarly composed presentation—footnotes and all—on the page. They also wonder, based on the translators' note, about the dynamics of an 8-year-old girl, Maria Curatolo, telling the story to Pitrè.

I present students with another tale—this time only in translation and print—to discuss in groups and in relation to "The Tale Told Time and Again." Drawn from A. K. Ramanujan's *A Flowering Tree and Other Oral Tales from India* (1997), "A Story and a Song" is a "story about stories," a category that Ramanujan suggests should be added to the international tale type index. It tells about the danger of not telling stories and how stories and songs can take revenge on or punish those who silence them. Students are quick to recognize that Pitrè's tale is also a story about stories and go on from there, with little prodding, to discuss dynamics of class and gender in both stories, ask questions about how the scholarly apparatus helps them or not to read unfamiliar traditions, and consider issues of genre and the transportability of genre. I point to how the written word is made to support the oral in Pitrè's tale; how stories, told and untold, within the tales intervene in the characters' lives; and how it matters that certain stories are more available than others and to whom. What we are beginning to see together, I hope, is how tradition or the passing down of stories involves responsibility, motivation, and change. These are crucial dynamics in the work of translation and adaptation as well.

Before the end of class, I briefly introduce the 11 (!) essays for the next ses-sion, "Traditions, Disciplines, and Responsibilities," and describe how we will be collectively responsible for them: each student will read three essays—one they want to read, another they kind of know or will reread, and a third that promises to stretch them—and be prepared to present takeaway points from them to the class. My selection of texts is especially meant to help activate a conversation between folklore and indigenous studies in relation to tradition, place, beliefs, and genre; the division of labor also sets the tone for taking on responsibility in the learning.

Have I so far even mentioned fairy tales in the course? Not directly, but I have sketched a framework for discussing traditional narratives that is interdisciplin-ary and transnational and one that foregrounds varied power dynamics of and contexts for retelling. When we do approach folktales and fairy tales in classes 3 and 4, we focus on them as late-nineteenth- and early-twentieth-century trans-lations of tales from the British colonies—translations that would more accu-rately be described as adaptations. A successful in-class activity has students in groups applying the critical questions and methods of Sadhana Naithani's book *The Story-Time of the British Empire* to read the paratextual apparatus (preface, introduction, notes, illustrations) that frames specific collections: *Old Deccan Days*, edited by Mary Frere (1868); *Tales of the Punjab*, edited by Flora Annie Steel (1894); and *Australian Legendary Tales*, collected by Katie Langloh Parker (1897). Later in the course, after discussing colonial translations and adaptations of Ocea-nian genres, we return to "folktales in/from Europe translated and adapted in the nineteenth century" (week 9) and contemporary film adaptations of fairy tales (in the final weeks). And by the end, I consider the course to have worked if most students are able and willing to approach folktale and fairy-tale translations and adaptations as sociohistorically and ideologically situated, and to approach the fairy-tale web as participating in a larger network of genres and people moving and adapting across cultures.

BIBLIOGRAPHY

Carter, Angela, ed. *The Virago Book of Fairy Tales*. London: Virago, 1990.

Conrad, JoAnn. "Folktale." In *The Greenwood Encyclopedia of Folktales and Fairy Tales*. Ed. Don-ald Haase. Westport, CT: Greenwood, 2008. 363–66.

Donoghue, Emma. *Kissing the Witch: Old Tales in New Skins*. New York: HarperCollins, 1999.

Frere, Mary. *Old Deccan Days*. London: J. Murray, 1868.

Gaiman, Neil. "Instructions." In *A Wolf at the Door and Other Retold Stories*. Ed. Ellen Datlow and Terri Windling. New York: Simon & Schuster, 2000. 30–32.

Giese, Shelby. "Feasting in Fairy Tales." Honors thesis. University of Hawai'i at Mānoa, 2014.

Glassie, Henry. "Authorship in Oral Narrative." In *Marvelous Transformations: An Anthology of Fairy Tales and Contemporary Critical Perspectives*. Ed. Christine A. Jones and Jennifer Schacker. Peterborough, Canada: Broadview Press, 2012. 523–28.

Hafstein, Valdimar. "The Constant Muse: Copyright and Creative Agency." *Narrative Culture* 1.1 (2014): 9–47.

Harries, Elizabeth Wanning. "The Case of the Disappearing Author." In *Marvelous Transformations: An Anthology of Fairy Tales and Contemporary Critical Perspectives*. Ed. Christine A. Jones and Jennifer Schacker. Peterborough, Canada: Broadview Press, 2012. 529–32.

ho'omanawanui, ku'ualoha. *Voices of Fire: Reweaving the Literary Lei of Pele and Hi'iaka*. Minneapolis: University of Minnesota Press, 2014.

Hutcheon, Linda. *A Theory of Adaptation*. New York: Routledge, 2006.

Jones, Christine A., and Jennifer Schacker, eds. *Marvelous Transformations: An Anthology of Fairy Tales and Contemporary Critical Perspectives*. Peterborough, Canada: Broadview Press, 2012.

Kern, Maya. *Redden*. 2013. www.mayakern.com/cshort.html (accessed March 26, 2018).

Lüthi, Max. *The European Folktale: Form and Nature*. Trans. John Niles. Bloomington: Indiana University Press, 1986 [1981].

Maggi, Armando. "Oral versus Literary Tales: A New Approach to Issues of Authorship." In *Marvelous Transformations: An Anthology of Fairy Tales and Contemporary Critical Perspectives*. Ed. Christine A. Jones and Jennifer Schacker. Peterborough, Canada: Broadview Press, 2012. 533–37.

Naithani, Sadhana. *The Story-Time of the British Empire: Colonial and Postcolonial Folkloristics*. Jackson: University Press of Mississippi, 2010.

Nogelmeier M. Puakea. *Mai Pa'a I Ka Leo: Historical Voice in Hawaiian Primary Materials—Looking Forward and Listening Back*. Honolulu: Bishop Museum Press, 2010.

Parker, K. Langloh, ed. *Australian Legendary Tales*. London: David Nutt; and Melbourne: Melville, Mullen & Slade, 1897.

Pitrè, Giuseppe, ed. *Fiabe, novelle e racconti popolari siciliani*, vol. 1. Palermo: Luigi Pedone Lauriel, 1875.

The Princess and the Frog. Dir. Ron Clements and John Musker. Walt Disney Animation Studios. USA. 2009.

Rak, Michele. "Il racconto fiabesco." In *Lo cunto de li cunti*. By Giambattista Basile. Ed. and trans. Michele Rak. Milan: Garzanti, 1986. 1055–1111.

Ramanujan, A. K. *A Flowering Tree and Other Oral Tales from India*. Berkeley: University of California Press, 1997. ark.cdlib.org/ark:/13030/ft067n99wt/

Shrek. Dir. Andrew Adamson and Vicky Jenson. DreamWorks Animation. USA. 2001.

Silva, Noenoe. *Aloha Betrayed: Native Hawaiian Resistance to American Colonialism*. Durham, NC: Duke University Press, 2004.

———. "Nā Hulu Kupuna: To Honor Our Intellectual Ancestors." *Biography* 32.1 (2009): 43–53.

Stam, Robert. "The Theory and Practice of Adaptation." In *Literature and Film: A Guide to the Theory and Practice of Adaptation*. Ed. Robert Stam and Alessandra Raengo. Malden, MA: Blackwell, 2005. 1–52.

Steel, Flora Annie, ed. *Tales of the Punjab*. London: Macmillan, 1894.

Tatar, Maria, ed. *The Classic Fairy Tales: A Norton Critical Edition*. New York: Norton, 1999.

Thoms, William J. "Folk-Lore" (1846). *Journal of Folklore Research* 33.3 (1996): 187–89.

Warner, Marina. "The Old Wives' Tale." In *The Classic Fairy Tales: A Norton Critical Edition*. Ed. Maria Tatar. New York: Norton, 1999. 309–17.

Willingham, Bill. *Fables: 1001 Nights of Snowfall*. New York: Vertigo DC Comics, 2006.

Zipes, Jack. *When Dreams Came True: Classical Fairy Tales and Their Tradition*. New York: Routledge, 1998.

Zipes, Jack, and Joseph Russo, eds. and trans. *The Collected Sicilian Folk and Fairy Tales of Giuseppe Pitrè*, vol. 1. New York: Routledge, 2009.

Spinning Fairy-Tale Webs in the Undergraduate Classroom

Suzanne Magnanini

Two studies published in 2013, Cristina Bacchilega's *Fairy Tales Transformed? Twenty-First-Century Adaptations and the Politics of Wonder* and Patricia Eichel-Lojkine's *Contes en réseaux: L'émergence du conte sur la scène littéraire européenne,* use the metaphor of the web or network to chart new relationships among fairy tales and their creators and thus challenge entrenched conceptions of the genre. In *Fairy Tales Transformed* Bacchilega spins numerous metaphorical webs as she explores how and by whom fairy tales have been adapted in the twenty-first century. First, she conceives of her methodological field as "an intertextual and geopolitical fairy-tale web of reading and writing practices" (Bacchilega, ix). Although webs recall spinning spiders and thus, by association, the classic spinning storyteller seated by the hearth, Bacchilega's web is more virtual than natural. By focusing on adaptations of tales that challenge the dominant triad of Perrault, Grimm, and Disney, she strives to decolonize fairy-tale studies by showing "how activist adaptations are wielding the powers of wonder to contest the hegemony of the European-American fairy-tale magic" and by calling "for the remapping of the fairy tale genre onto a worldly, not worldwide, web" (Bacchilega, x). Although they are not simply coterminous with the World Wide Web, the webs Bacchilega constructs, she explains, are more akin to the World Wide Web than to spider webs because they possess no identifiable center or starting point. These are hypertextual networks of tales in which Perrault-Grimm-Disney still figure but no longer assume the role of palimpsest or default pretext. These webs also exhibit a capaciousness that far outstrips any spider web, for there is space to gather and connect diverse genres and media. And as in the World Wide Web, although certain voices might dominate the conversation, disruptive voices and plenty of talking back can still be heard. Bacchilega subscribes to Donald Haase's view that we must see fairy-tale production as "translation, transformation, and transcultural communication" in order to decolonize our field (Bacchilega, 24; Haase, "Decolonizing Fairy Tale Studies," 30), and she makes these cultural exchanges visible in part through Steven Gin's intermedial illustrations that depict different tales and cultural artifacts on a black spider web. Perhaps it is not surprising that Bacchilega is using the metaphor of the web, because a number of her objects of study were created specifically for, or now exist on, the Internet.[1]

In *Contes en réseaux* Patricia Eichel-Lojkine focuses primarily on early modern French and Italian tales and their medieval antecedents. Yet she too adopts the metaphor of the web or network to chart relationships among texts. Eichel-Lojkine founds her concept of *réseaux* on Michel Foucault's theories of discursive fields, as articulated in his *Archaeology of Knowledge* and *The Order of Discourse*, though she also briefly references digital networked technologies (Eichel-Lojkine, 26). In many ways, her webs closely resemble those spun by Bacchilega. For example, Eichel-Lojkine adopts the organizing metaphor of the network to topple existing textual hierarchies and to question Perrault's dominance in French fairy-tale studies. Like Bacchilega's webs, her networks lack a privileged center, with each node possessing its own power to radiate outward. These networks are expansive, allowing space for tales previously excluded from study, forced into subordinate positions, or rarely considered in relation to canonical tales.[2] For Eichel-Lojkine, origins are less important than relationships, and Foucault's ruptures, thresholds, and breaks in the literary system are what demand examination. Whereas Bacchilega invokes Andrew Teverson's assertion that "fairy tales are fiction's migrants" (Bacchilega, 20; Teverson, 54), Eichel-Lojkine describes fairy tales as "écriture mouvante" (Eichel-Lojkine, 19), narratives that shift and change as they move across cultures either orally or in print.

One year after these two studies were published, Marina Warner adopted a similar set of metaphors in *Once Upon a Time: A Short History of the Fairy Tale*. For Warner, this history is a map on which two "prominent landmarks" are initially discerned, the tales by Perrault and the Grimms (Warner, xiii). But further inspection

---

1. For example, Bacchilega briefly discusses Donna Leishman's digital fairy tale *Red Riding Hood* (www.6amhoover.com) and Dina Goldstein's photo series *Fallen Princesses* (www.fallenprincesses.com).
2. For example, Eichel-Lojkine juxtaposes a Yiddish tale published in 1602 and Straparola's tale of Livoretto (*The Pleasant Nights* III.2 [ATU 531]) (Eichel-Lojkine, 12).

reveals a much more complex topography including "a whole web of routes from points east," Italian port cities where Giovan Francesco Straparola and Giambattista Basile penned their tales, and Hans Christian Andersen's Denmark (Warner, xiv). Warner imagines the history of the fairy tale as a "fictive atlas" with many windows, like those in an Advent calendar, that open onto "scores of storytellers and inventors gathering, interpreting and revisioning the material" (Warner, xiv).

Thus, in recent scholarship, fairy tales are texts on the move, best understood by analyzing their positions in expansive networks. The new maps drawn to guide our travels through the genre tend to expand outward and trespass the former spatial, linguistic, generic, and chronological borders that once circumscribed our inquiries. Because webs have been such productive metaphors in recent fairy-tale scholarship, how might we use webs in fairy-tale pedagogy? How might webs, maps, and networks inform not just the content but also the structure of our courses on fairy tales? How might we transform our own students into active collectors and spinners of tales and webs?

In this essay I imagine an introductory undergraduate course on early modern Italian and French fairy tales in which the readings and written assignments are structured by the metaphor of the web (see the syllabus "French and Italian Fairy Tales" in Chapter 6 of this volume). Taking a cue from digital humanists, who insist on the importance and necessity of "building things," I ask students to become both twenty-first-century tale collectors and fairy-tale web designers.[3] Specifically, I use a collaborative learning model and require groups of students to depict, analyze, and describe relationships among different versions of a single tale type (e.g., "Puss in Boots," "Sleeping Beauty"). The webs are essentially mind maps of a given tale type on which students position the tales we read in class, versions of the same tale type and related critical studies that they find through their research, and their own original versions of the tale type.

In class discussion and activities, we focus intensely on the close reading of primary texts by French and Italian authors, including Straparola, Basile, Charles Perrault, Marie-Catherine d'Aulnoy, Marie-Jeanne L'Héretier, and Jeanne-Marie Leprince de Beaumont. I also include, however, lesser-known texts that challenge the parameters of the genre either in form or content.[4] In addition, we read a small

---

3. In a roundtable discussion on digital humanities at the 2011 Modern Language Association convention, Stephan Ramsey stated, "Personally, I think Digital Humanities is about building things." See Gold, accessed online (February 10, 2015) at dhdebates.gc.cuny.edu/debates.

4. For example, I include Moderata Fonte's tragic animal bridegroom tale "Liocorno" (Unicorn), embedded in her proto-feminist dialogue *The Worth of Women* (1600), and Giulia Bigolina's prose romance *Urania* (after 1553), in which she rewrites Straparola's tale of a cross-dressing heroine who tames a satyr (*The Pleasant Nights* IV.1 [ATU 514**]).

number of theoretical texts meant to help students develop a critical vocabulary to define the fairy-tale genre (Warner), understand the concept of the fairy-tale web (Bacchilega), discuss early modern and contemporary theories of imitation and adaptation (Castiglione; Hutcheon; Murat; Straparola), and comprehend the social functions and uses of stories (Frank).

In the past, the domestic hearth was the imaginary locus for the production and consumption of fairy tales; one need only think of the frontispiece to Charles Perrault's *Histoires ou contes du temps passé* (1697). Now and in the future, our students will increasingly consume, share, discuss, and produce fairy tales in digital formats. And these digital spaces will welcome participation and interaction, as do reading digital fairy tales and using apps such as FairyTale that allow children (and adults) to create multimedia e-books. Furthermore, in academic settings, various digitization projects allow students easy access to texts once difficult to obtain, such as nineteenth-century pantomime scripts or eighteenth-century English translations of Perrault.[5] For these reasons, despite teaching early modern texts, I view my students as seated at a digital hearth. I assume that most of their research—although not all—will be carried out on the Internet and that their fairy-tale webs will be collaboratively constructed and shared online using Prezi software. Prezi is well suited for the task at hand because it allows for a nonlinear presentation of ideas that emphasizes relationships and interdependencies by visually linking videos, websites, images, sound, and pdf files. The Edu Enjoy version, free to students and teachers, allows for the simultaneous collaboration of up to ten individuals and for the use of privacy settings.[6]

Once the pertinent background material on the authors and their contexts and a basic critical vocabulary have been provided in the first two weeks of the course, students begin to formulate their own definition of the fairy tale. This definition is developed and reshaped over the course of the semester. Besides considering existing definitions of the genre, students also write an original tale that embodies their definition of the fairy tale through its characters, language, and key narrative

---

5. The pantomime scripts are available through the Center for Research Libraries Digital Delivery System; the translations of Perrault are available through the Eighteenth Century Collections Online.

6. Two caveats regarding Prezi. First, as I write this article in early 2015, Prezi is not ADA/508 compliant, meaning that it is not accessible to students requiring screen readers. Second, "digital natives," to use Marc Prensky's now ubiquitous term for students born after 1980, are not always "digital literates." It might not be practical or efficient for instructors to require that students learn to use Prezi if the learning curve is particularly steep and there is no institutional support for IT instruction outside the classroom. Students can nonetheless construct webs and present them to the class by using PowerPoint (which is ADA/508 compliant) or by creating posters that depict their assembled materials in webs.

features. This assignment of creating an original fairy tale is repeated at the end of the semester so that students can compare their two attempts at writing a tale, and both tales become a part of the fairy-tale webs.

After these initial lessons, the course proceeds according to tale type rather than in chronological order. Before dividing the class into groups and assigning each group a tale type, I spend two weeks modeling what will be required of students over the course of the semester. During these two weeks, the entire class works together as though it were one large group analyzing and constructing a web for the "Puss in Boots" tale type (ATU 545B). We replicate, in a condensed way in class, the activities and assignments the students will then complete in their groups. Specifically, during weeks 3 and 4 we conduct close readings in class of early modern versions of the tale type; we analyze a scholarly article that explores the relationship among different "Puss in Boots" tales; and we discuss contemporary versions of the tale. Once we have completed our work together on "Puss in Boots" and have built a collective web, the students can form their groups and choose their tale types. In what follows, I use the "Puss in Boots" tale type as an example to illustrate both the modeling of the assignments at the beginning of the semester and the actual work that the groups complete as they construct their own webs during subsequent weeks.

The first task at hand is to activate the students' prior knowledge of the tale type; they will repeat this activity with their group's tale type as the first stage of the construction of their fairy-tale web. What version(s) of this tale type do they know? Can anyone in the group recount the entire tale? If not, can anyone at least describe the main character or some motifs? Many students will know the Puss in Boots character from the DreamWorks' *Shrek* franchise, now the protagonist of an Xbox game, a feature-length animated film, and a Netflix series.[7] This prior knowledge of the tale provides the first elements inserted in the webs and can be represented in different ways: as a film of a group member or member recounting the tale, as the results of a survey of group members, or by simply including images to represent the versions. This prior knowledge will then need to be positioned and linked to the four examples assigned to the entire class: Straparola's "Costantino Fortunato" (XI, 1), Basile's "Cagliuso" (II.4), Perrault's "The Master Cat, or Puss in Boots," and d'Aulnoy's "White Cat." As each version enters the web, the group will need to renegotiate the relationships among them.

The second stage of construction has as its learning objective the acquisition and development of research skills, as each individual member of the group is

---

7. The Xbox Kinect video game was launched in 2011 in anticipation of the feature animated-film release *Puss in Boots* in 2012. In January 2015 Netflix premiered the original animated series.

asked to find other versions to add to their web. These versions can take any form: literary tales, picture books, translations of the early modern tales, films, advertisements, and so on. We can model robust research practices and encourage our students to move beyond the exclusive use of Google searches by pointing them toward well-respected websites in fairy-tale studies,[8] by instructing them on how to use the online library catalog, and by introducing them to key reference works in the field.[9] To further shape their research experience and to exert a minimum of control over the variety of texts in their web, I require that at least one of the versions they include in their webs come from the extensive fairy-tale holdings in the Department of Special Collections, Norlin Library, University of Colorado, which we visit early in the semester so that students can familiarize themselves with the resources. There, students can find an array of texts and visualizations of the cat, including Perrault's Puss illustrated by Gustave Dorè and Edmund Dulac and an early-seventeenth-century engraving for Straparola's "Costantino Fortunato." Undoubtedly, they will have no problems locating film versions on YouTube, such as the Japanese anime featuring a well-shod cat named Pero, or Walt Disney's and Ub Iwerk's *Puss in Boots* (Laugh-O-Gram Studio, 1922).[10] Each group discusses their initial findings regarding the versions of their tale type that they have uncovered through their research on the Friday of the week that we focus on the group's tale type (e.g., the Cinderella group presents their initial findings on the Friday of week 6).

Furthermore, for each group I also select and assign one additional version of the tale type that I think will shape their inquiry in interesting ways. It might be a text that simultaneously radiates outward toward contemporary and early modern versions of a tale, or one that asks students to consider tales outside the Euro-American context. For example, I might assign Angela Carter's "Puss-in-Boots" from *The Bloody Chamber*. Her Puss is a first-person narrator whose explicit animality and robust libido redefine the cat's role as described in the early modern versions we read, but he also seems a precursor for Dream-Works' *Puss in Boots*. Heidi Ann Heiner notes that in the DreamWorks film "the animators obviously found inspiration from Doré's illustrations of the tale" by Perrault.[11] In many other respects, however, the DreamWorks Puss in Boots

---

8. Here I am thinking of Heidi Anne Heiner's www.surlalunefairytales.com and Terri Windling and Midori Snyder's www.endicott-studio.com as particularly useful sites for this project.

9. These include Haase (*Greenwood Encyclopedia*), Zipes (*Oxford Companion*), and Uther.

10. The English title for the Japanese anime created by Töei Animation is "The Wonderful World of Puss in Boots" (1969). The protagonist's name, Pero, recognizes Perrault as an inspiration for the film.

11. www.surlalunefairytales.com/pussboots/index.html (accessed February 10, 2015).

resembles Carter's Puss: He tells his own story, his behavior often underscores his animality (lapping milk, chasing strings and lasers, coughing up hairballs), and he functions as the main character rather than simply as an animal helper.

The third stage of the web construction has as its learning objective developing critical thinking and clear communication skills. Although I am not at the point of completely abandoning the academic essay, as some digital humanists have suggested we do, I do agree that we can deconstruct the traditional final paper into smaller assignments that can then be abstracted and posted on the fairy-tale web in a shorter form of public writing that is combined with images, video, and sound files.[12] Each student completes three assignments that are intended to help refine the connections among the elements in the webs. These assignments task each student with choosing and analyzing a particular strand or group of strands in the web that unite different texts. First, students are asked to write a response paper to a critical article that explores one or more versions of the tale type. The student must summarize the scholar's argument and reflect on how the article might reconfigure the group's web.[13] Having now analyzed an academic model for discussing tales of this type, students are asked to develop a thesis from a comparative analysis of at least two of the early modern versions of the tale type and write a brief paper. Finally, students write an analysis of one modern version of the tale that explores how the contemporary version embodies, challenges, or rewrites the early modern versions.

For the final written assignment of the semester, students once again create a fairy tale based on the tale type of their group, in a format of their choosing (literary, e-book, film, graphic novel). They must include a brief preface describing where their tale should be located in the web. By this point in the course, students will have discussed multiple versions of their tale type as well as a number of contemporary and early modern theoretical texts meant to enrich their understanding of the practices of adaptation and imitation.[14] The goal is that students will be empowered to truly experiment with the genre rather than simply replicate the dominant (Disney)

---

12. On the fading utility of the academic essay and the value of public writing, see Sample.

13. For "Puss in Boots" students might consider reading the following critical chapters or articles: Harries, on "The White Cat"; Hennard Dutheil de la Rochère, on Angela Carter as translator of Perrault; Canepa, on Basile's "Cagliuso" as a critique of court life; and Zipes ("Of Cats and Men"), on "Puss in Boots" as a tale of acculturation.

14. To explore the issues around imitation and adaptation in the early modern period, one could assign Baldassar Castiglione's description of imitation in the first book (Chapter 26) of *The Book of the Courtier* (1528); Straparola's own denial of plagiarism in the dedicatory letter to Volume 2 in *The Pleasant Nights*; and Madame de Murat's admission that she and her fellow female authors all borrow from Straparola in her letter "To Modern Fairies."

models, as they tend to do in their initial attempt at writing an original. At the end of the course, each group presents their web to the class.

Asking students to construct webs in order to think and write about fairy tales offers numerous pedagogical and conceptual advantages. This approach allows us to scaffold assignments and weave together both individual and group work. Because students publish their writing on webs accessible to the class, the writing assignments are no longer a closed exchange between professor and student but contribute to a multivocal, public exchange among classmates. The writing assignments completed throughout the semester can be embedded in the group's Prezi presentation, thus making them accessible to the entire group and, potentially, if the students decide to publish the presentation by changing the privacy settings, to the entire class and the general public. The group might also decide to attach excerpts from individual assignments to the Prezi conversation to better explain the relationships, or edges, connecting the various tales, or nodes, in their web.

Conceptually, constructing webs allows students to discover for themselves the incredible malleability of the fairy tale and to articulate relationships among texts in the absence of a hierarchical presentation of authors and national traditions. Certainly, the webs reveal certain texts to be influential hubs densely linked to many other versions, whereas other texts are shown to radiate outward in fewer directions. At the same time, however, a dominant text or film loses some of its power as it becomes one of many nodes in the web. Rather than being focused on "firsts" or "bests," the students' attention is directed to analyzing and articulating relationships among texts and understanding the complex ways in which early modern French and Italian tales shape the contemporary Euro-American fairy tale. The connections and interdependencies traced on the web not only map a tradition but also visually render the fairy tale's exceptional mobility as a genre that passes freely across borders and media.

These webs can also be used to raise questions about scholarly practices, such as canon formation and classification: How did Perrault's "Puss in Boots" come to exert such a great influence on modern versions? Because three out of four of the early modern Pusses do not wear boots, would it be more accurate to classify these tales as "Shrewd Cat" stories, as Jack Zipes does (Zipes, *Great Fairy Tale Tradition*, vi)? Finally, the inclusion of the students' original tales in these webs permits them to participate in the field of fairy-tale studies, not simply as scholars but also as conscious creators of tales who understand the stakes of their storytelling. The students themselves become a part of the history of the fairy tale, intervening in the tradition as "storytellers and inventors, gathering, interpreting, and revisioning" fairy tales (Warner, xiv).

BIBLIOGRAPHY

Bacchilega, Cristina. *Fairy Tales Transformed? Twenty-First-Century Adaptations and the Politics of Wonder*. Detroit: Wayne State University Press, 2013.

Bigolina, Giulia. *Urania: A Romance*. Ed. and trans. Valeria Finucci. Chicago: University of Chicago Press, 2005.

Canepa, Nancy. "The Disenchantment of Power: Kings and Courtiers." In *From Court to Forest: Giambattista Basile's* Lo cunto de li cunti *and the Birth of the Literary Fairy Tale*. Detroit: Wayne State University Press, 1999. 111–54.

Carter, Angela. *The Bloody Chamber, and Other Stories*. New York: Penguin, 1993.

Castiglione, Baldassar. *The Book of the Courtier*. Ed. and trans. George Bull. New York: Penguin, 1976. 66–68.

Eichel-Lojkine, Patricia. *Contes en réseaux: L'émergence du conte sur la scène littéraire européene*. Geneva: Droz, 2013.

Fonte, Moderata. *The Worth of Women, Wherein Is Clearly Revealed Their Nobility and Superiority to Men*. Ed. and trans. Virginia Cox. Chicago: University of Chicago Press, 1997.

Foucault, Michel. *Archaeology of Knowledge and The Discourse on Language*. Trans. A. M. Sheridan Smith. New York: Pantheon, 1972.

Frank, Arthur W. *Letting Stories Breathe: A Socio-Narratology*. Chicago: University of Chicago Press, 2010.

Gold, Matthew K. "The Digital Humanities Moment." In *Debates in the Digital Humanities*. Ed. Matthew K. Gold. Minneapolis: University of Minnesota Press, 2012. dhdebates.gc.cuny.edu/debates/text/2 (accessed March 25, 2018).

Haase, Donald. "Decolonizing Fairy Tale Studies." *Marvels & Tales* 24.1 (2006): 17–38.

———, ed. *Greenwood Encyclopedia of Folktales and Fairy Tales*, 3 vols. Westport, CT: Greenwood Press, 2008.

Harries, Elizabeth Wanning. "Fairy Tales About Fairy Tales: Notes on Canon Formation." In *Twice Upon a Time: Women Writers and the History of the Fairy Tale*. By Elizabeth Wanning Harries. Princeton, NJ: Princeton University Press, 2001. 19–45.

Hennard Dutheil de la Rochère, Martine. "Doing the Somersault of Love: From 'Le Chat botté' to 'Puss in Boots' and 'Puss-in-Boots.'" In *Reading, Translating, Rewriting: Angela Carter's Translational Poetics*. By Martine Hennard Dutheil de la Rochère. Detroit: Wayne State University Press, 2013. 157–88.

Hutcheon, Linda. "Beginning to Theorize Adaptation: What? Who? Why? How? Where? When?" In *A Theory of Adaptation*. By Linda Hutcheon, with Siobhan O'Flynn. New York: Routledge, 2006. 1–32.

Murat, Henriette-Julie de. "Perrault's Preface to *Griselda* and Murat's 'To Modern Fairies.'" Ed. and trans. Holly Tucker and Melanie R. Siemens. *Marvels & Tales* 19.1 (2005): 125–30.

Sample, Mark L. "What's Wrong with Writing Essays." In *Debates in the Digital Humanities*. Ed. Matthew K. Gold. Minneapolis: University of Minnesota Press, 2012. dhdebates.gc.cuny.edu/debates/text/42 (accessed March 25, 2018).

Straparola, Giovan Francesco. *The Pleasant Nights*. Ed. and trans. Suzanne Magnanini. Toronto: Iter Academic Press, 2015.

Teverson, Andrew. "Migrant Fictions: Salman Rushdie and the Fairy Tale." In *Contemporary Writers and the Fairy Tale*. Ed. Stephen Benson. Detroit: Wayne State University Press, 2008. 47–73.

Uther, Hans-Jörg. *The Types of International Folktales: A Classification and Bibliography, Based on the System by Antti Aarne and Stith Thompson*, 3 vols. Helsinki: Suomalainen Tiedeakatemia, 2004.

Warner, Marina. *Once Upon a Time: A Short History of the Fairy Tale*. New York: Oxford University Press, 2014.

Zipes, Jack, ed. and trans. *The Great Fairy Tale Tradition: From Straparola and Basile to the Brothers Grimm*. New York: Norton, 2001.

———. "Of Cats and Men: Framing the Civilizing Discourse of the Fairy Tale." In *Out of the Woods: The Origins of the Literary Fairy Tale in Italy and France*. Ed. Nancy Canepa. Detroit: Wayne State University Press, 1997. 176–93.

———, ed. *The Oxford Companion to Fairy Tales*. New York: Oxford University Press, 2000.

CHAPTER FOUR

FAIRY TALES IN THE FOREIGN-LANGUAGE CLASSROOM

"I Cannot Understand You"

FOLKTALES AND FOREIGN-LANGUAGE PEDAGOGY

Maria Kaliambou

FOLKTALES AND FOREIGN-LANGUAGE UNDERSTANDING

In the folktale "I Cannot Understand You" (ATU 1700), a man traveling in a foreign country is impressed by all the new things he sees. He is curious to learn more about the people of the land and tries to communicate with them, though he cannot speak their language. Every time he asks them a question, he receives the same answer, "I cannot understand you." Ultimately, the traveler is led to believe that "I cannot understand you" is the name of an important local: someone with riches who got married and immediately thereafter died.

Other folktales also address, in a similar fun-loving manner, the problems inherent in linguistic and cultural communication. The jocular tale "Misunderstanding Because of Ignorance of a Foreign Language" (ATU 1699) refers vividly and humorously to the situations that occur between people speaking different languages. The folktale "Words in a Foreign Language Thought to Be Insults" (ATU 1322) speaks to cognitive misinterpretation caused by ignorance of foreign vocabulary.

How many times have we ended up in comical, frustrating, cross-cultural conflict just because we do not speak and understand one another's languages? The folktales just mentioned epitomize the centrality and necessity of foreign-language competence. When we learn a foreign language, we strive to communicate our thoughts and feelings and also to understand what other people are trying to convey to us.

How can we learn foreign language more effectively? And which dynamic pedagogical materials offer an engaging means for instruction? Instructors use varied texts to teach their students linguistic and cultural competency. Experimenting with folktales at all language levels can be rewarding. In this essay I propose that folktales constitute rich, multilayered material for foreign-language pedagogy. Based on my teaching experience (see Kaliambou, *Routledge Modern Greek Reader*), I give concrete pedagogical suggestions regarding the learning and teaching of a foreign language (and its culture) through folktales, which can enhance all four linguistic skills (reading, writing, speaking, listening) while sharpening students' sensitivity toward other cultures.

WHICH FOLKTALES TO CHOOSE FOR THE FOREIGN-LANGUAGE CLASSROOM?

Language textbooks from different times and places contain folktales as suitable material for language instruction. For example, French textbooks for elementary schools in eighteenth-century France include Charles Perrault's stories as reading material (see Velay-Vallantin); the teaching of French language outside France also draws on Perrault's stories (in areas such as Germany and Greece; see Ranke and Kaplanoglou, respectively). In this case, folktales transcend region and become an inclusively effective means of teaching language. Cultures outside Western Europe incorporate folktales for teaching language as well. Ulrich Marzolph describes a seventeenth-century Persian grammar book that includes oral narratives for teaching reading and translating, something that contributed to the book's success and popularity. Even today one can find folklore included in readers and spelling books for children; it is the perfect entryway to learning a first or foreign language. Current foreign-language pedagogy suggests that teaching a foreign language should encompass more than formal and structural principles and that the study of cultural context is indispensable for a student of foreign language (Kramsch, *Context*). Instructors in class should use authentic material embedded in the real context of the spoken language. Folktales, as part of the larger cultural picture, constitute useful material for foreign-language learning.

Which folktales should an instructor choose for the classroom? The answer is suited to the lesson at hand. Magic, religious, realistic, anecdotal, and formula tales all yield positive pedagogical results, each for different reasons. According to the level of the students and the learning outcomes the teacher wants to achieve, different tales can serve different pedagogical needs. For instance, with respect to the language level of the class, animal tales are usually shorter tales with limited vocabulary, which makes them more accessible to elementary students. Magic, religious, and novella tales provide longer texts and thus are appropriate for higher levels of language competency. Formula tales, because they are based on repetitions, can help with vocabulary tasks. Jocular tales and anecdotes, usually shorter texts, are useful for studying the cultural dimensions of wittiness and trickery and can be paralleled with personal culture stories of the students.

Language instructors are not necessarily folklorists and consequently do not know that folktales have various subtypes. One suggestion for instructors is to consult a catalog of tale types for the target country, so that they can gather folktales from several subtypes. Instructors should choose folktales from various regions where the target language is spoken and should consider using stories in dialect form for more advanced students to get them acquainted with variety in the foreign language; dialect tales should also be considered for advanced classes in dialectology. In addition to folktales, many genres have useful material for language instruction, for example, myths, fables, legends, urban legends, and other fantasy stories. The structure and content of these genres are similar to those of folktales and thus facilitate language acquisition. In addition to autochthonous material, foreign-language teachers can use texts in translation from other countries to provide context for the source material in the target language. For instance, teachers can present the same folktale from different countries after teaching the target-language tale. This will generate various class discussions about intercultural similarities and differences.

The main concern and challenge for an instructor is the level of foreign-language competence required by a given folktale. Usually folktales can be taught after the second semester of instruction. Students need to have acquired basic knowledge of a foreign language, such as the new alphabet, so that they can read short texts and be familiar with basic grammatical structures—such as verb tenses and nouns and their inflection (if any)—to be able to read and learn from folktales. Obviously, the editorial hand of the teacher plays a defining role in sculpting the lesson. The instructor can modify the texts according to the needs of a particular class. Edited and simplified versions can be taught at the elementary level of a language class; advanced language classes will have more options available to the instructor. The role of teacher is catalytic not only to language pedagogy but also to the general knowledge provided about the source material. The folktale material delivered in class demonstrates the teacher's perception of what a relevant folktale is; this will consequently influence the perception students have of folktales.

Multiple Learning Outcomes

Folktales in a foreign-language classroom help students enhance all four core language skills: reading, writing, speaking, and listening. Depending on the desired learning outcome, teachers can use certain stories to focus on a particular language skill. Folktales offer excellent material for learning and practicing grammar and acquiring specific vocabulary. Furthermore, folktales provide a tool for better cultural understanding and can be an invaluable means of bridging cultural differences. In the following discussion I suggest some pedagogical activities and tasks that target practicing the four language skills. It is not possible to entirely separate the skills from one another because they are so interwoven, and thus most of the activities integrate more than one skill. I have also chosen to include some tasks that target the practicing of vocabulary and grammar and the sharpening of cultural awareness.

Reading

Reading (extensive and/or intensive) is an integral part of foreign-language instruction, and folktales offer a useful means of practice. Extensive "free" reading brings positive results regarding acquisition of new vocabulary and grammar. Instructors can schedule a few minutes every week in class for students to practice individual silent reading. According to Eric Taylor, folktales are particularly suitable for silent reading because they are short and students can finish them quickly. Also, because there are many types of folktales, they can encompass various degrees of difficulty and taste. Finally, and perhaps most significantly, folktales are interesting to students (Taylor, 134).

The most common method of intensive reading focuses on smaller linguistic units (such as sentences) and targets language accuracy (such as grammar and syntax) over the complete understanding of a text. Folktales can be used for teaching grammar and syntax and as a means of focusing on particular vocabulary.

The instructor can assess reading comprehension in several ways. Some activities for students are to answer in either oral or written form concrete questions related to the facts of the folktale, to determine whether statements related to the tale are true or false, or to answer multiple-choice questions. These questions can refer to concrete episodes, motifs, and plot points of the folktale or to more general theoretical issues raised by the folktale (e.g., envy, greed, love, marriage). Students should learn the structure of a text, including temporal and spatial sequences, the logical order of actions and their effects, and so on. This helps students develop their reading and analytical skills, because they have to summarize, analyze, and express their opinion on varied matters.

Writing

Students' analytical thinking can be further enhanced while strengthening their writing skills. The instructor can create various exercises based on folktales to support the students' written production. A common writing assignment is summarizing the story. More complex activities include theoretical, abstract, and interpretive questions, which require an advanced ability to write in the foreign language. These are the "why" and not the "what" questions. Some examples of activities are:

1. Write about whether or not you like the particular folktale. Give your reasons.
2. Write your opinion about the significance of an abstract notion (e.g., the role of fate, beauty, family, religion, etc.) in the folktale.
3. Finish the story with a different ending.
4. Search relevant literary motifs and compare them with the folktale studied in class (e.g., the "Beauty and the Beast" tale in antiquity, the personification of Death in ancient and medieval texts).

With these sets of assignments, students practice writing in the foreign language, perform research, make comparisons, present arguments, and explore their creativity.

Another excellent activity involves creative writing in the foreign language, where students are asked to write their own stories. Students become inspired by the stories they read in class and the stories they already know and love. Even the less creative students are usually motivated to let their fantasy spin. In the spring of 2011 I assembled the creative writing assignments of students at all levels of Modern Greek study (elementary, intermediate, and advanced) into a publication; among their writings are modern fairy tales (Appendix A).

Speaking

Folktales are helpful in promoting the skill of speaking. For example, they can be used to practice correct pronunciation. Furthermore, folktales raise issues that can initiate lively conversations in the classroom. Depending on language level, students can orally respond to factual questions related to the plot or expand on abstract or theoretical issues where they must develop and express an opinion. Other ways of generating discussion in the classroom—besides answering factual or theoretical questions—are presentations or mini-lectures by students either individually or in small groups. Students can conduct research on a specific topic raised by the folktale (e.g., the role of fairies or food and nutrition in the world of the folktale), give a short presentation in class, and initiate further discussion with their classmates. The presenters should prepare vocabulary lists for their peers. With this presentation-style activity, students can touch on a variety of cultural, historical, religious, moral, political, and personal issues while honing their speaking and listening skill sets. Furthermore, students can be introspective as they discuss their own cultural experiences and compare them with those of a given folktale (see section on cultural awareness later in this essay).

Another way to engage students in speaking is to make them tell stories. For instance, they can "retell" the folktales studied in class by adding a different ending. They can narrate a story from their own culture or from their own personal experiences. Through retellings and personal tellings, the instructor can teach students how to become storytellers in a foreign language.

To further use the performative aspect of folktales, the teacher can assign theater skits or theatrical dialogues. Students can select different roles from the studied folktales and perform a small dialogue, a scene from the folktale, or the entire narrative. Usually students have fun with this activity and become more creative and improvisational in the foreign language. As mentioned, they can alter the ending of the folktale—or, if they are more ambitious, create their own version of the folktale. Perhaps this reinterpretation could even take the form of a full-fledged adaptation and performance of a tale. In the spring of 2012 several of my students were involved in a Yale undergraduate theatrical production of an English adaptation of a Greek Cinderella tale, written by a student of mine who saw in the small tale an opportunity for culturally immersive theater (Appendix B).

Listening

Listening practice is included in all the mentioned activities. However, if instructors want to focus only on listening comprehension, they can read folktales aloud to students or, alternatively, play recordings of performances of the folktales. It can be pedagogically effective when the teacher becomes a mini-storyteller and narrates the stories without reading them. Illustrations can facilitate this process for the teacher, distilling the sequence of the plot and outlining the order of episodes. Drawings and illustrations can help students, particularly beginners who understand but cannot yet produce speech in the foreign language.

Eric Taylor offers a variety of activities with drawings that test the listening comprehension of students without requiring them to speak. For instance, students can draw what they hear, place a series of drawings in chronological order according to the story, or mark the story's events on a map (Taylor, 53–71). Forgoing visuals, the assessment of listening can occur as does the assessment of reading comprehension: with questions ranging from minimal (yes/no, true/false, multiple choice, find the correct order of the sentences) to elaborate language production (opinion questions, analysis, prediction, etc.).

Vocabulary

Claire Kramsch argues that the words in folktales have a symbolic power, "bring[ing] about events in a 'magical' way," and thus students learn to play with symbolic forms (Kramsch, *Multilingual Subject*, 38). Through folktales students can learn a broad spectrum of vocabulary of a foreign language. They can learn basic content words (nouns, verbs, adjectives, and adverbs) and function words (articles, pronouns, conjunctions, participles, etc.). Words in folktales can be both specific (fireplace, cow, pit, golden coins, etc.) and of general and abstract nature (happiness, laziness, piety, etc.). An additional lexical asset to the standard vocabulary is the abundant colloquialisms and idiomatic phrases in folktales. Everyday expressions, in particular, are suited to the folktale context and offer authentic scenes of language use. For language learners at a more advanced level, words in archaic language or with multiple meanings are available as well. As Cora Lee Nollendorfs states regarding the use of similar expressions in German folktales, "Students may not need to *use* such expressions, but they should be able to *understand* them and recognize their source and style" (Nollendorfs, 293–94).

The best method for learning new vocabulary is discovering meaning from a word's context. As Taylor states, "Because of the predictability, redundancy, and repetition in folktales, unknown words are usually easier to guess than in many other types of texts. This makes folktales good for developing skill at inferring meaning from context—a very useful general reading strategy" (Taylor, 142). If translations of words are provided, then the glossing of unknown words should be limited to content words and only some high-register function words. In my opinion the footnote system is the most efficient method for learning new vocabulary because students can immediately locate selected words, their translation, and any additional information provided by the teacher.

There is infinite potential for teachers to create class activities and home exercises that test vocabulary. Depending on the character of a class and the pedagogy of the teacher, folktales can be taught in either a communicative or more traditional manner. The communicative style intends to foster free and unimpeded communication between speakers of the language, whereas more traditional exercises emphasize accuracy and perfection of basic language skills. Several activities that can engage students to master new vocabulary are finding synonyms, providing antonyms, filling in the blanks with words from the text, making sentences with some key words of the text, finding as many words as possible related to a topic, finishing half sentences, and solving crossword puzzles.

Grammar

Grammar, an inevitable part of every language class, can be taught in an entertaining manner through the use of folktales. A teacher can concentrate on specific grammatical phenomena (such as verb tenses, conditionals, nouns, comparatives—and degrees—of adjectives, diminutive forms, and indirect and direct speech), highlighting relevant passages to illustrate a point. Folktales are excellent material for practicing all forms of verbs. A standard activity for practicing verb tenses is to have students narrate a story in the present, past, and future tenses. Worth noting is a standard characteristic of folktales: the repetition of "three," offering an excellent opportunity to teach the degrees of adjectives: good, better, best; bad, worse, worst; etc.

An alternative method for studying German grammar is offered, for example, by the textbook GRIMMATIK: *German Grammar Through the Magic of the Brothers Grimm Fairy Tales* by Margrit Zinggeller (2007), who uses folktales to teach complicated grammatical forms and structures. Another study for German-language instruction examines the teaching of relative pronouns through German fairy tales (Brown).

Culture

Teaching a foreign language should encompass more than formal and structural principles; equally important is the use of "context and culture in language teaching" (Kramsch, *Context*). Language evolves alongside cultural and social practice, because language occurs in (inter)cultural interactions. Study of cultural context is thus indispensable for the foreign-language student.

Folktales offer richly textured material for students to develop their cultural awareness and knowledge of a foreign culture. Folktales are situated in reality—as Lutz Röhrich states in his seminal book *Folktales and Reality* (1991)—and can thus teach us much about the cultural and social context in which they are embedded. Simultaneously, given the subject matter being studied, "students remain entertained and interested while learning sophisticated things" (Obergfell, 446). Sandra Obergfell, in her article about using French folktales in a French-language classroom, mentions that "we are not only foreign language and culture teachers; we are also humanists, interested in the development of the students as a whole person" (441). Folktales are a jumping-off point for the discussion of culturally bound morals, values, and norms and thus foster a greater understanding of different perspectives. If the desired learning outcome is cultural awareness, students can, for instance, conduct extracurricular research on the region a given folktale comes from (alternatively, the teacher can bring additional information to class).

When I taught a version of the Greek "Cinderella" tale to an advanced Modern Greek class, its idiosyncratic expression of the culture and sociohistorical reality of the region initiated lots of discussion in class. For example, the story starts with a father who cannot stand his poverty, leaves his family, and goes abroad to find a better job so that he can send money to his relatives back home. This episode triggered many thoughts about unemployment and immigration, an old phenomenon in Greece and still relevant today. Religion and religious rituals were another topic of conversation. Cinderella, in contrast to the well-known Disney version, goes not to a royal dance but to church for midnight mass on Easter; it is there that she meets her prince. This cultural detail underlines the importance of religion in Greek rural society. Village life in rural environments—including traditional occupations such as farming and animal husbandry—exists in the context of the decay that has befallen many villages as Greece has metamorphosed into a conglomeration of cityscapes. The shift from these communities to modern societies offers vivid material for conversation. Through folktales, my students were given the opportunity to learn not only the glory of ancient Greece but also the reality of modern Greek socioeconomic life, which for some students was totally new and surprising (see Kaliambou, "I Stachtopouta," 665–68).

Another way to engage conversations about multiple cultures in a language class is to assign stories from various regions. To follow up on the previous example of the Greek "Cinderella," students can read versions of the cinder-girl folktale from different countries. Students can analyze, evaluate, and compare and contrast stories, thus using critical thinking while practicing their language skills (see Taylor, 255–72).

One step beyond the standard classroom is ethnographic fieldwork. An educational trip in the country where the target language is spoken is always beneficial. Students can experience from within the unfamiliar culture, conducting interviews with locals and asking them to narrate stories. This cultural immersion is not just for advanced students but can be beneficial to beginner students looking to get involved with, engaged in, and inspired by the foreign language and its culture.

I Can Understand You!

I am confident that every teacher and every student of a foreign language will love teaching and learning through folktales! Folktales can help students to expand reading, writing, speaking, and listening skills; they are effortless avenues for learning new vocabulary, understanding grammar, and being exposed to foreign cultures. All of this, in an alternative and entertaining way: That is the power of folktales. Let's try to deconstruct the jocular fairy tales in which the protagonists could not understand a word and misunderstood everything. The same folktales that parody the difficulties of not knowing a foreign language can actually help in overcoming those obstacles and enable communication with foreign peoples. So we may be able to say, at the end of the day, "Yes, I can understand you!"

APPENDIX A

Creative Writing in a Foreign-Language Classroom

OBJECTIVES

Students were completely free to express themselves in a foreign language (in my case, Modern Greek), and thus they practiced and developed their writing skills in a creative way. To engage teamwork and peer learning, introductory-level students were divided into small groups. One group wrote a short poem, another a text in dialogue form between friends, and the third a short story, all based on fairy tales. The intermediate- and advanced-level students each wrote a creative essay. Because they were more advanced in the language, this second group was able to write at greater length and thus make fuller use of fairy-tale structure, motifs, and plots. Some students also included drawings (with and without subtitles) to support their stories. For the introductory level, this activity was assessed as part of their home-work grade, whereas for the higher levels it was part of their final essay project (thus accounting for a larger percentage of their grade).

OUTCOMES

The results were rewarding. I concentrate here on one intermediate- and one advanced-level student. The student from the intermediate class wrote two short stories resembling fairy tales and myths. The first story tells of a male good spirit and the beautiful woman who demands his magic power. The spirit refuses, the woman screams, the sky darkens, and stream waters run as blood. Ultimately, the sky opens to shine light, and at the end of the tale the woman is transformed into stone. His second story, titled "The Fairytale of Love," begins with Eros, the god of Love, shooting his arrow at two little mice. In the end, all the animals of the earth become friends and there is no more fighting among them. The student read his stories in class, and another student wrote a critical analysis of them in Modern Greek! The second student did an excellent close reading and was able to write a short theoretical essay based on these two new fairy tales written by her classmate.

The student from the advanced class wrote her modern fairy tale ("The Princess in the Castle") to resemble Disney versions of tales. In addition, she used drawings of famous Disney protagonists and replaced their faces with the faces of her class-mates. This created a vivid reaction in class, where students recognized their faces as the princess, the prince, the villain, and the fairy.

At the end of the semester, I compiled all the creative writings of my language classes and published a booklet (Kaliambou, *Modern Greek*). This little publication was a beautiful crowning achievement of folktale storytelling techniques in the classroom.

Evaluation

The students' reactions to this activity were quite positive. They immediately embraced the idea of this project and launched into their creativity with joy. This attitude of joy brought about delightful results. Creative writing in a foreign language can be challenging. Students may have various nice ideas, but it is hard to express them eloquently in a foreign language. Students need the aid of a dictionary and a grammar book to support their writings, and many of them use online tools to translate and write, which can bring questionable results. Yet despite the challenges they faced, they managed to express their thoughts and feelings effectively. Particularly through the use of fairy-tale motifs, they opened themselves up to saying more than they would have in other forms of writing.

APPENDIX B

"Cinderella" on Stage

OBJECTIVES

This theatrical activity was born in my advanced Modern Greek class on Greek folktales. Among the various stories students had to read was a Greek "Cinderella" version; they then had to talk about the tale and write a short response essay. The Greek tale is radically different from the well-known Disney version. The Greek folktale depicts a mother, her two evil elder daughters, and Cinderella, the youngest. The father is away in a foreign land in search of a decent job, so that he can send money back to his family. The mother cannot endure the disobedience of her two elder daughters and is transformed into a cow, which the two malevolent sisters kill and eat. Cinderella buries her mother's bones and mourns for 40 days at the grave of her mother. After this period, the bones are transformed into gold coins. Cinderella brings the coins, unbeknownst to her sisters, into church for the Easter liturgy; she throws them into the congregation at midnight, when Christ is understood to rise from the dead, and then rushes out before anyone can sense it's her. She performs the same ritual the following year, but the third year, the prince of the region smears honey on the steps of the church to catch her. Cinderella's slipper gets stuck in the honey and the prince searches for the girl whose slipper he has caught. He learns it is Cinderella's shoe, hears the story behind the gold coins, and falls in love. He marries Cinderella.

The American students found the Greek version unfamiliar and especially strange and foreign. "It's a morbid story," wrote one student. They compared it with their familiar cultural repertoire, which was mostly shaped by Disney productions. The different cultural elements of the Greek version helped to ignite and develop their cultural awareness and capture their fantasy. Questions such as "Why does Cinderella meet her prince at church instead of at a royal ball?" initiated discussions about the role of religion in Greek society. The rituals around mourning and lamenting constituted another area for intercultural analysis. Perhaps most viscerally, the students responded to the transformation of the mother into a cow and her being cannibalized at the hands of the evil elder sisters.

Unexpected Outcomes
Theater Production

This standard reading comprehension activity had some wonderful unexpected results, which moved beyond the standard curriculum. One student was inspired to use the story of "Cinderella" as the underpinning of an interdisciplinary performance piece. He translated the tale and adapted the narrative by creating a logical reason for the folktale's fantastic circumstances. He used the motifs and plot to create his own "deconstructive" version in which there is no prince and no wedding at the end. Rather, he preferred to end the story with Cinderella casting out a demon from her sisters.

This student then directed a theater production performed by undergraduate students. He also enlisted a member of the Yale Women's Slavic Chorus to prepare songs to be performed live as a musical accompaniment to certain movements and worked with a group of painters to create icons of the play's characters, images that were strategically placed to emphasize the actions of a scene.

The play was performed for three nights at a theater in an undergraduate Yale college. This endeavor required a large crew of people involved in a variety of capacities, among them producer, dramaturge, kinetic consultant, technical director, lighting designer, musical director, and book designer.

Booklet

A playbill-style booklet accompanied the performance (Kaliambou, *Cinderella*). The playwright-director wrote an introductory note about the process of writing the play and the ideas underlying the adaptation and expansion of the source material. The dramaturge wrote a short piece on magic and morality in the new *Cinderella*, and a student in my literature class on folktales wrote a scholarly piece on internal and external space in the original tale.

Evaluation

The theater performance was a great success and was well received by other students and by the community. Students from various classes, not necessarily from my language or folktale classes, worked admirably together toward a production, which required huge time commitments outside the regular class time.

The performative aspect that fairy tales can offer is invaluable to any class—not just in language courses but also in regular literature classes. Particularly in a foreign-language class, by performing dialogues, observing repetitions, and appreciating the cultural context of the story in the target language, students can practice and promote their speaking and listening skills. In addition, theater play is an excellent opportunity for varied and intricate teamwork, fostering a strong feeling of community.

Bibliography

Brown, Roger. "A Practical Approach to Relative Pronouns." *Die Unterrichtspraxis: Teaching German* 10.2 (1977): 121–22.

Kaliambou, Maria, ed. *Cinderella: The Light of God.* New Haven, CT: Yale Printing and Publishing Services, 2012.

———. *I Stachtopouta paei sto mathima: Mathainontas nea ellinika meso ton paramythion* [Cinderella Goes to Class: Learning Modern Greek Through Folktales]. In *To paramythi: Apo tous aderfous Grimm stin epochi mas—Diadosi kai meleti* [The Tale: From the Brothers Grimm to Our Times—Diffusion and Study]. Ed. M. Meraklis, G. Papantonakis, Ch. Zafiropoulos, M. Kaplanoglou, and G. Katsadoros. Athens: Gutenberg, 655–73.

———, ed. *Modern Greek at Yale: Spring 2011*. New Haven, CT: Yale Printing and Publishing Services, 2011.

———. *The Routledge Modern Greek Reader: Greek Folktales for Learning Modern Greek*. New York: Routledge, 2015.

Kaplanoglou, Marianthi. *Elliniki laiki paradosi: Ta paramythia sta periodika gia paidia kai neous (1836–1922)* [Greek Folk Tradition: Fairy Tales in Journals for Children and Young People (1836–1922)]. Athens: Ellinika Grammata, 1998.

Kramsch, Claire. *Context and Culture in Language Teaching*. Oxford, UK: Oxford University Press, 1993.

———. *The Multilingual Subject: What Foreign Language Learners Say About Their Experience and Why It Matters*. Oxford, UK: Oxford University Press, 2009.

Marzolph, Ulrich. "'Pleasant Stories in an Easy Style': Gladwin's Persian Grammar as an Intermediary Between Classical and Popular Literature." In *Proceedings of the Second European Conference of Iranian Studies, Held in Bamberg, 30th September to 4th October, 1991, by the Societas Iranologica Europaea*. Ed. B. A. O. Fragner. Rome: Istituto Italiano per il Medio ed Estremo Oriente, 1995. 445–75.

Nollendorfs, Cora Lee. "Fairy Tales for Language Instruction: Poisoned Apple or Gold from Straw?" *Die Unterrichtspraxis: Teaching German* 16.2 (1983): 290–94.

Obergfell, Sandra. "Fairy Tales as a Cultural Context in the French Classroom." *French Review* 56.3 (1983): 439–46.

Ranke, Kurt. "Via grammatica." *Fabula* 20 (1979): 160–69.

Röhrich, Lutz. *Folktales and Reality*. Trans. Peter Tokofsky. Bloomington: Indiana University Press, 1991 [1956].

Taylor, Eric K. *Using Folktales*. Cambridge, UK: Cambridge University Press, 2000.

Uther, Hans Jörg, ed. *The Types of International Folktales: A Classification and Bibliography, Based on the System of Antti Aarne and Stith Thompson*, 3 vols. Helsinki: Suomalainen Tiedeakatemia, 2004.

Velay-Vallantin, Catherine. "Tales as a Mirror: Perrault in the Bibliothèque Bleue." In *The Culture of Print: Power and the Uses of Print in Early Modern Europe*. Ed. Roger Chartier. Trans. Lydia Cochrane. Cambridge, UK: Polity Press, 1989. 92–135.

Zinggeler, Margrit Verena. GRIMMATIK: *German Grammar Through the Magic of the Brothers Grimm Fairy Tales*. Munich: Lincom Europa, 2007.

LOUISIANA FAIRY TALES

LESSONS IN NATION BUILDING AND THE POLITICS OF LANGUAGE

Christine A. Jones

When I was asked to teach a "grammar in culture" bridge course for my French program, I decided to use French fairy- and folktale history. My approach to the course was twofold: to give students a primer in classical grammar and to expand their horizons by exploring French colonial history. To that end, I structured the course to begin with tales students would find familiar ("Cinderella," "Red Riding Hood," etc.). Then the syllabus set out from France to Louisiana, Quebec, and then on to Burkina Faso, Nubia, and Senegal. Students loved this voyage and learned, along with a host of great stories, the remarkable diversity of collected and authored tales in French. Pedagogically, each one of the tales provides a different way to think about storytelling and, rather than use definitions and principles to guide our appreciation, we interrogated each one on its own terms from three perspectives: language, poetics, and cultural allusion. Not surprisingly, this raw approach worked best on tales students did *not* know well, but it also allowed them to return to the plots they took for granted with a new vision. My pitch, then, is for the virtue of the road less traveled through fairy-tale history, which presents both the challenge of novelty and also the advantage of freedom to roam without the bread crumbs left by Disney, television, and Wikipedia charting an escape route for students.

The case study in this essay serves, ideally, as an example of interpretive techniques that are particularly effective on lesser-known plots and that can easily be adapted for dusty outliers from other world literary and ethnographic traditions. My example is a dense, touching tale for children by Louisiana writer Sidonie de la Houssaye, "Une poupée d'autrefois" (An Old-Fashioned Doll). The manuscript dates from ca. 1869–1875, but with a few exceptions, La Houssaye's tales were not published until quite recently, when 11 stories appeared under the title *Contes d'une grand-mère louisianaise* (Tales of a Louisiana Grandmother). Neither the text nor the author is well-known today and there currently is no translation, so students found no help on Wikipedia and had to read carefully to understand the story.[1] That handicap was helpful because, though its plot is simple, the tale is complex: Aimée, a young child born in New York, voyages to Quebec to visit her French grandmother. She carries with her a favorite French doll, Evangéline, and (thanks to an American history book) a host of stereotypes and fears about the land of her heritage, which is foreign to her. In Quebec she confronts these fears in the figure of a Native Canadian and processes them, as a child might, by dreaming up the imaginative story of what happened when old European dolls came to America.

Layered deep with cultural allusion to Francophone North America, the tale also makes clear call-outs to the European tale tradition and politicizes questions of language hybridity and multiculturalism in the United States and Canada. For these reasons and because of the number of fairy-tale tropes it repurposes, "Une poupée d'autrefois" serves as a fine example of just how many different angles a class could take on a lesser-known tale. Although the ostensible goal of these readings is to illuminate the poetic depth of the tale, a higher purpose is to offer a series of optics—poetical, cultural, and lexical—with which to present any fairy or folktale. The first lesson in textual analysis reads the tale within fairy-tale history. I take up the tale's few and pointed literary allusions and suggest it as a New World addendum to a course on European fairy tales. A second approach is cultural. It focuses on how the tale deals with the plurality of cultures that make up the modern Americas, which permit both a French-French and an American-Canadian dialogue about race, nation building, and fear of otherness. The last critical optic that I take up focuses on the multilingual roots of the French in the tale, which mingles effortlessly with English and Algonquin. Characteristic of many stories told or

---

1. La Houssaye is better known in Southern and Francophone literary circles now for her tetralogy *Les Quarteronnes de la Nouvelle-Orléans* (The Quadroons of New Orleans), about the social practice of *plaçage*, or placing mulatto women into marriages with white society men. *The Crisis*, the official magazine of the NAACP, cited La Houssaye in 1952 as an early chronicler of interracial love, and the Athénée Louisianais, a society for the preservation of French culture, awarded her a gold medal for her writing in 1890.

written in a colonial tongue, linguistic hybridity gestures in fascinating ways to the political tensions binding and dividing European descendants and First Nations in post–Civil War America.

ALLUSION AS A FORM OF TEXTUAL ANALYSIS

La Houssaye's tale calls out to the tradition of classical French fairy tales of the seventeenth and eighteenth centuries in many ways. Typically, the beginning of a fairy tale serves as an allusion of sorts to genre itself. It sets up the tone, the main players, and usually a key premise of the story, which is what students expect it to do, having heard or read tales before. Such a red carpet of meaning can be helpful, especially in foreign-language classes, where reading anything poetic poses a challenge. "Une poupée d'autrefois" delivers in three ways: In the opening paragraphs the narrator presents Aimée, then Evangéline, and then Aimée's godfather. Each description is chock full of vocabulary that types the characters morally and provides a sartorial lexicon that dates and socializes them, and these can be listed and compared. To take one example, Aimée is a pretty little girl, 6 years old, with big blue eyes, a mouth like a pink button, and long curly blond hair that falls down to her waist. Students have seen this fantastical racial profile before and could speak at length about the role she continues to play culturally in Disney's America.

A second allusion to classic fairy tales comes out of her verbal name, Aimée (beloved), a past participle—conveniently declined in French for her gender—that semantically foreshadows the happiness in store for such a child. But that is not at all how La Houssaye uses this protagonist in the 1880s. Her beauty, we discover, participates in a greater and more dangerous mythology of cultural superiority. The figure of the godfather helps illuminate this facet of Aimée. Aimée's godfather gives her gifts, as per the role of "fairy godparent" in a traditional fairy tale, but nothing of the kind students have seen before. He has gifted her the "gorgeous French doll" Evangéline, we learn, and not long before her trip she receives a U.S. history book about the conquest of North America, which highlights the "crimes" of the Indians against the colonists.

Both the doll and the book loom heavy over the tale as objects and also as myths. Students discuss both, following when each one appears and what it does for Aimée's character. They note that as much as the doll comforts her (she is inseparable from it), the book frightens her. One draws her to Quebec and her ancestry; the other repels her from it. Indeed, what she learns from the godfather's second gift makes her afraid to visit her grandmother: Rural Canada, like the America of narratives she has been fed, must be full of savages who seek revenge on poor colonists. The godfather thus functions at once as the bearer of a narrative of comfort in cultural survival, symbolized by the doll, and of a narrative of fear and hostility toward First Nations. Students note here that in these two gestures the godfather plays both the role of the good fairy and the role of the evil fairy, endowing Aimée and cursing her at the same time. The doubling of the gift is a unique feature of this tale and makes students rethink the subtlety of seemingly innocent gifting scenes such as Cinderella's pumpkin/coach.

Once the trip with her mother to visit her French grandmother in Quebec is underway and the plot unfolds at the grandmother's house, the narrator and Aimée make two explicit allusions to European tale matter: "Barbe bleue" (Blue Beard; ATU 312) and "Histoire d'Aladdin ou la lampe merveilleuse" (Aladdin and the Wonderful Lamp; ATU 561). "Blue Beard" was published alongside "Cinderella" and "Little Red Riding Hood" in Charles Perrault's 1697 collection *Histoires ou contes du temps passé*, known popularly in English as the Mother Goose Tales. The *Thousand and One Nights* came into France in the eighteenth century from Persia, and that translation by Antoine Galland (*Les Mille et Une Nuits*) was, for more than a century, the classic version of the story in Europe. Brief plot summaries researched and generated by students bring a moral dimension to La Houssaye's story.

Regarded as a caution against the perils of temptation and curiosity, "Blue Beard" features an eponymous protagonist who takes young wives, several so far, forbids them from entering one of his chambers, and then murders them for trying. The narrator makes a connection between the wife of Blue Beard and Aimée's curiosity about her grandmother's house: "But, like [the forbidden chamber for] Blue Beard's wife, there was one thing at the farm that sparked the curiosity of our little girl: a staircase almost as steep as a ladder, which stood straight up against the end of the back porch."[2] When she inquires, Grandmother explains to her that it leads to the attic. In the next sentence her mother forbids her from going there, engaging the "Blue Beard" plot and igniting burning curiosity in Aimée. Once inside the attic, it is Aimée who recalls Aladdin: "I just know, she said, that there must be something valuable in these old wardrobes and trunks—a treasure, diamonds maybe? Who knows, maybe I'll find Aladdin's lamp!"

At its most basic, Perrault's tale of marital horror recasts the biblical temptation and thus can be productively used in class as a vehicle for that epic theme. If so, then this seemingly simple allusion casts a long shadow over the young protagonist, whose question about stairs at the house turns into a moral transgression that carries in it the threat of severe punishment. Layering the story of Aladdin onto that of Blue Beard takes the edge off the latter because this story of temptation

---

2. As there are currently no translations of La Houssaye's tales, these are my own.

demonstrates that greatness can also be gained through curiosity—which, incidentally, is also how the wife ends in the "Blue Beard" tale.[3] Students can wonder what riches await Aimée once she undergoes her trial-by-curiosity and track this theme through the story, where they discover that she gains no material wealth but is instead awakened from her fears to a more mature enlightenment (as we will see).

The students are then asked to make many more connections between plot elements and stories they know: Little girl goes to grandmother's house and meets with danger ("Little Red Riding Hood"); the prettiest young girl you could ever see is the protagonist of the adventure ("Cinderella," "Sleeping Beauty," "Little Red Riding Hood"); young child faces down her fears to save her parents ("Little Thumbling"). Lesser-known stories provide a rare opportunity to engage students' attention to detail because readers focus differently on a plot they find unfamiliar. At the same time, hunting for recycled tropes set to a new purpose offers valuable insight into a primary motor of tale history: repetition and difference.

Finally, the doll's name, Mademoiselle Evangéline, hides a literary allusion not to European fairy tales but to Longfellow's *Evangeline: A Tale of Acadie* (1847). Students are not likely to find this allusion, but it provides an important anchor for the story and for a discussion about the layers of cultural suppression that created English-speaking North America. "Evangeline" is Henry Wadsworth Longfellow's epic poem about the eponymous heroine, an Acadian or French-speaking Canadian, who was cruelly separated from her fiancé Gabriel at the onset of the French and Indian War. To punish them for refusing to fight the French in 1755, the British expelled thousands of its French-heritage subjects from the territory of Acadia (now Nova Scotia), some of whom settled in Louisiana. Longfellow's poem takes its inspiration from a moment when the British brutalized the French, who had, by that time, farmed that land for more than 150 years. Students research this story on their own and come to see linguistic resistance embodied both in the doll and indeed in the Francophone fairy-tale tradition itself.

Unlocking a Tale's Internal Cultural Logic

The plot of "Une poupée d'autrefois" takes a flight of fancy into multiculturalism when in her grandmother's attic Aimée finds an old doll from Holland—called Hilda—that is even older than her French doll, Evangéline. The reader is privy to an ersatz cultural conflict when Aimée nods off and the dolls come to life; they no sooner begin

---

3. The wife, whom we follow through her ordeal, seems on track to suffer the same fate, but she craftily calls on her soldier-brothers to kill Blue Beard and inherits his vast fortune.

to speak than they fight about whose immigration experience and cultural values are more interesting. Hilda is 60 and it took her 66 days to cross the ocean. Evangéline, a generation younger, scoffs that it took her only six days. Hilda was purchased for about $1. Evangéline bursts out laughing—she cost $5. Hilda from Holland, who was turned in wood, had no clothes when she was purchased. Evangéline from France came with her own dresses, jewelry, parasol, and fan. *Bien sûr* (of course), Hilda traveled on horseback, whereas Evangéline took steam locomotives. And so on.

The exchange, which is both hilarious and cruel, catalogs an extraordinary array of vocabulary words from a time gone by. It identifies Hilda with the old world of history books and Evangéline with cultural and technological advancement. Because the dolls are situated, one with respect to the other, in different cultural moments, they offer an opportunity—as vivid characters do—to reflect on how each one's trappings construct not simply a physical portrait but also what the French call a *portrait moral*, a sketch of the personality. On the surface of the scene, students are able to see Hilda as the simple and humble image of a time gone by and Evangéline—her name of course means "good news"—as a symbol of the sophistication that comes with modernity, here associated specifically with France. Students engage easily with the lexicon of binaries that suggests the superiority of novelty over tradition, particularly in the area of technologies of transport and fashion. Because each doll also represents a conquering nation in the Americas, each one's era also evokes an instance of imperial conquest: First Nations on what became Canadian territory lost land and culture to the French, and those in what became the American Northeast were overrun by the Dutch with New Amsterdam. Of course, that city now bears the British name, New York, once again recalling Hilda's antiquity. Thus the dispute between dolls reopens a conversation about layering and erasure in the story of nationhood.

As the dispute heats up, the unsophisticated Hilda emerges as the most experienced and toughest of them all. She describes her life in Canada as one fraught with struggle, in which she survived repeated attacks by Indians, something neither Aimée-the-urbanite nor Evangéline-the-sophisticate can hear without terror. Hilda delights in their fear and adds greater detail of savages seizing women by the hair, of tomahawks, and of scalping. The more she speaks—students note—the more it seems that she is a story come to life from the American history book the godfather gave to Aimée. In fact, this fantastical scene of storytelling, where the power shifts from Evangéline to Hilda—from the new to the old and from the sophisticated to the simple—also enacts cultural supremacy as a battle of wits. What does storytelling have to do with political history? This discussion opens the door to a lesson in historiography: the people who write history create cultural memory, which lives on through transmission. Every instance of storytelling within a tale presents an opportunity to reflect on the power of story in our lives and in our national identity.

At that moment Aimée wakes in a panic, and, sure that she hears the tomahawk-wielding, hair-grabbing scalper of Hilda's frightening memory, she races down the stairs expecting to find her grandmother and mother dead on the floor. Holding on for dear life to the proof of her transgression in the attic—both dolls and a lovely old hat that she sports on her head—Aimée dives into her mother's arms and bursts into tears. When her grandmother sees the purloined goods, she cries out for the relics of her past: her wedding hat and old doll, the "pauvre Jeanette," she calls it. As it turns out, the doll has played the role of the Dutch in Aimée's imaginary, perhaps an effect of her U.S. history book, but has every bit the same sort of French name and, no doubt, origin as Evangéline. When she learns of the fantastical hallucination that sent her granddaughter flying down the stairs, the grandmother, with the aid of her daughter, convinces Aimée that it was all a dream.

The soothing by her grandmother harks back to the first scene at the house after Aimée arrives in Canada. The family sits down to lunch when there is a loud knock at the door. Aimée opens it and her worst nightmare stands before her: a "colossal" Indian, "armed to the teeth." Here students take time to recall stereotypes in more recent American (particularly Utahn) representations of First Nations: Why has it long served white U.S. culture to think about the peoples they colonized as aggressive and dangerous? In the tale, the grandmother recognizes the visitor as one of the village trappers, purchases game, and, in exchange, sends him away with some lunch she has made. Herein lies the source of Aimée's nightmare, displaced into a tall tale spun by an old talking doll to frighten the naïve French New Yorker. One salient point in this coming home to Canada of a girl whose family has left the farm for the city is that it takes the form of an American-Canadian dialogue that is fascinating for American students to think about: The French Americans (both the godfather and the child) have a racist and delusional approach to history, whereas the French Canadians have found a new mode of cohabitation through sharing and mutual interest. Students reflect on similar instances of cultural erasure perpetrated against other historical groups on American soil.

FINDING HYBRIDITY AND AMBIGUITY IN WORDS

Linguistic hybridity makes "Une poupée d'autrefois" rich and fascinating but by no means unique in the fairy-tale tradition. All tales offer an opportunity to compare and contrast the language associated with different figures, lifestyles, and habits. Using a dictionary to get at the variations in definition (and thus in textual meaning) of key terms associated with each character enriches students' experience of the story immensely. In the names Aimée and Evangéline collide a number of cultures whose proximity was made possible by the New World: Aimée is the feminine past participle of the French verb *aimer*, "to love." Evangéline comes from *évangile*, or "gospel" in Greek, which has a textual root in the stories of the biblical Jesus and France's Catholic heritage. Hilda is not Dutch but comes from the German *hild*, or "battle"—and endows the child character with the poetic sensibility to give that particular name to a magical doll who tells stories about Indian warriors.

That is, when students chart it, they find that in the figure of Aimée and her vivid imagination, multiple cultures collide: French Canada (her heritage), Anglophone America (her birthplace), European France (her doll), Holland (her grandmother's doll in her imagination), Germany (her name for the Dutch doll), and First Nations (her mortal fear of Indians). The cultural web is mightily tangled in her character and in her head. In that sense, the child is a crossroads for a unique North American cultural and linguistic amalgam, and yet she shows us how fragile these relationships are and how fraught they are with anxiety about survival. But she is also a testament to the depth of character that readers can find in a short tale if they take the time to unravel its linguistic threads.

Linguistically, La Houssaye's story is written in French but incorporates Anglophone words for fine things that demonstrate the influence of New World English on the French spoken in North America, such as *bicycle* (bicycle), *ombrelle* (umbrella), and *milles* (miles).[4] Then it incorporates a Native lexicon of technology and practices that we have already seen—the tomahawk and the idea of scalping—that moved from Algonquian into English and then into French. Herein lies an opportunity to reflect on language itself as a foundation of nation building. According to the chart we made plotting the crossroads of Aimée's character in this story, students were asked to note ways in which all people and all languages in the story are Creole at their core. For example, in her dream life Aimée draws words from several traditions that have significance in her birthplace and have each contributed to modern French. Louisiana, a seventeenth-century French conquest until the famed "purchase" that made it British/American and Anglophone, nonetheless changed French—as did the experience of the early Québécois. The Larousse of today lists the noun *tomahawk* and the verb *scalper* as properly French words to name these phenomena that did not exist in Europe. Thus the hybridity of New World culture appears in language itself, as do all other cultural confrontations in history. Students

---

4. Although these words exist as such in European French, the spellings and the meanings La Houssaye ascribes to them here are those they would have in English, which makes them easy for students to see and appreciate as a mark of hybridity.

can be attentive to the fundamental "borrowedness" of language—a parallel to tale matter itself—in everything they read.

On the level of language and plot, fairy tales engage the generational clashes, gender stereotypes, and racial politics of their day. In that sense, La Houssaye's complex American narrative mirrors well the generic preoccupations of its ancestral French *contes*. Because students feel well versed in the plots of fairy tales, treating a story that transposes "once upon a time" into a clearly marked North American context brings its cultural elements—details one in fact finds in each iteration of traditional plots as well—to the fore. My students are then better able to see nuance and idiosyncratic detail in what they had earlier perceived as standard and consistent tropes (the princess, the fairy, the young protagonist, the hostile antagonist) in West African folklore and French literary fairy tales. Reading for intertextual allusion helps them notice difference in the repetition. Thinking about cultural conflict, in particular, binaries of power, reveals myriad tensions in stories that can at first feel morally unambiguous. Finally, attention to language and its multiple sources and registers encourages close reading; work with dictionaries brings out the fullness of even familiar words when they expand into a writer's imagination. Opening students to perspicacious reading practices was perhaps the most gratifying by-product of teaching La Houssaye's stunning testament to Francophone American folk culture. These skills are transferrable and can be brought to bear to great effect on standard fare in the French tradition such as "Cinderella" or "Little Red Riding Hood." And because every tale tradition has outliers to the classics we tend to teach repeatedly, it is worth treasure hunting in the corners of the attic to see if you don't find Aladdin's lamp.

BIBLIOGRAPHY

Galland, Antoine. *Les Mille et Une Nuits: Contes arabes*, 3 vols. Ed. Jean-Marc Simonet. Paris: Classiques Garnier, 1949.

La Houssaye, Sidonie de. *Contes d'une grand-mère louisianaise*. Shreveport, LA: Editions Tintamarre, 2007.

Longfellow, Henry Wadsworth. *Evangeline: A Tale of Acadie*. New York: Thomas Y. Crowell, 1847.

Perrault, Charles. *Histoires ou contes du temps passé* [1697]. Ed. Jean-Pierre Collinet. Paris: Gallimard, 1981.

REPETITION IN THE TEACHING OF ITALIAN FAIRY TALES

CONSIDERATIONS FROM THE CLASSROOM

Cristina Mazzoni

Literature classes in a foreign language are commonly taught through a mixture of lecturing and discussion that, more often than not, abandons the emphasis on language-learning skills prevalent in foreign-language courses at the elementary and intermediate levels. The class I describe in these pages, "Italian Fairy Tales," is a language course as well as a literature course: Although there is no formal study of grammar, every activity is designed to improve students' language skills in speaking, listening, reading, and writing, in addition to expanding their literary and cultural knowledge of fairy tales. This emphasis follows the recommendations of second-language acquisition research to continue with the development of language skills in literature courses taught in a foreign language; although we upper-level language instructors are typically trained in literary criticism and not language acquisition, most students who go on to this level do so in order to improve their linguistic skills more than their literary skills (Frantzen, 120). Even though it may be true that language skills inevitably improve through passive exposure to texts and (mostly the professor's) voice, an intentional emphasis on the workings of language, in my experience, encourages a more student-centered and vibrant classroom. "Italian Fairy Tales" remains focused on content—the fairy-tale tradition in Italy from the sixteenth century to the present day—but it also deliberately and repeatedly offers students the opportunity to develop the linguistic tools necessary to not only read and write but also speak critically about the texts at hand and their connections to their own lives.

The course objectives of "Italian Fairy Tales" are therefore twofold: literary and linguistic. The literary objectives include being able to identify a fairy tale on the basis of its textual features (such as characters, setting, plot) and to distinguish it from related genres, such as fables, legends, and short stories; summarizing a literary and cultural history of the fairy tale in Italy from the sixteenth century to the present day and placing a number of Italian fairy tales in the correct literary period through their date of publication and literary characteristics; describing the interpretation of fairy tales by such specialists as Vladimir Propp and Italo Calvino and applying their theories to specific Italian fairy tales; accurately retelling the plot of a number of Italian fairy tales, both orally and in writing; and performing a basic narrative and literary analysis of an Italian fairy tale. The linguistic objectives include correctly using the present and past tenses of the indicative mood and the four tenses of the subjunctive mood; reading dates and time periods fluently; using orally and in writing an expanded vocabulary derived from the fairy tales of the semester, including a number of idiomatic expressions and proverbs; and summarizing orally and/or in writing a new fairy tale after reading it once. Objectives are achieved through at-home reading and writing assignments, in-class discussion, and in-class literary and linguistic practice; objectives are measured through graded class participation, oral presentations, written homework assignments, and in-class exams.

Each time I prepare for this course, the fact of language is foremost on my mind: Which fairy tales and which critical approaches to fairy tales will lead to the greatest linguistic improvements and rewards for the students, in addition to introducing them to the historical and literary aspects of the genre? The concept of repetition gathers together different strands of my pedagogical approach in this course, because its central role in the language of fairy tales underscores its presence in everyday speech. Repetition can inform the teaching of fairy tales from the details of each class to the overall structure of the course. In terms of text selection, repetition drives the choice of thematic clusters of readings, such as units on the doll (Giovan Francesco Straparola's "La poavola," Giambattista Basile's "La papara," Contessa Lara's "La bambola vanitosa," Donatella Ziliotto's "La bambola, la pazza"), religious syncretism (Emma Perodi's "La matrigna di Lavella," Grazia Deledda's "Nostra Signora del Buon Consiglio," Italo Calvino's "Bellinda e il mostro"), and the rags-to-riches tale (Basile's "La gatta Cenerentola," Luigi Capuana's "Spera di Sole," Guido Gozzano's "Piumadoro e Piombofino"). The repetition of themes and even, in some cases, of a basic plot eases students into the reading of potentially difficult texts, allowing them to focus on details that might otherwise go unnoticed: "Common sense and research indicate that three or four texts on the same subject will prove more readable for foreign language students than texts dealing with different topics and will help expand vocabulary and syntax in the language" (Swaffar, 161).

The unit discussed in this essay focuses on tales of transformation involving women and tree fruit—notably, citrons, oranges, and pomegranates. An overview of the Aarne-Thompson-Uther index—which examines repetition as it manifests itself in the thematic patterns of folktales and catalogs them accordingly—introduces students to the tale type that is primarily discussed in this unit: ATU 408, "The Three Oranges." This is an especially important tale type for a class on Italian fairy tales because, as Calvino states in his introduction to *Italian Folktales*, ATU 408, which is popular in Southern Europe and the Middle East but is entirely absent from Northern European collections, is the only folktale "that can be considered of probable Italian origin" (xxviii).

To this tale type belong Giambattista Basile's "The Three Citrons" ("I tre cedri") (in his *The Tale of Tales*, or *Pentameron*, published in Naples in 1634–1636), the earliest printed example of this tale type, and Italo Calvino's "The Three Pomegranates," a tale from the Abruzzo region collected in *Italian Folktales* (1957). In these two stories, a royal protagonist desires a wife the color of his own blood and of the cheese on which his blood falls at the beginning of the tale, and he travels in search of her; out of the third of three fruits he receives as a gift and cuts open emerges the woman he wants; she is soon thereafter killed by a dark-skinned impostor but returns in the third of another set of fruits, grown from another magical tree, so that at the end the truth is revealed and the impostor is executed.

After studying these two similar tales, students read Luigi Capuana's "Le arance d'oro" (1882). It tells of a Sicilian king whose magical golden oranges are repeatedly stolen and, eventually, restored through the intervention of a foreign king disguised as a merchant—but not before the Sicilian king tries time and again to avoid giving the merchant his daughter in marriage, the reward he had promised him in exchange for the safe return of his golden oranges. Capuana's tale is related to Basile's and Calvino's for its thematic emphasis on enchanted fruit and on a sexual connection between women and fruit and for its stylistic emphasis on repetition.

All three stories are major texts of the Italian fairy-tale canon and are written by authors whom the students encounter several times during the semester. Basile's *Tale of Tales* is the oldest printed collection of literary fairy tales in Europe; because it is written in a Baroque Neapolitan dialect, I use Benedetto Croce's translation into standard Italian and bring to class a few sentences in the original for explanation and discussion. Calvino's compilation of folktales is the most influential and best known in modern Italy, and he is regularly called "the Italian Grimm" (e.g., Beckwith, 260); and Capuana, famous for his *Verismo* literature for adults, is among the most prolific authors of literary fairy tales in Italy, with several volumes in this genre to his credit.[1]

The learning objectives of the course as a whole support Janet Swaffar's definition of the goal of the disciplines of foreign-language study, namely, "to enable students to recognize the various intentionalities behind verbal and written texts and to use language effectively to achieve their own purposes within a cultural community" (157). But what should the students get out of reading these three fairy tales in particular? First, a clear understanding of the tales—not to be taken for granted in a foreign-language literature class dealing primarily with noncontemporary texts. Then, students should be able to identify, analyze, and discuss the cultural and literary elements. These include the basic narrative development of each tale and some of its structural functions as well as the rhetorical use of repetition, metaphor, simile, and symbol—particularly as they help define the Baroque style in Basile and the genre of the fairy tale more generally. It would be fairly easy to present this information in a lecture format; the challenge, in teaching literature while working on language skills, is to construct classes in which these objectives are attained through discussion and active student involvement.

Repetition enters the classroom from the beginning, with warm-ups that push all students to use their voice in a low-stress and fun context. These "repeat-after-me" exercises, involving key phrases from the assigned texts (such as the passwords in Capuana's tale: "Secca risecca! Apriti, Cecca" and "Ti sto addosso: Dammi l'osso"), repeated with increasing speed, improve pronunciation, give the students a keen sense of the musicality of everyday language and especially of literary language, and help create a relaxed learning environment. The repetition of ritualistic phrases—with rhymes based on the repetition of sounds—is indeed a key component of fairy tales and contributes to their sense of magic. As Markman notes, "Far from resulting in monotony, such repetition produces the effect of fantasy by creating a sense of sacred ritual, and it contributes to the abstract, stylized effect of the tale that also serves to remove us from everyday life" (34).

From pronunciation practice we move to fast-paced drills, also based on the readings, where repetition of new verbs involves transformation of tense, person, and number. For instance, Basile's "Al re cade addosso la casa" and Capuana's "il

---

1. Useful introductions to Basile, Capuana, and Calvino can be found in, respectively, Canepa, Miele, and Beckwith.

Reuccio fa la nanna" lend themselves well to this practice. With the demise of the audiolingual method in the 1980s, grammatical repetition has fallen out of favor, but recent research points to its usefulness: "In more recent theory . . . and teaching methods informed by cognitive psychology . . . repetition is viewed as a way of providing learners greater access to language forms . . . and as a means of enabling learners to develop automaticity in the target language" (Duff, 109). Furthermore, regardless of the extent of its linguistic benefits, this brief use of repetition for the first 10 minutes of a 75-minute class provides an entrance into more complicated uses of language and, when performed with good humor, places students at ease and gets absolutely everyone to talk. Its advantages are psychological as well as linguistic: It is often the first thing that is the hardest one to say, in a class, and repetition gets that first thing out of the way immediately.

The repetition of single words, so common in fairy tales, can be used to remind students that everyday Italian also uses this type of repetition—most often adjectives and sometimes conjugated verbs—to indicate emphasis. Thus Basile writes, in his original Neapolitan, "Na vecchia vecchia ch'era secca secca e aveva la facce brutta brutta" ("an old, old lady who was skinny, skinny and had an ugly, ugly face"). Capuana likewise describes the princess's fear with the doubling of the adjective *small* as it refers to her heart as the traditional seat of emotions: "Il cuore le diventava piccino piccino" ("Her heart was becoming very small"). Capuana and Calvino also repeat verbs to indicate a continuing action. Capuana uses the repetitive phrase "Canta, canta, canta" ("after much singing") five times, and Calvino uses the common fairy-tale formula "Cammina cammina" ("after much walking"). For a speaking practice that is "meaningful and relevant to the learners" (Duff, 110) and to increase empathy with the literary characters, students can be asked at this point to answer such questions as "In quali situazioni il cuore ti diventa piccino piccino?" and to complete sentences related to their lives that can meaningfully start with, "Cammina, cammina . . ."

From the repetition of single words, the repetition of speech formulas, or formulaic sequences, moves the students closer into the text even as they practice useful vocabulary items. The formulaic sequence is defined as "a sequence, continuous or discontinuous, of words or other elements, which is, or appears to be, prefabricated: that is, stored and retrieved whole from memory at the time of use, rather than being subject to generation or analysis by the language grammar" (Wray, 9). Speech formulas are often used in communicative approaches to language learning, and this pedagogical strategy can be inflected to examine literary language through its relationship to everyday language. The students are given three or four speech formulas from the day's readings, both in their original context and modified into an example of how I might personally use each of them to describe my own life. The students are then asked to provide their own personalized example—through an "experiential activity designed to mobilize students' personal schemata and thereby increase receptivity to textual issues" (Schultz, 18). Examples of such speech formulas might include, from Basile, the expressions "entrare da un orecchio e uscire dall'altro" ("queste e altrettali parole da un orecchio gli entravano e da un altro gli uscivano"), and, from Calvino, "non promettere nulla di buono" ("pensò che quella palombella non prometteva nulla di buono").

The formulas practiced in class are chosen primarily on the basis of their usefulness in today's spoken language; their practice presupposes "that repetition leads to automatization and integration of linguistic patterns or chunks" (Larsen-Freeman, 199), but also, importantly, that repetition with variation gives students the chance to adapt what they know into a different context: "Giving learners an opportunity to do something a little bit different each time they engage in a (repeated) particular activity is good training not only for creating and perceiving alterity, but also for being able to make the adaptations learners need when faced with a different context or task" (Larsen-Freeman, 204).[2] Throughout the semester, we regularly go back to speech formulas from previously read fairy tales and come up with ways of using them to discuss new fairy tales—thus repeating the repetition and reinforcing learning. As linguist Deborah Tannen notes about the role of repetition in language, "Prepatterning (or idiomaticity, of formulaicity) is a resource for creativity. It is the play between fixity and novelty that makes possible the creation of meaning" (37). Especially concerning this activity, it is worth noting that repetition with personalization "unifies students (and teachers) in their common pursuit of learning within particular communities of language users and learners, . . . scaffolds their learning by means of their interactions with other learners and with the teachers, and . . . socializes them into other academic and nonacademic uses of language, such as for humorous, affiliative, or rhetorical purposes" (Duff, 136).

Speech formulas provide a useful and often humorous entrance into a discussion of the formulaic nature of fairy tales as a genre. Much like longer narrative formulas, speech formulas facilitate memorization and are the hallmark of orally transmitted texts and of written genres, such as literary fairy tales, that draw from the stylistic and thematic patterns of traditional folktales. Through group discussion, students can come up with the repetitive patterns present in each tale. For example, in "The

---

2. "For language learners, an initial personal reaction is particularly important because they do not necessarily have ready access to the cultural underpinnings of the text. Grappling with the text from their own perspective first avoids the short-circuiting of critical reflection that can occur if, for instance, texts are first presented solely as a product of the author's life and times" (Schultz, 20).

Three Citrons" the protagonist meets three ogresses with whom he has three similar exchanges, and from them he receives three citrons, which he handles in similar ways three times; and then he does the same three more times later in the tale with another set of three citrons. Capuana's repetitions are even more numerous and obvious, with entire dialogues recurring more than once almost word for word. It is precisely such features as repetition that make Basile's and Capuana's narratives recognizable as fairy tales, and students realize this right away. The repetition in these tales and the repetition between different tales of the same or similar types make them ideal texts for language students, who are rewarded again and again for having learned new structures and vocabulary—given that these new structures and vocabulary appear repeatedly in the same tale and across tales.

It is also thanks to repetition that fairy tales provide a gradual introduction to literary analysis for students without college-level experience in literary criticism. The brevity and formulaic nature of fairy-tale narratives allow readers to recognize a basic taxonomy of narrative elements—exposition, inciting incident, rising action, conflict, climax, falling action, resolution (this taxonomy, based on Gustav Freytag's work, is ubiquitous in Italian textbooks and in annotated student editions of literary works published in Italy). This can be the basis for an oral summary of the story read at home; the taxonomy simplifies recall, and students quickly become adept at this, eventually telling the tale in a variety of ways (narrative analysis, through Propp's functions, as though telling it to a child, from the viewpoint of one of the characters, etc.). Each time, the story is told more fluently and with fewer errors; studies have shown that, "as the story becomes more and more familiar, processing space is freed for speakers to attend to other matters. In addition, researchers have found that when learners are asked to perform the same task twice, their performance shows clear improvement in terms of complexity of the output" (Larsen-Freeman, 200).

Toward the beginning of the semester, I assign excerpts from Propp's *Morphology of the Folktale* (1928), in Italian translation, so that from a simple narrative scheme class discussion can move on to another repetition-based taxonomy. Propp's theories, though certainly not the most nuanced of literary interpretations, offer tools that can be put to work immediately while reading, easing even the shyer or less literary-minded students into participating in the discussion. Like fairy tales themselves, Propp provides stock phrases and standard interpretations that can be drawn from during classroom contributions (a case in which repetition "enables speakers to produce language, while they are formulating what to say next ... [which] makes the discourse easier to process ... [and] helps learners get and keep the floor," Larsen-Freeman, 197). It is not difficult for students to identify and describe to the class the protagonist, the antagonist, the helper, the magical object, and so on, as well as the major functions of the fairy tales they read. In the case of Basile and Calvino, the more straightforward functions include the hero's departure, testing, reaction, and acquisition of a magical item; the protagonist then changes, and the male hero is replaced by a female heroine, who struggles with the villain, is branded, arrives incognito to the palace, and is eventually recognized; the villain is exposed and punished, and a wedding concludes the tale.

The repetitive elements of fairy tales point to their possible origin in ritual and mythic discourse, as hinted at in the pronunciation warm-up; in this context, the work of Mircea Eliade and Bruno Bettelheim could be usefully brought in for expansion. Eliade's emphasis on rites of initiation in relation to fairy tales invites a discussion of the connection between fairy tales and psychological development, leading to the theories of Bruno Bettelheim on fairy tales and patterning—for example, through the repetition of the pattern of the quest, clearly at work in both "The Three Citrons" and "The Three Pomegranates." These ideas can segue into a discussion of the pleasure effects of repetition, starting in childhood and continuing in one's present life: When is repetition pleasurable, and at what point does it lead to boredom? Students can be asked to reflect on their own storytelling practices: What do they emphasize when telling of an event that happened to them? What do people around them emphasize, and who is a good storyteller, and why? How much patterning and repetition is necessary for the story to make sense, and when are patterning and repetition too much? When are they experienced by the audience as "repetitive"?

A study of the elements repeated across different texts drives home the point that "each fairy-tale text is intertextual, created within the context of the structures of the genre understood through its other exemplars" (Tiffin, 10). The comparison of women with fruit, for example, especially explicit in Basile and Calvino, encourages an exploration of the differences between metaphors and symbols—often confused in the minds of students, and not only students. Symbols develop over time to form a fairly stable shared language, and not much is uniquely literary about them (except, perhaps, in the way they initially came to be). Metaphors are created anew all the time and provide insight into the nature of language itself, and they produce a tension and energy that "exist only momentarily in a particular context and are an immediate expression of insight into relationships and feelings through external events and visible objects. . . . It is the ephemeral aspect of the metaphor that helps to create the aura of magic that one associates with fairy tales" (Markman, 33).

With exercises aimed at developing their awareness of the cognitive effects of literary language, students can be guided into the creation of metaphors that are generally understood. To show the repetitive persistence of the woman-as-fruit metaphor, I like to bring in a couple of 30-second television commercials for Sicilian oranges that feature actress Rosaria Russo advertising and embodying the orange being advertised—also named Rosaria by this particular consortium of Sicilian orange growers; we work as a class with the verbal and visual language of these commercials.

The repetition, in literary fairy tales, of themes common to folklore also brings up the theme of social class: Folk episodes of peasants and shepherds who find oranges made of solid gold, which are promptly taken away from them by their masters through a theft resulting in the oranges' loss of value, are often repeated in the books of Sicilian folklorist Giuseppe Pitrè and also recur in Capuana's narrative. How does "The Golden Oranges" deal, if at all, with the injustice operated by the king—who does not seem to get punished for his shockingly repeated acts of deception? (And why does the king-in-disguise keep falling for it?) And in what ways does the pleasure provided by fairy tales (repetitive, familiar, escapist) elide the aristocratic and often oppressive society they represent, the injustice at the basis of so much of their narrative power?

At this point, students may be ready to reflect on the concept of repetition itself. As Lucia Re puts it, "Narrative always makes the implicit claim to be a mode of repetition, a going over once again (or doubling) of a ground already covered in real life" (171). Telling a story means repeating a story; it means putting into words that which, in a sense, has happened in either the real or a fictional world. This is an opportunity to reflect on the fraught relationship between language and experience: What are the elements of each of the three tales that we are not told? What choices must one make when telling a story? Even though it is a form of repetition, narrative "depends on a type of repetition that implies difference. Narrative representation is not the 're-presentation' of real events, no matter what it may claim to be or to do; it employs modes of textual repetition (such as symmetry and parallelism) to create a plot, which is always a significant interconnection of events. It is therefore always also a (trans)figuration of reality" (Re, 171).

Although fairy tales do not lay claims to realism, students have already read, earlier in the semester, Calvino's introduction to his collection, where he states that "folktales are true," because they provide "the catalog of the potential destinies of men and women, especially for that stage in life when destiny is formed, i.e., youth" (Calvino, *Italian Folktales*, xviii).[3] I never tire of reminding my students, following

---

3. Calvino uses the adjective *vere*, which the translator changes to *real*. As Markman underscores, "Students must be encouraged to realize that what is unreal is not of necessity what is untrue" (32).

Calvino, that fairy tales are about *their* own stories, the stories of young adults, in "their infinite variety and infinite repetition" (Calvino, *Italian Folktales*, xviii). As a class, we regularly—indeed, repeatedly—return to Calvino's brilliant catalog, which we read and reread at the end of each fairy tale we encounter, because it points to the repetition intrinsic to fairy tales and the variety that each fairy tale brings to the genre.

The arbitrary division of humans, albeit in essence equal, into kings and poor people; the persecution of the innocent and their subsequent vindication, which are the terms inherent in every life; love unrecognized when first encountered and then no sooner experienced than lost; the common fate of subjection to spells, or having one's existence predetermined by complex and unknown forces. This complexity pervades one's entire existence and forces one to struggle to free oneself, to determine one's own fate; at the same time we can liberate ourselves only if we liberate other people, for this is the *sine qua non* of one's own liberation. There must be fidelity to a goal and purity of heart, values fundamental to salvation and triumph. There must also be beauty, a sign of grace that can be masked by the humble, ugly guise of a frog; and above all there must be present the infinite possibilities of mutation, the unifying element in everything: men, beasts, plants, things. (Calvino, *Italian Folktales*, xix)

BIBLIOGRAPHY

Basile, Giambattista. "The Three Citrons." In *The Tale of Tales, or Entertainment for Little Ones.* By Giambattista Basile. Trans. Nancy L. Canepa. Detroit: Wayne State University Press, 2007. 433–42.

———. "I tre cedri." In *Il racconto dei racconti.* By Giambattista Basile. Trans. Benedetto Croce. Ed. Milva Maria Cappellini. Milan: Baldini & Castoldi, 2006. 193–205.

Beckwith, Marc. "Italo Calvino and the Nature of Italian Folktales." *Italica* 64.2 (1987): 244–62.

Bettelheim, Bruno. *The Uses of Enchantment: The Meaning and Importance of Fairy Tales.* New York: Knopf, 1976.

Bygate, Martin. "Effects of Task Repetition on the Structure and Control of Oral Language." In *Researching Pedagogic Tasks: Second Language Learning, Teaching, and Testing.* Ed. Martin Bygate, Peter Skehan, and Merrill Swain. London: Routledge, 2013. 23–48.

Bygate, Martin, Peter Skehan, and Merrill Swain, eds. *Researching Pedagogic Tasks: Second Language Learning, Teaching, and Testing.* London: Routledge, 2013.

Calvino, Italo. *Fiabe italiane.* Turin: Einaudi, 1956.

———. *Italian Folktales.* Trans. George Martin. New York: Pantheon Books, 1980.

Canepa, Nancy. *From Court to Forest: Giambattista Basile's* Lo cunto de li cunti *and the Birth of the Literary Fairy Tale*. Detroit: Wayne State University Press, 1999.

Capuana, Luigi. "Le arance d'oro." In *C'era una volta . . . Fiabe*. By Luigi Capuana. Milan: Treves, 1885. 57–63.

———. "The Golden Oranges." Trans. Santi Buscemi. *Journal of Italian Translation* 1.2 (2006): 64–79.

Duff, Patricia A. "Repetition in Foreign Language Interaction." In *Second and Foreign Language Learning Through Classroom Interaction*. Ed. Joan Kelly Hall and Lorrie Stoops Verplaetse. Mahwah, NJ: Lawrence Erlbaum Associates, 2000. 109–38.

Eliade, Mircea. "Myth and Fairy Tales." In *Myth and Reality*. By Mircea Eliade. San Francisco: Harper & Row, 1963. 195–202.

Frantzen, Diana. "Rethinking Foreign Language Literature: Towards an Integration of Literature and Language at All Levels." In *SLA and the Literature Classroom: Fostering Dialogues*. Ed. Virginia M. Scott and Holly Tucker. Boston: Heinle & Heinle, 2002. 109–30.

Freytag, Gustav. *Technique of the Drama: An Exposition of Dramatic Composition and Art*. Trans. Elias J. MacEwan. Chicago: Scott, Foresman, 1900.

Larsen-Freeman, Diane. "On the Roles of Repetition in Language Teaching and Learning." *Applied Linguistics Review* 3.2 (2012): 195–210.

Lynch, Tony, and Joan Maclean. "'A Case of Exercising': Effects of Immediate Task Repetition on Learners' Performance." In *Researching Pedagogic Tasks: Second Language Learning, Teaching, and Testing*. Ed. Martin Bygate, Peter Skehan, and Merrill Swain. London: Routledge, 2013. 141–59.

Markman, Roberta Hoffman. "The Fairy Tale: An Introduction to Literature and the Creative Process." *College English* 45.1 (1983): 31–45.

Miele, Gina M. "Luigi Capuana: Unlikely Spinner of Fairy Tales?" *Marvels & Tales* 23.3 (2009): 300–324.

Pitrè, Giuseppe, ed. *Biblioteca delle tradizioni popolari siciliane*, vol. 17, *Usi e costumi, credenze e pregiudizi del popolo siciliano*. Palermo: Lauriel, 1889.

Propp, Vladimir. *Morphology of the Folktale*. Trans. Laurence Scott. Austin: University of Texas Press, 2003.

Re, Lucia. *Calvino and the Age of Neorealism: Fables of Estrangement*. Stanford, CA: Stanford University Press, 1990.

Saville-Troike, Muriel. *Introducing Second Language Acquisition*. Cambridge, UK: Cambridge University Press, 2012.

Schultz, Jean Marie. "The Gordian Knot: Language, Literature, and Critical Thinking." In *SLA and the Literature Classroom: Fostering Dialogues*. Ed. Virginia M. Scott and Holly Tucker. Boston: Heinle & Heinle, 2002. 3–34.

Scott, Virginia M., and Holly Tucker, eds. *SLA and the Literature Classroom: Fostering Dialogues*. Boston: Heinle & Heinle, 2002.

Swaffar, Janet. "The Case for Foreign Languages as a Discipline." *Profession* n.v. (1999): 155–67.

Tannen, Deborah. *Talking Voices: Repetition, Dialogue, and Imagery in Conversational Discourse.* Cambridge, UK: Cambridge University Press, 1989.

Tiffin, Jessica. *Marvelous Geometry: Narrative and Metafiction in Modern Fairy Tale.* Detroit: Wayne State University Press, 2009.

Wray, Allison. *Formulaic Language and the Lexicon.* Cambridge, UK: Cambridge University Press, 2002.

CHAPTER FIVE

Fairy-Tale Activities and Projects

"Once Upon a Canvas"

Organizing an Exhibit on Fairy-Tale Illustrations

Elio Brancaforte

Narrative

What should an exhibit on fairy-tale illustrations be called?

"Witches can come true!"
"Make a witch . . ."
"Witch upon a star!"

These were just some of the possible titles for a student-run exhibition at Tulane University during the spring term of 2013 before the class took a vote and selected "Once Upon a Canvas: Exploring Fairy-Tale Illustrations from 1870–1942." In this essay I describe the various steps

I would like to thank the various individuals and entities at Tulane University who provided support for this exhibit, including the School of Liberal Arts, the Newcomb College Institute/Collat Media Intern Program, CELT (Center for Engaged Learning and Teaching), MEMS (Medieval and Early Modern Studies), the Department of Germanic and Slavic Studies (all the administrative assistants and work-study students), Howard-Tilton Memorial Library (in particular the Director of Special Collections, the Circulation Department, the Bibliographer for Social Sciences, the Preservation Librarian, the Digital Initiatives and Publishing Coordinator, and the staff of the Rare Books Collection/LA Research Collection), and all the students in the class (with special thanks to Reese Osta, Frances Roche, Yasmine Marden, Lauren Clement, Amanda Stoltz, Christina Hildner, Katarina Dvorak, and our media intern, Lauren Dean). Finally, I am grateful to Maria Tatar for her advice and guidance on all things relating to fairy tales over many years.

that were involved in organizing the exhibit, in the hope that similar projects can be re-created at other institutions (the steps can be adapted, depending on institutional holdings, facilities, and opportunities for support).[1]

"Grimm Reckonings: The Development of the German Fairy Tale" was a course I taught in the Department of Germanic and Slavic Studies at Tulane University. It met twice a week, Tuesdays and Thursdays, for 16 weeks in the spring semester of 2013; each class lasted 75 minutes. The exhibit opening took place in week 14. There were 21 undergraduate students enrolled: 5 German majors/minors along with students majoring in a wide range of subjects, from English, anthropology, psychology, and sociology to communications, business, and marketing. The focus of the class was to provide a background and history of the fairy tale, to investigate different cultural inflections of canonical stories, in particular those of the Brothers Grimm, to discuss methods for interpreting tales, and to examine some more recent adaptations of the tales.

I had taught the fairy-tale course three times at Tulane, and I decided to try something new that semester, namely, to have the students curate an exhibit on fairy-tale illustrations at the Tulane Rare Books Collection. The aim was to have the students engage with the work of one particular illustrator and select one image from a fairy tale that that artist had produced in an illustrated book. In our day and age, with its emphasis on the moving image in cinema, video, animation, and online, I wanted the students to take a step back and consider what a single image that was produced in the past and derived from a specific fairy tale could tell a modern-day viewer. Why does an artist select a particular episode or moment from a tale for illustration? What choices are made in this process? What elements from the artistic vocabulary are used, and what kind of effect does the author strive to create on an observer of the image? I also wanted students to have the experience of interacting with a physical, "old" book from the library's collections, to practice basic research skills, and to learn how to present information about the book, the artist, and the image to a general public.

Having grown up with sumptuously illustrated European fairy-tale books (and then later with comic books and graphic novels), I had developed an appreciation of some of the ways in which images allied with text could be harnessed in the telling of a tale. In 2008 I had learned some of the basic steps needed to organize a successful exhibit, namely, how to raise money, how to approach museum curators and librarians for objects to be loaned, how to display the items most effectively, and how to present the information about the objects to visitors clearly and effectively in the space available. I also realized the need to have an online component that

---

1. Readers should open the following webpage as they read the essay, so that they can see the online version of the exhibit: exhibits.tulane.edu/exhibits/show/fairy_tales (accessed Sept. 1, 2018).

would document the objects in the exhibit.[2] These were some of the lessons I hoped to impart to the students in the fairy-tale class.

Laying the Groundwork

This enterprise had many moving parts, and I provide an overview of the many steps that were involved in the planning of the exhibit and the various tasks I assigned to the students. Depending on the facilities at another institution, the whole process could be streamlined—or could take even longer. I should mention that I had the assistance of several work-study students and a media intern together with secretarial help and the input of expert librarians.

About four months before the class began, I made sure that Tulane's Special Collections contained enough original editions of illustrated fairy tales to warrant an exhibit and that these primary sources included several of the more important illustrators. Because the class had been capped at 25 students, I wanted to ascertain that there were at least 25 works by different artists, so that each student in the class would be able to work on a single artist. We are fortunate in that the main library (Howard-Tilton Library) has a special collection devoted to children's books (Amoss Collection); between that collection and the Rare Books Collection/Special Collections Department, I determined that there were enough illustrated books for a successful exhibit. I started compiling a bibliography of possible primary sources that could be used in the exhibit.

Three months before the class began I approached the director of Special Collections to discuss the feasibility of such an exhibit and to ask whether their gallery would be available at the end of the following spring term. He was enthusiastic about the idea, and two weeks later, after having conferred with his colleagues, he confirmed that the project could proceed. Because the library did not have any special funding to mount an exhibit, I submitted a teaching grant proposal for an opening reception and exhibition materials—and later received the requested amount. I also met with a number of specialist librarians to discuss how students would have access to the rare books and about the possibility of having an online component affiliated with the exhibit.

Once it became clear that there were no major impediments, I researched the Howard-Tilton Library's collection of secondary literature relating to book illustrations, fairy-tale illustrations, and the best-known illustrators that we would

---

2. This previous experience was gained through a double exhibition at Harvard's Houghton Library and the Harvard Map Library, "From Rhubarb to Rubies: European Travels to Safavid Iran (1550–1700)" and "The Lands of the Sophi: Iran in Early Modern European Maps (1550–1700)," which I co-curated with a historian of science, Sonja Brentjes (Max Planck Institute, Berlin).

be featuring in the exhibition. After identifying some 50 books that were not in our library's holdings, I met with the acting bibliographer for German/Slavic at the library. He found the necessary funds to purchase all of those books in time to have them available by the beginning of the spring term. I spent the next month evaluating the new books as they arrived, putting them on reserve at the library, and preparing a second bibliography of the various secondary sources that the students would be using in the spring to research their illustrators.

One month before class began, I submitted an application for a media intern who would be responsible for the online component of the exhibit. The proposal was accepted, and the liaison person in charge of the internship program assisted in the search for a suitable intern, someone with experience in website design and Omeka software and who could also audit the class. By the beginning of January (one week before the start of the class), I had my intern, a senior in anthropology, and she became my go-to person for the digital component of the exhibit. Those were the main preparations before the class began.

During the Semester: Activities Related to the Preparation of the Exhibit

On the first day of class in week 1 (a Tuesday), after the usual formalities and introductions, I went over the goals of the course, discussed the syllabus, and then described the idea of the exhibit to the students. I told them that I had never done this kind of project before in a fairy-tale class and that it would involve extra work on their part—but if all went as planned, at the end of the semester there would be a lasting product, one that the class could refer to in the future. After receiving murmurs of assent, I explained what would be expected from them, namely, to provide content on one illustrator and three or four images for an actual exhibit and for an online exhibit. In other words, the students would be expected to complete the normal assignments for the class and to work on the exhibit. Their first assignment (for Thursday) was to start thinking about which illustrator of fairy tales they would like to research. Specifically, I suggested the following:

1. They should look at the secondary sources (on fairy-tale illustration and on illustrators) that I had put on reserve at Howard-Tilton Library, or at a website such as SurLaLune.[3]
2. They should come up with a first choice and a second choice for the illustrator.

---

3. www.surlalunefairytales.com/illustrations/index.html (accessed Sept. 1, 2018).

3. Using the Howard-Tilton catalog, they should make sure that Special Collections had the relevant fairy-tale work by their chosen illustrator, preferably in an "old" edition, instead of a recent reprint.
4. If item 3 checked out in the affirmative, they should e-mail me their first and second choices (on a first-come, first-served basis).

By week 2, 15 students had chosen the illustrator they wanted to work on and had received my approval.

In week 3 I submitted another grant request, this time to Tulane's Center for Engaged Learning and Teaching, and received additional funding for the exhibit.

By week 4 the students had chosen their illustrator and the book they wanted to use in the exhibit. They also needed to provide our media intern and me with all the bibliographical information about the book, using a specific format, so that the intern could begin entering the relevant information into a database for the online portion of the exhibit.

In week 5 the class had its first meeting in Special Collections. Two of the specialist librarians gave a presentation on how to handle rare books when doing research; they also explained the procedures for requesting rare books from their collection. By special arrangement we were able to consolidate the necessary secondary sources from the Amoss Collection and from Howard-Tilton's collections and have them all be available in Special Collections. That was done so that the students would be able to consult the original works in Special Collections and have access to all the necessary secondary sources as they conducted their research. During the meeting, the students were also given the opportunity to start selecting the images from the books that would be displayed in the exhibit.

In week 6 students were asked to pair up with someone else in the class, so that they could exchange feedback about the images they were going to select and about the texts they were going to write about for the exhibit.

In week 7 I met with Howard-Tilton Library's Preservation Librarian to discuss the dimensions of the eight exhibit cases and measure the size of the books in the exhibit, so that we could start thinking about the order in which books would be placed in the cases. Once we had a rough idea of the placement of the books, we could measure the space available for the labels (two labels per book: one for the illustrator and one for the image shown in the book).

In week 8, right after the midterm exam, we had our second meeting in the large reading room of Special Collections so that all students could work with the rare book they had chosen and begin the brainstorming process with their partner. Students were asked to look through the images in the book and begin selecting the image(s) for the exhibits—and for each image they wanted to select, they would also review the content of the tale and see how the image related to the text. Working alone, they were to start writing down preliminary ideas about the images: Was it a strong image, one that would have an impact on a viewer? What was particularly compelling about the image; was it remarkable for its content, its structure, design, colors? Were there certain details in the picture that should be pointed out to the viewer? The next step was to consult with their partner and start to put their thoughts down on paper: Did the resulting text provide an accurate, concise description of the image? These paragraphs were then refined and reworked several times over the following week until they were submitted for my feedback.

Students were also able to work on the background information about their illustrator, using the secondary sources that had been put aside for them on a special cart in the rare book room. Information about the artist needed to include pertinent biographical details: Did the illustrator belong to any particular artistic movement? Were there features about the illustrator's life that were particularly important? A useful resource was Haase's *Greenwood Encyclopedia of Folktales and Fairy Tales* (2008; print and online versions were available); for illustrators who were less well known, students conducted web searches and/or asked reference librarians for assistance.

In week 9 students were asked to generate and submit the following:

1. For the Jones Hall/Special Collections exhibit (i.e., the physical exhibit): one paragraph with background information about the illustrator; and one or two paragraphs with information about their "illustration 1," that is, the one from the rare book that would be shown in the exhibit.
2. For the online exhibit: an expanded version of the paragraph about the illustrator (up to four paragraphs); and one or two paragraphs for each illustration (i.e., "illustration 2" and "illustration 3").

I asked each student to have their partner look over the paragraphs before sending them to me, so that an informed outsider could give an opinion about them and make suggestions about what information was missing or not necessary. As one student noted, "Criticism from peers, in my opinion, is better received and heeded." The partners were told to put themselves in the place of a visitor to the exhibition—the texts had to give that person an impression about why the image (along with the information about the illustrator and the images) was worth a second look. Were the texts clear and informative? As they generated their paragraphs, students were also asked to keep track of the sources they used for the bibliography of the online exhibit.

By the end of week 9, I had received from each student the basic materials needed for the exhibit. Our Preservation Librarian started measuring all the selected books to make cradles for them (to support the spines of the books).

Over the next week (week 10), I edited the students' texts and met with certain students to discuss their submissions. By the end of that week, I had signed off on the texts that would be used for the exhibit in Special Collections and for the online exhibit. The main work for the exhibit—at least on the part of the students—had been completed. Our media intern was then able to begin the process of digitizing the images for each illustrator and compiling the texts for inclusion in the online exhibit. The media intern worked with the Digital Initiatives and Publishing Coordinator in Special Collections, who oversaw the project and provided technical assistance for setting up the project and training on the software.

In week 11 I asked for some volunteers to help prepare some extra exhibition materials for the opening. Two students created the poster design for the opening, using Gustaf Tenggren's 1912 depiction of "Beauty and the Beast" (Figure 1), and a work-study student was enlisted to produce an invitation for the opening, using Gustave Doré's striking engraving of "Little Red Riding Hood" from 1867. Two other students began compiling a four-page brochure for visitors so that they would have something to take away with them—a souvenir of sorts (Figures 2 and 3). Another pair of students offered to write an introduction to the exhibit. Their text was transferred onto two large foam-core panels (each 20 inches wide by 30 inches high) and then placed on stands at the entrance to the exhibit (Figure 4). Upon entering the gallery, a viewer was expected to pick up a brochure, read the introduction on the panels, and then tour the gallery.[4]

At the beginning of week 13 I arranged to have 250 copies of the brochure made at a local copy shop, along with 200 copies of the invitations and 150 color posters (11 inches × 17 inches). The invitations were sent to colleagues and interested parties around campus (students from the class were asked to help distribute them along with the posters). One week before the exhibition opening we had a brush with catastrophe! We received word from the head of the Louisiana Research Collection that "the gallery sprang a water leak overnight. The carpet is wet, and I'm not sure what the status of the leak repair is." Luckily, one day later we were told that "everything would be repaired by the opening, including replacing the ruined ceiling tiles."

---

4. The exhibition materials (poster announcing the opening, brochure, and introductory panels) are available at exhibits.tulane.edu/exhibits/show/fairy_tales/exhibit_materials (accessed Sept. 1, 2018). By clicking on each hyperlink, you can view the materials in greater detail.

ONCE UPON A CANVAS

Exploring Fairy Tale Illustrations from 1870-1942

AN EXHIBIT OF RARE BOOKS
April 19th–May 24th, 2013

Come experience the magic of fairy tales through age-old illustrations,

presented by the students of the German Studies Course

Grimm Reckonings: The Development of the German Fairy Tale.

Featuring fairy tales from Tulane's Special Collections and from the

Amoss Collection, Howard Tilton Memorial Library.

Opening Reception: April 19th, 4p.m.

Jones Hall Gallery, 2nd floor, Special Collections

Exhibit is funded by a Newcomb College Grant, CELT and MEMS. Contact information: Dept. of Germanic & Slavic Studies, 865-5276, ger-sla@tulane.edu
Poster design: Amanda Stoltz (assisted by Christina Hildner)
Image: Gustaf Tenggren –Beauty and the Beast, 1942

Figure 1. Poster for the exhibit opening of "Once Upon a Canvas" (with Gustaf Tenggren's depiction of "Beauty and the Beast," 1912); design by Amanda Stoltz, assisted by Christina Hildner.

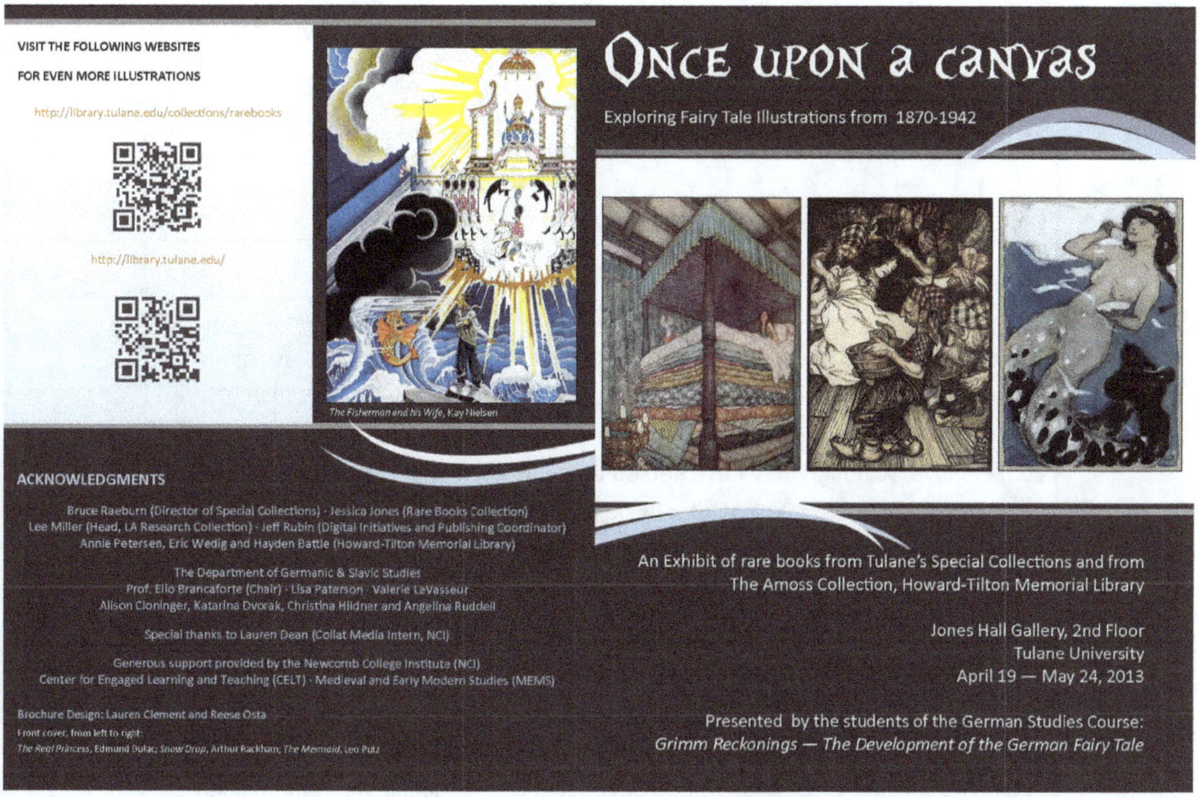

Figure 2. Brochure for exhibit, pages 4 and 1; design and text by Lauren Clement and Reese Osta.

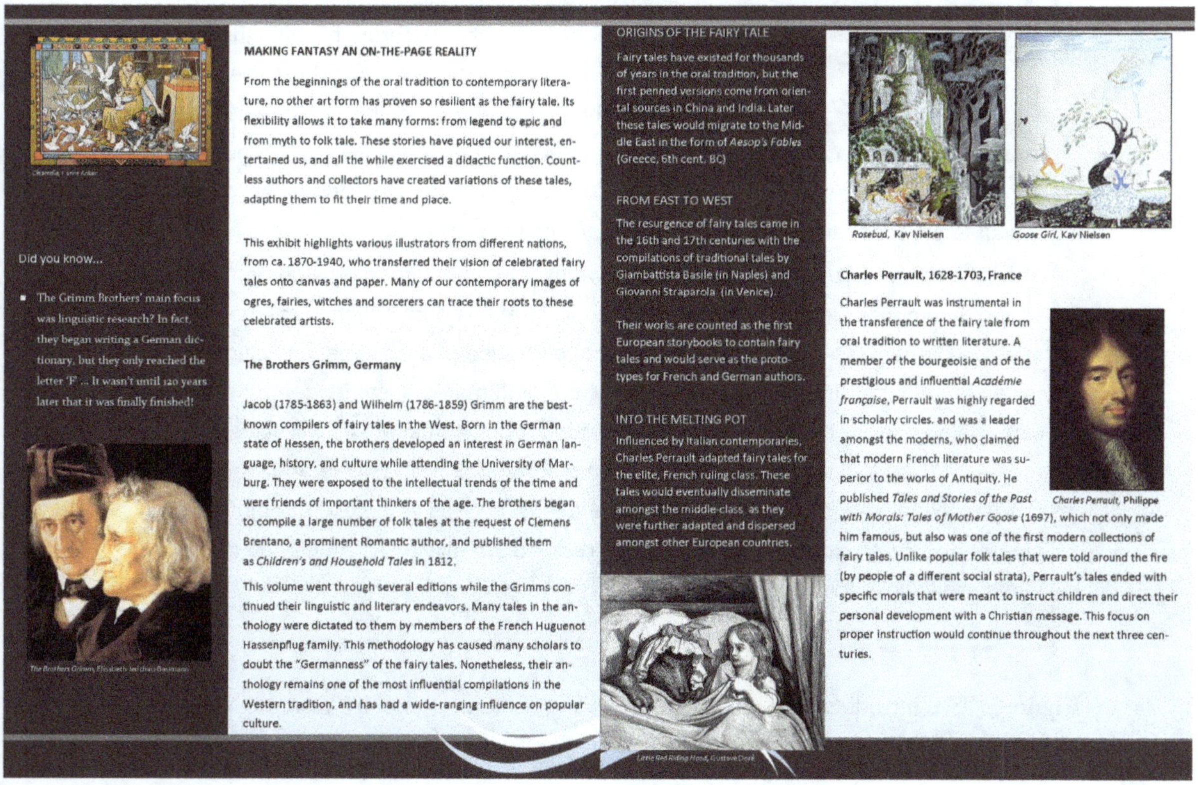

Figure 3. Brochure for exhibit, pages 2 and 3; design and text by Lauren Clement and Reese Osta.

Once Upon a Canvas...

Exploring Fairy Tale Illustrations from 1870 — 1942

Few things stoke the reader's imagination like a skillfully crafted image. Since the Brothers Grimm revolutionized the folk tale tradition with their collection of stories, illustrations have served to illuminate the characters and places readers have come to love. Although they have served to elaborate and clarify text, they have done something more magical: at a basic level, the fairy tale illustration has added to the mystique of simple tales, creating visual representations of characters and endowing simple phrases with unexpected beauty.

Bluebeard, Edmund Dulac

In the early 19th century, the Brothers Grimm published fairy tales in two volumes in order to commemorate German culture. Alongside this important oral-to-print transition, there was also a strong shift to visual representation (due in part to increased possibilities in the reproduction of images). The rich imagery in fairy tales was accompanied by evocative illustrations, and soon these illustrations became vehicles through which the story was told. The Grimms' decision to publish the fairy tales that they had heard from their bourgeois informants—some German, some French Huguenot—provoked artistic responses, and artists soon began to produce fairy tale illustrations in distinctive styles.

An illustrator utilizes technical skill and whimsy to fabricate an environment where the impossible can take place. Often illustrations depict fantastical moments such as Cinderella's transformation or the appearance of a prince at a secluded tower, but at other times they are pictures from nightmares, inspiring fear or revulsion. Using familiar dress, plants, animals, food, or customs, artists will visually represent tales to the readers in a way that resonates with their time and place. Frequently the images that accompany the tale fill in gaps in the text or paint a clearer picture. In executing this feat, illustrators often utilize skills they had learned in other artistic media.

Figure 4. Two introductory panels for the exhibit; text and design by Yasmine Marden and Frances Roche.

A fairy tale is a story of wonder. The images that accompany the text are undeniably part of a story's effect, and illustrators contribute to the story by creating a pictorial language. If one were to be shown an illustration of a graceful lady asleep surrounded by flowers, one would immediately identify it as an illustration from none other than Sleeping Beauty. We all have a visual idea of the "witch," and whereas these images may differ based on the version that we have read or listened to, the storyline is universal. Some may identify the witch as the evil stepmother, while others may call her Baba Yaga. Although the titles differ and call to mind a variety of images, the character often follows the same path in the narrative. It is cultural inclusions that distinguish one version of a tale from another.

Baba Yaga, Ivan Bilibin

Political satirists, caricaturists, and animators populate the field of fairy tale illustration. In order to visually represent tales and contribute to the plot, artists demonstrate their unique abilities. Illustrators display humor, originality, intricacy, and expertise in their craft. Often their command of the craft allowed for visually engaging experimentation with a variety of techniques. Although many of the illustrators are Western, take note of Eastern influences as well. One cannot examine fairy tale illustrations without acknowledging their antecedents.

Illustrators were inspired by their environments and made identifiable references to larger art movements. While browsing the illustrations on exhibit, look out for influences from Art Nouveau and abstract art, along with comedic and classical influences. Many of the illustrators on display became household names, contributing to sales of fairy tale collections.

Yasmine Marden and Frances Roche

Figure 4. (*continued*)

In week 14, on Monday, the final layout of books in the exhibition cases began under the supervision of the Preservation Librarian. We also found two more large cases that were available at the library, so we decided that we could add four foam-core panels to the exhibit (each panel was 20 inches wide × 30 inches high) so that scans of each student's second-choice illustration could be included (Figures 5 and 6). On the day before the opening, the labels were placed in the exhibition cases (blue card stock for the labels about the artist and off-white card stock for the labels about the illustration) (Figure 7), and I made sure that everything was in place for the next day.

Finally, on Friday, April 19, 2013, we had the opening reception for the exhibit in the Jones Hall Gallery of Special Collections. Students from the class had prepared fairy-tale-themed cookies and sweets (including a gingerbread house, Tom Thumb Finger Sand*witches*, and Three Little Pigs in Blankets) for the 100 or so visitors. The students also took turns standing by the exhibition cases, answering questions about "their" illustrator and explaining why they had chosen the artist and what they thought was particularly striking about the image on display. A local reporter from the New Orleans *Times Picayune* newspaper interviewed me and wrote an article on the exhibit that appeared in that Sunday's arts section, in print and online, which helped to attract visitors from the city to the gallery (see Walker).

Overall, the opening was a real success, and the students were proud of what they had accomplished in the class. The exhibit remained open until May 24, and the graduating seniors in the class were able to show it to their relatives who attended Tulane's graduation ceremonies. I also gave several tours of the exhibit to interested parties (which included small children with their parents and grandparents, some of whom recognized illustrations that they had grown up with). The online exhibit went live at the end of April, soon after the opening of the exhibition. The Digital Initiatives and Publishing Coordinator noted that

> *Once Upon a Canvas: Exploring Fairy Tale Illustrations from 1870–1942* was the first virtual exhibition created using Omeka on Tulane University's virtual exhibit platform, and that the nature of the web-based exhibit platform is perfect for these types of collaborative projects. Multiple people can be involved simultaneously, ideas can be visualized and critiqued quickly, and changes can be made in real time. The outcome for the students, faculty, and staff is a very tangible, although virtual, product. And because the policy for the library is to maintain all exhibit content in perpetuity, the exhibit can be cited by scholars without the worry of the web resource being removed.[5]

5. Jeffrey Rubin (Digital Initiatives and Publishing Coordinator at Howard-Tilton Memorial Library), personal communication, 2013.

"The Snow Queen" by **Honor Appleton**

Hans Christian Andersen, *Fairy Tales by Hans Christian Andersen* (London: George G. Harrap, 1916)
Rare Books, Special Collections, 839.818A546fXC59

"Sweet Annie Maroon" by **Dorothy Lathrop**

Walter De La Mare, *Down-adown-derry, a Book of Fairy Poems* (London: Constable, 1922)
Rare Books, Special Collections, 828 D336d

"The Valiant Little Tailor" by **Kay Nielsen**

Jacob Grimm, *Hansel and Gretel and Other Stories* (New York: Doran, 1925)
Rare Books, Special Collections, PZ 8 .G882Han

"Däumling (Tom Thumb)" by **Ludwig Richter**

Ludwig Bechstein, *Märchenbuch* (München: Winkler, 1967)
Howard-Tilton Memorial Lib., PT921 .B4 1967

"They walked side by side during the rest of the evening"" by **Viginia Sterrett**

The White Cat and Other Old French Fairy Tales by Mme. d'Aulnoy (New York: Macmillan, 1928)
Howard-Tilton Memorial Library, PZ8.A924 Wh

Figure 5. Supplementary panel with students' second-choice illustrations (by Honor Appleton, Dorothy Lathrop, Ludwig Richter, Kay Nielsen, and Virginia Sterrett).

Figure 6. Four supplementary panels with students' second-choice illustrations in the exhibit.

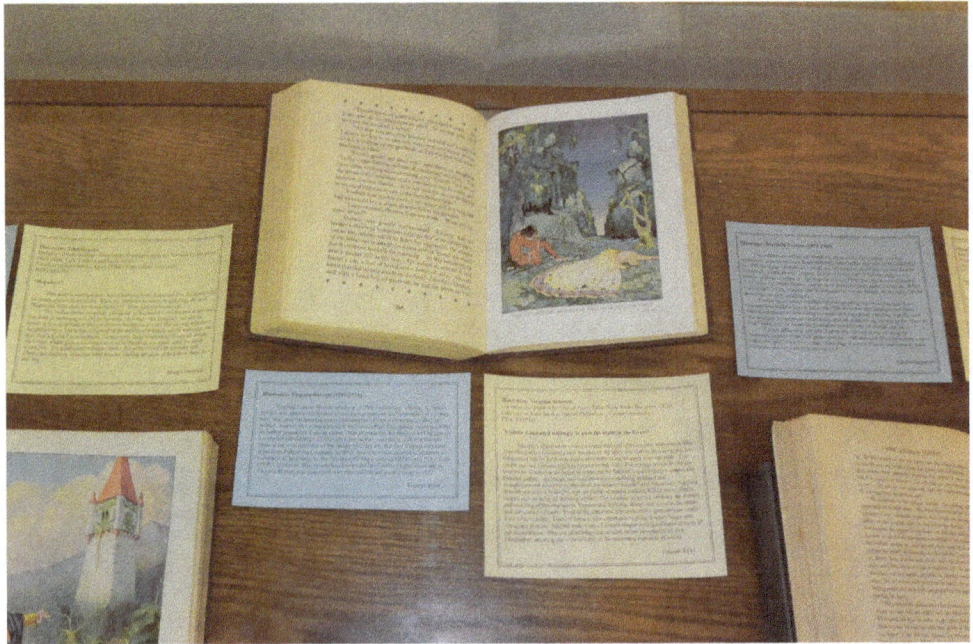

Figure 7. Exhibition case with illustration from the Comtesse de Ségur, *Old French Fairy Tales* (1920), illustrated by Virginia Sterrett. Information about the artist (blue label) and the image (off-white label) by Hannah Ryan.

Why Have an Exhibit on Fairy-Tale Illustrations?

Organizing an exhibit of this kind certainly places many demands on the instructor, primarily in terms of organization and coordination, especially with library staff and students. It is essential to have a good support network—in this case, the Tulane School of Liberal Arts, the various funding entities at the university, and administrators, secretaries, and work-study students all assisted in the endeavor in ways both large and small.

The biggest benefit of this type of activity is for the students, who are able to interact with fairy-tale literature in a different way. Through the analysis of images, they are able to engage with the material more deeply—they are asked to think about the illustration and try to find connections with the story. One student noted, "In creating the fairy tale exhibit I was able to get a better sense of how many layers there are to enjoying and interpreting a story." Another said, "Being responsible for choosing the information conveyed forced each of us to be a curator and decide through our own lens what was important for the audience." While learning about an artist, students practice their researching and writing skills; and working with partners allows them to present their ideas to a peer before it is submitted for review to the instructor and, eventually, to the outside world. A student observed that the "symbiosis of illustration and written word . . . not only strengthens the stories themselves, but the connection of readers to history and culture." In preparing the descriptions of the images, students had to give "explicit detail of the material being shown as well as setting it within the larger context of fairy tales and how all of the pieces related to one another."[6] This project also integrates student-faculty collaborative learning, because the instructor works individually with the students and as a group to select the relevant materials for the exhibit and to discuss the labels. Students present and talk about the individual artist they have chosen to the rest of the class and at the exhibition opening.

Finally, the exhibit has the potential to engage with the community. In our case, it drew the attention of the Tulane University community, neighboring Loyola University, and other local universities as well as of interest groups in the city of New Orleans. Students can combine this project with their public service commitments by giving presentations on fairy tales and illustrators at local schools and by giving tours of the exhibit to local student groups.

Overall, an exhibit of this type works on both a microlevel and a macrolevel: it provides students with an opportunity to create a final "product" at the end of the semester, one that allows them to engage with classroom material in a substantive

---

6. Personal communications from students in the class.

manner and that has an extended life in the form of an online exhibit. As a student commented, "We very much created a product in every sense. We planned, designed, drafted, edited, edited, edited, printed, marketed, and presented a product. . . . This was a great, albeit sometimes daunting experience."

A project like this also provides a showcase for what a language or humanities department can offer in a public forum—something that university administrators can appreciate at a time when it is important to demonstrate how scholarly content can be presented in an informative and entertaining manner. Fairy tales provide an excellent venue for this type of activity, with their ability to appeal to viewers of all ages and types.

BIBLIOGRAPHY

Dalby, Richard. *The Golden Age of Children's Book Illustration*. Edison, NJ: Chartwell Books, 2001.

Haase, Donald, ed. *Greenwood Encyclopedia of Folktales and Fairy Tales*. Westport, CT: Greenwood Press, 2008.

Harthan, John. *The History of the Illustrated Book: The Western Tradition*. London: Thames & Hudson, 1981.

Houfe, Simon. *Dictionary of British Book Illustrators and Caricaturists, 1800–1914*. Woodbridge, UK: Antique Collector's Club, 1981.

Menges, Jeff, ed. *Once Upon a Time: A Treasury of Classic Fairy Tale Illustrations*. Mineola, NY: Dover, 2008.

Meyer, Susan. *A Treasury of the Great Children's Book Illustrators*. New York: Harry N. Abrams, 1983.

Ray, Gordon. *The Illustrator and the Book in England from 1790 to 1914*. New York: Pierpont Morgan Library/Oxford University Press, 1976.

Vadeboncoeur, Jim. "Illustrator Biographies." Bud Plant Illustrated Books, July 4, 2008. www.bpib.com/illustra.htm (accessed Sept. 1, 2018).

Walker, Dave. "'Grimm' and 'Once Upon a Time' Fans Take Note: Tulane Exhibit Explores Fairy Tale Illustrations." April 26, 2013. www.nola.com/tv/index.ssf/2013/04/grimm_and_once_upon_a_time_fan.html (accessed Sept. 1, 2018).

The Story of "Myth, Folktale, and Children's Literature"

William Moebius

"Myth, Folktale, and Children's Literature"

Teaching fairy tales, or what I prefer to call "traditional narratives," has been a part of my own life narrative, as I have offered the course "Myth, Folktale, and Children's Literature" more than 40 semesters over a period of almost 40 years, and to well over 5,000 students. In its sixteenth year (1992) I described the course in a volume of the MLA's Options for Teaching series (Moebius, "Myth") and, in its eighteenth year (1994), I described it in an essay that appeared in *Reading World Literature: Theory, History and Practice* (Moebius, "Informing Adult Readers"), but I have always seen the class as a continuation of a course in myth and literature that I first offered in the late 1960s. Drawing on training in Classical Greek and with a strong interest in the web of Mediterranean and Mesopotamian myths, I had to take a next step.

The traditional tales (both fairy tales and myths) and children's literature that have become a key part of the course starting in 1976 had emerged from my experience as the father of three children, by then all flourishing on recitations of folktales and myths that had also become a part of my life. The beginnings of this course also happened to coincide with the offering of a graduate course in structuralism and an intense focus on the works of Algirdas J. Greimas, Roland Barthes, Vladimir Propp, L. S. Vygotsky, Jean Piaget, and Claude Lévi-Strauss, alongside works of Albert Lord, Milman Parry, Walter Ong, Gregory

Nagy, and Jean-Pierre Vernant and not a few formative works in the field of children's literature to which women were the primary contributors, from Barbara Bader and Francelia Butler to Sheila Egoff, the Opies, Jacqueline Rose, and later Maria Nikolajeva, Sandra Beckett, and Michelle Martin and also Jean Perrot, Jack Zipes, Peter Hunt, Perry Nodelman, and, in the critique of the tales of the Grimms, Ruth Bottigheimer and Maria Tatar. Although the large lecture course "Myth, Folktale, and Children's Literature" took its shape from the confluence of these streams, an unanticipated passion for children's picture books would play an increasing role in the evolution of the course, as would a lifelong friendship with Jean Perrot.

Another critical factor in the development of the course is its broad appeal to students. In 1976 no fewer than 250 students turned out for the first week, and even with several teaching assistants, the course would have to function as a large lecture course with discussion sections. It would soon (late 1980s) serve the needs of the General Education Program as a fulfillment of the literature requirement, drawing students from psychology, public health, and even engineering, as well as from the College of Humanities and Fine Arts. Two years ago, a student at the University of Bucharest persuaded me to let her attend the lectures (and view the course materials online) by means of a Google Hangout.

Some of these students to this day remind me of the impression the course made on them, somehow enriching their later experience as parents or simply as adults. To foster better understanding of the lectures, I offer a lecture synopsis (originally a transparency projected by an opaque projector, now an online document available before, during, and after each lecture); accompanying the lecture synopsis sometimes are maps or diagrams and, with PowerPoint, images taken from picture books from all over the world. I should not underestimate the contributions students themselves have made in enriching the content of this course; former students still send me picture books from China, Turkey, Sri Lanka, Japan, Romania, and elsewhere, and images from my ever-expanding collection find their way into many of the lectures. I have always meant for the dimensions of the course to be international, but little did I know how powerful the picture book would become as a vehicle of cultural exchange.

To make sure that the scope of the course is broad enough to embrace tales from traditions beyond the borders of the United States and Europe, I include tale collections from Hungary (with Finno-Ugrian language roots, not Semitic) and tales from across Africa as well as tales found in the Grimms and in Stith Thompson's *One Hundred Favorite Folktales*. Susan Feldmann's collection of African tales and Linda Dégh's *Folktales of Hungary* serve my purposes, because the tales they collected defamiliarize certain topoi and reaffirm others; they provide, in James Jerome Gibson's felicitous formulation, different "affordances." The Hungarian tales still resonate with the residues of shamanism, and the topography of the African tales offers not only a horizontal cosmos but also a vertical one, not as fully imagined in the Western fairy tale. The African tales also feature open-ended "dilemma" tales, such as "The Two Strangers." The ancient Egyptian tale of Anpu and Bata (found in Stith Thompson's collection) finds echoes in certain African tales concerned with the origins of fire, not to mention the stories of Potiphar's wife and of Hippolytos.

One of the intriguing aspects of both Thompson's and Feldmann's collections is the light shone on both the circumstances of the telling (in a factory lunchroom for some Hungarian tales) and their reception. "The Adventures of Mrile," found in Feldman's collection, was recorded by a Lutheran missionary; his account is the only one we have of this tale, and his interests as a Christian may have shaped his choice of tales and of tale fragments worth recording. The provenance of a particular tale, the gender or religious affiliation or social status of the teller, if determinable, inform our discussions of its meaning, as does the historical situation of particular writers of books for children, whether Roald Dahl, his nemesis Salman Rushdie, Hergé, Charles Dodgson, or Maurice Sendak.

Children's books are indeed the third dimension of the course, and one that has a refreshing effect on student response, whether as picture books, chapter books, or young adult novels. One of the earliest challenges in designing the course was the choice of pairings of folk narratives and books for children, because for the required readings I was determined not to depend entirely on books for children that more or less expressly adapt, subvert, enhance, or extend a familiar folk- or fairy tale, although there are plenty of these to work with. Thus, on the second day of class, students are introduced to what I call axes of transformation, which can be identified both in Maurice Sendak's *Where the Wild Things Are* and in "The Adventures of Mrile." One of the first exercises used in student discussion is to explore how these axes (play, power, cognition, place, and emotion) play out in both narratives as developmental patterns.

Although this axes-of-transformation exercise is described in more detail later in this essay, it is worth mentioning here the initial disbelief among students that a story in a popular mid-twentieth-century picture book for children could in any way be construed as parallel to a story related in a mythic tale from Kenya. With no history, no "source" or "influence" to link them, the connection seems arbitrary and capricious. Once framed within the axes of transformation, however, both stories suddenly share a number of congruencies, and what had begun as merely heuristic gradually becomes remarkably familiar and compelling. Had it not, I would probably have abandoned these axes of transformation as a group of tentative hypotheses not fated to be provable. That they continue to be presented as hypotheses and not as dogma spurs discussion, even today.

To sustain interest in the first half of the course, I focus on the question of identity in relationship to cognitive development and social recognition. I learned earlier in my teaching career that many students are particularly fascinated by their own journeys and can relate well to the trials and tribulations of someone who has some agency and wants some stability but who faces a number of stumbling blocks and needs assistance. The Greimassian actantial model and the Proppian sequences lack–lack liquidated and interdiction-violation-consequence become a starting point for an inquiry into strategies of violation, the key to which are acts of substitution. A second activity, described later, allows students to tally successful and less successful acts of substitution on the part of multiple stakeholders in a familiar fairy tale. This section culminates in the reading, or rereading for some, of Roald Dahl's classic *Charlie and the Chocolate Factory*, with attention to the differences between the first and subsequent editions, the resemblance to Menippean satire, the exploitation of the nominal fallacy, and particularly the quest for identity through acts of eating or acts of speech.

For the second half of the semester, we leave identity questions behind and focus on speech and cultural spaces, treating language as discourse and sign and examining power relations, cosmologies, systems of value, and historical perspectives. How is each storyworld constructed, and who's talking about it? What is speakable and what is unspeakable? What is prescribed and what is proscribed within the boundaries of specific spaces in each story? To anchor discussions in this section, I select three key literary texts: Lewis Carroll's *Alice's Adventures in Wonderland*, Hergé's *Prisoners of the Sun* (originally *Le Temple du soleil*), and, for a grand finale, Salman Rushdie's *Haroun and the Sea of Stories*. From this mix of traditional tale and modern fiction, several activities emerge, two of which are described in this essay.

One major change in the syllabus occurred around the tenth year (1986) in the history of the course. I realized that most of my students had little idea how to read a picture book with any attention to or appreciation of matters of design, stagecraft, or graphic conventions, matters I took to calling, after Horst Ruthrof, presentational process. I had to make space near the beginning of the semester for a two-week-long excursus on reading picture books and on the reading process itself. There is not room in this space to review the pedagogies that followed, but one can find an early version in my article "Introduction to Picture Book Codes" in either the original print version (Moebius) or online in the course "Children's Literature

Approaches and Territories," offered at the Open University of the United Kingdom, in cooperation with Palgrave.[1] My record of publication reflects the impact that picture books have had on me ever since, not necessarily because they echo the narrative content of fairy tales but because they exemplify the roots of tale recitation itself, still found today in, for example, Rajasthan, in which tellers recite stories against a background of images woven into a large carpet. Homer's description of Achilles' shield suggests a similar practice, and one can find it memorialized in Allen Say's picture book tribute to the pre-television "paper theater man," *The Kamishibai Man*, from his youth in Yokohama. A brief mention in Diderot's *Le Neveu de Rameau* suggests that such picture recitation was a staple of street life in Paris in the late eighteenth century, just as it was, according to Victor Mair, in India and China many centuries earlier.

The picture book itself has ties to theater and performance, whether an adult reader is reading the words out loud or the reader is experiencing what Barbara Bader famously described as the "drama of the turning of the page" (Bader, 1). Storytelling as an activity is one of the practices this course has always been intended to foster, along with sound interpretive strategies. When students in "Myth, Folktale, and Children's Literature" discover that the stories found in picture books actually speak to them as young adults, I think they learn another lesson about things that matter. The folktales read alongside picture books emerge as condensations of an experience that only needs to be told for its rich flavors to be fully available.

CLASSROOM ACTIVITY 1: AXES OF TRANSFORMATION

This activity is a heuristic exercise intended to ground students in narrative patterns derived from the perspective of both a leading character and the viewer's own experience. The axes themselves are presented as hypotheses, not as prescriptive binders. I have identified five worth exploring, but there could be more. Each axis is founded in moments of stasis that bookend the narrative. As a collection of nameable narrative patterns, these can and often do help ground students throughout the course.

The first step in this exercise is to acquaint students with these axes by introducing them to the experience of the character Max in Maurice Sendak's *Where the Wild Things Are*. During the first discussion session, we take at least 40 minutes to do a close reading, noting a number of visual paradoxes that encompass that which is wild and that which is deemed "mischief." We examine closely what is going on in Max's bedroom; we note the tent, the dangling naked doll, the nail going into the

---

1. The website for the online course is www.openuniversity.edu/courses/modules/ea300.

wall. We note the well-groomed couple on the title page retreating from Max, who is clad in his wolf suit. We also note later, and with care, that when Max, like the creature on the book's front cover, has assumed the academic pose of "the thinker," the narrator is telling us that Max "felt lonely and wanted to be where someone loved him best of all." We note many attributes of the book's design, the swelling and retreat of the images, the relative calm and tranquility of the creatures Max rules, and the isolation of the final words of the story in the absence of an image.

It isn't until the second discussion meeting, prefaced by a lecture on the axes of transformation, that students bring their reading of "The Adventures of Mrile" into their discussion. Like Max, Mrile has an issue with his mother and flees his family home; he performs a series of social and agronomic tasks, and, like Max, wishes to return home, having made a bargain, first with the moon and then with a bull, which agrees to transport him home if he promises not to eat its flesh.

The stories share certain explicit common features: Both make food and eating an issue; both feature runaway sons; and both record a journey home. Whether both mothers have the best interests of their sons at heart is not as easy to answer. Mrile is welcomed home with precious oil for his feet and a home-cooked meal. Max is also welcomed home with a meal. The meal cooked for Mrile happens to feature the flesh of the bull, so Mrile is said to sink into the earth for having violated the bargain or contract with the bull. One could say that the rules of hospitality observed by Mrile's mother trump the deal he made with the bull, but the conflict between two contracts is fatal to her son. We do not have any images of Max after he has consumed the simple meal his mother has prepared, but we do see him beginning to shed his wolf suit, his hand on his brow in the manner of Rodin's statue *L'Age d'Airain*, or John the Baptist.

Such a comparison may suffice for some. But the two stories share other dimensions, those marked by the axes of transformation, which can be usefully applied only to stories that permit change and development. What, after all, are these so-called axes? Is it enough to say that the pleasure principle is supplanted by the reality principle?

1. *Play*: At the start, a character will often be seen in a play relationship with the world, one in which the reality of the Other is subsumed in the imaginative construction of the self. At the end of the axis of play, the self is engaged in a social exchange with the Other.
2. *Cognition*: At the start, the character will link material objects according to the sensations they provoke; what is immediate, present, visible, or tangible

will preside, and similarities will be found to constitute identity; at the end, the character will recognize intangible, untouchable objects as real and important and will trust symbolic or figurative representations rather than relying on resemblance.

3. *Power*: At the start, the character will assume an absolute stance toward the Other that forces a distancing between self and Other; at the end, the character will accept compromise and enter into contractual relations with the Other.

4. *Place*: At the start, the character will construct the surrounding world as wild and dangerous; at the end, the character will favor a domestic space exempt from the laws of the jungle.

5. *Emotion*: At the start, the character's actions will be marked by rather turbulent emotions, whether of restlessness or rebellion. At the end, these actions will be marked by calmness and steadiness.

All five of these axes address a cycle of change that is not visible to the naked eye, only to the understanding. Learning about the ways these axes emerge again and again can help students recognize developmental patterns in themselves.

A brief legend found in Jack Zipes's translation of the Grimm brothers' collection offers even a legal "proof" of the understanding that underlies these axes. In "How the Children Played at Slaughtering," children at play butcher one of their own, as required by the rules of their play. They are brought to court and asked to choose between an apple and a gulden. If they choose the coin, they will be deemed culpable; if they choose the apple, they will be deemed innocent. The proof of their innocence lies in their inability to recognize the process of social exchange, which is the outcome anticipated in the axis of play. It should be made clear that narratives that involve tricksters or "numbskulls," stories such as "Tom Thumb" or the Hungarian "Csucskári," are excluded from this group of axes, because the main characters are "exceptional" and have no room for growth. The brutal legend just mentioned tells the story of children who have not yet experienced that necessary growth. I leave to the reader the challenge of reading these axes of transformation through the trials of Mrile and Max.

If your students have absorbed the tradition of folk- and fairy tales as the site of a lesson, punctuated by a moral, as a teaching moment for ethical behavior, the learning objective for this exercise is to expand and even challenge the simplicity of that kind of reading. Looking at the story as a site of several different arcs—one related to shifts in cognitive skills, another to the exercise of authority, and still another to power relations—renders the story a more holistic reflection on the development of the individual, of the fulfillment of the self. Just pressing students in the direction of multiple meanings can stretch their horizon of learning.

CLASSROOM ACTIVITY 2: SUBSTITUTIONS

As an introduction to the notions of "figure," "metaphor," "synecdoche," or "symbol," the study of substitutions in the traditional tale can be an eye-opener. Storytellers are bound in the course of the story to maintain the interest of the audience by offering variations of the same, which can, in the long run, enhance perception of an underlying pattern, culminating in a symbolic system that may or may not be consonant with social and cultural values in the storyteller's world. For example, who can account for the guidance offered to Hansel and Gretel by the dove, emblem of the Paraclete, a substitute for the divine, which enables the horror of the children's captivity? Folktales are often survival stories, and although survival requires action in physical space, it also requires strategies in the spaces between the threatening and the threatened. Reading "Hansel and Gretel" as a story of survival might lead us to discover how critical the choices each character makes are in shaping the perceptions of others.

In this exercise on substitutions and survival in "Hansel and Gretel" we play a game, using the chalkboard, small group discussions, and more. We put the names of all potential "substitutors" in the tale and behind it (diegetic or extradiegetic) in a row across the board. The substitutors include both of the children, their stepmother, their father, the witch, and, with the dove as the Paraclete, a divine spirit. We also consider the narrator herself as a substitutor, eventually replacing the figure of the stepmother with the figure of the witch, or in marking the travails of the children, having Hansel's efforts at substitution (e.g., of bread crumbs for pebbles) prove insufficient. Below the names of these agents all in a row, we put, in separate columns, acts of substitution (e.g., the stepmother's "children for food" or Hansel's "pebbles for parental guidance") and mark them as successful or not. After a painstaking inventory of all acts of substitution, we may come to the realization that some successful acts of substitution cease to be banal tropes of action and become sublime metaphors. We might also note patterns of success or failure according to age and gender.

The first challenge is to identify all the acts of substitution found throughout the story. Each small group of students can be assigned one small episode in the larger tale. One of the first substitutions to note might be "children for food," a substitution advanced by the parents and the witch. Obvious acts of substitution include chicken bone for finger and bread crumbs for pebbles. More subtle acts are

Hansel's gazing up and back at the chimney while dropping pebbles or crumbs on the ground, or the father's leaving a brush fire (short-term security) as a substitute for a fire of logs (long-term security), or the witch having a pastry house instead of a durable wooden one. Moonlight itself becomes a substitute for sunlight. In the pockets of the children, as tokens of security, substitute artifacts include pebbles, crumbs, and then jewels. In this exercise it is not necessary to foreground one agent over others, Hansel or Gretel over the father or stepmother, the witch or even God or the narrator, if one is considering "lack" or "need" in relation to interdiction, violation, and consequence. All parties are deemed to be needy, and all parties must be strategic, choosing their substitutions wisely.

Here is an "inventory" of sample substitutions:

Mother: words of rage for words of hospitality; suspicion or abusive language for deep trust; wife role for mother role; food for children

Father: fire of twigs and branches for fire of logs (brief and hot for long and warm); hanging axe windblown (making noise) for father's presence; second wife for first wife; stepmother for mother

Witch: house of glucose for house of protein or cement

God: Dove (Paraclete) for divine guidance, leading children to fire (?); duck (?)

Hansel: pebbles for parents; crumbs for parents; moon for sun; God for parents; jewels for witch; bone for boy; religious fervor for practical action; "the heavenly child" or false identity for true identity

Gretel: tears for both speech and action; self-pity for self-in-action; witch in oven for Hansel

Narrator: stepmother for mother; moon for sun; witch for stepmother; white duck for redeemer

Once all the acts of "instrumental" substitution have been noted, we evaluate them according to their "success" or "failure." Hansel's substitution of bread crumbs for parental guidance is an abject failure. His upward glance toward the chimney as a substitute for looking down at the pebbles he is strewing is a successful substitution, because it distracts the stepmother's attention from his survival strategy. But a longer list of Hansel's substitutions may demonstrate his vulnerability and susceptibility to the deceit of others.

We next consider factors such as age and gender in success rates. How does the storyteller dole out acts of substitution? The results may be surprising. Is the father a more effective substitutor than the stepmother? Is Hansel more effective than his sister, or than his father? Are the female characters better at substitution than the male characters? We might also consider which, if any, substitutions rise to another level, something more durable than a sleight of hand. Substitution is not unrelated to the creation of symbols and is a fundamental part of sacrifice. What does "Hansel and Gretel" tell us about hunger and sacrifice? All these factors engage us in thoughtful assessment.

I see three learning objectives here: (1) to come to terms with each of the stakeholders in the story, including in this case not just the two children but also the father and stepmother, the witch, and even the heavenly body that sends the Paraclete, and how they each use substitution for their own welfare; (2) to see how the storyteller parcels out acts of substitution according to age and gender; and (3) to come to terms with the power of the symbolic, or beyond that, to the power of sacrifice.

Classroom Activity 3: Speech and Topography

In this exercise we study story habitats and terrain as markers of particular kinds of discourse. Within this framework the African tale "How the Lame Boy Brought Fire to Earth" (Feldmann, 100–101) and the ancient Egyptian narrative "Anpu and Bata" (Thompson, 36–44) (the first third of this increasingly hermetic tale) reveal subtle cues about proper language use and function, grounded in particular domains or zones. This exercise is introduced by a close reading of a selection of dialogues in *Alice's Adventures in Wonderland*, dialogues in which Alice encounters, one after another, strangers whose rules of speech are not necessarily compatible with hers, given her peculiar training and upbringing. In each exchange students look for awkward moments and tease out the prescribed and forbidden elements of speech encountered in each domain. What, one may ask at each encounter, are the rules of access, the entry codes of speech?

A brief synopsis of one of the traditional narratives may help to clarify the measure of each of the steps. In "Anpu and Bata" there are three main human characters and an assortment of animals. The landowner (Anpu) and his brother (Bata) are seen to be powerful in different spaces. Anpu owns all the land and "owns a wife," but he does not visit the pastures, mind the animals, or enter the barn. His space is his house and his fields. On the other hand, Bata, Anpu's younger brother, has access to the barn, visits the pastures, and also the fields. Anpu tends to speak in commands, but his body is relatively unmentioned; the narrator delivers a number of favorable epithets about the body of Bata, and Bata himself has conversations with the animals. Animal speech is seen to be key to Bata's survival. When Bata is sent back from the fields to bring more seeds to the fields, he has to approach

Anpu's wife, who, it turns out, has command of the granary and lives in the house; the wife speaks rather passionately about Bata's body. Bata is offended by her overtures and orders her never to speak these words again. When Anpu returns, the wife uses Bata's speech to incriminate him and uses her clothing to suggest that she has been violated. Anpu then seeks to kill his brother, but Bata, warned by the cattle, escapes and then mutilates himself. It is in this context that we consider how the story deals with the speakable and the unspeakable, the monolingual and the multilingual, the spoken and the embodied.

The first step in this exercise is to tag all the spaces described in the first third of the story "Anpu and Bata." Who has access to which spaces? What is allowed or prescribed for each space? Answers to these questions follow a slow reading of the story as it unfolds. The second step is to pursue the question, To what extent are different kinds of speech acts reserved for different characters, both as they speak and as they are described by the narrator? The third step is to consider "speech environments" in the story—discourse grounded in particular domains—and the risks and benefits of multivocality, or what we might consider a version either of multilingualism or of "freedom of speech."

This three-step exercise can spur discussion of the African tale "How the Lame Boy Brought Fire to Earth." Some students may be familiar with the story of Prometheus, but few will recognize this "stolen fire" story. Many of the features uncovered in "Anpu and Bata" can be found in this story, which includes brief dialogues and markers of speech tone and register, even if one narrative is focused on issues of kinship (the language of which dictates who may sleep with whom), the other on ownership of fire. As the story unfolds, rather clear speaking environments emerge, a few of them quite unexpected.

The learning objective for this exercise is simply to open up a conversation on discourse, power, and place. How does the story establish relationships among speech, power, and place, and what qualifications are required of one who would have access in one place or another? Reading tales with this learning agenda has, in my experience, benefited students whose next assignment is to read *Alice's Adventures in Wonderland*. Alice's forays into spaces of the Other entail frequent misunderstanding, as Alice has to struggle to find the right words.

Classroom Activity 4: Sign, Use, and Exchange Value in the Cante Fable

The late-eighteenth-century painter Philippe Otto Runge's version of "The Juniper Tree," a written tale honored by its inclusion in the Grimm collection, draws

attention to the power of the image, both as an act of imagination and as a protec-
tive shield, and to its link with voice and song. In this tale a boy is conceived as a
result of his mother's seeing her own blood fallen on snow outdoors near a juniper
tree. He is then killed by his stepmother but returns to life as a bird, emerging from
the juniper tree and singing the tale of his suffering to villagers who rally around
its song. This exercise is designed to draw attention to how the tale structures a
value system, not only as a plot-driven revenge story but as an invitation for shared
ownership of a song and a vision. Certain African tales, such as "Let the Big Drum
Roll," also partake of this mixed-media act of social calibration and contribute to a
better understanding of a certain genre of traditional narrative, the cante fable, the
story with something in it for the storyteller to sing and for the audience to join
in singing.

To enter the parlance of sign, use, and exchange value, students need to understand the variability and arbitrary nature of both use and exchange value, each of
which depends on a circumstance and on multiple participants. In contrast, sign
value, as I am using it, is assigned by a single "sender" and dictates a designated
receiver, whose reading of the sign is uniquely empowering for that individual or
for the community that embraces that sign. In "The Juniper Tree," for example, a
mother, holding an apple and a knife, receives the appearance of her own blood on
the snow as the image of her son. She is the only person to witness this sign and the
only one able, so to speak, to embody it. (The exercise that follows requires more
time than the other three exercises described earlier unless a writing assignment
covering the first step is required in advance of class discussion.)

The first step is to identify the key "material objects" in the storyworld's first
manifestation, up to the reincarnation of the boy as a singing bird. Each of these
material objects must be recognized for its particular qualities as being seen or
envisioned. Here is a tentative list: a piece of property, the outside of a house, a
juniper tree, snow, apple, knife, blood. All of these mark what can be deemed the
world outside. With the passing of the mother and the entrance of the stepmother,
we view the inside of a house, a window, an apple bin with a lid, a dresser drawer,
a white scarf, a pot, a stove, a table, and a dinner. The world outside and the world
inside are competing for our attention and respect.

In the second step the material objects are singled out and discussed in terms
of their *use* or *exchange* value, or their potential as a part of a *sign*. Indeed, this step
requires that we take each object or element itself and consider, visualize, or recognize it in terms of its particular value. Some of these elements do indeed excite
the interest of a female subject in the story, whose sight of her own blood on the
snow, occasioned by her peeling an apple with a knife with which she cuts herself,

connects her with a vision of a boy. The mother's "unifying gaze" also connects visually with the juniper berries. Here the object world is rich in sign value. Although some of the material objects are decidedly useful, others appear to lie on a different plane as signs unto themselves or as a cluster of signs, one for the woman who "condenses" or groups them in the story and another for the narrator. This is a moment for the student to re-member the pieces that belong together (e.g., apple, snow, blood, all presumably "fallen"; mother and juniper). Even though these objects cluster meaningfully in the world outdoors, apple bin, bureau of clothing, drawer, and kitchen, as "containers," reflect the values of domesticity. In this first half of the tale, a unifying figure (the mother's vision of her boy-to-be) gives way to the boy himself and then to the death of his mother and the dismembering of the boy, from an "inclusive" scene in nature to a somewhat "exclusive" setting in a kitchen with windows.

The third step takes us through the dinner scene to the distribution of justice with which the story ends. We start by repeating the first two steps. We must take note of "new" elements—juniper tree with generative fire, bird that speaks, gifts (for the sister and father), and a deadly missile (for the stepmother)—and consider the links or clusters associated with these new items. But in this step we must also account for the song, a mode of delivery without precedent in the story, which calls attention to other kinds of utterances earlier in the story. What are those utterances? Some examples are the mother prays; the mother names the boy the apple of her eye; the stepmother curses; the stepmother orders; the stepmother prevaricates and misleads, producing a misleading image of the dead boy; and the father proclaims his satisfaction in eating the flesh of a son he does not recognize. But our notice of utterances is not limited to those in the story world. The song marks a transfer of authority from the voice of the narrator to the voice of the bird; although the song delights a community of listeners within the story, it may very well be sung by us, the community of listeners to the story itself. In singing this refrain, a retelling of the first half of the story apprehensible only to the audience of the story rather than to the audience in the story, we become active listeners and participants. We can share the unifying gaze of both the mother and the bird.

For this exercise to be useful, it is important to help students understand in advance the distinction between an object's sign value, something experienced as conveying a message for a specific recipient, and either its use value or its exchange value. The learning objective here is to face the challenge of how the fairy tale can perform justice, not only in terms of action but also in terms of vision, communication, and memory. Justice is grounded on the difference that sign value makes on memorability, whether transmitted as an image or as a song. Linking the boy to an apple, then to snow, then to blood, and finally beside a juniper tree seals the boy's status as one who will not go away, even when he has morphed into a singing bird, and each time the story is told, that bird sings the history of an unjust attack. In the course I teach, students relish the singing of the song, but they also begin to recognize how certain images conveyed in the folktale stick with them and somehow make the story unforgettable.

Bibliography

Aarne, Antti. *The Types of the Folktale: A Classification and Bibliography—Antti Aarne's Verzeichnis der Märchentypen*. *FF Communications* no. 3. Trans. Stith Thompson. Helsinki: Academia Scientiarum Fennica, 1961.

Applebee, Arthur N. *The Child's Concept of Story: Ages Two to Seventeen*. Chicago: University of Chicago Press, 1978. 64–71.

Bader, Barbara. *American Picturebooks from Noah's Ark to the Beast Within*. New York: Macmillan, 1976.

Barthes, Roland. *Mythologies*. Paris: Éditions du Seuil, 1970.

———. *S/Z*. Trans. Richard Howard. New York: Hill & Wang, 1974.

Benjamin, Walter. "The Storyteller." In *Illuminations*. By Walter Benjamin. Trans. Harry Zohn. New York: Schocken Books, 1969.

Bottigheimer, Ruth B. *Grimms' Bad Girls and Bold Boys: The Moral and Social Vision of the Tales*. New Haven, CT: Yale University Press, 1989.

Bourdieu, Pierre. "La Violence symbolique." In *La Domination masculine*. By Pierre Bourdieu. Paris: Seuil, 1998. 5–11.

Brémond, Claude. *Logique du récit*. Paris: Éditions du Seuil, 1973.

Calloud, Jean. *Structural Analysis of Narrative*. Philadelphia: Fortress Press, 1976. 24–27.

Carroll, Lewis. *The Annotated Alice: The Definitive Edition*, introduction and notes by Martin Gardner. New York: Norton, 2000.

Darnton, Robert. "Peasants Tell Tales." In *The Great Cat Massacre and Other Episodes in French Cultural History*. By Robert Darnton. New York: Basic Books, 1984. 9–72.

Dégh, Linda. *Folktales of Hungary*. Chicago: University of Chicago Press, 1965.

Erikson, Erik H. *Young Man Luther: A Study in Psychoanalysis and History*. New York: Norton, 1962.

Estés, Clarissa P. *Women Who Run with the Wolves: Myths and Stories of the Wild Woman Archetype*. New York: Ballantine, 1992.

Feldmann, Susan. *African Myths and Tales*. New York: Dell, 1963.

Frazer, James G. *The Golden Bough: A Study in Magic and Religion*. New York: Macmillan, 1922.

Genette, Gérard. *Figures: Essais*. Paris: Éditions du Seuil, 1966.

Gibson, James J. *The Ecological Approach to Visual Perception*. Boston: Houghton Mifflin, 1979.

Greimas, Algirdas J. *Sémantique structurale: Recherche de méthode*. Paris: Larousse, 1966.

Grimm, Jacob, and Wilhelm Grimm. *The Complete Fairy Tales of the Brothers Grimm*. Trans. Jack Zipes. New York: Bantam Books, 2003.

Kristeva, Julia. *Revolution in Poetic Language*. New York: Columbia University Press, 1984.

Lévi-Strauss, Claude. *The Savage Mind*. London: Weidenfeld & Nicolson, 1966.

Lüthi, Max. "Rapunzel, the Fairy Tale as Representation of the Maturation Process." In *Once Upon a Time: On the Nature of Fairy Tales*. By Max Lüthi. Bloomington: Indiana University Press, 1976. 109–19.

Mair, Victor H. *Painting and Performance: Chinese Picture Recitation and Its Indian Genesis*. Honolulu: University of Hawaii Press, 1988.

Moebius, William. "Informing Adult Readers: Symbolic Experience in Children's Literature." In *Reading World Literature: Theory, History, Practice*. Ed. Sarah N. Lawall. Austin: University of Texas Press, 1994. 309–27.

———. "Introduction to Picturebook Codes." *Word & Image: A Journal of Verbal/Visual Enquiry* 2.2 (1986): 141–58.

———. "Myth, Folktale, and Children's Literature." In *Teaching Children's Literature: Issues, Pedagogy, Resources*. Ed. Glenn E. Sadler. New York: Modern Language Association of America, 1992. 155–57.

Piaget, Jean. *The Child's Conception of the World*. Trans. Joan Tomlinson and Andrew Tomlinson. London: Paul, Trench, Trubner, 1929.

———. *Play, Dreams, and Imitation in Childhood*. New York: Norton, 1962.

Propp, V I. A. *Morphology of the Folktale*. Bloomington: Research Center, Indiana University, 1958.

Sendak, Maurice. *Where the Wild Things Are*. New York: Harper & Row, 1963.

Tatar, Maria. "Victims and Seekers: The Family Romance of Fairy Tales." In *The Hard Facts of the Grimms' Fairy Tales*. By Maria Tatar. Princeton, NJ: Princeton University Press, 1987. 58–82.

Thompson, Stith. *One Hundred Favorite Folktales*. Bloomington: Indiana University Press, 1968.

Vygotsky, L. S. *Thought and Language*. Cambridge, MA: MIT Press, 1962.

Warner, Marina. "My Father He Ate Me." In *No Go the Bogeyman: Scaring, Lulling, and Making Mock*. By Marina Warner. New York: Farrar, Straus & Giroux, 1999. 52–77.

Winnicott, D. W. "The Location of Cultural Experience." In *Playing and Reality*. By D. W. Winnicott. New York: Basic Books, 1971. 95–103.

———. "Transitional Objects and Transitional Phenomena." In *Playing and Reality*. By D. W. Winnicott. New York: Basic Books, 1971. 1–23.

From Mercantilism to Laissez-Faire

Teaching Economic Thought with French Fairy Tales

Benjamin Balak and Charlotte Trinquet du Lys

Economics and Fairy Tales

Teaching the past always benefits from contextualization because the relevance of history to contemporary issues is often lost on students living in a radically dehistoricized culture. For a class on economic thought, looking at the transformation from mercantilism to laissez-faire liberal classical economics from the literary perspective of the seventeenth-century fairy-tale canon adds a remarkable degree of nuance and provides a more rounded characterization of such key individuals as Jean-Baptiste Colbert, Bernard de Mandeville, and Adam Smith and their ideas and how they continue to be misunderstood today with significant consequences for critical policy debates in politics and economics. We propose to add another dimension to a traditional disciplinary course by looking at some surprising parallels between the fairy tales and the history of economic thought, adding a feminist twist by showing that the aristocratic women who wrote some of the first French fairy tales were well ahead of their time. This also foregrounds the important pedagogical role of interdisciplinary liberal arts education in connecting the arts and the sciences.

The first step in this module—or segment of the course—is to define the general concepts of zero-sum thinking in mercantilism (and all prior schools of thought since Aristotle) against non-zero-sum classical economics. The term *zero-sum* was first coined by John von Neumann and Oskar Morgenstern in their seminal *Theory of Games and Economic Behavior*, published in 1944. In the social sciences a zero-sum game implies that, for one party to gain, another must lose, and mutual benefit is impossible. Similarly in the context of fairy tales, zero-sum thinking manifests itself when the plots involve a finite sum of wealth or power, and for the protagonist to win, he or she has to trick the antagonist and take what belongs to him. Seven out of eight of Charles Perrault's tales indeed operate according to the zero-sum theory: Happy endings always happen through the ruin or the death of the antagonist. The rationale for examining these concepts is that, even though they are modern, they explain the fundamental paradigm shift that ushered in classical economic thought on which most of modern mainstream economics is still predicated. An easy way to explain it is by considering a pie: In mercantilism, to increase one's wealth, one has to secure a larger piece of the pie for oneself, whereas in classical economics one needs only to grow the size of the pie to earn more.

Perrault's production of eight short tales is just a small part of the French corpus, which is composed of more than seventy-five fairy tales written by a dozen tellers between 1690 and 1700. Moreover, Perrault's model of fairy-tale writing was at the time on the margins of the movement and was vastly supplanted by women's fairy-tale writing, which we refer to as the *aristocratic style*, in opposition to Perrault's *bourgeois*-mercantilist style and ethos. Perrault was an administrative aide to French finance minister Jean-Baptiste Colbert for almost twenty years, so it is not surprising to find significant traces of Colbertism and mercantilism in his worldview. The women's aristocratic style, on the other hand, was raging at the court of Louis XIV, where women tellers had been inventing and recounting a certain type of tale to the Versailles audience since the 1670s. The women's tales use a different economic view: Heroes and heroines do not need to ruin someone's life in order to better their own. Furthermore, in the selfish action of enhancing their own life, the protagonists also better the lives of their entourage, if not society as a whole. They basically make the pie bigger for everyone to profit, a proto-capitalist concept well ahead of Colbertism. In the elitist fairy-tale world of the seventeenth century, good people are often rewarded, but bad ones are not necessarily punished, a fact that goes against the political economy of Perrault's tales. These two styles of fairy-tale writing—the bourgeois and the aristocratic—reverse the received view that bourgeois adaptability drove the transition to market-based societies despite aristocratic intransigence (see, especially, Max Weber's *Protestant Ethic and the Spirit of Capitalism*) and suggest that the seventeenth-century female aristocratic writers of fairy tales were intriguingly well ahead of their time in challenging the bourgeois mercantilist economic zeitgeist.

In the 1690s corpus of French fairy tales, several tale types were written by both men and women tellers, and they are perfect examples of these two approaches, with reference to both the economy of the tales and the economic reality of the time (because the tales are often subversive and mimic the sociohistorical culture in which they were written). At the end of the activity outlined in what follows, students should be able to recognize several surprising reversals of commonly held concepts of this era, most notably regarding how the aristocrats seem to be ahead of the bourgeois in espousing the ethos of the new laissez-faire liberal market system.

A Classroom Activity

This activity uses eight fairy tales belonging to four tale types written by both men and women:

1. Perrault's "The Fairies" (1697) and Marie-Jeanne L'Héritier's "The Enchantments of Eloquence" (1695)
2. Perrault's "Little Thumb" and "Cinderella" (1697) and Marie-Catherine d'Aulnoy's "Finette-Cendron" (1697)
3. Perrault's "Riquet with the Tuft" (1697) and Catherine Bernard's "Riquet with the Tuft" (1694)
4. d'Aulnoy's "The Prince Marcassin" (1697) and Henriette-Julie de Murat's "The Pig King" (1699) (this pairing is a trick, as both women use a non-zero-sum approach to resolve the plot)

Students are provided with the eight fairy tales; however, they receive the list without the names of the writers (so they do not know whether they were written by men or women).

The class is then divided into groups. Each group takes one tale type. Students have to analyze the elements of the story in both versions of the tale type and do the following:

1. Identify the protagonist(s), antagonist(s), the problem to be overcome (by using Propp's functions), the elements that advance the plot, the use of the

supernatural, the resolution of the tales, and what happens to the characters at the end.

2. Decide which theory explains the progress of the protagonist: mercantilist or classical. How could the protagonist have won without using any of these theories?

3. Rewrite two modernized versions incorporating elements of modern economic thought and current policy issues (a neomercantilist version and a neoclassical version). What can be learned from comparing the two?

4. Bonus: Extend the rewritten modern economic fairy tale by using other economic theories (Marxian, Keynesian, Austrian, etc.) and tracing the zero-/non-zero-sum elements therein.

The groups then perform a dramatic reading of their modern fairy tales followed by a literary and economic critical analysis. This is done with groups competing against each other based on the tales themselves and the criticism.

This entire activity can be executed in a variety of ways and would be quite effective in a traditional classroom environment, especially with a relatively small class size. It is, however, multimodal in that it can lend itself especially well to a collaborative role-playing gamified pedagogy. We have discussed this pedagogical methodology extensively elsewhere (see Balak and Trinquet du Lys, "Cypherpunks"; Balak and Trinquet du Lys, "Teaching"; and Balak) and argue that it can not only enhance the relevance of the material and the enthusiasm of the students but also help overcome technical challenges, such as large class size, distance or blended learning, and diverse student learning styles. Whatever the technology and tools used to accomplish it, the pedagogical essence of this activity is that students master the concepts by applying them to the original texts, critically evaluate how worldviews operate in literature and economics, experience the actual creation process of both works of art and criticism, and engage in a collaborative effort to make sense of the social criticism and the dialectic between the arts and the sciences. This a perfect example of what Benjamin Bloom describes as higher cognitive levels of learning.

BIBLIOGRAPHY

Balak, Benjamin. "A Pluralistic and Gamified Senior Seminar in Economics: Capstone to a Heterodox Undergraduate Liberal Arts Economics Curriculum." *International Journal of Pluralism and Economics Education* 7.1 (2016): 7–21.

Balak, Benjamin, and Charlotte Trinquet du Lys. "Cypherpunks in the *Chambre Bleue*: A Twenty-First-Century Gamified Pedagogy to Teach the Social Networks of the Seventeenth

Century at the Intersection of Intellectual Culture and Political-Economics." In *Networks, Interconnection, Connectivity: Selected Essays from the 44th North American Society for Seventeenth-Century French Literature Conference, University of North Carolina at Chapel Hill & Duke University, May 15–17, 2014*. Ed. Ellen R. Welch and Michèle Longino. Biblio 17, v. 210. Tübingen: Gunter Narr, 2015. 203–13.

———. "Teaching Early Modern Fairy Tales to Disney Princesses; Or, If Only Mme. d'Aulnoy Had a Wiki." In *Origines: Actes du 39e congrès annuel de la North American Society for Seventeenth-Century French Literature, University of Nebraska-Lincoln, 10–12 mai 2007*. Biblio 17, v. 180. Tübingen: Gunter Narr, 2009. 311–21.

Bloom, Benjamin, ed. *Taxonomy of Educational Objectives: The Classification of Educational Goals*. London: Longman, 1984.

Von Neumann, John, and Oskar Morgenstern. *Theory of Games and Economic Behavior*, 60th anniversary commemorative ed. Princeton, NJ: Princeton University Press, 2007.

Weber, Max. *The Protestant Ethic and the Spirit of Capitalism*. Ed. Stephen Kalberg. New York: Routledge, 2001.

Following the Path of Cookies and Bread Crumbs

TAKING THE FAIRY-TALE COURSE ONLINE

Julie L. J. Koehler

It is the third week of class, and the class is divided. With all of them on their feet, they argue with impassioned voices on the topic of debate: Should Hansel and Gretel's parents have abandoned them, or should the family have starved together? There are, of course, no good answers, but, using textual evidence, students are working hard to make their claims. After class one of my students comes up to apologize for getting so into the debate. She realizes it was just an exercise, "but this class seems to be doing something to me. Yesterday I got in an argument with a stranger at the grocery store about the origins of Cinderella." This kind of passion, engagement, and excitement around the topic of fairy tales is the magic of the course that makes teaching it so rewarding. Although most students sign up because the course meets an undergraduate general education requirement, they leave as converts, under the spell of fairy tales, often saying they are sharing lecture notes with family members or renting course films to watch with their roommates on the weekend. And part of what engages them so thoroughly has much to do with the makeup of the course. The classroom, at a large urban university, usually holds students from different generations, faiths, races, socioeconomic backgrounds, and nationalities. Occasionally, there is even a student who is wholly unfamiliar with the genre of the European fairy tale. Students therefore have quite different experiences with the stories, even in the age of Disney, and in discussion they are sometimes shocked by the points of view of their fellow classmates. The course allows students to investigate their own experience and understanding of U.S. culture while studying the European fairy tale. The class is rich with aha moments.

So when it was suggested that an online version of the course be created, the instructors were a little hesitant. When students do not have to come face-to-face with the differing experience of their classmates or see the passion in the eyes of their opponents in debate, could they still have the same takeaway? Or would that same diversity even be represented online—would older students or students from a lower socioeconomic background avoid the course? All these considerations were in our minds as we began the process, but we found that taking a traditional face-to-face course online was much like adapting a book into a film. We had to reimagine the entire structure of the course from a new perspective, all the while doing our best to determine the essence of the course and how it could be translated into an online format. Through much discussion, work, and many trials, we found that, although the students would no longer be physically standing up in impassioned debate, online learning created a naturally more student-centered environment in which much of the learning happened not while students engaged with content but in their multimodal interaction with each other and the instructor. This interaction and, more specifically, these forms of discussion surrounding fairy tales are more evidence-based and more thoughtful than in-class discussion. It also allows for all students to speak and to be heard and to take more risks in both checking their peers and revealing their own development.

COURSE STRUCTURE

The development of the online course occurred over the 2014 summer semester and involved collaboration among instructors of two departments at Wayne State University: Abigail Heinger, of the Department of English (now of Bluefield College), and Anne Duggan and me, of the Department of Classical and Modern Languages, Literatures, and Cultures (CMLLC). Within the CMLLC Department, Duggan and I also represent two languages, French and German, and this course was cross-listed in those two departments. This collaboration across departments and language areas was key to the success of this multifaceted course. The development of the course was funded by a small grant from Wayne State University's Foreign Language and Technology Center. The course ran for the first time in fall 2014 and has been taught every semester since. The course has been adapted for a six-week accelerated semester and has been adapted by six instructors, who each taught it differently depending on their own research foci. A sample syllabus for this online course can be found in Chapter 6.

The course is structured as an introduction to French and German fairy tales, but Italian, British, Scandinavian, and Russian tales are also included, as are more recent retellings and films from across Europe, the United States, and Asia. In the traditional classroom, the major source of output is short analytical papers; although the online course includes these, students also create a group digital project. The course fulfills our philosophy and letters requirement, and therefore it is important that writing plays a role in the class. The traditional course had units structured around classic tales. In creating the online course, we structured the units around motifs and themes (often having much in common with classic tales), because this allowed us to include more tales outside the European structure and more tales written by women and minorities.

In addition to two essays, two blogs, a midterm, a final, and a group digital project, students had regular weekly assignments. In any given week students would complete readings, watch lectures, post six times on the discussion board, submit a personal journal entry, complete group project assignments, and take a reading quiz. Students were expected to put an average of nine hours a week into the three-credit course—three hours representing the time that we would have met in-person and six hours representing the time they would have spent preparing for class and completing assignments. Lectures were created with Explain Everything. Explain Everything is an app that uses slides, much like PowerPoint, and allows recording of voice and drawing on slides with a stylus. Lectures were not live but were recorded and put in each unit's folder to be watched as many times as needed. Students interacted with instructors during office hours, in conferences, and through feedback on their journals. In general, unless a grade needed explaining, instructors did not break into the discussion space but left that as a learner-learner interaction space. Students interacted with the whole class in the discussion board, and this space became the centerpiece of the course, where much of the learning took place.

Our top priority in setting up this course was to focus on creating interaction and presence. These two elements have been identified by many scholars as key to online learning success, and we relied on scholarship that demonstrated how to develop this in transition (e.g., York et al.). We wanted students to have ample opportunity to interact with each other and the instructor, and we wanted a variety of interactions as well, in formality, quality, duration, format, and worth (in the grading scheme). The goal was to create an online space that felt warm and full when students logged in, somewhere they might want to explore a bit. Interaction primarily focused around discussion, blogs, conferences, group wikis, and journal feedback.

Student perception of presence in online learning has been shown to have a powerful effect on their success. Although articles as recent as 2015 still surface claiming that online classes will eliminate instructors (e.g., Godsey), numerous studies have shown empirically that instructor interaction and presence are vital to student success in online learning (see Garrison et al.; Vaughan and Garrison; and Wicks et al.). Most recently, Huaihao Zhang and colleagues have shown that student perception of online presence increased outcomes in interactive and constructive learning (Zhang et al.).

Instructor presence is the student's perceived understanding of how involved the instructor is with the course; this can include the course's structure and content as well as instructor feedback, e-mails, announcements, and other interaction with students (Zhang et al.). Our goal was for students to feel as though the instructor was with them and available to them when they entered the online space. Through instructor announcements, lectures, and ThingLinks, the student would have to interact with instructor-created items each time the student entered the course and unit folders. Through journal feedback and conferences, students would interact with the instructor in a personalized one-on-one format. In conferences three times a semester, students chatted with instructors for 10 to 15 minutes about the course, their group, and their essay progress. This was an opportunity for instructors to touch base about student progress and issues and for students to ask for clarity about assignments as well as for letting the instructor know if group members were failing to participate.

Interaction is key to any online course, and we hoped to foster many forms of interaction, including instructor-learner interaction, learner-learner interaction in the large group, learner-learner interaction in small groups, and learner-content interaction. Although we certainly did not require students to divulge personal details about themselves in discussion, we did want to engage the varying experiences and viewpoints of students to create a rich discussion. In the classroom a younger student may look at older students and expect them to have a different life experience; in the online class, this was not so apparent. In many ways, this was a great equalizer. Students still recognized the diversity of the classroom but experienced it only through the discussion itself, not through their perceptions of other students based on appearance. Although student names were always viewable, assumptions based on names were tricky, as students often found out when assuming the gender of an Alex, for instance. Students interacted with each other through discussion, group wikis, and blog comments. Group wikis were wiki pages created for group interaction. Students wrote each other messages, held chats, produced partial elements of the project, and received feedback from the instructor on these pages. As a result of the nature of wikis, the instructor is able to track each student's participation and work, because the wiki records each time content is added. In whole-class discussion, students interacted by means of replies to each other's posts and comments on each other's blogs.

(Re-)Creating Rich Discussion

Creating discussion that exhibits the same richness and vigor of the traditional classroom was one of the major goals of the transition. Heiniger and I discussed at length the elements of in-class discussion we wanted to maintain and how to go about creating that. Some elements we transitioned into other parts of the course. Although the instructor is a key element of an in-class discussion, we understood that in the online space it would be best to have the discussion board be a student-centered place where students would learn through their own understanding of content and their interaction with their classmates' comments. Tisha Bender's *Discussion-Based Online Teaching to Enhance Student Learning* informed many of our choices, but other elements were particular to teaching fairy tales online. What we discovered was that online discussion actually had many benefits we had not anticipated. Mainly it allowed for a more student-centered classroom and gave every student more opportunities to speak and to hear from each other and to react and respond to each other and each other's work. Everyone had to speak, unlike a traditional classroom, and nearly everyone would hear what that student had to say. This meant that more voices were heard and more interactions were developed than would occur in a traditional classroom. Without a teacher at the front of the room, students were also responsible to each other. They would encourage each other, pose more in-depth questions to each other, and, when needed, even check each other.

Thinking about teaching fairy tales, in particular, we identified a few specific challenges to discussion. For some of these the online format was a benefit. For instance, studying fairy tales always requires students to engage with difficult topics, such as rape, murder, and child abuse. One element we appreciated about the online format was that it gave students plenty of space and time to process their reactions to these elements and to respond carefully and thoughtfully to discussion prompts and other students' comments. Having seen arguments develop out of debate in the classroom, I was concerned that in the impersonal world of the Internet, students would say unkind things to each other or not consider the feelings of the others in the class. What I had not considered, however, was the time factor. If there was a student comment that was particularly controversial, other students did not need to respond immediately or even that same day. There was time for students to compose responses. On the whole, the discussion was more thoughtful and civil.

One element that is both an asset and a difficulty in any fairy-tale course is that of pre-knowledge. Because many, if not all, of our students come into our courses knowing some fairy tales and also believing they know what a fairy tale is, it is not unusual for students to believe that they do not have to complete the reading. We thought that in an online class this would increase, because students would have access to each other's posts and plenty of time to compose a response that would sound as though the student had done the reading. To address this, we required students to quote a text during the discussion at least once a week and to compare texts at least once a week. Mostly, however, we relied on other pieces of the course to encourage reading.

Each unit included a pop reading quiz (students would learn about it at the start of the week) that was quite simple but difficult to pass without completing the reading. We also relied on other assignments to encourage reading. To produce quality blog posts, essays, and the group project, students would have to engage fully with most of the readings. In the second running of the course, a midterm and a final were introduced. Each exam was completely open book and quite simple for those who had been participating all along, basically asking students to make connections across major course themes, but through these tests it became clear when a student had not been reading.

Finally, we sought to get students excited to read using ThingLinks. These are images with hot spots placed in various locations. At the top of each folder we placed a ThingLink that highlighted readings and engaging facts about the tales to come. Several students told me that they shared the ThingLinks with friends, because they functioned as a sort of overview of interesting facts about particular tales but also as a preview of the readings.

The most unexpected outcome, however, was the way in which students themselves encouraged both engagement with content and thoughtful responses to difficult topics. Students owned the discussion board space and often spoke as though the instructor could not read it. It was not unusual for students to admit to not yet having read a text under discussion. For example, in a response to a student's comment another student wrote, "Your post may change my perspective a bit! I have not watched the film yet though." This student followed up that she was going to watch the film because of the interesting discussion point. Because students were both posting in discussion and completing readings over the course of the same week, they often came in at different points in their readings, meaning other students' comments and excitement would encourage them to complete the readings.

Another element arose when students acted as though they had completed the reading but had not; others would comment to correct them, as was the case in a discussion on aspects of consent in "Sleeping Beauty" tales. Although students were assigned Giambattista Basile's "Sun, Moon, and Talia" as the first reading of the week, one student posted, "I don't believe I see rape occurring outright anywhere." The other students in the class carefully crafted comments that pointed out their classmate's error while acknowledging the rest of her comment and moving the discussion forward. For instance, one student wrote, "Hey, I too am with you when you state that viewing these tales as rape is something you have never considered. I thought rape was [however] outright done in Basile's variant." And another said, "I believe in Talia, Sun and Moon [sic] rape does occur outright. The fact that the woman conceives children during her slumber is in my opinion enough evidence to show she was raped. What do you think?" Of course, all the evidence the student would need is the overt description of rape that does occur in the tale, but each of these commentators wrote almost overly politely, aiming to not humiliate the student while still checking her mistake.

Overall, it was harder for students to hide in online discussion. Students must post, and what they post is fair game to be analyzed and checked by any of the other students in the course. One student learned this the hard way when he wrote in regards to Perrault's "Bluebeard," "My first reaction is they got what they deserved. In Bluebeard he says, 'Open everything, go everywhere, but as far as the little office goes, you may not go in there' (165). The ladies were given specific orders and they disobeyed them so they have to face the consequences." Five thoughtful, well-argued, and referenced oppositions followed this post, each student building on the other's argument until the original poster had to respond back that he agreed that Bluebeard's actions were not acceptable and that "death would never be an option" for a proper punishment for disobedience. In the classroom the original statement may have led to heated discussion, but in the online forum it simply led to well-argued positions. One of the students who responded went on to structure an essay around her response.

This result was not uncommon. The essays in the online course were of a much higher quality than in the traditional course. Because we required students to include textual evidence every single week in discussion posts, they were naturally practicing the integration of citations more often than students in the traditional course and, importantly, not in a referential spoken form but in a properly composed and formatted written post. They also, therefore, received weekly feedback on errors in the use and formatting of this textual evidence, and they interacted with each other's evidence. Seeing weekly examples from their peers and beginning to recognize strong and weak examples of providing evidence, students regularly built on successful discussion posts to develop theses for future essays.

Visual Analysis and the Digital Gesture

Analyzing text was simpler in the online format, but analyzing images was significantly more difficult at first. Using her background in art history, Heiniger developed a unit based on visual analysis of fairy-tale illustration and film. In discussion, there was constant confusion about exactly what part of an image a student was discussing. In the traditional classroom we would simply project images and have students come to the front of the classroom and point to their illustration or scene. We needed a virtual gesture that could be expressed in the online format.

This is where ThingLink became a useful tool. Because students could place hot spots on the image itself and provide text, links, and even additional images and video in those hot spots, they were able to gesture to the image with their hot spots and make a clearer explanation to their classmates of their thinking. At first we relied on ThingLinks only in the visual analysis unit, but it became clear that it could have multiple uses. The students created a group project that was an analysis of a film, and ThingLink was a useful tool for group members to express to each other how they planned to visually analyze a scene. In addition, when students were brainstorming for their essays, we used ThingLinks to help them organize their interests in a tale or tale type and provide background information for others working on the same text. An example of one of those brainstorming assignments can be found in Appendix A.

Conclusion

Much of the online teaching experience was like this ThingLink example. We would take a successful and worthwhile activity from the traditional course—for example, visual analysis of fairy-tale illustration—and work to find a way to translate the most important concepts into an online format. Often this process, like all translation, was not a one-to-one transition. In fact, it was often much closer to adaptation, both in the way that every translation is an adaptation and in the way that the content and the lessons had to adapt to a new environment. In the case of the visual analysis, discovering ThingLink not only helped to solve this problem but also gave us ideas for other parts of the class, such as brainstorming and developing student interest in the content of a new unit. In this way, the online course slowly grew and morphed into something that ultimately met similar outcomes of the traditional course, but it was its own unique experience in comparison.

On the whole, the elements we most feared would be lost—passion, engagement, and those aha moments—were still there in spades. Although we could not know who did not take the course because of the online format, we still had a diverse group of students taking the course. And we had some surprise students from out of state, such as a woman who took the course to research her position as Belle at Disney World. For all students, however, because they posted every week and could not remain a silent mystery, their work demonstrated their individual growth in a much more complex and broad way. Significantly, not only was the instructor privy to this development, but also the whole class was developing and simultaneously observing each other's development together over the course of the semester.

In closing, I would like to relate one particularly rich example that brings clarity to this point. In our third semester teaching the course, there was one student who represented many of the qualities of a student who we expected might not take the online course. This student was going to college for the first time after retiring and taking her first online course ever. She brought some opinions into discussion that were a bit shocking to some of the younger students. For example, she once argued for the benefits of women maintaining a home while men went out to work. She had fond memories of her own traditional marriage and division of labor. She even wrote that she wondered why other students seemed to have given up on love and the happy ending. Although we feared other students might be harsh in their responses, they were often kind and patient with her while arguing honestly their own point of view. She actually came to me during office hours, saying she was depressed by how jaded the other students seemed and how she came from an entirely different perspective. She thought that the arguments in the class attacked her own happy marriage. I encouraged her to stick with it, and did my best to guide her. She asked for additional readings, and I tried to share some more examples that maybe put some of the jaded comments in context. Whether or not it was about sharing her true thoughts or simply beginning to think of fairy tales as something more than the children's stories she read as a little girl, her posts began to change. She wrote that the course was "eye-opening," and when we got to "Bluebeard" tales, she began to talk about how the fairy tales seemed to allow a place to discuss "barbaric thoughts" that people had in the past as well as now. In the last week of class, she wrote something that demonstrated how far she had come in her understanding. In response to someone's statement about the expectations put on women in fairy tales, she wrote, "I would ask, are they 'fairy-tale' expectations or just expectations that apply to a woman's life . . . Looking back on my life, I did a lot of waiting for a prince to come and kiss me and awaken me to life. Wow! And then something happened and I stopped waiting and started doing for myself." This post demonstrated to us that students could still develop their critical thinking skills, reflect on their own experience, and have those aha moments in the online format.

In the end, we discovered that in the online format the instructor must be willing to grow in the same way as the student and to move away from teacher-centered lectures or instructor-led discussions. The instructor cannot be present in the discussion board when every post goes up, but the learning is not happening because the instructor is there. The instructor sets the scene and learning begins when the students engage with each other. They can check in with each other about completing a reading, critique each other on how well they are doing, and together come to a bigger and broader understanding. They are more willing to take risks to seriously challenge each other online, but at the same time they have space to compose their thoughts and ideas. Ultimately, online courses, as with all courses, are a product of the time, effort, and thought that goes into them, and in the world of fairy-tale instruction, that means there was no less magic, only a new way of casting the spell.

APPENDIX A
ThingLink Activity

The essay fast approaches. For this journal, I would like you to list the two written variants and one film adaptation that you will cover in your essay. The film can be short or full-length, and the variants can be traditional or more modern or a mix. Think carefully about this choice. You do not have to give equal time to each in your paper. You could focus the paper on a film adaptation, for instance, and describe the written variants on which it is based. Or you could compare and contrast all three and give more equal time.

In addition to your choices, you should create a ThingLink using the following instructions:

1. Create a username at www.thinglink.com.
2. Click on "Create."
3. Upload a picture related to your story. A simple Google image search should show you quite a few options. Because this is only for a course and not publicly available, you do not need to be concerned with permission or copyright.
4. After uploading the picture, click anywhere to create a tag. The following are the rules regarding your tags:
   a. You must have at least six tags.
   b. One tag must be the illustrator or photographer of your image, the book, film, or series from which it comes, and the date of its publication.
   c. One tag must give some basic historical facts related to your tale.
   d. One tag must summarize one of the variants in which you are most interested in two or three sentences.
   e. At least one tag should be an image or a video.
   f. The remaining tags can be any information, link, image, or video related to your tale and/or your paper. Feel free to include unusual or fun references to fairy tales from pop culture or the Internet.
5. Once you have created your ThingLink, you must post it to your Week Four journal and to the Discussion Board Forum for Week Five. Because the journal is due Sunday, you will post the ThingLink to Week Five, so that other students will have the opportunity to see it. In order to do this:
   a. Click on "Share."
   b. Then either copy and paste the link into your journal or discussion, OR

c. You can paste in the embed code. If you would like to embed the image (make it available without clicking through to the link), you must first go into the HTML editor. To do this, click on HTML in the bottom writer of the text-editing toolbar in Blackboard. Then paste in the embed code from the ThingLink page. You should see your image appear in your post after submitting it.

Bibliography

Bender, Tisha. *Discussion-Based Online Teaching to Enhance Student Learning.* Sterling, VA: Stylus, 2003.

Garrison, Randy, Martha Cleveland-Innes, and Tak Shing Fung. "Exploring Causal Relationships Among Teaching, Cognitive, and Social Presence: Student Perceptions of the Community of Inquiry Framework." *The Internet and Higher Education* 13.1–2 (2010): 31–36.

Godsey, Michael. "The Deconstruction of the K–12 Teacher." *The Atlantic* (March 25, 2015). www.theatlantic.com/education/archive/2015/03/the-deconstruction-of-the-k-12-teacher/388631/ (accessed August 30, 2017).

Vaughan, Norman, and Randy Garrison. "Creating Cognitive Presence in a Blended Faculty Development Community." *The Internet and Higher Education* 8.1 (2005): 1–12.

Wicks, David, Baine B. Craft, Donghun (Don) Lee, Andrew Lumpe, Robin Henrikson, Nalline Baliram, Xu Bian, Stacy Mehlberg, and Katy Wicks. "An Evaluation of Low Versus High Collaboration in Online Learning." *Online Learning* 19.4 (2015).

York, Cindy S., Dazhi Yang, and Melissa Dark. "Transitioning from Face-to-Face to Online Instruction: How to Increase Presence and Cognitive/Social Interaction in an Online Information Security Risk Assessment Class." *International Journal of Information and Communication Technology Education* 3.2 (2007): 41–50.

Zhang, Huaihao, Lijia Lin, Yi Zhan, and Youqun Ren. "The Impact of Teaching Presence on Online Engagement Behaviors." *Journal of Educational Computing Research* 54.7 (2016): 887–900.

And They All Learned Happily Ever After

Activities for Teaching Language and Culture through Fairy Tales

Nancy L. Canepa

Many of the contributors to this volume have noted how fairy tales are a narrative form with which all students have experience, in some shape or form, and how integrating them into coursework as a springboard for discussing a cultural issue or as a framework for teaching grammar ensures that students share a familiar, common initial point of reference. Fairy tales can be uniquely adapted as teaching tools in contexts that range from introductory foreign-language courses to upper-level foreign-language seminars to large culture or survey courses offered by literature and other humanities departments to a general student audience (i.e., not necessarily humanities majors). Eric Taylor has noted how folk- and fairy tales are "well suited to the development of language and cognitive skills at nearly any level," skills such as "analyzing, drawing inferences, synthesizing, summarizing, and noticing underlying text structures" (Taylor, lx, 3). Furthermore, the relatively simple narrative structure of folk- and fairy tales may make them more "approachable" than other genres; they grapple with themes that students find inherently interesting, such as maturation and coming of age, family dynamics and interpersonal relationships, courtship and sexuality, the risks and rewards involved in socialization, and much more; and finally, they "provide a natural context for discussing cultural similarities and cultural differences" (Taylor, 15).

I have taught courses on the European literary fairy tale in the Comparative Literature Program and the Women's, Gender, and Sexuality Studies Program at my institution, Dartmouth College; I also regularly teach fairy tales at different levels of Italian language and literature classes, from introductory language courses to advanced seminars. In this essay I survey some of the ways I have incorporated fairy tales into my teaching in courses whose principal focus is the fairy tale and in units in language courses. I describe five fairy-tale activities that have, over the years, proved to be rewarding experiences for my students and me alike, activities that have expanded students' linguistic and cultural proficiency, enhanced their understanding of fairy-tale history, encouraged them to create their own fairy-tale narratives, put them in the role of innovative pedagogues, and overall made them more perceptive and critical readers and appreciators of fairy tales and of narrative in general.

Fairy Tales in the Foreign-Language Classroom

In courses in the introductory language sequence, I frequently use fairy tales to introduce or to review the use of verb tenses, in particular, the alternation of the past perfect (*passato remoto*) and imperfect in narration in the past (or, alternatively, the present perfect [*passato prossimo*] and imperfect). An excellent exercise involves asking students to read a tale aloud and make note of the correct verb tenses, assessing their understanding with a cloze test, and then, as a wrap-up activity, having the students tell the tale orally themselves. The narrative simplicity of (some versions of) fairy tales also makes them an ideal form to use when more generally reviewing vocabulary and parts of speech (see Appendix A). And, of course, any kind of culmination of these activities with a creative writing assignment ("My Favorite Fairy Tale," "A Postmodern Fairy Tale," "The Fairy Tale of My Life," etc.) is usually a hit. I have also experimented with more extended projects in the context of language classes, for example, a culture unit on fairy tales in Italian 2, a second-quarter language course (see later discussion).

The advanced Italian literature and culture courses that I regularly teach are on the fifteenth and sixteenth centuries, the seventeenth and eighteenth centuries, and the nineteenth century. All of these courses are taught in Italian, and in all of them I include a unit on fairy tales: for the first two time periods, we read the early modern forebears of the literary fairy tale, Giovan Francesco Straparola and Giambattista Basile; and for the last period, the Sicilian folklorists Giuseppe Pitrè and Laura Gonzenbach. In each case, studying fairy tales allows us to explore cultural history from an angle that students are not always familiar with. For the early modern period we discuss, for example, the Baroque literary fairy tale's similarities to and differences from the Renaissance novella and the unique ways in which an unconventional, fantastic literary genre could have engaged with social reality more aggressively than established genres. In the course on the nineteenth century, we discuss the emergence of folkloristics and the attitudes toward folk culture at a time of intense nation building as well as the passage of the fairy tale from an adult to a children's genre. I also teach a seminar on the Italian fairy-tale tradition from Straparola to the twenty-first century (see later discussion). In upper-level courses there is naturally more leeway for sustained creative work with fairy tales.

In the following sections I briefly describe a successful larger course unit that I have incorporated into a beginning language course (Italian 2) and an oral storytelling project in an advanced seminar on Italian fairy tales.

Italian Fairy Tales and Regions

Italian 2 is the second course in the three-quarter language sequence at my institution (the equivalent of a second-semester course); from the first day only Italian is used in the classroom, and all reading and writing are done in Italian. Although this is primarily a grammar course with a large number of structures to introduce and reinforce, culture is fully integrated into the course at every step. Besides the daily connections to Italian culture, there are also four mini-units on Italian culture that vary according to the offering (in the past, the mini-units, often coupled with a guest visitor or other special performance or event, have included opera, Futurism, Italian singer-songwriters, the culture of San Remo, Dante, and migration).

The last time I taught Italian 2, I invited a professional storyteller, Gioia Timpanelli (also a contributor to this volume). The initial reason for inviting her was to conduct a week-long storytelling workshop in my advanced seminar on Italian fairy tales, though she also gave several public performances, met informally with students, and visited one class of each of the language sections (Italian 1, 2, and 3). We often arrange to have a term-long cultural topic for all the language classes, and in this case, because of Gioia's presence, it was fairy tales and storytelling; each instructor thus devised a unit and related activities on this topic.

The fairy-tale unit extended over the last four weeks of the course, taking up four distinct days of class, and consisted of learning the basics about fairy tales and the Italian fairy-tale tradition, reading and discussing a fairy tale ("La Mammadraga") from Giuseppe Pitrè's nineteenth-century collection, attending Gioia Timpanelli's performance, hosting her in class for a discussion of her performance and of "La

Mammadraga," and the final project. The day students were to read "La Mammad-raga," they also read and prepared a handout, which included questions about their interest in and experience with fairy tales and activities more specific to the tale itself (see Appendix B). I prepared a short PowerPoint presentation for this same day, in which I reviewed common fairy-tale characters and plots and offered a short history of the Italian fairy-tale tradition.

After Gioia's performance the following week, the students discussed "La Mam-madraga" with her in greater depth. By that point, they understood the tale's plot quite well. "La Mammadraga" is a version of ATU 480, "The Kind and the Unkind Girls," a tale type that deals explicitly with determining what constitutes good and bad behavior and what the consequences of each are. The conversation with Gioia was an opportunity for the students to delve more deeply into the cultural and moral dimensions of the tale, as well as to discuss what its message and lessons were and whether they found these meaningful in the context of their own experiences.

The final project was done in groups of three and was two-pronged (see Appen-dix C for guidelines and timeline). Students chose an Italian region (their choices were limited to Piedmont, Tuscany, Abruzzo, Campania, Puglia, and Sicily) and one fairy tale from that region (I assembled folders of several fairy tales from each of the regions, all from Italo Calvino's *Fiabe italiane*). On the last days of class each group had 20 minutes to orally perform their tale, in any format they chose, and then to tell the class about their chosen region through a poster presenta-tion. They were asked to narrow their focus to a particular aspect of the region, such as geography and landscapes, arts and literature, cuisine, historical events, or famous monuments or people. Gioia returned for the final presentations, and students were encouraged to invite anyone else they liked.

Students had to come up with a basic working script for their storytelling, because I wanted to be sure that they had the essential words and structures necessary to tell their tales. I was, however, strict about the performance hav-ing to be oral—no cue cards, notes, or visual prompts—and I gave them some guidelines on how to prepare most effectively for oral narration. It was evident at the presentations that the students had practiced many times and that they had internalized and made the tales their own (as opposed to merely rote-memorizing them). Fairy tales are often formulaic; they tend to repeat episodes *and* the way key events and characters are described, and this repetition made the students' task both easier and more fun. It was also clear, from how they savored the rhythm of the language and the new and unusual words and expressions they had learned, that all their practicing had brought them to a new level of linguistic competency, and appreciation.

For the poster presentations, each group prepared a vocabulary list for their classmates beforehand, which I collected and compiled into a single document and handed out in class. Students were required to ask at least two questions apiece during each presentation day, and they were encouraged to use the new vocabulary from the lists when doing so. The poster presentations and the research that went into them sparked great interest in and surprise at the widely differing regional cultures of Italy, information which the groups were able to incorporate into their analyses of the culture-specific aspects of their tales. For example, one group focused on agriculture and peasant culture in the Abruzzo region. When speaking of living spaces, they used their chosen tale, an Abruzzese version of "Little Red Riding Hood" called "The False Grandmother," as an example. In the tale the grandmother lives on the second floor of a farmhouse and the animals are kept in the ground-floor barn space, a typical spatial arrangement in rural Abruzzo and one that plays directly into the plot of this particular tale.

Finally, the last short writing assignment of the quarter, keyed to one of the grammatical structures we had just studied, was "A Fairy Tale for the Future," which was to be written entirely in . . . the future!

Animal Spouse Tales in the Italian Tradition

I taught a very different sort of foreign-language class, the advanced literature seminar (taught in Italian) "C'era una volta . . . Italian Fairy Tales," in the same quarter as the Italian 2 course described in the previous section. As mentioned, storyteller Gioia Timpanelli's week-long residence at Dartmouth was a centerpiece of this course, in which she led a workshop in week 8 of the 10-week quarter. The raw materials for this workshop were Italian versions of the "animal spouse" tale type (students read a selection before Gioia arrived) along with secondary readings. During the week of the workshop, we discussed the tales—their contexts, symbols, and archetypes—as well as variants of the tales outside the Italian tradition, and practiced storytelling techniques. By the end of the week, students chose one of the tales as the basis for their final oral storytelling project, which required them to perform their tale in Italian in whatever form they preferred: a "straight" retelling, a song or rap, a dramatization, a puppet show, and so forth. The tales were performed at an end-of-term evening event sponsored by the Italian Club and open to the general public. Just as for the final presentations in Italian 2, the performance was required to be entirely oral and without textual support, and for this course, too, we brainstormed on effective oral storytelling. After their performance, students briefly commented on their tales—why they had chosen them and the questions and issues that the tales raised.

A week after the performance, students submitted a final paper (6–8 pages) in which they included an introduction to the overall tale type, compared several additional versions (including at least one non-Italian version), reflected critically on how their chosen tales refashioned the tale type in distinctive ways, and incorporated close readings of several significant passages from the tale. For this paper they had to consult, engage with in their analysis, and cite at least two critical works. The final prong of this project was a creative assignment: Each student wrote his or her own original animal spouse tale, and the tales were compiled and shared with the rest of the class.

Although these two projects involved students at different levels of language proficiency, students were able to exercise and improve their foundational skills in all areas (reading, listening, writing, and speaking), and the fairy tales proved to be an excellent vehicle for achieving this. As all foreign-language teachers know, impromptu speaking takes significant effort to develop, and even students in upper-level courses struggle with sustained oral production not related to short conversations about personal matters. Telling stories is one of the most common and appealing forms of extended discourse in which we partake in our daily lives—stories about our own experiences, stories that we hear or hear about and want to share, tales from our family or communal past. In the words of Arthur Frank, "Stories animate human life"; they "breathe life not only into individuals, but also into groups that assemble around telling" (Frank, 3).

These days, communal storytelling tends to be either textualized or generated in filtered or mediated form through television, cinema, or YouTube (I think of the many conversations I hear that involve description of a recently seen movie, TV show, or video). Re-creating, in the language class, a community of oral storytelling centered on the productively fantastic narratives of fairy tales gives students the opportunity to become creative storytellers in a way that they perhaps have not previously experienced, just as, of course, it engages them in the work of actively mastering the grammar and vocabulary of a new language. Moreover, just as fiction in general can encourage "freeing the mind from obligation and constraint" and stimulate "the free play of ideas in which innovative thinking depends," engagement with "imaginary worlds" in particular "allow[s] experimentation with possible eventualities which the mind, locked into a routine, might otherwise not have seen" (Cook, 42, 58). With their juxtapositions of familiar and unfamiliar worlds and tales of heroes and heroines pushing their limits as they embark on initiatory journeys, fairy tales present a striking parallel with the exhilarating, disorienting, and out-of-comfort-zone experiences that immersing oneself in a new language and culture offers.

HANDS-ON LEARNING IN FAIRY-TALE COURSES

In this section I consider activities that I have incorporated into two iterations of a fairy-tale survey course I teach in the Comparative Literature Program and the Women's, Gender, and Sexuality Studies Program. These courses have no prerequisite, tend to be large with respect to other humanities classes at my institution (30–50 students), and tend to attract students of diverse academic interests; a good number are non–humanities majors who take the course to satisfy a "Literature" distributive requirement. Even if many students are attracted to these courses initially as a way to reconnect with a form that they remember fondly from earlier in their lives, by the time the course ends, they have refined their competencies in critical reading and comparative analysis and have discovered new ways of engaging with cultural material and understanding cultural difference, all of which are easily applicable to many other contexts in their lives. An additional perk is that even students who do not consider themselves "literature types" are often inspired to continue their exploration of the humanities.

Little Red Riding Hood Goes to the Library: Exploring Fairy-Tale History Through Rare Books

I regularly teach "The Literary Fairy Tale" in the Comparative Literature Program at Dartmouth (see syllabus in Chapter 6). This course surveys the development of the fairy tale in Europe and North America, from the first collections in early modern France and Italy (Basile, Perrault), through the Brothers Grimm, to revisitations of fairy-tale subjects and motifs in the twentieth and twenty-first centuries. Over the course of the term, students also explore case studies of several of the best-known tale types, review critical approaches to the fairy tale, write and perform tales, conduct collaborative research, and visit our special collections library to explore the wide spectrum of material manifestations of the print fairy tale over the course of literary history.

I generally organize two of these library visits, the first in the third or fourth week of the quarter and the second around the sixth week. After a few initial remarks by the special collections librarian and me, the sessions are conducted as workshops in which students have ample opportunity to look at and handle the books and other materials. These classes are invariably a great success. For many students it is the first time they have visited this library and/or touched printed material that is over a hundred years old, and this experience in itself can be exciting (*especially* in our wired age) and mind-opening, inspiring students to imagine the environments in which the materials might have been used and by whom. One student from the last offering of this course commented, "I really enjoyed the various workshops we did as a class, especially the ones involving Rauner [the special collections library]. I found it fascinating getting to compare and analyze the differences between various versions of tales, purely by external characteristics. Seeing and touching copies of fairy tales from the 1800s is an experience I will never forget."

In the activity summaries in the following sections I briefly describe the objective of each of our visits, the materials we worked with, and the sorts of questions the students were encouraged to engage with during and after class. The texts we worked with are included in Appendixes E and G, and the worksheets that students used as guides are given in Appendixes D and F.

Activity 1: From Perrault to the Brothers Grimm— Changing Paradigms

In our initial visit to the special collections library we focused on studying editions of Charles Perrault's *Histoires ou contes du temps passé* (Stories or Tales of Times Past) and the Grimms' *Kinder- und Hausmärchen* (Children's and Household Tales), editions whose publication dates range from 1697 to 1909 with a predominance of materials from the eighteenth and nineteenth centuries. We had already started discussing in class how, in the passage from Perrault's collection to the Grimms' tales, the function of fairy tales shifted from adult entertainment to children's enjoyment and edification, and our first activity of the session was to compare the frontispieces (all involving the same scene of tale-telling at a hearth) of the first edition of Perrault (1697), two eighteenth-century editions of Perrault (one in the original French and one in English translation), and the first English translation of a selection of the Grimms' tales, *German Popular Stories* (1823 and 1826). Students enjoyed detecting the small but significant details that differed among the various frontispieces. They were encouraged to read these clues in terms of the changing function of the fairy tale as a genre but also in tandem with other material aspects of each book—size, binding, typography, pagination, illustrations, choice of tales, and so forth—in order to formulate educated hypotheses about the books and the contexts in which they were produced and about the transmission and reception of fairy tales over the 200-year period in question.

The questions on the worksheet were kept fairly general to encourage students to spend most of their time paging through the various editions and focusing on aspects of the books that they found most interesting. Dartmouth has a number of nineteenth-century fairy-tale editions from New England, some of them chapbooks or school primers, and students found it fascinating to note some distinguishing characteristics of the "local" materials and to offer their interpretations of these.

ACTIVITY 2: FAIRY-TALE TYPES

At this point in the course the students had already begun working on their final projects, which consisted of a collaborative group research project and class presentation (in Prezi format) on a single tale type. The second visit to the library was aimed at giving students the opportunity to model for themselves, in miniature, the sort of comparing and contrasting of different versions of a tale type that they would continue to do in the final projects, though in the library session the students were again encouraged to pay special attention to the physical characteristics of the works they were looking at. Students worked in groups of four or five, and each group worked with one tale type, though neither the groups nor the tale types were the same as those for the final projects. The materials in this case were much more diverse than during our first visit and included, besides more traditional picture books (both children's and more lavish collector's editions), novelty books (e.g., of tiny or shaped dimensions), a musical score, school primers, theater scripts, operas, and—my favorite—the wonderful "pictographic" renderings of fairy tales by Warja Honegger-Lavater, in which such classic tales as "Little Red Riding Hood" and "Snow White" are told through wordless panels of abstract geometric forms, necessarily requiring active interpretational effort on the part of the reader to reconstruct the tale. Students worked in their groups for most of the time, and at the end of the session each group shared with the whole class a few of their most significant findings.

For a generation of students whose principal contacts with books are sometimes limited to school texts and paperback editions (and/or e-books), these classes can be a thrilling initiation to the diverse forms and functions that books have had over time. In responding to the more open-ended questions (such as "What most struck you or impressed you about the books we looked at?" or "What did you look at during the free time in class?"), students often commented on the physical beauty or, in some cases, oddness of the books, and on how holding the books in their hands transported them to other times and places. With specific regard to the history of the fairy tale that we had discussed in the first part of the course, both sessions allowed students to observe firsthand the spectrum of ways that the fairy tale had been canonized, infantilized, hyperdidacticized, subverted, and in general continually reconceptualized over the course of barely 200 years, the time span represented by the books in this session.

Cinderella in a Dump Truck: Playing with Fairy Tales in the Elementary Classroom

In another course that I taught in the Women's, Gender, and Sexuality Studies Program, "Mirror, Mirror on the Wall: Gendered Images in the Literary Fairy Tale," students worked on two different creative assignments. The first was the culmination of a unit dedicated to fairy tales and/as children's literature that came after the midway point of the course, at the tail end of a historical survey of the European fairy tale. Students first read a selection of children's books along with writings on children's literature by Maria Tatar, Suzanne Barchers, and, above all, Gianni Rodari.

Rodari's *Grammar of Fantasy: An Introduction to the Art of Inventing Stories*, is a manual of active, creative pedagogical techniques and was the end-product of a seminar held in Reggio Emilia in 1972 on the valorization of creativity in preschool and K–8 schools. Its 44 short chapters describe activities designed to cultivate children's curiosity, imagination, and sense of play. Rodari's larger objective is to encourage children to have an active role in the construction of their own lives from the earliest age so that they can become, later in life, not only consumers but also active producers of culture. In his preface Rodari writes of the liberating potential of the creative word: "'Every possible use of the word for everyone' seems like a good motto, with a nice democratic sound. Not because we're all artists, but so that none of us will become a slave" (Rodari, *Grammatica*, 6). Chapter topics range from "The Word *Ciao*" to "Lenin's Grandfather" to "The Toy as Character" to "The Mathematics of Stories."

I assign most of the substantial section on fairy tales in the *Grammar of Fantasy* (Chapters 15–24 and 38). In these chapters Rodari underlines how fairy tales can so easily inspire liberating play, of which he gives various examples, such as asking students to retell a well-known fairy tale using a series of words or elements familiar to it along with one or two extraneous words ("Little Red Riding Hood in a Helicopter"), or presenting students with a reversal of the usual moral order of a tale and inviting them to re-create and extend the tale (in "Fairy Tales Reversed" Rodari posits a Cinderella who is "a good-for-nothing who drives her patient stepmother to despair and steals her virtuous stepsisters' boyfriends"). Lest these activities seem all too familiar today, we need to remember that Rodari's book dates to nearly 50 years ago!

Our work in class with the interactive and collaborative tale-telling and performance techniques described by Rodari served as preparation and inspiration for a one-hour activity that students designed and presented to small groups of second-graders at the local elementary school. Students submitted a proposal beforehand, and I also asked them to follow up our visit with a group reflection on how the second-graders reacted to the activity and what they themselves took away from the experience. One group wrote:

> We handed out various items: a broach, a gold and furry jacket, a jester's hat, a feather
> boa, chain, a necklace, a cowboy hat, and fairy wings. The characters that the children

came up with were fascinating: a magic swan, a girl with a pin that made every wish come true, a flying maiden, a power-hungry frog, a treasure-hunting bandit, the Greek hero Odysseus, and a powerful monster with laser eyes all around his head. It was interesting to see that the girls chose generally virtuous and good characters while the boys chose evil characters. . . . We had the kids draw pictures of their characters and to describe what it was that their powers were. They really got creative and transformed themselves into the characters that they had developed. We took all of their characters and the pictures they'd drawn and placed them in our own fairy tale, which they helped us to piece together.

The exercise was so fun and enlightening. I enjoy working with children because their imaginations seem to have no boundaries. This opportunity was something that I really took a lot away from. I want to make sure that I expose my children to fairy tales.

And another:

I have to say that going to the elementary school [and] seeing the second graders react to fairy tales was one of the most enjoyable experiences I've had in a long time. . . . Before going, our group had decided to use an exercise from Rodari's handbook, albeit a bit altered. . . . When we got to the school, we were presented with ten students, and decided that [one] group of five students would perform Little Red Riding Hood, while [another] group would perform a version of Cinderella. First, though, we asked each group to think of five words that the other group would have to incorporate into their telling of the respective tales. Some of the things the students came up with were imaginative and silly, like "snakes" and "dump truck," while others, like "cell phone," were more mainstream.

Our group ended up performing a version of Cinderella in which Cinderella was attacked by aliens, then taken to meet the King of Relish, and finally killed by being put into a dump truck filled with snakes. The other group's outcome was equally fantastic and imaginative. . . . What amazed me the most about doing this exercise was how creative and uninhibited the students were. They were also very good actors that took pride in their creations.

Cinderella Unplugged: Repitching Fairy Tales in Video Storytelling

The final project for the same Women's, Gender, and Sexuality Studies Program course was a 5–7-minute group video project. This was a time-intensive, scaffolded project that involved instructional classes, pitch and storyboard/shot list sessions, proposal and treatment worksheets, and final assessment forms. I gave students some basic guidelines on how to start thinking about their videos and on how to frame their approaches.

You'll be adapting or relating a fairy-tale type, paradigm, or set of motifs that you have encountered in the course to your own personal experience or to some aspect of modern life. The video may take a number of forms: theatrical/cinematographic dramatization of a fairy tale (in whatever temporal and spatial dimension you like); a dramatized telling (incorporating visual material); a musical rendition (e.g., MTV-type video); a dramatized interview with one or more characters from a tale; a narration in images, etc.! . . . Approaches to "retelling" the tale or reconfiguring the motifs you choose may involve reversals of fairy-tale patterns or character types we have seen, sequels or prequels to familiar tale types, shifts in narration, reframing the tale temporally and/or spatially, [and/or] reinterpreting or zooming in on single episodes, elements, or characters of a tale.

Overall, the results were impressive, and in a number of cases spectacular. In one video, *Behind the Happy Ending: Cinderella*, we encounter a Cinderella who, after marriage to a debauched and cynical prince (he calls the balls his father organizes "meat markets"), becomes miserable and "descend[s] into a whirlwind of drug and alcohol abuse," "searching desperately to fill the void that marred her ostensibly perfect life." After she cleans up at rehab, she decides to go to law school, where she meets and falls in love with the "noted prosecutor" Lisa White and refashions herself as a women's rights advocate. When he hears of this, the prince comments, "Uh, a what?" One of Cinderella's stepsisters replies, "A lesbian." Prince: "A lawyer." Stepsister: "Yes, that, but also a lesbian." Prince: "A lesbian lawyer." Stepsister: "Yes." Prince: "Wow! All right. Well, that's really interesting . . . I mean, I guess she's doing pretty well for herself. I mean, the lawyer part. I mean, the lesbian part, too. I don't . . . yeah, that's awesome!"

Another group also chose "Cinderella," adapting the formula of *E! True Hollywood Story* to showcase "a candid look at Princess Ella," "one of the nation's most notorious figureheads, the subject of ongoing scandal" due to "allegations of murder from slanderous reporter Giambattista Basile" (in the first literary version of "Cinderella" in Europe, Basile's heroine kills her first stepmother). Ella introduces herself while doing her nails in a luxurious bedroom suite: "Hello, subjects! So, there's been some kinky shit going around about me. But let me tell you, none of it's true! I swear, on the sacred soul of Donatella Versace! And if you don't believe me, then just shut up!" Her publicist is up next, with a sly reference to the process of fairy-tale canonization: "It's been an exhausting couple of weeks. That murder allegation came out of nowhere, and what with the monarchy's increasing unpopularity, my staff has been working overtime. By the end of the month we'll be publishing the official version of events, which refutes Basile's accusation. This will require me to euphemize much of Ella's character."

Another group, under the stage name "Princettes," created a rap video, "The Real Princess," to the music of Eminem's "The Real Slim Shady." It begins with the chorus

May I have your attention please?
May I have your attention please?
Will the real princess please stand up?
I repeat, will the real princess please stand up?
We're going to have a problem here.

The "problem" is that

There's probably a few of us waiting for our shiny prince
Tossing apples off of mountains and dropping hints
Or suffering silently because then she'll look cool
While her sisters walk all over her like some sort of fool
Little girl mopes and hopes for wedded bliss
Praying for her godmother to come and grant her wish
So that she can go to the ball and give the prince a kiss
Then he'll find her with a shoe cuz he's got foot fetish.

The piece ends with a series of choruses that ultimately complicate the notion of a "real princess."

So, will the real princess please stand up?
And put a ring-finger, empty or full on each hand up?
And be proud to be saving yourself and in control.
and one more time, loud as you can, how does it go?
I'm a princess, yeah I'm the real princess
All you other princesses are just dudes in dresses.
So won't the real princess please stand up,
Please stand up, please stand up? . . .
Ha ha, guess there's a princess in all of us.
Screw it, why don't we all stand up?

As its title suggests, another video, "Little Red Goes to Dartmouth," engages even more directly with the students' reality: in particular, rape culture on college campuses. The video's frame narrative features a red-cloaked young woman who talks about the dangers of "what happens to girls all the time, except nobody talks about it." She describes her own story of being raped after a fraternity party, ending her account with a citation of the moral that follows Charles Perrault's "Little Red Riding Hood" (the last lines of which read, "But watch out if you haven't learned that tame wolves / Are the most dangerous of all" [Perrault, 18]). *Plus ça change . . .* The rest of the video features interviews with students of differing viewpoints on questions that suggestively link the cultural narratives of fairy tales to societal attitudes, expectations, and behaviors of today; they are asked, for example, "Did you read fairy tales when you were younger?" "Were you aware of the sexual connotations in some fairy tales?" and "How do you think Little Red relates to gender dynamics at Dartmouth?"

In this course in particular, students became exceptionally adept not only at identifying the multiple ways in which fairy tales can underpin dominant ideologies and traditional patterns of socialization but also at appreciating how the elasticity and permeability of the genre allow for the rearrangement or deconstruction of these. The students' unequivocal enthusiasm about the opportunities the final project offered them for becoming tale-tellers themselves through collaborative and creative work also derived from a sense that they were intervening in larger conversations on topics directly pertinent to their own lives. Some final student comments exemplify this positive response and further underscore the potential of this project and the others that I have described here. One commented, "This is definitely one of the things that I am most proud of completing for a class at Dartmouth"; another, "The project was very important to all of us—not because of a grade, but because we spent so much time on it and liked our idea so much that we all became invested in making it the best it could be." At the end, the many hours the project required paid off. In the words of another student, "I had some doubts . . . about whether what we learned from the project was worth the hours of editing work, which had a fairly low learning-to-time ratio. Seeing the videos, however, changed my mind. They were all very polished, interesting products, and seeing them all together created a body of work that seemed larger than the sum of its parts—it said something about the way the class as a whole was thinking about fairy tales, and the very many ways in which fairy tales can be written, read, and rewritten."

APPENDIX A
Fairy-Tale Mad Libs: An Activity to Review Vocabulary and Parts of Speech

This exercise is done in Italian. I present here the English translation.

A MODERN CINDERELLA

My name is Ceni, and I live in a big house in _____ (*Italian city*) with my step-mother, _____ (*famous Italian woman*), and my two stepsisters, _____ and _____ (*two other women*). The old story that says that acquired families are _____ (*adjective*) is really stupid! _____, _____, and _____ (*names of the famous Italian woman and the other two women*) are totally awesome!! In fact, last weekend I went dancing with them. It was really _____ (*adjective*)!

To go dancing, I put on _____ (*article of clothing*) and _____ (*article of clothing*). _____, _____ (*names of the other two women*), and I met a really _____ (*adjective*) guy whose name is _____ (*famous Italian man*). He was _____ (*adjective*), too, since in his free time he plays _____ (*a sport*). He was wearing a _____ (*adjective*) _____ (*article of clothing*). I enjoyed talking with him for _____ (*number*) hours; we talked mostly about _____ (*type of animal*) and _____ (*interesting aspect of Italian culture*).

It was a _____ (*adjective*) evening, but I forgot my _____ (*article of clothing*) at the dance club. Fortunately, _____ (*same famous Italian man*) brought it to our house. First _____ (*name of first woman*) tried it on, but she didn't like its _____ (*adjective*) style. It seemed too _____ (*adjective*)! Then _____ (*name of second woman*) tried it on, and it was obvious that it wasn't hers, either. But then I tried it on, and it fit me _____ (*adverb*)! I thanked _____ (*same famous Italian man*), and I invited him to stay a little longer, for a snack of _____ (*food*). We have a lot in common! Who would have thought that a lost _____ (*same article of clothing*) could lead to a new friendship?

APPENDIX B

Italian Fairy Tales: "La Mammadraga"

[In this appendix I provide a translation of the version of the handout used in class, which is in Italian.]

Prepare the various sections as indicated below, and bring this handout to class.

Figure 1. Valentine Cameron Prinsep, *Cinderella* (1899).

PRE-READING ACTIVITIES (*REFLECT AT HOME*)

1. What has been your experience with fairy tales? When you were a child, did you read, listen to, or watch them? In what form (book, voice, movie)? When you were an adolescent? Now?
2. What are and were your favorite fairy tales, and why?
3. How can we define a fairy tale? What type of characters do fairy tales have, and what are typical fairy-tale plot elements?

THE FAIRY-TALE TRADITION IN ITALY (*READ*)

In Europe the literary fairy tale has its origins in the sixteenth century; the first written or authored fairy tales appear in Italy. (Before that fairy tales certainly existed but circulated orally.) Giovan Francesco Straparola is the author of *Le pia-cevoli notti* (The Pleasant Nights), published in 1550–1553, a book of 74 novellas that includes 13 fairy tales. The later collection by Giambattisa Basile, *Lo cunto de li cunti* (The Tale of Tales, 1634–1636), is made up entirely of fairy tales, of which there are 50. The fairy tales of Straparola and Basile are not for children but for an elite audience: people of letters and court and salon audiences. Much later, with the Brothers Grimm, who wrote *Kinder- und Hausmärchen* (Children's and Household Tales) in 1812–1857, the fairy tale becomes a children's genre. In 1956 Italo Calvino published *Fiabe italiane* (Italian Fairy Tales), the first "national" collection of Italian tales from every region of Italy.

An Italian Fairy Tale (*READ AT HOME*)

"La Mammadraga" (by Giuseppe Pitrè, *Fiabe novella e racconti popolari siciliani*) [distributed in photocopy]
N.B.: Below you'll find some of the new vocabulary from the tale. Use a dictionary to look up all the other words that you don't know. Pay attention to all the verbs in the passato remoto!
[Here I include a vocabulary list.]

Post-Reading (*IN CLASS*)

1. *Warm-up game* (in teams). Each team will have a packet of slips of paper; on each slip of paper is written an episode or moment of the tale. The first team to put all the slips in the right order wins and gets to read the tale out loud.
2. *Tale-telling.* Now we'll tell the tale again but without the text in front of you. One student begins the tale, and then, as we go around the room in round-robin fashion, each student continues the tale with one or two sentences. (Or alternatively, each student can repeat what has already been told, adding on his or her own several sentences.)

For Discussion (*PREPARE AT HOME*)

1. What most interested or surprised you about this tale?
2. Are you familiar with other tales of this type? What are they?
3. Does this tale have a moral or a "message," in your opinion? What is it? Can you imagine reading or telling this tale to a child?
4. Did you like this tale? Why/why not?

APPENDIX C

Italian 2 Final Project: Italian Fairy Tales and Regions

GUIDELINES AND SUGGESTIONS
What Are the Final Presentations?

- You will perform a *storytelling* of an Italian fairy tale and do a *poster presentation on the region* it comes from. For this project you will work in groups of three. Each presentation will be approximately 15–20 minutes long (storytelling and presentation combined) and in Italian. Your classmates will have 2 minutes or so to ask questions after each presentation.

Storytelling

- Each group will have three fairy tales to choose from. Once you have chosen the tale, read through it several times (with a dictionary!), until you understand it. Remember, there are a lot of verbs in the *passato remoto*! Then decide on how you'd like to retell the fairy tale: You may opt for a straight (re)telling, but you are also welcome to create your own version in verse, song, dramatized form, puppets, etc. You may divide the work, performing it in any way that you like. You should plan for your tale to last 10 minutes max.
- As you get to know your tale, try to reach a point where the characters and setting become as real to you as people and places you know. *Visualize your tale!* Imagine sounds, tastes, scents, colors. Only when you see the story vividly yourself can you make your audience see it! *Learn the story as a whole rather than in fragments.* Write a *basic working script* to hand in for correction (this will *not* be a script that you read from but a way for you to make sure that you have the basic words and grammar necessary to fashion your telling).
- Tell your tale without notes. This does not mean that you have to memorize your tale; on the contrary, it should not sound memorized but be told in your own words and delivered in a spontaneous style. Speak to your audience. *Other tips*: Your face and voice should be expressive and enhance the imagery of the story. Articulate clearly; don't speak too fast. Feel free to use movement and gestures, as well as props, and to elicit audience participation, inviting the class to join in with repetitive phrases, actions, questions, etc. Be animated!

Poster Presentation on Italian Regions

- The second part of the presentation can be on any aspect of the region your tale hails from (Piemonte, Toscana, Abruzzo, Sicilia, Campania/Puglia): geography and landscape, arts and literature, cuisine, historical events, famous people, etc. It's probably best to concentrate on just a few of these! Use several sources; the online regional tourist boards are a good place to start. And don't forget your textbook, which has a section on an Italian region after every chapter. You should plan for the presentation of your region to last 10 minutes max.

- You will first prepare and hand in (and then rewrite) a *working script* of your presentation (this will *not* be a script that you read from). Please differentiate between the text that will go on your poster and what you plan to say. Remember that no more than 25% of a poster should be text and that in any case you should not read from the poster but deliver the information in an oral, interactive way to your audience. This script will probably be no longer than a few pages. The group must submit one integral script, not separate pieces: This is a group project.

- When presenting, your goal is to be as *dynamic and interactive* as possible. The presentation must be without notes; you have your poster for support. Keep your Italian simple and well enunciated; the quality and comprehensibility of your presentation are important! Do not use structures that we haven't covered in class, as the rest of the class won't be able to understand you. Remember: The purpose of the presentations is not to impress me but to help your classmates explore an Italian region! They need to understand every single thing you're saying! Practicing the presentation out loud in a private "dress rehearsal" can also be useful.

- *Some notes on posters*: A poster is a graphic approach to sharing your ideas and interests with others and generating discussion. A poster must be visually engaging; limit your text, and use visuals (photos, drawings, charts) to tell your story. Make it clear to the viewer how to progressively view the poster. You can either number the individual parts or connect them through arrows. Type your text and use a minimum font of 18 points, using larger letters for the title. Be creative! The words in your presentation should be original. It goes without saying that everything you present must be in your own words, not taken verbatim from outside sources. Document all your sources on the back of your poster.

And finally:

- *Assessment* is based on your organization of the material into an informative, accessible, and interactive presentation. I'll also consider pronunciation, intonation, correct use of grammatical structures, delivery, and interaction with the audience.
- On presentation day, I will expect all of you to ask *questions* after each presentation. Each student should ask at least two questions in the course of the class.
- At the end of the presentation the class will nominate the best performance and the best poster, and there will be a prize for the group that wins!

TIMELINE

Week 7: Introduction
- Day 1: You choose a partner and region and communicate it to me. Your choice of fairy tales from your region will be on Canvas [course management system] in a Files folder titled "Fiabe e regioni."
- Day 3: Introduction to Italian fairy tales; discussion of Giuseppe Pitrè's "Mammadraga."
- Day 5: You choose fairy tale.

Week 8: Group Meetings and Beginning Work
- Days 1–5: Each group meets with me during office hours to discuss presentation.
- Day 2: Public storytelling performance by Gioia Timpanelli (7 p.m.).
- Day 3: Guest visitor and storyteller Gioia Timpanelli (discusses tales of performance and "La Mammadraga").
- Day 4: You hand in the first draft of your fairy-tale script and your cultural presentation (region) script. Distinguish between the text to be used on the poster itself and other material that you plan to include in your oral presentation of the poster.
- Day 5: I hand back your first draft with comments and requests for corrections.

Week 9: Revisions
- Day 1: You hand in a second draft (by e-mail).
- Day 3: I hand back your second draft.

Week 10: Presentations
- Days 1–2: Class presentations.

APPENDIX D

Special Collections Class 1: From Perrault to the Brothers Grimm—Changing Paradigms

Today we'll be looking at a series of editions of tales by Perrault and the Brothers Grimm. Although we haven't yet talked a lot about fairy-tale illustrations and how they may provide alternative interpretations of the texts in question, in today's session we will be considering, among other things, the differences in the way tales are illustrated. Also keep in mind that, as we move from the seventeenth century to the eighteenth and nineteenth centuries (i.e., from Perrault to the Grimms), the function of fairy tales changes radically: from court and salon entertainment to a didactic genre (often) aimed at young audiences.

Finally, a note on one of today's texts, which we haven't read yet (but will): "Bluebeard." This tale first appears in literary version in Perrault. It is the story of a woman who marries the mysterious Bluebeard, who she soon discovers has killed a series of previous wives for their curiosity, a fate that she too risks.

As you look at the various books on display for us today, reflect on the following questions, and take a few notes during class. (You'll also have the opportunity to revisit some of the materials we see in class, in the form of PDFs that I'll post on our course webpage.) Then hand in your answers to the questions at the next class (min. 300 words).

QUESTIONS

1. Look at the title page and the facing (or next page) illustrated frontispiece in the 1697 Perrault edition and in a number of the later Perrault editions (1777, 1785, and/or 1823 [English edition]). Although the illustrations are similar, there are also some significant differences. What do you see? What do you think about these differences?
2. What do you notice about the difference in size of some of the editions? Pay attention to the publication dates. How might we be able to explain some of these differences in size?
3. Are there other material "clues" that help you to determine the different functions that the different editions may have served?
4. Consider a number (two or three) of illustrations of one tale (from different editions) and when they were made. What do you notice about the differences and similarities among these illustrations? Do they offer different interpretations of the tales?

5. What most struck you or impressed you about the books we looked at? What new insights about the transmission and reception of fairy tales did they give you? What did you look at during the free time in class?

APPENDIX E
Special Collections Class 1: From Perrault to the Brothers Grimm—Changing Paradigms

LIST OF WORKS ON DISPLAY
1. Early Editions

Grimm, Jacob. *German Popular Stories*. London: C. Baldwyn, 1823 and 1826.

Perrault, Charles. *Contes des Fées*. Amsterdam: Jaques Desbordes, 1697.

Perrault, Charles. *Histoires du temps pass ou les contes de ma mere l'oye*. London and Brussels, [1785].

Perrault, Charles. *Histories, or, Tales of Past Times: Told by Mother Goose, with Morals*. Salisbury: Newbury, 1777.

2. Bluebeard

Perrault, Charles. *A New History of Blue Beard*. New Haven: Sidney's Press, 1805.

Perrault, Charles. *A New History of Blue Beard*. Albany, 1809.

Perrault, Charles. *A New History of Blue Beard*. Woodstock, VT: Watson, 1823.

3. Storybooks

Cruikshank, George. *Hop-o' My-Thumb and the Seven League Boots*. London: Bogue, 1853.

The Fairy Tales of the Brothers Grimm. London: Constable, 1909.

Grimm, Jacob. *The Prince Who Was Not Afraid: And Other Stories*. London: Collins' Clear Type Press, 1909.

The Sleeping Beauty and Other Fairy Tales. London: Hodder & Strouton, 1910.

The Story of Hans the Swapper. Boston: L. Prang, 1865.

APPENDIX F
Special Collections Books Class 2: Fairy-Tale Types

Today we'll be looking at many different fairy-tale materials, organized by tale type. After a brief introduction to the session, you will work in groups of four. Each group will look at four or five versions of one tale type (Sleeping Beauty, Little Red Riding Hood, Beauty and the Beast, etc.) and reflect on the differences and the similarities among the versions, in a way parallel to what you're in the process of doing for your third writing assignment and to what you'll do in your final project. (The tale type you're assigned at Rauner will not necessarily correspond to the tale type you're working on for your final project, nor will your groups necessarily be the same as those for the final project.) The various versions may present differences in the narrative (though not all do), different strategies of illustration, the adaptation of the tale type to a different genre (theater, song, art book, etc.), and so on. Approach your material creatively. For example, if one of the texts is a theatrical script, try reading some of it aloud! As we did in the first session, pay attention to the dates of publication of your materials, and ask yourself for whom your various texts may have been created.

In the last part of the class, each group will report back to the class on what they've found, using the questions below as well as any other information that you feel is significant.

As you look at your selection of books, reflect on the following questions. Then hand in your responses within one week (min. 300 words).

Please note that the books you see today will be on the "Comparative Literature cart" for approximately 10 days. Because any of these materials may be among the sources (= versions) you use for your final project, take advantage of their easy availability! There are also many other fairy-tale texts in the Rauner and Sherman (art history) libraries; explore the online catalog to find them!

QUESTIONS
1. Which of your versions (at least two) did you find most interesting, and why?
2. How are these versions different, in terms of publication date, size, genre, illustrations, and anything else you notice? Do the differences have something to do with the intended audience and function (make a hypothesis), in your opinion? To what else might you attribute these differences?

3. How do the different versions (at least two) offer different readings of the tales?

4. What is one significant thought or insight that you walked away with after this class in Rauner?

5. How did this activity help you prepare for the research for the final project?

APPENDIX G
Special Collections Class 2: Fairy-Tale Types

LIST OF WORKS ON DISPLAY
Group 1: Little Red Riding Hood

Crane, Walter. *Red Riding Hood's Picture Book*. London: John Lane, 1898.

Honegger-Lavater, Warja. *Imageries*. Paris: A. Maeght, 1965–1982.

Hyman, Trina Schart. *Little Red Riding Hood*. New York: Holiday House, 1983.

Little Red Riding Hood. Otley: J. S. Publishing and Stationery Co., ca. 1840.

Very, Lydia. *Red Riding Hood*. Boston: L. Prang, 1863.

Group 2: Bluebeard

Blue Beard and Puss in Boots. London: J. M. Dent, 1895.

King, Ronald. *Bluebeard's Castle*. Guildford: Circle Press, 1972.

Offenbach, Jaques. *Blue Beard Re-Paired: A Worn-Out Subject Done-Up Anew*. London: T. H. Lacy, 1866.

Perrault, Charles. *A New History of Blue Beard*. New Haven: Sidney's Press, 1805.

Perrault, Charles. *A New History of Blue Beard*. Woodstock, VT: Watson, 1823.

Group 3: Cinderella

Cinderella. London: George Routledge & Sons, 1873.

Cinderella; or The Little Glass Slipper. Providence: Cory, Marshall & Hammond, 1830.

Cruikshank, George. *Cinderella and the Glass Slipper*. London: David Bogue, 1854.

Honegger-Lavater, Warja. *Imageries*. Paris: A. Maeght, 1965–1982.

Moore, Marianne. *Puss in Boots, The Sleeping Beauty & Cinderella: A Retelling of Three Classic Fairy Tales Based on the French of Charles Perrault*. New York: Macmillan, 1963.

Group 4: Snow White

Heigh-Ho. New York: I. Berlin, 1938.

Honegger-Lavater, Warja. *Imageries*. Paris: A. Maeght, 1965–1982.

Sendak, Maurice. *The Juniper Tree, and Other Tales from Grimm*. New York: Farrar, Straus & Giroux, [1973].

Snow White. Boston: Little Brown, 1974.

Stories from Grimm. London, 1908.

Group 5: Tom Thumb

The Amusing History of Tom Thumb. Providence: Kendell & Stillwell, 1830.

The History of Tom Thumb. Otley: J. S. Publishing & Stationery Co., 1840.

Honegger-Lavater, Warja. *Imageries*. Paris: A. Maeght, 1965–1982.

Hop o' My Thumb. London: Blackie & Son, 1886.

Hop o' My Thumb and the Ogre. Boston: Degen, Estes & Co., 1860s.

Group 6: Sleeping Beauty

Honegger-Lavater, Warja. *Imageries*. Paris: A. Maeght, 1965–1982.

Mooney, George. *The Sleeping Beauty: An Entertainment for the Parlor*. New York: McLoughlin, 1883.

Planche, J. R. *An Old Fairy Tale Told Anew in Pictures*. London: G. Routledge, 1865.

The Sleeping Beauty. London: Raphael Tuck, 1917.

The Sleeping Beauty and Blue Beard. London: J. Lane, 1914.

BIBLIOGRAPHY

Calvino, Italo. *Fiabe italiane*, 2 vols. Turin: Einaudi, 1956.

Cook, Guy. *Language Play, Language Learning*. Oxford, UK: Oxford University Press, 2000.

Frank, Arthur. *Letting Stories Breathe: A Socio-Narratology*. Chicago: University of Chicago Press, 2010.

Perrault, Charles. "Little Red Riding Hood." In *The Classic Fairy Tales*, 2nd ed. Ed. Maria Tatar. New York: Norton, 2017. 16–18.

Pitrè, Giuseppe. "La Mammadraga." In *Fiabe, novelle e racconti popolari siciliani*, 4 vols. Ed. Jack Zipes. Trans. Bianca Lazzaro. Rome: Donzelli, 2013. 2: 132–39.

Rodari, Gianni. *Grammatica della fantasia: Introduzione all'arte di inventare storie*. Turin: Einaudi, 2001 [1973].

Rodari, Gianni. *The Grammar of Fantasy: An Introduction to the Art of Inventing Stories*. Trans. and introd. Jack Zipes. New York: Teachers & Writers Collaborative, 1996.

Taylor, Eric K. *Using Folktales*. Cambridge, UK: Cambridge University Press, 2000.

CHAPTER SIX

Fairy-Tale Courses

Sample Syllabi

The Fairy Tale

Graham Anderson

Course Description and Design

The following syllabus is based on a syllabus for a course I taught for several decades at the University of Kent from the 1980s onward, in what was a first-year foundation module for a comparative literary studies program but was accessible to other cohorts of students as well. The course was called "The Tale" and was actually a little fuller and broader than fairy tale as such. Here I have slimmed it down a little; the original syllabus contained sections on fable and biblical literature as well. The aim was to take students through a cross-section of narrative literature, familiar and less familiar, but also to allow an opportunity at the end for students to contribute short fairy tales of their own, reflecting their experience of the course. Students were given the option of retelling a familiar story with a significantly novel twist (in the manner of James Garner's *Politically Correct Fairy Tales*, for example) or forging a new tale in the manner of a familiar stylistic framework.

SYLLABUS

Week 1	*Introduction*
	Bring your own fairy tale and attempt a definition based on it.
	Try to construct a "minimalist" fairy tale. How few components do you need before a tale becomes recognizable as a fairy tale in the first place?
Week 2	*Some Fairy Tales in Homer's* Odyssey
	Polyphemus: one tale or two?
	Circe: Could Homer's version have been more economical? And *why* change men into swine in the first place?
Week 3	*Fairy-Tale Elements in Ovid's Metamorphoses*
	"A ragbag of almost-but-not-quite fairy tales." Do you agree?
	Why is metamorphosis so essential to Ovid's tales? Or is it?
Week 4	*Apuleius and The Golden Ass*
	Is the frame tale of the ass an effective container for the inset tales?
	Does Lucius deserve his fate?
Week 5	*Cupid and Psyche*
	"The first recognizable fairy tale." Do you agree?
	Allegory, myth, or "it doesn't matter what"? Discuss.
Week 6	*Straparola and Basile*
	"Violent, earthy, and vibrant." Do these authors create a convincing framework for the development of fairy tale?
	How important are differences of detail in the telling of fairy tales?
Week 7	*Perrault*
	"Fairy tales as we know and love them, and as they should be." Do you agree?
	"Perrault raises the key question of how far fairy tale should reflect society." Discuss.
Week 8	*The Grimms*
	"The nature of the Grimms' collections is inseparable from the question of nineteenth-century German cultural identity." How far is this the case?
	"The Grimms' collections raise the specter of cruelty in fairy tales in an extreme form." Discuss.
Week 9	*From Folk Tale to Art Tale (Andersen, Irving, Hawthorne, Wilde . . .)*
	How important is a writer's individuality in the reshaping of fairy tales?
	How important are pathos and emotion in the presentation of fairy tales?

Week 10	*Angela Carter, The Bloody Chamber*
	"Feminism in fairy tale is a distraction from narrative integrity." Do you agree?
	Compare and contrast any two presentations of the "Bluebeard" tale.
Week 11	*How Do We Account for the Success of Pullman, Dahl, or Rowling?*
	Is it still possible to break new ground in the development of fairy tale?
	How important is either the illustrator or the marketing process in the evolution of the successful fairy tale?
Week 12	*Now Write Your Own*
	Write your own version of a familiar fairy tale, importing a significant innovation in the handling of recognizable traditional elements.
	Write an original tale in the style of, for example, an Arabian Night or an Ovidian *Metamorphosis*.

Required Texts

The course relied heavily on handouts of the more recondite texts, such as Straparola and Basile, unfortunately in often antiquated and mannered out-of-copyright translations. But the choice of other materials has shown a dramatic improvement over the decades, with pride of place going to William Hansen's *Ariadne's Thread* (Cornell University Press, 2002) for ancient versions of international tales, supplemented by my *Fairytale in the Ancient World* (Routledge, 2000), in which I argue for more controversial examples and concentrate more narrowly on fairy tales as such. Marina Warner's *From the Beast to the Blonde* (Chatto & Windus, 1994) and *No Go the Bogeyman* (Chatto & Windus, 1998) present wide-ranging materials and deal with visual as well as literary examples over a wide chronological spectrum. Useful supporting resources include *The Oxford Companion to Fairy Tales* (edited by Jack Zipes; Oxford University Press, 2000) and A. Chaudhri and H. Ellis Davidson's *A Companion to the Fairy Tale* (D. S. Brewer, 2003).

General Evaluation and Comments

Apart from the creative storytelling options, students also have opportunities from time to time in seminars to try to re-create the process of transmitting tales, by giving two student versions of a short story and sending it around the class, in opposite directions, in the manner of Chinese Whispers or Telephone, to see how much it is altered by the time it has gone the rounds. The process exposes both tales to contamination with each other at the point where they pass and the listeners and retellers become confused. Various other games are devised from time to time, such as starting a tale with a single sentence, preferably embodying a "Once upon a time"–type cliché and having each student continue the tale with a further sentence, until each person in the seminar has had an opportunity to contribute. The exercise tends to invite comically absurd resolution as the last teller hastily winds up the tale ("with one mighty leap they lived happily ever after").

Results often depend on the composition of individual seminar groups, but there have been some distinctive contributions over the years. One resourceful take on "The Golden Ass" has the antihero Lucius begin and end as an ass, metamorphosing into a human in the middle and so inverting much of the material and calling for considerable adjustment en route. Another unexpected twist is to tell "Rumpelstiltskin" in the first person, raising the problem of how to deal with his splitting himself in two. The student narrator simply said, "I was so angry at the revelation of my name that I split myself in two" and then resumed "I have now recovered somewhat." Sometimes updating does not quite work: One reteller of "Cinderella" decided to update the prince into a celebrity pop star, which worked, but called him not Sid Vicious but Brad Dangerous, which somehow didn't! Opportunities are provided late in the course to test the analytical tools suggested by Aarne-Thompson on the one hand and Propp on the other; on the whole, students regard Propp with extreme suspicion, a tendency that may reflect the bias of the tutor!

One overarching theme that has interested me over the years is the basic level of civilization implicit in fairy tales. With few exceptions traditional fairy-tale heroes and heroines do not attend school or university, and there is much exploration of the often limited thought world as a result. In general, fairy tales do reflect an agrarian society rather than a hunter-gatherer culture, such as we find reflected in so many Aesopic fables. Humanities students seem slow to take this on board; a greater input of social science students might do better in picking this up.

Finally, two missed opportunities: I never devised a way to solicit the impressions of the pre–Harry Potter cohorts in comparison with those who have grown up taking this significant extension of fairy tale for granted. Nor have I managed to mobilize students to produce fairy tales with an academic background ("The Vice-Chancellor's New Clothes").

THE ORIGINS OF THE EUROPEAN FAIRY TALE

Jack Zipes

COURSE DESCRIPTION AND DESIGN

This course explores the origins of the literary fairy tale in Europe from 1550 to 1900 by analyzing the key texts by major writers in Italy, France, Germany, and England: Giovan Francesco Straparola, Giambattista Basile, Charles Perrault, Marie-Catherine d'Aulnoy, Charlotte-Rose de Caumont de La Force, Marie-Jeanne L'Héritier, Antoine Galland, Jeanne-Marie Leprince de Beaumont, Christoph Martin Wieland, the Brothers Grimm, Laura Gonzenbach, Andrew Lang, and Joseph Jacobs. An important focus is the relationship between the oral and literary tradition, and we explore how the interaction between oral and literary tales led to the formation of a specific literary genre. Consequently, I have designed and organized the course chronologically to demonstrate the gradual evolution of the fairy tale in different countries and how there were mutual influences. Using a sociohistorical approach, I relate the development of the literary genre to the civilizing process in each of the societies and countries where the fairy tale flourished. The most prominent and significant texts in each country have been chosen for analysis because they determined the course of the overall spread of the fairy tale in Europe.

Important questions are raised: Was the fairy tale a subversive form? What role did magic and the marvelous play in Europe? How did the Italian writers create a basis for the literary fairy tale through the novella? How did the French writers institutionalize the genre? Aside from studying the aesthetic and ideological meanings of the tales, connections are made to fairy-tale theater, ballet, opera, and drama in light of contemporary adaptations of the genre. Several fairy-tale films are shown to contrast the classical contexts with contemporary adaptations. Neglected Sicilian tales by the Swiss German collector Laura Gonzenbach are introduced to analyze the process of translation and transformation.

SYLLABUS

Week 1	*Introduction—Historical Background: Straparola, Basile, Perrault, d'Aulnoy, Grimm Brothers, Gonzenbach, Pitrè, Jacobs, and Lang*
	Jack Zipes, "Cross-Cultural Connections and the Contamination of the Classical Fairy Tale," in *The Great Fairy Tale Tradition*
	Zipes, "The Golden Key to Folk and Fairy Tales," in *The Golden Age of Folk and Fairy Tales*
	The Case of "Little Red Riding Hood"
	Charles Perrault, "Little Red Riding Hood"
	Brothers Grimm, "Little Red Cap"
	Film: David Kaplan, *Little Red Riding Hood*
	Alphonse Daudet, "The Romance of Little Red Riding Hood"
	Richard Henry Stoddard, "The Story of Little Red Riding Hood"
	Alfred Mills, "Ye True Hystorie of Little Red Riding Hood"
	Charles Marelle, "The True History of Little Golden Hood"
	Angela Carter, "The Company of Wolves"
	"Dangerous Wolves and Native Girls" section in *The Golden Age of Folk and Fairy Tales*
Week 2	*Straparola's Collection and Influence*
	Giovan Francesco Straparola, "Cassandrino the Thief"; Grimm, "The Master Thief"
	Straparola, "The Priest Scarpafico"; Grimm, "Little Farmer"
	Straparola, "The Pig King"; Marie-Catherine d'Aulnoy, "Prince Marcassin"; Henriette-Julie de Murat, "The Pig King"; Grimm, "Hans My Hedgehog"
	Straparola, "Pietro the Fool"; Giambattista Basile, "Peruonto"; d'Aulnoy, "The Dolphin"; Grimm, "Simple Hans"
	Straparola, "Constantino Fortunato"; Basile, "Cagliuso"; Perrault, "The Master Cat; or, Puss in Boots"
	Donald Beecher, "Introduction" to *The Pleasant Nights*

Week 3	*Basile's Collection and Influence*

Basile, *The Tale of Tales*, the frame tale

Basile, "The Ogre"; Grimm, "The Magic Table, the Golden Donkey, and the Club in the Sack"

Basile, "Vardiello"; Grimm, "Freddy and Katy"

Basile, "The Three Animal Kings"; Friedmund Von Arnim, "The Castle of the Golden Sun"; Grimm, "The Crystal Ball"

Basile, "The Seven Doves"; Grimm, "The Twelve Brothers"

Basile, "The Raven"; Grimm, "Faithful Johannes"

Basile, "Pride Punished"; Grimm, "King Thrushbeard"

Basile, "Ninnillo and Nennella"; Perrault, "Little Thumbling"; Grimm, "Hansel and Gretel"

Bendetto Croce, "The Fantastic Accomplishment of Giambattista Basile" in *The Pentamerone of Giambattista Basile*

Nancy Canepa, "Introduction" to *Giambattista Basile's The Tale of Tales, or Entertainment for Little Ones*

Week 4	*Charles Perrault and "Cinderella"*

Basile, "The Cat Cinderella"

Perrault, "Cinderella; or, The Glass Slipper"

d'Aulnoy, "Finette Cendron"

Joseph Jacobs, "Rushen Coatie" and "Cap O'Rushes"

Henri Pourrat, "Mary-in-the-Ashes"

"The Revenge and Reward of Neglected Daughters" section in *The Golden Age of Folk and Fairy Tales*

Lewis Seifert, "The Marvelous in Context," in *Fairy Tales, Sexuality, and Gender in France, 1690–1715: Nostalgic Utopias*

Week 5	*Charles Perrault and "Donkey Skin"*

Film: Jacques Demy, *Donkey Skin*

Straparola, "Tebaldo"

Basile, "The Bear"

Perrault, "Donkey Skin"

Grimm, "All Fur"

Laura Gonzenbach, "Betta Pilusa"

Jacobs, "Catskin"

	"Incestuous Fathers and Brothers" section in *The Golden Age of Folk and Fairy Tales*
	Patricia Hannon, "Corps cadavres: Heroes and Heroines in the Tales of Perrault," in *Fabulous Identities: Women's Fairy Tales in Seventeenth-Century France*
Week 6	**Mme. d'Aulnoy**
	D'Aulnoy, "The Island of Happiness"; "The Blue Bird"; "The Yellow Dwarf"; "The Green Serpent"; "The White Cat"
Week 7	**Mlle. L'Héritier**
	Marie-Jeanne L'Héritier, "The Discreet Princess; or, The Adventures of Finette"; Basile, "Sapia Liccarda"
	L'Héritier, "The Enchantments of Eloquence, or The Effects of Sweetness"; Basile, "The Three Fairies"; Perrault, "The Fairies"; Jeanne-Marie Leprince de Beaumont, "Aurore and Aimée"; Grimm, "Mother Holle"
	L'Héritier, "Ricdin-Ricdon"; Basile, "The Seven Pieces of Bacon Rind"; Grimm, "Rumpelstiltskin"; Grimm, "The Three Spinners"; Grimm, "The Lazy Spinner"; Gonzenbach, "Lignu di Scupa"
Week 8	**The Brothers Grimm**
	"The Frog King"; "The Companionship of the Cat and the Mouse"; "The Virgin Mary's Child"; "The Tale About the Boy Who Went Forth to Learn What Fear Was"; "The Wolf and the Seven Young Kids"; "The Three Snake Leaves"; "The White Snake"; "The Straw, the Coal, and the Bean"; "The Fisherman and His Wife"; "The Brave Little Tailor"; "The Bremen Town Musicians"; "Clever Else"; "The Tailor in Heaven"; "The Magic Table, the Golden Donkey, and the Club in the Sack"; "How Six Made Their Way in the World"; "The Wolf and the Man"; "The Goose Girl"; "Bearskin"; "Iron Hans"
	Siegfried Neumann, "The Brothers Grimm as Collectors and Editors of German Folktales," in *The Reception of Grimms' Fairy Tales: Responses, Reactions, Revisions* (ed. Donald Haase)
Week 9	**The Transformation of Fairy Tales in Germany**
	Johann Karl August Musäus, "Libussa" and "Melechsala"
	Christoph Martin Wieland, "The Philosopher's Stone"
	Johann Wolfgang von Goethe, "The Fairy Tale"
	Novalis, "Hyacinth and Roseblossom"
	Ludwig Tieck, "Eckbert the Blonde" and "The Runenberg"
	E. T. A. Hoffmann, "Little Zaches"

Week 10	*Luisa Gonzenbach, Giuseppe Pitrè, and Sicilian Folk- and Fairy Tales*
	Gonzenbach, "Sorfarina"; "The Green Bird"; "The Snake Who Bore Witness"; "The Sister of Muntifiuri"; "The Story About Ciccu"; "How St. Joseph Helped a Young Man Win the Daughter of a King"; "The Humiliated Princess"; "The Pig King"; "The Virgin Mary's Child"
Week 11	*Joseph Jacobs, Andrew Lang, and English Folktales*
	Jacobs, "Tom Tit Tot"; "How Jack Went to Seek His Fortune"; "Mr. Vinegar"; "Nix Nought Nothing"; "Jack and the Beanstalk"; "The Story of the Three Little Pigs"; "Jack and His Golden Snuff-Box"; "Jack the Giant-Killer"; "Molly Whuppie"; "Whittington and His Cat"; "Kate Crackernuts"; "The Ass, the Table, and the Stick"; "Black Bull of Norway"; "Tattercoats"
Week 12	*"Rapunzel"*
	Basile, "Petrosinella"
	Charlotte-Rose de La Force, "Persinette"
	Friedrich Schulz, "Rapunzel"
	Grimm, "Rapunzel"
	de La Force, "The Good Woman"
	Giovanni Fiorentino, "Dionigia and the King of England"
	Basile, "The Maiden Without Hands"
	Grimm, "The Maiden Without Hands"
	Gonzenbach, "Beautiful Angiola"
	"The Power of Love" section in *The Golden Age of Folk and Fairy Tales*
Week 13	*"Blue Beard"*
	Film: Catherine Breillat, *Barbe Bleue*
	Perrault, "Bluebeard"
	Grimm, "Fitcher's Bird"
	Grimm, "The Robber Bridegroom"
	Gonzenbach, "The Story About Oh My"
	Margaret Atwood, "Bluebeard's Egg"
	Carter, "The Bloody Chamber"
	"Bloodthirsty Husbands and Serial Killers" section in *The Golden Age of Folk and Fairy Tales*
Week 14	*"Beauty and the Beast"*
	Film: Jean Cocteau, *La Belle et la bête*

Apuleius, "Cupid and Psyche"

D'Aulnoy, "The Ram"

Jean-Paul Bignon, "Princess Zeineb and King Leopard"

Gabrielle-Suzanne Barbot de Villeneuve, "Beauty and the Beast"

Leprince de Beaumont, "Beauty and the Beast"

Grimm, "The Singing, Springing Lark"

Week 15	*"Sleeping Beauty"*

Basile, "Sun, Moon, and Talia"

Perrault, "Sleeping Beauty"

Grimm, "Brier Rose"

Straparola, "Cesarino, the Dragon Slayer"

Basile, "The Merchant"

Grimm, "The Two Brothers"

"The Fruitful Sleep" section in *The Golden Age of Folk and Fairy Tales*

Required Texts

Zipes, Jack, ed. *Beauty and the Beast and Other Classic French Fairy Tales*. New York: Signet, 1997.

———, ed. *The Golden Age of Folk and Fairy Tales: From the Brothers Grimm to Andrew Lang*. Indianapolis: Hackett, 2013.

———, ed. *The Great Fairy Tale Tradition*. New York: Norton, 2001.

Photocopied anthology of fairy tales, "Origins of the European Fairy Tale"

Assignments and Assessment

1. Class presentation (10 minutes) of an analytic approach to one of the fairy tales listed to initiate class discussion.
2. Each student will be expected to work on a collaborative project for a class presentation during the last two weeks of the semester.
3. Research paper (12–15 pages) on a fairy-tale project to be discussed and approved by professor. The research paper is due at the end of the semester.
4. Both the class presentations and the research paper are significant in this class because students learn to cooperate with one another, share ideas, and develop a final paper.

Fairy Tales in European Context

Linda Kraus Worley

Course Description and Design

Folktales and fairy tales entertain, but they also designate taboos, write out life scripts for ideal behaviors, and demonstrate the punishments for violating the collective and its prescribed social roles. In addition, tales pass on key cultural and social histories in metaphoric language. In the course "Fairy Tales in European Context" students examine a variety of classical and contemporary fairy and folktale texts from Germany and other European cultures and learn about—as well as critique—the primary approaches used to work with folklore materials and fairy-tale texts. Key issues, values, and anxieties of European (and U.S.) culture as they have evolved from the early modern period to the present are highlighted. Some of these issues are arranged marriages, infanticide, incest, economic struggles, the boundaries between the animal and human, gender roles, sexuality, and class antagonisms.

Several organizing principles guided my choices for the syllabus. The first weeks of the course are designed to acquaint students with some of the traditional theoretical tools used to read fairy tales. I thus use several well-known tales that readily lend themselves to these various critical approaches and include earlier versions of a particular tale to underscore the power (and limitations) of the various theories. Reading tales of the same tale type but from different eras and geographies helps students experience the interplay of core plot and motifs with changing sociocultural contexts. Once these core tools have been examined, the course is designed to focus on various themes as we continue discussing older tales. A third shift in the organization occurs when we begin to look at tales chronologically, beginning with nineteenth-century tales and continuing to the present. I do not see these shifts as ruptures in the course structure but rather as a way of building on the earlier approaches to the texts. An overriding goal is to help students understand the texts and, later in the course, experience how these earlier approaches and critiques can be challenged with new questions and through new media. I choose both well-known tales (to underscore how new insights can be gained by changing the questions asked of tales) and lesser-known tales (to expand the students' concepts of "fairy tales").

SYLLABUS

Week 1	Fundamentals: The Nature and Structure of Tales
Day 1	**Basic Concepts: Defining the Genre and the Origin of Tales** Brothers Grimm 200: "The Golden Key" Aarne-Thompson-Uther system: in-class investigation.
Day 2	**Basic Concepts: The Authors and Uses of Tales;** **the Formal Structure of Tales** Vladimir Propp, "Folklore and Literature" and "Morphology of the Folktale" excerpts Grimm, "Rumpelstiltskin," "The Three Spinners," and "The Lazy Spinner" Apply Propp's ideas to tales. Discussion: reading "Rumpelstiltskin"

Week 2	Social and Historical Interpretations
Day 1	**Ogres, Trolls, Cannibals, and Giants** Charles Perrault, "Little Thumbling," "Boots and the Troll," and "Hop o' My Thumb" Joseph Jacobs, "Molly Whuppie"; "Mutsmag," in *Grandfather Tales: American-English Folk Tales* (ed. Richard Chase)
Day 2	**Witches: Real Women and Fantasy** Grimm, "Hansel and Gretel" Eugen Weber, "Fairies and Hard Facts: The Reality of Folktales" Robert Darnton, "Peasants Tell Tales" Witches worksheet: How did real women and girls survive?

Week 3	*The Family Drama: Psychological Interpretations*
Day 1	**Freudian Interpretations**
	Grimm, "Hansel and Gretel"
	Bruno Bettelheim, "Hansel and Gretel" and "The Struggle for Meaning"
Day 2	**Mothers and Daughters**
	Giambattista Basile, "The Young Slave"; Grimm, "Snow White"; "Lasair Gheug"
	Sandra Gilbert and Susan Gubar, "Snow White and Her Wicked Stepmother"

Week 4	
Day 1	**Fathers/Masters and Sons**
	Giovan Francesco Straparola, "Maestro Lattantio and His Apprentice Dionigi"; Eustache Le Noble, "The Apprentice Magician"; Grimm, "The Thief and His Master"
	Disney, *The Master's Apprentice*—film shown in class
Day 2	**Jungian Interpretations: Stages of Development**
	Basile, "Sun, Moon, and Thalia"; Perrault, "Sleeping Beauty in the Wood"; Grimm, "Brier Rose"
	Grimm, "Iron Hans"
	Joseph Campbell, "The Monomyth: Prologue," excerpt from *Hero with a Thousand Faces*
	Jungian stages of growth applied to Grimms' "Iron Hans"; applying the heroic journey cycle to "Iron Hans"

Week 5	
Day 1	**Questioning the Heroic Quests**
	Grimm, "The Brave Little Tailor"; Jacobs, "Jack and the Beanstalk"; Appalachian Jack tales
Day 2	**Questioning the Heroic Quest: Animal Helpers and Fortune**
	Straparola, "Constantino Fortunato"; Basile, "Cagliuso"; Perrault, "The Master Cat"; Grimm, "Puss in Boots"
	Discussion: interplay of oral and literary traditions

Week 6	*Thematic Units*
Day 1	**Writers of the French Salon: Of Manners and Love**
	Marie-Catherine d'Aulnoy, "The White Cat"

	Beauties and Beasts: Jeanne-Marie Leprince de Beaumont, "Beauty and the Beast"; Peter Christian Asbjørnsen and Jørgen Moe, "East of the Sun and West of the Moon"
Day 2	Discussion of paper topics, how to write an outline

Week 7

Day 1	**The Power of Love**
	Basile, "Petrosinella"; Charlotte-Rose Caumont de La Force, "Persinette"; Grimm, "Rapunzel"
	Clips from Disney's *Rapunzel*
Day 2	**The Call of the Human**
	Straparola, "The Pig King"; d'Aulnoy, "The Wild Boar"; Grimm, "Hans, My Hedgehog" and "The Frog King"
	Lewis Seifert, "Animal-Human Hybridity in d'Aulnoy's 'Babiola' and 'Prince Wild Boar'" (excerpts)
	Moving a tale to film: Jim Henson's *Hans, My Hedgehog*

Week 8

Day 1	**The Inhuman Human**
	Perrault, "Bluebeard"; Grimm, "Fitcher's Bird" and "The Robber Bridegroom"; Jacobs, "Mr. Fox"
	Maria Tatar, "Bluebeard" and "Sex and Violence: The Hard Core of Fairy Tales"
Day 2	**Tales of Lucky Dummlings; Tales of Compassion and Self-Sacrifice**
	Grimm, "The Twelve Brothers," "Six Swans," "The Queen Bee," and "The Golden Goose"
	Return outline, discuss next steps in writing interpretive paper

Week 9

Day 1	**The Powerless and Abused**
	Straparola, "Tebaldo"; Perrault, "Donkey-Skin"; Grimm, "All Fur"
Day 2	**Virtue in Distress: The Abused Heroine**
	Basile, "Cat Cinderella"; Perrault, "Cinderella"; Grimm, "Cinderella"; Jacobs, "Catskin"
	Disney's *Cinderella*: end of film
	Writing workshop

Week 10

Day 1	**Biography of the Grimms and Typical Characteristics**
	Grimm, "The Story of a Boy Who Went Forth to Learn Fear"

Day 2	**Wildernesses: Of Wolves, Werewolves, and Girls—Rape, Sex, and Violence**
	"Story of Grandmother"; Perrault, "Little Red Riding Hood"; Grimm, "Little Red Cap"
	Reading illustrations: signifiers and signified
Week 11	*Thematic Units cont. (Day 1); Literary Tales of the Nineteenth Century (Day 2)*
Day 1	**Tales of Adults**
	Grimm, "The Magic Table, the Gold Donkey and the Club in the Sack" and "The Fisherman and His Wife"
Day 2	**Selkies and Other Mer-Creatures**
	Hans Christian Andersen, "The Little Mermaid"; Grimm, "The Swan Maiden"; "The Secret of Roan Innish," the "Dark One" segment
Week 12	
Day 1	**Characteristics of Traditional Folk Fairy Tales vs. Literary Tales**
	Andersen, "The Little Match Girl," "The Red Shoes," and "Ugly Duckling"
Day 2	Oscar Wilde, "The Selfish Giant," "The Happy Prince," and "The Nightingale and the Rose"
Week 13	*The Twentieth Century: The Dark? The Sentimental?*
Day 1	**The Uses and Abuses of Fairy Tales: Anti-Semitism, Racism, Nazis, and Fairy Tales**
	Grimm, "The Jew in the Thorns" and "The Bright Sun Brings It to Light"
Day 2	**Little Red Revisioned**
	Angela Carter, "The Company of Wolves"; Neil Jordan, *The Company of Wolves* (clip of wedding and final seduction scene); Roald Dahl, "Little Red Riding Hood and the Wolf" and "The Three Little Pigs"; Paul Patterson's musical interpretation of Dahl
Week 14	*Group Presentations on Revisionings in the Twenty-First Century*
Week 15	*Disney and His Films*
Day 1	**The Twenty-First Century: Fairy Tales for Children (for Girls?), Revised Tales for Adults, Disney and His Films**
	New media
Day 2	**Why Fairy Tales Stick**
	Jack Zipes, "What Makes a Repulsive Frog So Appealing: Memetics and Fairy Tales"
	Summary and review

Required Texts

Tatar, Maria, ed. *The Classic Fairy Tales*. New York: Norton, 1999. Zipes, Jack, ed. *The Great Fairy Tale Tradition: From Straparola and Basile to the Brothers Grimm*. New York: Norton, 2001. Other texts can be found on the course website.

Assignments and Assessment

1. Work in class (35%)
   A. Lecture sessions: attendance, one-minute papers: 10%
   B. Discussion sessions: contributions and mini-essays: 25%
2. Writing and speaking (30%)
   A. Analytic writing and peer editing: 20%

   Stages of paper: outline (5%); first draft edited by a peer (5%); final draft (10%). Students are asked to choose one of the interpretive tools modeled and critiqued in class and to apply this tool to one of a set of tales that we have not discussed in class (5–6 pages). Facts about the tale can be researched (with appropriate endnotes), but the interpretive analysis is to be original.

   B. Oral group report: 10%

   Each group of three students finds revisionings of fairy tales in contemporary culture. These modern versions can take the form of news stories, advertisements, cartoons, pictures, rumors, tabloid stories, celebrity issues and narratives, television shows, films, poetry, or fiction. Students focus on how the contemporary versions use or counteract the tale or tale type to which they refer as well as identify the values and presuppositions that underlie these contemporary artifacts. A short, 2–3-page written group summary is to be included.

An *alternative* to the group project can be an individual analytical paper of a tale not analyzed in class *or* a creative fairy tale that includes an explanation of how the tale uses the core structure and elements of fairy tales.

Of the various assignments, perhaps the most effective are the short essays students were assigned to write in response to questions designed to stimulate them to formulate and defend opinions during the weekly discussion sessions. These weekly assignments allowed students to apply the various theoretical approaches as well as engage directly with the tales.

3. Tests and exams (35%)
   A. Four tests (linked to Units 1–4): 20%
   B. Final examination (Unit 5 + comprehensive): 15%

General Evaluation and Comments

This format has proven to give the basic tools to the students early in the semester. After the first weeks, students critique the tools as well as use the tools as modified by culture-based interpretations (e.g., French salons, Nazi interpretations). Students are particularly engaged when critiquing Freudian approaches. The arrangement of the syllabus allows for new thematic units to be inserted as interests of the students and/or instructor change. Toward the end of the semester a chronological arrangement allows for a deeper understanding of the relationship of literary tales to their changing sociohistorical contexts. Students learn to read not only tales but also secondary literature. Many find scholarly discourse challenging, but they also seem to recognize that they have pushed themselves to new ways of knowing. The older and contemporary tales, in particular, generate a lot of student interest, because these tales are often radically different from their earlier views of tales, which were almost exclusively formed by their acquaintance with the Disney films or Disney spin-offs.

The Literary Fairy Tale

Nancy L. Canepa

Course Description and Design

"The Literary Fairy Tale" is an undergraduate course offered in the comparative literature program. The course surveys the development of the Western fairy tale, from the first literary collections in early modern Italy and France (Basile, Perrault), through the Brothers Grimm and the establishment of the field of folkloristics in the nineteenth century, to the innovative revisitation of fairy-tale subjects and motifs in the twentieth and twenty-first centuries. We discuss the defining characteristics of the genre, explore the role that a "marvelous" genre such as the fairy tale can have in interrogating everyday reality, and pay special attention to both the subversive potential of the fairy tale and the ways in which certain ideologies and narrative structures have been consolidated throughout the history of the Western fairy tale.

This course has no prerequisites, and I typically get an even mix of students from different class years and majors and with widely varying interests. I attempt to expose students to a range of primary and critical materials that give them a good idea of the history of the literary fairy tale as well as the critical questions that fairy-tale scholars have been posing over the past decades. I find that starting with a historical survey helps students to question their ideas about "classic" or "original" versions of tales (their terms), which for many of them go no further back in time than the Grimms' tales or even Disney films. The historical survey also revises the commonplace, for many students, that fairy tales are children's literature, by reviewing the various forms and functions that fairy tales have had through history as potent lenses through which to observe, reflect on, and critique society. At the same time, we review a number of the most common critical approaches to the fairy tale: structuralist, sociohistorical, psychoanalytic, feminist.

After studying the foundational texts of the European literary tradition, we move on to case studies of several of the best-known tale types. In each unit of this section students actively compare and contrast different versions of a tale, with an emphasis on modern and contemporary versions, in order to explore how the fairy tale has evolved and how the many voices—both literary and oral, authored and anonymous—that have contributed to the evolution of this narrative form have engaged in dialogue and discussion. We also have short units on fairy-tale films and fairy tales as children's literature and explore the fairy-tale resources of our special collections library. For their final project, students put their encounters with the fairy tale to dynamic use by collaboratively producing research on a tale type and by creating their own original versions of tales.

SYLLABUS

Week 1	
Day 1	**Introduction: Once Upon a Time . . .**
Day 2	**Telling Stories**
	Arthur Frank, from *Letting Stories Breathe*
	Neil Gaiman, "Instructions" (MT)
Day 3	**What Is a Fairy Tale?**
	Andrew Teverson, "Definitions"
	Maria Tatar, "Introduction" (MT)
	Max Lüthi, "The Fairy-Tale Hero" and "Abstract Style" (MT)
	Jack Zipes, "Spells of Enchantment: An Overview of the History of Fairy Tales"
	Selection of European tales: Giambattista Basile, "Petrosinella"; Charles Perrault, "The Sleeping Beauty in the Woods"; Brothers Grimm, "Cinderella" (MT)
Week 2	
Day 1	**The Ubiquitous Fairy Tale: Fairy Tales and the Contemporary Imaginary**
	Kate Bernheimer, ed., from *Mirror, Mirror on the Wall: Women Writers Explore Their Favorite Fairy Tales*, ix–xvi (Annotated Contents), xvii–xxiv (Introduction), and at least one tale of your choice
	Kate Bernheimer, ed. *Brothers and Beasts: An Anthology of Men on Fairy Tales*, ix–xv (Annotated Contents), xvii–xx (Foreword by Maria Tatar), and at least one tale of your choice

In class: Discussion of the role of fairy tales in your and others' formation, based on the tale(s) you chose, your own experience with fairy tales as children and young adults, and the presence of fairy tales and fairy-tale motifs in contemporary culture.

Day 2 **A Fairy-Tale Toolbox: Tale Types, Motifs, and Functions**

Hans-Jörg Uther, Antti Aarne, and Stith Thompson, from *The Types of International Folktales* (MT)

Vladimir Propp, "Folklore and Literature" (MT)

Vladimir Propp, from *Morphology of the Folktale* (MT)

Joseph Jacobs, "Jack and the Beanstalk"

Grimm, "Snow White" (MT)

[Optional: Hans-Jörg Uther, "Classifying Tales"]

Day 3 **Classifying Tales**

Small-group activity

Day 4 **From the Prehistory of Fairy Tales**

Apuleius, "Cupid and Psyche," from *The Golden Ass*

Anon., "The Story of King Shahrayar and Shahrazad, His Vizier's Daughter," from *The Arabian Nights*

Karen Rowe, "To Spin a Yarn: The Female Voice in Folklore and Fairy Tale" (MT)

[Optional: A. S. Byatt, "The Greatest Story Ever Told"]

Week 3

Day 1 **Early Italian Fairy Tales: Giovan Francesco Straparola and Giambattista Basile**

Giovan Francesco Straparola, "King Pig"

Basile, "Introduction to *The Tale of Tales*" and "End of the Tale of Tales," "The Tale of the Ogre," "The Old Woman Who Was Skinned," and "The Flea"

"Giovan Francesco Straparola," from *Greenwood Encyclopedia*

"Giambattista Basile," from *Greenwood Encyclopedia*

Day 2 Basile, "Cagliuso," "The Cockroach, the Mouse, and the Cricket," "Pretty as a Picture," and "Sun, Moon, and Talia"

Day 3 **Creative Tale-Telling**

Small-group activity

Day 4 **Early French Fairy Tales**

Perrault, "Introduction," "Little Thumbling" (MT), "The Fairies," "The Master Cat, or Puss in Boots," "Riquet with the Tuft"

Robert Darnton, "Peasants Tell Tales: The Meaning of Mother Goose" (MT)

[Optional: Jack Zipes, "The Rise of the French Fairy Tale and the Decline of France"]

Week 4

Day 1
Marie-Catherine d'Aulnoy, "The Ram"
Marie-Jeanne L'Héritier, "The Discreet Princess or The Adventures of Finette"
Catherine Bernard, "Riquet with the Tuft"
Anne Duggan, "Ideology and the Importance of Socio-Political and Gender Contexts"

Day 2
From Perrault to the Brothers Grimm: Changing Paradigms
Class meets at special collections library

Day 3
The Brothers Grimm
Grimm, "The Wolf and the Seven Young Kids," "Faithful Johannes," "Rapunzel," "The Six Swans," "The Bremen Town Musicians," "The Devil with the Three Golden Hairs," "The Queen Bee," and "The Three Feathers"
Zipes, "Once Upon a Time There Were Two Brothers Named Grimm"
Eugen Weber: "Fairies and Hard Facts: The Reality of Folktales"

Week 5

Day 1
Grimm, "Hansel and Gretel" (Tatar), "The Juniper Tree" (MT), "How Six Made Their Way in the World," "The Goose Girl," "Snow White and Rose Red," "Mother Trudy," "The Poor Boy in the Grave," and "How Some Children Played at Slaughtering"
Tatar, "Sex and Violence: The Hard Core of Fairy Tales" (MT)
Bruno Bettelheim, "The Struggle for Meaning" and "Hansel and Gretel" (MT)

Day 2
Hans Christian Andersen
"Introduction: Hans Christian Andersen" (MT)
Hans Christian Andersen, "The Little Mermaid," "The Little Match Girl," "The Red Shoes," and "The Emperor's New Clothes" (MT)

Day 3
Victorian Fairy Tales
George Macdonald, "The Light Princess"
Kenneth Grahame, "The Reluctant Dragon"
E. Nesbit, "Fortunatus Rex & Co."

Week 6

Day 1
Case Study 1: "Cinderella"
"Introduction: Cinderella" (MT)
Strabo, "Rhodopis" (MT)
"Yhe-hsien" (MT, pp. 146–48)
Basile, "The Cinderella Cat"
Perrault, "Cinderella, or the Glass Slipper"

Perrault, "Donkeyskin" (MT)

Jacobs, "Catskin" (MT)

Karen Rowe, "Feminism and Fairy Tales"

Day 2   Anne Sexton, "Cinderella"

Stacey Richter, "A Case of Emergency Room Procedure . . ." (KB)

Aimee Bender, "The Color Master" (KB)

Kelly Link, "Catskin" (KB)

Emma Donoghue, "The Tale of the Shoe"

Zipes, "Fairy-Tale Collisions, or the Explosion of a Genre"

Donald Haase, "Yours, Mine, or Ours?" (MT)

Day 3   **Case Study 2: "Beauty and the Beast"**

"Introduction: Beauty and the Beast" (MT)

Jeanne-Marie Leprince de Beaumont, "Beauty and the Beast" (MT)

Grimm, "The Frog King, or Iron Heinrich" (MT)

Grimm, "Hans My Hedgehog" (MT)

"The Swan Maiden" (MT)

Zipes, "What Makes a Repulsive Frog So Appealing"

Week 7	

Day 1   **Fairy-Tale Types**

Hands-on group work

Class meets at special collections library

Day 2   **Case Study 2: Beauty and the Beast (cont.)**

Angela Carter, "The Tiger's Bride" (MT)

Donoghue, "The Tale of the Rose"

Francesca Lia Block, "Psyche's Dark Night" (KB)

Day 3   **Case Study 3: "Bluebeard"**

Tatar, "Introduction" to "Bluebeard" (MT)

Perrault, "Blue Beard" (MT)

Grimm, "Fitcher's Bird" and "The Robber Bridegroom" (MT)

Jacobs, "Mr. Fox" (MT)

Day 4   Sylvia Townsend, "Bluebeard's Daughter"

Carter, "The Bloody Chamber"

Patrick Chamoiseau, "A Little Matter of Marriage"

Nalo Hopkinson, "The Glass Bottle Trick"

Week 8	
Day 1	**Revisioning the Fairy Tale as Film** Zipes, "Breaking the Disney Spell" (MT) Disney Studios, *Snow White and the Seven Dwarfs* (1937) Jean Cocteau, *La Belle et la bête* (1946) [Optional: Andy Tennant, *Ever After: A Cinderella Story* (1998)]
Day 2	**Case Study 4: "Snow White"** Tatar, "Introduction" to "Snow White" (MT) Grimm, "Snow White" (MT) Italo Calvino, "Bella Venezia" Sexton, "Snow White and the Seven Dwarfs" (MT) Sandra Gilbert and Susan Gubar, "Snow White and Her Wicked Step-mother" (MT)
Day 3	Robert Coover, "The Dead Queen" Gaiman, "Snow, Glass, Apples" (MT) Kim Addonizio, "Ever After" (KB)
Day 4	**Case Study 5: "Little Red Riding Hood"** Tatar, "Introduction" to "Little Red Riding Hood" (MT) "The Story of Grandmother" (MT) Perrault, "Little Red Riding Hood" (MT) Grimm, "Little Red Cap" (MT) Calvino, "The False Grandmother" (MT) Roald Dahl, "Little Red Riding Hood and the Wolf" (MT) Carter, "The Company of Wolves" Hopkinson, "Riding the Red"
Week 9	
Day 1	**Revisioning the Fairy Tale as Children's Literature 1: The Case of Maurice Sendak** Maurice Sendak, *Where the Wild Things Are* Maurice Sendak, *Dear Mili*
Day 2	**Revisioning the Fairy Tale as Children's Literature 2: Children's Books Today** Workshop/group activity with children's books
Days 3–4	Presentation of final projects (Prezi presentations or creative project)

Week 10	
Days 1–2	Presentation of final projects (cont.)
Day 3	**Happily Ever After?**
	Brothers Grimm, "The Golden Key"
	Walter Benjamin, "The Storyteller" (MT)
	[Optional: Zipes, "The Cultural Evolution of Storytelling and Fairy Tales: Human Communication and Memetics"]

Required Texts

Bernheimer, Kate, ed. *My Mother She Killed Me, My Father He Ate Me: Forty New Fairy Tales.* New York: Penguin, 2010. [KB]

Tatar, Maria, ed. *The Classic Fairy Tales*, 2nd ed. New York: Norton, 2016. [MT]

All other course readings are available electronically on the course management site.

Assignments and Assessment

1. Class participation: 15%
2. Short writing exercises: 15%

   These exercises are in the form of worksheets, study questions, participation in the course discussion board, in-class writing exercises, and mini-quizzes.
3. Writing assignments: 35%

   The first essay is an informal personal reflection on the role that fairy tales have had and do have in students' lives; the second essay is a reflection on and application of one of the critical approaches to fairy tales covered in class; and the third essay is a comparative reading of several versions of a tale type.
4. Final projects: 35%

   Final group projects are composed of a group Prezi presentation or a group creative project (students' choice), and an individual paper. Each group of three or four students chooses one tale type ("Jack in the Beanstalk," "Sleeping Beauty," etc.); groups conduct research on the tale type and collect a variety of different versions of the tale type, old and new, textual as well as in other media. Intermediate assignments involve various worksheets, an annotated bibliography, and a longer response to a critical article. The final presentation is based on analysis of the tale type, research on its versions, references to critical literature, and reflection on the significance and importance of the tale type. Those who opt for a Prezi showcase their research in a

15-minute presentation, with graded Q & A afterward; creative projects are presented in the same time frame and include an introduction in which students explain how their research and original analysis informed their creative choices (past creative projects have included videos, play scripts, handmade books, paintings, and puppet shows) as well as Q & A. All students must also complete a final 4–5-page paper: for the Prezi groups, either an original tale or a research paper that extends their Prezis; for the creative groups, a research paper (an original tale is optional). All students can receive extra credit by completing two individual components.

General Evaluation and Comments

This course generally enrolls 40–45 students, and the biggest challenge I have is balancing a lecture-style format with discussion (which I try to do during every class). During the last offering I had teaching assistants, and we often split the group into three sections for smaller discussions—either for part of a class, or several times for the whole class period, in this case usually for a specific activity. We also spend several classes at the special collections library, again working in small groups and with specific tasks (see my "And They All Learned Happily Ever After," in Chapter 5).

Students have their most sustained opportunity for small-group work in the final projects, which are generally considered fun for presenters and audiences but which also allow students to put to work the critical and research skills that they have been working on all term. Finally, students appreciate the variety of units, approaches, activities, appeals to different learning styles, and choice of different options for many of the assignments; they feel that there is something for everyone. The final projects, in particular, are a moment of validation for students, because they become active fairy-tale scholars (and/or creators) themselves, share in other students' scholarly and artistic discoveries, and through their presentations and contribution of feedback to others' presentations join in a more public conversation about fairy tales.

French and Italian Fairy Tales

Suzanne Magnanini

Course Description and Design

In the course "French and Italian Fairy Tales" we study Italian and French fairy tales written between 1550 and 1750, including early versions of "Cinderella," "Sleeping Beauty," and "Puss in Boots." We focus on the ways in which a single tale type is adapted and thus altered as it moves across time, space, languages, and cultures. Our goal is to map the relationships linking early modern Italian and French tales to each other and to the contemporary fairy tales we know best today in order to better understand the rich history and exceptional malleability of the literary fairy tale. Students try their hand at adaptation by writing original fairy tales and collaborate with classmates to create a web or map uniting multiple versions of a single tale type.

Two primary objectives shaped the design of this course. First, I sought to create a class that reflected a current critical trend in the field of fairy-tale scholarship that uses the metaphor of webs or maps to emphasize the interconnectedness of tales across national boundaries. Second, I wanted the course to be a first-year seminar. At the University of Colorado, these interactive seminars are limited to 19 students and aim to introduce students to both academic resources (the research library, special collections, digital tools) and academic practices (different types of academic writing, group projects, scholarly presentations). With these criteria in mind, I organized the course by tale types and focused on two national traditions, French and Italian, requiring students, however, to move beyond these two traditions as they collect and analyze additional versions of a tale type. Admittedly, the choice of national traditions was also influenced by my own training and my home department (French and Italian). The secondary readings, particularly those by Marina Warner and Cristina Bacchilega, provide models of fairy-tale maps or webs that students are asked to create as a final project.

Syllabus

Week 1	*Mapping Fairy Tales: Venice*
Day 1	**Introduction to Course/Review of Syllabus: What Is a Fairy Tale?**
Day 2	**Framing Fairy Tales: Framing Narratives, Riddles, Eclogues, Morals**
	Giovanni Boccaccio, *Decameron*, frame tale, 1–37
	Selection of Giovan Francesco Straparola's riddles (Straparola, *The Pleasant Nights*)
	Giambattista Basile's first eclogue (*The Tale of Tales*, 126–39)
	Charles Perrault's morals (selections)
Day 3	**Straparola's Venice**
	Dedicatory letters to Volumes 1 and 2, frame tale, *The Pleasant Nights*
	Andrea Calmo, "Letter to Signora Frondosa," in *Fairy Tales Framed* (ed. Ruth Bottigheimer), 47–53
Week 2	*Mapping Fairy Tales: Naples and Paris*
Day 1	**Basile's Naples and Court Culture**
	Baldassare Castiglione, *The Book of the Courtier*, bk. 1, ch. 26
	Girolamo Bargagli, excerpt from *The Dialogue on Games*, in *Fairy Tales Framed*, 55–60
Day 2	**Ancients and Moderns in Seventeenth-Century Paris**
	Henriette-Julie de Murat, "To Modern Fairies," 125–30
Week 3	*"Puss in Boots"*
Day 1	**Fairy-Tale Webs: Introducing "Puss in Boots"**
	Cristina Bacchilega, *Fairy Tales Transformed*, 1–30
	Straparola, "Costantino Fortunato," in GFTT, 390–93
Day 2	**Adaptations**
	Linda Hutcheon, *A Theory of Adaptation*, 1–32
	Basile, "Cagliuso," in GFTT, 394–97
Day 3	**French Cats**
	Perrault, "The Master Cat, or Puss in Boots," in GFTT, 397–400
	Marie-Catherine d'Aulnoy, "The White Cat," *Wonder Tales*, 19–63

Week 4	*"Puss in Boots" (cont.)*
Day 1	**Four Cats: Comparing Our Versions, Finding Scholarly Articles**
	Elizabeth Harries, "Fairy Tale About Fairy Tales," 19–45
Day 2	**Contemporary Cats**
	Angela Carter, "Puss in Boots"
	Film: Chris Miller, *Puss in Boots* (2011)
Day 3	**Mapping Our Versions**
	Marina Warner, *Once Upon a Time: A Short History of Fairy Tale*, xiii–xxiv
	Suzanne Magnanini, "Spinning Fairy-Tale Webs in the Undergraduate Classroom"
Week 5	*Group Formation/Special Collections Trip*
Day 1	*Group formation/work: Collecting modern versions of your tale type;*
	using online sources
Day 2	*Visit to library Special Collections to study versions of your tale type*
Day 3	*Visit to library Special Collections to study versions of your tale type*
Week 6	*"Cinderella"*
Day 1	**"Cinderella Assassin" and "The Glass Slipper"**
	Basile, "The Cinderella Cat," in GFTT, 445–49
	Perrault, "Cinderella or the Glass Slipper," in GFTT, 450–53
Day 2	**A Woman's Take**
	d'Aulnoy, "Finette Cendron," in GFTT, 454–67
Day 3	*Discussion of modern and other versions by "Cinderella" group*
Week 7	*Fairies and Their Spells*
Day 1	**Three Fairies**
	Straparola, "The Pig King," in GFTT, 51–56
	Basile, "The Three Fairies," in GFTT, 544–49
Day 2	**French Fairies**
	Marie-Jeanne L'Héritier, "The Enchantments of Eloquence," in GFTT, 550–63
	Perrault, "The Fairies," in GFTT, 564–66
Day 3	*Discussion of modern and other versions by Fairies group*
Week 8	*Dragon Slayers*
Day 1	**The Lone Slayer**
	Straparola, "Cesarino the Dragon Slayer," in GFTT, 361–65
	Basile, "The Merchant," in GFTT, 366–73

Day 2	**Teamwork**
	Straparola, "The Three Brothers," in GFTT, 337–38
	Basile, "The Five Sons," in GFTT, 339–42
Day 3	*Discussion of modern and other versions by Dragon-slayer group*

Week 9	***"Sleeping Beauty"***
Day 1	**Birthing Beauties**
	Basile, "Sun, Moon, and Talia," in GFTT, 685–87
Day 2	**Angry Fairies and a Fitful Sleep**
	Perrault, "Sleeping Beauty," in GFTT, 688–95
	Grimm, "Brier Rose," in GFTT, 696–98
Day 3	*Discussion of modern and other versions by "Sleeping Beauty" group*

Week 10	***Fools and Their Wishes***
Day 1	**Fishes and Wishes**
	Straparola, "Pietro the Fool," in GFTT, 101–5
	d'Aulnoy, "The Dolphin," in GFTT, 113–35
Day 2	**Dumb and Dumber**
	Basile, "Peruonto," in GFTT, 106–12
	Basile, "Vardiello," in GFTT, 435–38
	Basile, "The Ogre," in GFTT, 421–26
Day 3	*Discussion of modern and other versions by Fool group*

Week 11	***Tales of Incest and Abuse***
Day 1	**Incestuous Fathers**
	Basile, "The Bear," in GFTT, 33–37
	Perrault, "Donkey-Skin," in GFTT, 38–46
Day 2	**Abusive Stepmothers**
	Straparola, "Biancabella and the Snake," in GFTT, 406–14
	Basile, "The Maiden Without Hands," in GFTT, 512–18
Day 3	*Group discussion about modern and other versions*

Week 12	***"Beauty and the Beast"***
Day 1	**Beastly Bridegrooms**
	Straparola, "The Pig King," in GFTT, 51–56
	Murat, "The Pig King," in GFTT, 82–96
	Moderata Fonte, "Liocorno," in *The Worth of Women*, 161–65

Day 2	**Virtuous Beauties**
	Jeanne-Marie Leprince de Beaumont, "Beauty and the Beast," 805–15
	Jean-Paul Bignon, "Princess Zeineb and King Leopard," 800–805
Day 3	*"Beauty and the Beast" group's discussion of modern and other versions*
Week 13	***What Purpose Do Tales Serve?***
	Or, Why Tell Fairy Tales?
Day 1	Arthur W. Frank, *Letting Stories Breathe*, 20–44
Days 2 and 3	*Group work*
Week 14	*Presentations*
Week 15	*Presentations*

Required Texts

Zipes, Jack, ed. and trans. *The Great Fairy Tale Tradition: From Straparola and Basile to the Brothers Grimm*. New York: Norton, 2001. [GFTT]

Assignments and Assessment

1. First original fairy tale: 5%

   For this assignment, you will write a story that your classmates and I will easily recognize as a fairy tale. Suggested length: 3–4 pages.

2. Quizzes: 5%

3. Midterm exam: 15%

4. Scholarly article response: 20%

   A. Find a scholarly article that explores your group's tale type.

   B. Carefully read (and reread) the article.

   C. Write a 3–4-page response paper in which you: (1) concisely and clearly summarize the author's argument; (2) evaluate the scholar's argument; (3) reflect on how this argument shapes your group's fairy-tale web for your tale type.

5. Essay comparing two early modern tales: 20%

   For this essay, you will carry out a close reading of two early modern tales that belong to your group's tale type. How do the two versions differ? How does each author adapt, alter, and make suitable these tale types for themselves and their readers? What is the significance of (or how do you interpret) these differences? Do the two tales address the same themes or illustrate similar morals? Suggested length: 4–5 pages.

6. Analysis of modern version: 20%

7. Second original fairy tale: 5%

    For this assignment you will write an original fairy tale based on your group's chosen tale type. What motifs or actions must you include in order to make it recognizable as belonging to your tale type? I expect that, like the tales of the Italian and French authors we have read to date, your tale will reflect the cultural milieu in which it is produced; you may decide to use your fairy tale to express your political views, to criticize societal norms and expectations, or to offer your readers escapist fantasies. You may also choose to modernize the literary style of one of these authors. Please provide a brief preface to your tale that explains the tale type you are using and highlights the important motifs and features of your tale. Suggested length: 4–5 pages.

8. Final group presentation: 10%

    For the final group presentation you will create a map/web/network (in Prezi, Mindomo, or on an old-fashioned poster) that includes the assignments listed in items 1–7, our class readings, other versions you have found and/or analyzed, and scholarly articles related to your group's tale type. You cannot present every part of the map but will be expected to point out the most interesting points and relationships. Each member of the group should present one point or set of relationships on the map. Questions to consider: What version of this tale type do people tend to know today? Has one early modern version of the tale become dominant in contemporary culture? Why? Have contemporary fairy-tale authors avoided your tale type? Why? Has your tale type been represented equally in literature and film? Did you find any outlier or radically different versions of your tale type? When your fellow group members wrote their original versions of this tale type, did their versions resemble an early modern version or a dominant contemporary version? Neither? Remember to leave time for questions.

General Evaluation and Comments

The structure of the course and the required assignments reflect my attempt to translate recent theorizing of the history of the fairy-tale genre in terms of webs and maps into pedagogical practice. I have not yet had the opportunity to teach this course but imagine it as best taught as a seminar or midsized course (35–40 students) rather than a large lecture because of the oversight necessary for the group project and the requirement of group presentations.

Cultural Intersections of France and Italy

Allison Stedman

Course Description and Design

Taught in English, the course "Cultural Intersections of France and Italy" is an introduction to the intersections of French and Italian literary production from the Middle Ages to the end of the nineteenth century. Designed as a general survey, this course focuses on how French and Italian literature engage with similar cultural phenomena at different moments in their respective histories. For this reason, students study the literary evolution of France and Italy while simultaneously familiarizing themselves with the historical contexts in which these and related artistic movements developed. By the end of the course, students should be able to see how literature engages with the cultural context that produced it, both mirroring this context and acting as a powerful agent of cultural change.

SYLLABUS

Week 1	**Introduction; Courtly Love: France**
Day 1	Introduction
Day 2	Roger Price, *A Concise History of France*, 13–23, 30–48
	Marie de France: *Lais*; Prologue, "Lanval" (to p. 76)
Week 2	**Courtly Love: France (cont.)**
Day 1	Marie de France: "Lanval" (76–end)
	Visual art: The Lady of the Unicorn tapestries
Week 3	**Courtly Love: Italy**
Day 1	Christopher Duggan, *A Concise History of Italy*, 31–46
	The Hundred Old Tales, Proem, LXII, LXIII
Day 2	*The Hundred Old Tales*, LXIV, LXV
	Visual art: Giotto
Week 4	**Humanism in Italy**
Day 1	*A Concise History of Italy*, 46–59
	Visual art: Botticelli
Day 2	Giovanni Boccaccio, *The Decameron*, 4th day, 1st story
Week 5	**Humanism in Italy; Humanism in France**
Day 1	Boccaccio, *The Decameron*, 4th day, 2nd story
Day 2	*A Concise History of France*, 54–64
	Marguerite de Navarre, *The Heptameron*, Story 10
	Visual art: The Fontainebleau School
Week 6	**Humanism in France (cont.)**
Day 1	Marguerite de Navarre, *The Heptameron*, Story 10
Week 7	**The Civilizing Process: Italy**
Day 1	Exam I
Day 2	*A Concise History of Italy*, 61–75
	Giambattista Basile, "The Dove," 184–87
	Visual art: Gaulli, Pozzo
Week 8	**The Civilizing Process: Italy (cont.); The Civilizing Process: France**
Day 1	Basile, "The Dove," 187–94
Day 2	*A Concise History of France*, 64–75

	Marie-Catherine d'Aulnoy, "The Bee and the Orange Tree" (intro)
	Art: Cotelle
Week 9	**The Civilizing Process: France (cont.)**
Day 1	d'Aulnoy, "The Bee and the Orange Tree," 415–26
Day 2	d'Aulnoy, "The Bee and the Orange Tree," 426–37
Week 10	**The French Revolution: France**
Day 1	*A Concise History of France*, 75–95
	Visual art: David
Day 2	Isabelle de Charrière, *Letters of Mistress Henley*, 3–18
Week 11	**The French Revolution: France (cont.); The French Revolution: Italy**
Day 1	Charrière, *Letters of Mistress Henley*, 18–42
	A Concise History of Italy, 75–86, 87–116
	Ugo Foscolo, *Last Letters of Jacopo Ortiz* (Introduction)
Day 2	Foscolo, *Last Letters of Jacopo Ortiz*, 1–39
Week 12	**The French Revolution: Italy (cont.)**
Day 1	Foscolo, *Last Letters of Jacopo Ortiz*, 39–end
Day 2	Exam II
Week 13	**Romanticism in Art and Music; The Industrial Revolution: Italy**
Day 1	*A Concise History of Italy*, 143–70
	Antonio Fogazzaro, "An Idea of Hermes Torranza," 106–23
Day 2	Fogazzaro, "An Idea of Hermes Torranza," 123–47
	Visual art: Fontanesi
Week 14	**The Industrial Revolution: France**
Day 1	*A Concise History of France*, 97–98, 165–240
	Guy de Maupassant, "The Horla," 1–10
Day 2	Maupassant, "The Horla," 10–35
	Visual art: the Impressionists

Required Texts

Charrière, Isabelle de. *Letters of Mistress Henley Published by Her Friend*. New York: MLA, 1993.

Duggan, Christopher. *A Concise History of Italy*. Cambridge, UK: Cambridge University Press, 1994.

Price, Roger. *A Concise History of France*. Cambridge, UK: Cambridge University Press, 2005.

Coursepack

General Evaluation and Comments

Organizing the syllabus chronologically and with a parallel structure enables effective comparisons to be made between texts on a number of levels. Students can compare texts from different time periods in the same literary tradition to better understand how a particular concept has evolved over time. They can also compare texts from different literary traditions within the same time period to understand how the expression of a given concept varies depending on its cultural origin. This kind of work is particularly effective when the texts in question are of the same literary genre because it eliminates yet another variable of difference, allowing students to focus on the cultural nuances that come forth in the literary production and make France and Italy unique. I have found that students learn best when texts are close-read and analyzed in a comparative framework.

This class is taught in a large lecture setting, and exams provide the primary mode of evaluation. However, to ensure that students experience the same kind of intimate contact with a text that usually comes from writing papers and from discussing and analyzing quotes in a seminar setting, I assign short literature readings and spread them out over at least two classes. We spend the first class familiarizing ourselves with the historical period, the cultural phenomenon we are going to consider, the biography of the author, and the first few pages of the text. We spend the second class on the text itself, mapping plot sequences, analyzing quotes, and comparing these findings to the cultural and historical phenomena we have studied either in a previous class or in literature readings from other time periods.

To encourage students to keep up with the readings, I provide discussion questions in advance by means of Canvas. I also solicit virtual homework participation by having students answer one discussion question per course meeting on our blog. Blog entries must be submitted at least four hours before class begins, and I do my best to incorporate as many responses as possible into the lecture I have already prepared. There are at least three benefits to the blog submission requirement. First, students are apt to put more thought into their answers when they know that their responses are visible to their peers. Second, the four-hour submission deadline encourages them to complete their homework early. Third, a blog can be used to solicit class participation by calling on different students and asking them to discuss their entries with the class, a technique that can also help the instructor to learn people's names. Since blog entries can be easily copied, I avoid plot-summary questions, asking students instead to come up with original solutions to problems posed by the text.

Conversations Classiques

Faith E. Beasley

Course Description and Design

In today's world we are inundated with texts, voices, images, and real and virtual networks. How can one distinguish between the information and narratives that can benefit us and those that exist only to incite or elicit emotional responses or mislead us? In this course we return to the world of seventeenth-century France to examine how knowledge was created and disseminated. We see that, just as is the case today, social networking played an important role in the creation of texts and in the construction of knowledge. Conversation had an unprecedented place and played a unique role in French society during this period. We examine the different threads that constitute this social, literary, and intellectual conversation: books, but also letters, essays, newspapers, plays, and the institutions where conversation reigned supreme, namely, the academies and the salons. By examining how classical France was created and by whom, we become more attuned to the ways ideas circulate today and learn to interrogate how knowledge is created, by whom, and to what ends.

Syllabus

Week 1	*History of Conversation in France*
	Introduction: What is conversation? What was the social fabric of seventeenth-century France, and what was the role of conversation in this society? How was knowledge created and transmitted? What were the various communities of readers/conversants/intellectuals?
	Readings: Germaine de Staël, Nicolas Dew, Alain Viala, Joan DeJean, Roger Chartier, Norbert Elias.
Week 2	*Salons: A French Phenomenon*
	What is French "taste"? The relationship between the worldly public and the academies. The development of the novel and its inscription of this worldly public. Published conversations.
	Readings: Erica Harth; Madeleine de Scudéry, *Le Grand Cyrus*; la carte de Tendre; Scudéry, *Conversations*; Sapho à Erinne.
Week 3	*The Public and Literary Creation*
	Reading of Pierre Corneille's *Le Cid* and the quarrel that followed its production. Emphasis on the role of the worldly public in the debate. How the values of this public influenced the creation of the text and provoked the quarrel.
Week 4	*The Voice of Comedy*
	Plays and other works were often read aloud in the salons before being produced on stage. Students read Molière's *Le Misanthrope* in class together, re-creating the salon experience, to understand how one perceives a text differently when one encounters it in a salon versus in a theater.
Week 5	*Conversations and Narrative*
	Reading of Madame de Lafayette's novel *Zaïde*. Emphasis on the theme of conversation and communication in this text. This novel interrogates the role that language plays in the construction and transmission of knowledge, a theme that dominated intellectual discussions of the mid- to late seventeenth century.
Week 6	*Daring to Speak*
	A reading of the quarrel that surrounded Lafayette's novel *La Princesse de Clèves*, focusing on the debate over the heroine's use of language and the role of language and conversation in the novel.
	The second part of the week is devoted to the art of letter writing as practiced in seventeenth-century France. Emphasis is on the circulation of these letters in the salons and social circles. Readings are from Madame de Sévigné and Jean Chapelain.

Week 7	*Travel Narratives and the Epistolary Genre*
	François Bernier's travel narrative, composed primarily of letters, of his time in India. This work was developed while he was a member of Marguerite de La Sablière's influential salon, where he was joined by Lafayette, Sévigné, Bernard Le Bovier de Fontenelle, and Jean de La Fontaine, among many others. We approach this work as a product of conversations in this milieu and as a text that influenced conversations about India.
Week 8	*Philosophical Conversations*
	Analysis of Fontenelle's *Entretiens sur la pluralité des mondes*, which consists of conversations with a fictional marquise.
	The last part of the week is devoted to the *Mercure Galant*, a newspaper that has been termed a "salon en paper," that is, a written salon.
Week 9	*Fairy Tales*
	Marie-Jeanne L'Héritier, *Les Enchantements de l'éloquence* and *Le Marquise/ Marquis de Banneville*; the two Riquets. Tales as products of salon culture.
Week 10	*Conclusion*
	Visit to the Rare Books Collection. How do forms of texts affect our reception and understanding? Literary history: How do we construct the past? What texts are included, and how are they selected? The example of fairy tales.
	Final discussion: Knowledge and communication: yesterday and today.

GENERAL EVALUATION AND COMMENTS

My contribution to the present volume (in Chapter 2) describes in detail the way fairy tales were integrated into this particular course. When I first developed the course, I was tempted to include fairy tales at the beginning, but after having taught it, I believe that using them as the culminating example of narratives born of social networks is the best way to conclude the course. Students are able to understand how French society affected the creation of these tales. Fairy tales are often taught in isolation, as works that are somehow separate from mainstream literary culture. In this course students recognize that fairy tales are a genre that is intricately related to the century's literary culture as a whole. They thus take the tales much more seriously as a form of artistic expression than they would if they based their encounter with these texts on preconceived notions of fairy tales as oral narratives designed for children. By ending the course with the two Riquets, one composed by a man and the other by a woman, I am also able to raise many of the broader issues of literary production and history: Why do some texts become part of the literary canon while others are forgotten? What role does gender play in the creation of literary history? How do authors use texts such as fairy tales as social commentary? Many students in this course opt to do their final papers on fairy tales because they are so intrigued by these broader questions raised by our study of the tales. They leave the course with a new appreciation for this genre and its important role in the history of ideas.

Fairy Tales of Germany

Ann Schmiesing

Course Description and Design

"Fairy Tales of Germany" fulfills a lower-division literature and the arts requirement in the University of Colorado College of Arts and Sciences core curriculum and is also an elective for the German studies major. The course is a survey of the German fairy-tale tradition, although students spend the first two weeks reading Latin, Italian, and French fairy tales to better appreciate the history of the genre in Europe. In subsequent weeks students first learn about eighteenth-century German collections of fairy tales and folktales by Johann Karl August Musäus, Christoph Martin Wieland, and Benedikte Naubert and then study tales that exemplify Classicism, Romanticism, and Poetic Realism. Most of the course is then devoted to the Grimms' *Kinder- und Hausmärchen*. Students explore the manner in which the Grimms collected and edited their tales, the sociohistorical background to the tales, the many Others depicted in the tales, and various approaches to interpreting the tales, including psychoanalytic and feminist criticism. The course concludes with a unit on the reception of the Grimms' fairy tales in twentieth- and twenty-first-century society, including modern retellings of the tales in literature, film, and television. Although the course follows a largely chronological approach to the German fairy-tale tradition, within this structure it allows for ample discussion of genre considerations, interpretive approaches, and various themes.

Syllabus

Week 1	The Early History of the Fairy Tale in Europe
Day 1	What is a fairy tale?
Day 2	Lucius Apuleius, "Cupid and Psyche" (2nd century AD)
Day 3	Giovan Francesco Straparola, "The Pig King" (1553)
	Charles Perrault, "Riquet with the Tuft" (1697)
Week 2	From Seventeenth-Century France to Eighteenth-Century Germany
Day 1	Marie-Catherine d'Aulnoy, "Green Serpent" (1697)
Day 2	Johann Karl August Musäus, "Libussa" (1786)
Week 3	Eighteenth-Century German Tales (cont.); Goethe and Classicism
Day 1	Christoph Martin Wieland, "The Philosophers' Stone" (1789)
Day 2	Benedikte Naubert, from "The Cloak" (1789)
Day 3	Johann Wolfgang von Goethe, "The Fairy Tale" (1795)
Week 4	Romanticism and Poetic Realism
Day 1	Ludwig Tieck, "Eckbert the Blond" (1797)
Day 2	E. T. A. Hoffmann, "The Mines of Falun" (1819)
Day 3	Fanny Lewald, "A Modern Fairy Tale" (1841)
	Gottfried Keller, "Spiegel the Cat" (1856)
Week 5	Introduction to the Brothers Grimm; Psychological Approaches to the Grimms' Tales
Day 1	Jack Zipes, "Once There Were Two Brothers Named Grimm: A Reintroduction," and "The Origins and Reception of the Tales" (from Zipes, The Brothers Grimm: From Enchanted Forests to the Modern World)
Day 2	Brothers Grimm, "The Frog King or Iron Heinrich," "Hansel and Gretel," and "Little Red Cap"
	Maria Tatar, from Off with Their Heads!
	Bruno Bettelheim, from The Uses of Enchantment
Day 3	Sigmund Freud, "The Occurrence in Dreams of Material from Fairy Tales"
Week 6	Psychological Approaches (cont.); Rewards and Punishments; Child Abuse; Portrayals of Women
Day 1	Grimm, "The Nixie in the Pond"
	Verena Kast, "Nixie in the Pond: Fear of Overwhelming Emotions" (from Kast, Through Emotions to Maturity)

	Marie-Louise von Franz, "The Straw, the Coal, and the Bean (Grimm)" (from von Franz, *Archetypal Patterns in Fairy Tales*)
Day 2	Grimm, "The Maiden Without Hands" and "All Fur"
	Zipes, "Recent Psychological Approaches with Some Questions About the Abuse of Children" (from *The Brothers Grimm*)
Day 3	Grimm, "Cinderella," "One-Eye, Two-Eyes, and Three-Eyes," "The Juniper Tree," "The Stubborn Child," "Mother Trudy," and "The Virgin Mary's Child"

Week 7	**Women in the Grimms' Fairy Tales (cont.); Spinning in Fairy Tales**
Day 1	Donald Haase, "Feminist Fairy-Tale Scholarship" (from Haase, ed., *Fairy Tales and Feminism: New Approaches*)
	Grimm, "The Star Coins," "Snow White and Rose Red," "The Six Swans," "Old Hildebrand," "Clever Gretel," "The Clever Farmer's Daughter," and "King Thrushbeard"
Day 2	Grimm, "The True Bride," "The Goose Girl," "Snow White," "Rapunzel," and "Brier Rose"
Day 3	Grimm, "Rumpelstiltskin" and "Rumpenstunzchen"
	Ann Schmiesing, "Naming the Helper: Maternal Concerns and the Queen's Incorrect Guesses in the Grimms' 'Rumpelstiltskin'"

Week 8	**Spinning (cont.); Spinning Demonstration**
Day 1	Lecture on spinning with spinning demonstration
Day 2	Grimm, "The Three Spinners," "The Lazy Spinner," "Mother Holle," and "Spindle, Shuttle, and Needle"
	Ruth B. Bottigheimer, "Spinning and Discontent" (from Bottigheimer, *Grimms' Bad Girls and Bold Boys*)
Day 3	Exam I

Week 9	**Men and Trades; Soldiers and the Thumbling Character; Class Issues; Magic, Cunning, and the Political Background to the Tales**
Day 1	Grimm, "Lucky Hans," "The Magic Table, the Gold Donkey, and the Club in the Sack," "Iron Hans," "The Brave Little Tailor," "Puss in Boots," and "The Master Thief"
Day 2	Zipes, "Exploring Historical Paths" and "From Odysseus to Tom Thumb and Other Heroes: Speculations About the Entrepreneurial Spirit" (from *The Brothers Grimm*)

Day 3	Grimm, "Bearskin," "The Blue Light," "How Six Made Their Way in the World," "Thumbling," and "Thumbling's Travels"
Week 10	*Disability in Fairy Tales; Monstrous Birth Tales; The Simpleton/Dummy Character*
Day 1	Grimm, "Hans My Hedgehog" and "The Donkey"
	Schmiesing, "Cripples and Supercripples: The Erasure of Disability in 'Hans My Hedgehog,' 'The Donkey,' and 'Rumpelstiltskin'" (from Schmiesing, *Disability, Deformity, and Disease in the Grimms' Fairy Tales*)
Day 2	Grimm, "Brother Lustig" and "The Three Army Surgeons"
Day 3	Grimm, "Clever Hans," "The Three Languages," "The Queen Bee," "The Three Feathers," and "The Golden Goose"
Week 11	*Disease and Cure; Tales of Old Age and Death; Comparing Andersen and Grimm Tales*
Day 1	Grimm, "The Water of Life," "The Godfather," "Godfather Death," "The Bremen Town Musicians," "Old Sultan," "The Old Beggar Woman," and "The Old Man and His Grandson"
Day 2	Selected Hans Christian Andersen tales
Day 3	Final project discussion
	Original fairy tale due
Week 12	*The Reception of the Grimms' Tales in the Twentieth and Twenty-First Centuries (Nazi Era; Postwar East and West Germany); Twentieth-Century German Fairy Tales*
Day 1	Zipes, "The Struggle for the Grimms' Throne: The Legacy of the Grimms' Tales in East and West Germany from 1945" (from *The Brothers Grimm*)
Day 2	Zipes, "The German Obsession with Fairy Tales" (from *The Brothers Grimm*)
Day 3	Hermann Hesse, "The Forest Dweller" (1917–1918)
	Kurt Schwitters, "The Three Wishes" (1925)
	Franz Hessel, "The Seventh Dwarf" (1926)
	Günter Kunert, "Sleeping Beauty" (1972)
	Janosch, "Hans My Hedgehog" (1972)
	Rosemarie Künzler, "Rumpelstiltskin" (1976)
Week 13	*Special Collections Visit; Grimm Tales in Film*
Day 1	Visit to the Special Collections Department (Rare Books Room) to view original fairy-tale editions from the seventeenth to the nineteenth century and artist books on fairy tales

Day 2	Exam 2
Day 3	Zipes, "De-Disneyfying Disney: Notes on the Development of the Fairy-Tale Film" (from *The Enchanted Screen*); Disney fairy-tale film clips

Week 14	*Grimm Tales in Film and on Television, etc.*
Day 1	Bettina Kümmerling-Meibauer, "Marvelous Worlds: The Grimms' Fairy Tales in GDR Films" (from Joosen and Lathey, eds., *Grimms' Tales Around the Globe: The Dynamics of Their International Reception*); film clips from DEFA fairy-tale films
Day 2	Claudia Schwabe, "Getting Real with Fairy Tales: Magic Realism in *Grimm* and *Once Upon a Time*" (from Greenhill and Rudy, eds., *Channeling Wonder: Fairy Tales on Television*)
Day 3	Rebecca Hay and Christa Baxter, "Happily Never After: The Commodification and Critique of Fairy Tale in ABC's *Once Upon a Time*" (from *Channeling Wonder*)

Week 15	*Course Conclusion*
	Final project presentations

Required Texts

Readings are determined by what is available in English and by a desire to minimize the number of books students must purchase. I use Jack Zipes's *Spells of Enchantment* (Penguin, 1992) because it offers translations of numerous German tales from the eighteenth to the twentieth century; however, because it lacks tales by eighteenth- and nineteenth-century female German writers, I supplement it with other readings. Zipes's *The Complete Fairy Tales of the Brothers Grimm* (Bantam, 2003) remains the best translation of the 1857 standard edition of the *Kinder- und Hausmärchen* and also contains several unpublished tales collected by the Grimms and selected tales from the first edition. Because reading and discussing more than a few dozen of the 211 tales from the 1857 edition would be unwieldy in an undergraduate course, I vary the exact tales assigned from semester to semester; the tales listed in the syllabus illustrate what might be assigned in one but not all iterations of the course. Several Grimm tales are typically assigned for each day, but lecture and discussion focus on just one to three of the assigned tales and touch more briefly on how the other assigned tales exemplify patterns or exceptions. As secondary literature, Zipes's *The Brothers Grimm: From Enchanted Forests to the Modern World* (Palgrave Macmillan, 2002) provides excellent chapters on the Grimms' background and their editing of their tales, psychological approaches to and gender issues in the tales, and the reception of the Grimms' tales in the nineteenth and twentieth centuries. I supplement Zipes's monograph with scholarship by Maria Tatar, Ruth Bottigheimer, Donald Haase, and others.

Assignments and Assessment

In addition to essays and examinations, assignments include an original fairy tale written in imitation of a Grimm tale and a final research paper in which students analyze a twentieth- or twenty-first-century literary or visual adaptation of a Grimm fairy tale.

Other Activities

Activities beyond lecture and discussion typically include a demonstration of spinning and a visit to the Special Collections Department in the University of Colorado Libraries. The spinning demonstration and the Special Collections visit are included in part because of institutional and regional strengths: The Boulder area has a lively fiber arts community, and the Special Collections Department has an extensive collection of original fairy-tale editions. The spinning demonstration occurs during a week in which students discuss depictions of spinning in the Grimms' fairy tales. Students not only see firsthand how spinning wheels and drop spindles work but also handle flax line and tow and learn about the lengthy process involved in preparing flax for spinning. The demonstration enables them to better understand references in fairy tales to specific spinning terms and to appreciate the diverse attitudes toward spinning in the tales. During the Special Collections visit, students view important original editions of European fairy tales from the seventeenth to the nineteenth century, including a seventeenth-century edition of fairy tales by Marie-Catherine d'Aulnoy and the 1857 edition of the Grimms' *Kinder- und Hausmärchen*. Also on display are important illustrated works of the Grimms' fairy tales by George Cruikshank, Walter Crane, Arthur Rackham, and others, as well as twentieth- and twenty-first-century art books on fairy-tale themes.

GENERAL EVALUATION AND COMMENTS

This course uses the German fairy-tale tradition as a prism through which to acquaint students with various aspects of fairy-tale studies. To understand and contextualize the development of the German fairy tale, students are introduced, however cursorily, to the fairy-tale tradition in other Western countries and time periods and to a variety of interpretive approaches. After students become familiar with overall issues of genre and periodization, the basic features of twentieth-century psychological approaches are introduced. The assigned secondary literature in this portion of the course facilitates a discussion of portrayals of women and children in the Grimms' fairy tales, and this discussion in turn leads to an exploration of feminist approaches to fairy tales.

In studying the reasons for the popularity of the Grimms' collection in the nineteenth century and beyond, students survey what Jack Zipes has termed the "bourgeois entrepreneurial spirit" of the Grimms' tales, and, in so doing, they also study patterns typical in Grimm tales that feature male protagonists; in this segment of the course, a sociohistorical approach yields insights into portrayals of soldiers, thieves, tailors, and other tradesmen in the Grimms' collection. Discussion of the many Others in the Grimms' collection touches on representations of aging characters and of disabled and/or physically anomalous characters, and this discussion exposes students to lesser-known interpretive approaches, such as disability studies theory.

In all units featuring the Grimms' tales, students discuss the editorial changes the Grimms made to the tales they collected and the manner in which such changes convey their nineteenth-century bourgeois worldview. Although the course is called "Fairy Tales of Germany," students appreciate the opportunity to read selected tales of Hans Christian Andersen and to compare and contrast the tales he authored with the tales collected by the Grimms. In the last segment of the course, students discuss the reception of the Grimms' tales from the nineteenth century to the present, with an emphasis on the Nazi era, postwar East and West Germany, and contemporary popular culture.

Students' two favorite assignments in the course are invariably the fairy tale they write in imitation of a Grimm tale and the final research project. For the former, students are instructed to write an original tale that reads stylistically and thematically as though it could come straight out of the Grimms' collection, and they append a justification in which they discuss how the various features of their tale make it a sound imitation. Students are nevertheless allowed (and encouraged) to deviate from features typical of Grimm tales if they account for the deviation in their justification statement; taking this cue, students often update gender roles, for example, or modernize settings, trades, or magical tools. For the final research project, students choose any modern adaptation of a Grimm tale from any culture and any medium. They then use relevant secondary literature to analyze the differences between the Grimm version and the adaptation they chose, emphasizing what these differences reveal about the Grimms' nineteenth-century worldview and that of the culture or author/artist whose adaptation they chose. This exercise enables students to apply their knowledge of the Grimms and of various interpretive approaches to a topic of their choosing; in addition, it acquaints them with resources such as the International Fairy-Tale Filmography website (iftf.uwinnipeg.ca) and recent edited scholarly collections pertaining to the fairy tale in popular culture (e.g., Greenhill and Rudy's *Channeling Wonder: Fairy Tales on Television* and Joosen and Lathey's *Grimms' Tales Around the Globe: The Dynamics of Their International Reception*). Because most students begin the course having been acquainted with the fairy-tale genre only through their exposure to popular culture, the final project format helps them to connect what they have learned in the course with their prior (and now recontextualized) knowledge of the fairy-tale genre.

Popular Genres

THE FAIRY TALE

Jennifer Schacker

Course Description and Design

The course "Popular Genres: The Fairy Tale" is a 2000-level undergrad-uate course in the School of English and Theatre Studies at the Univer-sity of Guelph (Canada). This large lecture course introduces students to the multiple, varied, and unstable understandings of the "fairy tale": the history of the term in the English language; the various ways in which the genre's form, function, and meaning have been defined and debated over the past three centuries; and the range of forms (oral, written, the-atrical, cinematic, etc.) that have been considered part of the genre's intertextual web (sometimes retrospectively).

Over the course of the semester we examine the lengthy history of fairy tales as a popular genre, from the early modern period to the pres-ent day, but we give some special attention to literary tales and field-based collections of orally told tales that were enormously popular in nineteenth-century Britain. In this way, the course offers students a historical and critical perspective on the emergence of folklore study as a discipline, including its impact on popular literature (such as literature for children). Assigned readings are drawn from the anthology of tales and critical perspectives that I co-edited with Christine A. Jones, *Mar-velous Transformations*, which is organized chronologically to foreground historical connections and patterns that are sometimes overlooked in thematic approaches to fairy tales. In this course, our study of texts from fairy-tale history informs discussions of the genre in popular culture today.

Syllabus

Week 1	***Introduction to the Course***
	Jennifer Schacker and Christine Jones, "Introduction: How to Read a Fairy Tale," in MT, 21–40
Week 2	***Case Study: "Sleeping Beauty"***
	Walt Disney's *Sleeping Beauty* (excerpts viewed in class)
	Charles Perrault, "Sleeping Beauty" (2011 translation by C. Jones), in MT, 177–84 (also read the introduction to Perrault, in MT, 163–64)
	Giambattista Basile, "Sun, Moon, and Talia" (2007 translation by N. Canepa), in MT, 135–39 (also read the introduction to Basile, in MT, 114–15)
	Robert Coover, *Briar Rose* (excerpt), in MT, 390–93
	Overview of "genre" in fairy-tale studies, in MT, 487–88
Week 3	***"Classic" Fairy Tales I: Literary Tales from Early Modern Italy***
	Nancy Canepa, "The Translation of Enchantment," in MT, 560–65
	Giovan Francesco Straparola, "Costantino Fortunato" and "King Pig" (2011 translations by N. Canepa), in MT, 106–14 (also read introduction to Straparola, in MT, 99; "Crazy Pietro" is optional [MT, 99–105])
	Ruth B. Bottigheimer, "Geographical Translocations and Cultural Transformations," in MT, 555–59
	Basile, "Cinderella Cat" and "Cagliuso," in MT, 115–20, 130–34
Week 4	***"Classic" Fairy Tales II: Women Writers in Late Seventeenth-Century France***
	Marie-Jeanne L'Héritier de Villandon, "The Discreet Princess" (1729 translation by R. Samber), in MT, 139–56
	Catherine Bernard, "Riquet à la Houppe" (2011 translation by C. Jones), in MT, 157–63
	Sophie Raynard, "Sexuality and the Women Fairy-Tale Writers of the 1690s," in MT, 551–54
	Marie-Catherine d'Aulnoy, "Finette Cendron" (1892 translation by E. Lee and A. Macdonell), in MT, 188–200 (also read introduction to d'Aulnoy, in MT, 185; "The Fairies' Tales" is optional [MT, 185–87])

Week 5	*Classic Fairy Tales II: Charles Perrault*
	Perrault, "Cinderella," "Blue-Beard," and "Little Red Riding Hood," in MT, 169–74, 164–69, and 175–77 (reread the introduction to Perrault, in MT, 163–64)
	Perrault's tales and early animated films [excerpts viewed in class]
Week 6	*Oral Traditions and Nineteenth-Century Fairy-Tale Books: The Brothers Grimm*
	Jacob and Wilhelm Grimm, "Hansel and Gretel," "Worn-Out Dancing Shoes," "Snow White," and "Six Swans" (1987 translation by J. Zipes), in MT, 235–60 (includes introduction to the Grimms)
Week 7	*Oral Traditions and Issues of Authorship*
	T. Crofton Croker, "The Crookened Back," in MT, 260–64 (includes introduction to Croker)
	Overview of "authorship" in fairy-tale studies, in MT, 489–90
	Henry Glassie, "Authorship in Oral Narrative," in MT, 523–28
Week 8	*Early Experiments in Fieldwork and Tale Collecting*
	Peter Asbjørnsen and Jørgen Moe, "East o' the Sun, West o' the Moon," "Tatterhood," and "Little Annie the Goose Girl" (1857 translation by G. W. Dasent), in MT, 275–90
	John Francis Campbell, "The Story of the White Pet," in MT, 303–5
	Flora Annie Steel and Richard Temple, "Princess Aubergine," in MT, 348–53
Week 9	*Fairy Tales and Popular Literature: Hans Christian Andersen*
	Hans Christian Andersen, "The Tinderbox," "The Princess and the Pea," and "The Red Shoes," in MT (2004 translation by T. Nunnally), 264–75
Week 10	*Fairy Tales and Victorian Women Writers*
	Christina Rossetti, "Goblin Market," in MT, 306–21
	Mary de Morgan, "The Toy Princess," in MT, 333–42
	Rosamund Marriott Watson, "The Bird Bride," in MT, 354–57
Week 11	*Social Critique and Parody in Victorian Fairy Tales*
	George Cruikshank, "Cinderella and the Glass Slipper" (MT website: use your access code to read the full introduction and full story on the book's website)
	Victor Stevens, excerpts from "Little Red Riding Hood, or The Saucy Squire of Sunnydale" (pantomime script on the MT website)

Week 12	Modern and Postmodern Fairy Tales
	Sylvia Townsend Warner, "Bluebeard's Daughter," in MT, 367–80
	Anne Sexton, "Snow White and the Seven Dwarfs," in MT, 385–90
	Neil Gaiman, "Instructions," in MT, 404–7
	Kelly Link, "Swans," in MT, 407–16
Week 13	Oral Traditions in the Twentieth and Twenty-First Centuries
	Linda Dégh/Zsuzsanna Palkó, "The Serpent Prince" (1995 translation by V. Kalm), in MT, 435–50
	Hasan El-Shamy/Tahiyyah M., "Daughters of the Bean Vendor," in MT, 466–73
	Donald Braid/Duncan Williamson, "The Boy and the Blacksmith," in MT, 474–82
	Conclusions

Required Texts

Jones, Christine A., and Jennifer Schacker, eds. *Marvelous Transformations: An Anthology of Fairy Tales and Contemporary Critical Perspectives.* Peterborough, Canada: Broadview Press, 2012. [MT]

Assignments and Assessment

1. Quizzes: 30%
2. Short papers: 30%
3. Research assignment: 10%

    Over the course of the semester we will be discussing current cultural references to fairy-tale themes, motifs, characters, and conventions. In this research assignment your task is to locate one such reference or allusion—a recent one (2011–present). You can look at journalism, advertising, political rhetoric, any kind of publishing (print or virtual)—just keep your eyes and ears open. References to fairy tales are everywhere, so stay alert to ways in which some kind of understanding of fairy-tale conventions becomes part of non-fairy-tale discourses. In two or three sentences, describe what you find interesting or curious about your selection. What does it seem to assume about general understandings and assumptions about fairy tales, overall or about the specific fairy-tale element being referenced?

4. Final exam: 30%

General Evaluation and Comments

One of my primary goals in this large lecture course is to give students richly historicized contexts for canonical fairy tales while also introducing them to a wider range of texts than those referenced in popular culture today. I begin the course with a case study, "Sleeping Beauty," to allow students an opportunity to revisit a tale that feels familiar but whose history complicates inherited understandings of the genre's form, function, meaning, and potential audience. The remaining weeks move through fairy-tale history chronologically.

I have a particular interest in the interwoven histories of folklore study and literary production; by organizing readings historically rather than by tale type or national origin (two common modes of organization, both for anthologies and course design), students get a strong sense of these twin histories and start to see oral tradition as something ongoing and vibrant rather than as literature's prehistory. The course underscores the complexity and nuance of both oral traditional and literary tales. Our discussions also address the forms of performance, fine art, and cinema that have been and continue to be part of the fairy tale's multimedial history.

Folklore and Literature

Questions of Translation and Adaptation

Cristina Bacchilega

Course Description and Design

Within a framework that is interdisciplinary and attentive to the location of my university, my students, and me in the Pacific, in the course "Folklore and Literature: Questions of Translation and Adaptation" I focus on two connected cultural practices—translation and adaptation—that have, in different ways, shaped historical and current understandings of "folk" or "traditional" narrative genres (such as, in a Western genre system, folktales and fairy tales, myths, epics, and legends). Methodologically, the course presents students with the tools of a folklore and literature approach but does so in a self-reflective mode where disciplinary assumptions and methodological tools are both deployed and put into question, especially in light of the difference between "emic" (relevant within a community) and "etic" (descriptive from the outside) genre categories and of the imbricated history of folkloristics with colonialism and "coloniality" (Walter Mignolo) more broadly.

"Traditional" narratives considered in this course rest on oral tradition but are not limited to oral cultures; although many traditional narratives are authored, this is largely ignored when the tales are translated to represent an older or other culture and are adapted into "modern" literary texts. Why are they translated and adapted? How do translation and adaptation overlap? What are the methods and effects of colonial, postcolonial, and decolonial translations and adaptations of traditional narratives? What is gained and what is lost by differentiating between literary and traditional narratives?

By focusing on translation and adaptation as contact zones, in this course we pay attention to their politics (e.g., dynamics of othering, appropriation, and empowerment) and their poetics (e.g., translation as innovation, narrative strategies of adaptation). If traditional narratives are perceived as foundational to the construction of a language of the imagination, we can benefit from studying how structures of inequality inflect this language of the imagination; how the translation and adaptation of these traditional narratives inform children's, national, comparative, and world literatures; how these translations and adaptations function in globalized popular culture, especially fantasy film; and how social and ideological processes affect the production, transformations, and exchange of such narratives across cultures and history, without, however, determining a priori their ideological effects.

Decoding how translation often masks the practices of adaptation and appropriation in colonial and globalizing projects as well as making visible the work of translation in filmic adaptations are important goals as we approach these narratives with the tools of folkloristics, literary studies, cultural studies, adaptation and translation studies, and indigenous studies. More specifically, we ask how these dynamics have played out in the English-language translation of "folktales" from colonized India; *moʻolelo* from the Kingdom of Hawaiʻi and occupied Hawaiʻi; wonder tales from the European literary tradition and from *The Thousand and One Nights*; and other case studies students bring in.

Syllabus

Week 1	*Introduction to the Course; Personal Introductions; Orienting Ourselves to Resources*
	What are your thoughts about tradition, storytelling, translation, and adaptation now? What has been most productive for you in thinking about these cultural practices? What kinds of questions interest you and why?
Week 2	*Traditions, Disciplines, and Responsibilities*
	The readings for this week are individually selected according to guidelines given in class and the students' intellectual curiosity.
	Thomas King, ch. from *The Truth About Stories* (pdf and audio file)

Henry Glassie, "Tradition"

Dorothy Noyes, "Tradition: Three Traditions"

Keith Basso, "'Stalking with Stories': Names, Places, and Moral Narratives Among the Western Apache"

Jon Kamakawiwoʻole Osorio, "Memorializing Puʻuloa and Remembering Pearl Harbor"

Lisa Brooks, "Common Pot: The Recovery of Native Space in the Northeast"

Jill Terry Rudy, "American Folklore Scholarship, Tales of the North American Indians, and Relational Communities"

Daniel Heath Justice, "Renewing the Fire: Notes Towards the Liberation of English Studies"

Paul Lyons, "Introduction" to *American Pacificism*

Cristina Bacchilega, "Folklore and Literature"

In-class viewing: Brandy Nālani McDougall, "Ola (i) Nā Moʻolelo" (TEDx Mānoa lecture on YouTube)

In-class activity: Show, tell, and raise questions. Focus on a specific genre or concept of expressive culture/folklore and its translation into/from English. Length: no more than 3 minutes.

Week 3	*Translation as Adaptation: The Frame of British Colonialism*

Sadhana Naithani, *The Story-Time of the British Empire*, chaps. 1, 2, and 3 up to p. 64

[Recommended: Sara Hines, "Collecting the Empire: Andrew Lang's Fairy Books (1890–1910)"]

Activity: Comments on Naithani's approach in relation to colonial collections from India and Australia; focus on their prefaces.

Week 4	*Translation as Adaptation: Reframing Disjunctures*

Naithani, *The Story-Time of the British Empire*, finish ch. 3; read chaps. 4 and 5

Ngũgĩ wa Thiong'o, *Globalectics*

Activity: Putting Naithani's approach to colonial and postcolonial folkloristics in conversation with Ngũgĩ wa Thiong'o's discussion of orature and other colonial contexts with which you are more familiar; learning and unlearning. Instructor will discuss a few significant essays about and approaches to translation, including Gayatri Chakravorty Spivak's "The Politics of Translation," Puakea Nogelmeier's *Mai Paʻa i Ka Leo*, and Subramanian Shankar's "Postcolonialism and the Problem of Translation" as a transition to the next section of the course

Week 5	*Adapting, Translating, Experiencing Moʻolelo*
	Versions, adaptations, and translations of "Pele and Hiʻiaka" in various collections, including Emma Nakuina and N. B. Emerson
	Nogelmeier mā, selections, plus "Commentary," "The Art of Hiʻiakaikapoliopele," and "Editorial Notes"
	J. N. Kapihenui, Kaʻopio, and kuʻualoha hoʻomanawanui, "Hiʻiakaikapoliopele Destroys the Moʻo Panaʻewa"
	Noenoe Silva, "Pele, Hiʻiaka, and Haumea: Women and Power in Two Hawaiian Moʻolelo"
	Bryan Kuwada, "To Translate or Not to Translate: Revising the Translating of Hawaiian Language Texts"
	Amy Kuʻuleialoha Stillman, "Re-Membering the History of Hawaiian Hula"
	hoʻomanawanui, chapter of *Voices of Fire*
Week 6	*Adapting, Translating, and Experiencing Moʻolelo Under Colonialism*
	Emma Nakuina, *Hawaii, Its People, Their Legends* (be sure to read the preface and one or two stories, including "The Valley of Rainbows" [aka "Kahalaopuna"])
	Prefaces and introductions to Thrum and Westervelt's collections "Kahalaopuna" on Kawaharada's website and in Nakuina's book, Thomas Thrum's *Hawaiian Folktales*, and the Kalākaua-Daggett collection
	Noelani Arista, "Listening to Leoiki"; kuʻualoha hoʻomanawanui, "Moʻolelo as Social and Political Action"
	[Optional: Bacchilega, *Legendary Hawaiʻi*, chaps. 3 and 4]
Week 7	*Decolonial Adapting/Translating Moʻolelo and Other Traditional Stories in Films from Oceania*
	Viewing (ahead of time) and in-class discussion of *Holo Mai Pele*, *The Land Has Eyes*, and *Sinalela*
	Vilsoni Hereniko, "Cultural Translation and Filmmaking in the Pacific"
	Dan Taulapapa McMullin, "Sinalela" and "One-Eyed Fish"
Week 8	*Folktales in/from Europe Translated and Adapted in the Nineteenth Century*
	Brothers Grimm, *German Popular Stories*, as adapted by Edgar Taylor and edited by Jack Zipes: Introduction; selection of tales; two other translation/adaptations of the same tales (see www.surlalunefairytales.com) "Red Riding Hood" versions, including "Tale of Grandmother"

Karen Seago, "Nursery Politics: 'Sleeping Beauty' or the Acculturation of a Tale"

Kuwada, "How Blue Is His Beard? An Examination of the 1862 Hawaiian-Language Translation of 'Bluebeard'"

Donald Haase, "Framing the Brothers Grimm"

[Recommended: Ruth Bottigheimer, "Publishing History of the Grimms' Tales: Reception at the Cash Register"; Haase, "Response and Responsibility in Reading Grimms' Fairy Tales"; and Niklaus Schweizer, "Kahaunani: 'Snow White' in Hawaiian: A Study in Acculturation"]

Viewing (in class): Short film, David Kaplan's *Red Riding Hood*

Week 9	*Adapting Fairy Tales for the Twenty-First Century*

Emma Donoghue, *Kissing the Witch*

Essays by Hennard Dutheil de la Rochère, Ann Martin, and Jennifer Orme

Kay Turner and Pauline Greenhill, Introduction to *Transgressive Tales: Queering the Grimms*

Fables (comic book series), volume 1 or another of your choice

David Herman, "Towards a Transmedial Narratology"

Karin Kukkonen, "Popular Cultural Memory"

Haase, "Hypertextual Gutenberg"

Activity: The activity requires having read versions of at least two tales that Donoghue adapts; see www.surlalunefairytales.com.

In preparation for the fairy-tale film group presentation, instructor will discuss a few significant essays on and approaches to film adaptations of/and folk/fairy tales: Greenhill, "Film and/on Film"; Zipes, *The Enchanted Screen*, ch. 1; Robert Stam, "Beyond Fidelity: The Dialogics of Adaptation"; and Thomas Leitch, "Adaptation Studies at a Crossroads."

Week 10	*Arabian Nights: Translations and Adaptations*

The Arabian Nights, ed. and trans. Husain Haddawy, foreword and up to and including the 27th night

Edward Said, Introduction to *Orientalism*

Ulrich Marzolph, *Arabian Nights* and *Aladdin in the West*

Arista and Bacchilega, "*The Arabian Nights* in the *Kuokoa*, a Nineteenth-Century Hawaiian Newspaper: Reflections on the Politics of Translation"

Yousry Nasrallah, *Scheherazade, Tell Me a Story* (film)

Week 11	*Arabian Nights* Translations and Adaptations for the Twenty-First Century
	Andrei Codrescu, *Whatever Gets You Through the Night: A Story of Sheherezade and the Arabian Nights Entertainments*
	[Optional: Bacchilega, *Fairy Tales Transformed*, ch. 4]
Week 12	*More on Filmic Adaptations of Fairy Tales*
	Hans Christian Andersen, "The Snow Queen"
	Danishka Esterhazy, *The Snow Queen* (film)
	You are also welcome to read Patricia McKillip, "The Snow Queen" (1993) and one other adaptation
Week 13	*Group Projects on Fairy-Tale Films*
	We will choose three or four films to focus on. Some possibilities are *La Barbe bleue*, *The Juniper Tree*, *Hansel and Gretel*, *The Year of the Fish*, *Into the Woods*, and . . . well, it's up to you to agree in your group as to which film you will discuss. Everyone is responsible for watching all the films.
Week 14	*Regrouping, Querying, and Revisiting*
	What are your thoughts about tradition, storytelling, translation, and adaptation now? What has been most productive for you? Which questions interest you the most?
Week 15	*Showcasing Your Wonderful Projects!*

Required Texts

Critical texts include Sadhana Naithani's *The Story-Time of the British Empire: Colonial and Postcolonial Folkloristics* (University Press of Mississippi, 2010) and Ngũgĩ wa Thiong'o's *Globalectics: Theory and the Politics of Knowing* (Columbia University Press, 2012). In addition to essays on translation, adaptation, folklore, and indigenous studies that will be available on Laulima (the online course management system at the University of Hawai'i), we will read *Arabian Nights* (selections in English-language translation); *German Popular Stories* by the Brothers Grimm and adapted by Edgar Taylor (1823 and 1826); Emma Donoghue, *Kissing the Witch* (HarperCollins, 1999); nineteenth-century English-language translations of Indian and Australian tales in collections such as *Old Deccan Days* (1868) and *Australian Legendary Tales* (1895); translations of *mo'olelo* in *The Legends and Myths of Hawai'i by His Majesty Kalākaua* (1888); and Emma Nakuina's *Hawaii: Its People, Their Legends* (1904). Visual adaptations include David Kaplan's *Red Riding Hood*, Yousry Nasrallah's *Scheherazade, Tell Me a Story*, the PBS Great Performances multimedia presentation *Holo Mai Pele*, Vilsoni Hereniko's *The Land Has Eyes*, and Dan Taulapapa McMullin's *Sinalela*.

Other readings are posted on the course management site.

Assignments and Assessments

1. Informal assignments (leading discussion, contributing resources to a communal online library, translating/adapting activities): 25%
2. Oral presentation: 15%
3. Short paper with research component focused on a genre or critical concept: 20%
4. Final argumentative research paper: 40%

GENERAL EVALUATION AND COMMENTS

This course is ambitious but, although individual students are more or less invested in parts of it, I am not the only one to find the framework productive. Weeks 3 and 4, which focus on fairy tales in particular as part of a worldly consideration of translation and adaptation practices, provide an entry into the genre that is, on the one hand, a bit jarring and, on the other, helpful, especially later when the students consider fairy-tale translations in Europe (e.g., Taylor) and translations of the *Arabian Nights*. Given the framework of this course, I do not group folktales and fairy tales according to tale type or theme.

For a variation of this course offered in Fall 2016, "(Re)Mapping Tales of Wonder and Enchantment," I chose to think—always within a framework that is interdisciplinary and attentive to our location in the Pacific—of the fairy tale as one among many wondrous genres that hold different names and functions across cultures, and therefore I focused on how translation, adaptation, and scholarship shaped different understandings of "magic," "enchantment," and "wonder" in relation to systems of knowledge and matters of (dis)belief. As I wrote in the description of the 2016 course:

> The transcoding of "magic," "enchantment," and "wonder" in relation to systems of knowledge and matters of (dis)belief will be in focus as we study how socio-economic demands and cultural movements impact the popularization of different forms of the fantastic. In considering the work of translation and adaptation alongside scholarly discussions of tales of wonder from different locations and times, we will pay attention to when and how "magic" is constructed as counter-knowledge, or fantasy; how "enchantment" has been eroticized in Orientalist fashion, deployed to support consumer fantasies, and explored recently in readings that queer the generally heteronormative genre of the fairy tale; and how, while "fairy tale" applied to narratives of the non-Western world is a colonial concept, "wonder" *may* be an activist force

across genre and cultural systems. If ideology is what engages us in the discursive production of belief, it is crucial to focus on its workings in make-believe—the telling, collecting, translating, studying, retelling, and adapting of tales predicated on the suspension of disbelief or on the beliefs of others—and to become aware of how the economy of magic, enchantment, and wonder can serve heteronormative and queer as well as colonial and decolonial projects.

Here are some of the new texts we read: *Grimms' Tales Around the Globe: The Dynamics of Their International Reception* (edited by Vanessa Joosen and Gillian Lathey; Wayne State University Press, 2014); Christopher B. Teuton's *Cherokee Stories of the Turtle Island Liars' Club* (University of North Carolina Press, 2012); Neil Gaiman and Chris Riddell's *The Sleeper and the Spindle* (HarperCollins, 2014); and Helen Oyeyemi, *Boy, Snow, Bird* (Riverhead Books, 2014). Essays included selections from *Phantom Past, Indigenous Presence: Native Ghosts in North American Culture and History*, edited by Colleen E. Boyd and Coll Thrush (University of Nebraska Press, 2011); and two special issues of *Marvels & Tales*: "Queer(ing) Fairy Tales," edited by Lewis Seifert (2015); and "Rooted in Wonder," edited by Bryan Kamaoli Kuwada and Aiko Yamashiro (2016).

Among the assignments for the 2013 course was a short paper (20% of final grade) to be shared with the whole class.

About the Short Paper and Informal Assignments

I hand out the following information to students to explain the short-paper assignment.

The paper itself is short (5 pages of text), but it should have a substantial bibliography and its purpose is to set the foundation for working on a genre or problem or construct/concept—"something" that is important to your work in this course. Let's say you are focusing on a genre: By historicizing, mapping, and contextualizing it, you will discuss critical approaches that you have read about and identify questions that interest you as well as directions that the scholarship is taking. The same goes for a construct (e.g., "witch") or a problem/approach (e.g., "folklore as resistance"). In all cases, the point is for you to historicize, map different meanings or interventions, and identify questions and directions that interest you.

These are not argumentative papers. They are verbal maps that synthesize and showcase your research into a specific genre or problem and your finding your way in that research forest. What have you found out so far, and who/what is your resource? What are the "must read" texts or "must know" things about your topic? The map will be doing some historicizing as well: Which critical questions or directions emerged and when? How have the debates or the focus changed? The last paragraph may very well focus on the path that you may want to take based on what you found most interesting in your exploratory readings and discussions.

The bibliography tells what you have read (including texts you may not be highlighting in the paper). You may include a Further Readings list of what you know you should be reading next based on your work so far.

This assignment works well for some students, but for others it is hard to approach because it does not connect with a primary text. For 2016, I modified the assignment, as follows.

WHAT SHOULD YOUR ESSAY DO?

1. Explain a critical concept that one or more of our readings so far raise, propose, theorize, or exemplify, and briefly discuss the method, issues, stakes, or questions that hinge on it.
2. Outline what this critical concept, issue, method, or question enables you to do. Specifically, how does it provide you with new insight into approaching a specific tale of wonder or a set of wonder tales?

The wonder tale(s) need not be texts we have read, but there is no reason to exclude these. I am including folktales and fairy tales, *ka'ao* and *mo'olelo* (which are quite different from fairy tales), and other wonder genres as well as their translations and adaptations.

This is not an argumentative paper. Neither is it a fully worked out analysis of a text. It is an essay about taking in (grappling with, understanding, reflecting on) a critical concept or method and articulating what makes it useful to you and where you envision it can take you.

You asked if you could discuss more than one critical concept; if it is something as broad as "translation," yes—meaning that you'd want to be specific about which aspects of translation practice, poetics, and politics got your attention and are most enabling.

EXAMPLES

Globalectics   Poor Theory   Orature   Coloniality

Wonder   Enchantment

Fairy tales as wonder tales   *Mo'olelo* as wonder genre

Folkloresque   Paratext

Fairy tales/tales of wonder as:

Worldly tales	*Children's literature*	*Literatures of the world*
"Capital of resistance"	*Literary commodities*	*Multimedial genre*

Translation as colonial tool   Culture of translation   Translation as adaptation

Connected with the short-paper assignment is building the class's *communal online library* or *shared resources* (this is 25% of the student's grade). I set up a document in Google Docs for this. Students simply add the full reference (MLA style) for two critical texts (article, book, documentary, interview, etc.) that they really learned from and annotate the reference with one short descriptive sentence and one sentence about what is most useful and amazing about it. If they have a link or even better a pdf, they are encouraged to share that as well.

For both versions of this course, I include an assignment focused on film, and for the 2016 course students selected four films: *Blancanieves* (dir. Pablo Berger, 2012), *The Tale of Princess Kaguya* (animated; dir. Isao Takahata, 2013), *Tale of Tales* (dir. Matteo Garrone, 2015), and *Pan's Labyrinth* (dir. Guillermo del Toro, 2006).

About the Oral Presentation

The guidelines for the oral presentation (15% of the students' grade) are provided in another handout.

Each group presentation will discuss how fairy-tale or wonder-tale elements are adapted in the film; possibilities include plot and themes, characterization, setting, magic or wonder, symbols, family dynamics, gender relations, narration and focalization, happy ending, mixing of genres, etc. *The point of the analysis is (1) to get at the adaptation's relevance to or appeal in contemporary culture; and (2) to explain how the film affects not only your understanding of a specific tale but that of the fairy-tale/folktale genres or of fantasy in contemporary culture.*

Each person in the group will focus on one aspect of the film and prepare a brief handout or a PowerPoint presentation to accompany the presentation. You are welcome to use one *short* clip as a group (no more than 2 minutes) or a few screenshots to focus our discussion. To ensure the success of your presentation, it is important to coordinate your efforts by meeting face-to-face or communicating online.

On the day of the presentations, you will individually turn in your outline for the presentation, notes, and a bibliography of works you consulted or drew on.

IMPORTANT: Each group presentation should last no more than 20 minutes to ensure that we have some time for discussion. Please rehearse and time yourselves—I will have to interrupt you if you go over, because we want 10 minutes for Q&A.

You do not all have to agree on how to interpret the film, but you should coordinate, organize, and make use of relevant essays, handouts, or reviews. *And I hope you have fun realizing in the process of preparing how much you know about fairy tales, wonder, and adaptation!*

A particularly successful in-class activity in 2016 included an adaptation exercise of sorts, with students in small groups sketching an alternative cover image for Oyeyemi's novel.

Understanding the Fairy Tale

Julie L. J. Koehler

Course Description and Design

"Understanding the Fairy Tale" fulfills the Philosophy and Letters requirement at Wayne State University and also fulfills the short fiction requirement for German minors. This course introduces students to the interdisciplinary context of major French and German fairy tales. The literary fairy tale developed as a specific genre in the eighteenth and nineteenth centuries in France and Germany. This course explores the evolution of fairy tales, emphasizing the transformation of this literary genre into various media. Positioning specific fairy tales in their linguistic, national, and sociocultural context will allow students to map both the evolution and the cultural impact of these narratives. Fairy tales will be paired with major fairy-tale theories, introducing students to different veins of critical thought about these texts. The course was developed specifically for the online format based on a popular traditional course that has been taught at Wayne State for decades. Although the traditional course revolved around short essays and in-class discussion, the online course requires a variety of assignments in addition to essays and exams, including discussion, journals, a digital group project, conferences, and blog posts.

Syllabus

Week 1	Introduction
Week 2	Introduction to Fairy-Tale Studies
	Fairy-tale vocabulary
	Jack Zipes, *Fairy Tales and the Art of Subversion*, chaps. 3–4
	Donald Haase, "Dear Reader" (MT)
Week 3	Little Red Riding Hood
	Charles Perrault, "Little Red Riding Hood" (MT)
	Brothers Grimm, "Little Red Cap"
	"The Story of Grandmother"
	Egbert of Liège, "About a Girl Saved from Wolf Cubs"
	Roald Dahl, "Little Red Riding Hood and the Wolf"
	Angela Carter, "The Company of Wolves"
	Nalo Hopkinson, "Riding the Red"
	Matthew Bright, *Freeway* (F)
	David Kaplan, *Little Red Riding Hood* (F)
	Zipes, *Trials and Tribulations of Little Red Riding Hood*
Week 4	Cinderella: Tale Type and Structuralism
	Zipes, AoS, ch. 2
	"Tale Type," *Greenwood Encyclopedia*
	Vladimir Propp, "Morphology of the Folktale"
	Giambattista Basile, "Cinderella Cat" (MT)
	Perrault, "Cinderella, or the Little Glass Slipper" (MT)
	Marie-Catherine d'Aulnoy, "Finette Cendron" (MT)
	Grimm, "Cinderella"
	Alexander Afanas'ev, "Vasilisa the Beautiful"
	Marie de France, "Le Fresne" (MT)
Week 5	Cinderella (cont.)
	Algirdas Greimas, *Structural Semantics*, 200–209
	Working Girl, "A New Cinderella"
	Anne Sexton, "Cinderella"
	Tanith Lee, "When the Clock Strikes"
	George Méliès, *Cinderella* (F)
	Lotte Reiniger, *Cinderella* (F)

		Disney, *Cinderella* (F)
		Jane Yolen, "American Cinderella"
		David Pace, "Beyond Morphology: Lévi-Strauss and the Analysis of Folktales"
Week 6	*Visual Media*	
		Abigail Heiniger, Notes on Visual Analysis
		Zipes, AoS, ch. 9
		Naomi Wood, "Domesticating Dreams in Walt Disney's Cinderella"
Week 7	*Lady-Killers: Sociohistorical Theory*	
		Anne Duggan, "Ideology and the Importance of Socio-Political and Gender Contexts" (MT)
		Zipes, AoS, ch. 1
		Perrault, "Bluebeard" (MT)
		Grimm, "Robber Bridegroom"
		Grimm, "Fitcher's Bird"
		Joseph Jacobs, "Mr. Fox"
		Anne Thackeray Ritchie, "Bluebeard's Keys" (MT)
		Hopkinson, "Glass Bottle Trick" (MT)
		Méliès, *Bluebeard* (F)
		Helma Sanders-Brahms, *Pale Mother*, robber bridegroom scene (F)
Week 8	*Lady-Killers (cont.)*	
		Sylvia Townsend Warner, "Bluebeard's Daughter" (MT)
		Emily Carroll, "Out of Skin"
		Catherine Breillat, *Bluebeard* (F)
		Zipes, "Remaking 'Bluebeard,' or Goodbye to Perrault"
		Maria Tatar, "Monstrous Wives: Bluebeard as Criminal and Cultural Hero"
		Rose Lovell-Smith, "Anti-Housewives and Ogres' Housekeepers: The Roles of Bluebeard's Female Helper"
Week 9	*Enchantments and Curses; Feminism and Gender Studies (midterm week)*	
		Cristina Bacchilega, "Fairy Tales and the Ideology of Gender" (MT)
		Haase, *Feminism and Fairy Tales*
		Summary of Apuleius's "Cupid and Psyche"
		Jeanne-Marie Leprince de Beaumont, "Beauty and the Beast" (MT)
		d'Aulnoy, "The Ram"

Week 10	*Enchantments and Curses (cont.)*
	Grimm, "Frog King"
	Grimm, "Six Swans" (MT)
	Ludovica Brentano Jordis, "The Lion and the Frog"
	Pester Christen Asbjørnsen and Jørgen Moe, "East o' the Sun and West o' the Moon" (MT)
	Afanas'ev, "Frog Princess" (MT)
	Gary Trousdale and Kirk Wise, *Beauty and the Beast* (F)
	Kelly Link, "Swans" (MT)
	Carter, "Tiger Bride"
Week 11	*Enchantments and Curses (cont.)*
	Ron Clements and John Musker, *The Princess and the Frog* (F)
	Jean Cocteau, *Beauty and the Beast* (F)
	Jeanna Jorgenson, "Queering Kinship in 'Maiden Saves Her Brothers'"
	Bacchilega, "In the Eye of the Beholder: Where Is the Beast?"
	Susan Hayward, "Gender Politics: Cocteau's Belle Is Not That Bête: Jean Cocteau, *La Belle et la Bête* (1946)"
Week 12	*Fairies, Elves, and Sprites: Reception Theory*
	Haase, "Response and Responsibility in Reading Grimms' Fairy Tales"
	de France, "Sir Launfal"
	Jacobs, "Tamlane"
	Grimm, "The Elves"
	Ludwig Tieck, "The Elves" (MT)
	Christina Rossetti, "Goblin Market" (MT)
	Shepherd, "Fairies, Devils, and Witches"
	Jessica Lofthouse, "Fairy Lore"
	Molly Hillard, "The Fairy Tale in Victorian England" (MT)
Week 13	*Fairies, Elves, and Sprites (cont.)*
	Perrault, "The Fairies"
	Grimm, "The Three Little Men in the Woods"
	Karoline Stahl, "The Godmothers"
	Basile, "Sun, Moon, and Talia" (MT)
	Perrault, "Sleeping Beauty" (MT)
	Grimm, "Brier Rose"
	Letitia Elizabeth Landon, "Sleeping Beauty"
	Robert Stromberg, *Maleficent* (F)

Week 14	Tales of the Orient and Orientalism: Translation Theory
	Ruth Bottigheimer, "Geographical Translocations and Cultural Transformations" (MT)
	Nancy Canepa, "The Translation of Enchantment" (MT)
	The Arabian Nights, ed. and trans. Husain Haddawy, "The Story of King Shahrayar and Shahrazad, His Vizier's Daughter" (MT)
	The Arabian Nights, trans. Richard Burton, "The Story of King Shahryar and His Brother" (BB)
	Haddawy, trans., "The Merchant and the Demon"
	Tahiyah, "The Daughters of the Bean Vendor" (MT)
	Muhsin al-Musawi, "The Wonder of the Arabian Nights in English" (MT)
Week 15	Tales of the Orient and Orientalism (cont.)
	Elisabeth Ebeling, "Black and White"
	Reiniger, *Prince Achmed* (F)
	Fleischer brothers, *Popeye the Sailor Meets Ali Baba's Forty Thieves* (F)
	Bill Willingham, *1001 Nights of Snowfall*
	Bryan Spicer, "Fruit of the Poisonous Tree," *Once Upon a Time* (F)
	Bacchilega, "Resituating *The Arabian Nights*: Challenges and Promises of Translation," 143–78

Required Texts

Schacker, Jennifer, and Christine A. Jones, eds. *Marvelous Transformations: An Anthology of Fairy Tales and Contemporary Critical Perspectives*. Peterborough, Canada: Broadview Press, 2013. (MT)

Zipes, Jack. *Fairy Tales and the Art of Subversion: The Classical Genre for Children and the Process of Civilization*, 2nd ed. New York: Routledge, 2001. (AoS)

All other readings and films (F) are available on the course management system (Blackboard) website.

Assignments and Assessments

On a weekly basis, in addition to the readings and lecture, students are required to complete one journal entry and six discussion board posts (3–5 sentences each). Twice in the semester students will be asked to write a blog post (about one page typed).

1. Journals (12.5%)

   Journal questions are reflective and about personal experiences and ideas. In addition, students will use the journal as a place to begin brainstorming for their papers and to do some related activities. These will generally be about one-half to one page long.

2. Blogs (10%)

The blog posts are responses to short-answer questions about the readings and lecture. These will generally take 1–2 typed pages.

3. Discussion Posts (12.5%)

To get full credit for discussion, students will have to complete a minimum of six discussion posts. Discussion posts should be productive and further the conversation. In order to get a full 10/10 for the week, students must do the following over the course of the week: participate six or more times during the week; post at least twice on or before Wednesday and at least twice after Wednesday; post three to five sentence-long posts; make less than two spelling or grammatical errors; mention at least one specific point from the readings, film, and/or lectures over the course of the week (students *must cite this quote or point with a page number*); relate current readings, films, or lectures to previous readings, films, or lectures in the course to date and/or to personal experience or knowledge at least once in the week; and take part in discussion at a critical level, not just recitation of information from readings.

Over the course of the semester there will be a midterm, a final, reading quizzes, a group project, essays, and conferences.

1. Reading Quizzes (10%)

Once per unit students will have a reading quiz. These quizzes are open book but must be completed within 10 minutes once started.

2. Midterm Exam (10%)

The midterm exam will be a short-answer written exam with questions similar to those in discussion and in the blogs. It will be a timed exam on Blackboard. Students will have 2 hours to complete the exam once they begin it. The exam will be completely open book.

3. Final Exam (13%)

The final exam will be a short-answer written final with questions similar to those that students blogged about. It will be a timed exam on Blackboard.

4. Group Project (12%)

The project is outlined and will take place on the wiki. There are multiple stages to the project: (1) Groups will be assigned in Week 5. (2) Students will meet with their entire group via Skype or similar program by Week 6. (3) The group will choose a fairy-tale adaptation to analyze (link to wiki) in Week 6. (4) The group will post main variants, periods, and authors to the wiki in Week 7. (5) Group members will post four ThingLinks (one per person) related to the visual analysis (link to wiki) during Week 8. (6) The group will post an outline of their visual analysis to the wiki in Week 10. (7) Finally, the group will create an online presentation using Jing or Prezi or PowerPoint. They will record the presentation and upload it to the group wiki page in Week 12. The presentation should be 16–20 minutes long (4 minutes per person in the group).

5. Essays (8% + 12%)

There will be two essays over the course of the semester. The essays will each be a comparative analysis of *at least* three written tales and one film from a particular unit. There will be mini-assignments in the lead-up to each paper in the students' journals and discussion board posts. The first paper will be due in Week 8 and should cover one of the following units: *either* "Little Red Riding Hood" tales *or* "Cinderella" tales. The essay should be 2–3 pages long. The second paper will be due in Week 15 and can cover any unit not covered in the first paper. It should be 3–5 pages long. The following lead-up assignments will be completed in the student's journal before each essay:

A. List of the student's stories and film choices due in Week 3 and Week 10.

B. ThingLink using an image of the student's story to provide background information, due in Week 4 and Week 11. This is a journal grade but must be shared on the discussion board that week.

C. Summary of secondary source(s), due in Week 5 and Week 12.

D. Short outline and thesis, due in Week 6 and Week 13.

6. Conferences

Three times during the course of the semester conferences are held via Skype. We will use this time to talk about the student's papers and to try to resolve any issues before submission. Conferences will be about 10–15 minutes long. The first round of conferences is held in Weeks 3 and 4; the second round in Weeks 6 and 7; and third round in Weeks 13 and 14.

GENERAL EVALUATION AND COMMENTS

This online course was structured in such a way as to meet the same objectives as the traditional classroom course, but transferred those elements into an online format. All of the various assignments and assessments in the online course were chosen to ensure that students had the same rigor and opportunity as that afforded them in the traditional classroom. Two of the big foci of the course were for students to not only learn theory but also use it in their essays, group projects, and blog posts. Although students found this difficult and even overwhelming in early units, their final papers demonstrated not only their understanding of a particular theoretical perspective but also their ability to apply it in their analysis. The second focus was for students to learn about the German and French traditions and to use this knowledge to think critically about their own cultural understanding of fairy tales. Although the content and lectures were focused around the European fairy tale and though students were to master this content, the ultimate goal of the course was to give students the tools to critically reflect on cultural constructions, including their own. For this reason, personal journals were as important as whole-class discussion in building these skills. As students debated their arguments with each other in discussion, and reflected on their new understanding of their personal experiences in journals, they began the heavy lifting of the course that was then demonstrated more formally in blogs, essays, and the group digital project. The quizzes, midterm, and final were meant only to assess understanding of content, whereas these other assignments sought to assess development of skills. When students commented at the end of the course that they would never see their favorite fairy tales from childhood the same way again, we knew that we had at least cracked the surface of their own cultural understanding.

CHAPTER SEVEN

FROM TEACHING FAIRY TALES TO CREATIVE TALE-TELLING

Nine Weeks of Adventures in Storytelling

Kay Stone

As an academically trained folklorist specializing in women and fairy tales, I taught classes on folklore topics for almost 30 years in the Department of English at the University of Winnipeg, in Manitoba, Canada. For the last 15 years of my career I added the 13-week course "The Art of Storytelling," which met three hours each week. The "Introduction to Folklore" course, which familiarized students with oral narrative genres, was a prerequisite for the storytelling class. Instead of learning *about* traditional stories, we would be learning to *tell* them. The class was limited to 25 students, which allowed for individual and small-group work. In the actual course the students had 13 weeks to learn two stories in depth, with various tools for bringing this about. These included readings from two texts, *World Folktales* (Clarkson and Cross) and *Creative Storytelling* (Maguire), and several resources available on hold in the library. In addition, they did written assignments, exams, and two performances in the class. Many of my students were in the education program and hoped to use their storytelling skills for telling stories and for teaching story techniques in their classes.

In this essay I create a virtual 9-week noncredit class based on the actual courses I taught, drawn from the most effective teaching methods I used. Textbook readings, written assignments, and exams are omitted in order to focus on the dynamics of story preparation techniques. In the nine weeks of this projected "class" students would learn and prepare two stories for class performance, using practical, imaginative methods for bringing stories to life inside and out. The two texts mentioned earlier could be used as resources. A few summarized stories would be used to model various story-learning methods for the students' stories. The students would be finding internal, imaginative ways of developing their own stories rather than more straightforward, practical, how-to approaches. The intense focus on only two stories would allow them to use perspectives and approaches that could be developed for their own further work. Do keep in mind that this is a hypothetical class.

WEEK 1: IN THE BEGINNING— THE OLDEST STORIES IN THE WORLD

I open the first class by drawing a large circle on the board and dividing it into four sections representing different time periods. The circle represents 100,000 years, when our species, *Homo sapiens*, has been peopling the earth. Each of the four segments in the circle represents 25,000 years. I ask if anyone knows how long people have been using writing to communicate. A few linguistics students can trace writing back only 5,000 years at most. So what were we doing for the other 95,000 years? Communicating orally! Books have never been an absolute require-ment for storytelling, as students already know from the folklore classes. We discuss the many narrative possibilities in these ancient times—for example, stories of the hunt, strange beings and happenings, spiritual experiences, and "teaching tales" on how to survive in a hostile environment. This gives students a more down-to-earth sense of human verbal creativity as they go far deeper than the overworked cliché about stories "going back into the mists of time."

Stories on papyrus from 2000–1700 BCE began to be discovered in the late 1880s, but we do not find fairytale-like stories until 1250 BCE. "The Two Broth-ers" is a complex tale of two loyal brothers and their treacherous wives and how the brothers survive dire circumstances by using wisdom and magic. The full text can be found in Stith Thompson's masterwork, *The Folktale* (275–76), where he notes that oral tales can be considerably older than written versions, but of course oral tales can be preserved in writing and also told. Without writing it is difficult to date and trace old tales. For example, we would know far less about the Grimms' tales if they hadn't been written down. However, written and oral narratives exist together. Stories similar in plot to "The Two Brothers" have been found throughout Europe, as listed in the invaluable index in Aarne and Thompson's *Types of the Folktale*. Some narratives the students will be using, then, will most likely be far older than the books in which they appeared.

We have an extensive question and answer period about oral and written tales, the nature of fairy tales, and anything else the students think to ask. This three-hour class ends with The Name Game, in which each student in a circle of 25 says their name loudly to the whole group and then quietly to the person next to them. The next person tells their own name and repeats the name of their neighbor, until the class has gone around the whole circle. It is more challenging than expected, because in focusing on saying their own name loudly they often forget their neighbor's name. They are allowed to ask. After everyone has finished, they know first-hand three basic skills they will need for the next few weeks: to speak up, to listen carefully, and to repeat accurately. I then hand out stories of about five minutes in length from the Clarkson and Cross collection *World Folktales*. They will describe them next week.

Week 2: New Viewpoints—"Dog Builds a House"

The story "Dog Builds a House" comes directly from oral tradition, told by a 13-year-old boy from Laos in an ESL class I was visiting. Students are also asked to bring a story from their tradition that they can read or tell and are surprised at stories from other traditions that echo their own. That is, in fact, what intrigued early narrative scholars more than 200 years ago and set them on the illusive search for origins. This particular story seems to be unique to Laos and perhaps to the boy's village.

> *Dog builds a house with a door but no windows. Cat knocks on the door and is let in. Elephant wants in too but is told he (or she) is too big. In anger Elephant kicks over the house and walks away. Dog optimistically builds a new house, with windows and a door, and puts a notice over the door that says, "No Elephants, PLEASE!"*

In groups of three, students retell this simple story from another perspective. I point out that the story has been told from Dog's point of view and that each student is to choose either Cat, Elephant, or House as their character and to redo the story from the first-person sympathetic point of view of this character. It seems to be an innocent game, but they learn a great deal about the possibilities of even a simple tale. House and Elephant, the two most mistreated characters, offer suggestions for improvement. Some elephants suggest that Dog build a park behind his house where they could all meet together. House approves.

Students then form new groups of three to describe the stories they have chosen from the list. They take turns describing their choices but do *not* tell the story as a whole. First, each tells the opening of their story, then the central action ("And then Cinderella went to the ball . . ."), and then the resolution. This is an attempt to break down reliance on the printed word, not trying to learn a story from beginning to end as a whole piece. To emphasize this further, they are asked to tell their three sequences in reverse order, again taking turns. There is a lot of laughter as they go backward. I also suggest alternatives to the beginning, middle, and end formula that they are most familiar with by explaining turning points, the places where the plot changes direction. When they understand and can identify turning points in the stories they have just told, they have a new way of looking at story structure. They can see the turning points in "Dog Builds a House"—the invasion of Cat, the rejection of Elephant, building a new house—and then decide which one is the most significant turning point. I note that even a simple story can have several places at which the story turns in a new direction, even if they are not of equal importance.

Then we play The Name Game again. But this time each student chooses an onomatopoeic animal name that will be used for the rest of the term and may even turn up in story-play. (I still remember Foxy Philippe, Anteater Andrea, and Leopard Leona from my actual classes.) Next week, they will tell their chosen stories in full.

WEEK 3: SIGHT, SOUND, FEELING—"DIAMONDS IN THE SNOW"

In the legendary Jewish village of Chelm, a village of fools, four "wise men" were chosen to find some way of giving hope to the villagers who were disheartened by the long winter. The "Wise Men" spent all night talking but found no solution and fell asleep. When they awakened, they saw that new snow had fallen in the night and that the reflection of the rising sun had created diamonds, rubies, and emeralds in the snow. Thinking that the jewels were real, they woke the entire village to see the miracle. Instead of collecting the jewels, they decided to celebrate—dance, sing, talk, and eat. The jewels disappeared as the snow melted, but the villagers didn't mind—they now had the miraculous jewels in their minds and were no longer downhearted.

I heard this story from Len Udow, a Winnipeg cantor, musician, and storyteller. Working with what they learned from The Name Game (speak up, listen, retell), students work in groups of four to retell the story, each taking a section and passing it on to the next person. Help is allowed because this is not an exercise in memorization.

Next, they are asked to recall moments in the story that caught their attention—sights, sounds, feelings—and share these with their group. This is further encouragement to understand that stories are more than words and that what they hear, see, and feel inside the story helps them to understand it more fully. They are moving further away from memorizing, from depending on the text, from "getting things right." Their stories are coming to life as they are told and retold.

Students then tell their own prepared stories, this time giving voice to their characters. They are loosening up. They are to practice telling their stories aloud outside of class, perhaps using a pet if they can't find a willing human listener. Someone suggests that plants would be good too. I agree.

Week 4: Into the Forest—"The Angel of Death"

An old woodcutter went into the forest to cut wood for the coming winter and cut so much that he could not carry it home. Discouraged, he sat down on his pile of wood and prayed to The Creator to send the Angel of Death. "I'm so old that I can't even carry my own wood anymore. No use to go on living." But when he heard Death coming, he had second thoughts. When Death appeared and said, "You called?" the old man thought quickly and said, "Yes, can you please carry my wood home for me?"

I heard this story told as a joke by my husband and in more serious form from a friend many years ago.

Students retell this brief tale in groups of four and decide for themselves how it might end. They agree that the turning point is when the old man gives up. Using imagination, they try to "see" the old man when he cheerily goes out to the forest, when he sits down discouraged, and when he slowly stands up and asks Death to help.

They apply this by "seeing" the main characters in their own stories, imagining themselves actually following behind them, and observing what this might tell them about their characters. I point out that they themselves had been in the forest with their character, feeling and hearing what was around them. They are surprised by how effective this experience is, how much they have learned about their stories.

The students then each tell their stories to the class and do a quick written evaluation emphasizing what they might change if they tell it again. I read each of these and comment but do not evaluate. This takes pressure off the tellers.

As the class draws to an end, I hand out larger texts with ten-minute fairy tales (also from Clarkson and Cross), which they will summarize next week.

Week 5: Imaginary Journeys—"The Mouse Wife"

A woodcutter's three sons were given axes and told to go outside, toss their axes into the air, follow the direction their axes took, and find someone willing to marry each brother. The winner would be the heir to the property. The two older brothers followed their axes west and east to the farmlands, but the youngest brother—the fool, of course—threw his too far and it landed somewhere in the great forest to the north. His brothers laughed as they set out, calling back, "You'll never find a wife in the woods." He walked until he came to a little white cottage, but the only inhabitant was a mouse. "Oh well," he said, "will you marry me?" And Miss Mouse agreed. When the brothers returned home to report their successes, they were told to have their wives-to-be bake bread and weave a fine piece of cloth. On hearing this, Miss Mouse had all her rodent friends gather grain for the bread and flax stalks for the weaving. Her work was finer than the two human women. Now, all three had to appear in person before the father. When the fool came in with Miss Mouse, his brothers laughed, but the father said nothing. Instead he proposed riddles, and only Mouse was able to answer them. The final riddle was, "Tell me what I'm thinking right now," and Mouse answered, "You're thinking that I'm only a mouse, but that's not so." She became a fine young woman, and she and her husband became the heirs.

This complex Finnish fairy tale, starkly summarized here from Jan Andrews's *Out of the Everywhere* (10–17), is the students' introduction to fairy tales. It will serve as a model story for the next five weeks as they work on their own stories. The group as a whole retells the story by telling a part and then passing it on to the next person. They can ask for help, because the point is sharing. I point out that their differing interpretations are useful in seeing how they have taken in the story on its first hearing. Then we adopt another method, using an imaginary journey to put us into the forest itself. They have the option of closing their eyes to shut out visual distractions. They walk into an imaginary meadow and into a dark forest. They are asked to feel the path under their feet, listen to birds singing and small creatures moving around them, to smell the earth and the trees. They walk until they come to a small white cottage with an open door. Inside is a small table with a box sitting on it. They are to study the box, pick it up carefully and feel its weight. Inside is something that belongs to them, and they are to slowly open the box, look inside, and see what it contains. They can lift this object out and study it for details. (If nothing is inside, it means the box is a door to somewhere else.) When they "return" to the classroom, they describe what they've experienced in as much detail as possible. Partners can question one another on elements of sight, sound, and touch, finding new details as they go. Most are surprised by the contents of their boxes and are eager to describe them. They are becoming a community, working together with ease and humor ("I found a rat in my box. What do I do with it?" "Ask it to marry you."). The usual competition of a university class is absent, and because they are doing things they have never done before, they fall into the adventure of it all—with little idea how much they are learning.

The same group shares their chosen stories in summary and tries to "see," "hear," and "feel" the stories, helping each other with details: "What did she look like when she fell into the well?" They are to know their tales thoroughly by next week. Practice, practice, practice.

Week 6: Meeting New Characters

By now the students know their story as a whole and are ready for some new twists. They have noticed how the stories they've heard from the other groups have motifs, actions, and characters similar to their own. With a partner they share their story in full, and when they have each finished, they choose a character from the other's story and find a place for it in their own story. Imagination is the challenge here, not getting it right. Then they split up and find another person to share their "new" story with. They have now told their stories more than once and are looser and more comfortable with them.

The students are then instructed to find another partner and work on the *antagonist* in their stories, as they did in "Dog Builds a House" with the house-wrecking Elephant. This negative character is to be presented positively and sympathetically and in first person: "They just didn't understand me" is a possible place to begin. If there is time when they finish, they choose an inanimate object from their story—a ring, a shoe, a cooking pot—that has its own viewpoint on the story, and describe it. The stories are getting wider, deeper, and more entertaining.

Next week they will draw a map of the different places in their story.

Week 7: Story Tour

I begin by sending the students on a journey outside the classroom with a partner, using their maps and taking turns leading guided tours of their stories. They have 30 minutes to find a quiet place in the university big enough to walk through their stories: "So here's where the bridge was, and there's the house." When they return, they choose another partner and each talks about what they learned from their tours. The stories become more solid, more convincing as characters and landscapes become more vivid. There is also a clearer sense of timing, as the students have had to be able to summarize as well as amplify and to feel the difference between summarizing a story and telling it.

The class as a whole then discusses the different methods we have used for learning and developing stories and which ones work best for them. Because this is the last class before their performances, they are enthusiastic and responsive. One student remarks that "it wasn't like cooking from a recipe but learning from other cooks." They are more excited than nervous that for the next two weeks they will be performing their tales in full.

Weeks 8 and 9: Performances for the Class

Each student has ten minutes to tell the story they now know well, inside and out. There is a pause between stories to let the action settle in, giving them time to relax before another story begins. Because they all know all the others' stories as well as their own, there is a feeling of comfort and support. When the performances are over, each student writes suggestions for themselves on what they might do if they tell the story again. As before, I read and comment but do not evaluate. We still have time left for an open discussion on what worked and what could have been better—in a word, their evaluation of my teaching. In my actual classes this was valuable information that I used each year.

Last Words

I have used some of these methods in shorter courses and workshops and in individual mentoring, so I know that they can be adapted to different situations and age groups. With these tools, students can continue working on their own, learning new stories and new methods of learning and telling them.

Bibliography

Aarne, Antti, and Stith Thompson. *The Types of the Folktale: A Classification and Bibliography.* Helsinki: Suomalainen Tiedeakatemia, 1964.

Andrews, Jan. *Out of the Everywhere: New Tales for Canada.* Toronto: Groundwood Books/ Douglas & McIntyre, 2000.

Clarkson, Atelia, and Gilderbert B. Cross. *World Folktales.* New York: Scribners, 1980.

Maguire, Jack. *Creative Storytelling: Choosing, Inventing, and Sharing Tales for Children.* New York: McGraw-Hill, 1985.

Thompson, Stith. *The Folktale.* New York: Holt, Rinehart & Winston, 1946.

A Week of Notes from a Storyteller

From Folktale to Fiction

Gioia Timpanelli

Monday

Careful living in a specific place is the foundation of our old folktales; this mountain, that tree, this badger and her friend coyote, that golden fish, Raven, the women coming in with the baskets, the North wind, March, and the stars, and on and on and wondrously on. One story holds us among the many things of the world. It does this while nurturing the Imagination, which is not a superfluous gift but a necessity for seeing with the material into the structure of our real lives. What seems outside and inside is experienced in the same place; what seems small and hidden is an entire world.

Tuesday

Nature is prone to remarkable complexity, and because nature is not outside us, we humans, however different we believe ourselves to be, are also prone to this complexity. A culture, while maintaining its own integrity in its varied stories, also reveals in them a universal interest in

This essay is in part based on my earlier essay, "The Sacred Does Not Shun the Ordinary," which includes "The Old Couple" with commentary on folk stories, in Charles Simpkinson and Anne Simpkinson, eds., *Sacred Stories* (New York: Harper Collins, 1993).

what makes a communal life and what makes a human being. These traditional folk stories, bare to the bone, do not shirk the human dilemma. They reflect every aspect of our nature and the laws of nature, our cultures, our moral codes. They are about hunger and plenty, leaving home, adventures on the way to finding love and work. Empathy, courtesy, generosity to others—strangers, animals, mineral and plant life, including trees and stones—are all universally rewarded in the folktale and especially in the fairy tale. How do compassion, sympathy, and empathy appear in the stories? What happens when they are missing? What makes a fair and just individual, a fair and just community? What is considered valuable? What is the difference between emotions and feelings? Is the culture one that gives a place for feelings?

Do traditional stories have a system of meaning? In general, what excites our interest or inspires us is the place where we tend to search for meaning. Are we interested in human nature, the laws of nature, ecology, moral laws, cultural conventions, philosophy, history, anthropology, language, gender studies, spiritual studies, sociology, psychology, and the journey of the psyche and the self? After we hear a story, respond intuitively, and at the same time look at it through the communal or our individual sense of values, we see what good judgment—or what poor, even terrible judgment—human stories can reflect. Stories were created by humans who, like us, were/are not immune to this danger. But when one finds a story that has wonder and wisdom, is measured with poetry, and balanced by common sense and good judgment, then one can join the line of tellers who went before and who will come after and tell that good story. In the beginning of a fairy tale something is missing; in the end it is found. We are part of this great connection of being. As it is in a wilderness, balance, mutual exchange, and life's creative connection is everything.

WEDNESDAY

> "Speech is not of the tongue, but of the heart. The tongue is merely the instrument with which one speaks. He who is dumb is dumb in his heart, not in his tongue . . . As you speak, so is your heart."
>
> —*Paracelsus (cited in Hillman, 133)*

After a story, or something in the story, chooses us, we are in the place of connection. When we know about the land and the people who tell the story, respect for both follows. When we learn more about human nature, we see how connected we all are to both the place outside and the place within. Choose stories from all the corners of the Earth and a great education follows. The story is dependent on the local and speaks of the universal. It is the heart that feels empathy, and it is the educated heart that knows what is happening in different situations and engenders appropriate behavior. It takes time and experience to get to that educated heart, but once there, a conversation is begun that is both outward and inward, in one language and in all languages.

Talking is on the spot and surprising, open and here; the voice speaking is immediate and natural. To be present is to be aware, and the story touches and reflects the experiences in both listener and teller. The heart is the place where we understand the natural connection, and seeing and feeling this is the beginning of a new life.

Thursday

"Tell all the truth but tell it slant," said Emily Dickinson.

Storytelling, with its entertaining narrative, is our first theater. Like poets, novelists, and playwrights, storytellers are not always, sometimes, or ever telling only literal, material truths. The unseen, unknown part of our lives is hiding in the story's plot, in its characters, and in the places that echo consciousness: our hearts and minds.

Before the story begins, there is a traditional, telltale frame that tells the listeners we are beginning a story and then a traditional ending that tells the listener the story is over. A variety of cultural frames surround the story, getting us to pay attention to important aspects of the place of old stories in people's lives:

"Once upon a time . . ."—This takes place in eternal, mythic time.
"It is told and retold . . ."—In Sicilian, *Si cunta e s'arricunta*. The teller is in a long line of tellers.
"Far beyond the edge of the world . . ."
"Back when the world was young and the humans and animal people could talk to one another . . ."
A Sudanese teller commonly begins with this audience participation: "I'm going to tell you a story." "Right!" shout the people. "It's a lie." "Right," they say again. "But not everything in it is a lie." "Right!"

Let's look at a few ending frames from different cultures:

"The mouse has run, the tale is done, let's put it back where we found it." (African)
"They remained happy and content and here we are sucking our teeth." (Romany and Sicilian. Now that we have dealt with universal issues, let's remember that we have to get our real food for dinner.)

"They remained happy and content / And here we are without a cent" ("Iddi arristaru filici e cuntenti / E ca semu nuautri senza nenti").

My Great Grandmother, Angelina Milano, used to say, "Iddi arristaru felici e cuntenti / E ca semu nuautri circanu u veru travagliu" ("They remained happy and
content / And we're still looking for our true work").

What about, "And they lived happily ever after"? Have some people misunderstood this to mean that the fairy tale is promising that *we are going to live happily
forever*? But it does not say that. Our ancestors were not deluding us into thinking
that *we* would live happily ever after. The ending frame says that *they* would live
happily ever after; it does not say that we would live happily ever after. The characters in the story are not real, ordinary people but archetypes, the communal large
figure of the mother, father, the third child, and so on. (The stories are for those
who have ears to hear them now or later.)

FRIDAY

Storytelling comes from the art of language, its music sung and felt, its words
spoken and heard (Timpanelli, "Stories and Storytelling"). By its very nature it is
communal; the teller and the listeners are together in a shared space. The storyteller
sensually sees the details of the story unfolding—as though for the first and *always*
time—and then creates and re-creates the story so vividly that the listeners imagine it and, by their attention, feelings, and responses, become part of the moving
experience. It is this shared speaking and hearing that makes such a memorable
impression. At the beginning there are listeners and tellers; in the end there is
the story and the experience of an alive presence. Traditional stories are works of
art that in each generation are continually being reinvented and reinterpreted com-
munally and personally. Even in our own life, the Cinderella story we heard at 10 is
not the same one we hear at 20 or 50 or 70. The story's simple form and complex
images have not changed . . . but *we* have.

SATURDAY

The famous teacher Maharishi Mahesh Yogi once wrote that stories "promote
world harmony by enlivening within the listener that field of pure consciousness
that is the source of all stories."[1] There are ways of hearing stories at any age that

---

1. Maharishi Mahesh Yogi, from the 1995 Maharishi Award presented by the Ministry of Cultural
Integrity and World Harmony to Gioia Timpanelli.

make them still relevant and even essential. Stories are entertaining, show awe and beauty, are humorous, are heavy and slow, and are quick and enlightening. They are surprising and cause the new and unexpected to appear. In some nothing seems to happen, and then, later, in retelling, something appears. But for a growth in consciousness, experience is essential. It is this experience that opens understanding and brings the awakening of consciousness. It is a work in progress like life itself.

Dante refers in his *Vita Nuova* to moments of life that "you cannot completely understand if not experienced" ("che 'ntender no la può chi no la prova") (Dante, 58). The understanding that comes from experience does not come only from the intellect or feelings or history or cultural know-how. There is something in our experience that can go beyond our usual ways of knowing. Once we have experienced something, even if we temporarily forget it (in stories humans are constantly falling asleep or forgetting), we have been changed in a place that we cannot explain completely. We have learned something that exists between doing and knowing, where the perimeter of seeing has now become larger. The stories are often about getting through a dangerous event or surviving a series of trials and coming away with a new way of seeing. To understand an experience, we have to observe carefully, truly be present, and then understand the Other or others as well as ourselves. Gaining wisdom depends on knowing this larger situation, and for this *way of being* you need knowledge of the whole experience. Ultimately, what one gets hold of from a complete understanding of experience, including the wise experience of others, is not a continual memory of a real trauma (a blow or the feeling of being in a cage) but the deep knowledge of felt pain and the value of freedom after flying away from a cage (see Timpanelli, "Indian Bird Story," for the full narrative). And now the story is for the value of others as well as oneself. There is no system; it wouldn't help. Words such as pain and freedom are not abstract ideas but are made up from our experiences, the stuff of the world. We are now in the field of consciousness that is the source of stories.

SUNDAY

Profane stories rely on what happens, how and why. They give a vivid sense of our living, our journey, our mortality. These stories speak extemporaneously from the moment, from personal experience and understanding, from error and mistake, from a windfall picked up after a storm. They are common/uncommon treasure boxes of the human mind and mirrors of its soulful life. The old folktales especially have a sneaky logic found in poetry, metaphor, and dreams. They believe in balance: What is missing at the beginning will be found at the end. Full of lively images, these old tales carry with them the magic of the created world. We can be thankful that they are not given to large statements on meaning, for like the heart to which they constantly speak, they prefer experience to concepts, unity to separation. Everything in them has weight, even a feather blowing here and there. They are best understood by hearing them told aloud in a shared place of telling and listening where the story is deeply felt and understood in its most alive and present state. They live in the particular while trying to talk politely about everyone. Although humble, they hold the possibility of experiencing the miracle of an ordinary day.

Here is a Sicilian folktale, from Alcamo, found in Giuseppe Pitrè's *Studi di leggende popolari siciliane* (311).

S. PETRU E LU VECCHIU

Na vota lu Signuri caminava cu l'Apostuli, e vitturu un vecchiu chi chiantava viti. S. Petru cci dici: "E chi jiti chianttannu a st'età?" Lu vecchiu arrispuni, "Lu benfattu nun è persu mai." S. Petru si vota cu lu Signuri e cci dici: "Maistru, possibili chi stu vecchiu voli arrivari a manciari racina di stu chiantitu?" "Senti, Petru: ssu vecchiu pri ssa bona parola chi dissi antura, havi a manciari racina di ddocu."

ST. PETER AND THE OLD MAN

Once the Lord was walking with the Apostles, and they saw an old man who was planting grape vines. Saint Peter said to him, "What are you doing planting at your age?" The old man answered, "The Good [figuratively *lu benfattu*, the beautifully made] is never lost." Saint Peter turns to the Lord and says, "Teacher, is it possible that this old man wants to live long enough to eat grapes from this vine?" "Listen, Peter: because of the good word he said before, this old man *will eat grapes from there.*"

Everyone who hears the story in Sicilian knows that it takes years to get mature grapes, and so the old man would not likely be able to enjoy a glass of wine from his labor. Here is this sparse story of an ordinary act seen in a practical, laughing (the old man must be foolish), and maybe even cynical view—it seems quite modern. And then the story takes a turn that ends with a transformation of the student and an unexpected gift, given to the old man and perhaps to us who are listening. And perhaps it has been a story acted out for our benefit—all the characters take their places and enact the whole thing again—if we have the heart and ears to hear it this time.

Then the images in the folktale turn into a story (I lived for years in an Italian countryside where every home had a family garden and planting a small home vine was common). When I saw (in my mind's eye) an old woman and her husband, without any thinking I wrote a fiction based on the simple narrative of "S. Petru e lu vecchiu" and on the lives of a number of other wonderful old couples whom I had experienced in life.

The fiction was also inspired by stories, one especially from poet and scholar Charles Martin's beautiful translation of Ovid's *Metamorphoses*. Here is his translation from "Baucis and Filemon," "Seek / no servants in that house, nor masters neither, / or there were only two there, and the one / commanding was the same one who obeyed" (Ovid, 289).

Do Angels Like Potatoes?
FOR R. B.

She knew she had dreamt angels, not a frightening dream but not quite a comforting one either. For, after all, she and her husband were so old, so very old. "We're at the bottom of the hill," he had said just last evening. "But that's where we've always lived," she answered, and they had both laughed. "Besides, Sweetheart, there are many things to do at the bottom of the hill." "Yes, *Tesoru*, like planting the new grape vine tomorrow."

She smiled when she thought that after all these years, she still called him Sweetheart and he still called her Treasure. "Why do you call me *Tesoru*?" she had asked him once, long ago. "Ah," he said, "when I was a boy wild grape vines grew like treasures in the woods. You are like those vines to me, an unexpected treasure." That evening while she was peeling potatoes she thought of his words and was so moved that tears came to her eyes, so that from then on potatoes, tears, and love all shared a common place in her heart. Now when she thought of her dream, she called out to him, "Do angels like potatoes?" *All'angiuli ci piaciuni li patati?*

"What? Did you say Angelo is here?" He stepped out the door to search the hillside above for their nephew who often came to visit them. When he saw no one on the road, he shrugged and called back, "I think you're mumbling, *Bedda*. I can't hear you." Later he would ask her to repeat what she had said. He touched the handle of his shovel and went back to a worry he'd been having since dawn: How long would he be able to pick up a shovel, or even do the simplest thing? A pain that had been lurking became present: he made a fist against it and waited. By the time the pain left, the worry was gone as well and he felt able again. *The animals are blessed, without useless worry; in this the animals are blessed.* Again he shrugged, but this time he picked up the shovel at the door and began to walk down the steps.

How funny, she thought, *angiulo—Angelo*. He didn't hear me. And then she remembered that her dream angel had not said a word to her; it probably knew that they were both quite deaf by now. Suddenly it was all too much for her, and she just had to sit down. At the same moment something made him turn so that he saw her fall back into the chair—as though someone had gently pushed her. "What is it? *Chi c'è? Chi c'è?* What do you need?" He asked anxiously. "Nothing I'm fine. I don't need anything." "*Nenti, nun vugliu nenti.*" "Do you want a glass of water?" "No, please Sweetheart, I'm all right; I just had to sit down for a minute. Thank you." She touched his hand. "Please don't worry. I'm really fine. Let's go out and plant those little vines. It's the right time. Don't you think the roots have been in water long enough?" He came back to her carrying a glass of water shaking in his hands. She took the cold glass from him, smiled, and sipped a bit of water to please him. He made a satisfied sound, nodded, and then waited while she looked around for a safe place to settle the glass. She found the spot and put it down. What does this spot mean? He helped her up and then he moved back to the door. She walked over to the stove and picked up a few sticks of wood. "You know," he said, "I was just thinking we might make ourselves a nice plate of potatoes and eggs for dinner." "That's funny, I was just wishing for the same thing."

While this was going on in the little house below, by chance two travelers were about to round a bend in the road, which would give them a view of the little house and the valley beyond. One was a curious fellow who looked around, taking in as much as he could, gesticulating as he walked, hitting one side of the road and then the other. He spoke the whole time in a running commentary about everything he was seeing. The other walked quietly without curiosity, his step deliberate and quite steady, like a native of the place. Much escaped the animated talker. On the other hand, nothing escaped the silent companion who was barely noticeable except for a triangular bit of light that came from the back of his neck, perhaps from something that the low sun caught and reflected. A donkey in the field below saw it and turned; the silent man looked up briefly and their eyes met, neither surprised. The donkey looked on, waiting to see if the newcomers were real news for him or not. As the two men came to the top of the hill, they saw an ancient couple working at something in the field below. The talker stopped and watched.

The old man had just finished digging, and the old woman was gently placing each plant with its delicate wet roots into the new holes. This now done, the old man quickly covered the plants while the old woman patted the earth. Everywhere along the branches new buds had opened or were about to burst into the familiar leaf of the grape vine. When they were sure the new plants had just enough water, they looked at the beautiful row.

Verifying his suspicion, the traveler turned with a sly smile on his lips and in a sarcastic tone said, "Teacher, look at that old man. What is he doing planting grape vines at his age?" (It would take five years at least to get some grapes out of those roots—it was plain to see that the couple were too old, too old, to ever see that vine mature.) The teacher looked up; the donkey shifted its weight and waited. "*Maistru*, isn't that old man truly foolish?"

"Why don't you just ask them what they are doing," said the teacher and the student immediately walked down the hill. The student came up to them and asked the old man, "What in the world are you planting grape vines for at your age?"

"*Buona sera*," said the old man.

"*Buona sera*," said the old woman.

"*Buona sera*," said the student looking at them both for the first time. He repeated his question to the old man: "*Chi stai faccinu chianttannu racina alla vostr'eta?*"

A warm wind came up and the two stood swaying a bit like two gnarled trees grown together in sympathy and years. "The good," began the old man, "is never lost," finished the old woman. She repeated the old saying under her breath getting real pleasure from hearing it again, "*Lu benfattu nun è persu mai.*" The old couple looked at the young man and waited.

"Would you and your companion like to stop with us for a rest or some water?"

"No, thank you, we are on our way to join friends," he said in a sweet voice.

They exchanged good evenings again and the traveler hurried away.

When they were alone again, she asked, "What do you suppose he thinks the good is?"

"Only God knows, but he did seem to understand what we said."

"That's true. He was in better humor when he left."

The old woman went to water a bit of wild mint. A bright reflection caught her eye, and she looked up in its direction.

The student ran up the hill to where the Teacher stood waiting.

"Teacher," said the student, "the old man said, 'The good is never lost.'"

"And the old woman, what did she say?"

"The old man started the saying and the old woman finished it. I guess we can say they are of one mind." After reflecting for a minute, he laughed good-naturedly at himself.

"For their good words to you, the old couple will drink wine from that place."

"From that vine, *Maistru*?"

"Yes, from there."

The travelers walked out of hearing, the donkey turned and found something delicious to eat, the old man looked at the row satisfied, and humming to himself, looked up in the distance at the new oaks they had planted five years ago. Maybe he would walk to the woods tomorrow to look for wild grape vines.

The old woman looked up at the sky. It was so beautiful; so many running sheep clouds. She started for the steps, felt her dream for a second. She had no doubt that somewhere near the angel of chance was present.

BIBLIOGRAPHY

Cox, Marian Roalfe. *Cinderella: Three Hundred and Forty Five Variants of Cinderella, Catskin, and Cap o' Rushes, Abstracted and Tabulated, with a Discussion of Medieval Analogues and Notes*. London: Folklore Society, 1893.

Dante Alighieri. *Dante's Vita Nuova*. Trans. Mark Musa. Bloomington: Indiana University Press, 1973.

Hillman, James. *"The Thought of the Heart."* In *Eranos Yearbook* 48. Frankfurt am Main: Insel Verlag, 1981. 133–82.

Ovid. *Metamorphoses*. Trans. Charles Martin. New York: Norton, 2004.

Pitrè, Giuseppe, ed. *Biblioteca delle tradizioni popolari*, vol. 12, *Studi di leggende popolari in Sicilia e Nova raccolta di leggende siciliane*. Turin: Carlo Clausen, 1904.

Timpanelli, Gioia. "Indian Bird Story," retold with commentary in "Notes and Pieces on Speaking Poems and Stories: Learning by Heart." In *Robert Bly in This World*. Ed. Thomas R. Smith and James P. Lenfestey. Minneapolis: University of Minnesota Press, 2011. 149–59.

———. "The Old Couple." In *Walking Swiftly*. Ed. Robert R. Smith. New York: Harper Collins, 1993. 193–97.

———. "Stories and Storytelling, Italian and Italian American." In *The Italian American Heritage: A Companion to Literature and Arts*. Ed. Pellegrino D'Acierno. New York: Routledge, 1998. 131–48.

CONTRIBUTORS

Graham Anderson is Emeritus Professor of Classics at the University of Kent, Canterbury. He has written widely on ancient fiction and the cultural history of the early Roman Empire and is the author of *Fairytale in the Ancient World* (2000), which won an Aslan Award for Mythopoeic Scholarship in 2003. He has just completed an anthology of ancient fairy tales (*Who's Been Telling My Tale?*) and a study of fantasy in the Greek and Roman world. Further projects include a study of *paideia* and *pepaideumenoi* in the first two centuries CE.

Cristina Bacchilega is a professor in the Department of English at the University of Hawai'i, Mānoa, where she teaches fairy tales and their adaptations, folklore and literature, and cultural studies. She has published three books: *Postmodern Fairy Tales: Gender and Narrative Strategies* (1997), *Legendary Hawai'i and the Politics of Place: Tradition, Translation, and Tourism* (2007), and *Fairy Tales Transformed? Twenty-First-Century Adaptations and the Politics of Wonder* (2013). With Bryan Kamaoli Kuwada and Donatella Izzo, Bacchilega also co-edited "Sustaining Hawaiian Sovereignty," a special issue of *Anglistica*, an online journal of interdisciplinary studies. Her recent essays appear in *Narrative Culture*, the *Routledge Companion to Media and Fairy-Tale Cultures*, the *Journal of the Fantastic in the Arts*, and *The Fairy Tale World*. With Anne Duggan she co-edits *Marvels & Tales: Journal of Fairy-Tale Studies* and co-organized the conference "Thinking with Stories in Times of Conflict" at Wayne State University (August 2017).

Benjamin Balak earned his PhD in economics at the University of North Carolina at Chapel Hill. He has held positions at Washington & Lee University and, since

2002, at Rollins College, where he is Associate Professor of Economics. His areas of specialization are the history, methodology, rhetoric, and ethics of economics and comparative economic systems. He has written a book on the rhetoric of economics: *McCloskey's Rhetoric: Discourse Ethics in Economics* (2006). His recent work is increasingly focused on the teaching of economics; he has spent more than 15 years experimenting with technologically enhanced pedagogy to breathe life into the teaching of the dismal science of economics and to facilitate interdisciplinary and transdisciplinary education. A computer geek and gamer since the late 1970s, he has been using computer games to teach economics and is researching the topic with the help of students. Outside the classroom, he works as a public intellectual and engages in various forms of activism, blogging, podcasting, and radio.

Faith E. Beasley is a professor of French and women's and gender studies at Dartmouth College. A specialist of early modern French culture, she is the author of numerous books and articles in which she resurrects the works and influence of French women writers and puts them in dialogue with those of their contemporaries. In *Revising Memory: Women's Fiction and Memoirs in Seventeenth-Century France* (1990) and *Salons, History, and the Creation of Seventeenth-Century France: Mastering Memory* (2006) she interrogates the effect that women's actions have had on the cultural field in general and analyzes how and why the historical record has been constructed to erase this influence. In her most recent book, *Versailles Meets the Taj Mahal: François Bernier, Marguerite de La Sablière, and Enlightening Conversations in Seventeenth-Century France* (2018), she explores how one salon served as the focal point for the encounter between France and India during France's Grand Siècle and the effect of this encounter on early Enlightenment thought, material culture, and literature. Beasley is also the editor of *Options for Teaching Seventeenth- and Eighteenth-Century French Women Writers* (2011) and co-editor with Katherine Ann Jensen of *Approaches to Teaching The Princess of Clèves* (1998). She was a Guggenheim Fellow in 2012–2013.

Elio Brancaforte is Associate Professor of German at Tulane University, specializing in sixteenth- and seventeenth-century German literature and culture. He regularly offers a course on the history of the fairy tale—"Grimm Reckonings"—in the Department of Germanic and Slavic Studies. His scholarly interests include early modern travel literature, translation, cultural exchange, theories of representation, the history of the book, German Baroque drama, and the history of cartography. Past publications include *Visions of Persia: Mapping the Travels of Adam Olearius* (2003) and a translation into English of Sperone Speroni's *Canace (1542)* (2013).

The relationship between word and image informs his current book project: *Europe Discovers Iran and Azerbaijan: Dutch and German Representations of the Safavid Empire (1635–1712)*. From 2019 to 2021 he will be working on *The Epistemology of the Copy in Early Modern Travel Narratives* with Stephanie Leitch and Lisa Voigt while on an ACLS Collaborative Research Fellowship.

Nancy L. Canepa is Associate Professor of Italian at Dartmouth College. Her research and teaching center on early modern Italian literature and culture, fairy tales, folklore and popular culture, dialect literature, and translation. Among her publications are the edited volume *Out of the Woods: The Origins of the Literary Fairy Tale in Italy and France* (1997) and the critical monograph *From Court to Forest: Giambattista Basile's* Lo cunto de li cunti *and the Birth of the Literary Fairy Tale* (1999), which received the Modern Languages Association Marraro and Scaglione Prize for best book in Italian studies. She has translated Carlo Collodi's *The Adventures of Pinocchio* (2002), the film *Pinocchio* (dir. Roberto Benigni, 2002), and Giambattista Basile's *The Tale of Tales* (2007, reprint 2016). Current works in progress include a critical anthology of Italian fairy tales in translation, *The Enchanted Boot*; a study of linguistic and literary experimentation in seventeenth-century Naples, *Baroque Metamorphoses*; and a critical translation of Castore Durante's *Il Tesoro della sanità* (The Thesaurus of Health, 1586), an early modern "wellness" manual.

Anne E. Duggan is Professor of French and the chair of the Department of Classical and Modern Languages, Literatures, and Cultures at Wayne State University. Her most recent books include *Queer Enchantments: Gender, Sexuality, and Class in the Fairy-Tale Cinema of Jacques Demy* (2013), which appeared in French as *Enchantements désenchantés: Les contes queer de Jacques Demy* (2015); and *Folktales and Fairy Tales: Traditions and Texts from Around the World* (4 vols., co-edited with Donald Haase, with Helen Callow, 2016). She has also published on French early modern women writers, with a focus on Madeleine de Scudéry and Marie-Catherine d'Aulnoy.

Donald Haase is Professor Emeritus of German at Wayne State University. He is the editor of *The Reception of Grimms' Fairy Tales: Responses, Reactions, Revision* (1993); a dual edition of Joseph Jacobs's *English Fairy Tales and More English Fairy Tales* (2002); *Fairy Tales and Feminism: New Approaches* (2004); the three-volume *Greenwood Encyclopedia of Folktales and Fairy Tales* (2008); and, with co-editor Anne E. Duggan, the four-volume revised and expanded second edition of that work, newly titled *Folktales and Fairy Tales: Traditions and Texts from Around the World* (2016).

For 16 years he was editor of *Marvels & Tales: Journal of Fairy-Tale Studies* and currently is general editor of the Series in Fairy-Tale Studies for Wayne State University Press.

Christine A. Jones holds a PhD from Princeton University and is Professor of French at the University of Utah. She writes on fairy tales and material culture in early-modern France. She has co-edited two anthologies of world tales, *Marvelous Transformations* (2013) and *Feathers, Paws, Fins, and Claws* (2015), with Jennifer Schacker (University of Guelph). As a sole author, she published new annotated translations of Charles Perrault's fairy tales under the title *Mother Goose Refigured* (2016) and a monograph on porcelain (*Shapely Bodies*, 2013) that mentions fairy tales too. Her current work includes a translation volume of tales by the little-known Louisiana writer Sidonie de la Houssaye and a blog (www.cacaosophy.com) on the early reception history of chocolate in Europe.

Maria Kaliambou is Senior Lector in the Hellenic Studies Program at Yale University and teaches folklore and Modern Greek language. She earned her PhD in folklore studies at the University of Munich, Germany. She held postdoctoral positions at the University Charles-de-Gaulle Lille 3 and at Princeton University. In 2006 her dissertation received the Lutz Röhrich Prize in Germany as the best dissertation in oral literature, and in 2011 the European Commission elected her Erasmus Student Ambassador of Greece. In 2006 she published her first book, *Home—Faith—Family: Transmission of Values in Greek Popular Booklets of Tales (1870–1970)* (in German), and in 2015 *The Routledge Modern Greek Reader: Greek Folktales for Learning Modern Greek*. She is currently working on her third book with the tentative title *The Book Culture of Greek Americans*. Her research focuses on the dialogue between folklore and book history, particularly in the diaspora. Also, she is interested in foreign-language pedagogy, particularly teaching Modern Greek.

Julie L. J. Koehler is a lecturer of German and coordinator of the Basic German Language Sequence at Wayne State University. She holds a PhD in modern languages and an MA in German from Wayne State University, and an MA in education from the University of Michigan. Her recent publications include the article "The Persecuted History of Cinderella: A Case for Oral Tradition in Western Europe" in *Gramarye*, and the "Fairy Tales and Folktales" entry in the Oxford Bibliographies Online from Oxford University Press. At Wayne State University, Dr. Koehler is a member of Ethnic Layers of Detroit, a digital storytelling project funded by the National Endowment for the Humanities, and she serves on the faculty advisory board for Women and Gender Studies. Dr. Koehler is currently working on an anthology of fairy tales written by European women in the nineteenth century together with colleagues in French and English. The anthology is tentatively titled *Women Writing Wonder*.

Suzanne Magnanini is an associate professor at the University of Colorado, Boulder, where she teaches courses on early modern Italian and French fairy tales, Dante, Boccaccio, and early modern women writers. She earned her PhD in romance languages and literature at the University of Chicago. She is the author of *Fairy Tale Science: Monstrous Generation in the Tales of Straparola and Basile* (2008) as well as articles on early modern instances of plagiarism, the practice of *riscrittura*, and Italian Renaissance comedy. As a translator and editor, she has published Giovan Francesco Straparola's sixteenth-century collection of tales titled *The Pleasant Nights* (2015), three fairy tales from Lorenzo Selva's prose romance *The Metamorphosis* (in *Marvels and Tales*, 2011), and theoretical writings on the fairy tale by various early modern Italian authors in *Fairy Tales Framed: Forewords, Afterwords, and Critical Words* (2012), edited by Ruth Bottigheimer.

Cristina Mazzoni holds a PhD in comparative literature from Yale University and teaches Italian studies at the University of Vermont, where she is a professor of romance languages and linguistics; she regularly teaches a course on Italian fairy tales in Italian and another on European fairy tales in English. In addition to articles and book chapters on European fairy tales, she has published essays and books on neurosis and literature (*Saint Hysteria*, 1996), holy women writers (*Angela of Foligno's Memorial*, 1999, with John Cirignano; and *The Voices of Gemma Galgani*, 2003, with Rudolph Bell), motherhood in literature (*Maternal Impressions*, 2002), food studies (*The Women in God's Kitchen*, 2005), and the Roman she-wolf (*She-Wolf*, 2010). Her latest book is *Golden Fruit: A Cultural History of Oranges in Italy* (2018).

Gina M. Miele, Assistant Professor of Italian and former director of the Coccia Institute for the Italian Experience in America, both at Montclair State University, holds a PhD in romance languages and literature from Harvard University. Her research focuses on nineteenth- and twentieth-century Italian folk- and fairy tales. She has published in *Italica, Marvels and Tales, Fabula, Marvelous Transformations: An Anthology of Tales and Contemporary Critical Perspectives*, the *Greenwood Encyclopedia of Folktales and Fairy Tales*, *The Literary Encyclopedia*, and the *Paterson Literary Review*. With Elvira DiFabio, she co-authored the fourth and fifth editions of the activities manual that accompanies the Italian textbook *Parliamo italiano!* She is currently at work on an annotated translation of Luigi Capuana's fairy-tale collections.

For some 40 out of 51 years at the University of Massachusetts, Amherst, William Moebius has offered "Myth, Folktale, and Children's Literature" as a general education course in comparative literature, and thousands of students have completed the course. Moebius's work on children's picture-book narratives has earned him a national award and has been published in French, English, Spanish, and Chinese, both in the United States and in Belgium, France, Germany, the United Kingdom, Venezuela, Taiwan, and Canada. As a student and translator of ancient Greek, Moebius launched his career with translations of Sophocles' *Antigone* and the poetry of Philodemos. At the keyboard, Moebius has performed all of Bach's Brandenburg Concerti with orchestra, and for 18 years played Mendelssohn's *Songs Without Words* and a medley of Broadway songs twice weekly at the Green Street Café in Northampton, Massachusetts. As the parent of three children, Moebius was often on call as the storyteller.

Maria Nikolajeva is Professor of Education at the University of Cambridge, where she teaches children's literature and literary theory. She is the author and editor of numerous books, including *Power, Voice, and Subjectivity in Literature for Young Readers* (2010), *Reading for Learning: Cognitive Approaches to Children's Literature* (2014), and *The Edinburgh Companion to Children's Literature* (2017). From 1993 to 1997 she was the president of the International Research Society for Children's Literature. She was also one of the senior editors for *The Oxford Encyclopedia of Children's Literature* and received the International Grimm Award in 2005 for lifetime achievement in children's literature research. Her current research interest is evolutionary literary criticism.

Jennifer Schacker received her PhD from the Folklore Institute at Indiana University and is an associate professor in the School of English and Theatre Studies at the University of Guelph, where she has taught since 2002. Her teaching and research engage with developments in several related but distinct disciplines: folklore, anthropology, performance studies, children's literature, material culture, and fairy-tale studies. Schacker is the author of *Staging Fairyland: Folklore, Children's Entertainment, and Nineteenth-Century Pantomime* (2018) and *National Dreams: The Remaking of Fairy Tales in Nineteenth-Century England* (2003), which won the 2006 Mythopoeic Scholarship Award. She has collaborated with Christine A.

Jones and Belgian artist Lina Kusaite on *Feathers, Paws, Fins, and Claws: Fairy-Tale Beasts* (2015), an illustrated critical anthology of tales featuring animal characters. Schacker and Jones are also co-editors of *Marvelous Transformations: An Anthology of Fairy Tales and Contemporary Critical Perspectives* (2012), a volume that historicizes both oral traditional and literary tales and includes a series of original essays written by specialists from varied disciplinary backgrounds.

Ann Schmiesing is Professor of German at the University of Colorado, Boulder, where she also serves as Dean of the Graduate School and Vice Provost for Graduate Affairs. She received her PhD in German from the University of Cambridge in 1996 and joined the University of Colorado faculty in 1995. Her teaching includes the core curriculum course "Fairy Tales of Germany." She is the author of *Disability, Deformity, and Disease in the Grimms' Fairy Tales* (2014) and *Norway's Christiania Theatre, 1827–1867: From Danish Showhouse to National Stage* (2006), in addition to articles on German and Norwegian drama and narrative fiction, theater history, book illustration, and fairy tales. She has also co-authored an article on the use of rare books and special collections in humanities pedagogy. She is currently writing a biography of the Brothers Grimm.

Lewis C. Seifert is Professor of French Studies at Brown University. His research interests include early modern French literature and culture, folk- and fairy-tale studies, gender and sexuality studies, and environmental humanities. He is the author of *Fairy Tales, Sexuality, and Gender in France, 1690–1715: Nostalgic Utopias* (1996) and *Manning the Margins: Masculinity and Writing in Seventeenth-Century France* (2009); co-translator of *Enchanted Eloquence: Fairy Tales by Seventeenth-Century French Women Writers* (with Domna Stanton, 2010) and *Fairy Tales for the Disillusioned: Enchanted Stories from the French Decadent Tradition* (with Gretchen Schultz, 2016); and editor of the special issue of *Marvels & Tales* "Queer(ing) Fairy Tales" (2015). His current research projects include a study of the trickster in the folklore and literature of the French Atlantic world and, with Pierre-Emmanuel Moog, a critical edition and comparative translation of Charles Perrault's fairy tales.

Victoria Somoff is Associate Professor of Russian at Dartmouth College. She was born in Ukraine and received an MA in folklore and a PhD in Slavic languages and literature from the University of California, Berkeley. Her research interests include Russian and European novels, narrative theory, folklore and oral poetics, and Bakhtin studies. She is the author of *The Imperative of Reliability: Russian Prose on the Eve of the Novel, 1820s–1850s* (2015). She is currently working on a book devoted to the transformation of folklore plots in literature and conducting research on an Eastern European folk narrative, "Egle, Queen of Grass Snakes."

Allison Stedman is Associate Professor of French at the University of North Carolina at Charlotte. She has published articles on early modern French literary portraits, psalm paraphrases, novels, and fairy tales and on pedagogical strategies for teaching French and Italian literature and culture at the university level. With Perry Gethner, she is the co-editor and translator of *A Trip to the Country* by Henriette-Julie de Castelnau, Comtesse de Murat (2011). She is also the author of *Rococo Fiction in France, 1600–1715: Seditious Frivolity* (2013) and of a modern French edition of Murat's 1699 experimental novel, *Le Voyage de campagne* (2014). She is currently completing a book project on representations of the mind-body connection in early modern France as thematized in the writings of Montaigne, Descartes, St. François de Sales, Giulo Cesare Vanini, and Blaise Pascal.

Kay Stone, folklorist, storyteller, writer, and artist, heard her first stories in the 1940s when her father told her very tall tales about the animals he saw while driving his gasoline tanker across the wild Florida Everglades. Her training as a folklore scholar specializing in Anglo-American traditional tales led, in 1969, to the start of her teaching career at the University of Winnipeg, where she taught folklore, children's literature, and storytelling. It was an exciting multidecade adventure that she has happily shared in workshops and performances for all ages. Stone has written numerous articles and three books: *Burning Brightly: New Light on Old Tales Told Today* (1998), *The Golden Woman: Dreaming as Art* (2004), and *Some Day Your Witch Will Come* (2008). She is presently working on a collection of her own stories.

Maria Tatar is the John L. Loeb Professor of Germanic Languages and Literatures and Folklore and Mythology at Harvard University. She is the author of *The Annotated Brothers Grimm* (2012), *Enchanted Hunters: The Power of Stories in Childhood* (2009), and *The Annotated African American Folktales* (2017), among many other volumes. Her work has appeared in the *New York Times*, *New Republic*, *The New Yorker*, *Slate*, and other media outlets, and she is a frequent contributor to National Public Radio. She served as Dean for the Humanities at Harvard University from 2003 to 2006 and is currently a senior fellow at Harvard's Society of Fellows. She is the recipient of the NAACP Image Award for Outstanding Literary Work of 2018.

Gioia Timpanelli, along with other storytellers, is a founder of the current worldwide revival of storytelling. She has presented evenings of stories and has taught classes and courses on world folktales and medieval poems, at times alone and at times in collaboration with poets, mythologists, scientists, and storytellers, at places small and large, for foundations and libraries, conferences, and colleges. Before storytelling, she created, produced, and broadcast eight series of programs for Educational and Public Television; one series, *Stories from My House*, won an Emmy citation for "Tales from Viet Nam," and another, *African Anthology*, a 30-program series on ancient stories and modern African literature, featured interviews with African authors. She wrote *Sometimes the Soul: Two Novellas of Sicily* (1998), which won an American Book Award, and *What Makes a Child Lucky* (2008), with drawings by Fulvio Testa. She also received an award from the Women's National Book Association "for bringing the oral tradition to the American Public." Currently she broadcasts *Story Traveler*, a 5-minute story program for Public Radio, distributed by PRX, heard on Public Radio stations and especially on North Country Public Radio, which broadcasts the series.

Charlotte Trinquet du Lys is Associate Professor of French and director of the French program at the University of Central Florida. She specializes in early modern fairy tales and the relationship between European texts from high and low cultures. In her first monograph, *Le Conte de fées français (1690–1700): Traditions italiennes et origines aristocratiques* (2012), she explores the sociohistorical context of female and aristocratic literature, while reinstating the often neglected influence of Italian tellers on the creation of the French corpus, and examines the importance of literature in the elaboration of the folkoric fairy-tale genre of the nineteenth and twentieth centuries. Her other contributions to the field include many articles, and a NASSCFL conference held in 2016, titled "Creations, Recreations, and Entertainment During the Long Seventeenth Century," the proceedings of which are in press. Trinquet du Lys also hosted a radio show for a year, "Secrets of the Fairies," on WPRK 91.5 FM in Winter Park, Florida. Some of the recordings can be found at secretsofthefairies.org/.

Linda Kraus Worley is Associate Professor of German Studies at the University of Kentucky with a focus on nineteenth-century literature and culture. Her publications have concentrated on eighteenth- and nineteenth-century German women writers viewed through various feminist and sociocultural theoretical lenses. Her ongoing background preparations for the course "Fairy Tales in European Context" have led her to publish on aspects of the Grimms' tales in the article "The Horror! Gothic Horror Literature and Fairy Tales: The Case of 'The Robber Bridegroom.'" She is currently researching the fairy tales of Marie von Ebner-Eschenbach. She regularly teaches graduate courses on the literary constructions of gender identities, German fairy tales, and issues in higher education. She is co-editor of the international journal *Colloquia Germanica*.

Jack Zipes is Professor Emeritus of German and Comparative Literature at the University of Minnesota, and an active lecturer, writer, and storyteller. Some of his recent publications include *The Enchanted Screen: The Unknown History of Fairy-Tale Films* (2010), *The Irresistible Fairy Tale: The Cultural and Social History of a Genre* (2012), *Grimm Legacies: The Magic Power of Fairy Tales* (2014), *The Sorcerer's Apprentice: An Anthology of Magical Tales* (2017), and *Tales of Wonder: Reading Fairy Tales Through Picture Postcards* (2017). He has also translated the first 1812–1815 edition of the Grimms' tales, *The Original Folk and Fairy Tales of the Brothers Grimm* (2014). Recently, he has published *Fearless Ivan and His Faithful Horse Double-Hump* (2018), his own political version of a Russian folktale; *Slap-Bam, or The Art of Governing Men: Édouard Laboulaye's Political Fairy Tales* (2018); and, as editor, *The 100 Riddles of the Fairy Bellaria* (2018), written and illustrated by the neglected folklorist Charles Godfrey Leland (2018).

INDEX

www.ingramcontent.com/pod-product-compliance
Lightning Source LLC
Chambersburg PA
CBHW081401090726
47908CB00012B/2750